"I don't think I have ever read anything quite so compelling. Everything was woven together beautifully and could only have been done so by someone who had actually lived through similar experiences in the courtroom."

—PennyTerk.com

"Move over John Grisham!"

—Denton A. Cooley, M.D., world-renowned pioneer heart surgeon

"Seldom does a first effort at courtroom fiction find itself in the class of such notables as *Inherit the Wind, The Verdict,* and *The Rainmaker.* But Larry Thompson's *So Help Me God* belongs there. I predict it will become a modern-day classic courtroom tale."

—Jim M. Perdue, nationally renowned trial lawyer and author of *I Remember Atticus*

"I hated to finish that last page of *So Help Me God....* The courtroom scenes are both realistic and spellbinding."

—Hartley Hampton, former president of the Texas Trial Lawyers Association

SO HELP ME GOD

LARRY D. THOMPSON

A TOM DOHERTY ASSOCIATES BOOK
NEW YORK TOR®

This is a work of fiction. All of the characters, organizations, and events portrayed in this novel are either products of the author's imagination or are used fictitiously.

SO HELP ME GOD

Copyright © 2004, 2008 by Larry D. Thompson

Originally published in 2004, in somewhat different form, by Live Oak Productions.

A Tor Book
Published by Tom Doherty Associates, LLC
175 Fifth Avenue
New York, NY 10010

www.tor.com

Tor® is a registered trademark of Tom Doherty Associates, LLC.

ISBN-13: 978-0-7653-5753-3
ISBN-10: 0-7653-5753-4

First Tor Edition: April 2008

Printed in the United States of America

0 9 8 7 6 5 4 3 2 1

This is for my children, Casey, Kel and Ryan,
and in remembrance of my brother, Thomas Thompson,
a great author and a greater friend.
Tommy, I hope this lives up to your standards.

Author's Note

The most experienced trial attorneys know that our role in the legal process is unique and invaluable. We do not determine the outcome of our cases, how the public views the issues or even how the laws of the country apply in any given cause. Those matters are determined by the witnesses, the scientific evidence, the jury's perspectives, the judge's inclinations and the finality of appellate review. Yet as trial attorneys we are called upon to bear the burden of presenting the best, most persuasive, direct evidence supporting but one side of any cause. We advocate for views we may not share, but will fight to the death for the right of each position to have a full voice in our society, to have full exposure to the heat of public debate, to have its place in the shaping of the mores of our society and to succeed or fail on its own merits. It is therefore, with the pride of more than thirty-five years of advocating before juries, that I bring the process, the science and the art of advocacy of controversial issues to the fiction reading public to share the joy, exasperation and wonderment of the civil courtroom in America today. It is not ours to change opinions, but to test and challenge those opinions in the light of great advocacy.

Respectfully submitted,
Larry D. Thompson
Lorance & Thompson, P.C.
Houston, Texas

"I will give no deadly medicine to anyone if asked, nor suggest any such counsel; and in like manner I will not give to a woman a pessary to produce abortion."
—Hippocrates (460–377 B.C.), *The Hippocratic Oath*

We need not resolve the difficult question of when life begins. When those trained in the respective disciplines of medicine, philosophy, and theology are unable to arrive at any consensus, the judiciary, at this point in the development of man's knowledge, is not in a position to speculate as to the answer . . .

With respect to the State's important and legitimate interest in potential life, the "compelling" point is at viability. This is so because the fetus then presumably has the capability of meaningful life outside the mother's womb. State regulation protective of fetal life after viability thus has both logical and biological justifications.

This means, on the other hand, for the period of pregnancy prior to this "compelling" point, the attending physician, in consultation with his patient, is free to determine, without regulation by the State, that in his medical judgment, the patient's pregnancy should be terminated. If that decision is reached, the judgment may be effectuated by an abortion free of interference by the State.
—*Roe v. Wade*, U.S. Supreme Court (1973)

SO HELP
ME GOD

Prologue

The storm raged in from the Gulf of Mexico. Only thirty minutes earlier, the stars shone through a dark blue autumn sky. Claps of thunder, like a drumroll, heralded the tempest's arrival shortly before it struck the small city on Galveston Bay. Wind howled through the treetops and drove the rain sideways. Windows rattled in their casements. Hail pinged off the pickup trucks and cars. Great bolts of lightning struck the neighborhood, illuminating the small form of a teenage girl, shuffling down the middle of the street, clothes soaked to the skin as she clutched her shoes. The rain matted the girl's hair and cascaded down her face where it was joined by tears streaming from her eyes. Shoulders slumped, she wiped her eyes with one hand and touched the right side of her lip to check for bleeding. Lost in thought, the girl ignored the storm, the lightning and the overflowing streets. As she turned the corner and walked up the sidewalk, she put her shoes on, straightened up and used both hands to wipe her face before opening the door. She hollered to her parents, "I caught a ride home. I'm going to bed."

After closing the door, she collapsed on the bed and buried her face in a stuffed bear.

LUCY BAINES BRADY WAS a seventeen-year-old junior at Texas City High School. With short brown hair and brown eyes, her facial features were not classically beautiful. Nothing about her really attracted attention. Maybe her chin protruded a fraction of an inch too far or her mouth could have been slightly smaller. Even studying her closely, it would be hard to pinpoint the problem. Whatever the reason, when she walked down the halls, the boys at school never turned as Lucy went by. She was too shy to flirt or otherwise attract their attention. And with an evangelical upbringing, Lucy's mother would not permit her to wear tight-fitting sweaters, shorts and skirts or use more than just the slightest makeup.

Texas City was a suburb of Houston, thirty miles south and perched on the edge of Galveston Bay, a stone's throw from the Gulf of Mexico. Decidedly blue-collar America, its skyline was one of petrochemical smokestacks, refinery cracking towers, the superstructures of ships and church steeples. Most families lived in standard three-bedroom, one-bath houses and nearly every driveway had a pickup truck and a bass boat parked in front of the attached garage. The men were well paid for their work at the petrochemical plants and on the docks. They spent their leisure time fishing and hunting. Friday nights were reserved for high school sports, preferably football. Most Saturday nights were spent at the local roadhouses where the music came from bands hoping for a shot at Nashville and the Opry.

Lucy had lived in Texas City her entire life. She had gone from kindergarten through the eleventh grade with the same four hundred classmates. After graduation, she was destined to work at one of the refineries or the mall, marry a petrochemical worker like her father and spend life as a working mother. If asked if she was disappointed with such a life and its prospects, she would have said no. In fact, it was not something that entered her mind. She accepted life in Texas City. She knew little else and expected nothing more.

It was at church where she first met Jason. Early in the school year, seated in her usual front row seat in the choir loft, she saw him staring at her from an aisle seat in the congregation. New boy in town was her first thought. Her second was big, good looking, probably a football player. Then he smiled and she quickly looked down at her hymnal. That evening at youth fellowship, Jason grabbed the seat beside her and introduced himself. Afterward, Lucy was a half block from the church on her walk home when a new, black pickup slowed beside her.

"Want a lift?" Jason asked.

"No thanks," Lucy answered. "I only live a few blocks from here."

"Cool. See you tomorrow."

Jason threw it in low and burned a little rubber as he sped away.

Lucy's eyes followed the truck until it turned the corner two blocks down the street. During the next week, they passed each other several times in the hall. Jason always looked her way as he smiled or waved. Embarrassed by the attention, Lucy rarely acknowledged him. More often she would look down at the floor.

On the following Sunday evening after youth fellowship, Jason grabbed her arm. "Let me give you a ride home?" he asked, flashing his best smile.

"No thanks. I'm used to walking. It's a nice night."

"Well, then, I'll just walk you home and come back after my truck."

"Suit yourself," Lucy said, somewhat embarrassed. "Seems like a waste of time to me."

Lucy was not accustomed to being alone with a boy and felt uncomfortable with small talk. He was content just to have someone listen as he re-created his great plays from the previous Friday night. He left her at her front door without even a handshake, turned and jogged back up the street toward the church. Lucy wondered if he noticed that she couldn't think of a thing to say.

Over the next three weeks Jason became more aggressive. One morning when she got off the school bus, Jason pulled her away from her girlfriends as he insisted on escorting her into the building. Soon, Lucy began to find him waiting outside her classroom door. He walked with her to most of her classes and talked with her in the hall until the next bell rang.

Each Sunday evening he continued to walk her home even when she tried to refuse. Then his persistence paid off when, on the next try, Lucy relented. After all, she thought, what could possibly happen on a five-minute drive from the church to her house. As they left the fellowship hall, they walked around the church to the back parking lot as Jason explained that he didn't like the lighted lot in front. A new pickup was too tempting to car thieves. As Lucy got in on the passenger side, Jason started the engine, turned on the stereo and fiddled with the various knobs, slides and buttons until he was satisfied with the sound. They listened silently for several minutes to Garth Brooks singing about his friends in low places before Lucy said that she had to be going home. Without protest, Jason put the truck in gear, backed out and drove slowly out of the parking lot. When they got to her house, he shut off the engine and before she could turn for the door handle, Jason slid over, pulled her toward him and kissed her. It wasn't long and certainly not passionate, but it startled Lucy. Instead of returning the kiss, she got the door open and closed it behind her, not knowing how to react or what to say. Jason started the engine and disappeared down the street. If Lucy could have read his thoughts, she would have known that he expected to have her bra off and his hand in her panties in another two or three weeks. Unfortunately for Lucy, she was not a mind reader.

Jason planned his assault carefully. First came more kissing in front of Lucy's house. By the third time, Lucy was a willing participant and eager to return his youthful passion. Then he began to brush her breast with his hand and that was followed with the unbuttoning of her blouse, and she felt his hand under her bra, massaging her nipple. At first Lucy resisted, worried about the fires of hell, but more so about the wrath of her mother if she were found out. Then she gave in to the caress of his hand as it made her nipples rise to his slightest touch. When Lucy's mother began to notice that her daughter had a regular ride home on Sunday night, she started watching for the pickup. She gave them five minutes before the porch light came on, instructing Lucy that if she didn't want to be embarrassed by her father standing under the porch light, she better be in the house within a minute after the light came on.

Not satisfied with what he could accomplish in five minutes, Jason came up with a new plan. They would just stay parked behind the church longer. No one would notice since he was the only one that parked back there on Sunday evening anyway. At first Lucy objected but then relented when Jason convinced her that she could just say she stayed over a few minutes to discuss a new solo with the choir director. Accepting the excuse, she reached up to kiss him and almost immediately Lucy felt his hands fumbling at the buttons on her blouse and then at the hook on her bra. She fought momentarily and then gave in. Knowing that she would have to pray for forgiveness, she couldn't help but enjoy it. Jason rubbed his hands on her breasts. When she felt them start to drift lower, she came to her senses.

"No, Jason, I won't do that. Take me home." She put her bra back on. Jason acquiesced in silence and drove while she buttoned her blouse.

As she exited the truck, he said, "I'm sorry, babe. I got carried away. It won't happen again. I promise."

Lucy said nothing in reply but slammed the door shut. After saying good night to her parents, she went to her room and, instead of undressing, she kneeled and prayed for forgiveness of her sins, promising God that if He would forgive her, nothing close to that would happen again until she was married. She also promised God that these Sunday night adventures in the parking lot were over. She was going to remain a virgin until her wedding night. Satisfied that she was forgiven, she read her Bible until she fell asleep.

Her resolve was firm until the end of the next Sunday's fellowship. That was when the storm rolled in over Texas City. Lucy was in line to call her parents when Jason caught up to her. "Lucy, this storm is bad. No point in calling your parents. I can give you a ride. Just a ride home. Nothing more. It'll save them from having to get soaked."

Thinking of her parents out in the storm, she finally agreed. As they left the fellowship hall, Jason told her to wait while he made a dash for his truck. When he drove back to where Lucy stood, she burst from the door and ran through the rain.

As she climbed in, Jason turned on the stereo. Then he said, "I think we're going to have to give it a few minutes for the storm to pass and let the water go down."

The Gulf Coast was well known for streets that suddenly flooded, often making them impassable and leaving cars stranded. Jason did not have this problem. His pickup had big tires that would have no trouble forging through the rising water. He only had to convince Lucy otherwise.

"Jason, I've been riding in pickups my whole life. Don't lie to me."

"No, Lucy, you don't understand," Jason replied, as he looked her right in the eye. "This is a brand new truck. We might make it. We might not. I'm just scared to try. If we get stalled in high water, my old man will kill me and park the truck in the garage until spring. I don't want to be riding the school bus for the rest of the year."

As Jason drove the truck away from the door to a parking space in the dark lot behind the church, Lucy had to concede that this was a real "frog strangler," as her dad would put it. She weighed her alternatives and decided that ten minutes inside the truck was better than ten minutes walking through the downpour. She sat on her side of the truck, listening to the music and watching the windshield wipers as lightning flashed and rain filled the streets. It wasn't long until Lucy began to shiver in her wet clothes.

Seizing his opportunity, Jason said, "I'll hold you and warm you up. Nothing more, I swear."

Reluctant at first, she finally slid over to his outstretched arm and snuggled against his chest. Suddenly, Jason grabbed her chin in his hand and forced her to kiss him. She tried to pull away but couldn't shove him off. When he started to unbutton her blouse, she screamed. Jason backhanded her across the face. "Shut up, Lucy. You want this as much as I do."

Afterward, he commanded, "Get dressed. I'm taking you home."

Whimpering as she put on her skirt and buttoned her blouse, Lucy retreated to her side of the seat. She couldn't find her panties in the dark. When she finished dressing, her back stiffened. She reached over and slapped Jason as hard as she could. Jason looked startled for a moment, then shoved her toward the passenger door.

"For that, bitch, you can walk home."

He opened the door, pushed her out, and left her standing in the parking lot as he roared off into the night. Lucy stared at the fading taillights, then pulled off her shoes and started the walk home. Uncertain about what she could do, the only thought that came through clearly was what she couldn't do—and that was to tell her mother.

1

For twelve years the faithful had journeyed from around the world to view the comatose man whose life depended on the feeding tube in his abdomen. This Christmas Eve morning was no different. They began arriving at the City of Miracles on the west side of Fort Worth at dawn. The parking lot resembled Universal Studios. Young men and women in tan slacks and white shirts directed traffic.

By nine o'clock, hundreds were gathered. When the gates opened, a guide escorted the first group inside. The young woman who led them resembled a college cheerleader, blond, blue-eyed, a face filled with eagerness and religious fervor. As they walked, she explained where they were going and what they would see. "My name is Naomi. Twelve years ago today, a demented woman stabbed Reverend Thomas Jeremiah Luther, the Chosen, in the heart as he left a revival at the Cotton Bowl in Dallas. They rushed him to the hospital where he was not expected to live. He refused to die. After months, they could do nothing more so we brought him back here where we could care for him and wait for him to be born once again. You will see him where he lies in state. He has been in a coma for twelve years, fed by a tube and cared for by those of us who believe in him. Five years ago, we took him off life support at the directive of the City's board of governors. Since then, the doctors have repeatedly declared him clinically dead, but each time a miracle has brought him back.

"The finest doctors in the world have evaluated his condition over the years. They have reached the same conclusion. He will never wake up. He will always be in a vegetative condition and there is nothing we can do except care for him until his death.

"We know the doctors are wrong. They do not understand the power of prayer or believe in miracles. We know that he will not die. Our Father has much more work for him to do in this life. When the time is right, he will awaken and take his rightful place as the spiritual leader of the City of Miracles. Once again, his voice will be heard throughout the world."

They arrived at the center of the city and found themselves standing in front of an unimpressive, round dome that rose twenty feet above the ground. It could have been a tomb or a bunker or a landed spacecraft. The young woman asked the assembled group to form a single-file line and to bow their heads as they entered. One by one, they vanished into the shadows of the dome. Smoky oil lamps provided a faint light. The circular walkway surrounded a smaller, slightly glowing glass dome, thirty feet in diameter.

"Please be silent and follow your guide along the walkway. There will be room for each of you to view the Chosen. As soon as you position yourselves facing the dome, we will begin," a voice commanded through loudspeakers.

The glass dome covered a modern and fully functional intensive care unit fifteen feet below the level where the visitors stood. In the middle of the unit was a hospital bed. On it lay the frail, almost lifeless body of Thomas Jeremiah Luther, a.k.a. the Chosen, covered in white linen with only a red blotch carefully placed over his heart where the knife had entered twelve years earlier. His face was the picture of serenity. A light shone on it, forming a halo above his head. A close look revealed a barely perceptible rise and fall of his chest. To his right a young man dressed in a white robe sat ceremoniously on a rock, reminiscent of the scene that Mary Magdalene and Mary, the mother of Jesus, had seen three days after Jesus had been crucified.

As the visitors took their places, the nurses stopped what they were doing and stood off to the side. A portrait of Jesus hung on one wall. Eyes filled with compassion, he seemed to stare at the man in the bed. Reverend Luther himself had done the portrait when he was a resident in the Tarrant County jail many years before. The portrait had been moved to the City when the Chosen was at the height of his power.

The faithful silently witnessed the scene before them for five minutes before the young man on the rock started speaking.

". . . as he cared for us in life we care for him as he lies in limbo before you. The ladies in white provide physical and pulmonary therapy three times a day. He does not need life support. He is on no regular medication. Occasionally, he blinks his eyes. Otherwise, he shows no sign of life. Yet, we know he lives and someday will rise to lead us again. It has been prophesied that on an anniversary of his near-death he will awaken. For twelve years, people like you have gathered here on that anniversary and prayed for his return. For whatever reason, God has not given him back to us. Now the lights are going to dim and you will be in total darkness. Do not be afraid. For the one minute that you are in darkness, think instead about the twelve years that the Chosen has been in darkness and pray silently to our God to return him to us."

The lights dimmed as the lamps were snuffed out and the room went black. The visitors could not see their families beside them. They could only reach out and clasp hands. After about thirty seconds of silence, a woman in the crowd started crying, quietly at first before her crying turned to wailing and gasping for air. Then she sank to her knees as grief overwhelmed her.

"Woman, why are you weeping?" A voice, soft and weak, asked the question.

At first no one knew where it came from until the young man on the rock shouted, "Turn on the lights. It's him!"

2

Lucy awoke from a horrific night of tossing, turning and nightmares. She lay in bed and wondered whether to tell her mother that she was not feeling well and needed to stay home. Fearing that would only arouse a series of questions, she changed her mind, made her bed and put on a robe for the trip to the bathroom and breakfast table. Her dad, Randall "Bo" Brady, would have left for work an hour earlier.

Lucy's mother, Joanna, worked as a bookkeeper and cashier at the Texas City Cafeteria in town. Each morning she left before Lucy boarded the school bus and returned home by five o'clock. Within minutes, she would be joined by her mother at the kitchen table before she had to leave. On this particular morning, breakfast was the last thing on Lucy's mind, but she followed her routine and was soon seated in front of a bowl of cereal with *The Miracle Morning Hour* on the television in the adjoining family room. As she toyed with her food, Joanna joined her.

"Good morning, dear. You're running a little late this morning. The bus will be by in fifteen minutes."

"I know. I'll make it." Glancing at the television, she added, "Mom, I know that Aunt Jessie's on the board of the City of Miracles, but do we have to watch that show every morning?"

"That ministry is my sister's life and I like to be able to discuss it with her when we talk. You can change the channel when I leave. What's that on your lip?"

Lucy hesitated and replied, "Oh, it's nothing. Just a fever blister starting."

"You get some ointment on it before you go to school. By the way, who gave you a ride last night?"

"You know, Mom. Jason."

"Seems to me like you were a little late getting home. What were you and Jason doing?"

"Nothing, Mom. We had to wait a few minutes in the parking lot for the storm to let up."

"Exactly what were you and Jason doing in that parking lot?" Joanna demanded, once again recalling how many times she had spent the evening on her back in a pickup and hoping to nip in the bud any possibility that her daughter might develop similar habits.

Putting on an innocent and incredulous look, Lucy replied, "Nothing, Mother. We listened to Garth Brooks for ten minutes. That's all."

"Well, darling daughter, see to it that there really is nothing more. If there is, the Good Book says you will be damned to hell." With that parting comment, Joanna rose, kissed her daughter on the cheek and left for work. Lucy sat at the table with a mixture of emotions, thoughts and questions rampaging through her mind.

Had she caused it?

Was she responsible?

Did she want it as much as Jason did, like he told her?

Should she report it to the police?

Would anyone believe her?

Could she be pregnant? He had barely gotten it in and most of the liquid had gone down her leg. She also remembered conversations with her best friends, whom she considered experts on the topic of sex. According to them, a girl couldn't get pregnant the first time.

She sat in her classes that day, although her mind could just as well have been in outer space. The thoughts of the early morning kept popping up, one by one, like the words in one of those little black fortune-telling balls, only these were questions, not answers. During lunch she sat with her usual group of friends. Surveying the table, she considered whether she could tell any of them. As lunch ended, she concluded that not one would keep her mouth shut. She quietly left the table for her next class.

Lucy wanted to confide in her mother. Then she remembered people up in front of the congregation, confessing their sins and asking for forgiveness from the membership, the church, Jesus and God. She had convinced herself that her mother would not believe what had actually happened. She wasn't sure that her mother would make her confess; yet she couldn't be certain, and she wasn't willing to take that risk. She considered her aunt Jessie in Fort Worth where she spent several weeks every summer, but gave up the idea when she thought of the weekly conversations between Jessie and Joanna.

Over the next several days, Lucy began to heal, at least physically. Her soreness went away. She slept a little better. She was able to pay attention in class and she joined in the conversations at lunch. On Saturday, her dad took his Boston Whaler out in Galveston Bay. His buddy, Al, met him at five A.M. and they fished until midafternoon. When they got back to the house, Al hung around, helping Bo clean the fish and wash down the boat. Al was a policeman and Lucy had known him all of her life. By now, Lucy had almost decided that Jason had raped her. Al could tell her for sure. She wandered out to the garage.

"Well, there's my best girlfriend. How're you doing, kid?" Al asked as he gave her a hug.

Al was one of the biggest men she had ever seen. He stood at least six feet, six inches tall and had to weigh three hundred pounds. In full uniform, "Respect" was his middle name. With Lucy, he was like a favorite uncle.

"I'm fine, Al. How was the fishing?"

"Good day, sweetie. We each caught our limit of reds and a couple of snapper to boot. Our families are going to eat good tonight." As soon as her dad went into the house, she broached the subject.

"Al, I'm writing a research paper on the decline in crime

over the past several years and the reasons for it. Can you give me some ideas?"

"Sure, honey, violent crime is way down. It's largely due to our cities waking up and putting more money into law enforcement. Part of it is because Texas built more prisons a few years ago. If they're locked up in the crossbar hotel, they can't bother you and me."

"What do you consider violent crime?"

"Murder, assault, armed robbery, rape. Those are the main ones."

"Are they all down?" Lucy asked.

"Well, sweetie, all but rape. That one's not really affected by anything I mentioned."

Seeing her opportunity, Lucy seized it. "How do you define rape?"

"I'd have to go to the penal code to give you the exact definition. With adults, it's usually a man forcing a woman to have sexual intercourse against her will."

"How can you tell if there's been a rape?"

"We've got ways. The first thing is the credibility of the person reporting it. It's particularly important that the woman, and usually it's a woman, report it immediately. The relationship of the victim and the alleged perpetrator is right up there. It's hard to get a conviction if they knew each other before the complaint. The longer she waits, the more likely a jury is going to conclude that she consented, then just got mad at the guy. Physical evidence is important. If there is a rape, we have police officers trained to recognize it. They get the woman to the hospital where they use a rape kit to gather evidence. They look for proof of violence, bruising, tearing, etc. They also take samples, searching for semen."

Al sensed that Lucy was directing the conversation.

"Lucy, do you have something you want to talk to me about?"

"Uh, no. Not me. I'm just doing research. Thanks for your help." She turned and quickly went back into the house before Al could say anything else. In the quietness of her room, she compared his comments to her situation. It had been a week. The soreness between her legs was gone. If there had ever been any semen, it had long since washed away. To make it worse, she hadn't told anyone. The kids at school knew they walked together in the halls. If Jason said that they had agreed to have sex, it would boil down to his word against hers. From what Al had said, the chances were slim that a jury would find him guilty. And there would be the publicity. The thought of being in the Texas City newspaper and having people stare at her was the last straw. She would just have to keep her mouth shut.

On Monday, she returned to school with the events of that Sunday night still in her mind. She managed to push them to the back where they would stay—at least for now.

3

Lester Higdon, the neurologist on call, arrived at the City in less than an hour. He was whisked through hidden tunnels to the bedside of the Chosen who had lapsed back into a sleep. The doctor was fearful that Luther wouldn't speak again. Dr. Higdon checked his vital signs, listened to his heart and lungs and determined that his reflexes were intact. Fortunately, the round-the-clock nurses had done their job. While the limbs were thin, muscle was present, and more importantly, there were no contractures.

"Dr. Higdon, what is going on? Is it a miracle?" one of the nurses asked.

"Carol, I'm not even sure that I know. I've been practicing neurology for twenty-five years and I've never seen this. There are reports in the literature of patients who were thought to be comatose and turned out to be in what is known as a locked-in state. They appear to be completely unresponsive, and after months or years, something happens to trigger their recovery. For the most part, it remains a medical mystery. Is it a miracle when it happens? I'm afraid I'm not the one to make that call. I'm a physician, not a theologian. I can't even tell you if he'll wake up again or if he will die tomorrow. All we can do is watch and wait."

And so they did.

Within a week, Reverend Luther woke again and he responded to simple questions with blinks of his eyes. Soon, he moved each of his limbs. Next, came short sentences. While it may not have been a miracle, the improvement in the condition of the Chosen was remarkable. In the fourth week, they moved him to a chair where he sat for thirty minutes. He slept twelve hours each night and took a nap every afternoon. Then, he asked for a TV. When he wasn't sleeping or undergoing therapy, he was glued to it, interested in all of the news shows. He asked for magazines and books that discussed world events that had occurred while he had slept.

As his recovery continued, Reverend Luther's doctors outfitted one floor of the Miracle Tower as a rehabilitation facility. The Miracle Tower rose above the City. Twenty stories tall, it was covered in glass the hue of a good Kentucky bourbon. It housed the administrative and accounting offices, archives, a research and religious library, suites for the members of the board, and a boardroom on the nineteenth floor. The twentieth floor penthouse had been designed for Reverend Luther. When the Chosen was moved to the newly redone rehabilitation facility, the City was sealed off from visitors and T.J. was taken on a tour. He was pleased to find that his work had not been allowed to lie fallow. Many of his original ideas were completed with more on the drawing board. Miracle College had an enrollment of three thousand students. Miracle Foundation, the think tank for the Right Side, occupied its own six-story building, housing some of the best and brightest right-wing minds that money could buy. The television ministry had tripled during the twelve years. The Crusade schedule was booked solid for years in advance. The various theme sections of the City were fully operational. T.J. whistled under his breath at the amount of the City's net worth, so much money that the City employed a staff of managers to oversee investments. In studying the City's stocks, one of them caught the attention of the Chosen. It was a company called GreenForest Utilities. He took particular note of the investment because he had seen a business talk show where two analysts were discussing a lawsuit involving that company in Houston.

As T.J.'s recovery progressed, Reverend Jimmy Witherspoon faced a dilemma. He had been a young minister twelve years earlier when the Miracle Board plucked him from his growing ministry in West Texas. They named him "temporary pastor" at the City of Miracles, moving him and his family into T.J.'s penthouse. While not the equal of the Chosen, he was carefully molded with speech and acting coaches until he could stand with the best. He may not have measured up to T.J.'s performance before he was stabbed, but he was at least in the same lineup with the finest that Sunday morning had to offer. It wasn't long before Reverend Witherspoon praised the Lord, cursed the devil and drove out demons as well as any man on television. He had ratings to prove it. As one year became two and two became twelve, he was still called the temporary pastor at the City of Miracles. Yet, he was the one who had substantially completed the vision of the Chosen. He began to think of it as his city, not that of the vegetable in the hospital bed.

He would have never admitted that early in his ministry he had prepared a proper eulogy for the Chosen, which he had polished each time that T.J. was pronounced clinically dead.

4

The thoughts didn't come on like a runaway freight train on a downhill grade. Instead they began as tiny nagging worries that would pop up like balloons over a cartoon character's head. When they worked their way to the front of her mind,

Lucy would try to shove them to the back and, hopefully, out of her consciousness.

Am I pregnant?

Is my period late?

When exactly did it last start?

The questions came at the oddest times—at the breakfast table, riding on the school bus, sitting in church. Most often they occurred just before she went to sleep at night and always when she awakened in the morning. At first it was easy to ignore them because Lucy had the prior counsel of her assembly of lunch table experts on sex and pregnancy. Besides, her periods were rarely regular. At the end of the second week after the rape, she anxiously awaited the start of her period.

Nothing happened.

As the weeks wore on Lucy began to consider the possibility of pregnancy. While she tried to convince herself that it wasn't possible, her mind stubbornly refused to dismiss the subject for longer than a few minutes. One night she woke up with her mother at the side of her bed.

"Child, whatever were you dreaming about? You were moaning, yelling and thrashing about. You woke the dog and I suspect half the neighborhood."

"I don't know, Mom. I'm all right now. I'll get back to sleep."

Her mother left the room. Lucy had lied. She wasn't all right. She was relieved that her mother could not interpret her screams. Her dream, as so many had been in recent weeks, replayed her struggle with Jason. In her dream, no matter how hard she tried she could not get Jason off her body or his erection out of her vagina. At the end of the fifth week, Lucy estimated that she was three weeks overdue. She argued with herself now, not about whether it had been a rape, but whether she was pregnant. Every morning she hoped that her period would start. When it didn't, it was usually lunchtime before she could concentrate. By the seventh week she could think of nothing else. She had seen pregnancy tests advertised on television, those commercials with the couple smiling when they got the result. Lucy decided it was time for one of those tests.

After the school bus dropped her at the corner, she walked four blocks to a drugstore. Satisfying herself that nobody recognized her, she picked the cheapest test kit, paid for it, and stuffed it in the bottom of her backpack. She walked through her front door at four-thirty, pleased that the only sound was that of a rotary sander coming from the garage. Going to her room, she hid the test kit under clothes in the bottom dresser drawer.

Dinner was even quieter than usual that evening. Lucy volunteered nothing. Joanna noticed and attributed it to worry about an algebra test. Bo talked about some lawyer up in East Texas who just got a judgment of over two hundred million dollars for a bunch of chemical workers who had been exposed to asbestos. The verdict had been the main topic of conversation at the plant that day. After dinner, Joanna and Lucy did the dishes and Lucy kissed her mom good night.

"I'm checking in early."

"You feeling all right, hon? You've hardly said a word since I got home."

"I'm okay. I just need to hit that algebra for a little while longer and then I'm going to try to get a good night's sleep before the test tomorrow."

When the house was quiet and her parents were asleep, Lucy opened the bottom dresser drawer and withdrew the kit. She tiptoed to the bathroom, shut the door, and turned on the light. The box contained a small cup, a device wrapped in cellophane that was about six inches long with a handle at one end, a hard brushlike device at the other and a small window in the middle. She followed the instructions. In two minutes she would learn if she was pregnant by looking at the lines that appeared in the window. She laid the test stick on the bathroom counter and filled the urine cup to the top. Next, she put the urine cup on the counter beside the stick and froze. Never in her young life had she been so petrified about performing such a simple task. With a shaking hand she reached out, picked up the stick and dipped the absorbent tip into the urine, counting slowly to five. Then, she laid the stick on the counter and waited, watching the bathroom clock for a full two minutes. After the second hand completed two rotations, she took a deep breath and looked at the stick. There was a pink line in the window. Her eyes widened with fear. Her heart raced. Her head throbbed. She was eight weeks pregnant. Sinking slowly to the floor, tears filled her eyes. Time passed and she didn't care.

5

The next two weeks disappeared and Lucy never knew they were there. She went through the motions of her life. She got up, talked briefly to her mother, caught the school bus, attended classes, and went to choir practice and church. The only thing she remembered was passing Jason in the hall. He was always smiling and talking to a couple of friends. When he saw her, he quickly looked the other way.

It was when she woke up nauseated one morning that she realized that there was a clock ticking inside of her body and she had a decision to make. There were only two options, have the baby or get an abortion.

Before this had happened to her, she would never have considered an abortion. Everything in her upbringing shouted against it. Yet, if she told her mother, Joanna would condemn her to hell. Then, she would demand that Lucy have the baby and put it up for adoption. Having known two girls who had gotten pregnant and still attended school, Lucy couldn't face the gossip and whispers that would follow her. She would forever be branded as "one of those girls."

Lucy made the lonely decision to learn something about abortion and turned to the Internet. On the next Friday, after her parents left for the football game, she logged on to the computer. When the computer was ready, she paused, then slowly typed in the word: ABORTION. Shocked at the number of hits that appeared, she scrolled through them. There were pro-life sections, pro-choice, message boards, articles from women who had abortions and those who had chosen not to do so, scientific articles, sermons from priests and lectures from philosophers. Only then did she realize the magnitude of the debate that was raging throughout the country. The idea that she would become the center of the debate could never have entered her mind.

She looked for something that would give her advice about her decision and spotted a site by Population Planning. Having seen a billboard with that name on it somewhere, she started there.

Population Planning had its roots in the segment of the environmental movement that feared a population explosion. A small group of hippies at Berkeley started it in the late fifties and it spread to college campuses throughout the country by the mid-sixties. They believed that people were going to overpopulate the earth in a hundred years, causing famine, starvation and war. They urged birth control and limiting families to 1.6 children, a number that brought some kidding from their opponents, primarily the Catholic Church. Abortion was not on their agenda until 1973 when the United States Supreme Court decided *Roe v. Wade*. With that decision, the leaders of Population Planning quickly saw abortion as the chance to jump-start their cause. The feminist movement joined them, seeing the right to abortion as a giant step in their equal rights agenda. Soon Population Planning centers around the country were performing legal abortions, thus becoming the primary target of the pro-life movement.

When she arrived at the section titled "What To Do If I Am Pregnant," she slowly began reading and thinking. It said that there is no right choice for every person. This was the first time she had ever seen or heard anything that suggested that abortion might be okay. The writer said that her choices were to have the baby and raise the child, to have the baby and place the child for adoption, or to terminate the pregnancy. Somehow, "terminating the pregnancy" sounded much nicer than "having an abortion." She read on and concentrated on a series of questions designed to help her decide which choice to make.

Which choice can I live with?

What are my spiritual and moral beliefs?

What is best for me in the long run?

What can I afford?

As she looked at the screen with these questions, Lucy pondered. *How can I have a child? I'm just seventeen. My parents may throw me out of the house. I can't get a job to support myself, much less a baby. If I'm a mother, no boy will ever want to date me, much less marry me. How will I explain it to the members of the church? If I do have an abortion, it'll be over with soon. If I can do it in Houston, no one will ever have to know except me and God. What about God? What about the fires of hell? Will I have wasted the rest of my life and given up any chance for Heaven? God is supposed to be a forgiving God. Can he forgive something like this? Is it murder? Is the baby alive? Will an abortion hurt? Will I miss school? How sick will I be afterward? I wish I had someone to talk to.*

The article encouraged her to find someone to help—her boyfriend, her best friend, her parents, her minister. She had already been down that path and hit a dead end. As a last resort, she saw that Population Planning offered counseling which they said would be absolutely confidential and gave an 800 number. She memorized it rather than risk writing it down. The last thing she read at the Population Planning site was a warning about "crisis pregnancy centers," which they claimed were anti-abortion. According to them such centers were not going to counsel her. Instead, they would try to frighten her away from abortion with films and lies about the emotional effects of the procedure.

She logged off the site and found another from a pregnancy crisis counseling center. Population Planning was right. The crisis center was definitely anti-abortion. Their site also made strong arguments that fit with how she had been raised and her religious beliefs. The author of this site talked about science and medicine: that there are two bodies in pregnancy; that the pre-born human beings cry, hiccup, dream, and urinate; that they have brainwaves and heart-beats; that they can kick and suck their thumbs; that they have hands and feet. As she read, Lucy carefully moved her hand to her stomach and felt around. No sign of life yet.

With a mind crammed full of confusing thoughts, Lucy logged off the computer. Soon she wandered out into the backyard. Like most yards in the neighborhood, it was small and surrounded by a six-foot fence. Her mother found time to grow a few flowers there and her dad planted a garden behind the garage, growing potatoes, beans, peas, carrots and tomatoes. Her favorite place was the old swing set, left over from her childhood days. Not a year went by that her parents didn't decide to throw it away or donate it to a char-ity. The next year it was still there and Lucy didn't mind. She did some of her best thinking while sitting on the little swing beside the trapeze bar, slowly rocking to and fro and drag-ging her feet on the ground. On this evening, the sky was filled with stars. She looked up at them, seeking an answer and asking for divine guidance. If there was any answer from above, it must have been that it was her choice because she heard nothing else.

For several days she debated the decision that she had to make. With nowhere else to turn, she decided to seek advice from Population Planning. After school she searched the house, garage and backyard to make sure that her dad was not home. Satisfied the house was deserted, she sat at the kitchen counter and slowly dialed the number. It rang twice. As someone picked up on the other end, she lost her nerve and hung up. She stared at the phone and walked around the house a second time, pausing to look out the front window to make sure no one was coming.

Then she returned to the kitchen and dialed again. This time, she stayed on the line when someone answered.

"Population Planning, can I help you?" It was a woman's voice, pleasant, soft and friendly. Counselors, usually social workers, manned the telephones. Everyone who worked there believed in a woman's right to choose. They had to because they worked in the eye of a social and political storm. Not only was their work controversial, but they were reminded of the potential danger every day. They parked in a guarded lot across the street from the center. As they approached, they saw a two-story building surrounded by a six-foot wrought-iron fence. Rooftop security cameras scanned each corner, positioned so that no one could get close without an image being recorded on videotape. Workers at the center often forgot about the importance of security until they walked through the one door that permitted access. Once there, they were confronted with an off-duty policeman and the most sophisticated metal detector available. While the officer was friendly and helpful, it was nearly impossible to walk through the metal detector without being reminded of the important reasons for security. When the war over abortion had escalated to violence years before, such centers had to adopt a bunker mentality. In Houston alone, they had to spend over one hundred thousand dollars to install the detector, bulletproof glass, security cameras and other devices to try to ensure the safety of the clinic's employees and their clients.

"I . . . uh . . . would like to talk to a counselor."

"My name is Sylvia. I can help you."

Lucy hesitated and finally said the words out loud. "I think I'm pregnant."

"Would you like to come to the center and talk? If you'll tell me your name, we can schedule an appointment," Sylvia said.

"My name is Lucy. I've already looked at the calendar and next week on Friday the teachers have a workday. Could I come in then?"

"That's fine, Lucy. Our address is 4432 Space Shuttle Drive in Houston. When you get here, ask for Sylvia."

"One more thing, ma'am, is there any charge?"

"There's no charge for counseling, but if you want a procedure done, the fee is three hundred and seventy-five dollars."

As Lucy put down the phone, she went to her closet and pulled a Mason jar from the top shelf. That's where she saved the proceeds from babysitting along with birthday and Christmas money. When she spread the money out on the bed and counted carefully, she had exactly $305.55. Next, she retrieved a large freezer bag from the kitchen, stuffed the money into it, and placed it on the top shelf of her closet next to the jar.

6

Born in Fort Worth shortly after World War II, Thomas Jeremiah Luther was called T.J. He drifted through high school and graduated near the bottom of his class, his only distinction being voted the class clown during his senior year.

With a certain amount of charm and charisma, T.J. thought that he could make his way through life without ever breaking a sweat, and he soon discovered that the easy money was in what the police called the "character" world of hoodlums, pimps, prostitutes and drug dealers. He fell into life on the underbelly of society and relished it. Starting as a small time drug dealer, it wasn't long before T.J. became hooked on his own products. To supplement his income, he robbed an occasional convenience store and passed hot checks. It was the trail of hot checks that eventually led the police to his fleabag apartment. He surrendered peacefully. None of the checks was over one hundred dollars, making them all misdemeanors. Without the benefit of a lawyer, T.J. quickly pled guilty to the check charges, preferring that the D.A. not paddle through the backwaters of his brackish life. He agreed to eighteen months in the county jail, figuring good behavior would get him out in nine.

Prisoner # 214C53, according to the identity card with the Tarrant County jail, was the sum of these parts: Name: Thomas Jeremiah Luther; Weight: 157; Height: five feet, nine inches; Race: Caucasian; Complexion: Sallow; Date of Birth: April 18, 1946; Identifying Marks: tattoo of coiled serpent on right bicep. The photo in his folder revealed a man at nadir. His eyes were dead, more sad than sullen. His hair, sideburns and mustache were the trimmings of a nineteenth-century desperado, once gunmetal black, now streaked with gray.

To ensure he got out as soon as possible, T.J. was a model prisoner, kissing the ass of anyone who wore a badge. "Yes, sir," and "No, sir," "Can I get you some coffee, sir?" "Here, sir, let me mop that hall, sir." "Can I help you pass out the dinner trays, sir?" While he didn't have an official "trustee" status, T.J. unofficially became one. His jail cell was opened in the morning and he didn't have to return to the iron cage until after the evening news.

Thinking the guards would look favorably on a prisoner that demonstrated worthwhile use of his time, he asked a social worker if he could purchase a sketch pad and colored pencils with his savings from the dollar a day he earned for his jailhouse duties. At first, his efforts wouldn't have placed in a third grade art show. After a few weeks, the guards started to comment, "Ain't bad," when they walked by. It wasn't long before they were posing for portraits to take to their wives and girlfriends.

On Sunday mornings, a Baptist preacher led a small service in the dayroom on the eleventh floor of the jail. T.J. was up and sitting in the dayroom with sketch pad in hand as the preacher spoke to half a dozen inmates. After the service, T.J. gave the preacher a portrait of himself, hands raised to the heavens. The preacher was so impressed that he pulled a Bible out of his briefcase and handed it to T.J., who accepted the gift, thanked the preacher and carried it back to his cell. On the cover was the basic Sunday school fantasy of Jesus, true blue eyes, silk honey hair, and the same sort of mustache and scraggly beard that T.J. had on admission to the jail.

After a nap, T.J. took a shot at duplicating the picture of Jesus on the wall of his cell. It was against the rules but he figured that he'd wash it off if one of the guards complained. Using a lead pencil, he sketched a giant face, taller than a man. He worked until well past dark, adding layers of charcoal and crayon. Before lights out, he sat on his bunk and stared at the gloomy countenance that stared back, comparing it with the picture on the front of the Bible. It was definitely not a gentle savior with a halo and choir robe. Instead, he had drawn a foreboding figure of authority with no compassion. Its hollow eyes were darkened pits of gloom.

The next morning, T.J. got a bucket of soapy water and another mixed with ammonia and lye, telling the guard he had to wash out his toilet. As he returned to his cell, a second guard followed him with a young black man, struggling as the deputy dragged him down the corridor. Shoving him at T.J., the guard said, "I want you to babysit this peckerwood. I'm shorthanded and this one is threatening to commit suicide. For me that might be a cause for rejoicing, but it might also get me fired, so you watch him while I do his paperwork."

The door clanged shut. As the guard disappeared, the black man suddenly attacked T.J., throwing him to the floor. As T.J. struggled to his feet, the other man picked up the bucket and threw the half-gallon of ammonia and lye into T.J.'s eyes. T.J. sagged to the floor and said, quite softly, "I'm blind. Oh God, I'm really blind."

Above him, Jesus, similarly soaked, wept ammonia tears.

Thus was born "The Miracle of the Tarrant County Jail." The face that T.J. had painted the day before had been replaced. Now, an eerily beautiful face of Jesus Christ filled the cell. Later, art experts would say the portrait resembled that of a Renaissance master. Most of all they exclaimed about the half-open eyes of Christ, mirrors of sorrow, pain, compassion and hope. Later, T.J. also pronounced it a miracle because he had not painted Christ's eyes the night before. Jesus had finished his own portrait.

Another miracle occurred that day. As suddenly as T.J. lost his sight, it returned. Within three hours he could see again. A local ophthalmologist said he suffered severe scarring of corneal tissue and retinal burns that should have left him permanently blind. T.J. later told others that while he was blind he heard a voice speaking to him, saying, "I will heal thee for thou hath done Me honor."

When they released T.J. from jail, Jerry Abraham, a tent revivalist, was quick to track him down, offering him a hundred-dollar bill to appear at his revival on the outskirts of Dallas. Abraham sensed a box office draw if there ever was one, and T.J. was paid to tell his story, loosening the purse strings of Abraham's flock.

One night, the damnedest thing happened. As T.J. stood at the front of the stage talking about being blind and regaining his vision, a voice came from the back of the room, "I can see! Praise God, I can see!" The woman pushed her way through the audience and fell at T.J.'s feet, embracing his legs. Somewhat embarrassed, T.J. broke away and whispered to Jerry, "I didn't do anything."

Jerry knew different. What he saw was a charismatic man in his mid-thirties exuding sexual magnetism. He had a star attraction. Even the dark glasses that T.J. constantly wore to hide the damage to his eyes added to his mystique. That night he dubbed T.J. "the Chosen" and signed him to a contract as an assistant healer at three hundred dollars a week plus 10 percent of the collection buckets. Within one short year the banners changed from JERRY ABRAHAM—SPECIAL APPEAR-ANCE BY THE CHOSEN to JERRY ABRAHAM REVIVALS PRES-ENTS THE CHOSEN to JERRY ABRAHAM AND THE CHOSEN.

The next year, the Lord took Jerry Abraham. T.J. assumed the deceased preacher's ministry, including possession of his tent, organ, kettledrum, and most important, his mailing list. T.J. considered it to be the will of God.

If a historian followed the trail of evangelists from the beginning of the twentieth century, from Billy Sunday through Brother Jack Coe and A. A. Allen to Oral Roberts and finally to the Chosen, no one rose as fast or climbed as high as T.J. Oral Roberts first recognized the value of the electronic pulpit, stringing together his own network of independent stations. T.J. decided that he could duplicate the efforts of Oral Roberts, Jerry Falwell and Pat Robertson. Better yet, he would outdo them. Whether it was his charisma and sexual magnetism, luck, timing, God's will or all of the above, his ministry took off like a meteor across the southern sky. Within a few years, his ministry expanded from tents to basketball arenas to football stadiums. His Sunday morning service broadcast to all fifty states and one hundred and eighty-seven countries. While it was perhaps a late evening star, the star of his celebrity rose rapidly when it came over the horizon.

The money rolled in. All T.J., now known as the Chosen, had to do was ask, and ask he did. At first there were mailbags delivered daily. Eventually, the post office had to send an entire truck. His name was so well known that if a letter was addressed to "The Chosen, U.S.A.," it was delivered to him in Fort Worth, Texas. As the bank account began to overflow, T.J. conceived the City of Miracles, his opulent announcement to the world that he was the foremost messenger of the Lord. It started with the donation of eighty-five acres in the hills west of Fort Worth. Within five years several buildings were complete. The first was the Miracle Sanctuary. It resembled a Las Vegas showroom, only three times the size. Next came the Miracle Tower. Beside it stood the Miracle College. Like Disney World, various other areas were plotted.

T.J. decided to emulate his contemporaries in every way. It was not enough to just have power over the religious thinking of his followers. He wanted to put his believers in positions of leadership throughout the United States and the world. When he thought about it, power was the word that most often came to mind, more power than the world had ever known in a religious leader. He wanted presidents, kings and dictators to find their way to Fort Worth to seek his advice and blessing. In his mind the pope would eventually take second place behind Reverend Thomas Jeremiah Luther. The people working for the Miracle Foundation planned such a political overtaking, dubbing T.J.'s political action arm "the Right Side." They did so quietly at first, merely issuing press releases that a certain politician in Georgia was on the right side, or a governor in Michigan was on the right side. When the press release came from the City of Miracles, it drew the attention of the faithful who began to carry T.J.'s message to the ballot box.

What led to T.J.'s comatose condition could not have been predicted, not even by the best of soothsayers or fortune-tellers. He had just said the final prayer on the fifth night of a Christmas revival at the Cotton Bowl in Dallas. The average attendance for the five nights was sixty thousand people. The revenue generated each night was over one million dollars. As T.J. concluded the prayer, the lights dimmed and he was escorted from the stage, surrounded by guards. When he exited the stadium, a short, middle-aged woman, dressed in an old gray coat and wearing a floppy red hat stepped from the shadows. The guards assumed that she merely wanted to touch the hand of the Chosen and did not block her way. As she approached, she pulled a knife from her blouse and shouted, "You charlatan! You liar! You thief! You convinced my husband and me that if we gave all of our money to the City, you would heal his cancer. We did what you demanded and my husband died anyway."

Before T.J. could reply and before the guards could react, she plunged the dagger into the heart of the Chosen. As the guards rushed to his side, she disappeared as suddenly as she had come. She was never seen again.

The Chosen should have died. He lost a massive amount of blood. He threw an embolism to his lungs and his heart stopped beating. Even though the EMTs revived T.J., he remained comatose. After months in the hospital, he was moved to the City of Miracles.

The day dawned brighter than Lucy. Listening to two country disc jockeys bantering about the Houston Rockets, she stripped off her pajamas and stood in front of the mirror, front view first and then side. While there was no doubt that her jeans were getting tighter, she convinced herself that her abdomen wasn't bulging. Lucy showered quickly and put on a brown T-shirt and clean jeans. After pulling on her hiking boots, she applied a small amount of lipstick. She put the money bag in her purse, hoping that it would be enough if she decided to go through with an abortion. She made her bed, rinsed the breakfast dishes, loaded the washing machine, turned it on and headed out the front door for Population Planning. At the bus stop, she prayed no one would see her.

Upon arriving in downtown Houston, she transferred to a local bus. Lucy had no preconceived expectations about the center. When the bus approached the forty-four hundred block of Space Shuttle Drive, the scene frightened her. She knew that she was at the right stop as she saw the name POPULATION PLANNING on the building. What she had not expected was a throng of thirty or forty people, walking up and down the sidewalk. Fate had dealt her another unkind hand. The Houston pro-life forces had picked that day to picket the center.

The protestors were an eclectic group, young and old, male and female, Anglo, Hispanic and one or two African-Americans. Some walked up and down with signs. Others stood at locations where the Population Planning clients were most likely to approach. Two carried rosaries and quietly prayed. One kneeled on the driveway. Mixed among them were clinic volunteers, wearing orange bibs with the center's logo and name on the front. Other than the bibs, they looked about the same as the protesters, but so strong were their convictions that neither side spoke to the other. The job of the volunteers was to spot prospective clients as they arrived. Whether they parked in the fenced Population Planning lot or arrived by bus, the volunteers intercepted their clients and escorted them through the protesters to the building's entrance.

Lucy's bus rolled to a stop at the corner across the street. Seeing the demonstrators, she considered staying on the bus until she saw a young girl and an older woman, probably the girl's mother, get off. Her courage renewed, she walked down the aisle, thanked the bus driver and stepped onto the curb. As the bus pulled away, she surveyed the scene before her. Standing at the corner, she was not sure what to do or how to break through the picket line to get to the building. Suddenly, a woman in an ordinary blue dress and orange bib appeared at Lucy's side. She was large, three inches taller than Lucy, and weighed well over two hundred pounds. Her hair was gray and her face was kind. Her voice was strong.

"Young lady, I'm a volunteer and I'm here to help you. My name is Margaret. These people are out here six or eight days a month. They are peaceful demonstrators and will not harm you. The law will not permit it. See that big officer over on the corner. He's here to make sure that you are safe. Now, I'm going to take your arm and we're going to cross the street. They will try to get you to stop and talk. You see that young woman pushing a baby carriage. She's likely to plead with you, something like, 'Don't let them kill your baby.' They'll also try to force you to take their literature. The best thing to do is ignore all of them. Pretend that they aren't there. Just walk beside me. They will back off as soon as they see that you're not going to stop. Ready?"

With a trembling voice and a lump in her throat, Lucy replied, "Yes, ma'am."

They stepped from the curb. Margaret walked briskly and with determination. Her instructions proved correct. Several of the protesters converged on Lucy, including the young woman with the baby carriage. They waved their signs and attempted to frighten her away.

"What's going on in that building is murder," shouted a man wearing a clerical collar.

"Look at my beautiful baby. Yours will be just as wonderful," said the young woman with the carriage.

"You'll be branded a murderer if you go through with it," a man in laborer's clothes yelled.

"Here, take this pamphlet. Don't do anything until you visit the pregnancy planning center down the street," an elderly woman said.

They did not touch her and parted to let her through as the two quickened their pace. To say that Lucy was intimidated by it all would have been an understatement. If she could have walked away without having to pass through them again, she probably would have done so. Besides, Margaret already had her at the front door of the center. Lucy hesitated when she saw a metal detector looming in front of her. In her mind, metal detectors were only for one purpose: to keep bad people with weapons away. The people in the center had to be more concerned than Margaret let on.

Seeing the startled look on her face, Margaret explained, "I'm sorry, dear, I should have told you about this. It's just a precaution. We haven't had a violent incident in this center in five years. Those people out in front are peaceful. However, there are some who will resort to violence. We take every precaution. You don't have a thing to worry about."

Lucy was not convinced, but after a moment's hesitation, she handed her purse to the guard and walked through the detector.

Subdued colors lined the reception area. There were pictures on the wall with captions proclaiming, EVERY CHILD A WANTED CHILD, a sign that said, THE DECISION TO BEAR CHILDREN IS PRIVATE AND VOLUNTARY, and plaques reflecting that some of the biggest foundations in Houston had donated funds to the center.

Margaret led Lucy to a desk where another woman asked how they could help her.

"I'm here to see Sylvia. Is she available?"

"Let me check," the woman replied as she dialed the

phone. After a brief conversation, she said, "Sylvia is winding up a meeting and will see you in about ten minutes."
Margaret excused herself and went back out to the street,
ready to assist the center's clients and, in her own way, to do
battle with the pro-life forces. Lucy found a seat and waited.
Shortly, the elevator door opened and a woman walked over
to her. "I'm Sylvia. Can I help you?"

"I'm Lucy. I'm here for my appointment."

"Of course, Lucy." Sylvia smiled. "Please follow me back
to my office."

They walked past the elevators to locked double doors
that could only be opened by swiping a magnetic card
through a reader. Then they walked down a hallway past a
library and into Sylvia's office. The room was small, decorated to avoid the look of an office. Instead it contained a
couch, a comfortable chair and a coffee table. The picture
on the wall was a mountain valley in summer, flowers in
bloom.

"Have a seat. Can I get you anything?"

"No, ma'am. I'm fine," Lucy said, as she perched uncomfortably on the edge of the couch with her hands folded in
her lap.

"Tell me a little about yourself, Lucy."

After a moment of silence, Lucy replied, "My name is
Lucy, Lucy Baines Brady. My mother liked President Lyn-
don Johnson when she was growing up and I'm named after
one of his daughters."

"Where do you live?"

"I'm from Texas City and I'm a junior in high school."

"What do you plan to do after graduating? College or get
a job?"

"I don't know yet. I'm thinking about community college."

"Well, that's okay. I can tell you a lot of people are not
sure what to do after high school. And you told me on the
phone that you're pregnant."

Lucy stared at the mountain scene and wished for a moment that she could be there, sitting among the flowers beside

the stream that flowed through the valley. There or anywhere but here.

"Lucy?"

"Yes, ma'am."

Sylvia could not have estimated the number of times that she had heard those words, at least twenty times a week. Each time she had to think of the right response. She had spent a total of about ten minutes in conversation with this girl, part of it on the phone. Sylvia considered her approach. Questions went through her mind. Was this girl mature enough to make this decision? Is abortion an option for her? Is it something she can recommend today? Should she suggest the involvement of her mother in making the decision?

"Lucy, I know what's going through your mind. You're frightened. You don't know why this is happening to you. You're scared of an abortion, and you're not sure that you are ready to be a mother."

"I'm really scared, ma'am," Lucy replied, relieved to hear someone express what she had been feeling.

"Let me get some basic information. First, how long have you been sexually active?"

"Just one time."

"You mean you've had sex with just one partner?"

"Yes, and only one time. I don't know how I could possibly be pregnant."

"When did this one time occur?" Sylvia asked.

"About three months ago. I've been getting a little bit confused lately."

"That's okay, Lucy. I know that this has been a difficult time for you. How old was your partner?"

"My age. He goes to my high school."

"Is he your boyfriend?" If marriage were on the horizon, she would steer Lucy toward carrying the baby.

"No, ma'am. He and I haven't talked since that night."

"What about your parents? Do they know about it, or that you're possibly pregnant?"

"No. My mother is a born-again Christian."

Sylvia had no problem sizing up the situation. "There are basically three alternatives. First, you appear to be young and healthy and would probably have no major problems during pregnancy. You could have the baby and raise it as a single parent. We can arrange for prenatal care if necessary. You would have to be willing to take on the obligations of a single parent, which would include providing food, clothing, medical care and a home for your child. Or, you could have the baby and we can put you in contact with an adoption agency that could find a good home with people who would love to raise your child as their own. Both of those options involve carrying your pregnancy to term. Obviously, you would have to tell your parents, and your friends would probably know. The third option is abortion. An abortion will end your pregnancy, today if you choose.

"Lucy, do you want an abortion?"

"Does an abortion hurt?" she asked, as she stared at the mountain scene and heard almost nothing except the last question.

"You will be given some pain medication at the start, and any pain will be minimal. Afterward, you may be sore for a few days and there may be a menstrual-like flow that occurs on and off for a couple of weeks. If you have the abortion today, you should be able to go to school on Monday."

"Will I be able to have children later on?"

"An abortion at your stage should not affect your ability to have children. There are some possible complications that will be explained by the medical staff. I can tell you that abortion is one of the safest medical procedures. In fact, there are greater medical risks in carrying a baby to full term and giving birth."

Lucy looked down at her feet before speaking again. "I'm worried about what will happen after the abortion, too. My preacher says that it's a sin."

"That's a moral issue that people have different opinions about, and I'm not the one to try to advise you. Most young women who have abortions are depressed for a few days and then they get on with their lives. You have to weigh those feelings against having the baby and all the things that we just discussed."

Lucy thought for several seconds and then asked, "Do my parents have to know?"

"No. At this time in Texas, they do not. What you do here today is absolutely confidential."

Lucy finally verbalized the decision that she had been working toward for several weeks, almost since she suspected she was pregnant, the one that she had finally made when she stepped off the bus and entered the center. "I'd like to terminate my pregnancy."

As she was saying those fateful words, she prayed to God, asking Him to forgive her for what she was about to do. Backed into a corner, she had no other choice. She hoped that God would understand.

"Are you absolutely certain that this is what you want to do? You can go home and think about it for a few days if you're not." After a pause, Sylvia continued. "If you really want it done, now is better than later."

"Yes, ma'am. I'm certain. But there's one problem. You told me on the phone that the cost was three hundred and seventy-five dollars." As she mentally subtracted the bus fare to and from the clinic, she continued, "I only have two hundred and ninety and that's all the money I have in the world. Can I still have the abortion?"

"We can take care of that. We have a fund that will make up the balance. Then, you can sign a note to pay the fund back at ten dollars a month. Can you handle that?"

"Yes, ma'am," she responded, figuring that somehow she would find a way to do it.

"Then, let's go upstairs and start the processing."

Lucy never suspected that this decision would haunt her for the rest of her life.

8

Lucy woke when the bus driver slammed on the brakes to avoid a car that had cut in front of him. She had been dreaming about children swinging in her backyard. They were her children. The oldest had fallen off the swing and Lucy rushed to pick up her daughter. When she got to the swing and reached down, the little girl had disappeared. She was frantically searching for her child when she heard a horn honking. At first she didn't know where she was. As the fog lifted from her brain, she recognized the street and realized that she was about three stops from her corner. Then she noticed the cramping. It was still there. She would take some Advil as soon as she got home.

Lucy left the bus and tried to be nonchalant, as if she had just returned from a day of shopping. When she got to her driveway, she said a small prayer of thanksgiving.

Her parents weren't home, so she went directly to the laundry where she changed the clothes from the washer to the dryer. She had more chores to do, but the cramping was worse. She went to the medicine cabinet in the bathroom, took two Advil and lay down for a few minutes. Then, she heard her mother's voice.

"Lucy? Lucy, where are you?"

The door flew open. Joanna was surprised to see her daughter lying on the bed fully clothed.

"What's going on, Lucy? The house is still a mess. You haven't even cleaned the kitchen or started dinner." Looking at her more closely, she continued, "Are you feeling all right? You look a little pale."

"Sorry, Mom. I think I'm coming down with the flu that's been going around. I managed to get the clothes washed, but I've been sleeping all day," Lucy fibbed, thinking to herself that she was going to have to do something really good so the Lord would forgive all of her lies.

Joanna put her hand on Lucy's head. "I don't think that you have a fever. Have you checked your temperature? You probably need to take some Advil."

"I don't feel hot. I had a headache and took some Advil about an hour ago. I was lying down to get rid of the headache when I fell asleep again."

"Okay, Lucy. You stay there and rest. Put on your pajamas. I'll take care of the kitchen and dinner."

When Lucy heard her mother in the kitchen, she undressed, gently removing the feminine pad from the clinic. She was shocked when she saw the amount of blood. She took the instructions from her purse and read: *Often there is a dark, menstrual-like flow that occurs off and on for up to two weeks. Blood clots may be passed for ten days after the abortion.* While it was a lot of blood, Lucy interpreted it as normal. She replaced the pad with a clean one, put on her pajamas and robe and went to the bathroom. The cramping had returned.

After dinner, Lucy kissed her mother and father good night and taking a glass of water with her, she went to her bedroom. Sitting on the bed, she got out the packet that contained the antibiotic bottle. After reading the instructions, she took one white pill and downed it with a glass of water. She hid the packet and instructions in her dresser before crawling into bed, exhausted after the second most harrowing experience in her life. Before she could sleep, rumbling started in her stomach. Then the room started to spin. She sat on the edge of her bed, hoping it would settle things down. It didn't. She dashed down the hall to the bathroom and barely made it before everything in her stomach came up. Her dinner, the water and the antibiotic.

On the way back to her room, Joanna stopped her. "Lucy, your flu is getting worse. Call me during the night if you need to. You sleep late tomorrow. I'll take care of things."

When Lucy finally got to sleep, she slept hard and had the same dream of her children in the backyard, only this time they all kept falling off of the swing and disappeared before she could pick them up.

Saturday morning, she woke with even more pain. When

she got out of bed, there were bright red stains on the sheets. Petrified and unsure what to do, she decided to call the clinic as soon as her mother left. Her mother would be gone until after lunch. Her father went fishing and wouldn't be home until dark. She pretended to sleep until her mother opened the door.

"Lucy, I have to go to work. How are you feeling?"

Joanna sat on the side of her bed, her hand on Lucy's forehead, as Lucy frowned. "Mom, I'm feeling worse than yesterday. I'm just going to take it easy. I may try to do a little homework between naps."

"Sure, hon. Sleep as much as you need to." She took her hand from Lucy's forehead. "You don't have a temperature yet. Take it easy and drink lots of water. Call me at work if you need anything."

Joanna kissed her on the cheek and closed the bedroom door. Lucy heard her car start and leave the driveway. She waited about ten minutes and then surveyed herself and her bed. Her pajama bottoms were bloody and the stain on the sheet went through to the mattress cover. The first thing to do was to clean herself up and then wash her pajamas and bedding. She took two Advil and her morning antibiotic. Next, she showered and loaded the washing machine.

It was eight o'clock. The idea of calling the clinic was repugnant. She wanted nothing to do with that clinic, not ever. Again, she read the instructions and figured that she better at least make one call. The phone rang five times, and she was about to hang up when someone answered.

"My name is Lucy. I had a procedure done yesterday and I think that I should talk to a nurse."

"Hold on, Lucy. I'll get someone right with you."

Nurse Sylvester came to the phone. She was an L.V.N., a licensed vocational nurse. She could call herself a nurse in Texas, but her training consisted of one year after high school followed by a test that would grant her a license and title. Her license severely restricted what she could do, and she always had to be under the supervision of a doctor or registered nurse.

"This is Nurse Sylvester, Lucy, how can I help you?"

"I had a procedure done yesterday. This morning I woke up with some blood on my pajamas and on my sheets."

"A lot of blood, Lucy?"

"Well, I'm not sure what a lot is. I've washed the sheets and pajamas and put on a new pad."

"Do you have any fever?"

"I haven't taken my temperature, but I don't feel hot."

"How about cramping?"

"Yes, ma'am. I'm cramping. Advil seems to help."

"Let's see, your chart says you live in Texas City. Do you have any way to get to the clinic today?"

"Only by bus and that will take about two hours."

Nurse Sylvester debated what to do. Lucy's symptoms were borderline and a four-hour round-trip bus ride certainly wouldn't do her any good. "Okay, Lucy. Keep taking your medicine. If you are still bleeding this afternoon, or if your cramping gets worse or if you start running a fever, you call back. Do you understand?"

"Yes, ma'am."

"Stay in bed and take it easy. Drink plenty of water. Be sure to call if you need to. You can ask for me or any nurse here at the clinic."

"Okay. Thank you."

Lucy hung up, not sure if she was relieved or not. She pulled out the fact sheet and read again about the complications of an abortion. Surely she couldn't be one of the few that had a problem. That nice black doctor said she would be fine. When the bedding and pajamas were washed and dried, she changed another soaked sanitary pad and put on her pajamas. After making her bed, she pulled the covers up and fell asleep. While she was sleeping her body did what it was supposed to do. It clotted off the area of the bleeding in her uterus. When she awoke she looked for blood on her bed and found none. Then she checked her pajamas and they were dry. The pad had some blood but not nearly as much as before. Even though the cramps were still there, she began to feel reassured. Unconsciously, she touched her forehead. It felt a little warm. She attributed it to having been under the covers and refused to think it was caused by anything else. She was going to be okay.

Putting on some loose fitting sweatpants, Lucy wandered out to the backyard, half expecting to see children playing. The sun felt good as she relaxed on the swing. Her mind wandered back to what she had done. She felt relief and sadness, but overriding all the other thoughts were those of sin. Was she barred from Heaven now? Was she a murderer? Was the fetus alive before yesterday? The questions were there. Still no answers surfaced. One thing was certain. She would have to live with it and no one else would ever know.

The next day was Sunday. Complaining of a sore throat, Lucy told her parents she needed to stay home from church but would watch *The Miracle Morning Hour* on television.

An hour later, she felt hot and took her temperature. It was one hundred and one degrees. Again, she called the clinic. This time she got an answering service. She explained that she was a patient and needed to talk to someone. It took nearly an hour before the phone rang.

"Is this Lucy?"

"Yes, ma'am."

"This is Nurse Simms, I'm on call this weekend. I don't have your file in front of me, so tell me when you had a procedure done and how you're doing."

Lucy gave her the complete rundown of events.

"Are you taking your medicine?"

"Yes, ma'am," replied Lucy. "Just like the instructions say," neglecting to mention that she had thrown up the pill from the first night.

"Well, I'm a little concerned about your temperature. The fact that you have almost stopped bleeding is a good sign. Push on your abdomen. Is it tender?"

"It's a little tender, but not much."

Again, a nurse had to make a judgment call on a patient she had never seen. To make her come to the clinic on Sunday would require Nurse Simms to drive in from Katy, thirty miles away, and she would have to page the doctor on call.

He would be upset if he arrived and found a normal postoperative patient. Weighing the alternatives, she came down on the side of waiting a few hours. Most likely, there would be no problem, and if there was, a few hours shouldn't make any difference.

"Lucy, take three Advil, not two, and go to bed. When you wake up, if your fever is over one hundred and one degrees, call me back."

Unfortunately, Lucy had no way of knowing what had happened. On Friday, two of the complications of an abortion had occurred. The doctor had not successfully removed all of the fetal parts. He also had perforated her uterus, probably while he was using a vacuum cannula. It could have happened to the best of gynecologists under the best of circumstances, or it may have happened because his coordination was off just slightly after a sleepless night. No one would ever know for sure, yet within months, it would be part of the debate that would rage throughout the country.

As Lucy slept, armies of bacteria and armies of white cells waged a war inside her body. Whether the infection was caused by the retained fetal parts that had become necrotic, or whether it was from the perforation in the lining of the uterus, would never be known. Like most infections, it started with just a few bacteria. Later, the doctors would call it endometritis, an infection of the endometrial lining of the uterus. The bacteria were anaerobic and thrived in the dark moist environment. The antibiotic on the first evening was intended to fight just this type of infection. Whether it would have succeeded was now a moot point since Lucy had thrown up the antibiotic and it never had a chance. The bacteria had already grown and multiplied so that the antibiotics taken on Saturday were too little and too late. Lucy's body discovered the invading forces and sounded a warning to assemble the army of white cells to kill off the bacteria. Her white cells responded by increasing their numbers. Unfortunately, the bacteria loved their environment and multiplied so rapidly that the white cells could not kill them quickly enough. Soon the number of bacteria grew large enough to launch other attacks on the battlefield that her body had become, using the bloodstream as their super-highway. Lucy had developed sepsis, a blood-borne infection that could cause brain damage, organ failure and death. As she slept, her temperature rose, and for some reason, the clot that had stemmed the flow of blood broke loose and blood began to ooze from the uterus.

Lucy's parents came home from church and found the house quiet. Assuming she was asleep, Joanna quietly opened the door to check on her daughter. The hallway light allowed her to see the form in the bed. She walked over and sat beside Lucy who didn't move a muscle. Lucy was sleeping. Her breathing was rapid. Joanna touched Lucy's forehead and jerked her hand back, as if she had touched a hot stove.

"Lucy, wake up. You're burning up!"

Lucy only stirred.

Joanna hurried to the bathroom and returned with a thermometer. This time she turned on the bedroom light and put the thermometer under Lucy's tongue. Lucy didn't move. Joanna stared at her watch for three minutes. It felt like a lifetime. At three minutes, she withdrew the thermometer. It read 104.5 degrees. Horrified, she forced Lucy to sit up.

"Come on, Lucy, you've got to wake up. I'm going to put you in a cold shower." This time, Lucy murmured something that Joanna could not understand, something about children falling off a swing. She pulled back the bed covers and saw that Lucy's pajamas were soaked with blood.

"Oh, my God, Lucy, what's wrong with you? I'm calling an ambulance."

9

Joanna ran to the kitchen phone and dialed 911. She found Bo in the garage and explained Lucy's condition on their way back to her room. As soon as they heard the siren, Bo raced to the door to meet the two young EMTs.

"Mrs. Brady, I'm Jack Alford. Tell me what you know about your daughter's situation."

While she did so, he walked to the bed and started his examination. He put an automatic thermometer in Lucy's mouth, at the same time checking her pulse. The thermometer beeped. "Her temperature's now one hundred and five degrees with a pulse of one hundred and ten." Wrapping a blood pressure cuff around her arm, he said, "Eighty over fifty-five." Looking at the blood on the pajamas and sheets, he turned to Joanna and Bo.

"Mrs. Brady, this is not the flu. It's much more serious. She has a raging infection and internal bleeding. I don't see bleeding from anywhere but her vagina. Has she had serious kidney or bladder problems?"

Getting a negative response, he continued, "How about problems with her uterus or a recent abortion?"

Shocked, Joanna replied, "She's never had any unusual female problems and she certainly hasn't had an abortion."

"Well, ma'am, we've got to get her to the hospital in a hurry. She's a very sick little girl."

His assistant had already returned with a stretcher and they carefully lifted her onto it while her parents watched, the horrified looks on their faces not beginning to express their feelings.

"Mrs. Brady, you can ride with us. Mr. Brady, I suggest that you follow along in your truck."

Within two minutes Jack and his assistant were in the ambulance with Lucy and Joanna. As they pulled away from the curb, the red lights reflected off the houses and the siren filled the neighborhood. Jack started an IV using Ringer's lactate. Next, he called the emergency room, describing his patient and making sure that the emergency room doctor was available.

Dr. Sean Kelley, the emergency physician, met the ambulance at the door, and started checking Lucy as the attendants wheeled her into the hospital. He ordered a stat complete blood count as he repeated what the ambulance attendants had done. Her temperature remained at one hundred and five degrees; her erratic pulse bounced between one hundred and five and one hundred and twenty and her respiratory rate was twenty-eight. Within minutes he had the blood work results. Her white count was twenty-one thousand and her hemoglobin and hematocrit were nine and twenty-six, indicating that she had lost a significant amount of blood and needed a transfusion. Lucy faded in and out of consciousness. For the few moments when her eyes were open, she was delirious and confused, not understanding where she was or why. She didn't even recognize her parents. Dr. Kelley's mind raced over the medical possibilities.

"Lucy, did you have an abortion? Lucy, can you hear me? Answer me!" He shook her gently. "Lucy, tell me about your abortion!" He shouted.

Joanna almost intervened. It was not possible. Then Lucy stirred and murmured, "Friday."

Joanna collapsed and Bo led her to a row of chairs where he lowered her into one.

The pieces of the puzzle now fit together. Dr. Kelley was convinced that Lucy had a botched abortion. He gave orders to the emergency room nurses. "I think this girl has sepsis caused by something that went wrong with an abortion. We need a gynecologist who also handles infectious diseases and a hematologist. We need to get her to the medical center in a hurry. Call Life Flight. Take one of those vials of blood to type and cross match. Maybe we can get a transfusion started before Life Flight gets here. Give her Zosyn, three point, three seven-five grams; Gentamycin, one hundred and twenty milligrams; and Clindamycin, nine hundred milligrams. Start oxygen by mask, then a heart monitor and pulse oximeter. Also, draw blood to start cultures."

The blood would replace what Lucy had lost and help stop the bleeding. The three medications were broad-spectrum antibiotics. Without knowing the specific bacteria, Dr. Kelley had no way of knowing exactly which antibiotic would be effective. The blood cultures would help the medical center physicians determine the exact bacteria and the correct antibiotics to fight it. In the meantime, Dr. Kelley could use a shotgun approach and hope that he would get lucky. As to what was happening in the uterus, the gynecologist would need to evaluate that condition. His worst fear was that Lucy would develop septic shock. As he completed his instructions, a nurse approached the bed, and after a brief, quiet conversation with her, Dr. Kelley turned to speak to Lucy's parents. His reassuring voice hid his concerns. "Mr. and Mrs. Brady, I've done what I can for Lucy right now. The nurses are taking good care of her. In the meantime, I've just been told that we have a man here who is complaining of severe abdominal pain and I need to check on him. I'll only be a few seconds away. The nurses know exactly what to do. They'll call me if there's a problem. Life Flight should be here in about thirty minutes."

"Is she going to be all right?" Joanna asked, trying to control the quiver that had taken over her voice.

"I hope so, Mrs. Brady. Once we get her to the medical center, she will have the best care in the world. She's very sick, but if anyone can pull her through, they can."

He could have added that she had only about one chance in three of making a recovery without some significant, lifelong medical problem. Now was not the time for such straight talk. Dr. Kelley excused himself to take care of the other patient. Joanna and Bo watched as the nurses went about their assignments, starting antibiotics, hooking up various machines, drawing blood and placing an oxygen mask over Lucy's mouth and nose.

Then Joanna turned to Bo and quietly said, "We need to be praying."

She walked over to Lucy's bed, got down on her knees on the hard floor, and touching Lucy's arm, started praying for her daughter's life. Bo saw what she was doing and kneeled beside her, head bowed, with his arm around the shoulders of his wife of twenty-five years. The nurses' voices were stilled and they silently joined in the prayer. Unlike the Bradys, they knew the odds were against Lucy. While the nurses were doing all they could, they were willing to hope that prayers might save Lucy's life.

Joanna continued to watch the nurses checking vital signs every ten minutes and the monitors. They asked about the helicopter and they waited. Dr. Kelley came into the cubicle, checking Lucy with a grim look on his face, then hurrying back to the patient next door. After about twenty minutes, a nurse started a blood transfusion. The Bradys saw it as a sign of some progress and some hope. Then the head nurse approached.

"The helicopter will be here in five minutes. We're beginning preparations. Your daughter is stable. We're going to temporarily disconnect the monitors. She will still have the IV and blood bag attached. Once the transfer is made, the EMTs will be monitoring her in the helicopter. Mrs. Brady, you can ride with her and I suggest that your husband drive to Hermann Hospital where they will be taking over her care. Mr. Brady, do you know how to get to the medical center and find Hermann?"

"Yes, ma'am." He nodded.

As he spoke, they began to hear the *thump, thump, thump* of a helicopter as it made its approach.

Unexpectedly, the nurse called Bo over to a quiet corner of the emergency room. "Mr. Brady, I'm a nurse and I despise malpractice cases, but something happened to Lucy that never should have occurred. You may need a lawyer. Years ago, I used to work at Parkland Hospital in Dallas with a nurse named Mildred Montgomery. She left there and moved to Palestine where she became a paralegal for a lawyer named Tisdale. I don't talk to her much anymore, but she tells me that he's one of the best plaintiff lawyers in the country. In fact, he just handled a big asbestos case that's been all over the news lately. Here's her name and phone number in Palestine and her boss's name. If it becomes necessary, call and tell her you're a friend of mine."

The nurse handed Bo a slip of paper that he stuck in his pocket and returned to Joanna.

"It's landing now," she continued. "We have a space marked off on the parking lot as a helipad where it will land. If you don't mind, I'd like for both of you to go out and stand under the carport entrance. There's nothing you can do here. You can observe from there."

The modern medical helicopter was one of the marvels of the late twentieth century. Initially developed by the military, it soon became a mainstay in nearly every major metropolitan area in the country. In Houston the Life Flight helicopters flew for Hermann Hospital, one of the major hospitals in the sprawling Texas medical center, located about five miles south of downtown. By the late nineties Hermann had three fully equipped helicopters that ranged throughout southeast Texas twenty-four hours a day, seven days a week. Their nurses were among the most capable and experienced trauma professionals in the country. When the emergency called for it, a trauma surgeon often went along. Their pilots were the best in the business. Usually denied the luxury of setting down on a helipad, they had to drop their craft on narrow streets, in unlit forests with only the smallest of openings between swaying pine trees, among storm-whipped electrical power lines or on crowded freeways. They flew in wind and driving rainstorms with lightning streaking the sky. Only hurricane-force gales would keep them on the ground.

Captain John Peterson was the pilot of the helicopter dispatched to pick up Lucy. Undoubtedly the most skilled and dedicated on the Hermann Hospital crew, he was in his fifties and had been flying helicopters since Vietnam. Life Flight had been his passion for fifteen years. His kindly face featured blue eyes above a bushy graying mustache, giving him the appearance of a good-natured grandfather that belied the conviction he had for his job. It was about saving lives and if there was a need, he could put his helicopter down in an area not much wider than the blades that whipped above it. He looked out of the cockpit as the nurses opened the doors, dropped out of the helicopter and dashed for the girl on the stretcher in Texas City.

The Life Flight nurses pushed a stretcher toward Lucy and two hospital nurses. They coordinated their efforts to transfer the patient and her IV bags of fluid, antibiotics and blood to the helicopter stretcher. Joanna and Bo watched with fear etching their faces until one of the nurses waved at Joanna to follow. She gave Bo a quick hug and ran toward the helicopter.

Bo turned to the parking lot, determined to be at the hospital by the time his daughter got to Hermann. As he reached his pickup, he glanced at the red pickup parked beside his and its license plate briefly caught his attention. The frame around the license read, MY LAWYER IS J. ROBERT TISDALE. He paused long enough to pull the paper the nurse gave him from his pocket and, after comparing the names, he jumped into his pickup, backed out of the parking space and was soon out of sight.

Captain Peterson watched a scene similar to those he had witnessed so many times before, including the mother running along behind the stretcher and the father getting into a blue Ford pickup and speeding out of the parking lot. The nurses loaded the stretcher and patient, locked the wheels in place and directed Joanna to a jump seat. They were starting to hook up the various monitors when they gave Peterson the okay to take off. Checking to make sure that everything was clear, he radioed his base and lifted the chopper into the air, rapidly directing it toward the Gulf Freeway.

Between them, the nurses had more than forty years' experience and they wasted no time in assessing the patient, determining that they needed immediate help on landing. The older of the two radioed Hermann, "We've got a seventeen-year-old female in severe distress; pulse thready at one-twenty; blood pressure of eighty over fifty; temp of one-hundred-four-point-five, even after antibiotics; respirations of thirty-two; on oxygen by mask; H and H are nine and twenty-five. She's being transfused and is on Ringer's, Zosyn, Gentamycin and Clindamycin. Bleeding vaginally; she's in and out of consciousness. We need to ready an O.R. for immediate surgery. Preliminary diagnosis is complications of abortion, sepsis and possibly the beginning of DIC."

After receiving an affirmative from the nurse at base, she turned to join in Lucy's care. Joanna understood most of the nurse's report, but DIC was something new.

"Excuse me, but what is DIC?" she asked over the thumping of the helicopter blades.

The nurse didn't pull any punches. "DIC stands for disseminated intravascular coagulopathy. It's a problem with the clotting factors in the blood that can be caused by many things, including sepsis and blood loss. If it can't be stopped, it can be fatal, but I hope we have your daughter on the way in time. The most important things are to keep blood products and the right antibiotics infusing while the doctors correct whatever is causing the problem. If the abortion caused it, a gynecologist will have to fix the underlying problem. We hope that the blood products and antibiotics will help her turn the corner."

The use of the word "fatal" shocked Joanna. Until that moment, she had never considered that her only daughter might die before she did. She expected to see Lucy married, to make her a grandmother. She couldn't picture herself crying at Lucy's funeral. She prayed harder than ever before, tears streaming down her face and sobs racking her body.

Up front, Captain Peterson was pushing the chopper toward Houston parallel to the Gulf Freeway when he spotted the father's pickup going at least ninety and being tailed by a police vehicle with lights flashing as they both weaved in and out of traffic. Seeing what was happening, he radioed the police dispatcher.

"Ann, one of your boys is chasing a blue pickup on the Gulf Freeway northbound. It looks like the number on the top of the patrol car is two-eighty-three. The pickup is being driven by the father of a girl I've got in my chopper on the way to Hermann. It's a life or death situation. That pickup driver needs an escort, not a ticket."

"I hear you, John. I'll take care of it," Ann replied as she switched frequencies to radio Unit 283.

Peterson watched from above as within a minute Unit 283 moved over two lanes, put on a burst of speed to pass a truck and pulled in front of the pickup. It took Bo a moment to recognize that he now had an official escort and not a potential speeding ticket. Soon, he was following the police officer as he weaved in and out of traffic toward the downtown skyline, lights flashing and siren wailing. He would never see the look of satisfaction on Captain Peterson's face as the pilot veered from the freeway and angled over to the helipad adjacent to the hospital.

10

J. Robert Tisdale left the throng inside the courthouse and lumbered to his fire-engine-red Dodge Ram pickup. It was the biggest and finest that Dodge made, a quad cab with dual wheels on the back and a giant diesel engine. A light rack rose above the cab and a roll bar extended to the truck bed. The lawyer had installed a big red box directly behind the cab. When the door to the box on the passenger side was unlocked, it revealed storage space for his briefcase, files and law books. On the driver's side the box contained a specially made refrigerator, fed from the battery but designed to keep beverages cold as long as the truck ran at least an hour a day. The lawyer dropped his briefcase in the right side box and walked around to the driver's side, unlocking the refrigerator to find his usual supply of Lone Star beer along with sodas for his grandchildren. He picked out a cold beer, popped the top and took a giant swig even though he was on the town square right in front of the courthouse. Letting forth a loud and long belch, he climbed into the cab and started the engine. As he drove from the courthouse, Lone Star in hand, he turned on a siren that pierced the town square. It could be heard for six blocks in any direction. J. Robert Tisdale had won another case, and he wanted everyone in town to know it.

HE CAME INTO THE world at the community hospital in Palestine, Texas, a small town about one hundred miles southeast of Dallas where his father worked for the railroad. His parents named him John Robert Tisdale, but as a small town boy from Texas, he quickly became Johnny Bob. His nickname, "Tank," came from his size. As a sophomore in high school, he was six feet, four inches tall and weighed two hundred and eighty pounds.

Until his senior year, Johnny Bob assumed he would work for the railroad after high school. College didn't enter his mind until the coach over at East Texas State in Tyler called, offering him a scholarship to play football. What the heck, Johnny Bob figured, might as well give college a try. Besides, it would postpone having to look for a job. Four years later, he completed his stay at East Texas State, graduating with a C average. After college, he moved back home and loafed for the summer, hanging out with his old friends and drinking beer. When August came, his dad announced that Johnny Bob either had to move out or start paying rent.

After receiving the ultimatum, Johnny Bob borrowed his dad's pickup and drove around town, thinking and weighing his options. Nothing interested him except the few big houses on a tree-shaded street where the rich people lived . . . the doctors, lawyers, railroad executives and a banker or two. He drove up and down that street half a dozen times before making his decision. He would be an attorney. He'd live in one of those big houses where he could sit out on a shaded veranda at the end of the day and drink a beer or whatever it was that rich lawyers drank when they got off work. How to become a lawyer was a question he could not answer.

The next day he wandered down to the courthouse and

asked to see Judge Arbuckle, a lifelong resident of Palestine and an attorney for thirty years, the last ten of which he had served as the local district judge. A big supporter of Palestine High School football, he never missed a game and had followed Johnny Bob's athletic career since he played in junior high school.

After sitting uncomfortably in the outer office watching the secretary type on an old Underwood for twenty minutes, Johnny Bob amused himself by trying self-hypnosis, staring intently at the ceiling fan. Not exactly a candidate for hypnotism, he had dozed off when Judge Arbuckle opened the door to his chambers. A slight man with white hair, the judge radiated a no-nonsense personality, particularly when on the bench. Having no court duties that day, he wore a white short-sleeve shirt and thin black tie. Mopping his brow with a red bandanna, the older man greeted his visitor with a smile. "Well, Tank, what brings you here? You're not in trouble, are you?"

"No, sir," Tank replied forcefully to emphasize his point as he rose from the chair. "I just need some advice."

"Then come on into my office and let's see how I can help you. Have a seat."

Johnny Bob sat in a hard, straight-backed chair across from the judge's desk as the older man walked around it and settled into a large, comfortable chair with a black leather seat. Behind him was an open window facing the courthouse square.

"Boy, it's a hot one, ain't it, son? I've been trying to get the commissioners to air-condition this courthouse, but they won't do it. Maybe the next time I have a three-week trial in July, I'll subpoena every one of their fat asses and make them serve jury duty in that oven of a courtroom. Maybe that'll do the trick. Meantime, I may just have to dig into my own pocket to buy a window unit for this office. How're your mom and dad?"

"Just fine, sir."

"You tell them I said hello. Now what do we need to talk about?"

Johnny Bob didn't hesitate. "Sir, I want to be a lawyer and I don't know how to do it."

"Well, well, ain't that just fine." The judge chuckled. "Tank Tisdale for the defense. Not sure we have a courtroom in these parts big enough for you. Just kidding, son. How were your grades up at East Texas?"

Johnny Bob looked down at the floor as he responded, "Not very good, sir. I spent a lot of time playing football and most of my grades were C's with an occasional B."

Judge Arbuckle spun around in his chair and stared out the window while he pondered a moment before he spoke. When he swiveled back around, he leveled with Tank. "Then, I suspect that the better law schools in the state, Texas, Baylor, S.M.U., are probably out. They require pretty good grades and a good score on the LSAT to get in. You even know what the LSAT is?"

"No, sir."

"That's the Law School Admission Test. All these damn schools are requiring it these days. Not like in my day when you just showed up on the first day of class, paid your fees and became a law student. There's a law school down in Houston that's probably your best choice. It's called South Texas College of Law. It started in the basement of the YMCA and used to be strictly a night law school where people working full time could go and eventually become lawyers. It didn't have much of a reputation for a lot of years but it's improving and, from what I've seen, it has turned out some damn fine trial lawyers. It's a private school, pretty expensive. You'd probably have to work in the daytime and go to school at night. Might take you an extra year."

"That's okay, sir. I can handle it."

"Tell you what, Tank, the first step is that LSAT. I'll have my secretary call and get the forms. When they arrive, you can get together with her and complete them. I suspect the test will be available sometime this fall and you might be able to get into school by January. That suit you?"

Johnny Bob almost climbed over the judge's desk to shake his hand, saying, "Yes, sir. Thank you, sir."

Two weeks later, with the help of the judge's secretary, Johnny Bob completed the forms, and the following month he drove to Dallas where he took the test along with several hundred other lawyer hopefuls. In November, he got the results. While he didn't quite understand everything that he read, it was clear that he scored in the bottom third of the examinees. When he took the results down to Judge Arbuckle, he was in for a disappointment. The judge looked over the test results and then looked up with a solemn expression.

"Son, I'm afraid this score and your college grades won't get you into any law school in the state." He could see the dismay on the face of the big old boy sitting across the desk.

"Well, sir, I guess I better get down to the railroad yard and try to get on there. I appreciate all that you did for me." As he rose to leave, Judge Arbuckle stopped him.

"Tank, let me try one more thing. The dean down at South Texas is an old classmate of mine. Maybe with my recommendation, you could get in on probation. Hold on there a minute while I see if I can get him on the phone."

The judge turned and thumbed through a Rolodex until he found the right number. When he got the dean on the phone, they exchanged pleasantries, talked about their families, kids, and grandkids and then Judge Arbuckle got to the point. "Dick, I've got a young man sitting across from me. His name is Johnny Bob Tisdale. I've known him and his family all his life. He wants to be a lawyer but his college grades and LSAT, frankly, are piss-poor. If I gave you my solemn word that he's willing to work his ass off to be a lawyer, would you let him in on probation for just one semester? If he doesn't cut it, kick his butt all the way back up here to Palestine."

After listening to the reply on the other end, he gave Johnny Bob a thumbs up, thanked the dean and hung up the phone. "You're in, son. It's probationary. If you don't make it the first semester and every semester thereafter, you're out on the street. I put my name on the line for you and I damn sure don't want to be eating crow because of you. You start in two months. You best get on down to Houston, find yourself a job and get settled in. Classes start in January. You understand all that I've said?"

"Yes, sir, and I won't let you down," Johnny Bob replied as he circled the desk and came close to pulling Judge Arbuckle off his feet as he grabbed the judge's right hand.

Johnny Bob moved to Houston in a matter of days. Unfortunately, Johnny Bob's law school grades were no better than those he earned at East Texas. He managed to attend most classes, studied as much as he could with the work schedule that he had and scraped by. Other than passing his courses, his only law school accomplishment was placing second in a mock trial competition. He graduated in the four years Judge Arbuckle said that it would take. He was in the bottom quarter of his class, but he had a law school diploma. Three months after surviving the petrifying experience of the bar exam, he had a license to practice law.

After getting the results, Johnny Bob put on his best suit and started interviewing with the big firms in Houston. A waste of time. They took one look at his law school grades and decided that he wouldn't make it in a major Houston law firm. He couldn't compete with the top graduates of the best law schools hired by such firms. Besides, his East Texas redneck appearance and vocabulary would make it tough to sell any case to a jury.

After two months of job hunting, Johnny Bob began to think that he had wasted four years, a lot of money and even more grief in law school. He was faced with staying where he was, working at a menial job. Tail between his legs, he drove home to Palestine to see if Judge Arbuckle had any ideas. After spending the weekend with his mom and dad, he showed up at the judge's office on Monday morning. It hadn't changed. Mable, the judge's loyal secretary, typed at the Underwood. The same uncomfortable chair. The same ceiling fan. He waited until the judge arrived. Arbuckle greeted him like a prodigal son.

"Tank, my boy, how goes life in the big city? Come on in."

Johnny Bob didn't waste time in getting to the point. He

explained why he hadn't landed a job and asked for suggestions.

"Well, Tank, your timing may be just perfect. I'm retiring from the bench at the end of this year. My pension is enough to live on, but I enjoy the law and want to keep my hand in it. I've rented some space in the bank building across the street with an extra office. It's not much. I'll let you have it for nothing if you will help out on whatever business I bring in. I'll try to throw you some overflow when I can. It won't amount to much at first, but it's a start. Interested?"

Johnny Bob could not suppress a grin. "Judge, that's the best offer I've had so far. I'll take it. When can I move in?"

"Up to you, son. I've got three more months on my term, but the bank says the space is available and I can have it now."

A week later Johnny Bob moved some used furniture out of his old pickup and into the tiny back office on the third floor of the bank. His office was so small that his size filled it almost to capacity, but it was his and he was now a lawyer. Judge Arbuckle came over at lunch to see how he was doing. He found Johnny Bob hanging his law license on the wall behind the desk.

"Well, Tank, looks like you're settling in. Mable will start moving my stuff over here little by little. In the meantime, if you have anything for her to type, just ask. Now we're going to need to put our names on the hallway door, mine on top, of course. How do you want yours to read? John Tisdale? Johnny Bob Tisdale?"

"No, sir. I've been thinking about that. I'm a professional man now, and people in this town need to know that old Johnny Bob is now an attorney. They may still call me Johnny Bob or Tank, but from now on they need to know that my professional name is J. Robert Tisdale, Attorney at Law."

So it was. The judge arranged for the bank's painter to put the two names in gold on the glass-paneled door: ARTHUR "BUCK" ARBUCKLE AND J. ROBERT TISDALE, ATTORNEYS AND

COUNSELORS AT LAW. When the painter finished, Johnny Bob sat on the floor outside the door and stared at the sign for an hour.

From that day forward he never introduced himself as Johnny Bob again. It was always J. Robert Tisdale. When he appeared before a judge, it was, "Your Honor, J. Robert Tisdale for the plaintiff." When he met a client for the first time, it was, "Name's J. Robert Tisdale. Pleased to meet you." Even when he met his future wife, he handed her his card and said, "I'm J. Robert Tisdale, attorney at law."

After he moved in, he put an ad in the local newspaper:

J. Robert Tisdale
Attorney and Counselor at Law

is pleased to announce the opening of his office
for the practice of law

Palestine State Bank Bldg.
Phone: 555-5562
Palestine, Texas

On the day after the ad ran, Johnny Bob arrived early, wearing his best suit, white shirt and tie, halfway expecting people to be lined up out in the hallway. It was deserted. The young lawyer waited around until late morning, convinced that the phone was going to ring any minute. Instead, all he heard was the sound of silence. Having nothing better to do, he crossed the street to the courthouse and found the judge arraigning prisoners who had been arrested over the past couple of days.

As Johnny Bob took a seat in the courtroom, now in one of the chairs in front of the rail with the other lawyers, Judge Arbuckle called the name of the next prisoner, a skinny, middle-aged man dressed in jeans and a dirty white T-shirt. He pled not guilty to a charge of theft. Johnny Bob saw the judge looking at him before returning his gaze to the prisoner.

"Well, sir, can you afford a lawyer?"

The prisoner put on his most pitiful expression and replied,

"No, Judge, I ain't got enough to feed my family. I cut timber for a living when the weather's good and we been havin' too much rain lately."

"Then, sir, I'm going to appoint one of the finest young lawyers in this part of the country to represent you. Mr. Tisdale, would you approach the bench?"

Thus began the legal career of one J. Robert Tisdale, Attorney at Law.

11

The return of the Chosen was imminent, though not without problems. The board of directors of the City, called the Miracle Governors, faced a major dilemma. Jimmy Witherspoon had performed ably as temporary pastor, growing into his role more than anyone had a right to expect. Only the king had returned and made it clear that he expected to reclaim his throne. A special board meeting was called for a board that would make General Motors, Exxon, Microsoft or the Carnegie Foundation jealous. Composed of thirteen seats, the chair at the head of the giant conference table remained vacant, awaiting the return of the Chosen. It was originally T.J.'s idea to have twelve governors other than him. The symbolism did not have to be explained. Among the twelve were a former president of the United States; the heads of two major international foundations; two retired chairmen of Fortune 500 corporations; a four-star general of the U.S. Army, retired; an African-American woman who had risen to prominence in the Republican Party; one of Hollywood's wealthiest producers; the chairman of the largest e-commerce corporation in the world; a third-generation West Texas rancher who just happened to be the only descendant of a family near Wichita Falls, Texas, and also owned two million acres of land as well as all of the oil under it; the host of the most popular conservative talk show in the country; and

Jessie Woolsey, a rich widow, Lucy's aunt, and the only board member from Fort Worth.

While each of the twelve members had their individual reasons for serving on the board, they had certain common interests. They were part of the political and religious right. They believed that the left wing media dominated the country. They believed in the Second Amendment and were supporters of the National Rifle Association. They were concerned about the power of the United Nations and the possibility of one world government. They supported Republican candidates from dogcatcher to president since they never met a Democrat that could be trusted. They believed that prayer belonged in schools, as long as the prayers ended in Jesus's name. They fought to keep the government out of private lives except in one area: abortion was murder and the federal government, acting through good Christian conservative congressmen, had the duty to overrule *Roe v. Wade*. If Congress couldn't get it done, they intended to use their considerable power to elect a Republican, pro-life president and pray that he could put a pro-life majority on the Supreme Court during his term in office.

The special meeting of the Miracle Governors began at ten A.M. on a Saturday morning. The governors came from all over the country, most landing their Lear jets on the private landing strip adjacent to the City. They were met by limousines and taken to their private suites in the Miracle Tower to freshen up for the meeting. The boardroom filled the floor directly below the penthouse that was designed for the Chosen and still occupied by Reverend Witherspoon and his family. An architect, who had been a James Bond fan since his youth, had designed the room. The boardroom would make one of Bond's adversaries proud. It occupied twelve thousand square feet on the nineteenth floor with windows facing all directions. The view of the sunset reflecting on the hills west of Fort Worth was spectacular.

A giant oval table, twenty-five feet long and eight feet wide, dominated the room. The table was made from pecan, the Texas state tree, and stood on pedestals of pink granite, chiseled from a quarry in central Texas. The leather on the thirteen chairs came from the hides of cattle born and raised in Texas. The floor was polished Texas oak. Under the table was a giant white oval carpet with red trim. Perhaps a little out of place, the intent was to glorify the purity and blood of Christ. Gold curtains bordered the burnished bronze windows. In front of the governors' table was a sitting area facing a giant fireplace, furnished with couches and easy chairs.

Jessie Woolsey was the only board member who didn't arrive by jet. She merely drove her Jaguar from the Rivercrest section of Fort Worth west to the City of Miracles. She arrived early and sat in the boardroom alone, drinking coffee, reviewing her packet of materials and contemplating the decision facing the board.

The second to arrive, ten minutes before the scheduled time, was General Horace Mallory, tall, silver-haired, lean and in his sixties, with a military bearing that commanded attention the moment he entered a room. The remainder of the board, some coming straight from limousines and some from their personal suites, followed him. As the chairman of the board, the general called them to the governors' table, the general at one end with the others seated in order of seniority on his right and left. After making sure that each governor had an appropriate drink, he excused the staff.

"Thank you all for coming on such short notice. I know that you all have busy lives and too much to fill your days. It's an imposition to ask you to attend these meetings monthly and to serve on our various committees. However, it is the opinion of the executive committee that this is a matter that needs immediate attention. We are faced with a critical dilemma, and, I might add, a most remarkable one at that. For twelve years, we have hoped that the Chosen might rejoin us. I don't think that there's a person in this room who really thought that it was even a remote possibility. We received advice from the best doctors in the world. They considered it hopeless. Why he didn't die is one for the books."

"Well, I, for one, can tell you why he didn't die," interrupted Berlina Symonds. The only black person on the board, she never hesitated to state her opinions, whether behind closed doors or appearing before Congress and the nation. "All you have to do is read the Good Book to know that God has a plan for this man. He isn't about to let the Chosen die until He is good and ready. It's apparent to me that He just let Reverend Luther sleep until we needed him again. While I'm talking, let me point out, Mr. General, that you started this meeting without even one word of prayer. Asking for a little guidance from above might make our job easier."

"My apologies, Mrs. Symonds. My mind was occupied by the matter at hand. Would you be so kind as to lead us in prayer?"

"Be happy to, Mr. General," Berlina Symonds replied as she looked around the table to make sure all heads were bowed. "Let us pray. Most kind and loving Heavenly Father, we all have many reasons for your guidance. On this occasion, it is particularly important. You have returned Your servant and our spiritual leader, the Chosen, to us. Those of us assembled here have to make decisions that could affect him, our ministry, our nation, and even the world. It's a big job and we need Your help. Grant us Your wisdom throughout this day and the coming months. Amen."

"Thank you for those inspiring words, Mrs. Symonds," the general said. "As I was saying, we have a most unusual dilemma. If you haven't seen them, in the packet before you are the latest reports on the health of the Chosen along with the most recent press releases from him. He wants to take back the ministry as soon as he is able, which appears to be any day now. You also have a letter from Reverend Witherspoon. He expresses his desire to remain as our primary minister and lays out very convincing arguments supporting his position. I have purposely avoided discussing this matter with either of them, thinking that we needed to have this meeting first. We need to make a decision and I invite your comments."

A discussion ensued. Jimmy and T.J. each had their champions. As the debate continued, voices were raised. Tempers flared. One side argued the ministry wouldn't have existed without the Chosen. Now they were positive that he had divine guidance. Reverend Witherspoon's friends argued that without him, the ministry would have failed long ago. With him as their spiritual leader, not only was the ministry one of the top five in the world, but the political strength of the Right Side became more powerful with each election.

As arguments filled the room, the former president of the United States said nothing. History would place him as only a mediocre president upon being defeated after one four-year term. Yet, twenty years after leaving the White House, he stayed involved in international charities and served from time to time as an interim ambassador. On more than one occasion, he had been the president's personal envoy, negotiating peace in those parts of the world where war was an everyday part of life. When he spoke, his soft voice carried the authority of making life and death decisions for twenty-five years.

"General, may I say a few words?"

The governors stopped their discussion and turned to the president.

"Yes, Mr. President. We were wondering when you might offer us the benefit of your experience."

"Thank you, General. A strong case can be made for either of these fine servants of the Lord. Both have proven that they can do the job. Judging from the comments in this room, the issue is divisive. In addition to our ministry, we must also think about what is best for the country. If our decision caused a split among our followers, the ministry could probably recover. However, it could set our political agenda back several years. I propose that we ask both of these fine ministers to remain; that they be co-ministers or something of that sort; that they share the pulpit, alternating services. Maybe it will work for the long haul, maybe not. With two ministers of their stature, certainly there is hope that they could carry our message even further. Still, I don't want to be unrealistic. There is a good chance that one will eventually leave, hopefully, though, not until after the next election."

"Thank you, Mr. President," replied the general. "I certainly agree that is a solution, and it would certainly be best for all concerned if we could advise the press that our decision is unanimous. Anyone opposed to the president's plan?"

"Well, General," drawled the rancher from Wichita Falls, "I'm not going to stake out any opposition, but I would like it to go on the record that in my experience, there ain't no pasture big enough to hold two bulls."

12

Jessie Woolsey had been a Miracle Governor for five years, although she had not been an active churchgoer when her husband died. She wasn't sure she had ever had a religious experience. The one experience that definitely left her with strong feelings was paying the taxes on Warren's estate. Shocked at how much the government took, she began to study the various ways that it intruded upon her life and was appalled. With nothing other than a few charities to occupy her time when she wasn't visiting her children, she turned to television, searching for a solution to the government's interference in her life. Instead she found the televangelists. She discovered that they not only had religious programming, but also news programs, variety shows and talk shows, all with religious undertones, each one taking the conservative view of politics.

When she realized that one of the major spokesmen for the religious right emanated from Fort Worth, she studied the local television guide and arranged her days around programming coming from the City of Miracles. Shortly thereafter, she attended Sunday morning services. When she gave the first of several one-million-dollar donations to the City, she had a reserved front row seat. When her donations hit five million, the board invited her to fill a vacancy at the table of Miracle Governors. Soon, the City was her major charity, and next to her family, it became the most important part of her life.

She had remained silent during the long debate about which preacher to choose. A strong, intelligent woman, she was somewhat in awe of the minds that shared the boardroom with her. Her practice was to comment occasionally; however, at most of the board meetings, she tried to listen, absorb what others said and vote her conscience. This day was no different. As she listened to the advocates for each of the ministers, she was swayed to their respective points of view. When the meeting ended, though, she agreed with the president who had made many decisions that were bigger and more important than this.

At the conclusion of the meeting, the general called a press conference to announce their decision. The board members shook hands, wished each other well until the next month and departed. Jessie took the opportunity to excuse herself, claiming that she had to powder her nose, and returned to the nineteenth floor to await the sunset and contemplate the day's events.

EARLY IN HER SERVICE on the board Jessie had discovered how spectacular the sunsets could be from the Miracle City boardroom. She was so smitten by them that she would often drive her Jaguar out to the City at sundown. Using her pass key for the private elevator, she sat alone on the nineteenth floor, watching the changing panorama of the setting sun as God covered the western sky with reds, pinks and oranges that could never have been matched from an artist's palette. Usually she did so as she sipped on her bourbon and branch water, the bourbon coming from a small flask she carried in her purse.

With her drink in hand, she watched the sun disappear as it painted the clouds with pink and yellow stripes. When the fiery glow dropped below the horizon, Jessie was startled to see an apparition reflected in the glass, standing beside her. She had heard no door open or footsteps, but standing there was the figure of a man, medium height, wearing all white.

Not being one to believe in ghosts and certainly not one to fear them, she turned to see a man, dressed in a white linen shirt, open at the top, white pants and white running shoes. She recognized him immediately. Dark glasses covered his eyes. His face looked like the one in his pictures that were prominently displayed throughout the City, although in the pictures his hair was wavy and dark. Now, while still thick, it was entirely white. His body was that of a boy, small arms and legs, thirty-inch waist and a chest not much bigger.

"Good evening, Mrs. Woolsey," Reverend Luther said. "Ever since I was a boy growing up here in Fort Worth, I always thought that God favored Texans with the most marvelous of sunsets. I used to watch them from my front porch on Cloverdale as a kid, and after this tower was complete, I spent many an evening in a chair just like that one you're sitting in, thinking about His majesty and wondering what He had in store for me. Mind if I join you?"

Rarely at a loss for words, Jessie didn't respond. What do you say to a man whom you have never met, who had been dead, for all practical purposes, for twelve years? After too long of a pause, she gathered herself together. "Why no, Reverend. Please pull up a chair."

"Ma'am, my friends call me T.J. If it's okay, please call me that and I'll call you Jessie, if it suits you."

"By all means, T.J." She looked around for a place to hide her drink. No one ever caught on to her sunset toddy and she certainly didn't want the Chosen to be offended.

"You don't have to be embarrassed about your drink, Jessie. Bourbon and branch water is a great Texas tradition. I drank an entire lifetime's measure of whiskey before I was thirty-five, far in excess on too many occasions. After I was born-again and became a follower of the Lord, while I stayed away from booze in public, I certainly didn't mind a drink in the privacy of my quarters. I'm not one of those people who thought that Jesus and the disciples drank grape juice when the Bible called it wine. It's been twelve years since I've had a taste of spirits. If you have any left in that flask in your purse, I'd be obliged if you would let me share a little with you."

Regaining her senses, she realized that this was just a man beside her. Besides, twelve years is a long time between drinks. "Please, T.J., get yourself a glass and some ice. Be my guest."

T.J. excused himself to the table where an ice bucket, glasses and assorted beverages remained from the meeting. As he settled into a chair beside Jessie, she handed him her flask and watched as he poured Jack Daniel's over ice.

"To your health, Mrs. Woolsey," T.J. toasted as he raised his glass.

"No, Reverend, to yours and to your miraculous recovery."

T.J. sipped at the bourbon and smiled as the liquid burned its way into his stomach. "Whooee, I'd forgotten that taste. Brings back memories, most of them bad, along with a few good ones."

"T.J., are you sure your doctor would approve of this?"

"Well, ma'am, I guess what he don't know won't hurt him. After what I've been through, I expect that one little ol' drink isn't going to send me back into a coma."

"Can I ask you about that?"

"You certainly can ask, and I'll tell you all I know about those years. It's not much. I have recollections of doctors and nurses, therapy, people around, a lot of people. I can't tell you if what I remember is real or just dreams. I don't re-call anything about getting stabbed. I remember everything about growing up on Cloverdale. You know where that is, don't you, Jessie? It's on the poor side of Camp Bowie Boule-vard, actually just a few blocks from your mansion in River-crest. Do you like serving on my board, Jessie?"

A little surprised that he knew anything about her, she challenged him. "How is it you know anything about me? We certainly didn't know each other years ago and I've only been on the board for five years."

"Jessie, I make it a point to know about everyone who is important in my life, and I guarantee you, I have studied the backgrounds of every one of my board members. You wouldn't know this. Before your husband Warren died and before my long sleep, I tried to recruit him for my board. He declined, saying he was too busy. He did donate ten thousand dollars, which meant a lot to me in those early days. So, what did you think about today's meeting? I kinda liked it when old Josh made that statement about no pasture being big enough for two bulls."

Jessie was stunned. "Reverend Luther, I was told that these board meetings were absolutely private and nothing ever left this room. Just how is it you know what Josh had to say?"

"Why, Jessie, nothing left the room. If you must know, I designed this building. I did it so that nothing that goes on here gets past me. Let's just say that some walls really do have ears."

Jessie was offended by the eavesdropping. She sat in silence as the sun's reflection danced from cloud to cloud. Finally, T.J. figured he had to explain and continued, "Look, Jessie, everything here is mine. I conceived it. I built it. I put together this board because I needed to give legitimacy to my cause. Many years ago, when they decided the board had the right to have occasional meetings without me at the head of the table, I made damn sure that I knew what was going on. I do the Lord's work, Jessie, and I'm not going to let any man or board get in my way."

Silence prevailed. Jessie was still upset with T.J. Her thoughts drifted off as the last rays of the sun reflected from a sky that was dotted with stars. "So, Reverend, what do you think about the decision to go with two ministers as soon as you're able to resume preaching?"

"Frankly, Jessie, to paraphrase a famous old Texan, it's worse than a warm bucket of spit."

"I remember those famous words of our country's former vice president from Uvalde, T.J. The question is whether you are going to accept it?"

"And the answer, Mrs. Woolsey," T.J.'s voice was rising, "is not only 'no' but 'Hell No!' I didn't build this ministry to share it with anyone. I am the Chosen and only I speak for the Lord. Just you wait and see. It won't be long before there's only one bull in this pasture and it won't be the one named Jimmy."

13

The Chosen returned to the pulpit two weeks after the board meeting, dressed in a white satin robe adorned with a gold collar and gold trim at the bellowing sleeves. A gold sash bound his waist. Dark sunglasses covered eyes that resembled a road map of West Texas. If truth be known, T.J. was disappointed that lightning didn't crash, that clouds didn't part and a voice didn't announce, "This is My son, My faithful servant, with whom I am greatly pleased. Rejoice in his return!"

His followers overflowed the sanctuary, requiring another several thousand people to watch on giant television screens located in the parking lot. A worldwide television audience joined them. The press occupied the first ten rows. After a fifteen-minute standing ovation, T.J. acknowledged the praise of the general, who introduced him. T.J. embraced the general and then shook the hand of Reverend Witherspoon. T.J.'s approach to the two men with whom he shared the stage was not missed by the media. He waited for the applause to fade before he began.

His preaching was that of a first-year divinity student. Like a baseball player who was going to bat for the first time in spring training, T.J. was rusty and it showed. He started by thanking his doctors and those who had been faithfully awaiting his return. As he warmed up, the audience could almost see the rust fall away as he found his groove.

"Most of all I want to thank my Heavenly Father. I was born-again and received the miracle of restored sight in the Tarrant County jail, just a few miles from here. Before that time I had lived a life of shame, committing sins far worse than any of you could possibly imagine. That my Father could forgive me of those sins and put me on the path of righteousness should be a clear sign that He is a compassionate and often forgiving God. When I was born again, I was given ten years to carry out my Father's mission. I carried His word to small towns in Texas and ultimately to the capitals of the world."

A voice from the back of the auditorium shouted, "You the one, preacher! You're the messenger from God!"

T.J. acknowledged the comment with a wave of his hand and continued. "He gave me the vision to understand what was wrong in our society and a plan to correct those wrongs, not just from the pulpit but also through the power of political change. We called mayors, governors, senators, and, yes, even presidents, to join us on The Right Side. Many of them answered that call as we worked to restore family values, eliminate the epidemic of pornography from our society, maintain our constitutional right to bear arms, and, most of all, stop killing the pre-born through legalized abortions. We saw progress on all fronts when God called me back to His side where I spent the past twelve years.

"A few months ago my Father resurrected me, and once more, I have been born-again. I must admit I was confused at first. I didn't know what God expected of me. Eventually, I became aware of my surroundings and gained an understanding of what has happened in the world while I slept. It is not a better place. All of the challenges that faced me twelve years ago are still here. As I have watched television, not just the news stations, but the so-called sitcoms and other programming, I am shocked at the immorality of our society. We have no leadership at the statehouse or the White House. Someone must step forward to restore our society to what our forefathers intended. I now know that is my Father's will. I will preach my message from this pulpit, and I will do all I can to make sure that our national leaders are on the Right Side of our moral issues. I cannot tell you how long I will be on earth this time. That is known only to my Father. Whether it is days or weeks or years is for Him to decide. While I am here, I will work every hour of every day to carry out His will.

"Let us pray. My Father, and the Father of all in this audience, I thank You for resurrecting me at this most important time in the course of history. Give me the strength to carry out Your Commandments, the voice to make Your message heard, and the power to bring about Your changes, not just in this country but throughout the world. Amen."

The commentators on the evening news marveled at the performance from one who was so near death only months before. They picked up on his theme of the message of the Right Side being foremost in his sermon. And, of course, they commented about his description of "his resurrection," "his Father," and his days being numbered with the exact number being known only by his Father. As one commentator put it, "Is this guy a savior or a charlatan?" In the months that followed, many voices would raise similar questions, but only one would have the final answer.

14

Over the next three months, things could not have gone more smoothly. If the Chosen took the Sunday morning service, then Reverend Witherspoon preached in the evening. The next Sunday they reversed their roles. T.J. deferred to Jimmy on the Wednesday night healing service, announcing that he had to wait for his healing to be complete before he could heal others. The board asked Jimmy to permit T.J. to return to his penthouse and Jimmy graciously agreed to move into a townhouse while crews turned a part of the eighth floor of the Miracle Tower into suitable living quarters. The board met monthly and marveled at how wonderfully things were going, and more importantly, how revenue had increased by 50 percent since the return of the Chosen. At the end of each meeting they shook hands and patted each other on the back in praise of their decision, concluding that it must have been divinely inspired. Only Mrs. Warren Woolsey had any reservations, and she kept them to herself, never mentioning T.J.'s comment about "one bull."

T.J. was pleased to return to his penthouse in the Miracle Tower. One evening after the servants had been dismissed and the sun had disappeared over the horizon, he bathed and surveyed what he saw in the mirror. He refused to admit to the sin of vanity, at least not in public, yet as he studied himself in the mirror, he liked what he saw. For a man in his fifties, he was well preserved, with only a few lines around his mouth and eyes. True, he needed to add a few pounds and some muscle, but the reflection was that of a vigorous middle-aged man, the white hair being the only real indication of his age. He toyed with the idea of darkening it, then had second thoughts. The white hair gave him credibility and a presence that he found appealing.

As soon as he was able, T.J. took to wandering the complex, particularly in the evening after the gates were closed. He found that his master plan, conceived many years before, had not only been implemented, but had been expanded. On the way out one night, he stopped his elevator on the third floor where the City's accounting offices were occupied twenty-four hours a day. Getting some help to log onto a computer, he found his way to the list of Miracle City contributors where they were registered according to the size of their contribution, largest ones first. T.J. studied the computer, trying to match faces with names, knowing that it wouldn't be long before he was making a personal appeal to his biggest donors. After scrolling through the million dollar givers, he soon found the half-million-dollar contributors. One caught his eye and he turned to the accountant at the next desk.

"Bruce, there's a donor here who says that his half-million-dollar donation is a tribute to his lawyer, J. Robert Tisdale, who he calls the best plaintiff lawyer in the country. He's tithing ten percent of a judgment that this Tisdale fellow got for him. I assume that means that he collected five million. You ever heard of a lawyer named Tisdale?"

"Reverend, if he's the one I'm thinking about, he's from East Texas . . . Palestine, I think. I don't know about him being the best in the country, but he's supposed to be damn good."

"Interesting," T.J. mused as he shut off the computer. "I'll try to remember his name in the event I need me a good lawyer sometime."

If there was a single advancement that he did not anticipate, it was the age of computers. He thought he understood computers and their potential before his near-death experience. Now, what they could do was beyond his imagination.

As the weeks went on, he spent more and more time in the recording studio, the building that housed all of the computers, video equipment, mixers and other paraphernalia that gave him a worldwide ministry. He found it remarkable that the technicians could dub over his mistakes on Sunday morning and make it appear that he never missed a beat or stumbled over a word. If this was the Miracle City, then the studio performed the magic. He spent evenings observing the technicians and editors preparing video and audiotapes of sermons, lectures, classroom presentations and appeals for money in forty-two languages. As he did so, a plan evolved.

Talking to one of the young technicians, he broached the subject. "Tell me, Jerry, can you dub one person's voice over another's so that it sounds realistic?"

"Sure thing, Rev. That's not a problem."

"How about changing one person's face for another?"

"Again, no problem. Watch this." Jerry pulled up a video of Reverend Witherspoon and clicked a couple of times, replacing his face with that of Mickey Mouse talking with Witherspoon's voice.

After they had a good laugh about Mickey preaching about hellfire and damnation, T.J. asked, "Is that very difficult?" He paused and then continued, "I mean, if I wanted to surprise a friend on his birthday, could I learn how to do that?"

"Rev, it's a snap. Pull up that chair and I'll teach you in an hour." An hour was a start, but it took several more weeks, showing up after midnight when the technicians had gone home, before T.J. perfected the craft. Late one evening, he left the City, driving a new, white Lincoln Continental, bearing his favorite custom license plate, CHOSEN 1. Disguised only with his dark glasses and a Texas Rangers baseball cap to cover his silver hair, he drove to downtown Fort Worth and then out North Main toward the stockyards until he found an all-night adult video store. He parked in the dark parking lot, feeling a little conspicuous about driving a new Continental, and entered through the rear door. Relieved that the place was almost deserted, he evaluated a few of the videos, selecting several and paying with cash. He kept his head down and never exchanged a word with the attendant.

Over the next several nights, he dismissed the servants and retired to his bedroom where he watched the movies until he found the ideal one. Even after choosing it, T.J. played the videos again, no longer searching for a certain one. Instead, he enjoyed the sensations that coursed though him and settled in his loins as he sipped a California Syrah and amused himself by trying to count the number of sexual positions on the videos. The feeling in his loins told him that his recovery was complete. Fortunately, his God did not preach celibacy. Soon it would be time to find a woman to share his bed, at least for an evening. The next night, waiting until long after midnight, he put the video in the pocket of his jacket and walked to the studio. He sat at the mixer and cued up one of the most pornographic scenes, featuring a blond woman with big breasts performing oral sex on a well-endowed young man. It would be easy to substitute the face of Jimmy Witherspoon for that of the man on the video. T.J. cued up several of Jimmy's sermons until he found just the right look of ecstasy. Taking a view of Jimmy's head, T.J. worked until five A.M., replacing the head of the porno star with that of the Reverend Jimmy Witherspoon.

15

With a smug look, the attorney in the expensive Armani suit
concluded the direct examination of his client, the CEO of
GreenForest Utilities, a major Houston energy trading company. The federal court case involved allegations of manipu-
lation of revenues, called round-trip trading, and alleged
fraudulent accounting practices that caused the company's
stock to tumble to the basement in only a matter of weeks.
The plaintiffs in the lawsuit were stockholders trying to
recoup their losses from the company and the man on the
witness stand. His lawyer was surrounded by a cadre of associates who were barely able to conceal their awe as their
senior partner led his client, seemingly unscathed, through
the labyrinth of alleged shady dealings.

As he was about to start his last series of questions, he
heard sounds of a briefcase opening and papers being moved
at the adjoining counsel table. Tod Duncan, the attorney for
the stockholders, had lifted his heavy briefcase to the table,
opened it and, one by one, he noisily emptied it of briefs,
depositions and assorted papers. Noticing that the company
lawyer was glaring at him, he fished into his briefcase once
more as he said, "Oh, I'm sorry, Your Honor. I found what I
was looking for."

No one noticed the twinkle in his eye as he moved the
briefcase from the table and the questioning continued.

"Mr. Fitzgerald, I want you to look each one of the jurors
in the eye," GreenForest's attorney said. "Tell them whether
you knowingly permitted fraud of any kind, were dishonest
in any way, or personally engaged in any wrongdoing."

The man on the witness stand drew the attention of the
hushed courtroom. Dressed in his three-thousand-dollar
suit, his gold Rolex watch reflected an overhead light as he
adjusted his glasses. As chairman of an international con-
glomerate, he expected complete attention to his every word.

Further, he expected to be believed. He turned in the witness chair so that he could face the jury as he responded:

"I grew up as the son of a widowed schoolteacher. I worked my way through college as a busboy and waiter. I started GreenForest from nothing and spent thirty years building it. Until the unfortunate series of events of the past year, it had been number ten on the Fortune 500 list of companies. I provided thousands of jobs to people in this community and around the country. I chose GreenForest as the name because I also wanted to protect the environment and endangered species. I have served on the boards of at least a dozen charities. I have donated millions of dollars of my own money to provide for the poor, the sick and disabled."

He paused for dramatic effect.

"The fraudulent acts of our accountants were what brought my company down. I trusted them to audit operations within GreenForest. Instead, they encouraged practices that, in hindsight, should never have been permitted. By the time those practices were brought to my attention, it was too late."

He took off his glasses to permit the jury to observe the credibility in his steel blue eyes. "At no time did I do anything dishonest or fraudulent. Nor did anyone else at GreenForest. We were honest and forthright with our stockholders and the public. I permitted nothing less."

His lawyer knew Mr. Fitzgerald had ended his speech. They had practiced it at least a dozen times, including the gestures with the glasses. The lawyer rose. "No further questions of this witness, Your Honor."

Ben Hand, the senior judge in the Southern District of Texas had unruly white hair and a goatee. He was known as a legal scholar and a judge who gave considerable latitude to attorneys when it came to jury trials. He enjoyed the drama of the courtroom.

"Let's take our midafternoon break. See you all in fifteen minutes. Mr. Duncan, you'll be coming to bat when we return."

Tod Duncan appeared to be mismatched in this battle with the army of lawyers at the other table. In his late forties, he looked at least ten years younger. Others described him as boyish. Only the gray in his mustache and the need to pull reading glasses out of his coat pocket to glance at his notes gave away his real age.

Tod turned to his associate and his paralegal and said, "Wayne, you and Joyce clean everything off the counsel table. Get rid of every notebook, pad, pencil and paper clip. When we get back, I want you to take a seat out in the audience. I don't want anything to distract the jury from this little show I'm about to put on."

Puzzled looks crossed the faces of Wayne and Joyce as they followed his instructions. Tod excused himself and left the courtroom. A few minutes later he was rearranging the chairs around the counsel table when Judge Hand returned and his bailiff called the court to order.

When Tod left the courtroom, a woman in the audience stepped into the hallway, pulled her cell phone from her purse, and dialed a number. "Let me talk to T.J. Make it quick," she whispered. After a brief conversation, the spectator returned to the back bench.

As Tod took his seat, GreenForest's lawyer remained standing and addressed the court. "Your Honor, this is most unusual. I object to the demeanor of opposing counsel."

The judge covered his mouth to hide an amused look. "Well, counsel, I don't see that Mr. Duncan has broken any rules yet. We'll see where this goes. Your objection is overruled."

"Mr. Fitzgerald," Tod began. "During the last year before your company's collapse, you cashed in three hundred million dollars in options and pocketed the money, didn't you?"

"Mr. Duncan, that was part of my compensation package. I earned every penny of that money because our stock rose over fifty dollars during that time."

"The biggest reason that it rose so dramatically, Mr. Fitzgerald, was because of those phony trades that we all learned about after you had sold your stock?"

"Sir, I never saw anything to indicate that those trades

were improper at the time. I learned about them at the same time as everyone else did."

"Mr. Fitzgerald, we've heard about all of your charitable contributions; however, you still managed to have enough left to maintain a mansion in River Oaks here in town and a ten-million-dollar house in Vail?"

"Yes, sir," the witness replied, a slight smirk accidentally appearing on his face as he thought that no one else in this courtroom could afford the bathroom in one of those houses.

"And, let's see." Tod glanced at the paper in his hand. "As I understand it, you also own a villa in the south of France."

"I do, sir."

Glancing at the paper again, Tod continued, "And a beach-front house in Maui?"

"I travel a lot, Mr. Duncan."

"Matter of fact, Mr. Fitzgerald, you travel so much that in that last year, you were never in the corporate office when your quarterly earnings were reported, were you? Always off in some exotic place and unavailable to talk to your shareholders, the media or Wall Street?"

Small beads of perspiration began to form on the witness's bald head. "There was no need for me to discuss the earnings reports with anyone. I had public relations people and staff to handle those matters."

The company lawyer rose in an effort to break the flow of Duncan's cross-examination. "Again, Your Honor, I must object to the demeanor of counsel."

Judge Hand smiled at him. "Sir, if that's the best objection you can muster, it's overruled. Mr. Duncan's questions seem to be quite easily understood. I don't see that he is disrupting this courtroom. Proceed."

"Did you even review those financial reports before they were released?"

The CEO took a handkerchief from his coat pocket and nervously swiped it around the edges of his glasses. "No, sir. I was quite satisfied that they were in order."

Tod looked down at the paper in his lap again. "How about

this, Mr. Fitzgerald. We've established that you didn't study the financials and that you were always unavailable to talk about them. Before you left for Vail, or Maui, or the south of France at the end of each quarter, did you call your vice presidents and those outside accountants into your office for a discussion of what you were going to report to the public?"

The witness shifted in his chair as he sputtered, "Mr. Duncan, I didn't find that necessary."

"Sir, isn't it true that the ultimate responsibility for running GreenForest rested with you? As Harry Truman used to say, 'the buck stops here'?"

"Counsel, I wish I had known then what I know now. If my outside accountants had only done their jobs. By the way, Mr. Duncan, could I see what you are reading from? It's very difficult for me when you are seated, facing the rear of the courtroom with your back to me."

Tod grinned as he rose to face the witness, the judge and the jurors. "Why, Mr. Fitzgerald, all I'm looking at is the sports page of this morning's *Chronicle*. I turned my chair to face the back wall, though, to illustrate what I understand to be your defense. Isn't it true that your defense in this lawsuit is that you were looking the other way the whole time and all of these shady dealings were done behind your back?"

Several jurors laughed out loud as Tod turned his chair to face the witness.

"No, sir, it is not." Fitzgerald tried to regain some composure.

"Mr. Fitzgerald, you can't have it both ways. Either you turned your back as your company collapsed or you were like the captain of the *Titanic,* taking full charge as you ran it into an iceberg. Which is it?"

"Objection, Your Honor. He's harassing the witness."

This time, the judge looked sternly at GreenForest's lawyer.

"Overruled. Mr. Duncan is entitled to an answer. Also, I might add, so are the shareholders and the jurors."

Turning to gaze at his lawyer for help and receiving none,

Fitzgerald said, "I don't know the answer, Mr. Duncan. You'll have to ask my lawyer what our defense is."

Tod slowly tapped a pen on his empty table, giving the jurors time to assimilate everything they had heard. "One last thing," he then added.

"Isn't it true that you play classical guitar, Mr. Fitzgerald?"

"Sir, I'm not sure of the relevance of that question, but the answer is yes. I've done so for many years. In fact, I keep one in my office and play it frequently at the end of the day. It helps me unwind."

"Then, Mr. Fitzgerald, as I understand it, your final defense is that you were in your office, door closed and strumming your guitar while your accountants were cooking the books. Kinda like Nero fiddling while Rome burned, right, Mr. Fitzgerald?"

"Objection, Your Honor."

"Never mind, Judge." Tod smiled. "I withdraw the question."

In the crowded courtroom, a big man left his seat in the back row. J. Robert Tisdale took an elevator to another courtroom where he was scheduled for a hearing, chuckling to himself at Tod's cross-examination. He thought: *I couldn't have done better myself.*

16

Jimmy and T.J. rarely saw each other except on Sunday mornings when they went out of their way to smile and act like long lost friends. Otherwise, it was like two people who occupied the same apartment building in New York City, living across the hall from one another, with each one never knowing the other's name. That came to a halt after four months of sharing the pulpit. At the conclusion of the Sunday morning service, T.J. invited Jimmy to meet with him in his penthouse on Monday.

Promptly at ten A.M. on Monday morning, Jimmy knocked on T.J.'s door. Dressed in jeans and a white golf shirt, T.J. opened the door with a smile. "Reverend Witherspoon, please do come in."

Jimmy entered the quarters that had been his for twelve years and took the seat that T.J. offered.

"Can I get you a cup of coffee, Jimmy?"

"No, thanks, I'm just fine," Jimmy said as he surveyed the apartment, looking for signs of anyone else.

T.J. took a seat across from him. "Well, then, let me get right to the point . . . if you don't mind my avoiding meaningless polite conversation. You've been living in my home for the past twelve years. I appreciate all that you have done to carry on my ministry while I was gone. However, I have been resurrected for a purpose, and that purpose does not include you. To put it in the terms of my earlier life as a two-bit mobster, it's time for you to hit the road, to establish your own ministry. This one's mine."

Jimmy stared back at T.J., just as confident and replied, "You're wrong, T.J. This one is ours. I spent twelve years building it. I'm fifteen years younger than you. The word that I get from my friends on the board is that in three years they are going to ask you to retire, to assume the role of Pastor Emeritus, and the pulpit will be mine. I'm willing to wait it out. If that means playing second fiddle for three years, so be it. I'll inherit one of the biggest teleministries in the world. It's worth the wait."

T.J. sat in silence for so long that Jimmy began to think that he had won. He rose to leave as T.J. responded. "Well, my friend, I suppose that means that it's hardball time. I didn't really want to play this card, but you give me no choice." T.J. turned on the VCR and watched as Jimmy saw himself starring in a porno flick while a voluptuous blonde with enormous breasts performed oral sex on what appeared to be his erection.

Jimmy's eyes first narrowed, then widened. As a shocked expression filled his face, he shouted, "T.J., you know that's not me. I'm a happily married man with four children."

T.J.'s expression didn't change and his face was a mask of determination, as he countered, "Jimmy, I don't deny your marriage. I can only tell you that this arrived in a brown envelope, marked 'Personal, to be opened only by the Chosen.' Those of us who are servants of the Lord are also victims of the flesh. I prefer not to have to use this video; however, if you force my hand, it will arrive in an unmarked envelope at all the major networks next Monday. It's your choice. I would suggest that it's time that you find your own pasture."

"Fuck you, T.J.! I've got more friends on the board than you do. Let's see what they have to say."

T.J. only smiled as he pitched another envelope on the coffee table in front of them. "Okay, if that video is not convincing enough, take a look in that envelope. It's a detailed analysis of your stock trades and profits in GreenForest Utilities along with your e-mails to our investment managers, pushing them to buy GreenForest stock. Only, you didn't tell them to sell when you did. I'm sure the board and maybe even the Feds would be most interested in how you participated in driving the stock up, particularly since it cost the City ten million."

On the following Sunday, Reverend Witherspoon announced his resignation.

17

Like so many other preachers, T.J. never really understood the healing part of his ministry. When it happened the first time while he worked as an assistant healer with Jerry Abraham and the blind woman claimed that she could see again, Jerry gave him his best advice about the subject.

"Don't matter, boy. I don't know how it works either. Not our job to figure it out or to check tomorrow to see if the healing is still there. Could be temporary, could be that the ailment was more in the mind than in the body, could be our preaching gave them the strength to overcome whatever ails them, could be they'll wake up tomorrow with the same aches and pains that they said were healed tonight, could be tomorrow they will be dead. And it could be that God has something to do with it. Whatever the reason, healing is what draws them to us like insects to a porch light. Don't matter what you do. Just follow the script. The people will think the afflicted are healed and they'll fill the offering buckets."

T.J. followed Abraham's advice and found that he was right. He also discovered that the better the show, the more the healing and the bigger the take at the end of the night. So, T.J. started giving his followers a show full of lights, sound, thunder and lasers, topped off with a generous dose of charisma. Still, he was more than slightly shocked when he started having people line up at the stage to receive his healing touch. The first time he cupped his hands on the head of a woman with migraine headaches, demanding that the headache devils be gone, the woman passed out at his feet. He worried that she had stroked on him right there on stage. Soon, it became so common that he had ushers standing behind the person who was accepting his healing, knowing that there was at least a fifty-fifty chance that he or she would pass out for a few seconds or minutes. They even had blankets available to cover the prostrate bodies until the people awakened.

After Jimmy Witherspoon's departure, it was another two months before T.J. was ready to try healing again. Having spent hundreds of hours watching television as he recuperated, he found that the airwaves were chock full of preachers, pastors and evangelists of every shape, size, ethnicity and religion. These twenty-four-hour channels were not the place for Catholics, Methodists and Episcopalians. The fundamentalists filled these airwaves. They praised God, damned the devil and the most popular of them seemed to include healing as a part of their service. As T.J. studied them, he saw that they all played to packed houses but none had captured the national limelight. He watched the downfall of

Jimmy Swaggert and Jim and Tammy Faye Bakker. Pat Robertson and Jerry Falwell were still as strong as ever. A black preacher named T. D. Jakes seemed to be gaining popularity. Otherwise, none of these modern-day preachers had what it took to captivate the imagination of the entire country, much less the world. There was a void. T.J. intended to fill it.

Two months later, T.J. announced that the next Sunday would be his first healing ministry since his resurrection. Ads were placed in major metropolitan newspapers. The event was an item on the evening news in several markets. How many times does a preacher awaken after twelve years to announce he is ready to start healing the masses?

When Sunday arrived, the Chosen could not have looked or sounded better. He had been fanatical about his therapy and it showed. In addition to added weight and muscle, his step was strong and his voice resonated with strength and power. He began speaking in a voice not much more than a whisper, knowing that if his voice was soft that people would strain to hear.

"My fellow believers, it's been a long journey. There were times that I was ready to give up the ghost. Just when I was weakest and ready to let go, a voice would bring me back, saying, 'I didn't resurrect you to spend a few weeks recovering and then leave this earth. I have work for you to do. Get out of bed and heal yourself so that you can do My bidding.' So I did, all the time hearing that voice pushing me on to return to this place. I wanted to make sure that God had healed me completely before I used His power to heal others. Today, I stand before you completely healed and ready to do the work of my Lord."

The congregation rose to its feet, cheering, clapping and waving hands in the air. T.J. let the celebration go on for five minutes before he motioned for them to be seated. "If anyone doubts that God can heal through man, I invite you to turn to the text of my sermon in the Book of Acts, Chapter Nine, where a good woman named Tabitha fell sick and died. Her family laid her in an upper room. Hearing that Peter was nearby, they summoned him, entreating him to 'please come to us without delay.' Peter rose and went with them to the upper room and asked the mourners to leave. When they were gone, he knelt down beside Tabitha and prayed; then, turning to the body, he said, 'Tabitha, rise.' When she saw Peter she sat up and it became known throughout all the area and thereafter many believed in the Lord."

As his sermon continued, T.J.'s voice rose to that of an army drill instructor, commanding and then demanding that the audience believe, not just in their Lord but in him as the one anointed to do His work. Suddenly, he began to shout.

"Devils, I know you are out there! I can feel your presence. I can smell your evil breath. I can see your eyes glowing like embers from the fires of eternal damnation. I intend to drive all of you out of my temple. For those of you who are inflicted with the devils of arthritis, heart disease, high blood pressure, or any other ailment that has been tormenting you, including the devil of cancer, listen to my voice. If the doctors have told you there is no hope, I tell you that if you believe in God and His miracles, there is hope. There is the power of His healing. All of you who are in need, I tell you to rise up. Stay in your place. Stand so that I may look into your eyes and into your soul. For I can tell you that my power is so strong that I need not to lay my hands upon you. The power of my healing has gone untapped now for over twelve years. It's like a thunderstorm, filled with electricity and ready to light up the sky."

As he spoke, one by one, people in the audience started rising. Soon there were hundreds standing, some swaying, some with their hands in the air. A few rose, only to collapse onto the floor.

"For those of you who are so crippled that you cannot stand, don't worry. I can see you. I can see right into your heart. Now, you devils, I want to talk directly to you. You demons have come to the wrong place. You followed these good people into my house and I am here to drive each of you out. I demand that you release your hold on my people! Get out of this house and out of their lives! These people are my people and God's people. As strong as you devils may be, you're no match for my Father and me. Be gone!"

18

Jessie Woolsey had just returned to her Rivercrest mansion from a City of Miracles board meeting when she got the call from her younger sister, Joanna. After a bad experience early in her life, fate dealt Jessie a good hand, and she was smart enough to know how to play it. As a senior in high school, she became pregnant. It definitely wasn't a rape. She had been dating the father for two years and they both took great joy in their youthful sex. They took precautions. He used condoms. She refused his advances for about ten days between each period, but somehow she became pregnant. She tried to talk him into marriage. He begged off. By the third month, she told her parents. Abortion never entered her mind. She wasn't embarrassed about it. She recognized it as something that she would have to deal with. Before the *Roe v. Wade* decision, abortions were available with the right connections, but the two primary alternatives were to have the baby at home or to go to what was known as a "home for unwed mothers." The staff would care for the young mother and arrange for the baby's adoption, especially if the mother was white and reasonably attractive.

Esther Johnson in Fort Worth ran one of the best known of these homes where some of the finest families in the state adopted their children. After getting Jessie's agreement, her mother called Fort Worth and arranged for Jessie to become a resident. The next day Jessie, kissed her parents good-bye, hugged her little sister and boarded the bus to Houston where she transferred to a Greyhound bound for Fort Worth. Jessie had never been that far from home, but at age seventeen she looked on her life as an adventure and this was the next chapter. She thought about the idea of giving the baby up for adoption. Assured by her mother that the child would have a good home, she had no reservations. Besides, she wanted to write a few more chapters in her book of life before she settled into motherhood.

When Jessie arrived at the Fort Worth Greyhound station, she asked directions and within half an hour the local transit bus dropped her in front of the Johnson Home. Jessie saw before her a campus dominated by an old redbrick mansion, four stories high with each floor at least three or four times the size of her entire house in LaMarque. Behind it were several newer and smaller one-story buildings, also redbrick. A black wrought-iron fence surrounded the entire complex. Jessie walked through the gate, up the stairs, and without knocking, pulled open one of the two big double doors. Inside, she found herself in a nicely appointed living room with several sitting areas and one black-and-white TV. There were girls about her age and a little older, talking, watching television and reading magazines. Some were obviously pregnant. Others weren't showing yet. To one side was a desk and behind it sat a lady with gray hair and a pleasant expression who smiled and said, "Can I help you?"

"Yes, ma'am. My name is Jessie and I'm going to be staying here for a few months."

"Jessie, of course. We've been expecting you. Come have a seat. Let's get some paperwork out of the way before I show you to your room."

Thus, the Johnson Home became Jessie's home. The next months went by much more rapidly than Jessie anticipated. The home provided her with a nice room and meals. She attended school for six hours every day. At first she had doctor appointments once a month. As her time grew near she saw the doctor every two weeks. She earned her high school diploma shortly before her baby was born. When she went into labor, she told one of the attendants who drove her to Harris Hospital near downtown where everything went smoothly. Jessie had a seven-pound, twelve-ounce boy. She got to see him once and thought that he would grow up to look like her dad. Then, he was gone and out of her life, to be adopted by a family that she would never know. While she would miss him and he would always be somewhere in the far reaches of her mind, she never regretted her decision.

Finding that she liked Fort Worth, Jessie was ready to find a job and get on with her life. In the sixties, the *Fort Worth Star Telegram* separated its employment section into male and female categories. Under the female job listings were waitresses, retail clerks, secretaries and cooks. She scanned the listings until she saw one for a Ford dealer, looking for a "girl Friday" to answer the telephone, greet customers and do some light typing. She called and got an appointment on the same day that she saw the ad.

Warren Woolsey, a thirty-five-year-old divorcee with no children, owned Cowtown Ford. He had started in the car business at the age of eighteen and soon became a top salesman. Working his way up to sales manager more quickly than anyone in the history of the region, he was able to buy his own franchise before he was thirty. At six feet, two inches tall, he had the lean build of a college athlete and the face of a movie star. He did his own television commercials and aired them in Fort Worth and Dallas. With a Stetson set firmly on his head, he convinced people throughout the area that Cowtown Ford was "where deals were done." He was well on his way to becoming a wealthy man.

Warren Woolsey was looking for a girl Friday. When he saw Jessie, he found exactly what he was looking for and much more. At eighteen, Jessie was a striking young woman. She had long strawberry blond hair, opaline green eyes, a bosom that caught every man's eye and a personality that made it clear that she was a match for anyone, man or woman. She still had a few extra pounds around the middle and didn't hide the fact that she had just had a baby, had put him up for adoption and needed a job. Warren hired her on the spot. He wanted her not just for his girl Friday but also for every other day of the week. Within three months, they were sleeping together. Jessie saw nothing wrong with sleeping with her boss and it didn't bother her that he was seventeen years older than she. Warren gave her orders during the day and worshiped at the temple of her body at night. After another three months, Warren flew her to Hawaii where they were married in a ceremony by the sea with a waiter and waitress from their hotel as best man and maid of honor. Jessie never worked another day for the rest of her life.

Jessie and Warren had four children, two boys and two girls, and Warren kept buying car dealerships. He kidded Jessie that every time he bought a dealership she got pregnant; or maybe it was the other way around. After the fourth dealership they moved to a mansion in Rivercrest, across the street from Rivercrest Country Club where the old rich played golf and the pot in the men's grill poker games was often thousands of dollars. As their children grew into teenagers, they bought a ranch in Palo Pinto County, fifty miles west of Fort Worth, where they raised horses and took friends on deer hunts in the fall. Jessie became a good shot and pleased Warren when she killed a buck from three hundred yards. Jessie's life could not have been better.

Warren was standing by the fireplace in their mansion, scotch in hand, telling Jessie about the exotic deer that he was going to import to their ranch for the next season when he suddenly gasped, clutched his chest and collapsed on the floor. Jessie rushed him to the hospital. His left anterior descending artery had occluded. Warren died instantly.

Jessie grieved for months before she closed the best chapter of her life and contemplated what destiny would bring next. Her children were grown. In addition to the car dealerships, Warren had made some wise stock investments over the years and had joined some of his friends in successful oil ventures. Jessie was a wealthy woman. She sold the car dealerships to pay estate taxes. When she surveyed what Warren had left her, she concluded she could not possibly spend it all if she lived to be two hundred. After his death, she filled her time with charities, visited her children who were scattered around the country, traveled and generally led a quiet life. Although there were plenty of men in Fort Worth who would have loved to have this still-beautiful lady at their side or in their bed, she refused to date. She and Warren had something very special and, in her mind, he was irreplaceable. If asked, she would have said that she was content but bored. She stayed that way until two things happened. The first involved Thomas Jeremiah Luther and the City of Miracles. The second was the call.

19

"Jessie, this is Jo."

"What's the matter, Jo?"

"Lucy's very sick. She's in Hermann Hospital in the medical center. She had an abortion and developed an infection and lost a lot of blood. We didn't know anything about it until I found her in bed with a temperature of one hundred and five."

"Is she going to be okay?"

"We don't know, Jessie. They operated on her." Joanna paused, took a breath and continued. "They say she could have brain damage or even die."

"I'm coming down, Jo. I'll fly into Hobby and rent a car. Get me a room at that hotel across from the medical center. In fact, get two rooms and I'll pay for them. You and Bo will need a place to rest, too."

Jessie took charge as she always did. She and Jo had not been close growing up. She was eight years older and left home when Joanna was just a kid. After Jo graduated from high school, they began to spend more time together. As adults they talked on the phone at least once a week. Jessie often marveled at the turns in their lives. If she hadn't gotten pregnant and gone to Fort Worth, she might have been just like Joanna, married to a refinery worker, living in a frame house and working for ten dollars an hour. Fate plays a strange and unpredictable game. Now an unwanted pregnancy had once again entered their lives. This time she feared the result might be far different.

Then, her mind turned to Lucy. Why did Lucy have to get an abortion? She could have come to live in Fort Worth. Besides, Lucy had to know abortion was wrong. Those thoughts and many others whirled through her head as her housekeeper drove her to Dallas to board the Southwest Airlines shuttle to Houston. As she sat in the plane, she shoved them aside and concentrated on how she could best help her family. Deep down she liked having a crisis to manage, if only it had not involved Lucy and Joanna.

20

After drinking coffee and picking at food in the hospital cafeteria, Joanna and Bo returned to the waiting room outside the post-anesthesia care unit. Joanna walked to the nurse's station and asked if they could see their daughter yet. A few minutes later Dr. McIntosh came through the double doors. Joanna tried without success to read her face.

The doctor's voice was calm and reassuring. "We are transfusing blood products and I have Lucy on high doses of antibiotics. She's still bleeding internally. Her hemoglobin and hematocrit are low but not critical. That's a good sign. We have her heart monitored and she's on a ventilator to help her breathe. You can come in for about five minutes. Don't be shocked by what you see. We've got tubes and wires almost everywhere."

With grim expressions on their faces, Joanna and Bo followed Dr. McIntosh into the unit. There were patients in every bed separated by curtains, each one in some stage of recovery. Some were moaning quietly. Others were pulling on the tubes attached to them. Some were staring at the ceiling and a few called to the nurses.

They found Lucy in the fourth bed on the right. Until the doctor stopped at the foot of the bed, they wouldn't have recognized her. The ventilator masked her face. There were tubes in her arms, one infusing blood products and another dripping a clear liquid into the other arm. Wires went to monitors that gave constant readings of her blood pressure, heart, pulse, oxygen and temperature. Tears filled Joanna's eyes as she looked at her baby girl. Bo clenched and unclenched his fists.

Finally, Joanna spoke. "How long will she be like this?"

"I wish we could give you a definite answer," Dr. McIntosh replied. "Once the anesthesia wears off, we'll have to see what her responses are. That ought to be in the next hour or so." She decided not to tell them her concerns because the anesthesia should already have been wearing off. They should have been seeing some response. She erred on the side of caution and excused herself to wait awhile in hopes that she would not have to further alarm Lucy's parents.

Dr. McIntosh came back an hour later. "Well, there's no real change. Lucy's blood count seems to be stabilizing some. Her temperature and her white count are high. She hasn't regained consciousness. I think we have the right antibiotics for now. We won't have the blood culture results back until at least tomorrow morning. It may be that there is another antibiotic that will be more effective to fight the infection. We won't know until then."

"Is it still the effects of the anesthetic, Doctor?" Joanna asked with a hint of hope in her voice.

"No, Mrs. Brady. The anesthetic has worn off and we are getting ready to move her into the intensive care unit one floor down. Because she hasn't improved, I'm going to ask a neurologist to consult. We're doing everything we can for her."

"Well, Doctor, you might try one more thing."

"What's that, Mrs. Brady?"

"Prayer, Doctor."

"Joanna, I'm Catholic and I pray for all of my patients. My prayers are already up there with yours."

"Thank you, Dr. McIntosh."

As the doctor walked through the double doors back into the unit, the elevator opened and Jessie burst out. Dressed in brown slacks, a tan cashmere sweater and Nike running shoes, she wore a heavy gold necklace and diamond earrings that would have made Elizabeth Taylor proud. Jessie's wealth, combined with her headstrong personality, convinced her that there was no situation that she could not dominate and control by the sheer force of her will. She marched over to where Joanna and Bo were seated and almost physically lifted her sister out of her chair, hugged her and then turned to Bo for a kiss on the cheek.

"Lucy's better, right, Jo?" she said with confidence although one look at the two parents told her that it wasn't so.

"No, Jessie, the doctor just left here and there's been no real change since I talked to you."

"Joanna, are you sure you've got the right doctors involved? I know about doctors and hospitals. I'm going in there and talk to them."

She started toward the unit and before she reached the double doors, a nurse who stood as tall as Jessie and outweighed her by fifty pounds blocked her way.

"Excuse me, ma'am. Is there some way I can help you?" the nurse said.

"No thank you, nurse," Jessie countered sternly. "I'm just going in there to check on my niece and talk to the doctors."

The nurse had handled this situation too many times to count, and in a low but self-assured voice, she said, "I'm sorry, ma'am. That won't be possible. You'll have to wait out here."

Not accustomed to being told no, Jessie was momentarily taken aback. Recovering quickly, she commanded, "Then get one of those doctors out here. I want to talk to him or her right now."

"Ma'am, they have very sick patients in there. I'll try to get your niece's doctor out as quick as I can."

The nurse walked through the doors and Jessie returned to sit beside her sister.

"I'll give them five minutes," she warned.

Fortunately, it didn't take that long before Dr. McIntosh came out. Sizing up Jessie, she decided that deference was the best approach.

"Joanna, I understand that this is your sister."

Before Joanna could introduce them, Jessie interrupted, "I am Mrs. Warren Woolsey from Fort Worth. I sit on the board of the largest hospital system in the metroplex and my foundation is a heavy contributor to most of the hospitals in this medical center, including this one. I want to make sure that you have the best doctors in Texas taking care of Lucy. Do I need to get on the phone and call Dr. DeBakey or Dr. Cooley?"

The doctors in the Houston medical center were not surprised by Jessie's attitude. As a renowned center of medicine, they regularly operated on and cared for princes, potentates, presidents, celebrities and politicians from all over the world. Each of them demanded excellence and they got it. However, it wasn't because of their money or station in life. These doctors considered themselves the best in the world, and they were going to provide the same care for Lucy as they would for the president.

"Mrs. Woolsey, I'm sure that if I thought that Dr. Cooley or Dr. DeBakey could help, they would be here. Your niece doesn't have a cardiovascular problem and I am certain that they would defer to the team that we have assembled. Frankly, I don't think that all the money in Texas is going to buy her better care."

"Then tell me what in tarnation is going on with my niece."

"I'm a gynecologist and an infectious disease specialist. Lucy had to be brought via Life Flight here from Texas City. She'd had an abortion and had two complications, her uterus was perforated and there were some retained fetal parts. She lost a lot of blood and had developed sepsis, an infection in the blood. I operated, removed the fetal parts and then sutured the perforation."

"That means she's going to be just fine, right, Dr. McIntosh?"

"I'm sorry, Mrs. Woolsey, but I'm afraid it's not that easy. She lost a lot of blood and I had to get Sam Hunt, a hematologist, involved. We've got her on antibiotics but I can't be sure they are the right ones until we get a culture back from the lab. Meantime, her temperature is still high. Trust me, Mrs. Woolsey. We're doing all we can do. If Lucy can be saved, I'll do it."

Jessie sized up Dr. McIntosh and recognized that Lucy was in good hands.

Smiling, she replied, "Thank you, Doctor. We'll be waiting."

Dr. McIntosh returned to the unit and Jessie turned to her sister who described what happened before she arrived. Shortly, a nurse let them know that Lucy had been moved to intensive care. They went one floor down and were permitted to see her briefly. She was being cared for by a short, stocky, black nurse who had an aura of proficiency about her.

"I'm Nurse Bancroft. I'll be responsible for your Lucy from three to eleven every evening. Which one of you is her mother?"

"I am," replied Joanna, dismayed to find that Lucy still had the same tubes and lines as she had upstairs. "This is Lucy's father, Bo, and this is my sister, Jessie, from Fort Worth."

"Well, I'm pleased to meet you all. My job is to take good care of Lucy and I'll do just that. This is the intensive care unit and until Lucy gets better, she'll have one nurse with her at all times. You're allowed to visit for about five minutes once an hour, family members only. That can include you, Jessie. The doctors are telling me that she is not going to change much during the night. If you all live close by, I suggest you go get some rest."

"Well, they don't live close by. We have rooms at the Marriott across the street," Jessie interrupted.

"Why don't you go over there to your rooms? We have that number and will call you if there is any change."

Although she was reluctant to do so, Joanna bowed to

Nurse Bancroft's suggestion. She squeezed her daughter's hand, told her she loved her and followed Jessie and Bo to the hotel. Joanna slept a few fitful hours. At five A.M. she got up, dressed and went back to the hospital. This time a different nurse told her there was no change. To Joanna that was no solace. With a heavy heart, she returned to the waiting room.

Everyone was quiet. Some of the men had two days' growth of beard. Some slept. Many had haggard, worried looks, fearing the worst yet hoping for the best. The surroundings did nothing for her mood. As Joanna absentmindedly gazed at the television, the elevator opened. Bo and Jessie, carrying food and coffee from McDonald's, joined her. After eating two breakfast tacos, Bo left to go to their house to pack a suitcase. Clearly, the crisis would last several days.

Behind the closed doors, the doctors were making their morning rounds. Dr. Hunt, the hematologist, found that the blood drawn at seven-fifteen showed some slight improvement. He knew he was only succeeding in stabilizing the patient and he could not hope for real improvement until Dr. McIntosh could find the right antibiotics. He had to keep her DIC in check until that time. At Lucy's bedside, Dr. McIntosh joined him, disappointed to find that her fever hovered around one hundred and three and had spiked a couple of times to one hundred and five. And, her white count was going up, not down. They did not have the right combination of antibiotics on board, but the lab had not reported on the culture. Her choices were to try something different, another shot in the dark, or to give the lab a few more hours. She regularly had to make such judgment calls and elected to give the lab more time. If she didn't have a report by early afternoon, she would reevaluate Lucy.

Returning to the professional building across the street, Dr. McIntosh saw patients until early afternoon when she called the lab again. They had nothing to report. Dr. McIntosh hung up the phone and weighed her options. She could wait no longer. Considering the various possibilities, especially the aggressiveness of the bacteria, she concluded that it was most likely a Group D strep, one of the most virulent and potent of bacteria assaulting patients in the modern era. Once it established a beachhead, the army of bacteria multiplied and moved with the swiftness and cunning of the Allies attacking Normandy on D Day. Sometimes people had been known to die within seventy-two hours from their first symptoms. Dr. McIntosh had an uphill battle. At least the antibiotics were maintaining a holding action. Now, she would change the battle plan, substituting massive doses of Vancomycin, one of the most potent of antibiotics and one that good infectious disease specialists saved for the worst of bacteria. She called the ICU and changed the order, discontinuing the previous antibiotics and ordering one gram of Vancomycin IV every twelve hours. She also ordered a stat white count to allow her to measure the impact of the new drug. The nurse reported the change to Joanna, Bo and Jessie.

"Does this mean she is going to get better now?" asked Joanna.

"Mrs. Brady, I'm not the doctor. What I do know is this is a powerful drug and we can hope for the best," not adding that this patient was going downhill so fast that she might soon be classified as "a train wreck," a term used by the medical staff when talking among themselves about a potentially terminal patient. Very few people survived a train wreck.

Their hopes raised, Joanna, Bo and Jessie went downstairs to the cafeteria, confident that when they got back, Lucy would be awake and recognize them. Their hopes turned out to be no more than dreams. Nothing had changed. They called Dr. McIntosh who explained, "If we have the right antibiotic, as sick as Lucy is, it will be forty-eight to seventy-two hours before we will notice any improvement."

Jessie demanded to know what was going on. Did they need more doctors? Did they need to send her to Johns Hopkins or the Mayo Clinic? Should she charter a jet?

Two days after Dr. McIntosh had switched the antibiotics,

she found the family in the waiting room after her morning rounds. "Are you guys holding up okay? Joanna, your eyes tell me that you're not getting enough sleep. We have a little good news. The antibiotic seems to be working. Lucy's white count is going down. While her temperature is high, it's moving down. I can't say that she has turned the corner. Nonetheless, there is room for a little optimism. Also, it looks like we are going to save her uterus. If she hadn't started improving on the antibiotics, we might have had to perform a hysterectomy. Fortunately, I think that risk has passed. On the negative side, we still are unsure of the extent of the DIC since we have been keeping her packed with blood products. Also, we're calling in a nephrologist, a kidney specialist, because of some of the complications that can result from being on the blood products. That's not unexpected and I think that we can handle it."

Joanna had quietly absorbed all of this as she mentally counted all of the specialists, residents and interns involved in her daughter's care, then asked, "Doctor, I suppose I know the answer to this, but is she waking up at all?"

Dr. McIntosh's face clouded as she replied. "No. I promise, though, that I'll tell you the minute we see any signs of her coming out of it. Realistically, I think that we are looking at two or three days at the earliest."

Dr. McIntosh's prediction proved to be too optimistic. Two days later, Lucy's white count approached normal and her temperature hovered around one hundred degrees. The antibiotics were working. The hematologist started backing off on blood products as he became satisfied with Lucy's blood count. In spite of the improvement, Lucy didn't respond. Dr. McIntosh again discussed Lucy's status with her family.

"Joanna, Bo, Jessie, as you know, Dr. Gerald Rosenthal, a neurologist, has been monitoring Lucy with us. He and I have agreed that it's time for him to get more involved."

For several days Jessie had done a good job of keeping her mouth shut and her thoughts to herself. Now she erupted again. "Dr. McIntosh, what kind of games are you people playing? Your team of so-called experts chose the treatment plan. You pumped her full of antibiotics and blood products. You tell us that the antibiotics are working and her bleeding is under control, but you still have tubes running everywhere, have her breathing through a ventilator because she can't do it herself and worst of all, you can't wake her up. Isn't it about time that you doctors quit practicing and get on with getting this girl well?"

"Jessie, calm down," Joanna interrupted. "These doctors are doing their best and your temper is not helping anything." She turned her attention back to Dr. McIntosh. "What's Dr. Rosenthal going to do now that you can't?"

"We think that we need to be looking for signs of central nervous system problems that could be resulting from the DIC or the infection."

"Now, I think that we have too goddamned many doctors involved," Jessie said. "What we need is one good country doctor like the one that I use in Fort Worth. He wouldn't need all these pedigreed specialists and professors."

Having her fill of her sister's comments, Joanna yelled, "Shut up, Jessie, or go back to the Marriott and watch soap operas."

"If you like, I'll just go back to Fort Worth," Jessie threatened but kept her seat as Dr. McIntosh excused herself.

Dr. Rosenthal was originally from the East Coast and still spoke with a slight Brooklyn accent. He had been trained in New York City and sought residencies at Johns Hopkins, Stanford and Baylor. Accepted at all three, he elected Baylor to enjoy the warm weather for a few years and never went back. As a doctor who took care of children with muscular dystrophy and adults with diseases like multiple sclerosis and Parkinson's along with victims of all ages who suffered from strokes and paralysis, he had to be good as well as compassionate. Now in his fifties, he combined the excellence of his training with close to thirty years experience in caring for such illnesses and injuries. With a grandfatherly appearance, most people he met took an immediate liking to him, including Joanna and even

Jessie. Up until now, he had remained in the background since he and Dr. McIntosh had decided that it was better for Lucy's primary physician to interface with the family. This time, after he had examined her again, he introduced himself and made some slight small talk. Then, he told them his findings and what he proposed.

"The other doctors have done a good job. The infection and DIC are under control. My job is to figure out why Lucy is not waking up and what we can do about it. I don't find any clinical evidence of swelling in the brain. Her pupils are reactive and her reflexes seem to be intact. That's all good. DIC can cause hemorrhaging in a variety of places. I've done one CT scan of her brain, but it's time to do another. Hopefully, that will provide us with more information."

Joanna asked the same question once more, hoping to get a different answer from another doctor. "She is going to wake up and be all right, isn't she?"

"Mrs. Brady, we are going to continue to be optimistic, but there are no guarantees. I think the chances are good that she will wake up. Assuming she does, I need to warn you that she could have some brain damage and may require months of physical therapy. Even with therapy, she may still be left with some residual disability. Let's hope for the best."

Dr. Rosenthal excused himself and told them he would be back after the CT scan. Joanna lost herself in thoughts of her teenage daughter with long-term brain damage. Will she wake up? Will she be able to talk? To walk? To get back to her classes? To sing? To have babies? Those were questions that she would need to ask the doctors when Lucy woke. Once again she turned to prayer.

Late that afternoon, Dr. Rosenthal returned with the news. The DIC had caused some hemorrhaging on the left side of the brain that was causing her continuing problems. It had stopped but the blood was still present. It would eventually be absorbed. If they were lucky, when the blood was gone, Lucy would start responding. Over time there was the possibility of a recovery, but Dr. Rosenthal warned that it would be days to weeks before they would know the full extent of any damage. Just when Joanna thought she could see the light at the end of the tunnel, it dimmed and flickered. Fortunately, it did not go out.

21

Dr. Rosenthal did four more CT scans over the next two weeks, each showing less blood. In the intensive care unit, Joanna had just spent her five minutes talking to Lucy. As she got up to leave, she squeezed Lucy's hand and told her she loved her when she felt Lucy squeeze her hand in response. At first she thought that she imagined something until it occurred again. When she looked, Lucy's eyes were open.

"Nurse, nurse," she cried. "Come quick. Lucy's awake!"

The nurse came to the bedside, evaluated her patient and paged Dr. Rosenthal who was there within twenty minutes. While Lucy was in and out of consciousness, there was no doubt that she was awakening. Joanna was convinced that the nightmare was over. She was right, of course. She was also wrong. The nightmare of the hospital with her daughter teetering on the brink of death was about to end, but a new public nightmare was about to engulf the whole family.

Once she woke, Lucy's otherwise healthy young body responded quickly. Within days the physicians were able to wean her from the ventilator, as she was able to breathe on her own. Her reflexes were generally intact. She tried to talk, but her words were slurred. Dr. Rosenthal was unsure of the cause. It could have been the result of being on the ventilator for so many weeks, or it could have been some continuing neurological involvement.

It was late in the afternoon when Dr. Rosenthal found Joanna and Bo in the waiting room. Lowering himself into an easy chair beside them, he grunted and then said, "I may never be able to get out of this chair again. You may have to start taking care of me." He shut his eyes for a few moments and then looked at the expectant faces. "Here's her status. She's made a lot of improvement. We need to give her two or three weeks of intensive physical and speech therapy. Hopefully, you'll be able to take her home after that. You'll need to work with the physical therapists to learn what to do because you'll have to continue the therapy for quite a few more weeks once she gets out of here."

The therapy started the next day with Joanna and Jessie observing at first. Two days later they started assisting. Even though Lucy cooperated, Joanna saw that she was merely going through the motions. When the physical therapist would try to push her a little further, there were times that she would just shake her head, stop and refuse to go on. Speech therapists worked with her in the afternoon, and again there was only partial cooperation. No one was pleased with her progress. Soon everyone recognized that her recovery might drag on for months.

Joanna was convinced that Lucy was still experiencing severe emotional trauma. Even when she was in her room she generally ignored her family, staring at whatever sitcom was on the TV instead. Within a few weeks, the rehabilitation specialists told Joanna that there was nothing they could do for her that could not be done at home. They suggested a discharge if she could continue the therapy and care. Jessie rose to the occasion.

"Look, Joanna," Jessie argued, "you've been off work for nearly two months now. I've got a big house that is empty except for me and a housekeeper. And I've got nothing to do. Let me take Lucy to Fort Worth. I've been watching the therapy and I can do it as well as anyone. I'll also have therapists come to the house. As soon as she's ready, she'll come home."

The mother in Joanna cried no. Ultimately, the logic of her sister's argument won her over. Besides, she could drive the five hours to Fort Worth to be with Lucy most weekends.

Jessie immediately called Anita Jimenez, her housekeeper of thirty years, and told her to rearrange the sunroom to make it a suitable bedroom for Lucy. French doors opened from the downstairs study to a thirty-by-thirty-foot room with floor to ceiling windows on three sides, and double french doors opened to a patio and garden. The room was filled with cushioned wicker furniture. The view of the patio and garden was spectacular, and beyond the garden was the green expanse of Rivercrest Country Club. The room faced west, catching the late afternoon sun and reflecting it onto bookcases filled with crystal glassware and what Jessie called her knickknacks from the four corners of the world.

Jessie told Anita to get the gardeners to store some of the wicker furniture, bring a bed from upstairs, raid her daughter's former room to fill the bed with stuffed animals and put pictures on the walls that would please a girl of seventeen. She also had the gardeners build a ramp to the patio doors for Lucy's wheelchair.

Anita met Jessie and Lucy at Dallas Love Field and the three women drove the forty-five minutes to Fort Worth. It was a warm, bright March day in North Texas, a day when spring was doing its best to shove winter aside. Anita and Jessie talked while Lucy silently looked out the window. Arriving at the house, Anita wheeled Lucy to the side entrance and up the ramp to the sunroom. Opening the door, she proudly displayed her work.

"So, how you like this, Lucy?" Anita exclaimed, obviously pleased with the transformation. "The best room in the house, just for you."

"Why, Anita, this is perfect," Jessie replied.

Lucy said nothing.

The room still had a wicker couch and two wicker chairs along with the bookcases full of Jessie's prized possessions. It now contained a double bed almost hidden by stuffed animals, a nightstand with a bell, telephone and TV remote control, a large television and a small refrigerator, loaded with bottled water, fruit juice and various soft drinks.

"Lucy, what do you think?" Jessie asked.

Lucy stared off into space and finally replied, "It's okay."

"Lucy, when you're in bed, you have your own remote for

the television. You can use that bell to get my attention, or Anita's," Jessie added. "If that doesn't work, the telephone is on a separate line and you can call the main phone number. It will ring on the other phones in the house and out in Anita's apartment over the garage. You know where the bathroom is and either of us will help you when it's necessary. I've got a physical therapist lined up to start with you tomorrow. She'll take up where they left off in Houston. Anita and I will assist her however we can." She smiled as she concluded, "It won't be very long before you'll be up and around and on your own again."

The therapists worked with Lucy twice a day to strengthen her muscles. It worked as planned. Only Lucy's mind did not respond. Lucy went through the motions with the therapists. When they left, Lucy got out of bed only to get in her wheelchair. Anita brought her meals and tried to engage her in conversation. All she got were responses of "Yes, ma'am," "No, ma'am," and "Thank you." When the therapists were not there, Lucy spent her time watching cartoons or sitting alone on the patio.

After a few weeks, one of the therapists told Jessie that there was nothing to prevent Lucy from walking. Jessie considered telling Lucy that therapy was over. If she wanted to eat, she would have to walk to the dining room to join them. If she wanted to go to the bathroom, it was right there. Then Jessie reminded herself of what Lucy had been through and that she had almost died.

Instead, she decided that she would get Lucy out of the house. There was plenty to see and do in Fort Worth. They started their daily expeditions with a visit to the zoo and followed with almost daily excursions to the botanical gardens, the art museums, and the tourist areas of the old Cowtown stockyards. On Saturdays they went to Jessie's ranch, where Lucy's parents often joined them. On most Sundays they drove from the ranch to the City of Miracles to attend church.

22

As the weeks went by, T.J. began to notice the girl in the wheelchair sitting beside Jessie each Sunday. When he made discreet inquiries and learned that Jessie was her aunt, he looked for an opportunity to learn more about the girl and found it one evening at sunset.

T.J. appeared on the nineteenth floor as he usually did. There was no sound until his reflection appeared in the window. Jessie was no longer surprised to see him. In fact, she actually enjoyed his company, although she had yet to figure out how much of him was real and how much was showmanship. This time before he had a chance to speak, she said, "Welcome, T.J. You know where the glasses are. It looks like we're in for a spectacular sunset and I'm pleased to share it with you."

T.J. did as he was told and returned with a glass and ice, helping himself to bourbon from a flask bigger than the one that Jessie had first carried. They sipped their drinks and enjoyed the sunset until T.J. broke the silence. "Tell me about your niece, Jessie."

Jessie stalled for a few moments, not sure where to begin or how much to tell. After a moment's reflection, she decided that the man beside her was a minister and he might as well hear it all. "Well, to start, she's the daughter of my sister in Texas City. She's seventeen and she had an abortion. We learned in the hospital that she had been raped, but by then it was too late to do anything about the assault."

"Did she tell anyone about the rape?"

"No, T.J., she kept it quiet. I better give you a little family history that may help you understand Lucy. My sister calls herself Joanna. That wasn't her birth name. Our parents named her Abigail; Abigail Addison. She's eight years younger than me. I was already in Fort Worth, married to Warren, when she was entering puberty. I heard from some friends back in Texas City that my little sister was becoming a hell raiser. Turns out she was smoking at twelve, drinking beer behind a neighbor's garage at thirteen and lost her virginity to the first boy that tried after she turned fourteen. I tried to talk to her only she wouldn't listen. My friends told me she drank and screwed her way through high school. The boys in her senior class appreciated her so much that they voted her most popular girl."

"Jessie," T.J. interrupted with an astonished voice and a gleam in his eye, "did Lucy follow in her footsteps?"

"Heavens, no!

"I'm not near through. After she graduated from high school, Joanna became a born-again Christian. You'll like this story. A high school buddy wanted to get laid and took her out for a sunset sail on Galveston Bay. After they made love, he promptly fell asleep. Sometime, T.J., after we know each other a little better, maybe you can explain why men seem to associate sex and sleep. Anyway, as Joanna told me later, while her lover slept, she lay nude on the deck and started counting stars as they filled the night. As she studied the heavens she began to realize that the universe couldn't be an accident. There had to be a greater power to have created all that she saw above her. Like that she was a Christian and I can tell you that no greater believer walks the planet than my sister."

"What about her name, Jessie?"

"Ah, yes. Her name. You remember in the Book of Luke, Jesus healed some women of 'evil spirits.' They were called Mary, Joanna and Susanna. Joanna went to church the day after her rebirth and was given a Bible by the minister. That afternoon she discovered the story in Luke and tried each of the names in front of the mirror in her room. She settled on Joanna and never let anyone call her Abigail again.

"That fall she got a job in one of the plants and met Bo. They married, bought a little three-bedroom house and Lucy's brother, Junior, came along. Lucy was born a few years later."

"Sorry, Jessie. I'm still confused. What does this have to do with Lucy's rape and abortion?"

"T.J., just bear with me. Lucy's mother became the most fundamentalist Christian you ever saw. It wasn't that she was a poor mother. She was a very good mother. However, when you combine her misspent youth with an Evangelical Christian, you get a mother that did more preaching than listening. Lucy told me later that when she was raped and even when she found out she was pregnant, she couldn't tell her mother for fear that she would be forced to confess in front of the congregation, and her mother would make her carry the baby—something she wasn't ready to do at seventeen."

"What about her dad? A lot of girls have strong bonds with their fathers."

"Bo's a good man. He's like thousands of fathers in South Texas, maybe all over the country. He's always been faithful to Joanna. He brings home a steady paycheck as a supervisor in his plant. He coached Junior in Little League. His passion is the outdoors. He wants to be hunting dove, duck and deer in the right seasons. Otherwise, he's got a twenty-two-foot Boston Whaler that he takes to Galveston Bay nearly every weekend. You know what a Boston Whaler is, T.J.?"

"No, ma'am. They must not have had them out on Eagle Mountain Lake when I was growing up."

"It's a fishing boat. Pretty much the Cadillac of fishing boats from what I understand. Most houses in Texas City have one of those and a pickup in the driveway. Anyway, Bo's attitude has always been that he'll put a roof over his family's head and give them three squares a day, and it's up to Joanna to raise Lucy. You understanding now why Lucy didn't talk much to her parents?"

"I'm beginning to, Jessie. Tell me what happened."

"First, let me make it clear that what I'm telling you is coming from Lucy. She's told me bits and pieces and we'll probably never get the whole story. She met this boy, Jason, at the start of the school year at her church's Sunday evening youth fellowship. Some place to meet a rapist, huh, T.J.?"

"Now, Jessie, God gave ample quantities of testosterone to most men. Even us Christians sometimes have trouble controlling it," he said with a grin.

The grin took Jessie aback since she considered this to be a most serious conversation. Frowning at T.J.'s grin, she continued. "Jason chased her for weeks. He hung around outside her classes at school and began to walk her home from the youth fellowship on Sunday evening. Then he got her into his truck for some mild petting until one Sunday evening when it was raining so hard that he talked her into waiting in the church parking lot until the storm passed. That's when he assaulted her. According to Lucy, he only barely got it in before he ejaculated down her leg. You can imagine how hard I had to work to get her to tell me that much.

"Once it happened she wanted to tell her mother but was scared to do so. Bo probably would have gone after the boy with a shotgun. Anyway, she kept it to herself and a few weeks later found that she was pregnant. She called Population Planning in Houston and arranged for an abortion on a Friday teachers' work day. The abortion went bad and she almost died. The doctors in Houston saved her life."

It took Jessie nearly an hour and a refill of each of their drinks to tell the whole story. She concluded with her frustration about a girl who remained so emotionally scarred that she had no interest in walking or anything else that life had to offer.

"What about the young man, Jessie?"

"All I know is his name is Jason. Nothing else." Jessie's jaw clinched. "But, I can guarantee you that if I ever get him in my sights, one bullet will be enough."

Startled by the anger in her voice, T.J. took her hand and beckoned her to kneel with him, facing the disappearing sun and saying, "Let us pray. Lord God, first we want to give You thanks for bringing Lucy back this far. Like the chances You have given me, she has an opportunity for a second life. Her parents and her aunt have exhausted their abilities and Lucy has yet to be completely healed. We need Your help and Your guidance, Father. Help her find emotional peace so that she may get on with her life. Grant her that peace, dear God, and soothe the anger in her aunt's heart. Amen."

"Amen," echoed Jessie, as they rose to their feet.

23

The conversation about Lucy's rape and her mother's wild youth was too much for T.J. to handle. "Jessie, let's go up one floor to my penthouse. I doubt you've ever seen it. I have a great balcony and an even better selection of red wines."

Jessie hesitated as her mind quickly ran through the implications of such an offer. Finally, she concluded that it was merely an invitation for another drink from a friend and accepted. T.J. led her to an oak-paneled wall with no door. She was about to say something when he pushed on the panel that opened to reveal a spiral stairway to the next floor. T.J. stepped aside and motioned her to lead the way. The stairs were illuminated by a soft blue light. At the top Jessie pushed on a panel and it opened into T.J.'s penthouse. The sofas were gold; the drapes were gold; the chandelier was gold; the carpet was gold. The lights were dim and Frank Sinatra crooned from hidden speakers.

"I hope you like Sinatra, Jessie. He was my favorite before I took my long sleep."

"Give me him or Tony Bennett and I won't complain," Jessie replied, "although I have taken a liking to Jimmy Buffet in recent years."

Almost before she finished the sentence "My Way" became "Cheeseburger in Paradise." Jessie smiled as T.J. sorted through his rack full of red wines and settled on a Shiraz from California's central coast. He picked two large wineglasses and filled them to the brim. Handing one to Jessie, he escorted her out to his balcony that faced west.

"Would you look at that, T.J.?" Jessie said as she leaned over the balcony. "Every star seems to be shining just for the occupants of this balcony. Just think. Those are the same stars that led to my sister's rebirth nearly thirty years ago."

She sipped the red wine as she contemplated what would happen to her sister and her family. T.J. set his glass on the iron rail and turned her to face him. As he leaned forward to kiss her, Jessie pushed him away.

"No, T.J. I know that your testosterone has gone untapped for twelve years, but I won't be the one to turn the spigot. I assume that you find me to be an attractive woman, even at my age. Still, I had a husband that no one can replace and I'll stay faithful to him until I see him up where those stars are shining."

"Forgive me, Jessie," T.J. replied. "I got carried away by the spirits and the moment. I value your friendship. Have a seat and let's talk about something different, like your ranch that I understand is not too far out there in the distance."

"Apology accepted, T.J. Let me tell you about the ranch."

After they finished their wine, T.J. went with Jessie down the elevator to the garage and walked with her to her Jaguar, blessing her for the sacrifice she had made for her niece. As Jessie drove away, a plan started to evolve in T.J.'s ever-fertile mind. He could use Lucy as the centerpiece of another miracle, a very important one at that, because she almost died from an abortion.

24

In the months since T.J. had returned to his ministry, things could not have gone better. The money kept rolling in, and his television ratings demonstrated that he once again had become one of the top three televangelists in the country.

During this election year, the presidential candidates were quizzed about their stand on abortion at almost every campaign stop. Even congressional candidates were not immune to litmus test questions. The religious right condemned abortion. If a candidate would not support their belief that abortion anywhere, anytime, anyplace and under any circumstance was wrong, he or she could depend on the religious right to attack with a vengeance not seen since Jesus threw the money changers out of the temple.

Unfortunately for the Chosen, his long absence from the political arena put him out on the fringe of many of the fundamentalist political causes and his Right Side political action committee was not nearly as rich or as effective as he demanded. He needed something to focus national attention on him. The more he studied the issues of the religious right the more he realized that abortion generated more heat, anger and debate than nearly all other issues combined. If he could make abortion his personal mission, it would serve to catapult him back to the forefront of the religious conservatives where he belonged. Although he had not completed his plan, it must begin with national attention converging on him as he healed Lucy. Of course, he could not discuss any of this with Mrs. Warren Woolsey. While a rich woman, she was also a person who valued her privacy. She would not permit her niece to be used, no matter how noble the purpose.

Two weeks later, T.J. crafted a sermon on the power of God, ending it with God's power to heal. As was his custom, he waited backstage until the assistant pastors had made announcements and warmed up the audience. The Miracle Singers followed them. Their songs and music were intended to entertain and to get the faithful on their feet. If a few danced in the aisles, so much the better. The formula had been tested. Jerry Abraham had not invented it. He had only improved on it. The Chosen came close to perfecting it. After the offering buckets were passed, there was time for one more song before T.J. made his appearance. After the singing there was silence. Followed by darkness. Then, a red spotlight directed the audience's attention to the upper stage where the Chosen stood on a circular platform, apparently suspended in midair, dressed in his white robe with the gold braid sash, the light flashing from his dark sunglasses. He raised his hands and the audience began to cheer. The platform, still bathed in the spotlight, began to descend through the darkness until it stopped at the back of the stage where the Chosen stepped down and slowly walked to the pulpit. With the power of God as his message, he launched into an oratory that lasted thirty minutes before he turned to God's ability to heal all of man's illnesses. As he touched on various maladies and infirmities, he held up first one hand and then the other, counting them off on his fingers, with the tenth finger reserved for healing the lame and crippled. As he finished the ten, he walked toward the governors' circle. A white spotlight shined on Jessie and Lucy. At first Jessie was uncertain about what was happening. Then she started shaking her head. T.J. ignored her as he approached.

"My friends, for the past several weeks I have watched this lady and her niece, sitting here every Sunday. I have seen this beautiful young woman in a wheelchair and I have asked God why? Today God has given me an answer, but not to my question. Instead He has answered by telling me that if I have the strength and faith in Him, I can make this young lady rise up out of her wheelchair and walk again."

The spotlight and cameras showed Lucy as a frightened teenager with nowhere to hide. T.J. approached, placing his right hand on her head and lifting his left hand to God as he began to speak in tongues. He paused, looked at the television cameras and commanded, "Lucy, stand up!"

When Lucy didn't move, he commanded again, "Lucy, in the name of God, forsake that wheelchair and rise on your own two legs!"

Mesmerized by the situation, Lucy gulped and pushed herself out of the wheelchair. Gasps from the audience were followed by cheers. T.J. demanded silence and walked back to the pulpit, turning as he reached it and commanded, "Lucy, come to me!"

This time Lucy hesitated only a moment before walking slowly to the preacher. When she reached the pulpit, T.J. placed his hand on her head and turned to the congregation, crying, "Behold the power of God!"

The clapping, cheering, yelling and stomping of feet were deafening. Lucy tried to blink back tears and stood beside

T.J. as he said the final prayer and the stage went dark. When the house lights came up, T.J. and Lucy were gone.

The ushers led a furious Jessie backstage. The Chosen and Lucy were surrounded by his entourage who were praising him for the most brilliant performance since his resurrection. Jessie pushed her way through the staff members, and getting right in the face of the Chosen, she screamed, "How could you do that? How could you take advantage of my niece and make a spectacle of her? How could you betray the trust I had in you? You're no man of God. You're nothing more than a self-serving hypocrite!"

Jessie's tirade stunned the crowd around the Chosen into silence. For once T.J. was also at a loss for words.

A quiet voice interrupted. "Aunt Jessie, it's all right," Lucy said. "Something happened out there. When he put his hands on me, I felt forgiven for the first time since I had that awful thing done. It's like I woke from a long sleep. I'm fine. Don't blame the Chosen."

Jessie paused in midbreath, turning to look at Lucy. In the months since her niece's surgery, Jessie had rarely heard her speak more than three words. Jessie took two steps to face her niece and hugged her as she said, "Welcome back, Lucy. We've missed you."

As he looked at the attractive seventeen-year-old, T.J. said, "Jessie, what I have done here is just a beginning. When Lucy is ready, I think I can further improve her mental outlook with some pastoral counseling."

Not sure what had happened, Lucy looked at T.J. who only smiled in return. Jessie took her niece's hand and left. Maybe there had been a minor miracle that day. Maybe it was God's will. Maybe it was the powerful presence of the Chosen that had brought Lucy out of her shell.

As T.J. watched them walk away, he turned to continue receiving the acclamation of his staff as his mind leaped to the next day. His plan was beginning to come together.

25

On Monday morning at nine o'clock T.J. met with his public relations people. He ordered the staff to take the video clips of his "miracle" with Lucy and add a voice-over, describing her near-death experience. Next, he directed them to disseminate the videos to every network, cable news service and religious channel in the country, along with every television station in the country's top hundred markets. Of course, not all of them would feature the video. But, if it were a slow news day, this kind of human-interest story would garner attention. He had important reasons for wanting Lucy's name to become a household word. ´

At ten o'clock, he called the receptionist at the City's "think tank" and asked her to send for Albert Hammond and Riba Clibourn, the two staffers who studied and analyzed the abortion debate. Albert was forty, thin, with greasy red hair, and wore old-fashioned black horn-rimmed glasses that made him appear akin to an emaciated owl. Riba was about the same age. In contrast to Albert, she was short and dumpy with brown stringy hair and a face that occasionally saw lipstick and little else. What they lacked in appearance they made up in fervor for their cause. Both came from families of strong religious faith, one Catholic, and one Assembly of God. They had adopted abortion as their cause while still in college and had dedicated their lives to ending abortion in the United States. They gathered evidence, compiled statistics, catalogued the daily influx of newspaper clippings that mentioned anything about abortion and reviewed radio and television clips where abortion was debated or discussed. Additionally, they compiled a dossier on every politician who achieved at least the rank of state representative and tracked the status of any bill anywhere in the country where abortion was the topic.

The receptionist announced their arrival, and T.J. met

them at the door of his office, escorting them to a sitting area overlooking Fort Worth in the distance. After exchanging small talk, T.J. got to the point. "Tell me the status of our pro-life movement."

"Reverend Luther," Albert said, "I'm not sure where you want me to start. The war is being waged on so many fronts. I suppose, since this is an election year, we might as well start with the politics of abortion. On the Democratic side, it's easy. All of the Democratic candidates for president are pro-choice, meaning, of course, they favor a woman's right to choose abortion without limitation. On the Republican side, it's a hodgepodge of rhetoric. One or two candidates are against abortion in any form for any reason. Some are saying that abortion should be banned except in cases of rape, incest or the health of the mother. Another takes the position that abortion should only be allowed if the life of the mother is threatened. Even among the Republican candidates, they often have a hard time keeping their position straight, particularly if asked how they would advise their own teenage daughter if she became pregnant. As to Congress, they pretty much line up the same way except that a number of the Republican women in Congress come down on the pro-choice side, as do a few Republican men. I don't know of any Democrats in Congress who are pro-life."

"Is there any hope of a favorable bill getting through Congress and having it signed into law by the president?" questioned T.J.

"Not in our lifetime. At least not in mine, Reverend, since I'm not sure exactly how many lifetimes you have," replied Albert.

T.J. smiled and turned to Riba. "How about the media, out on the picket lines or the judicial system—any better hope?"

"Hope springs eternal, Reverend. We are fighting the battle on all fronts and we take our victories where we can get them. Our media attacks on abortion clinics and doctors are having some impact. Sadly, most of the media are liberal and usually pro-choice. They look for opportunities to paint us with a big black brush. As to the judicial system, even with our conservative Supreme Court, I don't see *Roe v. Wade* being overturned anytime soon. We have had some success in backing a few medical malpractice cases around the country. I must tell you, though, they're difficult to win. The bottom line is that the abortion debate has been around for twenty-five hundred years or more and I don't see it going away."

That piqued T.J.'s attention. "What do you mean, twenty-five hundred years? I thought that *Roe v. Wade* was only about thirty years old."

"You're right," Riba continued, "at least partially. The Supreme Court announced the *Roe* decision in 1973. Only that didn't start the debate. It's at least as old as the Hippocratic oath. Hippocrates wrote his oath over four hundred years before Christ. Physicians have been taking some form of that oath ever since then. Some have modified it or taken it out. I promise you though, Reverend, that you aren't onto something new. Just the opposite, as a matter of fact."

"Well, I'll be damned," T.J. exclaimed. "Pardon my language. Doesn't look like the issue is going to go away anytime soon then, is it?"

"No, sir, it's not," Albert answered.

"What about funding? Do those of us on the pro-life side have sufficient funds?" T.J. asked.

"The answer to that would be a very strong yes," Riba said. "Both sides are well-funded. It's the single most divisive social issue of our time, and the true believers, no matter which side they're on, are willing to dig deep when the occasion calls for it. There are at least a dozen strong national groups on both sides, with hundreds of local chapters. 'Passionate' is not a strong enough word for the people who have taken this as their cause, no matter which side they choose."

"Well, now," T.J. pondered, "it looks to me that if we were to get out in front on this issue, we might just take over the leadership of the religious right. The Right Side could become the biggest and most well-funded political organization in the country."

"I don't think that's unreasonable, Reverend Luther, if you could find a way to galvanize public opinion." Riba smiled at the thought of working for the organization that would be leading the way on the single most important issue in her life.

"If I needed a million dollars up front for the right reason and, additionally, the backing of these so-called, well-funded pro-life organizations, you figure I could get it?"

"For the right cause, Reverend, in a heartbeat."

"Then, I reckon I better get me a lawyer and a damn good one at that," T.J. mused. He excused his consultants and contemplated the plan that had been simmering in his brain. Fortunately, he knew of a damn good one.

26

Judge Arbuckle hollered down the hall, "Tank, you in there?"

"Yes, sir, Judge. Be right there," Johnny Bob yelled as he left his office and appeared at the judge's door.

"Sit down, son. I have a little case here that you might be interested in. It's a plaintiff case. The bank's lawyer downstairs signed it up. He doesn't do trial work and referred it up here. Gonna be a tough case on liability but the damages are respectable. Our client had a stop sign out on the north edge of town at Highway 79. It was night. He saw lights way down the road and figured he had plenty of time. Turned out he was wrong. The lights were on the front of an eighteen-wheeler that clipped the tail end of his pickup before he got out of the intersection. The collision spun him around and he ended up in a ditch against a telephone pole. He suffered a compound fracture of the left leg and a bad concussion along with some cuts and bruises. Eighteen-wheeler left a lot of skid marks. You might be able to put speed on their driver. There's one other thing. Our man had just left the roadhouse at that intersection. He might have had a little too much to drink. It's a long shot, but I suspect you don't have much else to do. We have it on a forty-percent contingent fee and have to pay a quarter of that to the referring lawyer. If we collect anything, you'll be in for half of our piece."

Johnny Bob leaped at the chance. According to the police report, the truck left over three hundred feet of skids. The medical bills totaled $15,340 and the client, one Danny Potts, had been off work as a switchman at the rail yard for six months while his leg healed. That added another $8,000 in damages. Johnny Bob called the client and told him he was on the way to visit. He was not surprised to find that the house was a two-bedroom frame with rocking chairs on the small front porch. However, he didn't like finding his new client sitting on the porch, drinking a beer at ten in the morning.

As he climbed the steps, he introduced himself. "Danny, I'm J. Robert Tisdale. I'm going to try your case for you."

Potts set his beer on the porch rail and got to his feet. "Glad to see you, Mr. Tisdale. I don't know how you are as a lawyer," he said as he looked the big man up and down, "but I sure would want you on my side in a fight. Pull up a chair. Can I get you a beer?"

"No thanks to the beer, and as to fighting, I expect to do that in the courtroom, but I don't want to lie to you. This is going to be my first trial."

"Hell, everybody's got to start somewhere. I expect you'll just work harder than anyone else. What do you need to know?"

Johnny Bob thought a minute as he sized up the little man in front of him, a beer bottle in hand and the start of a beer belly on an otherwise slender frame. "Let's start with what is in your hand. How much did you have to drink that night?"

"Let me tell you something, Mr. Tisdale. What do I call you anyway?"

"You might as well call me Johnny Bob. That's what most folks around here do."

"I was in that roadhouse playing shuffleboard for three

hours and only had three beers the whole time. You can check with Jake, the bartender. He'll tell you the truth."

Johnny Bob looked his new client right in the eye and said, "Now, Danny, don't lie to me. I'm your lawyer. I can deal with whatever the facts are. Only, I don't want any surprises at the courthouse."

"God's truth, counselor. I'll swear on a stack of Bibles."

"Forget the stack of Bibles. I'll check it out with the bartender," Johnny Bob responded as he changed the subject. "How come you didn't make it across the intersection?"

"Listen, Johnny Bob, that trucker had to be flying like a bat outta hell. Lot of those truckers don't notice that the speed limit changes just about there, drops down to forty-five as you're coming into town. Either that or they don't give a damn. If he'd been driving the speed limit, I would have been two blocks away before he got to that intersection." Danny's voice rose as he relived the incident, "I could've been killed!"

"All right, Danny. You just take it easy. We're going to trial at the end of next month. And, watch your beer drinking, particularly in public. This is a small town. No telling who may end up on the jury."

When Johnny Bob reported to the judge, the older man stroked his chin and looked out the window before speaking. "Tank, we have a shot here. Our client's local and the trucking company and its driver are from the East Coast. You and I both know that folks around here don't care much for Yankees, particularly Yankee trucking companies. Let's do one more thing, and we'll have to hurry. Let's get the driver's log and see what that old boy had been doing a few days before the wreck."

They sent a formal demand for the log. The defendant then had thirty days to respond. That was cutting it short so the judge had Mable get the necessary paperwork done and in the mail that very day. Johnny Bob returned to his office and called the lawyer for the trucking company. His name was Kermit Gautreaux, a Cajun from Louisiana who migrated across the border when he graduated from Tulane Law School. A few years older than Johnny Bob, he had tried auto and trucking personal injury cases for five years. Unknown to Johnny Bob, he was actually dreading this call.

"Kermit, this is J. Robert Tisdale from over at Palestine. I'm officing with Judge Arbuckle, and he's given me this Potts case to try at the end of next month."

"Nice to talk to you, J. Robert. Is that what I call you?"

"Well, I grew up here in Palestine, and outside of the courtroom most folks call me Johnny Bob."

"Fine, Johnny Bob. I saw that Judge Arbuckle had substituted for that bank lawyer. I was actually looking forward to being on the opposite side of a case from him. I appeared in his court a number of times when he was on the bench. A fine judge. You tell him I said that. I figured I might learn a few tricks from him. Anything we need to do before we go to trial next month?"

"Well, there's just one thing. The judge said that we should request your driver's log and we'll have that request in the mail today. I was just calling to introduce myself and give you a head's up that the request was coming so you could get it from your client if you didn't already have it. I damn sure don't want to do anything to delay the trial."

Lawyers have to be poker players. Even though their hand doesn't even hold two-of-a-kind, the good ones will never let you know it. In this case, Kermit knew what was in that log. It was in his file. Truck drivers are required to maintain such logs, showing where they started their trip, where and when they stopped and, most importantly, that they did not drive an excessive number of hours in any twenty-four-hour period. The obvious intent of the law was to make sure that long-haul drivers got ample sleep. In this case, Kermit's client was in gross violation of the regulations. It was a common practice. Trucking companies pushed their drivers hard, and the drivers were paid by the mile. There were strong economic reasons for both companies and drivers to break the rules.

The log documented that in the previous forty-eight hours

the truck driver had wound his way from the East Coast, stopping four times to drop and pick up loads. During that time he had slept seven hours and that had been more than twenty hours before the collision with Danny Potts. At the time of the accident he was on his way to Laredo, down on the Mexican border. He had to be there at five A.M. to transfer his load to a Mexican trucker who was to take it on to Monterrey. The travel time from Palestine to Laredo was no less than six hours, not including stops for coffee and fuel. The driver had to be living on coffee and uppers, both readily available at most truck stops. As he was driving into Palestine, he was speeding and, on top of that, his sense of perception and reaction time were way below normal.

Kermit said in his best matter-of-fact voice, "No problem in you having those records, Johnny Bob. I'll have to request them from my client's dispatcher."

Little white lies and occasional whoppers were common among the trial bar, expected and understood by both sides. Knowing, though, that if this evidence ever saw the light of day, the risk of trial as well as the settlement value of the case was going to double or triple, Kermit continued. "While I'm getting those records, we're pretty close to trial. I suspect your client's made a good recovery and is about ready to go back to work. At least, that's what it looked like the last time I saw his medical records. Maybe we ought to be talking a little settlement. I might get the insurance company to pay his medical bills and time off from work and throw in a little extra for you and the judge to make a decent fee. What do you figure it'll take to wrap this case up and save both of us having to take the time to get it ready for trial?"

"Don't rightly know, Kermit. I'll talk it over with Potts and the judge and get back to you."

"That's fine, Johnny Bob, but while you're coming up with a number, remember that your client was drunk and ran the stop sign." They ended the conversation and Johnny Bob walked down the hall to report to the judge. Arbuckle had his feet up on his desk and was dozing when Johnny Bob entered. Johnny Bob coughed loudly and the judge's eyes opened. "So tell me, Tank, what does our friend Kermit have to say?"

After describing the conversation, the judge didn't say anything for a couple of minutes and then he gave Johnny Bob a surprise. "Tell him our demand is two hundred fifty thousand dollars."

"Judge," Johnny Bob responded, "isn't that just going to force a trial? I want my first trial as soon as I can get it, but if we could get fifty thousand dollars to settle this case, wouldn't that be a pretty damn good settlement?"

"Most of the time, Tank, I'd say you're right on. But there's something else here. This case has been on file for nine months. As ol' Kermit rightly points out, our driver did have a couple of beers and for sure had the stop sign. There's not much reason for the trucking company to pay us any money on those facts. As soon as you tell him we want the driver's log, up pops a settlement discussion. We just need to keep the pressure on and wait to see what's in that log. We'll get it two weeks before trial and all the cards will be on the table. We can afford to wait."

Johnny Bob started getting weekly phone calls from Kermit, wanting to talk settlement. Initially he said, "You and the judge talked yet? Why don't I try to get twenty-five thousand and we'll wrap this one up?" Then the offer went to thirty-five thousand. A few days before he was required to turn over the driver's log, it was raised to fifty-five thousand with the added requirement that if that amount was not accepted in seven days, the offer would be withdrawn and the case would be tried. Johnny Bob was eager to take it. Judge Arbuckle, speaking from thirty years of experience, told him just to keep his powder dry. If fifty-five thousand dollars were available this week, it would still be there on the morning of trial. His advice was to sit tight and wait on that log. Johnny Bob reported all of this to Danny Potts whose eyes grew big at the amount of money being offered. After thinking about it, he said he would go along with the judge. So they waited a week. It was worth the wait. Johnny Bob and the judge took one look at the log and the judge let out a low whistle.

"Tank, this is even better than I expected. We just got into gross negligence and a distinct possibility of punitive damages. We're still two weeks from trial. Go tell Mable to add a gross negligence paragraph to our petition and to plead for two hundred fifty thousand dollars in actual damages and a million in punitives."

The petition now read that the truck driver and the trucking company had consciously and recklessly disregarded the safety of others, including Danny Potts. Further, punitive damages should be awarded against the defendants to punish them and set an example so that other similar defendants would be discouraged from such conduct in the future.

27

Constructed at the turn of the century, the old, gothic courthouse with a domed roof and spires at each corner dominated the town square. Johnny Bob was at the courthouse by seven-thirty. His footsteps echoed as he walked down the first-floor hallway and up the stairs to the district courtroom. Like his footsteps, thoughts echoed through his mind about what was about to occur. He had to please the new judge, his client and, more importantly, twelve people from around the county. He didn't know if he was up to the task. Nothing in law school or in the few months since he had been licensed could possibly prepare him for trying a lawsuit.

As instructed by the judge, Johnny Bob was the first in the courtroom. The first attorney to arrive on the opening day of trial got his choice of counsel tables. Judge Arbuckle told him to take the one closest to the jury box, facing the witness stand. Old trial lawyers always wanted to be as close to the jury box as possible. Given their preference, they would have taken a seat right in the middle of the first row of jurors. Kermit came in a little after eight o'clock, big briefcase in hand and accompanied by the truck driver, dressed neatly in a starched plaid shirt, clean jeans and shiny black boots. Kermit sat his briefcase down at the other counsel table and pointed to a chair for his client.

"Johnny Bob, let's talk. Step outside with me for a minute," Kermit said, motioning him out the back door of the courtroom. When they walked out into the hallway, Kermit kept his voice low since others, perhaps prospective jurors, were now beginning to filter into the corridor. "I've been beating on my client all weekend and I've got another twenty-five thousand dollars. That makes eighty thousand. A lot of money for a broken leg and a few bumps and bruises, particularly when your drunk busted a stop sign."

By now, Johnny Bob was learning how to play the game. "Now, Kermit, I admit that's a lot of money for a broken leg and some headaches. But, that doesn't near begin to cover the punitive damages that I expect twelve good citizens of this county to put on your Yankee trucking company. I'll talk it over with my client and Judge Arbuckle. My guess is that when the jury sees that driver's log, they ain't gonna be very happy about it."

Johnny Bob turned and walked down the stairs to the front of the courthouse to wait for Danny and Judge Arbuckle. As he waited, he mulled over the options. He would have jumped at eighty thousand dollars only a few weeks ago. Now he was in agreement with the judge. It wasn't enough. He was bouncing figures around in his head when Danny walked up, dressed in a white shirt, khakis, and brown boots.

"Well, how's my lawyer doing? Ready to go kick some trucking company ass, Johnny Bob?"

Before Johnny Bob could reply, Judge Arbuckle joined them and Johnny Bob explained the latest offer. This time Danny's eyes grew even bigger as he mentally calculated his percentage. Once again, Danny acquiesced to the judge's recommendation to reject it.

Johnny Bob's voice cracked several times on voir dire

examination of the jury, that part of the trial where he got to explain a little about his case and question the prospective jurors. However, he said it was his first jury trial. The jurors smiled. The testimony flowed as expected. Judge Arbuckle said that they needed to call the truck driver as their first witness to get the jury on their side before Danny's drinking came into evidence. It was a good move. The driver conceded that he had been on the road for more than forty-eight hours with only seven hours sleep. He admitted he was loaded up on caffeine but denied taking uppers. Still, just the question planted the thought in the jury's mind. He readily agreed with Johnny Bob that he could not have made his schedule if he had taken the mandatory rest stops. That testimony brought looks of disgust to the faces of a number of the jurors. The witness admitted that he had not seen the speed limit sign just up the road from the accident. Still, he was certain that whatever the speed limit, he was not over it. The jury didn't buy what he was selling.

The next witness was the highway patrolman who had come over to the side of the plaintiff. Of course, he conceded that Danny had left the stop sign. However, based on the skid marks, he would have been out of the intersection if the truck had been traveling within the speed limit.

Then, Danny's doctor testified that although Danny's leg had almost healed, as he got older it was likely that he would develop arthritis in that leg and might need a cane to get around. The older he got, the more trouble he could expect.

The plaintiff's last witness was Danny Potts who did a good job. By now, Johnny Bob was feeling more comfortable with his lawyering skills and walked his client through the night in question, even bringing a chuckle from the jurors when it came out that Danny had lost five dollars playing shuffleboard. Of course, Danny saw the big truck. No one could miss it. He had been at that intersection hundreds of times. It was a major highway, but the lights on that truck were hundreds of yards up the road. No doubt in his mind that he had plenty of time to make it across. He denied the accusation from Kermit that his depth perception was impaired by alcohol. After all, he volunteered, he had at least three beers every night and they didn't affect him. Johnny Bob winced at that testimony. After the accident Danny spent ten days in the hospital with the broken leg, a concussion and other injuries. Although it took longer than expected for the leg to heal, it was doing pretty good now and he hoped to go back to work at the railroad soon in spite of a noticeable limp.

Kermit's argument was right out of the can. Stop sign, drinking . . . the accident was the fault of Potts. If anyone needed to be punished, it was Danny Potts for getting out on the highway after drinking for three hours. Certainly, nothing his client did caused the accident or was grounds for punishment. Kermit made the argument very well even though it was hollow and he knew it.

Johnny Bob's cracking voice returned on closing, causing grins from a couple of jurors. This time he just smiled, apologized and went on with his description of the events, damage to his client and the long-range implications of the severely broken leg. Then, he closed with a stirring damnation of trucking companies who would do what this one did to its drivers and to the Danny Pottses of the world, making even the truck driver a victim of the greed of the East Coast corporation. He asked for two hundred fifty thousand dollars in actual damages and a finding of gross negligence with punitive damages one million. The defendants needed to be taught a lesson.

The jury had been deliberating about three hours when Judge Arbuckle walked to the courthouse. He found Kermit, brow furrowed, talking earnestly with Johnny Bob. Kermit left as the judge approached.

"What's going on, Tank?"

"Judge, the jury just sent out a question and asked if they were limited in their damage award by the amount of money that I asked for on closing argument."

"Well, I'll be damned, son," the judge exclaimed. "Looks like we're fixing to kill a fat hog."

About that time the bailiff came out and announced that the jury had reached a verdict. The parties and the lawyers filed back into the courtroom and the judge took the bench. As the jurors took their seats, several of them looked at Johnny Bob and nodded. When the verdict was read, Johnny Bob could hardly believe what he was hearing. The jury found both negligence and gross negligence on the driver and his company; none on Danny; and awarded five hundred thousand dollars in actual damages and one million in punitive damages. As the foreman told Johnny Bob afterward, they wanted to send a message to trucking companies that they damn sure better obey the law when they come through Palestine in the future.

28

On the evening after the trial Johnny Bob, Judge Arbuckle, Mable and Danny celebrated at the Davy Crockett Steakhouse, located on the highway south of town. This time they all drank, keeping the waitress busy bringing beer, scotch and margaritas. Word of the verdict traveled rapidly. A number of the other restaurant patrons stopped by the table to shake Johnny Bob's hand, toasting him and congratulating the others. After devouring the biggest steaks in the place, Judge Arbuckle told them it was time to talk.

"All right, Danny. Let me explain what can happen from here. We'll prepare a judgment and probably get it entered tomorrow. They will file a motion for a new trial and then the case will go up on appeal. As a former judge, I think I can tell you that there aren't any errors in the case that would cause a reversal. Nonetheless, they'll keep it on appeal for two or three years. We'll be earning interest on the judgment. In the end we will win, but you won't get your hands on the money until the appeal is over. The alternative is for us to talk settlement now. There's something to be said for knocking ten or fifteen percent off the judgment to get our hands on the money. If we did that, say we took ten percent off and they agreed to it, then you would get sixty percent of one-point-three-five million or about eight hundred thousand dollars. We lawyers would get about five hundred fifty thousand as our fee and expenses."

Johnny Bob didn't have to think about it. He wanted the money in his hands, now not later. He was tired of living on beans and hamburgers. His share would buy a lot of steak. However, it was Danny's choice and Johnny Bob didn't want to influence him.

A smile filled his face as Danny said, "Judge, that ain't hardly any decision at all. Eight hundred thousand dollars is a lot more than I ever thought that I would see in my whole life. It'll buy me a new house, a fine bass boat and an even finer pickup. I might even buy the old lady a new Buick. Let's take the money and run."

They did. The defendant negotiated a little harder than the judge anticipated. After two weeks they settled on one-point-three million. It took two more weeks for the check to arrive from New York and another five days for it to clear the banking system. It was a Monday morning when the judge called Johnny Bob into his office.

"Well, Tank, this is the day. I just confirmed with the bank that the check has cleared. You can take Danny's check out to him shortly. I wanted to personally give you your share of the fee. Here's a check for two hundred thousand dollars. I threw in a little bonus for the fine work that you did."

The judge handed him a check payable to "J. Robert Tisdale, Attorney at Law." Johnny Bob stared at the check, his name and the numbers. Then, he sat down in the hard-backed chair and looked up with tears in his eyes. "Judge, I never figured that the law practice would be like this. I don't know what to say."

"Tank, you don't have to say anything. You did your talking in the courtroom. Let me say a few things. First, you earned this money. You're a natural trial lawyer. Forget your law school grades. Forget all those fancy Houston law firms. Before your career is over you'll make more money than all of their partners combined."

Johnny Bob's eyes widened as he listened to Judge Arbuckle's praise. Up to this point in his life, compliments from teachers, coaches and professors were few and far between.

"I've tried cases for thirty years and I know what I'm talking about. You've got the knack. You can connect with a jury like very few lawyers I've ever seen. It's a little like a preacher who becomes one with his congregation. By the time you finished the first day of that trial the jury was in the palm of your hand and was ready to believe whatever you told them. Not to say that you won't have to work your butt off for every trial, and you've got to make sure your case is credible. That it can pass the smell test. If you pick the right cases, jurors are going to do your bidding. Don't mean you won't occasionally lose a case. Any lawyer who's never lost a case just ain't tried very many, but you're going to win more than your fair share and win them big. Stick to the plaintiff's side. Go look for victims. That's where the money is. I'm going to hang around for a few more years and second chair you, not that you need it. I figure with you as my partner, my retirement can be on easy street. If it's okay with you, we'll change the lettering on the door to read Arbuckle and Tisdale, Attorneys and Counselors at Law.

The first thing that Johnny Bob did was trade in his old beat-up pickup for a brand new red Ford pickup, loaded with every bell and whistle the dealer offered. On a spur-of-the-moment decision, he also picked out one for Danny. Leaving his new pickup behind, he drove Danny's out to his house, parked the new truck in Danny's driveway and was climbing the steps to the porch when Danny came bursting out of the house.

"There's my lawyer now. Best goddamn lawyer in East Texas. No, make that the whole state of Texas. See you've already been out buying yourself a new pickup."

"Came to bring you your money, Danny," Johnny Bob replied as he handed his client a check for almost eight hundred thousand dollars. He watched as Danny looked down at the check, then danced around the porch waving the check over his head before stopping to grab him in as much of a bear hug as a little man could achieve with one the size of his lawyer. Johnny Bob pulled away from Danny, saying, "And there's one more thing. That's not my truck. It's yours. My present to you for putting me on the fast track in my legal career."

"Just a minute, Johnny Bob," Danny protested. "I damn sure can afford to buy my own pickup now. Matter of fact, I ought to be buying you one."

"Nope, Danny. I won't hear of it. Let's pile in your new truck and go by the bank to deposit that check. Then you can take me back out to the Ford dealer where my new truck is waiting for its owner."

29

After that first trial, Johnny Bob had started a tradition. As the years went by, every time he won a case in excess of seven figures, or as the judge put it, "killed a fat hog," he bought himself a new pickup and also gave one to his client. He did so to show his gratitude to a client for entrusting him with an important part of the client's life. The tradition became a great marketing tool, as he became known as the Texas plaintiff's lawyer who was so generous that he bought his clients a new red truck, a gift in Texas more meaningful than a new Cadillac or Lincoln. He even had a license plate frame designed, announcing, MY LAWYER IS J. ROBERT TISDALE.

Word about the new plaintiff lawyer in Palestine began to spread throughout East Texas. It didn't hurt that Danny Potts was a railroad man and bragged about his lawyer to every railroad worker within two hundred miles. Soon, the little waiting room in the third-floor office was filled. Johnny Bob turned down all of the criminal matters and divorces, now referring them to other lawyers in the area. It wasn't long before Johnny Bob began to have his pick of cases. Bad truck accidents, usually involving death or serious injury; products liability cases where the victim was paralyzed; and medical malpractice cases, preferably where someone went into the hospital for some minor elective surgery and the outcome was a disaster. If there were a victim with a serious injury or death and, of course, a deep-pocket defendant on the other side, he would take the case. He preferred to stay in East Texas where he was known and knew the ways of the people. For the right case, though, he would venture to Dallas or Houston, even out of state. He found that his country boy manner could easily out-slicker the city lawyers, at least in the early years before his winning reputation became known. As the years rolled by, he married, helped his wife, Bernice, raise three children and saw the passing of Judge Arbuckle. He hired a few associates along the way, but the firm name would always be Arbuckle and Tisdale with the judge's name first even after he was gone. After all, it was the judge who got him into law school and gave him his chance as a lawyer, and it was the judge's wisdom that guided him in the early years. In fact, while Johnny Bob couldn't be positive, when he had a tough decision to make about a case, even after the judge was gone, he would swear that he could hear the judge's voice, lending his counsel. Whenever he sensed the voice, Johnny Bob took the advice, just as if the judge were sitting in his office, feet propped up on his desk and sharing his wisdom of forty years.

The years also gave him the trappings of wealth. He bought one of the big old houses in Palestine on that shaded street where the rich folks lived. Once his kids were grown, Johnny Bob and Bernice, then his wife of nearly thirty years, spent more and more time on their ranch fifteen miles east of town. With three thousand acres, he had room to roam, raise a few cattle and horses and relax after a heavy trial. As he passed his sixtieth year, about the only deference he gave to his age was that after a big trial he retired to the ranch for a week or two of rest and relaxation. If possible, he would lure his grandkids out for fishing, tromping in the woods and, in the right season, deer hunting. While his house in town was big, at least by Palestine standards, the ranch house was opulent. Set back in the woods ten minutes from the highway, it was a rambling fifteen thousand square feet, including three two-thousand-foot apartments for each of the three kids and their families. Directly behind the house was a barn full of gentle horses, a swimming pool fit for a luxury hotel, and a covered basketball court, lighted for nighttime play.

Johnny Bob had no way to predict that his long string of victories would lead him to a Houston courtroom where Reverend Thomas Jeremiah Luther would use Lucy Brady in an attempt to capture control of the country's religious right wing. Nor could he predict that his adversary would be Tod Duncan, another legend among Texas trial lawyers, who was dubbed "the Magician" for his uncanny ability to consistently pull a win out of thin air.

30

Johnny Bob was doing cannonballs into the swimming pool with his grandchildren when Bernice hollered that he had a phone call. Johnny Bob climbed out of the pool, dried himself and picked up the portable phone. "This is J. Robert Tisdale, attorney at law. How can I help you?"

"Counselor, this is Thomas Jeremiah Luther, and I'd like to hire you."

"Why, Reverend Luther, I'm pleased to hear your voice. You and I have never met, but I've followed your career in the media ever since that day fifteen or twenty years ago when you were a resident of the Tarrant County jail. I saw that you pulled off another miracle recently and woke up like ol' Rip Van Winkle himself. I hear you're back to full steam. Can't imagine why you would need an old lawyer like me. You interested in suing some doctor for putting you to sleep for twelve years? If it's something like that, I might be able to help."

"No, counselor. It's nothing like that," replied T.J. "I'd

rather not discuss it on the phone. Would you mind if I drove down to Palestine in the next couple of days?"

"Preacher, you sure you don't want one of those good lawyers in Fort Worth or Dallas? I could recommend you to some fine ones. You know, I'm just an old country lawyer."

"Come on, Johnny Bob. Is it okay if I call you Johnny Bob and you call me T.J.? I need the best plaintiff lawyer around for what I have in mind and you don't need to try to 'country boy' me."

"Okay, T.J., I didn't really want to have to call you 'the Chosen,' anyway. I'd be afraid that I might have to kiss your ring or something. Tell you what. I've heard of your City of Miracles but I've never seen it. We've got our grandkids with us for a few days. Why don't my wife and I and the grand-kids drive up to Fort Worth tomorrow? They can take a tour of your place while you and I talk."

"Sounds good," T.J. agreed. "Just give us a blast on that siren when you get to the parking lot and we'll have an es-cort there immediately, say around eleven in the morning?"

"Oh, you know about my siren and my little red pickup truck, do you, T.J.?"

"To be honest, Johnny Bob, there's not much I don't know about you. I had my staff do a thorough background check before I decided you're the man for the job."

"Well, Reverend, now you do have my interest piqued. See you tomorrow."

They left in the pickup at nine the next morning. Bernice had a Lincoln Continental Town Car, but Johnny Bob re-fused to drive it. Too small and too cramped. Instead, they loaded the three grandkids into the backseat of the quad cab and drove the two hours to Fort Worth. Johnny Bob didn't intend to use his siren at the gates of the City of Miracles, but when he mentioned it to the three kids, they insisted so that as he approached the parking lot, he let out a long whis-tle. Within thirty seconds, a car appeared, looking like a metropolitan police car that was occupied by two large young men, clean cut and carrying side arms.

"Welcome, Mr. Tisdale. We've been expecting you. If you

would, please follow us around to the back. You'll be parking in the garage under the Miracle Tower in one of the spaces reserved for the Chosen."

As they entered the garage, Bernice counted three Lincolns, one red Jaguar, one navy blue Mercedes-Benz and one black Corvette, all in spaces marked RESERVED FOR THE CHOSEN. They piled out of the pickup. A young woman in her twenties told them that she would be the tour guide for Bernice and the kids while Mr. Tisdale met with the Chosen. She said she would bring them back to the penthouse of the Miracle Tower in time for lunch at one o'clock. The two security guards escorted Johnny Bob to T.J.'s private elevator. At the penthouse, the doors opened and the Chosen welcomed Johnny Bob. He was dressed in his usual public attire, white linen suit, white shirt, a red tie and his ever-present sunglasses.

"Mr. Tisdale, I'm pleased that you could come."

Johnny Bob looked around at the opulence of the penthouse. He had been in some fancy places in his days. This one took first prize at the county fair. In fact, looking around at the setting and seeing T.J. dressed in his custom-made suit made him feel a little embarrassed, especially since Johnny Bob was wearing his usual non-courtroom attire, a blue jumpsuit, one of many that he bought at the local Wal-Mart. He replied, "Shucks, preacher, looking around here, I feel a little like the country mouse that came to town. I guess I didn't know this was a formal meeting."

"Not to worry, Johnny Bob, and call me T.J. Besides, I expected you to be wearing one of those. I would be dressed in jeans and a golf shirt myself except I've got a board meeting this afternoon and have to look the part of the Chosen. Come and admire the view before we sit down. Matter of fact, if you look almost straight down, you'll see a fancy, red, oversized, covered golf cart. Your wife and grandkids are in it. We reserve it for visiting dignitaries."

T.J. pointed out various sights in all directions, including downtown Fort Worth off in the distance. He invited Johnny

Bob to sit in one of two easy chairs facing west. A maid appeared and left them a tray of soft drinks, bottled water and coffee.

"All right, T.J., just why is it you need this old country lawyer?"

"Johnny Bob, I don't need an old country lawyer. What I need is the best medical malpractice plaintiff lawyer I can find and your name is the one that keeps popping up. I want you to sue an abortion doctor down in Houston for ruining a young lady's life."

T.J. spent the next hour telling Lucy's story, starting with the abortion and ending with the miracle of her recovery for which he gave himself full credit.

"T.J., let me tell you what you're getting into. I've tried about every kind of medical malpractice case there is, and there's flat no tougher case for a plaintiff to win. Most people start off by putting doctors up on pedestals. They just assume that a doctor can do no wrong. When one of their own gets sued, doctors tend to circle the wagons. I usually have to hire an expert from out of state who may or may not impress a Texas jury. Then you are talking about abortion. I actually took on one of those cases many years ago, not too many years after *Roe v. Wade* came down. Wanted to see what a jury would do with one. I lost that case and decided that I would never touch another abortion case again. Can't make any money with them. Frankly, even with bad injuries, I think a jury may hold it against a woman, even a young rape victim, for terminating her pregnancy."

Johnny Bob paused and T.J. interrupted. "Come on, Johnny Bob. I've checked you out. There's no better plaintiff lawyer in the state, or probably the country for that matter. And name me one defense lawyer that could even polish your boots. With these facts, it's gonna be about as sure a win as you ever had."

"Just a minute, preacher. We got some damn fine defense lawyers in this state. If you want me to name just one, I'd pick Tod Duncan to go up against me. You don't need to be mouthing about polishing boots if he's on the other side. He's capable of kicking any witness in the ass so hard that they won't be able to sit comfortable for a week."

T.J. stared out the window for a time and then added, "There's one other thing you need to know. I don't just want to sue the abortion doctor, but I also want you to sue Population Planning along with him. I want you to sue for enough punitive damages to put Population Planning out of business and maybe scare a few more of these murder factories into closing their doors."

Johnny Bob poured himself some coffee, added three cubes of sugar and stirred for a long time before he spoke. "T.J., you have just quadrupled the problem. You don't want just a malpractice case. You want to tackle the whole pro-choice movement. I don't like abortions although I'm not one of your fanatics. What you're suggesting is going to take up probably two years of my life with not much chance of success. In my younger years I might have considered it. While I may not quite be in my twilight years, I can work my regular docket and know that each year I'll put a couple million in my pocket, ten percent of which, by the way, will go to the Baptist Church in Palestine. I expect you better go fishing for your lawyer in some other pond."

T.J. pondered a few minutes, sizing up the big man before him. "Suppose that I get a group together that will pay the expenses of the litigation, get you some talented legal support, and guarantee you two million against your usual forty percent contract. Would that get your attention?"

Johnny Bob grinned and replied, "Well, you're certainly beginning to speak my language. But you better understand that in addition to the two million, the expenses will proba-bly be another half million. We'll need the usual experts and depositions, which are always expensive. Then, I'm going to need office space and a staff in Houston along with apart-ments for everyone for up to a year. You're talking big-time litigation and it carries a big-time price tag. By the way, do you have the agreement of this girl and her parents?"

"Hadn't even discussed it with her and her parents yet.

I'm fairly sure she'll do whatever I ask her to. I just don't know about her parents or her aunt who's no pushover and has significant influence over our girl's parents. If you take on the case, you can meet with them and it'll be my job to do the convincing."

"Tell you what, then, T.J. You get me the medical records from the abortion clinic and the hospital in Houston along with the rehabilitation records. Let me take a look at them. I've got a first-class nurse-paralegal, Mildred Montgomery, who can dissect them and if necessary, I'll consult with the obstetrician who delivered my grandchildren. Then, if I think that we have a reasonable medical malpractice case, I'll have you get me together with the girl and her parents and her aunt, if you want to include her. I don't want to make any promises, understand? I'll look at the records and we'll go from there."

T.J. wondered at a lawyer who would hesitate at making at least two million dollars for one case, maybe more. "Deal, Johnny Bob. Timing couldn't be better. It's about one o'clock and we need to meet your family in the dining room. I'm anxious to meet your wife. I understand she's a faithful viewer and I want to offer her a front row seat some Sunday. Matter of fact, if we get you on board, we'll probably see you lots of Sundays. I'll even arrange for you to have a suite here in the Miracle Tower. Let's go to lunch."

31

Johnny Bob and his family went back home to Palestine, and T.J. put his plan in motion. First, he asked Jessie to get the signatures of Bo and Joanna on medical releases for Lucy, telling her only that he wanted another doctor to have a look at the records to determine what more could be done for Lucy. Within thirty days he had the clinic records, the records from Hermann Hospital, the rehab records and all of the doctors' records in a package that he messengered to Johnny Bob's office in Palestine.

When he received the foot-tall stack of records, Johnny Bob set them on the floor beside his desk. He would take a Saturday when the office was quiet to study them. It was a job that he had done literally hundreds of times in his career, maybe thousands. Every case he had ever handled had medical aspects to it. Over the years he began to understand what the records meant, what to look for, what might be missing, and even how to do a reasonable interpretation of a doctor's henscratching. What he didn't understand he would hand to Mildred Montgomery, his nurse-paralegal of twenty years. She had been an ICU nurse at Parkland Hospital in Dallas before burning out. She moved to Palestine, expecting to get a less demanding job in the local hospital. Instead, she ended up with Johnny Bob. Together, they missed very little.

Johnny Bob started with the various medical records early on the next Saturday morning. He could see damages big enough to ring the cash register well into seven figures if he could just establish liability. He was satisfied that he could paint Lucy as a victim in every sense of the word. According to her aunt, she had been raped. Her decision was that of a seventeen-year-old girl with nowhere to turn. She almost died from the complications of the abortion. The medical bills were in the hundreds of thousands of dollars. The emotional scarring would be with her for the rest of her life. She might not be able to have children.

What about liability? Who breached the standard of care? The information that T.J. had obtained on Dr. Moyo, the physician who performed the abortion, showed him to be competent. Both complications, perforation and retained fetal parts, were known risks of the procedure. However, it was very unusual for a good doctor to have both complications in one abortion. That was worth further analysis. What about the antibiotics? He would have Mildred check them out on Monday, although he didn't really expect to find anything. Surely, Population Planning, an agency that did abortions all over the country, would know which antibiotics to use. What about Saturday and Sunday? Should they have gotten her to the clinic? Would it have made any difference? These were questions that would have to be answered by an expert. Still, chances were good that somewhere he could find an obstetrician to swear that the clinic failed in its standard of care when Lucy made those two phone calls.

By the time Johnny Bob waded through all of the records, it was dark and he was ready to call it a day. He locked up the office, the same one that he and Judge Arbuckle had first occupied thirty years ago, only now he had the whole third floor. Before climbing into the pickup, he unlocked the refrigerator and extracted a Lone Star tall boy. As he drove through the piney woods, Lone Star in one hand and listening to Willie Nelson on a CD, he let his mind surf through what he had learned and thought about the questions that needed to be answered. He still wasn't sure that he wanted the case, not even for two million dollars.

Suddenly, it hit him like a Texas tornado, right out of nowhere. He slammed his fist on the steering wheel, let out a whoop, and turned his siren on as high as it could go. He had himself a lawsuit. A damn good one at that. He kept the siren on all the way home and bursting through the ranch house door, beer in hand, he yelled, "Bernice, we've got ourselves a lawsuit and a ring-tail-tooter of one at that."

Bernice was the quiet one of the family. She really had little choice after being married to Johnny Bob for more than thirty years. As she gave him a kiss on the cheek, she replied, "Well, I kinda figured that there must be something exciting happening. It's not very often that I hear your siren from a mile away."

"Bernice, you're not going to believe this. I spent all day going over those abortion records and came up with some good questions and possibly some good answers. Only it didn't hit me until five minutes ago. This little lady, Lucy, was seventeen when she had that abortion. These clinics claim it's okay to perform an abortion on a girl of her age, and like any other medical procedure, they made her sign a consent form. That consent form lists every possible risk of abortion, including death, paralysis and the complications that she developed. Shit, I'm surprised that it didn't advise her of what could happen if she didn't pay her taxes."

"Johnny Bob, don't cuss in the house. You know I don't like it."

"Sorry, dear. I just got carried away. Anyway, she signed off on the consent form, but her parents didn't. Hell—whoops, sorry dear—her parents didn't even know about it. A child can't consent to anything in this state. When you get to be eighteen, you can sign a contract, go off to war, and consent to a medical procedure. Without a valid consent, that doctor and that clinic committed an assault on her. If they assaulted her, we can collect actual damages, punitive damages, too. Now, we're kinda sailing in uncharted waters here since I don't think there's ever been an appellate case about a minor consenting to abortion. Still, the legal theories are sound as a five-dollar gold piece. Hang on, Bernice, this may be the case to cap my career. Now what's for supper?"

Johnny Bob had a case, and his gut told him that it would only get better once discovery was underway. After dinner he picked up the phone and called the City of Miracles. At first the operator didn't want to put him through to T.J., advising in no uncertain terms that the Chosen would not take phone calls after nine on Saturday night since he had to rest and pray in preparation for the next morning's service. After hearing Johnny Bob's threat to drive all the way to Fort Worth and blast everyone in the place awake with a siren at midnight, she switched to another line. T.J. picked up.

"What's up, Johnny Bob? It's a little late to be calling a preacher on Saturday night."

Johnny Bob thought he sounded like he had been dipping a little too heavily in the sacramental wine. "T.J., you get that family up to your office on Monday morning. I'm ready to sign them up. We've got us a lawsuit. Also, you be thinking about where you want to deposit that two million, pending the likelihood that I'm going to get more. See you Monday morning at ten in your office."

After he hung up the phone, T.J. took his wine out to the balcony and sat in one of the wrought-iron chairs as he contemplated the events that were to unfold. While he found Lucy to be a very attractive young woman, he was not really interested in her welfare. He saw her only as someone he could use to further his quest for power. He would befriend her and use her, then drop her back into her aunt Jessie's lap when he achieved his goal. He raised his glass to the nighttime sky and toasted himself, "Here's to the Chosen. He's come a long way from the county jail, but it's only just the beginning."

BO, JOANNA, AND LUCY were nervous as they stepped off the elevator with Jessie. She told Bo and Joanna to fly to Fort Worth on Sunday night because Reverend Luther wanted to see them on Monday morning. They were greeted by T.J. and a big man wearing a dark, pinstriped suit and red tie. Johnny Bob dressed for the occasion.

Lucy had made remarkable outward improvement since the Chosen had healed her. She joined in conversations, enjoyed going for walks with her aunt Jessie, and seemed to be in good spirits. By mutual agreement, she continued to live with Jessie, being tutored by teachers who came daily to Jessie's house.

"Lucy, how fine you're looking," complimented T.J. "Thanks for coming, Mr. and Mrs. Brady. This is J. Robert Tisdale, a lawyer from over Palestine way. Mr. Tisdale and I have a proposal for you. Please sit down. Go ahead, Johnny Bob." As he spoke to Lucy, T.J. could not see Jessie glaring at him.

After they had taken their seats, the lawyer began. "Lucy, Mrs. Brady, Mr. Brady, I'm a plaintiff lawyer. That means I represent victims of wrongdoing. Reverend Luther asked me to look at your case. He wanted me to see if what happened to you was just a complication of the procedure or whether it involved medical negligence. I spent most of the weekend going over your medical records, and I'm satisfied that you were a victim of substandard care on the part of the doctor and Population Planning. Additionally, Lucy, you're only seventeen and didn't have the authority to consent to the procedure without a parent's approval."

Bo and Joanna didn't know what to say and turned to Jessie with blank looks on their faces. Never at a loss for words, Jessie jumped in.

"First of all, T.J., I'm upset with you because you didn't tell me the truth about why you wanted those medical authorizations."

"Forgive me, Jessie," T.J. responded as he wiggled around the accusation. "I assumed that Mr. Tisdale would be having the medical records reviewed by a doctor. I'm certain that is still to come."

"Mr. Tisdale, let's get to the bottom line here," Jessie continued. "I know you and your reputation. You sued one of my husband's dealerships when he was alive. The case involved a salesman who took his demonstrator home on a Saturday night. He stopped a little too long at his neighborhood icehouse, busted a red light and smashed into a car occupied by your four clients. As I recall, you collected about half a million dollars from our insurance company. All that tells me is that I'd rather have you on our side than against us. There's no doubt that Lucy has been badly hurt by this whole incident and the damage will be with her for the rest of her life. What kind of money are we talking about here?"

"Mrs. Woolsey, I've reached that stage in my career where I don't take on small cases. If I didn't think that this one had the potential for a verdict well into seven figures, I wouldn't be here."

That got their attention.

"There are some other issues that need to be discussed and I think that Reverend Luther is the one to address them. T.J.?"

"I want Lucy to recover damages and I want them to be big. No amount of money can compensate her for what she has been through. I also have other reasons for taking on this mission. I don't want any other girl to go through what Lucy has suffered. I'm against abortion. My church is against abortion. The issue is a major one in the current presidential election and has been simmering on the front burner in our country since the *Roe v. Wade* decision in 1973. At times it's flared up only to die down to a simmer again. I want to turn up the heat so that it becomes a roaring fire. I want this to be the catalyst that will cause public opinion to come down against abortion once and for all. If we can use what happened to Lucy to focus our efforts and make our politicians take a stand, we can force a vote on *Roe v. Wade* and kill this abortion monster. If not, I want your case to send a message to every abortion doctor and clinic in the country. They need to know that they may be next. I want to drive a stake through the heart of this devil, and I want Johnny Bob here to be the one with the sledgehammer."

T.J.'s speech got Joanna's attention. As a devout born-again Christian, she was staunchly anti-abortion. Knowing what abortion had done to her child and her family, she didn't want any other girl to go through Lucy's nightmare. She turned to Johnny Bob.

"Mr. Tisdale, Lucy has already been through more than any girl should have to. What's going to be involved in this?"

"Well, Mrs. Brady, I wish that I could tell you that it will be easy. I can't. Lawsuits are emotionally draining. The lawyers on the other side will be top notch. They'll throw up every obstacle they possibly can. Lucy will have to testify at a deposition and at trial. So will you, Bo and Jessie. To accomplish what T.J. wants, it will become a media circus. As we get close to trial you'll run into reporters and television cameras everywhere you turn. I'll tell you not to worry about it. You will. I'll tell you not to lose sleep over it. You will. While it's nothing like what Lucy has already been through, it won't be easy."

Lucy had been silent. She raised her hand. "Can we sue Jason along with the doctor and the clinic?"

"Lucy, honey, I assume that Jason is the boy that attacked you. I know that you would like to punish him, and there's no doubt that he deserves it. If I'm to be your lawyer, I would advise against it," Tisdale replied. "He is still only a teenager and doesn't have any money. To sue him would just serve to divert attention away from Dr. Moyo and Population Planning. Besides, if we did, we'd have to get into the debate about whether you consented or were raped. I don't see any good coming out of that fight."

Lucy looked to T.J. for support for her request. When she saw that he was shaking his head, she lowered her eyes and stared at the floor.

"And how do you get paid, Mr. Tisdale?" asked Jessie.

"My standard contract is for forty percent of any recovery. Reverend Luther has generously guaranteed my expenses and a minimum attorney's fee. Your family won't be out one penny. Lucy, do you understand what we have discussed? You'll be eighteen soon and will be the one with the final say-so by the time this gets to trial."

"Yes, sir. I think I understand. My mom and dad and Aunt Jessie will be the ones to make the decision for now. I'll do whatever they say. Also, considering what the Chosen did for me, I'm one of his biggest admirers and I would do anything to help him out." As she spoke, she turned to smile at T.J. He returned her smile with a quick wink.

Jessie intervened once more, again noting Lucy's smile at T.J. "We'll all go back to my house to discuss it. We may even have a little prayer. We'll let you know our decision tomorrow. If we decide to do it, we'll be out here in the morning to sign the papers."

As T.J. and Johnny Bob watched Jessie's Jaguar leave the City, Johnny Bob asked, "Well, T.J. where do you place your bet?"

"Being a man of the cloth, of course, I'm not a betting man. However, I can tell you the fix is in. I've already spoken to my Father and He has assured me that they will join our little crusade." And that wasn't all that Reverend Luther would fix over the next several months.

32

As if directed by prophecy, the family was back at ten the next morning. Contracts were signed all around, with Johnny Bob cautioning Lucy that the day she turned eighteen she would have to sign one herself.

T.J. and Johnny Bob had work to do before the suit could be filed. Texas law required that before a health care provider could be sued, the provider had to be given sixty days written notice. Johnny Bob prepared two letters, one to Dr. Moyo and one to Population Planning. The letters were similar and very standard. Dr. Moyo's read as follows:

Dear Dr. Moyo:

I represent Randall "Bo" Brady, Joanna Brady, and their daughter, Lucy Brady. You performed an abortion on Lucy Brady at the Population Planning clinic in Houston, Texas. As a result of that procedure, Lucy and her parents sustained damages arising from various breaches of the appropriate medical standards of care by you and the personnel at the clinic. Additionally, because Lucy was under the age of eighteen at the time, you and the clinic will be charged with assault.

Please accept this letter as notice under Article 4590i that I will be bringing a claim for medical malpractice and damages on their behalf. I am enclosing a copy of this letter for you to provide to your insurance company. I invite you, your attorney or your insurance company to contact me within sixty days. If this matter is not resolved in that time, then suit will be filed against you and Population Planning without further notice.

Very truly yours,
J. Robert Tisdale
Attorney at Law

Texas law also required that if Johnny Bob was going to sue a health care provider, he had to file a report with the court from an expert who was critical of the defendants. If he could get the report by the time he filed suit, he would attach it as an exhibit to the petition. Might as well show the defendants that he was damn serious. He called on his friend, Doc Rusk, for this task. They had fished and hunted together for twenty years and Dr. Rusk had delivered Johnny Bob's grandkids. Doc Rusk didn't like malpractice suits and had little use for plaintiff lawyers, Johnny Bob excepted. Still, he didn't want Rusk to testify against another doctor, just to write a report. Johnny Bob picked up the phone and called the doctor's office.

"Alice, Johnny Bob here. Is the old sawbones around?"

"Johnny Bob, I wish you'd quit calling him that. He's a woman's doctor. He hasn't sawed a bone since medical school. Hold on. I'll see if he can come to the phone."

Momentarily, Dr. Rusk picked up the phone. "Hey, Tank. How's it going? I bet you heard about the bass starting to hit over at the reservoir. You want to take a drive over there Saturday morning?"

"Sounds good to me, only that's not what I'm calling about. I need a little help on a malpractice case I'm fixing to file down in Houston."

"Tank, you know I don't like malpractice cases. I've been delivering babies for twenty-five years now and I never deliver one without worrying that if this one doesn't have all ten fingers and toes and doesn't come out looking like John Wayne or Marilyn Monroe, I'll get my ass sued. I've been fortunate that the worst I've had was a clubfoot or two that could be fixed with a little casting or surgery. But since it's you, I'll listen. What do you want me to do?"

"Bud, you're showing your age there a little. John Wayne or Marilyn Monroe? How about Tom Cruise or Julia Roberts instead? My case involves a botched abortion. You ever performed abortions?"

After a pause, his friend lowered his voice. "It's not something that I like to talk about in public. I'm generally against abortions and send women elsewhere if they just don't want the kid. Two or three times a year, I have a patient where there's a significant risk to the mother if she continues a pregnancy. Then I'll do one, but only if it's in the first eighteen weeks."

"That'll do. I just need for you to be able to say you're familiar with the medical standards for performing an abortion. All I want you to do is review the medical records. If you agree with what I think is malpractice, write a letter and say so. The defendants are a Dr. Moyo and Population Planning, both down in Houston. Let me tell you what happened and I'll send you the records."

Johnny Bob described the events surrounding Lucy's abortion, using medical terms that were actually as familiar to him as to Dr. Rusk. When he finished, Bud agreed that if the medical records supported what Johnny Bob told him, it was malpractice. He would be willing to write the letter, particularly since it was an abortion case. Additionally, the defendant doctor was one hundred and fifty miles away. Nonetheless, he made it clear that no amount of money or friendship would cause him to testify against another doctor. They worked out the arrangements for fishing on Saturday and ended the call. J. Robert Tisdale was making just the progress he expected.

33

Back in Fort Worth, T.J. also had a job to do. He found the cause that would put him in the center of the abortion debate and at the front of the right wing political movement. With Johnny Bob on board, he had to raise the two million dollars plus another half million for expenses. It wouldn't be easy, but he figured he could get it done. After all, wasn't it God's will? He asked his secretary to pull the top twenty pro-life organizations off the Internet. He made the calls himself, figuring that most of them would not turn down a personal call from the Chosen. Out of the twenty, he wanted to get at least ten of the leaders of the pro-life movement to Fort Worth for a meeting in two weeks. Where lawyers were concerned, money talked. T.J. would ensure that Tisdale got the message loud and clear.

T.J. told them only that he had an issue that would serve to galvanize the pro-life forces and highlight the national abortion debate with the idea of making it a central issue of the fall presidential campaign. Fourteen of the organizations accepted his offer of an all-expense paid trip to Fort Worth and the City of Miracles.

They were an eclectic group who came from every geographical area in the United States. They were split equally between the sexes. Anglos predominated. There were three Hispanics and only one African-American. Two were wealthy. One thing was absolutely clear. This issue cut across all political, social and economic lines. While these people might differ on other issues, they were united in their fight against abortion.

They represented groups with names like "Save the Babies," "Executives for Life," "Operation Save-a-Life," "Organization to Ban Fetal Tissue Research," "Life is Right," "Give a Child a Chance," "Viva Bambino" and "Christian RIGHT Coalition." Most were sufficiently funded to have a presence in all fifty states.

The meeting was scheduled to start with lunch at noon, followed by an afternoon conference. One by one they arrived. Some were dressed in jeans, some in business-casual attire. Only the director of the Executives for Life wore a three-piece suit. T.J. wanted to use the lunch to size up his guests and to ensure that they would have confidence in him and what he was about to propose. To that end, he turned on the old T.J. charm. As he made his rounds, T.J. settled on four organizations that had potential for big money, one of them being Executives for Life, headed by Walter Thaddeus McDade. A slim man, with silver hair and a matching mustache, he was the former CEO of a Fortune 500 company.

After lunch, the group adjourned to the governors' board-room where T.J. called the meeting to order. "First, please let me welcome you to my city and my home. Thank you for coming. I know your schedules are full and a number of you came quite a distance. I appreciate it. As I look around this room I see a great cross section of people with varied ethnic, economic and social backgrounds. We all have a variety of issues and problems that are in our daily lives. The one issue that binds us together is the plague that is upon our land, the plague that takes more babies than all of the diseases of mankind combined. Pharaoh's murder of the firstborn of the Jews pales in comparison with what we have tolerated in this country. We all know the statistics. Two million babies a year are killed in our society. All of your efforts, worthy though they have been, have not been able to stop the slaughter."

T.J.'s voice rose as it did on a Sunday morning. "It's time that we put the issue under a magnifying glass so that when the sunshine of public opinion focuses on it, the heat will become so hot that it will burst into a flame that will burn throughout America. We want it to destroy every abortion clinic, every abortion rights organization and every murdering abortion doctor in the country."

"Preacher, I've heard all of that rhetoric before," one older woman spoke up. A tall woman with her hair in a bun, she wore no makeup. T.J. recognized her as the leader of one of the most adamant of the invited organizations. She continued, "You're preaching to the choir. Why don't you save all of that for another day and get to the reason that we're here?"

Two other women were offended by her rudeness. Still, they expected it since they had attended other meetings with her. One of them chimed in, "Reverend Luther, we've come a long way and we're willing to hear all that you have to say. Feel free to continue."

"Well now, I certainly do appreciate the points of view of both you fine ladies. Perhaps I can hit a middle ground and satisfy each of you. A miracle occurred in my church recently. Some of you may have seen it on television or read about it. A young lady of seventeen was wheelchair bound." He was careful not to say crippled. "The grace of God shone upon her and He used me as His instrument of healing. That day she walked for the first time in several months. For those of you who did not see it, I'd like for you to see her and witness what happened."

The lights dimmed and the scene on that Sunday morning appeared on a screen. Then, the lights brightened and T.J. continued.

"She became pregnant and made a bad decision. She called Population Planning and was forced into an abortion at their center in Houston. If that wasn't bad enough, things got worse."

T.J. proceeded to tell Lucy's story. Next, he described his plan to attack Dr. Moyo and Population Planning with a multimillion dollar lawsuit. The lights dimmed again and Lucy appeared on the screen.

"Hi. My name is Lucy Brady. Thank you for being here. Thanks to the doctors at Hermann Hospital in Houston and to the healing powers of God and the Chosen, I'm recovering. I want to make sure that no other girl has to go through my nightmare, ever again. My parents and I have joined with the Chosen to launch this crusade against Dr. Moyo and Population Planning. I hope that you'll find it in your hearts to assist us."

T.J. continued. "Like any crusade, this is not going to be cheap. If we can prove an assault and convince a jury to award punitive damages, we can bankrupt Population Planning. Once they realize the battle that they are in, we can expect nothing less than all-out war, not just in the courtroom, but in the national media. We have to be prepared to fight on all fronts and winning is going to be expensive. We've employed the services of one of the best plaintiff attorneys in the country. His office is in Palestine, Texas, a small town about a hundred miles from here. By the way, maybe it is coincidence that our advocate lives in a town called Palestine, or maybe God put him there for us to find. Whichever way it is, he's on board."

T.J. handed out Johnny Bob's resume and a list of big cases that he had successfully handled over the years. "The bottom line is this. We have Population Planning right in our cross hairs. The plaintiff and her family could not be more appealing, and we have the man to take us to victory at the courthouse. To do it, we're going to need two and a half million dollars."

T.J. paused to let the number sink in. Several people around the room looked astonished. Others merely stared at the table. T.J. was pleased to see that three or four continued to meet his gaze, waiting for him to go on. "I know that's a lot of money—"

The same rude woman interrupted T.J., "How do you expect to spend that money?"

"Ma'am, Mr. Tisdale expects this case to take at least two full years out of his life, not counting an appeal that could drag on for another three or four years. His fee in this case is forty percent of any recovery. I've guaranteed him a minimum of two million dollars in advance. Additionally, he estimates that the expenses of this litigation will be a half million. The best don't work cheap. There's one other thing that I should add. I've agreed to lead the national publicity campaign at no cost to anyone. With the power of my pulpit I figure that I can get on just about any talk show in America."

"Personally, Reverend Luther," the woman continued, "I think that if we had two million dollars, we could find better ways to spend it than on a lawsuit. I think you're wasting all of our time. If you'll excuse me, I'm flying back to New York. Count me out." She excused herself and marched from the room.

After she was gone, Walter McDade, the director of Executives for Life, joined the conversation. He spoke with a deep, resonant voice, one accustomed to commanding attention. "With all due respect to the lady who just left, I disagree with her. Properly orchestrated, I can see this trial rivaling that of the O. J. Simpson case. Lucy, bless her heart, is the perfect victim. From what I hear, Mr. Tisdale certainly is the right man for the job. Seeing that list of cases he's won, I'm just glad that we didn't have to face him when I was CEO of my company. Population Planning, as well funded as it is, may not be able to withstand a multimillion-dollar verdict. My guess is that they probably have a million in insurance and would have to pay the rest out of their own budget. If we can bring them down, you can bet that other doctors and other clinics may quietly get out of the abortion business. Then, there's the courtroom of public opinion. I agree with Reverend Luther. This could be the catalyst that we need to overturn *Roe v. Wade*. Reverend Luther, I like the idea. Can I inquire as to how much your organization is putting up for this project?"

"Not a problem, Mr. McDade. I've talked to my board and we are in for five hundred thousand dollars. We're hoping that around this table, there's another two million, and please let me point out that if Mr. Tisdale is right, this is nothing more than a loan. He'll be paid by the defendants when he wins the case and collects on the judgment."

The people around the table were pleased by the financial commitment of the City of Miracles. McDade continued, "Reverend Luther, I'm impressed with your conviction in this undertaking. I'll have to go back to my board. With my recommendation, I think that we can match you."

Others began to talk. T.J. went to a chalkboard and started writing down the figures as they expressed what they might be able to do. Nobody came close to T.J. and Mr. McDade. Two people thought that they might convince their organizations to dig deep and come up with one hundred thousand each. Another apologized as he offered ten thousand. T.J. treated him like it was a king's ransom. When everyone had spoken, the total was $2,100,000.

McDade looked at T.J., asking, "You think your lawyer is proud of this case, right?"

"Mr. McDade, from what I understand, he's about as proud as a papa whose daughter was just crowned Miss America."

"Then, I'll tell you what, T.J., I'm a businessman and I know that most people go into negotiations not really expecting to get exactly what they want. Why don't you and I each put up another hundred grand? You go tell Mr. Tisdale that we've got two million, three hundred thousand. That's the best you can do. I know human nature. He'll go for it."

McDade was right. Johnny Bob agreed that the money was close enough. They added a one-paragraph supplement to their contract, changing the amount of the retainer and listing the various organizations to which T.J. would give periodic reports. Four weeks later, T.J. called Johnny Bob to tell him he was sending two checks, one for $1,800,000 as his fee and one for $500,000 to be deposited in his trust account for expenses.

After he completed the call to Johnny Bob, T.J. made one more call, this one to a female lawyer in Ohio, the one he had in mind when he told Johnny Bob that he would also provide some talented legal support.

34

Within three months after he had performed the abortion on Lucy Brady, Mzito Moyo quit Population Planning. It had been his intent all along although it had nothing to do with Lucy. His plan was to do abortions at the clinic only until his obstetrical practice could support his family. It was coincidental that his practice reached that level shortly after terminating Lucy's pregnancy.

When he received the notice letter from the lawyer in Palestine, he was dismayed, although not particularly upset. He knew when he went into obstetrics that he was going into a branch of the medical profession that was at high risk for claims and lawsuits. He had talked to other obstetricians, many of whom had been practicing far longer than he, and they all told him that it was just a part of the practice. Do your best, carry insurance and let the insurance company deal with it, should the need arise. His dismay arose from the fact that this claim was from an abortion and not a delivery. To his knowledge, he never made mistakes at the clinic.

As to a patient named Lucy, he had no recollection of her, no surprise since he usually did fifteen abortions a day. He couldn't be expected to put a name with a face when he was only with the patient for about ten minutes. When he saw the letter was from some country lawyer in East Texas, he concluded that it was nothing more than a nuisance claim. Whoever Lucy was, she obviously couldn't find a lawyer in Houston to represent her. Dr. Moyo put the original of the letter in a file folder and sent the attached copy to his insurance company, figuring that it would either go away or the insurance company would settle the matter for a few hundred dollars. Nonetheless, Dr. Moyo drove home that night, thankful that he had gotten out of the abortion business. He did abortions because they were legal in this country and he needed the money. Never again.

Sixty days later the formal petition was served on Population Planning and on Dr. Moyo. Styled Randall and Joanna Brady, individually and as next friend of their daughter, Lucy Baines Brady v. Population Planning, Inc. and Mzito Moyo, M.D., it was filed in the district court of Harris County, Texas. The first ten pages laid out the factual scenario, from the rape, to the abortion at the clinic, to the involvement of Life Flight, and the near-death experience at Hermann Hospital. It included Lucy's stay in Fort Worth and the miracle performed by the Chosen. It described her future damages, including her emotional scarring and alluded to the possibility that she would no longer be capable of bearing children. After that, it went into the various counts of negligence, referring to the letter from Bud Rusk, M.D. that was attached as an exhibit. The petition closed with the charge that the procedure performed on a minor without her parent's consent amounted to an assault.

Dr. Moyo's receptionist called him to the waiting area to see a visitor.

"Are you Dr. Mzito Moyo?" the deputy asked.

"Yes, sir, I am."

"I have these papers for you, Doctor." He handed the petition over and turned to exit the reception area as he said, "Oh yes, you have a nice day, hear?"

He could feel the eyes of his patients as he folded the petition and stuck it in the pocket of his white coat. Trying to act nonchalant, he strode back through the door to his clinical area where he had five patients waiting. At the end of the day, when the last patient was gone and the last of his staff had told him good night, he sat at his desk and unfolded the petition. As he read, shock began to set in. He could not have done such a horrible thing to a patient. She almost died. Surely not from his hand. As he turned to the letter written by a board-certified obstetrician, his shock turned to panic. Retained fetal parts? A perforated uterus? Profuse bleeding? A staph infection? Septic shock? DIC? Questions raced through his mind. He could understand the possibility of retained fetal parts. But, she never returned to the clinic. Perforated uterus? To his knowledge, in all of the abortions that he had performed a perforation had never occurred. Infection? Didn't she take her antibiotics? Who was this patient?

He went to his calendar to make sure that he had even been at the clinic on that day. He had. As he studied the calendar he remembered that had been the day when he hadn't slept in thirty hours. He was pleased that he had gotten through it without a problem. What was this thing about an assault? Didn't minors have a right to have an abortion in Texas? Didn't the clinic get her to sign the consent form? He didn't remember for sure, but he was certain he would have discussed the procedures with her and would have satisfied himself that she understood what was happening and that the various risks had been discussed with her before he even entered the room. Dr. Moyo slumped in his chair, and taking his handkerchief from his pocket, wiped the sweat from his brow.

That evening he told his wife what had happened and showed her the petition. If a truck had run over him, he didn't think that he could feel any worse. He pictured losing his medical practice, maybe his license; losing his house and cars; having to file for bankruptcy; being thrown out on the street; having all he had worked for since the age of eighteen destroyed. Sleep did not come that night. Following the instructions in his insurance packet, Dr. Moyo reported the lawsuit to the claims department of Physicians Reliant Insurance Company. He talked to a young lady who asked that he fax the petition to her. The insurance company would hire a lawyer who would answer the petition and would be in contact soon.

POPULATION PLANNING TREATED THE petition routinely. While a lawsuit was not a regular occurrence for the clinic, it certainly was not the first time they had been sued. The director looked over the petition and noted the letter from Dr. Rusk. Otherwise, she calendared the answer date, faxed a copy to their insurance company, and faxed one to Janice Akers, an attorney and one of their board members.

Janice was a former nurse who went to law school in her early thirties and had a solo practice with an office not far from the clinic. Primarily a trial lawyer, she knew her way around most of the civil, criminal and divorce courthouses. Because of her background as a nurse, she was designated by Population Planning to represent them in any medical malpractice suit. She firmly believed that a woman had a right to choose what to do with her own body, and the government and religious fanatics should stay the hell out of any decision involving abortion. It was for that reason that she had been on the board of Population Planning for ten years. Now in her early forties, as she made the rounds of the various courts in the Harris County Courthouse complex, she still attracted the attention of male attorneys and judges. Not only could she hold her own with any trial lawyer in town, but she also worked out vigorously three times a week, assuring that there was hardly an ounce of fat on her five-foot, two-inch frame. She never hesitated in negotiations to speak softly, smile and offer a come-hither look. Yet, if push came to shove, she could push with the best.

Janice received the petition by fax and promptly flipped to

the last page to see who the plaintiff lawyer was. The prominence of the plaintiff lawyer would tell the defense lawyer much more than the words in the petition. When she saw J. Robert Tisdale's name, she knew she was up against one of the best. She flipped to the front page and very carefully analyzed the facts that he enumerated and his counts of negligence, paying particular attention to the charge of assault. She was impressed that he had even attached a letter from a doctor that laid negligence at the feet of both Dr. Moyo and Population Planning. To say she was scared, awed or even intimidated because Johnny Bob was on the other side would be wrong. She stood in fear of no man. Instead, she felt challenged. If anything, she looked forward to assisting in the defense against Johnny Bob Tisdale. Bring him on! She would have a major, though secondary, role in the defense of the case. Provided the insurance company for Dr. Moyo had any sense, they would also get one of the best and he would be first chair. Far better to have the doctor out in front, with Population Planning taking a backseat. Her first job was to make sure that the doctor's insurance company sent the case to a damn good malpractice defense lawyer, not to some schmuck who wined and dined the adjuster often enough to get business.

Picking up the phone, she called Population Planning and asked for the director, who immediately got on the line. "Gloria, just read the Brady petition. This one's liable to be a barn burner. I want you to get on the phone to Dr. Moyo's insurance company and track down the adjuster. Tell them that we insist that Tod Duncan be assigned to this case for Dr. Moyo. Don't take no for an answer. Got it?"

35

The three divers dropped from the boat into the water and gave each other the "okay" sign. Raising their left hands to the sky and holding the air hose attached to their buoyancy compensator, they each pressed the release valve and descended below the surface of the Caribbean. The water was crystal clear with visibility in excess of one hundred feet as they entered the undersea world and drifted slowly to the ocean floor sixty feet below. If they had pictured the largest aquarium made by man, multiplied the numbers, sizes, varieties and colors of fish and other aquatic life by ten, added rainbows of coral, sponges, ferns and other undersea vegetation, then stirred in a vivid imagination, it might have come close to resembling the world through which they descended.

At the bottom, Tod Duncan checked to make sure that his two sons were with him. Then he led the way through the coral filled with schools of small fish that fled as they approached. When they rounded the end of a reef, they saw it: a shark coming right at them, no more than twenty feet away. They watched with curiosity and excitement as the six-foot monster approached to within inches, glanced at them and with a swish of his tail silently passed by. It was the first time they had ever seen a shark up close. It was not the first time that the shark had seen divers. In fact, he had been expecting them. Ahead, they saw the rest of their group kneeling in a circle on the ocean floor around the dive master. As they closed the hundred feet, Tod and his sons could see at least three other sharks lurking off in the distance, their attention on the man in the middle of the circle. Like the divers, the sharks knew what was coming. It was feeding time, and they were hungry.

Fortunately, they were expecting to eat pieces of fish fed to them by the dive master. They had no interest in a human feast. Not that they were incapable of taking off an arm or leg with one bite, but these were Caribbean nurse sharks, never known as man-eaters. Nonetheless, the dive master had warned the group to keep their arms folded in front of them as he fed the beasts. He opened the bucket and speared a piece of fish with a four-foot rod. More sharks began to assemble and circle. Up to seven feet long, at least ten of them had arrived for breakfast. They were joined by a handful of giant groupers weighing several hundred pounds ready to battle the sharks. As the dive master raised the fish over his head, a five-foot shark, mouth open, baring rows of razor sharp teeth, burst through the assembled divers. As he approached the dive master, another shark came from the other side of the circle. They met at the top of the spear where they collided before one was victorious and both swam away. The piece of fish disappeared.

The feeding frenzy went on for twenty minutes with sharks and groupers fighting for the fish as fast as the dive master could spear them from the bucket. The sharks swam around the divers, over their heads, and between them, often brushing human shoulders with fins or tails as they broke through to the spear. This is what the divers had come to see and they got their money's worth.

When the bucket was empty, the dive master motioned upward and started back toward the boat. The fish and the divers recognized that breakfast was over and the dive had ended. The sharks and groupers wandered off to cruise the reefs while the divers slowly made their way to the surface, making a safety stop fifteen feet below sea level as the boat rocked on gentle Caribbean waves above their heads. Tod's youngest son, Chris, used the three minutes to hang upside down in hopes of getting one more glimpse of a shark before they surfaced. Handing their flippers to the captain, they climbed the ladder into the boat and removed their air tanks, masks and scuba gear. The boat was awash with conversations that bubbled with excitement. The dozen people could now say they swam with sharks and lived to tell about it.

"Hey, Dad!" It was Tod's oldest boy, Kirk. "Wasn't that wild? Did you see me with that little grouper between my knees?" While the sharks and giant groupers were battling for breakfast, a baby grouper, no bigger than ten inches, had swum between Kirk's legs and stayed there, watching the others, knowing that he would have to add three feet and about a hundred pounds before he could join the game.

"I saw it, Kirk," replied Chris, at fifteen, two years younger than his brother. "Dad, can we do it again before we leave Nassau?"

Tod appreciated the excitement and enthusiasm in his two sons. He enjoyed it as much as they did. "Sorry, boys. This is our last dive. We leave tomorrow and head back to Houston. You know the rules. No diving within twenty-four hours of boarding a plane, but we're playing golf this afternoon and I'll spot you a stroke a hole. Anyone that beats me wins twenty bucks provided neither one of you wears that T-shirt."

"Which one, Dad?" Kirk asked, a grin on his face.

"You know exactly which one, that ugly green one with the old duffer on the front and the language on the back about 'Old Golfers Never Die. They Just Lose Their Balls.' Now you guys go join the others at the front of the boat. The captain has put out a tray of fresh fruit. I've got to check in with the office."

The boys headed to the front of the boat, arguing about who had seen the biggest shark. As Tod spoke, he was digging into his bag to find his cell phone. When he turned it on, he was surprised to find a message from Janice Akers. He and Janice had been friends for ten years, almost as long as she had been practicing law. They started off as adversaries when Janice had a medical malpractice case against Tod's client, an orthopedic surgeon. They fought through four days of trial like some of the sharks and groupers that Tod had just seen, finally settling the case just before it went to the jury. Afterward they became friends, and had frequently co-defended cases, still arguing over who would have won that first case.

"Hey, Jan, it's Tod. What's up?"

"Tod, where the hell are you? Your secretary told me you

were out of town. Don't tell me you're off on another wild adventure with your boys?"

"Jan, you know me too well. We're in the Bahamas. Been here for five days, diving and golfing. I'm calling you from the dive boat about two miles offshore. We've been down at the bottom, diving with sharks. Please, no cracks about lawyers and sharks. I've heard all the jokes."

"Well, you need to get your ass back here. We've got us a case with J. Robert Tisdale and it may be a whopper. I've got Population Planning. You're going to represent the doctor. Tisdale's client was seventeen and had an abortion. Almost died. Damages are big and he's even claiming we assaulted the girl."

"My doc do anything wrong?"

"Don't know. He perforated her uterus and there were some retained fetal parts. You and I both know those are complications of the procedure."

"I don't mind one complication. Two get my attention."

"When are you coming back?"

"Tomorrow night. Why don't you send a copy of the petition and the clinic's chart over? I'll look at them when I hit the office on Wednesday."

"You got it. By the way, it may be that you were safer down there with the real sharks."

After the call, Tod considered Jan's last comment. J. Robert Tisdale, he mused. He'd been playing in the litigation big leagues for more than twenty years and this would be his first case with Johnny Bob. Not that they were strangers. Tod had been on the trial lawyer lecture circuit for years and frequently shared the same panel with Tisdale. He looked forward to the challenge. In his mind, he pictured Randy Johnson pitching to Barry Bonds. The best against the best. He had no doubt that he was Johnny Bob's equal. Hell, he was probably better.

36

Thomas Oswalt Duncan inherited his names. Thomas came from his father. Oswalt was his mother's maiden name. It was only natural that with his father's first name and with those initials, he would be dubbed "Tod." He was born while his father, then a colonel in the Air Force, was based in San Antonio at his last duty station. Shortly thereafter, Colonel Tom Duncan retired from twenty-five years in the military. Tod had the advantage of two parents who worked hard at raising him right. While he lacked for very little, his military father made certain that Tod appreciated everything he got. It was understood that school came first. An occasional B was accepted but two on one report card brought a quiet, strong message from his father.

Tod was destined to be an attorney. His grades were outstanding, his command of written English was near perfect, and he captained his high school debate team that placed second in the country. He convinced his parents to send him to San Diego State, figuring that he would get a decent education, experience a different lifestyle and then be ready for three hard years in law school.

The four years in San Diego were just what Tod expected. San Diego State was certainly not the Harvard of Southern California. Still, he graduated with a 3.7 average, good enough to get "cum laude" on his diploma. Along the way he learned to surf with the best of the Californians and brought his golf scores down into the middle seventies. After graduation he put away his surfboard and clubs, returned to Austin and entered the University of Texas Law School, considered one of the top law schools in the country, not far behind Harvard, Yale and Stanford, at least in the eyes of Texans.

His law school career was good enough to attract the attention of the big three Houston firms, the same ones that some years before had shown J. Robert Tisdale the door. He accepted a job with Sanders and Watson, then a firm of one hundred and fifty lawyers in downtown Houston. At twenty-four he was a licensed attorney, drove a Corvette and had the world by the tail. Sixty-hour workweeks were common in the firm and he accepted them. What he couldn't accept was the fact that he was expected to spend the next three years in the library, researching esoteric points of law without ever seeing the inside of a courtroom.

At the end of the first year, he said good-bye to big firm life and joined a three-lawyer trial firm. The pay and prestige couldn't match where he had been. However, Tod witnessed a trial in his first week as he assisted the firm's senior partner at the counsel table. It was during that trial that the senior partner kidded him about looking sixteen even though he was now twenty-five. That evening, Tod studied himself in the mirror and realized that the partner was right. If he was to convince a jury that his future clients should win their lawsuits, he couldn't look like the president of the high school debate club. He pictured the face in the mirror with assorted types of facial hair before deciding that a mustache would give him just the right look. Shortly, one appeared on his upper lip where it remained throughout his career.

Eight months after he joined the new firm, he tried and won his first case. It would be the first of many courtroom victories over the next twenty years as he took his place in the upper echelon of Texas trial lawyers. Over the years, medical malpractice defense became his specialty and his real love as he studied and understood the nuances of medicine as well as the workings of the human body. Unfortunately, it was the insurance companies for the doctors that selected counsel and Tod's reputation soon commanded fees that were far beyond what a doctor's insurance company would authorize. So, except for an occasional case where the company was worried enough about a multimillion dollar loss that they were willing to pay for Tod's expertise, he left medical malpractice defense behind. While he would not turn down a really good plaintiff lawsuit, he became known as one of the best defense lawyers in the state. National and international companies began to seek him out when they had a multimillion dollar case in Texas. Although he did not really plan to do so, by the time he was in his late thirties, he was on the way to building a giant firm. Then tragedy struck.

37

Tod was thirty when he married Amy, a statuesque blonde who worked as a paralegal for another firm in his building. Within a few years they had Kirk and Chris and moved to a rambling ranch house on two acres in northwest Houston. Tod's life revolved around his work and his family. Then, Amy found a lump in her breast. By the time it was diagnosed, the cancer had spread to the lymph nodes. Then it hit her bone marrow. She fought for a year before she died. The boys were ten and eight.

Tod surveyed his life and decided that it had to be simplified. Simplicity did not include managing a firm with forty lawyers. There was no choice. The boys came before his firm. Two weeks after Amy died, he invited seven attorneys to join him in leaving the burgeoning firm to start a smaller, more streamlined litigation boutique, handling only select cases where the stakes were high and the fees were big. Certainly, it was a rare occasion when the attorney whose name was on the door packed up and left, but the change enabled him to spend even more time with his boys.

While it took two years for Kirk to overcome the effects of his mother's death and more than three for Chris, they both learned to live with their loss. As the boys grew older, they each picked their respective sports. Kirk chose soccer and Chris wanted to be the next Michael Jordan. Nearly every evening there was a practice or a game. Tod coached each boy's team until they entered high school when he reluctantly settled for the role of spectator.

Summer was their time for adventure. Tod arranged his schedule so that he and the boys could take three or four adventure vacations. Canoeing, mountain climbing, white-water rafting and scuba diving filled their summer schedules.

All three of the Duncans had adjusted to life without Amy. While they never closed her out of their lives, eventually they were able to accept her death. Although Tod could never replace the boys' love for their mother, he came as close as a father could. The boys reciprocated.

Tod was satisfied with his life. He didn't have a serious romantic involvement. There were occasional dates, usually resulting from an attempt at matchmaking by another lawyer's wife. He had a law practice, long known as a jealous mistress, and he had two boys to raise. He figured there would be time for romance when the boys went off to college, and in the meantime he served his boys and his mistress well.

38

On the Wednesday morning after returning from the Bahamas, Tod was eager to get to the office. An adventure of a more familiar kind awaited him. He left the boys, knowing they would get themselves up and find breakfast around the house or at McDonald's. Life had become easier since Kirk had gotten a driver's license. Once he was satisfied that Kirk had no major wild streaks to endanger him, Chris or other Houston drivers, he bought Kirk a four-year-old Toyota pickup to get him and Chris to school, movies and friends' houses. A used pickup with sixty thousand miles was also a calculated parental decision. While money was not an issue with Tod, he refused to join so many of the other wealthy parents in playing a game of who could outdo the other in outfitting their children with Corvettes, Porsches and new pickups. For a seventeen-year-old kid, a four-year-old Toyota ought to be treated like a gift from the gods. Fortunately, Kirk felt the same way.

As part of his strategic planning, Tod chose not to office downtown. Instead, he located on Washington Avenue, just two miles west of the courthouse. It was an older part of town that was originally about half Hispanic and half black. Now, it contained a variety of houses converted into small offices along with a growing number of yuppie town houses.

The office had originally been a City of Houston fire station, left behind as fire trucks grew bigger. It had been abandoned for years with only a small sign among the weeds, offering it for sale. Tod spotted it one day, not long after Amy died, and immediately placed a call to the Realtor. The outside of the building was in reasonably good shape. Viewing it from the front, there were two large garage doors and a small pedestrian entry. The brick veneer appeared to be in near-perfect condition. As soon as the Realtor unlocked the door, they found water, mold and fungus everywhere. Remnants of a campfire remained in the middle of the garage where, long ago, some winos had lived. Behind the station was an asphalt parking lot, full of holes and covered with weeds. About the only thing that seemed to still be functional was the fireman's pole that ran from the second floor to the first. After closing on the building sale, he hired an architect to convert it into a law office.

It was six months later when Tod, seven other attorneys and their staff moved in. The outside had been sandblasted, revealing a burnt red color on the hundred-year-old brick, intended to match fire trucks in the early 1900s. The two garage doors were replaced with giant windows, curved at the top with planter boxes at the base. The entryway was covered with a brass awning. The reception area was decorated to maintain the fire station motif. The wall to the right of the door held hooks for coats and hats, including two from which hung a firefighter's hat over a firefighter's breakout coat from early in the century. A fireplace was on the opposite wall with pictures of old fire trucks above the mantel.

The pole remained. Always polished like King Tut's gold, the pole was enclosed by a brass rail with a sign, DANGER! FALLING OBJECTS. The younger attorneys took particular delight in greeting first-time clients by sliding down the pole, landing with a grunt and extending a hand in introduction.

Tod bought a vacant lot beside the building for parking and converted the weed-infested lot in back into a garden, complete with wrought-iron sitting areas, a waterfall and a fishpond. Behind the reception area on the first floor were file rooms, a copy room, three conference rooms, a kitchen and a war room. The war room was nothing more than a large room with folding tables, old file cabinets, a few chairs, a computer and a telephone. When a big case got close to trial, the files, depositions and exhibits were moved to the war room so that the lawyers and staff could have everything in one place as they prepared for the courtroom battle to come. Upstairs were the lawyers' offices, paralegal offices and secretarial cubicles. Tod's office was in the back, overlooking the garden and away from the traffic on Washington. When he was stressed about something going wrong in a case, he found some tranquility in staring out the window and watching the water cascade down the falls to the pond below.

Tod drove a metallic gray Chevrolet Suburban that was usually covered with a heavy coat of dirt and mud from weekend outings with the boys. He still had his old Corvette in the garage at home, driving it on weekends only enough to keep the battery charged. The Suburban better served his dual lives.

Before seven A.M. on Wednesday morning, Tod turned into the driveway, parked his car and walked next door to the office, entering through a wrought-iron gate that led to the garden and the back entrance of the building. He unlocked the door and noted that the alarm was off.

Grace Hershey had been Tod's secretary for fifteen years. In her early forties, she was an attractive woman, with long brown hair and an eternal smile. More importantly, she was the best damn secretary alive. She lived in the far western part of Harris County with her husband and two boys, close in age to Kirk and Chris. She worked out every morning at five A.M. and was the first one in the office. Tod was pleased to see her smiling face at the top of the stairs, a steaming cup of coffee in her hand as she greeted him. "Well, I see the sharks didn't get you but the sun did."

"Right on both counts, Grace. We saw the sharks up close. I'm pleased to say that they would have nothing to do with Texans, at least not those with the name of Duncan. What's been going on around here?"

Tod rounded the stairs to his office and Grace followed, replying, "Josh and Alicia are in the second week of the Blackburn trial. From what I hear, things are going okay. Bill is in New York on depositions. The rest should be here shortly. I figured that you'd be here early. Jan has been bending my ear about this new malpractice case with ol' Johnny Bob whatshisname on the other side. You know him?"

Tod went around his desk, turned on his computer and, while waiting for it to warm up, answered, "Sure do. Known him for about fifteen years. We run across each other at seminars and bar meetings. He was finishing his three-year term as a director on the State Bar Board when I was starting mine. We overlapped a year. He's a big, burly fella, booming voice, outgoing personality. Hides one of the best legal and tactical minds in the country behind an old shit-kicking grin. He'll country boy you to the poorhouse if you give him half a chance. This lawsuit ought to be a helluva ride."

"The petition's on your desk. I've already logged the case in. Answer's due Monday next week. Who do you want working on it with you?" Grace expected Tod to have at least one associate and one paralegal assisting him. Three of the other lawyers in the firm were partners, but of a lesser stature than Tod. That left four associates to choose from.

"With Jan involved, we won't have quite as much need for a lot of associate time. For good measure, ask Wayne if he has time to work with me on this one. And since the case involves medical malpractice, that's Marilyn's ball game."

Wayne Littlejohn was Tod's brightest associate. Five

years out of law school, he had the trial skills of a lawyer who had practiced three times as long. Marilyn Parker was Tod's response to Johnny Bob's Mildred Montgomery. A registered nurse, she had once been a part of Denton Cooley's heart surgery team. When she decided on a midlife career change, she sought out Tod and convinced him that after scrubbing in on six to ten heart surgeries a day, she could learn how to be a paralegal without breaking a sweat. She was right.

"As usual, I've been reading your mind. Figured you'd want those two. I checked with them yesterday. They're both available. Wayne said that he hoped you wouldn't hog all of the good depositions. He'd like to see how he measured up to J. Robert Tisdale, too."

"When they get here, tell them to plan on lunch with me. We'll go to the Spanish Flowers. I've been in a place that wouldn't know a burrito from a taco for a week and I'm craving Tex-Mex. A Texan shouldn't go this long without a stomach full of enchiladas, beans and rice. Could ruin the digestive tract."

"I'll tell them. I'll also tell them to leave you alone until lunch so you can get through your mail and return phone calls. The phone messages are on your computer. Should I call Jan and see if she can join you for lunch?"

"Good idea. Tell her eleven forty-five."

"One more thing. Dr. Moyo has been calling daily. He's upset and is gonna be a handful. He'd like to meet with you as soon as you can."

Glancing at his computer calendar, Tod told Grace to get the good doctor in at three on Friday afternoon, if it worked with his schedule. Grace returned to her desk. Tod settled into his chair and began reading the Plaintiffs' Original Petition in the Brady case. As he got to the end of the fact section, he propped his feet up on his desk and stared out the window at the waterfall.

Okay, what's going on here? Tod mused. Usually there's nothing more than a general allegation of negligence on the part of the doctor, a claim that his conduct caused damages and not much more. Johnny Bob didn't spend the time to lay out all of these facts in such detail for nothing. He's probably trying to get the attention of the insurance company, hoping to encourage a quick settlement. On the other hand, he could be laying it out for the media. But, he's got a seventeen-year-old client. He wouldn't want to broadcast her troubles to the world. Or would he?

Tod filed the questions away and continued reading. When he got to the section dealing with assault, he read it more carefully. He'd never really seen a medical malpractice case where assault was a serious allegation. After reading the facts as alleged by Mr. Tisdale, he made himself a note to have Wayne research this issue of a seventeen-year-old being allowed to have an abortion when she was not yet at the age of consent. He puzzled over that dichotomy and didn't arrive at an answer. There may not be one. Maybe this is a case of first impression. The rest of the petition was standard, closing with a request for actual and punitive damages. He would have to ask Johnny Bob to amend his petition and set forth a maximum amount that he was seeking in damages. He had to know that information to properly advise Dr. Moyo as well as his insurance company.

Setting the petition aside, he turned to his credenza and found the *Harris County Medical Society Directory*. Thumbing through it, he found Dr. Moyo's picture and brief biography. He saw the countenance of a pleasant black man. Tod was impressed with the limited credentials listed in the directory. They were the credentials of a well-qualified specialist. Why was such a competent physician performing abortions at Population Planning? He would find out shortly.

Tod assumed that what Tisdale had recited in the detailed factual description in the petition was reasonably accurate. He was eager to have the Hermann records for analysis. Well, thought Tod, as he looked at the clock, I might as well see if Johnny Bob is an early riser.

"Law office of Arbuckle and Tisdale," answered a female voice with an East Texas twang.

"Morning. Is Mr. Tisdale in?"

"Can I say who's calling?"

"Yes, ma'am. Tell him that T. Oswalt Duncan is on the line."

The next voice was the deep East Texas drawl of Johnny Bob. "Tod, my friend, good to hear from you. How are things down in the big city?"

"Doing just fine down here, Johnny Bob. How are you and your kids and grandkids making out?"

"Couldn't be better for a tired, old country lawyer. Do wish you city boys would send a few more defective products and overworked truck drivers up my way. How are you and your boys making out? I know you lost your wife some years back. That's tough on a man and his kids." One thing that Johnny Bob and Tod shared was a love of family.

"We're making it, Johnny Bob. It was hard for the first two or three years. Now, the boys are doing fine. My oldest son graduates from high school this year and his brother is two years behind. Thanks for asking."

Johnny Bob turned the conversation. "So, tell me, Tod, what are you calling this old country lawyer about today? You calling me to give a talk at some seminar, or are we gonna make us some money?"

"Well, Johnny Bob, you just sued one of my clients. First of all, I want to tell you I appreciate the business." Tod remembered the old defense lawyer's adage that "He who sues my client is my friend."

"Am I going to get to show you a little East Texas hospitality? I've filed three or four new cases up in this neck of the woods lately. I'd be pleased to have you on the other side."

"No, Johnny Bob. Looks like I'm the one that's going to have to be hospitable. I'm going to represent Dr. Moyo in Lucy Brady's case."

"So, you've got Dr. Moyo. Congratulations. You strap on your chaps and spurs 'cause this one's gonna be one fine rodeo."

Tod pondered the enthusiasm in Tisdale's voice and continued. "I've only read your petition and the clinic records. By the way, I was highly impressed with your petition. Not often that I see one with the facts so detailed. I was calling just to say I'd be on the other side and to ask two things. First, would you amend your petition to put a cap on the amount of damages? Second, can I get you to send me a copy of the Hermann records, at my expense, of course?"

"Tod, you know that the answer is yes to both. I'll get my nurse to copy the records and you should have them in a couple of days. It'll take a little while since they are about a foot and a half tall. As to damages, I'll amend shortly. I can tell you that I am suing for five million actual damages and a hundred million in punitives."

Tod let out a low whistle under his breath. "All I can say is you must be mighty proud of your case. Pretty tough to get punitive damages these days. Our Houston juries are pretty damn conservative."

"Well, Tod, once you understand the facts, I think you'll understand that I'm being very reasonable, considering what happened to this poor child. You know who'll be representing the clinic?"

"Sure do. Name's Janice Akers. She's an ex-nurse and a real pistol. I'll be taking the lead, but she'll be one fine second chair. Anything I can do for you?" Tod had asked for a favor and wanted to show courtesy in return.

Johnny Bob replied, "Can you tell me whose court we're in? It's been awhile since I've tried a case in the big city. Maybe you can give me some idea of when we can expect to go to trial in that court."

Tod glanced at the petition and noted the court number. Pulling out his court directory, he answered, "We're in Ruby O'Reilly's court. Good judge. Been on the bench for twenty-plus years. Smart, no-nonsense jurist. I'll give you a little advice, though, Johnny Bob. She doesn't tolerate bullshit. Be prepared and you'll get along fine with her. As to a trial date, it's usually about eighteen months in her court. If she takes an interest in the case, she could set one in less than a year. As long as we play by the rules, she'll stay out of our way."

"Appreciate the info, Tod. Let's see if we can aim for about fifteen months for a trial setting. Sound okay with you?"

"Sure thing, Johnny Bob. I'll be getting an answer on file next week."

"Sounds good to me, partner. Look forward to working with you."

While some might be surprised at such a conversation from two modern day gladiators, if the lawyers respected one another, such conversations took place every day. Both sides understood the rules. At some point in the development of the case, or in trial, tempers could flare. At the start of the process, there was no reason to hassle over minor matters. And there was one other aspect to such a relationship. Good lawyers knew when to draw swords and when to extend the olive branch. It was a strange relationship among attorneys. The good ones could separate their courtroom battles from their professional relationships. It was not unusual for them to argue to the point of fisticuffs in the courtroom and then adjourn for lunch together where they discussed politics and baseball in modulated and friendly tones. Like gladiators of old, it was nothing personal.

JOHNNY BOB HUNG UP the phone and wandered over to the window. He pondered the fact that Tod Duncan was going to be on the other side. It ought to be a fair fight. He only had two reservations. In looking at the courthouse across the street, he wished that it were on his home field and not Tod's. There was nothing he could do about that. He had to file suit in Harris County. The second that popped into his mind was about Reverend Thomas Jeremiah Luther, a.k.a. the Chosen. He was the joker in the deck. How big a joker, Johnny Bob could not have possibly imagined.

AS TOD HUNG UP, he pondered the fact that Johnny Bob was seriously going to ask for one hundred million in punitive damages. While he couldn't yet put his finger on it, another idea simmered in the back of his mind. Maybe there's something more afoot than a routine malpractice case. Certainly, Johnny Bob had a reason for everything that he did. Time would tell.

He turned to preparing an answer to the petition, pleading a general denial and raising defenses of various kinds that would probably amount to nothing at the time of trial. The only one he reserved for later analysis was the issue of consent to the procedure. That would require research.

At eleven-thirty, Wayne appeared in his office door. Wayne was tall with sandy blond hair, a natural born trial lawyer who was destined to take Tod's place as head of the firm someday. He was dressed in slacks and a long-sleeved sports shirt, the standard office attire for the firm of Duncan and Associates. "Hey, Tod, welcome back. You ready to head out for lunch? Marilyn's going to meet us."

"You bet. Good to see your smiling face." Tod shook his outstretched hand like he had been gone for a month. As Tod started down the stairs, Wayne stopped him. "Come on, man. You haven't been down the pole in a week."

Turning, Tod followed him toward the front of the building, pausing at a large brass bell mounted on the wall and rang it three times. The sound echoed through the building.

Wayne responded to the three rings, saying, "You mean this new case is only a three alarm? Shit, I was hoping it would be at least a four bell or maybe five." The bell was added to the building a couple of years after the firm moved in. Tod had found it at a garage sale and established another firm tradition. When a lawyer was hired on a new case, he announced it with the ringing of the bell. One ring was equivalent to a one-alarm fire. When the occasional case came in that justified five clangs of the bell, it brought lawyers and staff from all directions to listen to a shorthand rendition of a five alarmer.

"This one has J. Robert Tisdale on the other side. Other than that it looks to be a pretty routine medical malpractice case. Three alarms ought to be plenty."

39

To get to the Spanish Flowers they drove two miles north of downtown. It was almost like going to another country. After turning off the North Freeway, drivers found themselves in the middle of the Hispanic barrio where Houstonians could find some of the best Mexican restaurants in the state. Tod's favorite, the Spanish Flowers, was five or six blocks off the freeway. Housed in a large brick building built sometime in the twenties, it was family owned. In fact, the family still lived on the second floor. By the time they arrived, the parking lot overflowed with the Cadillacs and Infinitis of downtown executives parked next to the pickups of construction workers. As they entered the restaurant, the pungent aroma of spices, cheese, garlic and a variety of cooked meats greeted Tod and Wayne. Tod took a deep breath, inhaling all of the aromas, saying, "I've been starving for this for a week."

Of course, in Texas he was not alone. Mexican food was as much a staple as barbecue. Tod looked around the room and saw Jan and Marilyn, waving at them from a corner table. They worked their way through the packed dining room. Tod gave Marilyn a pat on the shoulder and leaned down to kiss Jan on the cheek.

"Hi, boss. Welcome home. Glad you're back in the world of the real man-eating sharks," Marilyn said.

As she spoke, the waiter brought two margaritas and placed them in front of the ladies. "Now, Tod," Jan jumped in. "Don't blame Marilyn for these drinks. I forced her into it, telling her that I refused to drink alone. I just had to have one of these. You guys want to join us?"

Tod was definitely not a teetotaler. Rarely, though, did he have anything to drink at lunch. Wayne followed his boss's lead as they each asked for iced tea.

"You read the petition yet?" Jan continued.

"Read it this morning already and prepared my answer. Even picked up the phone and called Johnny Bob."

"Well, tell me, how's the pulse of the most famous plaintiff lawyer in East Texas? Why the hell is he coming into our territory with an abortion case of all things? He's made enough money. Damn sure doesn't need to take on a case like this."

Tod took a sip of his iced tea and dipped a corn chip into the chili con queso. "Ah, that's good," he said with a crunch. "Can't wait for an enchilada. I haven't got this one figured out yet, Jan. Some serious damages, probably with medical bills of hundreds of thousands of dollars. The girl seems to have made a pretty good recovery. Johnny Bob's pretty damn proud of his case. I asked him to plead his damages and he said he's asking for five million in actuals and a hundred million punitive. He seems to like this assault theory. You ever run across that in representing Population Planning?"

"Tod, you know that we run a first-class operation. We don't get sued very often. As far as I can recall, we've never had a lawsuit in Texas where the minor was the only one to give consent. It may be an open question in Texas. And I've got to tell you, I know Dr. Moyo and he's a top-notch gynecologist. Still, I don't like two complications in one procedure. We may have our work cut out for us."

As she finished, they ordered "their usual," which for Tod was the beef enchilada plate with a beef taco on the side. Rice and refried beans came with it. Mexican restaurants in Texas were not places for people on diets.

"Tod, there's one thing you should know about," Jan said, wiping a drop of cheese from the corner of her mouth. "There seems to be a new national strategy developing in the continuing war of the pro-life versus the pro-choice forces. The battle has been waged in Congress, the various legislatures, in the media and on the streets. Violence has even become a weapon for some of the more extreme groups. Now the anti-abortion forces are taking the fight to the courthouse.

There have been several of these cases around the country. So far, the damages haven't been much and the plaintiff lawyers were usually ones who were mediocre on their best day. This seems to be the first one where there's been a lawyer of Tisdale's ability, not to mention the appeal of a seventeen-year-old girl who has been a victim of events beyond her control."

"Well, I'll be damned," exclaimed Tod. "Tisdale just may have some help somewhere on this one. Maybe he's going to play this case for the national media. Hell, this one may make five alarms." As the waiter brought their food, Tod continued, "Okay, let's get started. First, I've got Dr. Moyo coming to the office on Friday. Marilyn, I'll need you to go to the medical center library and pull all of the most recent articles on abortion. I'm looking for techniques, risks and complications, warning signs of problems, the usual. Have those for me by one o'clock, Friday afternoon. Jan, can you meet with your folks at Population Planning and get me statistics on abortion, numbers performed annually in this country, serious complications, including death, and most important, any information on other medical malpractice cases involving abortion anywhere in the country? I'm looking for any common strategies that Johnny Bob may borrow, not that he needs any help. Wayne, your first job is to research this assault issue, and I'll need for you to meet with me and Dr. Moyo on Friday afternoon."

Understanding their assignments, the others changed the subject and asked about the Bahamas, especially the personal confrontation with sharks.

When Tod and Wayne returned to work, they climbed the back stairs. Tod entered his office and Wayne walked down the hall, pausing to clang the bell two more times. "Shit," Tod muttered under his breath. "I've only had this case for six hours and it's already gone from three alarms to five." As he said it, he was grinning as he glanced out the window. Pondering the waterfall, the grin spread across his face when the waterfall was replaced by another scene. He saw himself on a great white horse, armor in place, lance pointed over his horse's head, thundering toward a giant black knight on a black horse racing toward him with lance lowered. May the best man win!

40

On Friday morning Tod switched off the alarm at five A.M., wiped the sleep out of his eyes and reached for his running gear to get ready for his morning jog. Tod usually ran five or six miles, three days a week and a ten-miler on weekends. At one time, he had done his workouts in under seven minutes a mile and had even broken three hours in several marathons. Now he was content to cruise along at eight minutes per mile. Running had been part of his life for twenty years and he expected to be doing fourteen-minute miles when he was ninety. For years he had preferred to run in the evening. No matter how stressful the day, after about three miles, sweat broke out, his breathing became more rapid and all his thoughts were focused on the next step and the beer that he earned at the end of the run. But, after Amy died, evenings were reserved for the boys. That meant an early morning during the week if he were to get his run in. He had five, six, eight and ten-mile routes laid out on the streets around his neighborhood. Not having been out for ten days, he chose the five-mile route and took it slowly, using the time to think about the Brady case and his meeting with Dr. Moyo in the afternoon. When he finished, he found both boys dressed for the first day of a new school term and devouring cereal.

"Morning, boys. You guys sleep okay?"

"Sure, Dad. How about you?" Kirk responded as Chris focused on the comics in the morning paper.

Tod opened the refrigerator and poured himself a glass of Gatorade. "Yeah, I did fine. Woke up once thinking about this new case. That's about par for the course. You boys need to tackle the yard this weekend. It hasn't been mowed or edged since we left for Nassau."

"Yes, sir," came the reply, sounding like two recruits answering a drill sergeant.

"Okay. At ease, men. I'm going to shower and shave. You've got a pre-season game tonight, right, Kirk? Home game?"

"Yes, sir. Seven-thirty."

"Okay, take Chris with you and I'll see you both there. We'll go out to eat afterward."

One o'clock came and Marilyn had a file folder on Tod's desk containing a stack of medical journal articles on abortion, the procedure for doing one and known risks and complications. Taking a yellow highlighter, Tod spent the next two hours reviewing and analyzing the materials. He had to know almost as much about the operation as the doctor who was performing it. He was more attentive when he got to sections on complications, how to recognize them and what to do if they manifested. By three o'clock he was ready to meet with his client.

Tod knew what to expect. Anger. Resentment. Shock. Disappointment. Disgust. Concern. And often fear. Physicians were angry about being sued, especially at first. Some were righteously indignant. Eventually, they became concerned as the case approached trial. It was the fear of the unknown.

At five minutes after three, Grace let Tod know that Dr. Moyo was downstairs. Dr. Moyo stood in the reception area, looking at the pictures of fire trucks on the walls and puzzling over the fire pole going through the ceiling to the second floor.

"Dr. Moyo, I'm Tod Duncan. How are you doing today?"

"Fine. Fine, Mr. Duncan. Of course, I would prefer not to be here," Dr. Moyo said as he extended his hand and firmly shook Tod's. Tod took an instant liking to his new client. He judged Dr. Moyo to be close to forty, with a smooth black face and curly black hair with a few strands of gray starting to show. Dr. Moyo had a pleasant smile and a few laugh lines around his eyes. Most impressive was a British accent with just a hint of another country. "Might I inquire about the fire trucks and the pole through the ceiling, Mr. Duncan?"

"Sure. First of all, call me Tod."

"Then, if you please, call me Zeke."

"Okay, Zeke. This was an abandoned fire station when I bought it and as we redesigned it as a law office, I had it decorated to remind visitors of its original purpose. We still call it the fire station. The pole is the only thing inside that still remains from the original building. Follow me and we'll go up to my office."

Tod led him upstairs, stopping to introduce him to Marilyn and Grace, pointing out that they were both important members of his defense team. Wayne was already in Tod's office when they arrived.

"Dr. Moyo, this is Wayne Littlejohn. He'll also be working with me in your defense. Please have a seat there at the table with him. Can I get you something to drink?"

"Thank you. I'm fine."

Tod seated himself at the place where he had been reviewing the medical records and began. "Zeke, you didn't choose me. Your insurance company did. So, let's start with a little about my background. I want you to feel comfortable with me as your attorney on a case like this. Next, I want to know something about you and your personal background."

Tod outlined his career. He touched briefly on the firm he led to rapid growth, the death of his wife and the decision to streamline his life with a small firm. He closed by mentioning that he had tried over two hundred cases in nearly twenty-five years of practice, winning about 90 percent of them.

"Any questions, Zeke?"

"Just one. What's your experience in defending doctors who perform abortions?"

"For about ten years, I did nothing but defend medical malpractice cases, with a docket at any given time of about fifty. As to abortion, I can only recall one and it didn't go to trial. I would encourage you not to worry about that. In every malpractice case there's a learning curve. With the help of my client and experts and by reading a lot of medical literature, I have yet to find a medical area that I could not understand well enough to cross-examine witnesses and get our defense across to a jury. This one should be no different. Now, tell me about yourself."

"I was born in Nigeria where my father is still a family doctor. I was fortunate enough to go to medical school in England and then came to Baylor College of Medicine here for my ob/gyn residency. I'm board certified and have an obstetrical and gynecology practice in the medical center. And, by the way, I met my wife in England and we have two daughters."

As he concluded, Tod asked the one question that had been on his mind for most of the week. "With all of your very impressive training, why were you doing abortions?"

"It wasn't an easy decision, Tod. I was just getting started, and for a black man from another country, it's hard to establish a practice. I had loans to pay plus a wife and two young children to support. Working at the clinic a few hours a day, three or four days a week paid my overhead, my house payment and put food on the table at home. I suppose I could have moonlighted in an emergency room, only this seemed more suited to my training. If a woman is going to have an abortion, she's going to be much safer in my hands than those of a lot of other doctors who perform them. I did them for more than three years, starting in the last year of my residency. I quit when my practice had developed to the point that I didn't need the additional income. I probably performed around two thousand abortions in that time and, as far as I know, never had a problem until this one."

"Did this procedure on Lucy Brady have anything to do with your quitting the clinic?" Tod asked.

"Absolutely not. I didn't even know she had a complication until I got the letter from the lawyer. I'd already quit the clinic."

"You still do abortions?"

"Occasionally. Only when there is a risk to the mother.

Otherwise, I send a patient down the street to Population Planning."

"Good. Score one for our side. It's going to make it easier for us in front of a jury if the other side cannot point the finger at you as a doctor who still makes his living doing abortions."

"Excuse me for interrupting, Tod, but were you aware that there is something about this girl being healed by some preacher in Fort Worth?"

"Only what I read in the petition."

"I don't really know much about it either. After I was served, one of my nurses commented that she watched a preacher called the Chosen nearly every Sunday. She saw a girl that she thought was this Brady girl being healed or something of the sort on national television."

"Well, I'll be damned. When we talk about the 'healing arts' in medical malpractice cases, we're not usually talking about preachers."

Tod spent several minutes outlining the various stages of a lawsuit and what Dr. Moyo could expect. Zeke took all of this in with an amazed and puzzled look. "Are you saying that we just can't get this case dismissed and be done with it? I didn't do anything wrong."

"I'm afraid that it's not that easy. You saw from the petition that Mr. Tisdale has already obtained one expert from his hometown. I doubt if he will use that one as his testifying expert. But, don't underestimate Johnny Bob Tisdale. He'll have a whole stable of experts before too long."

"I guess I don't understand. Can some lawyer named Johnny Bob Tisdale from Palestine be a good lawyer?"

"Not to disappoint you, Doc, but I can't name a better plaintiff lawyer. Frankly, I'm good and so is he. He won't miss a trick. In fact, he's been known to invent a few. Now I have a couple of questions. We haven't seen the Hermann records, but if what Johnny Bob says is true, there were two complications. How could two things go wrong in the same procedure?"

Dr. Moyo thought a moment before he replied, "You have to understand that this is a blind procedure. We can't see into the uterus. We have to do it on the basis of experience, training and feel, if that's the right word. The pregnant uterus is thin and we are inserting various instruments. We do our best to avoid a perforation. Still, no matter how careful we are, once in every few hundred times it happens. Often we don't even know it since the perforation is so small that it will heal itself without complications. As to retained fetal parts, again, we do everything possible to make sure we have extracted all of the products of conception. The best of gynecologists occasionally leave something behind. Can both of those happen in the same procedure? Although I haven't searched the medical literature, I'm sure that there are other reported cases. I can tell you that in every abortion that I've done, I've been extremely careful. I've never had one complication that caused a serious problem, much less two."

"Tell me your thoughts about the calls to the clinic afterward, Zeke."

"Of course, I wasn't there. From reviewing the clinic record, the first call was probably not that significant. Some bleeding and cramping are to be expected. Of particular importance is that there was no sign of fever. As to the second call, I would be a little more concerned. By then, it was about forty-eight hours post-op. I don't like the fever. If the nurse had called me, I would have had the patient come to the clinic. While it's a judgment call on the part of the nurse, the clinic may have a problem there."

"What about the bleeding, Zeke? At first there's bleeding and then it stops. The next thing we know, it's Sunday afternoon and her mother finds her lying in a bed soaked with blood."

"Remember, I haven't seen the Hermann records. If she had a perforation, it can seal itself off, just like a cut on your arm. It can also break loose again. That's what could have happened. Then, from the petition we know that she developed DIC. Are you familiar with disseminated intravascular coagulopathy? The blood loses its ability to coagulate and once it does, it's a cascading medical event. Frankly, she's lucky to have survived. One of the issues you will need to explore is whether she took her antibiotic. It is designed to prevent the routine infections. If she didn't take the medication, she could have created some of the problems herself."

Tod made himself a note and looked at his watch as he did so. "Oops, Doc, it's six o'clock. I've got to be at a soccer game at seven. Are you a soccer fan?"

"As a matter of fact, I am. I played goalkeeper in my younger days, even professionally while I was in medical school in England."

"My oldest boy is goalkeeper on his high school team. They're playing a pre-season game tonight. I think that we've made a good start this afternoon. Let's call it a day. Things will be quiet for a couple of months while we exchange paper discovery. I'll forward the medical records to you as I receive them."

41

True to his word, Johnny Bob sent the big stack of medical records to Tod and Jan by the end of the following week. Tod skimmed through them, looking for anything out of the ordinary. He made notes to carefully question the Brady family about the days surrounding the abortion. He found it strange that Lucy would be so sick without her mother knowing anything about it. He was pleased to find that even though she came close to dying, she made a recovery in a matter of months. In fact, after she was discharged from Hermann, she had regained the use of all of her limbs, had no cognitive defects and was fully capable of walking yet chose not to do so. The attending physician recommended that she might need psychiatric counseling on an interim basis. At least, she could walk and talk and think. Maybe he had some hope of keeping the damages down.

After he evaluated the records, he turned them over to Marilyn for a thorough analysis. Like her counterpart in

Palestine, if there were anything of importance to be found in the records, she would do it. He then took standard discovery from the computer and prepared a Request for Disclosure along with Interrogatories and a Request for Production to all three of the Brady plaintiffs. This part of the lawsuit, particularly between plaintiffs and a doctor, was routine. The documents asked everything about Lucy from the day she was born, including hospital of birth, attending physician, all medical providers for her entire life, every school she attended and her grades, all physicians and health care providers since the abortion, including counselors, psychologists and psychiatrists, all medical bills caused by the abortion and, of course, a question as to whether she had other abortions or pregnancies. Johnny Bob sent similar discovery to Dr. Moyo and Population Planning. Each party had thirty days to file answers to the discovery and was under a legal duty to amend any answer as new facts developed.

Tod met with Dr. Moyo once more to discuss his opinions about the medical records from Hermann and get his suggestions about gynecology experts. This time he went to Dr. Moyo's office across from Methodist Hospital in the Houston Medical Center. He found his client in a somber mood.

"Looks like you don't appreciate visits from lawyers, Zeke," Tod started the conversation after he was shown to the doctor's private office.

"Tod, I've just finished reading through these Hermann Hospital records on Lucy. I could hardly believe what was written. She came close to dying at least four times. If they hadn't gotten her to the medical center, she probably wouldn't be here. The only good news is that she seems to be all right now. Deep down, I know I didn't do anything wrong. I did her procedure just like hundreds of others. Still, there's no doubt that her problems came from my operation. Is there any way we can win this case?"

"Doctor, calm down. Let me start off by explaining that the only malpractice cases I handle have terrible outcomes—death, brain damage, paralysis, quadriplegia, to name a few. I wouldn't be needed if the results were perfect. Is the fact that she almost died going to weigh heavily with the jury? Of course. Does that mean we lose? Absolutely not. We'll line up a couple of the best experts in Houston or maybe somewhere else in the country if needed to support our position that what you did was exactly correct. What happened could have resulted no matter who did the abortion and no matter how great the skill of the physician. So let's talk about possible experts. We need at least two gynecologists to review this case for us. We may need an infectious disease specialist to explain that in this type of procedure, infections can occur even under the best of circumstances. That's the reason that you put the patient on antibiotics afterward. Also, I'll consult an expert on DIC. What I would hope to do is develop a theory that the perforation and retained fetal parts, known complications, could have caused the infection, but that this particular bug was so strong that the standard antibiotics could not destroy it. Then the DIC resulted from the infection. That's my starting point. Do you agree?"

"Although you have said only a few words, I am quite impressed with your understanding of medicine, not just gynecology but infections and antibiotics also. You are to be commended. Yes, that's a plausible theory. It's complicated somewhat with both the perforation and the retained fetal parts. However, it's certainly worth exploring."

Tod left Dr. Moyo's office with the names of three gynecologists, two in Houston and one from Harvard. Dr. Moyo also added one infectious disease expert and an expert on DIC to the two names that Tod's paralegal had found.

JAN HAD TO DECIDE which of Johnny Bob's questions would be answered and which would receive objections. Her approach was to keep it a simple malpractice case. The plaintiffs had the consent form and the medical records. The documents had everything they needed to know about the abortion, the antibiotic and her two calls. They didn't need any more information to prosecute the case. Johnny Bob damn sure didn't need to know such things as the number of abortions that her client performed every year at every center in the country.

That kind of information would only be used to try to inflame the jury. For that reason, with the exception of standard questions about witnesses and experts, she objected to the remainder of the discovery.

Johnny Bob was not surprised at Jan's responses and objections. He hollered at Mildred to call the court and get a hearing on her objections. It was about time that he met this Judge Ruby O'Reilly.

42

Sunday morning, a few weeks after Tod and Jan had filed their answers, the Chosen decided to launch the first of his media missiles directed two hundred and fifty miles south toward Houston. He spoke about the moral decay of the country and the need, in this presidential election year, to have leaders of strong moral character who would do what was right and stand on the right side of issues, with emphasis on the phrase "Right Side."

"My friends, here and across the nation," he concluded the sermon, looking into one of several television cameras, "the one issue that will define the character of a politician, be it man or woman, be it Republican or Democrat, is the issue of abortion. If a candidate for any office, whether it's president or county commissioner, won't come out publicly and condemn abortion in any form, promising to do all in his power to eliminate it from our society, then that candidate doesn't deserve the support of right-thinking Americans. Abortion causes the death of two million babies a year and a lifetime of physical and emotional scarring for the two million mothers who are also victims of this tragedy. My friends, I have experienced the travesty of abortion firsthand in recent months. A member of my own congregation was butchered and left for dead by one of these murder clinics in Houston."

As he spoke, the cameras panned over to Lucy and her family, seated in the first row.

"Lucy, come up here on this stage so I can introduce you to my friends."

Lucy squirmed in her seat and didn't move. Finally, T.J. walked down the steps to her, grabbed her hand and pulled her out of the chair. Holding her hand, he walked back up to face the audience and cameras. As they turned around, he put his arm around her and drew her to him.

"This is Lucy."

Suddenly, Lucy realized that she was with T.J. In her mind, anything he asked she would do. So, she straightened her shoulders, looked up into T.J.'s face with a beaming smile and then smiled at the audience.

"This young lady almost died after an abortion. She spent weeks in a coma and couldn't walk until I commanded her to do so. She may never be well, but she's a fighter. She and her family decided to strike back and filed a hundred-million-dollar lawsuit against that clinic and its butcher doctor. We and our forces of the Right Side intend to put that place of mass murder and its murdering doctors out of business. If we can't get it done at the statehouse, then we will do it at the courthouse!"

After applause and "Amens," T.J. ended the sermon with a prayer for Lucy, her family and her valiant lawyer who had taken up the sword of battle against the forces of evil.

On Monday morning, Tod got to the office. Before he could get a sip of coffee, Dr. Moyo called.

"Tod, I thought you said that everything was going to be quiet and routine. Did you see *The Miracle Morning Hour* yesterday? My wife had it on television. I was shocked. Where does he get the right to talk like that?"

"Calm down, Zeke. I haven't seen the program, but Jan Akers, the clinic's lawyer, called me yesterday and told me about it. She's sending over a copy of the tape, and as soon as I look at it, I'll give you a call."

The tape arrived within the hour and Tod called Wayne into his office to watch it. He fast-forwarded to the beginning of T.J.'s abortion tirade. They watched it three times before clicking off the television.

"What do you think, Wayne?"

"To start, I can see why Zeke's mad. Fortunately, he and the clinic aren't mentioned by name. My big question is how does this bozo fit into the picture? This lawsuit has only just been filed and we just answered a few weeks ago. This guy is acting like he knows more about the case than we do. You picked up on that part about 'we' and 'our forces'?"

Before Tod could reply, Jan called. Tod put her on the speaker. He couldn't even say hello before she began. "What did I tell you? You remember me saying that the pro-life forces were sponsoring some of these lawsuits? I smell something like that going on here."

"You may be right. It's still a straightforward medical malpractice case. The issues don't change."

"But, Tod, this joker has a national pulpit. If he keeps this up, he's going to impact on public opinion, which will affect our jury somewhere down the road. Can't we put a stop to him?"

"Can't do a damn thing right now. He hasn't mentioned any names, so he hasn't libeled anyone. We can't enjoin him from his preaching. That's a prior restraint and a violation of the First Amendment. Maybe it's an isolated sermon that will be long forgotten by the time we get to trial. If not, we'll have to figure out a way to launch a counterattack in the media. Or, if he steps over the line into defamation of our clients, we may have some options. For now, just tell your client to remain calm. I'll do the same with Dr. Moyo, although he won't take my advice. Let's just leave it alone and hope it doesn't happen again."

ON THAT SAME MONDAY morning in Palestine, Johnny Bob rewound the tape for the fifth time. T.J. had promised the consortium—as Johnny Bob now called the pro-life organizations that had put up the $2.3 million—that he would handle the media campaign. Certainly, he was wasting no time in launching the attack. If Johnny Bob had his druthers, he would have preferred that T.J. moderate his rhetoric. He might as well try to put a muzzle on an alligator.

TWO WEEKS LATER, THE lawyers had their first hearing before Judge Ruby O'Reilly. Johnny Bob made his way through the metal detector and up the elevators to the third floor of the Harris County Courthouse where he spotted Tod Duncan talking to an attractive lady outside Judge O'Reilly's courtroom. As he approached, he stuck out his hand. "Tod, my good friend, how's the best defense lawyer in South Texas this fine Monday morning? And you, darling, must be Ms. Akers, my worthy opponent today."

"I intend to be your most worthy opponent today and every other day, but I'm damn sure not your darling," Jan replied.

"Please, Ms. Akers, no harm intended. I'm just from East Texas and it's hard to break old habits."

"Then why don't I just call you Johnny Bob and you call me Jan, and we'll call it even."

"Well," Johnny Bob said, "again, I apologize. Can either of you fine lawyers tell me how Judge O'Reilly runs her motion docket? This is my first time before her."

Tod spoke up, "She'll sound the docket promptly at nine. The courtroom's packed with lawyers. I've checked and we're number six out of twenty this morning. The good news is that she doesn't waste much time. She will have already read all the motions and briefs. Expect her to pretty much have her mind made up."

Looking at the hallway clock, they decided they had better find seats. As they entered the courtroom, Judge O'Reilly took the bench. Ruby O'Reilly was a striking woman. She was only thirty-five when she took the bench as one of the first female judges in Harris County. She had been re-elected without opposition now for nearly twenty-five years. Many politicos had encouraged her to advance up the judicial ladder to the Texas Supreme Court, or perhaps through the federal system. She declined their suggestions. She had found her calling as a civil trial judge and had no higher ambitions. Even in her late fifties, her hair was still a flaming red and no one dared ask if something from the drugstore helped maintain the color.

Intelligent, fair and compassionate, she treated lawyers and litigants with courtesy. She expected the same from everyone who entered her courtroom. To be unprepared or to be other than absolutely professional to one's opposition were two things that would incur her wrath. Wasting her time came in a close third. She wouldn't hesitate to tell a lawyer that she had heard enough and was ready to rule. If she made such a pronouncement, every trial attorney in Houston realized they better shut up and listen.

She went through the first five cases in thirty minutes and called "Brady v. Population Planning and Mzito Moyo, M.D." The judge spoke as the lawyers approached her bench. "Good morning, Ms. Akers, Mr. Duncan, and you must be Mr. Tisdale."

"Yes, ma'am. J. Robert Tisdale, here for Lucy Brady."

"Welcome to my court, Mr. Tisdale. Your reputation precedes you. I've had the pleasure of having Mr. Duncan and Ms. Akers in my court on many occasions. I look forward to seeing you from time to time but hopefully infrequently before trial." The judge made it clear that she expected good lawyers to resolve most of their discovery disputes without her intervention.

"I certainly understand, Judge O'Reilly, and we'll try not to take up your time very often. However, you must understand that this is a most serious case."

"Mr. Tisdale," Judge O'Reilly cut him off, "every lawyer who stands before this bench tells me exactly the same thing. All cases are serious to the litigants. Otherwise, you lawyers would be laying bricks or doing something else. I've read your petition and I must say that you have laid out your facts extremely well. When I cut through the chafe, this is a malpractice case and I've tried hundreds of them. Unless you or the defense lawyers have anything to add, I'm ready to rule on Population Planning's objections to your discovery."

Quickly getting the lay of the land, Johnny Bob said that he had nothing further. Jan agreed.

"Then, my ruling is that the local Population Planning clinic is a separate corporation from the national one. For that reason, whatever is at the national level is irrelevant. However, the plaintiffs are entitled to know the policies and procedures of the local clinic from the time of the first phone call until the last contact with the patient. Personnel files of everyone who came in contact with your client are to be produced. The plaintiff is entitled to know the number of abortions performed a year by the Houston clinic only. I think five years should be more than enough to allow you to determine their competence in performing the procedure. The credentialing file of Dr. Moyo is privileged, but in looking at his answers to discovery, I doubt that you would find that he is anything other than a capable physician. Any questions?"

Solomon-like, Judge O'Reilly had split the baby. Each side both won and lost. The attorneys would accept the decision and not threaten appeal. She had not been on the bench for twenty-five years for nothing.

43

Money was not T.J.'s objective in this courtroom struggle. He sought power. He had no illusions about being president or even a United States senator. Besides, if things went according to plan, any national political office would be a step down. He wanted to be the kingmaker, the power behind the throne, the puppeteer who pulled the strings of his puppet who occupied the White House. He wanted a voice so strong and so powerful that those who would be president would seek him out to obtain his blessing, his endorsement and of course, money from his political action committee. To gain that lofty status, he had to be *the* spokesperson for the religious right. He intended to vault to such a lofty pedestal, using Lucy Baines Brady as a springboard.

The next Sunday morning, he decided the time was right

for a direct frontal attack. The platform descended, with T.J.'s feet planted firmly in the middle. As it came to a stop at the stage, he stepped from it and moved to the pulpit. With a great flourish, he closed the book that contained his sermon notes and threw it to the floor. Then he stalked across the stage and back toward the pulpit, saying nothing while the audience sat in silence. He turned and walked down the steps extending from the center of the stage until he was no more than two feet from the first row. In a low voice, almost a whisper, he started, "My brothers and sisters, I don't need sermon notes for what I am about to say. I don't even need to refer to the Bible. My message this morning is about killing and the Bible sums my message up in four very simple words." His voice rose to a thunder as he shouted, "Thou Shalt Not Kill! Is that difficult to understand? Does that commandment need interpretation? Does anyone here or out there watching on television need me to explain that simple commandment?"

The audience erupted, "No!"

"Well, I must say that some of you are lying. Some of you don't understand God's word. For we are a society of killers. Look around you. Read the daily papers. Watch television. We have drunk-driver killers. We have drug-dealer killers. We have people shot just driving along the freeway. We have convenience store operators who work in fear for their lives. We have serial killers. We have domestic violence that leads to the murder of loved ones. We have mass murders in work places, McDonald's, post offices and, yes, even in schools.

"My friends, no society can survive if it does not place the highest value on human life." For the next fifteen minutes T.J. sermonized on the decadence of society, that if it continued, the United States could not survive. He had the audience right where he wanted them. "My brothers and sisters, I purposely left out the single greatest cause of death in our country. If we are to become the kinder, gentler, more compassionate society that we all desire, we cannot have abortion for sale. I've told you before and I'll say it again.

Two million babies are murdered every year right here in this country, and it's all as legal as buying a candy bar at your neighborhood grocery."

A chorus of "No's" filled the auditorium. Lucy chose to leave her seat without prompting from T.J., walked up to stand beside T.J. and took his hand as he continued.

"We all know that giant companies have sprung up across the country that claim to offer other services, but they serve one purpose—to murder innocent babies. In the past, I've backed off from naming names. The time has come for me to step up to the line and call out our enemies, call them out so that you, too, may know who they are and the evil that they are doing. They are murderers, killers of babies, and their names need to be known. The largest and most evil is Population Planning. I know about them from our studies on the abortion murders here at the City of Miracles. I also know of them on a firsthand basis for it was at the Population Planning clinic in Houston where Lucy Brady, this young lady beside me and one of the young members of our congregation, was butchered and almost lost her life. And if we are going to put the doctors out of the abortion business, then their names must be known. The butcher who almost killed Lucy was one Dr. Mzito Moyo. A mass murderer, he makes his living killing babies. On this occasion, he killed Lucy's baby and he botched the abortion so badly that Lucy teetered on the brink of death for weeks. It took a miracle to make her walk again.

"It's up to each of you to honor God's commandment," T.J. continued. "The first step must be to shut down these murder clinics and put these murdering doctors out of business, at the ballot box, on the streets and at the courthouse. Let us pray."

IN PALESTINE, JOHNNY BOB walked through the kitchen where Bernice had the television tuned to *The Miracle Morning Hour*. Getting a cup of coffee, he sat at the kitchen table and watched the spectacle, actually admiring the skill with which T.J. was able to control and manipulate an audience.

When T.J. got to the part about abortion and even broadcast the names of the defendants in the lawsuit, his expression changed, "Shit. Sorry, Bernice. Why did he have to do that?"

"Johnny Bob," Bernice replied, "I don't understand. Isn't what he is saying the truth and isn't that what you are trying to prove down in Houston?"

"That's not the point. This isn't a murder trial. Besides, the evidence in a trial must be presented to the jury in the courtroom, not on national TV. Judge O'Reilly is going to blow her redheaded stack when she sees this. Expect me to have to appear at a command performance in her court before the week is out. And it ain't going to be fun."

In Houston, Dr. Moyo found Tod on his cell phone as Tod and his two sons were playing basketball in the driveway beside their house. "Yes, Zeke, I saw the spectacle this morning. I'm as shocked as you are."

"Tod, this is a catastrophe! This kind of thing will destroy my practice. I might as well pack up now and go back to Nigeria. None of my current patients know that I worked at that clinic. You've got to put a stop to this," he pleaded.

"Zeke, I'll do my best. I'll be on the phone to the court first thing in the morning. I've got to warn you, though, that we have a major problem in that this preacher isn't a party to the lawsuit. The judge really doesn't have any jurisdiction over him. I'll see what can be done."

Tod didn't have to call the court on Monday morning. By the time he arrived at his office there was a message from Judge O'Reilly's clerk, demanding that the lawyers in the Brady case be in her court at eight o'clock on Tuesday morning. No excuses would be accepted.

Three solemn lawyers stood before her as the judge's wrath spilled over an otherwise empty courtroom. She normally kept her temper under control, but when it erupted, it was like a dormant volcano exploding. Nothing in its path was safe. "Counsel, I don't remember when I have been so mad as Sunday afternoon when my court reporter dropped off the tape of Reverend Luther's latest sermon. Mr. Tisdale, who is this Reverend Luther and what is his connection to this case? I presume that you know him."

Johnny Bob had to tread carefully. He couldn't tell what he knew. At the same time, he had to be truthful with the court. "Judge, he's a preacher up in Fort Worth."

"Mr. Tisdale," interrupted the judge, "I know that. Don't waste my time. Answer my question."

"Sorry, Your Honor. He's a friend of the family. My clients are members of his church and he's very much interested in Lucy's welfare. I certainly agree that he has, perhaps, let his personal feelings for Lucy get carried away."

"That's probably the understatement of the year, Mr. Tisdale. He's not a party to this lawsuit and I've never had this situation come up in all my years as a district judge. I presume that you have had some contact with him. I'm going to give you the benefit of the doubt that you have not encouraged such outrageous conduct. I want you to contact him and advise him that I'm more than just a little upset. If this continues, I'll find some way to haul him into my court, and I'll figure out a way to sanction him. Do I make myself clear?"

"Yes, ma'am," Johnny Bob responded meekly, knowing this certainly was not an opportune time to take issue with the judge. "Please understand, Your Honor, that I can only talk to Reverend Luther and relay the court's comments. I have no control over him."

Up to this time, Tod and Jan had remained silent. As good trial lawyers, they knew when to keep their mouths shut, and one of those times was when the other side was getting a judicial chewing-out.

Tod interrupted, "Your Honor, if I may have just a word. I think that the court needs to understand that if this conduct continues, it will be impossible for my client or the clinic to get a fair trial anywhere in this country."

"I understand your position, Mr. Duncan. Impossible may be too strong a word. I've tried too many cases where the media circled the courthouse like flies around honey. However, I hear what you are saying. We'll just have to rely on

Mr. Tisdale to convey the message and hope that Reverend Luther follows the directions of the court. You are all excused. Have a good day."

The only other person in the courtroom that day occupied the back bench, taking notes as the judge and the lawyers spoke. It was the courthouse reporter for the *Houston Chronicle*. Afterward, he filed a short story that appeared the next day on one of the back pages of the *Chronicle*. It described the basic facts of the lawsuit, the judge's anger and her instructions. It was the first news coverage of the case.

Johnny Bob grabbed his cell phone as soon as he hit I-45 north of Houston. "T.J., you're getting us in a mess of trouble. I just left Judge O'Reilly and she's madder than a whole nest full of hornets. You've got to cut out this crap about the defendants being murderers and killers. You hear me?"

"I hear you loud and clear, Mr. Tisdale," Reverend Luther replied, "and I appreciate you conveying the message from the judge. What you don't understand is that I only take orders from my Father, not any man or any woman. It is His wish that I continue my attacks on abortion clinics and the murderers who perform abortions."

Frustrated, Johnny Bob yelled into the cell phone, "Goddammit, T.J, I've warned you! That's all I can do. Keep it up and there may be hell to pay."

Not wanting to hear a reply, he clicked the button on the phone and ended the conversation. He cussed T.J. all the way back to Palestine.

Back in Houston, Tod called Dr. Moyo. "Zeke, the judge has warned this two-bit Fort Worth preacher and that's all that can be done."

"But, Tod, it's too late; twenty-three patients have already cancelled."

On Sunday, T.J. ignored the judge and his lawyer, cranking it up a couple of notches, particularly when he saw his television ratings were up 12 percent. He called out the names of his enemies, Population Planning and Dr. Moyo. This time he concluded with a prayer for "our forces" to triumph in the Brady lawsuit and in the fight against abortion.

For Tod and Dr. Moyo it was the last straw. On Monday Tod issued a notice to take the deposition of Thomas Jeremiah Luther, a.k.a. the Chosen, on the following Friday in Fort Worth. Tod had to get to the bottom of Luther's involvement, and the best place to start was to put him under oath. Johnny Bob immediately filed a motion to quash the deposition and asked for an emergency hearing on Thursday morning.

"Your Honor," began Johnny Bob, "this deposition is totally uncalled for. This is a malpractice case. The deposition of Reverend Luther cannot possibly lead to anything relevant to this lawsuit. He wasn't even in the picture when most of the events occurred. We haven't even begun the depositions of the real witnesses in the case."

"Your response, Mr. Duncan?"

"Yes, Your Honor. I'll be brief. I could argue that he is a material witness since he clearly has knowledge of young Ms. Brady's physical condition. He even claims to have healed her. However, I don't want to mislead the court. He has publicly intervened in our proceeding here in Houston for some reason that's unclear to me. He talks about 'our forces' without naming them. He has defamed my client and Population Planning. You will note that I have also designated this notice as one to investigate a claim. Frankly, I want to get to the bottom of his interest in our lawsuit."

Janice Akers chimed in, "Your Honor, Population Planning joins in Mr. Duncan's motion and his argument."

"I assumed you would, Ms. Akers," the judge replied. "Here's my ruling. I'm going to let you have your deposition, including videotaping it, Mr. Duncan. I'm not going to limit your questioning. However, I recognize that this is most unusual and I can see that Mr. Tisdale could raise a number of objections at the deposition. So, I'm going to make myself available by telephone here in the courtroom. If you have an objection or another matter to take up with the court, give me a call and we'll try to resolve it on the spot. Maybe that will save you a few trips back and forth to Fort Worth. Any questions?"

Once again, the *Chronicle* reporter was in the back of the courtroom. This time he filed a very small story that was used as filler in the metropolitan section of the next edition. Only two column inches, the Associated Press picked it up. The small story caught the eye of several editors around the country who calendared the deposition for follow-up. The Chosen was a national figure whose deposition might be newsworthy.

44

When Tod got back to his office, he found Zeke Moyo waiting for him, dressed in jeans and a golf shirt. Tod had never seen him look so solemn. He almost expected the doctor to break out in tears.

"Come on up to my office, Zeke."

When they were seated at the table overlooking the garden, Tod waited until Dr. Moyo spoke.

"Tod, I don't know what to do. All of my patients canceled again today. I've only got two appointments left for tomorrow. Half of my patients have requested that their records be transferred to another doctor. At this rate, I won't be able to feed my family or pay my rent. What am I to do?"

Tod had grown to like his client. In the back of his mind a plan was brewing. It grew from Jan's comment about the pro-life forces using the courthouse as part of their battle plan. But he had to develop the facts to implement his plan and he didn't want to give his client false hope. "Zeke, I have an idea that I prefer not to discuss until I have some facts to support it. I'll be taking that two-bit preacher's deposition tomorrow and maybe we'll get to the bottom of this. Can you find other work? Although it could impact on our lawsuit, you could go back to doing abortions."

"No, sir! That's what got me into this predicament. I am applying to do some emergency room work. It doesn't pay much. If I can put in a lot of hours, I hope that I can pay my rent and keep food on the table. I've already cut my staff down to one nurse, and I'm worried that she'll be looking for another job soon."

"Zeke, I know that it's not much consolation. All I can tell you to do now is tough it out. I'll give you a call after the deposition in Fort Worth tomorrow."

AT TEN O'CLOCK ON Friday morning, the deposition began at a court reporter's office in downtown Fort Worth. Johnny Bob introduced everyone. "Reverend Luther, this is Tod Duncan, the lawyer for Dr. Moyo, and this is Janice Akers, the lawyer for Population Planning."

"Johnny Bob, are you representing Reverend Luther in this proceeding?" inquired Tod.

Before Tisdale could answer, T.J. interjected, "Counsel, it's not necessary for me to have an attorney for this proceeding. I can handle myself quite well, thank you."

"He's right, Tod, at least about the part of not having a lawyer. I suggested that it would be best for him to have one and he declined. So, we're ready to go."

The court reporter confirmed that everyone was ready, then turned to the witness and spoke. "Reverend Luther, would you raise your right hand? Do you solemnly swear to tell the truth, the whole truth and nothing but the truth, so help you God?"

T.J. looked at the reporter and the lawyers for a moment before replying, "I do."

Tod started the questioning. "Reverend Luther, do you understand that you have just taken an oath to tell us the truth today?"

"I do. But the oath is unnecessary. I always speak the truth."

"Do you know a young lady named Lucy Baines Brady?"

"With respect, sir, I must advise you that I will answer none of your questions. I answer only to my Father, not to you or to your judge."

Tod looked at Jan. Jan looked at Johnny Bob. Johnny Bob

just shook his head. Tod tried once more, "Sir, can you tell us who are the forces for whom you were speaking when you preached last Sunday morning?"

"Again, sir, I will answer questions only from my Father."

"Are you saying that no matter what questions that I ask, that will be your answer?"

"That is correct, sir."

Tod turned to Johnny Bob. "This is not exactly the kind of thing that I suspect the judge had in mind when she said she would be available, but I suppose we might as well put in a call and get her advice."

"I agree." Johnny Bob nodded.

Shortly, Judge O'Reilly said, "My goodness, counsel, you couldn't have been going more than fifteen minutes. You mean to tell me that you already have questions that are objectionable, or at least Mr. Tisdale thinks they are objectionable?"

"No, ma'am. Not exactly," Tod said as he proceeded to outline the events that had led to calling the judge.

"Mr. Tisdale, did Mr. Duncan describe the events accurately?"

"Yes, ma'am. I'm afraid he did."

There was a pause on the other end of the phone as Judge O'Reilly considered her options. After all, this was not some average Joe Citizen being deposed. Whatever she did was likely to hit the media, but she had ordered the deposition, and she damn well expected her orders to be carried out, no matter who the witness was. Even President Clinton had to sit for a deposition. She made up her mind. "Reverend Luther, can you hear me okay?"

"Yes, Judge. Your voice is coming through quite well."

"Very good, then. I want to make sure you understand what I am saying. Reverend Luther, I am ordering you to answer the questions in this deposition. You have no more nor fewer rights under our system than any other citizen of this state. Our rules do not permit a witness to decide whether or not to answer questions. If you do not answer Mr. Duncan's questions, then I will entertain a motion to have you held in contempt. That means you may be fined or potentially jailed until you are willing to answer questions. The latter is a harsh remedy that I have never had to invoke in more than twenty years on the bench, but I've never had a witness who refused to answer the most basic of questions. If you are jailed, you will stay there until you change your mind or until the trial. Have I made myself clear?"

"I understand, Your Honor, but I do not answer to you or any person on this earth. I answer only to my Father."

"So be it. Counsel, do whatever you think best."

Tod disconnected the call and turned to T.J. "Reverend Luther, on the record one more time, I want to confirm that you understood the judge. Further, you understand that if you continue to refuse to answer my questions, I will be filing a motion to hold you in contempt of court. Are you still refusing to answer any of my questions?"

T.J. looked into the camera and replied, "I understood the judge and I understand you, Mr. Duncan. I have nothing more to say."

The deposition ended. T.J. went back to his penthouse. The lawyers returned to their respective offices to contemplate their next moves. At the conclusion of the deposition, the *Chronicle* reporter called the court reporter for an account of the proceeding. On Saturday morning, the story of the preacher who would answer only to his Father made the front page of the metropolitan section. This time the story described the Chosen, the history of his long sleep followed by his awakening, and the Brady lawsuit. It ended with a comment the reporter had gotten from Tod who said he would be filing a motion to hold the Chosen in contempt. When the Associated Press picked up the story, it made headlines across the country. CNN mentioned it on the evening news. T.J. wanted publicity and he knew how to get it.

ON THE WAY BACK to Palestine, Johnny Bob was in a bad mood. Each lawsuit had a life of its own. It ebbed and flowed like the tide. When a lawyer was on the crest of a wave, he rode it for as long as possible, knowing full well that eventually he would end up in the trough with the wave pounding over his head until the next crest came along. Such highs and lows were expected by seasoned trial lawyers. Yet, he couldn't recall ever having a case with a problem this big almost before it was underway. T.J.'s rantings had the distinct prospect of torpedoing Lucy's entire lawsuit. There was now no doubt that T.J. had an agenda different from his. Johnny Bob had not anticipated just how different.

The big lawyer parked his truck in front of the bank building and climbed the stairs to his office, feeling his age for the first time while thinking that maybe it was time to build an office that did not require climbing to the third floor. As he entered the front door, a visitor, a tall black woman in her mid-thirties, greeted him. She had short black hair and an almost perfect face framed with gold, loop earrings. She accented her black dress with a solid gold necklace. A gold figure of a small child hung from the necklace. Three-inch heels accentuated her natural height. She rose as he entered.

Johnny Bob looked her over before speaking. "I'm sorry, I didn't realize I had an appointment with a new client. Please forgive me, Ms. . . . ?"

"Well, first of all, Mr. Tisdale, I'm not a new client. My name is Claudia St. John Jackson. I'm an abortionist's worst enemy and I'm here to help you."

"Very kind of you to offer, Ms. St. John Jackson. If you're talking about the Brady case, first, I'm surprised you even know about it, and second, we have several lawyers here. I'm not looking to hire another one."

"I understand what you're saying. Hear me out. Do you mind if we go into your office?"

"Of course not. Please forgive my lack of manners. Can I get you some coffee or a Coke or water?"

"Water will be just fine, bottled if you have it."

They entered Johnny Bob's office and sat at the coffee table, Johnny Bob in the big easy chair and Claudia on the old leather couch. Sara, his secretary of fifteen years, brought coffee and bottled water.

After she poured her water, Claudia began. "Let me explain. My last name is Jackson. The St. John part wasn't given to me by my parents. I just thought it had a nice professional touch, so I added it when I graduated from law school."

Johnny Bob smiled, thinking back to his becoming J. Robert instead of Johnny Bob.

"I grew up in the Midwest, the daughter of a Baptist preacher and a schoolteacher. I went to Stanford on scholarship where I graduated with honors and made Phi Beta Kappa. From there I was accepted at Harvard, not because of the color of my skin but because I earned admission. I wrote for the *Harvard Law Review* and made Order of the Coif. I had more job offers than I could count but returned to the Midwest to work for the Midwest Pro-Life Legal Defense Fund. You don't find many blacks who take up abortion as their life cause. Not only is my father strongly anti-abortion, but it goes even further. I had an older sister who died at the hands of an abortionist when I was in high school. I've been practicing law for ten years. I know every appellate case in the country, state or federal, that touches on abortion, and I've been involved in fifteen abortion cases in the past five years. Besides, you've got a black defendant, and pardon the expression, but you look like an East Texas redneck. You need some balance on your team. Now, how did the deposition go this morning? I presume that Reverend Luther took the holy Fifth Amendment, or something of that sort."

The last comment took Johnny Bob by surprise. It had only been two hours since he left Fort Worth, hardly enough time for word about the deposition to make its way to Palestine. "I gotta admit, Claudia, if I may call you that, now you really have me stumped. I'm impressed with your credentials, but I damn sure would like to know how you learned what happened in Fort Worth this morning."

"You remember one of your first meetings with T.J. when he told you that he would not only provide you with two million dollars, but he would give you legal support. Well, I'm the support that he was talking about, and better yet, you don't have to pay for it. I talked to T.J. earlier this week and he told me what he was going to do. I tried to talk him out of it. You can see that I was not very persuasive. Looks like you got a tiger by the tail."

Johnny Bob looked at the striking black woman before him and stroked his chin, a habit that he had picked up from Judge Arbuckle many years ago, before he spoke. "Welcome aboard, Claudia. You call me Johnny Bob. Whether you're a gift from God or T.J. don't rightly matter. I'm not prone to looking a gift horse in the mouth. Are you here for the duration?"

"You bet. Got my clothes in the car and my case law in my laptop. I just need a desk and a place to stay. Got any recommendations?"

"As to a desk, my old office down the hall is available. We use it for storage, but under all the boxes, there's still a desk and chair. Sorry to say that there's no view, though. As to a place to stay, you come out to my house. I've got three apartments for my three kids. One of them lives up in Colorado and doesn't use it much. It's two thousand feet and fully furnished. It's got its own entrance. You can come and go as you please and you're welcome to eat with me and Bernice as much as you want. We always enjoy company."

"Sounds good to me, particularly the part about using your old office. It'll make for a good story back in Ohio. You may not realize it, but your reputation has traveled all the way to Harvard. In torts class when they talk about the great plaintiff lawyers, you're always in the top five."

"Must be some Yankee prejudice working. I kinda figured I'd earned the number one spot."

45

As soon as he got back to Houston, Tod dictated a motion to hold Thomas Jeremiah Luther in contempt. It tracked what the judge had told T.J. and asked that he be incarcerated in the Harris County jail until he agreed to answer questions under oath. He faxed it to Jan for approval and filed it that same afternoon. Judge O'Reilly glanced over it and saw nothing out of the ordinary, assuming, she thought, that a request to throw a nationally known religious leader in the hoosegow is not out of the ordinary. She had already decided that she would set the motion in two weeks. She wanted to give Reverend Luther plenty of time to seek the advice of counsel, hopefully one that would beat some sense into his head. She didn't realize that two weeks would also be enough time to assemble what would become the first act of a three-ring media circus. She would have preferred not to be the ringmaster, but fate would have it no other way.

OUT FOR HIS MORNING run the next day, Tod contemplated what had transpired. Concerned that T.J. would never answer questions, he considered his options and finally settled on one. When he got to the office, he filed a second motion, this one requiring the Brady plaintiffs—really Johnny Bob—to divulge the forces that were backing the lawsuit. Such a motion wouldn't normally have a prayer except that he also requested T.J.'s deposition for the purpose of investigating a potential claim. If T.J. continued to refuse to answer questions, the motion would be a backup plan. Tod had no strong basis in law. Still, the judge wouldn't be happy with the conduct of the Chosen. If Johnny Bob couldn't identify T.J.'s forces, he could say so. If he knew them, the judge might be inclined to require disclosure. This time they were all sailing on uncharted waters.

The second motion was also set at the same time as the motion to hold T.J. in contempt.

Claudia read the two motions and marched into Johnny Bob's office. Flinging the documents on his desk, she angrily took a seat and launched into a verbal attack on Tod Duncan. "What kind of shit is this? I understand the first motion. As to the second one, how the hell can he possibly think that a judge will grant a motion requiring you to disclose a privileged matter like who is funding your fees? That's got to be attorney-client privilege."

"Now, Claudia, just you calm down. I learned years ago that when it comes to planning lawsuit strategy, getting angry only muddles the mind. The motion wouldn't stand a chance if T.J. had just answered questions. Remember, in Texas we have this discovery process called a deposition to investigate a claim. Tod threw that into his original motion. The judge may just be mad enough at T.J. to give Tod this information in another way. We'll fight it. Eventually, the names of the forces that T.J. kept alluding to are going to come out if he has to depose every pro-life group in the country. Don't be surprised if we lose. Tod Duncan's a shrewd lawyer and has something up his sleeve. I just haven't quite figured out what it is. You go on and prepare responses to both motions."

As Claudia returned to her office, Johnny Bob hollered down the hall, "And throw some of those Harvard words in there. Maybe they'll impress the judge."

Next, he picked up the phone and called Fort Worth. When T.J. came on the line, he barely said hello before Johnny Bob barked. "Now you've done it, T.J. You've got to be in Judge O'Reilly's court on this contempt motion in less than two weeks. Let me give you the names of a couple of lawyers in Fort Worth and Houston who will give you first-class representation."

"Won't be necessary, Johnny Bob. I'll represent myself."

"T.J., for once would you listen to me? That's the one sure way for you to end up in jail for contempt of court."

"Jail doesn't bother me. It won't be the first time."

"Then you best bring your toothbrush to the hearing, T.J., and while you're at it, probably a change of underwear."

When Johnny Bob ended the call, T.J. smiled to himself. His plan was developing nicely. He had not contemplated a jail term when he first conceived the idea of using Lucy's lawsuit as the centerpiece of his great leap to the forefront of the religious right. However, when he listened to the judge's admonition on the speakerphone at his deposition, he realized that he could become a martyr. He would not be the first religious leader imprisoned for his beliefs yet he was convinced that he could capitalize on such a situation far better than any of his predecessors. Of course, he was right. Unfortunately, he neglected to consider one thing. With all the plans afoot, he failed to consider that Tod Duncan was a match for any man when it came to the strategy of a courthouse battle.

On Monday morning two weeks later, the court reporter stuck her head into Judge O'Reilly's chambers. "Judge, you're not going to believe this. We've got a courtroom full of reporters and other media types. There's not a seat to be had. They've filled up the jury box and the back of the courtroom. They're even spilling out into the hallway. All four networks along with CNN have remote trucks out in the street. Even the *New York Times* is here. I gotta go to my office and check my makeup."

The door slammed, leaving Judge O'Reilly to evaluate her options. As to Reverend Luther, she was satisfied that she had none. She was not about to let him set himself above the law, not in her court. As to the second motion, except for T.J.'s obstructive behavior, she would deny it. On the other hand, his behavior led to the motion. She put on her robe and glanced at herself in the mirror on her bathroom door. Finding everything in place, she opened the courtroom door promptly at nine. As she made her appearance, everyone in the courtroom rose.

"Please be seated. We have before us the matter of Brady

versus Population Planning and Dr. Moyo. I assume all parties are ready. Reverend Luther, I recognize you from your television shows. Do you have counsel?"

T.J. responded, "No, Your Honor. I have no need for counsel. I am quite certain I can represent myself."

His reply caused a murmur from the assembled reporters, which in turn caused an admonition from the judge. "Ladies and gentlemen in the audience, we are pleased to have you in my court. However, you will not be permitted to interfere with court business. If there are any outbursts or even whispers that reach my ears, I will instruct my bailiff to have you removed. Do you understand?" She continued, "The first matter will be the motion to hold Reverend Luther in contempt. Reverend Luther, you, of course, recall that I warned you that this could occur when you refused to answer questions at your deposition. I must advise you before you speak that if you continue to refuse to obey the orders of this court, I will find you in contempt and hold you in the county jail until you change your mind. Now, are you willing to answer Mr. Duncan's questions?"

T.J. rose and replied, "With the utmost respect to you, Your Honor, and to your court, my Father has advised that I should answer to no man, only to Him. For that reason, my position has not changed and I fully understand the consequences."

Silence filled the courtroom. The judge paused, took a noticeable breath and spoke. "Then, Reverend Luther, you leave me no choice. I find that you are in contempt of court and I commit you to the Harris County jail until you are willing to answer questions of counsel in this case. The court will not entertain any motion for bond. Bailiff, take Reverend Luther away."

As the bailiff led T.J. into the hallway, the reporters crowded out the door, holding microphones in T.J.'s face and asking for comments. The camera crews in the hallway also tried to get a comment, but the bailiff had prepared for this event and had three more deputies waiting beyond the door.

They formed a flying wedge, with T.J. in the middle, and pushed their way through the phalanx of reporters and cameras to a waiting elevator where they took T.J. to the first floor and escorted him from there to the jail two blocks away. The networks and CNN led off their evening news with the story of the powerful televangelist who had come back from death only to be incarcerated for his beliefs.

T.J. watched the telecasts from the dayroom of the jail that night with a slight smile. He figured that with his fertile mind and a little luck, he could keep himself on the nightly news for however long it took to get the case to trial. He thought of Nelson Mandela and his years in prison before he emerged to claim a Nobel Prize. He certainly didn't expect twenty years in jail and didn't want a Nobel Prize. He would settle for a few months and the leadership of the religious right. His plan was working.

Back in the courtroom, neither T.J. nor the reporters understood the importance of Tod's second motion. In fact, the reporters didn't even stick around.

"Mr. Duncan, Mr. Tisdale, Ms. Akers . . ."

"Your Honor, forgive me," Johnny Bob spoke. "I failed to introduce my associate on this case. May I introduce Claudia St. John Jackson from Ohio. I'll be filing a motion to admit her to practice in this court for the limited purpose of participating in this case."

"Welcome, Ms. Jackson. I'm sure there'll be no opposition to Mr. Tisdale's request. Here's my ruling. In light of the refusal of the Reverend Luther to answer the question regarding his forces, and only because of that, Mr. Tisdale, I am directing you to turn over the names of any organizations that may be assisting Reverend Luther in this matter. I'll go on record as telling you that I am not sure where this is all going, and I concede that my ruling is most unusual. Mr. Tisdale, you are welcome to appeal, if you desire. If you do so, I must remind you that while this issue in on appeal, Reverend Luther will be a resident of the Harris County jail. You will have ten days to turn over the names of the forces or to give notice of appeal. That's all, ladies and gentlemen."

As Johnny Bob and Claudia drove back to Palestine, they debated their next move.

"Look, Johnny Bob, this is the first time I've seen this Judge O'Reilly in action. I don't quarrel with her decision to throw T.J. in the slammer, but I think she's dead wrong when she required us to give up the names of our pro-life organizations. We need to appeal the decision."

"Claudia, Tod knows there are some other organizations out there. We can thank T.J. and his big mouth for that. Even if we win on appeal, in the meantime, Tod will be deposing the head of every major pro-life group in the country until he learns who 'our forces' are. By now, he damn sure knows that this is something more than just your everyday, garden-variety malpractice case. I know him well enough to guarantee you that he won't stop until he finds what he's looking for. We might as well give him the names and be done with it."

As they approached Palestine, Claudia finally gave in to the experience and courthouse savvy of J. Robert Tisdale, a decision they would live to regret.

46

When Tod got the list of the organizations that had apparently supported T.J. in the funding of the litigation, he could not control his excitement. He called Jan and asked her to meet him and Wayne at his office as quickly as she could get there. When she arrived, Tod slid down the fire pole to meet her, a grin spread across his face. He gave her a hug exclaiming, "Come on up. This is going to be fun."

Wayne waited at the table by the window. Jan took a seat and spoke first. "All right. What the hell is going on? So we got the names of a bunch of pro-life organizations. Pardon my language, but big fucking deal. What does that do for our defense?"

"Ah, Jan, my most honorable colleague, you clearly have

not divined the moves that I have been making for the past several weeks. That's good. If you haven't figured them out, neither has the other side. Let me explain. As you know, when you're a defendant, it's always best to try to go on the offensive. Much better if the other side has something to lose as well as something to win. Next, as you know from my ancient past, I happen to know something about libel and slander, having successfully defended a number of such cases. Defamation law makes it clear that whatever is said in a court of law is absolutely privileged, even if it is wrong. If a witness accuses me of murder, as long as it is said from the witness stand, such statements are generally protected by our Constitution. Such statements carry no such protection if said outside a court of law.

"You told me early on that the pro-life forces were using the courthouse as a weapon. I suspected, when T.J. began blasting the defendants in this case, that they had chosen this for a major battle. They hired J. Robert Tisdale to get them a giant verdict, and that's why T.J. started attacking us almost every Sunday. The pro-lifers want to focus national attention on our malpractice case, and with T.J., they're succeeding. What he said was absolutely slanderous and I've known it from the start. I wasn't just interested in the one fish with the big mouth. I wanted to cast a wider net in hopes of landing the whole school, and now we have done so. All we have to do is haul them in."

"Wait a minute, Tod. Quit talking about fishing and let me try to understand what you are saying. Are you suggesting that we are going to sue T.J. and all of these other organizations?"

"Ah, my confidence in you was not misplaced," he smiled. "You have seen right through to my admittedly devious plot."

"Tod, do you realize what's going to happen if we add ten or twelve more players to this thing, particularly pro-life organizations? World War Three might as well break out."

"Not so, Jan. Look at it this way. They're already players. They're just not defendants. Remember when we first got involved, you told me that the pro-life forces were using the courthouse to try to put the pro-choice movement out of business. Let's put the shoe on the other foot. They have already succeeded in destroying the career of my client, whom I have grown to respect. He's a damn fine doctor and may never be able to practice his specialty again, all because T.J., as spokesman for *His* forces, called him a murderer, a baby killer and a butcher. That's slander per se. Don't you see? As a matter of law he has been defamed, and so has your client. It's just a question of damages. They've succeeded in putting my client out of business even without a trial. The next move for them is to push your client into bankruptcy, not just in Houston, but nationwide. If they want a fight, let's give them one. Let's sue them for a hundred million dollars for the damages to our clients. They need to know that this lawsuit may also put all of them into bankruptcy and out of business."

Jan buried her face in her hands and peeked through her fingers, looking out at the garden as she contemplated what she was hearing. Finally, she spoke. "Boy, remind me to never get on the opposite side of a lawsuit from you. I don't want you ever plotting against my clients. I was kidding about World War Three, but that's what we're in for. My client has had to defend these malpractice cases around the country. Maybe it is time to go on the offensive. I'll have to clear it with my local board and also with the national board. What you're fixing to do may have the greatest impact on this issue since *Roe v. Wade*. Well, you get Dr. Moyo in for a heart-to-heart, and I'll meet with both my boards. Give me two weeks for an answer."

Jan left the office with a determined look. As she walked past the hallway bell, she clanged it once. Was there such a thing as a six-alarm fire?

It took two days to catch Dr. Moyo when he was not working in the emergency room. Zeke arrived at the fire station not knowing what to expect. As Tod explained his plan, Zeke's eyes grew big. "Are you saying that this will give me the opportunity to restore my name and also the opportunity to recover all that I have lost?"

"Zeke, I don't want to promise you anything," replied

Tod. "There are no guarantees or warranties that come with lawsuits. If we win, you will have a finding that the slanderous statements of the pro-life forces have defamed you. From what I know about what has happened to you, I have no doubt that you have been damaged. Hopefully, we can convince a jury that your damages are well into the millions of dollars. Again, I can't make any promises. I can't even promise that the judge will let us do this or that there will be any solvent organization that will be able to pay a judgment. I want your name and reputation to be vindicated and I'll do everything in my power to make that happen. One last comment. If we do nothing, the best we can hope for is that a jury will find that you were not negligent and that won't do much to restore your name."

"You're my lawyer, Tod, and I have grown to have confidence in you. My life is in shambles now. If you think this may improve our chances, I trust your judgment. Let's go for it."

Tod smiled as he heard his client's response. He liked being the aggressor.

A week later he heard from Jan. She had gotten clearance from her client's national board. Tod and Jan wanted to bring this action in the original Brady case although there were strong legal arguments against such a tactic. Even conceding that they could maintain such a cause of action, which was not an issue in their minds, they could expect Johnny Bob and Claudia to fight to make it a separate lawsuit. They would push for a different judge and a different trial schedule, one that would put them in front of a jury long after the Brady case was over. Besides, Brady was a malpractice case. It should not be cluttered up with an action for slander that had nothing to do with malpractice.

Tod and Jan had to figure out a way around such an argument. Jan had an idea that led to the theme of their motion. The Texas Rules required that if a third-party action were to be joined with another predecessor lawsuit, it had to arise out of the same set of facts. It also helped if an argument could be made that it would make for judicial economy if both cases could be tried before the same judge and jury. Jan carefully crafted a motion, pointing out that the slander that had been inflicted on Dr. Moyo and Population Planning arose out of the same factual scenario that led to Lucy Brady's lawsuit. The underlying facts would be exactly the same. The only addition would be the slanderous comments of Reverend Luther as spokesperson for the pro-life forces, and they all tied back into the abortion performed by Dr. Moyo at the Population Planning clinic. It would be a close call. Judge O'Reilly had a tendency to try multiple issues at one time. It was worth a shot. With a little luck, they would hit a bull's-eye.

When Johnny Bob saw the motion to sue the pro-life forces, he understood all of the maneuvering that Tod had done. "Well, I'll be a goddamned country lawyer if I ain't been slickered," he said to Claudia. "That's one fine move that Tod has put on us. I haven't seen such a nice move since Michael Jordan played for the Bulls. Claudia, we have a chance at winning this motion. There's not a real basis for attaching this slander lawsuit to our malpractice case. You ought to find plenty of law to support our position. Go to it, girl. The hearing is in seven days."

While Claudia's brief was brilliant, it wasn't good enough. Probably what carried the day for Tod and Jan was nothing that Johnny Bob could control. Another courtroom full of reporters with even more remote television vans parked outside watched as the judge listened carefully to both sides and then ruled that the defendants could sue T.J. Luther, the City of Miracles, and the dozen other pro-life organizations in the Brady lawsuit. As she made the ruling, she commented, "Gentlemen and ladies, I like circuses, but I prefer the kind that have elephants, tightrope walkers and clowns." Glancing at the audience of reporters, she continued, "While we may have an abundance of clowns, I don't like media circuses in my courtroom. If I don't combine these cases, I'll have two circuses. In my mind, that's one too many."

Turning back to the lawyers, she continued, "Mr. Duncan, you get your citations served pronto. I presume that you gentlemen and ladies have heard of a fast track. Well, you ain't seen nothing yet. Consider that you are all on one of those

European high-speed bullet trains. It's going to arrive at the station in four months. I expect you all to be ready for trial. Mr. Tisdale, I feel certain that you have some contact with the new third-party defendants. I recommend that you get on the phone with them today. Tell them to get their act together in a hurry and not to waste their time in asking for a continuance. However, you can also advise them that I'll entertain a motion for summary judgment for any of them that can show me that they were not involved with Reverend Luther and his comments. I don't want anyone who doesn't truly belong in this fight."

The print reporters scurried to use their phones. The television reporters raced to broadcast the story throughout the country. Tod commented to one reporter as he left the courthouse, "The price of poker has just gone up."

Johnny Bob and Claudia used the back door of the courthouse to avoid reporters and cameras as they walked the two blocks to the Harris County jail to inform T.J. of the development.

When they took the elevator to T.J.'s floor, a deputy met them at a reception desk. Discovering that they wanted to see T.J., his eyes brightened. "Oh, you want to see the preacher man. That won't be very hard. He's in the deputy lounge on the telephone. I think it's to Fort Worth." Seeing the surprised look on their faces, he continued, "Well, you know, it's not like he's a murderer or even a robber. He's here because of what he believes. He's not gonna go anywhere. So, we pretty much let him have the run of the place until lights-out at ten. He's a real helpful fella, too. Matter of fact, a bunch of us used to watch his Sunday morning service even before we got to know him on a first-name basis. You want to see the Bible he personally autographed for me? I'm saving it to give to my wife on our anniversary."

Declining the invitation, they were shown into the lounge where they found T.J. sitting in an easy chair, feet propped up on a coffee table and talking on a cell phone. When he saw them, he ended his call and rose. "Howdy, Johnny Bob.

Who's this lovely lady with you? On second thought, I know who she is. I talked to her a couple of months ago. I was just on the phone to the *Fort Worth Star Telegram*. They're running a front-page story on me being in jail in their Sunday edition and wanted a few quotes. I gave them an earful. That's the fifth interview I've done this week. I'm really trying to limit interviews to national media, *Time, Newsweek, USA Today* and the networks. This, though, is my hometown paper and I always feel obliged to help my friends."

Johnny Bob and Claudia sat on the couch opposite T.J. and filled him in on the morning's events. As he explained the lawsuit to be brought against the City of Miracles and the others, Johnny Bob saw a flicker of concern cross T.J.'s eyes as he mentioned one hundred million dollars. Then it was gone and T.J. spoke. "So, tell me the truth, Johnny Bob, did you underestimate this Tod Duncan? Is he out-lawyering you?"

"Nothing of the sort, T.J. Like a good prizefighter, Tod saw his opening and landed a good blow to the body. I gotta tell you, though, I didn't expect you to be quite so vicious in your attacks on Dr. Moyo and the clinic."

"Just did what I had to do. They are murderers and there's no way to sugarcoat the truth."

"Well, T.J., sometime you and I just might debate that, but not now. We've got to do some planning. You're about to be served with a petition along with the rest of your forces. The first decision is whether there's a conflict of interest among the consortium. While some of the others may not like how you said things, not one of them has disagreed, at least not to my knowledge. Besides, they all agreed that you would be the person to galvanize public opinion and expected you to be speaking from the pulpit on this lawsuit. So, while they may not like getting sued, particularly for a hundred million, my recommendation is that you all have one lawyer. I'd like that much better since I don't want to have to get a consensus from a dozen other lawyers when decisions have to be made."

"Don't disagree, Johnny Bob. Who'd you have in mind?"

"Far as I'm concerned, the pro-life groups' lawyer is sitting right here. Frankly, I don't know of another lawyer who has as much standing with them as Claudia, and I can tell you she is first-class."

Claudia sized up the situation and quickly decided that she liked the idea of being something more than second chair to Johnny Bob. "Assuming we have a meeting with the rest of the groups and they agree, I'm available."

As they left the deputy lounge, Johnny Bob paused and turned at the doorway. "By the way, T.J., you may want to cut down on those interviews. If things heat up much more, we're going to get a gag order from the judge. Not only will you be locked up, but there'll be a zipper on your mouth. Won't be pleasant."

THREE DAYS LATER THE general chaired another meeting of the consortium in the Miracle City board room. Johnny Bob and Claudia were there to brief them. All of the various representatives recognized that they were in the middle of the fight now, no longer just observing from the sidelines. They were well aware of Claudia's reputation and agreed that she could represent the group, including T.J. and the City of Miracles. They were concerned about T.J. He already had created enough trouble. Johnny Bob assured them that he would be locked in the Harris County jail for a while. As a party to the lawsuit, he wasn't going to say anything. As a matter of fact, he advised the group that he expected Judge O'Reilly to put a gag order in place at the first opportunity, probably when all parties were in the case, and were subject to her mandate. Johnny Bob failed to recognize just how pissed off T.J. was. Had he known, he just might have tried to put a muzzle on that alligator himself.

47

Lucy burst out the door of her room to the garden where she found Jessie reading. "Aunt Jessie, we need to go to Houston to see T.J."

"Lucy, you know T.J. is in jail."

"But, that's just why we need to see him. I just got off the phone with him and he says he's lonely. Besides, he says that he's really in jail because he's trying to help me."

"Look, Lucy, it's too long a drive for a short visit. The judge will probably let him out soon enough."

"Aunt Jessie, you know that I don't have any friends right now besides T.J. He's the reason I'm doing so much better. His counseling is what convinced me that even though I was raped and had an abortion, I'm still a woman and entitled to live a normal life. I'm entitled to have a husband and maybe even kids and a dog. *Please,* Aunt Jessie. We can even visit Mom and Dad."

The last plea finally convinced Jessie. The next day she and Lucy loaded her Jaguar with a few snacks and soft drinks and pointed the car south toward Houston.

Not surprisingly, they found T.J. in the deputy lounge. T.J. gave them both a hug and thanked them for coming.

"I really miss seeing the people I cherish," T.J. continued. "Jessie, you and Lucy and Lucy's family have become like family to me. I don't mind being in jail. Still, it's good to see familiar faces occasionally. Tell me, Lucy, how are you holding up with all of this?"

Lucy hesitated as she collected her thoughts. "I know that we're doing the right thing. I'm scared of being involved in the trial and having to get on a witness stand. I just want it over so I can try to have a real life."

Jessie interrupted. "Don't you worry, honey. I've told Mr. Tisdale this is taking a toll on you. With his help and T.J.'s we'll all get through it. I just hope it's worth it in the end."

"Jessie, I can promise you that is not even an issue," T.J. replied. "We will prevail."

As he finished, there was a knock on the door and a deputy told them that time was up. As Jessie got up to leave, Lucy turned to Jessie and said, "Aunt Jessie, can I have one minute with T.J. alone?"

A puzzled look flitted briefly across Jessie's face before she nodded and left the lounge.

48

It was the second Saturday after T.J.'s incarceration when it started. Several of the local pro-life groups decided that they needed to show their support for the Chosen. After alerting the local media on Friday evening, about forty of them showed up on the sidewalk in front of the Harris County jail where they were met by the *Chronicle* reporters and crews from two local television stations. Their signs were not particularly original. FREE THE CHOSEN. WHATEVER HAPPENED TO RELIGIOUS FREEDOM? LET OUR LEADER LOOSE. WHY IS THE FIRST AMENDMENT ONLY FOR MURDERERS? They waited until the cameras were rolling and began circling the sidewalk, chanting, "Free the Chosen Now!"

After a few minutes, a local Baptist minister picked up a bullhorn and delivered a short sermon focusing on the depravity of a society that would jail such a great man as the Chosen yet allow abortionists to walk the streets. He made sure that he kept it short enough for a good sound bite on the evening news.

From a window high above, T.J. looked down on the small assembly. Few though they were, it was a start. Grabbing his cell phone, he called the City of Miracles' public relations department to make sure that they picked up any local stories and forwarded them for national distribution. He also directed one other event for the following weekend. If he were to be a martyr, it was time for more attention.

On the next Saturday morning, an assortment of motor homes, minivans, passenger cars and pickups filled the parking lot of the City of Miracles. Nearly all of them had writing about T.J. and the lawsuit on the windows. At six-thirty the message over the loudspeaker told them to move out. The vehicles followed a large motor home owned by the City, with permanent lettering on the sides and back, inviting others to FOLLOW US TO A MIRACLE. The caravan was on its way to Houston. With headlights on and horns blaring, they left the parking lot and fell in line behind the motor home. This time the national media were in attendance, complete with helicopters following the several-hundred-vehicle caravan. Five hours later, they arrived in Houston and filled the parking lots around the Harris County Courthouse. Soon a thousand protestors shouted, "Free the Chosen." The caravan and demonstration were on the national news for the rest of the weekend. Now the whole country recognized that Reverend Luther sat in jail because he stood up for his religious beliefs.

On the Monday after the Miracle City caravan and demonstration, Judge O'Reilly's clerk called each of the lawyers. She ordered a command performance at five o'clock Tuesday afternoon. At the appointed hour, Johnny Bob and Claudia arrived from Palestine. Tod, Jan and Wayne joined them in the judge's chambers.

"Good afternoon, counsel," she began. Her demeanor was solemn and determined. "Please be seated. When I first saw this case, you all know that I anticipated that it had the potential to be a media circus. Under the circumstances, I don't want to be called a prophet, but it looks like I was exactly right. However, I did not anticipate that I would be accused of religious persecution and I don't like that accusation one damn bit. Mr. Tisdale and Ms. Jackson, I want you to make it perfectly clear to your client that all he has to do to get out of jail is to act like any other citizen of this state and answer questions in a deposition."

"Yes, ma'am. We have made that very clear to him," Johnny Bob responded.

"Frankly," the judge continued, "I have more than a strong suspicion that your client is orchestrating all of this as a means of attracting attention to himself and to this case, but there's nothing I can do about that. I'm not letting him out of jail. However, in light of what happened here on Saturday, I'm imposing a gag order on this case. I have no doubt that all I have to do is to tell such fine counsel as yourselves not to talk to the media and you will follow my instructions. For the benefit of your clients, most notably yours, Mr. Tisdale and Ms. Jackson, I will issue a written order by nine A.M. in the morning and that order will remain in effect until this case is over. I can't stop the media from their feeding frenzy, but I can make damn sure that the parties don't throw chum in the water. Anybody disagree?"

Knowing they had no choice in the matter, each lawyer agreed.

"Very well. The order will be in written form in the morning. Please advise your clients that it is effective immediately."

Tod and Jan used cell phones to call their respective clients while Johnny Bob and Claudia took the short walk over to the county jail. When they arrived, they found T.J. helping the guards pass out the evening dinner trays. After he finished, he joined them in the deputy lounge.

"Do you have the exclusive use of the guard's lounge, T.J.?" asked Johnny Bob.

"No, of course not, although I spend a good bit of time in here when I'm not ministering to the other prisoners. The guards are kind enough to leave me alone when I have visitors or when I am using my cell phone. They've been very gracious to me. I've even agreed to be a visiting pastor at a couple of their churches when this is all over."

"We've just come from Judge O'Reilly's court and she's now issued a gag order. That means that you can't talk to the press anymore, no contact with the media by you or anyone at the City of Miracles."

"Well, ain't that just a damn fine kettle of fish," T.J. replied, not hiding the anger that was seething through clinched teeth. "I'm just more than a little pissed off with this judge and what she's doing. I'm doing God's bidding. It's that damned Dr. Moyo and the murder clinic that are the criminals in the eyes of God. Instead of punishing them, she throws me in jail and now I'm not even allowed to talk about my case. I had *60 Minutes* coming in here for an interview, and you're telling me I can't talk to them. Damn it, my whole purpose is to get the media and the public on our side. I want twelve jurors who already have their minds made up when you put them in the box."

"Well, T.J., you see, that's the whole problem," Johnny Bob said. "This judge is one smart cookie and she's wise to your plan. You can remain in jail and play the role of the martyr. The media is onto the case, and it's not going away. You just can't call the shots."

T.J. reluctantly agreed to do what he was told, knowing that he was going to ignore his promise. Unfortunately, no one thought to advise the deputies of the judge's ruling only the evening before. T.J. told them that a *60 Minutes* crew would be there on Wednesday morning. That led to every inmate—T.J. excepted, of course—spit-shining the entire floor. The guards personally straightened up the deputy lounge and two guards brought flowers from their wives to brighten up the place.

The cameras arrived at nine A.M. and were rolling by ten o'clock. The producer explained that they would lead with a segment on T.J.'s life, leading up to his years in a coma, his awakening and his return to the pulpit. That would be followed by his miracle that caused Lucy to walk again and then the lawsuit, including the claims and counterclaims. The last part of the introduction would be the decision of the Chosen not to answer questions in the deposition. Then the reporter would start the interview from the lounge. After a series of softball questions, the reporter asked T.J. why he had refused to answer questions and T.J. took over.

"Let me start by saying that after I was resurrected, I was

directed by my Father to answer to no man. I have a mission here on earth and I must fulfill it before I return to my Father's side. I answer to God's law, not to the law of man. Even as we sit here today, I may again be violating one of man's laws. The judge in this case has issued a gag order. Since we had this interview scheduled before her order, it is my position that I am not violating her ruling. If I am wrong, I am willing to accept whatever sanctions the judge imposes. I will not have my freedom of speech taken away. I was put here because I would not subject myself to man's questions in a deposition. I have not changed my mind. It is shocking to me that I can be persecuted and incarcerated for my stand against abortion as well as my religious beliefs. We put that behind us two hundred years ago when our forefathers drafted the Constitution. I can only hope that my incarceration will serve to focus the attention of our national leaders to such persecution. I am willing to stay in this jail until trial and beyond, if that is necessary."

"Will you testify at trial?"

"Fair question. I don't know. I'll cross that bridge when I come to it. It may be that I'll have something to say in my defense at that time. Let me remind you that I should not be the prisoner here. The ones behind bars should be those who are running the abortion clinics and doing the killing."

Seeing where the interview was going, the producer terminated it. In another sentence or two, T.J. would launch an attack with his claim of the defendants being butchers and murderers. Certainly, she didn't want her program to be accused of taking sides. Nor did she want *60 Minutes* involved in the lawsuit.

ON SUNDAY NIGHT THE judge really blew her stack. This time she was at home, having seen a promo that *60 Minutes* would have a segment about the Chosen. The promo didn't bother her one bit. She couldn't control the media. It was when the reporter mentioned that Reverend Luther had been interviewed on the day after she had entered her gag order that she burst out a string of profanity. After watching *60*

Minutes, she called her clerk and told her to chase down J. Robert Tisdale and have him, Ms. Jackson and their client in her court by ten A.M. on Monday. Johnny Bob had also seen the promo and watched the same program. While he understood that T.J. was potentially in trouble, he was more than a little surprised to get a call from the judge's clerk on Sunday night. It was beginning to look like he might wear out his pickup on the highway to Houston.

Judge O'Reilly took the bench. With no advance warning, somehow the word had gotten out and the courtroom was almost full of reporters. Johnny Bob, Claudia and T.J., dressed in his jailhouse-orange jumpsuit, sat at one counsel table. Tod and Jan were seated at the other. "Ms. Jackson, this is going to be brief. I do not want to interfere in any attorney-client privileged communications, but prior to last Wednesday, did you apprise your client of the order I entered on Tuesday evening?"

Claudia said only two words. "Yes, ma'am."

"Reverend Luther, would you please stand?" While she waited for him to rise, she took a sip of coffee from a cup emblazoned with a warning: "You will never know a woman until you meet her in court."

"Reverend Luther, I have been checking on your living conditions in the county jail and find that they have certainly been above average. I'm going to change them. You have intentionally violated my orders, not just in refusing to answer questions in a deposition, but now my specific order that you not discuss this case with the media. To top it off, you did it on national television. I'm taking away all of your jail privileges. You are going to be placed in solitary confinement and you will be permitted to speak only with your counsel until further order from this court. Bailiff, return him to the jail and see to it that my orders are strictly enforced. That's all, counsel."

The judge stormed from her bench and slammed the door to her chambers.

49

As T.J. returned to jail, Johnny Bob stopped Tod at the elevator. "Tod, why don't you and me go down to the cafeteria and get a cup of coffee? Claudia's going over to the jail to check on your favorite client's living conditions. We need to talk anyway."

"Only if I buy, Johnny Bob. I want you in my debt even if it is for a dollar." The two lawyers rode in silence to the basement and then chatted about families, kids and grandkids as they walked through the courthouse tunnel system to the cafeteria. Finding a quiet table in the corner, they sipped their coffee, which was like the coffee in most county cafeterias, very hot and bearing only a faint resemblance to the real thing.

"Look, Tod, first I want you to know that I had no idea that T.J. was going to violate the gag order. I've been around him off and on for a while, and the more that I see of him, the more I understand that he listens to a voice that apparently only he hears. Whether it's the voice of God or just voices, your guess is as good as mine."

Tod accepted the apology. Johnny Bob was as tough an opponent as he had ever faced and generally played by the rules. Tod described in a limited way the impact that the lawsuit and, particularly, the verbal attacks had had on his client and mentioned that Dr. Moyo's practice had dried up, forcing him to do emergency room work. It was a fairly candid discussion between two professional lawyers, each, of course, being careful not to divulge something that wouldn't come out anyway.

"Let's talk about discovery," Johnny Bob said, focusing the discussion on what lay ahead. "The judge, bless her little red head, has us on a damn short fuse. We've got a lot to do. We ought to be limiting depositions to only the key witnesses. Then we'll line up any experts we gotta have for deposition and be ready for trial when the judge says this train has to be in the station."

"Don't disagree. Who do you have in mind as the key witnesses?"

"Well, on your action for defamation, one of them is across the street in solitary. So, I suppose we eliminate him unless some voice directs him to speak up. You've got what he said on videotape anyway. I need Dr. Moyo. I don't think that for a medical malpractice case it'll be a long deposition. The procedure is not complicated and we know what problems developed. By the way, that was one slick move you pulled in filing that third-party action and then getting the judge to keep the two cases together. Sure leveled the playing field and got some people's attention on my side of the table."

Tod nodded his thanks at the compliment.

"I've got to take some of the people at the clinic, probably the counselor and those two weekend nurses. You're going to want Lucy, her parents and, I'm sure, Aunt Jessie."

"And, I may want to depose a couple of the treating doctors and that psychologist that Lucy's been seeing," Tod said as he took over the discussion. "I'll need one or more of the groups who joined together to fund this lawsuit. I need some admission that T.J. was speaking for them when he made those speeches from the pulpit."

"I suspect that they would prefer, at this point, not to have T.J. tied to them like a tin can to a groom's car, but I'll line someone up for you. Why don't we work out a written agreement to get these fact witnesses done in sixty days? I think I can speak for Claudia and I suspect you can for Janice. About the experts, you think that you and Janice can designate sixty days from now?"

"I suspect we can, Johnny Bob. The problem is that then you would have to designate in thirty days. You'll have to tell me if you can have your experts lined up that quickly."

"Good point, Tod. Let's make it forty-five days from today for me to designate experts and then you give me your list of experts thirty days after that. That'll be pushing it real close to get expert depositions done. Again, maybe we won't need to depose them all. Matter of fact, the older I get, the more often I just wing it at the courthouse with experts anyway."

"Come on now, Johnny Bob, it's not a question of age. You're just so damn good that you don't need some of those depositions. Call it experience, not age, and I'll believe you."

Tod's compliment brought a smile from the old fox across the table. Johnny Bob and Tod worked out a few other details, and Tod agreed to have a draft of a discovery agreement faxed to Palestine by the time that Johnny Bob got back to his office.

"One last thing, Tod. I'm going to need some living quarters down here for the next few months. It's time to get out of hotel rooms. Got any ideas?"

"Sure do, Johnny Bob. If you've noticed as you have driven around Houston lately, every old building downtown is being converted into loft apartments. Let me have Grace make a few calls and she'll call your secretary to give her a list of what's available. Some of them may even be walking distance from the courthouse. How many do you need?"

"Probably four. One for me, one for Claudia, one for my legal assistant and secretary and an extra one for witnesses. Well, make it five. Maybe by then, T.J. will wise up and he can get out of the graybar hotel for trial."

NOT KNOWN FOR SILENCE, Johnny Bob was lost in thought as he and Claudia drove back from Houston. Claudia recognized the best she could do was to leave him alone and stared out the window, wondering what twist the lawsuit would take next. When they got back to Palestine, Tod's proposed agreement was waiting for Johnny Bob on the corner of his secretary's desk.

As he walked back to his office, he hollered down the hall and asked Claudia to join him. She yelled back that she was going to get out of her courthouse clothes and would be there in five minutes. It only took about three minutes before she entered his office, coffee mug in one hand and yellow pad in the other. Claudia had quickly adapted to Palestine's example of business casual attire. She was wearing jeans, not designer but just plain old Wranglers, cowboy boots with the highest heels she could find, and a blue T-shirt with gold letters across the front, entreating, MAMAS, PLEASE LET YOUR BABIES GROW UP TO BE COWGIRLS! She plopped down in the chair across from Johnny Bob and propped her boots up on the corner of his desk.

"So, what's our move, Johnny Bob?"

"Well, we damned sure can't do much for the Chosen. He's out of choices. He's in solitary and Ruby's got the only key. You know him as well as I do; so, don't be surprised if he's still there when we start trial."

"Well, I, for one, was not the least bit surprised. When I heard what he had done, she had to bring the hammer down on him, God rest his holier-than-thou soul. You think we should make any effort to spring him?"

"Naw," Johnny Bob said. "Hopefully, he can't get into any trouble in solitary. Let's leave him there so we don't have to worry about him. After the hearing, Tod and I worked out an agreement. See what you think about it."

Glancing over the proposed deadlines, Claudia replied, "Damn short timetable. I don't suppose that we have any choice, though, do we? Let's talk about experts.

"I know a first-class obstetrician in Ohio who has good academic credentials. Knows how to do abortions. He only does them when the mother's got a serious problem. I think he'll help us on the malpractice, both against Dr. Moyo and the clinic. He may be able to offer an opinion that Lucy will not be able to have children. We've got the treating doctors on damages and the psychologist on Lucy's emotional state, past and future. Speaking of damages, that brings me to a real concern of some of my organizations. They are damned scared of this slander action. They now understand that T.J. could very well have gone too far in some of those comments about murder and baby killing."

"Well, they might as well get ready to worry some more," Johnny Bob responded. "Tod told me that Moyo's practice has gone down the tubes. He's having to do emergency room work now."

"Shit," Claudia exclaimed. "Too damn bad we didn't rein in T.J. the first time he started talking about baby killing and before he started calling names."

"I agree, Claudia, but there's an old country saying in these parts, 'Once the cow's peed in the milk, you can't strain it out.' T.J.'s done pissed all over Dr. Moyo and Population Planning, and we're just going to have to defend it."

Smiling at another of Johnny Bob's East Texas sayings, Claudia asked, "What's your experience in the defamation area? I was interested in the First Amendment in law school. Since then I haven't really had any practical experience in handling libel and slander for either the plaintiff or the defendant."

"It may be that I have just a little more learning on this subject than you do. I've looked at a few plaintiff defamation cases over the years and had to go update myself on the current state of the law each time. Never actually agreed to take one, though. Defamation is not that hard to prove. The plaintiff just has to prove that the statement was made; that it was false; that it was defamatory, meaning the ordinary person would consider that it would do damage to the reputation; and that the statement caused damages to the plaintiff. The problem usually is damages. Some wiseass can call someone every name in the book and accuse him of all manner of evildoing, all of it absolutely false, and there's usually no real economic loss. I never figured that a jury would award a lot of money for damaging someone's reputation, regardless of what Shakespeare says when he compares stealing a purse to a good name. I'd much rather have a death or an amputated leg that my client is suing about."

Claudia concentrated like she was sitting on the first row of a Harvard torts class.

"Now, let's talk about Dr. Moyo. First, when he's accused of being a murderer and a baby killer and so forth, that's going to be slanderous per se. Last time I looked, murder was a crime and if you accuse someone of committing a crime, it's slander as a matter of law. As to damages, T.J. broadcast his comments all over the world, and if what Tod told me today is true, Moyo can show some significant economic damages and the jury just might choose to punish T.J. and his forces. As to Population Planning, while T.J. may have slandered them, my guess is that they can't show any real economic loss. I doubt if a jury is going to get up in arms about some damage to their reputation. Bottom line is that Moyo just may have a pretty damn good case against the Chosen and his forces. The only thing that we haven't talked about is truth. Even if a statement is slanderous, if it's the truth, that's a defense. Call your neighbor a horse thief and accuse him of stealing your prize stallion, you've slandered him. If the stallion is found in his barn, you're gonna win because what you said was true even if it was defamatory."

Claudia sat quietly for a long time and Johnny Bob gazed out the window at the courthouse until she spoke. "I've got an idea. Why don't we prove that what T.J. said was true?"

"You lost me there, Claudia. Moyo didn't commit a murder," Johnny Bob replied, as a quizzical look came across his face.

"The hell he didn't! You need to be thinking like a pro-lifer. We believe that life begins at the moment of conception. If we're right, and I know we are, he has killed a pre-born human being, lots of them. That makes him a murderer and a baby killer and whatever else T.J. called him. Same goes for Population Planning."

Johnny Bob got out of his chair and paced the room, then stroked his chin as he stared out the window again before he spoke, obviously absorbing and debating in his own mind what Claudia had just proposed. "Boy, now ain't that just an interesting theory. Texas usually doesn't give a pre-born human being, as you call it, much in the way of rights in a civil lawsuit. You got any law to support your theory?"

"Not a shred out there that I know of, Johnny Bob, not on either side of the issue. You opposed to trying to make law?"

"Not something that I've had to do very often, although this wouldn't be the first time in my long and semi-illustrious career. You realize, though, that if we do this, we're going to put the pro-life/pro-choice debate right in the middle of our lawsuit. You also know that just because you try to make law, you don't always succeed. On the other hand, if you don't try, you damn sure will fail."

As he turned from the window, Claudia could tell from his expression that he had made up his mind. "What the hell? We might as well try to get a jury to go along with us, then worry about it on appeal. After all, I've got me a Phi Beta Kappa, Harvard Law graduate to handle my appeal. Now, I wasn't figuring on trying such issues in this case; so, you better start by giving me a little education on the abortion debate and then we'll talk about what experts you think we'll need."

Claudia was pleased to see that it was her turn to be the teacher. "First, you know that this debate goes back thousands of years."

For the next hour, Claudia led Johnny Bob through the years of debate, from Rome to old England to early state legislation against abortion in the 1800s until she reached the pivotal decision of the United States Supreme Court.

"In 1973, the Supreme Court decided *Roe v. Wade,* and the doors to the abortion clinics were thrown wide open. The majority of the court bought into the plaintiff's position that an anti-abortion statute abridged a woman's right to personal privacy, protected by various constitutional amendments. Justice Blackmun wrote the opinion, finding that such a right of privacy is found in the Fourteenth Amendment's concept of personal liberty and its attendant restrictions upon state action, as well as the Ninth Amendment's reservation of rights to the people. Both, he said, were broad enough to encompass a woman's decision as to whether or not to terminate her pregnancy. He also concluded that the definition of the word 'person,' at least as used in the Fourteenth Amendment, does not include the unborn. And, by the way, with what we are about to do, we can expect his language to be thrown into our faces. We'll have to come up with an argument around it. Bottom line is that the Supremes said that a state couldn't regulate abortion prior to viability."

Johnny Bob had settled into his chair and propped his feet

on his desk as he tried to absorb all that Claudia was telling
him. After staring up at the ceiling with his hands folded
across his ample belly, the trial lawyer in him took over.
"Now wait just a damn minute, here, Claudia. The pro-life
side is grabbing a lot of attention with something called
partial-birth abortions. Sound pretty damn bad from what
I've read. Can we stir that into our pot and heat up the jury,
maybe even make them mad?"

"You're talking about a procedure called dilation and extraction, D and X for short. You're damn sure right that it's
likely to upset most everyone if they hear how these are done.
Nebraska described it as a procedure in which one partially
delivers a living unborn child before killing the baby and
completing the delivery. The abortionist often has to tear off
various parts, including arms and legs. Usually, the head is
the last part remaining and because it's the biggest part of
the fetus, he then sticks something sharp into the uterus and
punctures the head, drains out the fluid and pulls the head
out."

Johnny Bob leaped from his chair, a smile on his face as
he thought of a witness describing in vivid detail such a procedure to perform an abortion. "That's it. That's what we
need. Jury'll be pissed all to hell with that kind of stuff going on."

Claudia shook her head as Johnny Bob was talking.

"What're you shaking your head about? We get the jury
good and angry, we're halfway home."

Claudia rose to face Johnny Bob across the desk. "No
doubt you're right that this kind of abortion gets people's
blood to boil. Unfortunately, the Supreme Court just ruled
the Nebraska statute trying to outlaw the D and X procedure
was unconstitutional because it didn't provide an exception
for the health of the mother. They also found that the statute
was so broad that it could be interpreted to include the dilation and evacuation procedure used earlier in the pregnancy.
That exposed every doctor who performed an abortion of
any kind to fear of prosecution, conviction and imprison-
ment. That also violated the Constitution. You never saw

more dissents and concurring opinions in your life. They took out the knives and were trying to cut each other to pieces, verbally you understand. But, there's a problem that we can't get around. If you take off your plaintiff lawyer's hat for just a minute, you'll figure it out."

Johnny Bob was silent as he folded his body back into his chair and twirled around very slowly one time. When he again faced Claudia, he very quietly said, "I understand. Dr. Moyo didn't use a partial birth procedure, did he? This was a first trimester abortion and he used the vacuum extraction."

"You got it, Johnny Bob," Claudia nodded. "The partial-birth abortions usually start at about sixteen weeks. I don't see any way that Judge O'Reilly will let you get into the subject. So, I could go on, but I think I've said enough since we have a first trimester abortion.

"On second thought, let me make one more comment when it comes to trying to make law. Don't forget that in the eyes of our founding fathers, because I'm black I would not have been considered a person. It took a Civil War and over two hundred years before I could be sitting across the desk from you as an equal."

"Boy, you just said a mouthful. You know your stuff and I'm damn glad you're on my side. So, let's talk about experts. Who do we need to establish that life begins at conception?"

"Prepare yourself, Johnny Bob. There's gonna be a bunch. I'll line them all up. I either know most of them or know people who do. Once we line them up, you and I can decide which ones to use. We could call ten experts in ten different fields. From what I've seen of Judge O'Reilly, she's not going to let us do that. To give you some idea, I'll line up experts in embryology, a pediatric neurologist, a neonatologist and a geneticist, which by the way could be most interesting. We'll want a medical ethicist and probably a theologian. Even Justice Blackmun alludes to the fact that this has also been a theological and philosophical debate. And that probably brings us to our last one, a philosopher."

Johnny Bob was accustomed to having cases with multiple experts involved. As he pondered Claudia's list, he recognized that this case had more diverse experts than any in which he had been involved in thirty years of law practice.

"Okay, Claudia, get on your horse and ride. You've got less than forty-five days to line all these folks up and get reports out of them."

Then he broke out in a laugh.

"What's so funny, Johnny Bob? We're in a damn serious case here," Claudia said, puzzled at the big man's reaction.

"Claudia, my young friend, don't take everything so seriously. Every day has to have a little fun in it, no matter how serious the case. I was thinking of two things. First, the look on Tod's face when he gets our list of experts, reads their reports, and figures out that this is not just a malpractice/slander case; that we're trying the issue of when life begins. He figured he got the best of us when he filed the counterclaim and sued your pro-life groups for a hundred million. As we say in Texas, that gun kicks as hard as it shoots. He's gonna have himself about two weeks to round up rebuttal experts on the beginning of life. Next, I was just thinking about Ruby O'Reilly's comment that she really didn't want this case to turn into a three-ring circus. Well, she's not gonna get her wish. While I don't know the world record for the number of rings in a circus, I can damn well tell you that this is one where old P. T. Barnum himself would gladly pay admission."

50

Knowing that they were riding on a bullet train with Ruby O'Reilly at the throttle, over the next several weeks the lawyers hastened to schedule their first depositions. Tod had agreed with Jan that he and Wayne would handle the depositions while she searched for experts. They had deposed Lucy, Joanna, Jessie and Lucy's psychologist. Johnny Bob had completed the deposition of Dr. Moyo. The depositions had gone as the lawyers had anticipated with a couple of exceptions. Tod learned from Jessie's testimony that the consortium had funded nearly two million dollars plus expenses to pay Tisdale. No wonder he took the case. Johnny Bob was able to trace Dr. Moyo's steps leading up to the morning of the abortion and learned that he had not slept in over thirty hours. Tod silently groaned when he heard his client admit to that, at the same time wondering why Zeke had not told him about something so important in their numerous meetings. Tod learned from Lucy that she had thrown up the first antibiotic. Whether it would have changed the outcome was uncertain, but it became an issue in the case.

WHEN T.J. REALIZED THAT the trial was imminent, he asked the guards to arrange a visit with his lawyers. Claudia showed up alone. They met in a small room reserved for attorney-client conferences, furnished with a metal table and two metal chairs. He rose as she entered.

"Welcome to my humble castle, counselor. I'm sorry that I cannot offer you caviar and champagne, but it seems that my wait staff is off for the week and the cupboard is bare."

"Well, T.J., I'm pleased that you haven't lost your sense of humor in all of this," Claudia replied.

"Actually, Claudia, I would much prefer being in the thick of things. However, I'm forced to observe the action from this proverbial seat in the bleachers. Perhaps I can get into the game in the late innings. Maybe even save the day."

"T.J., does that mean that you're thinking of testifying at trial?"

"Thinking about it would be the proper phrase, I believe. Actually, I'm still waiting on word from my Father as to how best to serve Him in this whole matter. I promise that you will be among the first to know of our decision. Now, if you would, please tell me what's going on and how the lawsuit is progressing. By the way, let me commend you on your decision to put the pro-life debate on trial. It will certainly serve to generate even more attention to our cause. I feel certain that we can convince twelve people that life begins at conception."

Claudia opened her briefcase and pulled out a legal pad as she began to brief T.J. on the status of the case. "Johnny Bob gave me the assignment of lining up our experts. I had forty-five days to get it done. We're still about ten days out from having to list them and provide reports. I'm close to being finished. Since you're interested in the abortion debate witnesses, let me skip over the malpractice experts. Just take my word for it that they'll be strong. T.J., these pro-life experts are going to blow them away. I'm not going to bore you with the details, but I've got a Nobel Prize–nominated geneticist, an embryologist, a fertility specialist and a theology/philosophy professor, all of whom can conclusively prove that life begins at conception. All of these experts have written and lectured widely on the subject. They know their stuff, and I've got more on the way. Tod thought that he had thrown us a curve when he added this defamation issue to the case. Well, just watch him call time-out when he sees our array of experts to prove that you spoke the truth. Our only problem will be deciding which ones to actually call. Johnny Bob is pretty certain that Judge O'Reilly won't let us parade all of them to the stand. He thinks we'll probably have to go with our best two or three. We can make that decision as we get closer to trial."

"Claudia, I couldn't be more pleased," T.J. remarked with obvious pleasure. "Get me copies of their reports as soon as they're done. I'll be most interested in their final opinions. And it just might be that I'll have to join such an illustrious lineup. Looks to me like you could use a good cleanup hitter, one, of course, who is capable of knocking the ball not only over the center field wall, but out of the park."

As she got up to leave, Claudia replied, "Well, T.J., if that hitter decides to get off the bench and get into the game, you be sure to let me know."

51

It wasn't long after Judge O'Reilly told the lawyers that they had four months to get the train to the station that Johnny Bob moved his whole crew to Houston. Leaving behind associates, secretaries and paralegals to keep his other cases moving, he took five loft apartments about three blocks from the courthouse. He and Bernice, who was delighted to spend a few months in Houston, occupied a large two-bedroom loft, with one bedroom reserved for his office. Claudia moved into a one-bedroom large enough to give her sufficient workspace. Sara and Mildred shared a two-bedroom condo, which became the base of operations since it contained the largest living area, sufficient to provide room for two computers, two printers, a fax, a copy machine and several file cabinets. Another two-bedroom condo was reserved for out-of-town witnesses. Johnny Bob set aside one for T.J., just in case.

On the evening before they were to designate experts, Johnny Bob and Claudia sat in his apartment while Bernice prepared green beans, a salad and a tuna casserole. Johnny Bob sipped on a tall scotch and water while Claudia did the same with a glass of Chardonnay.

"Claudia St. John Jackson, you've done us proud. I've never seen such an imposing array of experts in such a wide variety of disciplines, all to confirm what we all know, that life begins at conception. I might also add that I am most impressed with our expert on obstetrics, and my old boy from Fort Worth seems to have come through for us on the emotional scars that our client will suffer for the remainder of her days. Looks to me like we've got our case pretty well in hand. I need to depose a couple more of the clinic's fact witnesses. Tod has already told me that he wants the deposition of Walter McDade, the director of Executives for Life. Then he has a few weeks to counter what we have done. Do you think he sees it coming?"

Claudia took a sip of Chardonnay before replying. "Johnny Bob, one thing I've learned in this case is not to underestimate our opposition. Tod's as good a lawyer as I've run across in my brief career. If he wanted to do a series of lectures as a visiting professor at Harvard, I'd be the first to recommend him. On the other hand, do I think that he has anticipated what is coming? I'd have to say no. He first treated this as a malpractice case and then came up with the idea to add defamation as a counterclaim; a brilliant move, I might add. As good a lawyer as he is, Tod's not as attuned to the abortion controversy as I am. He's going to assume that, particularly with an abortion of a twelve-week fetus, there's not even an issue. He's going to think that life begins at birth, or at the earliest, viability. I'll bet you a thousand dollars that it never occurred to him that we might try to defend his slander case by convincing a jury that life begins at conception. I'd like to be a fly on the wall when he reads our expert reports tomorrow."

"Well, then," Johnny Bob spoke as he rose from his chair, "I propose a toast. Bernice, hon, come in here and bring your glass." After Bernice rounded the corner from the small kitchen area, wearing her newest Chanel outfit from Neiman Marcus, Claudia rose, drink in hand. "Here's to the confusion of our enemies and the lives of the babies that we are about to save."

"Hear, hear!" Bernice exclaimed.

"Amen," said Claudia and then followed it with a question. "I know we're under a gag order. We're also getting close to trial. Do you think that I might leak a copy of this list of experts and their reports to one of my friends in the media? We've got a lot of attention already. When the media learns what's going to be tried in this case, we're going to need the Astrodome to hold the crowds. They might as well start lining up."

"Claudia, my dear, you know what the judge said. On the other hand, as I recall most reporters are not prone to revealing their sources. If one of them has our list of experts slipped under the door in the dark of night, I presume that he would rather join T.J. than reveal the source. If you do any such thing, just hope that Ruby doesn't make a big issue out of it. She could put us on the stand, you know. But, my guess is that there are bigger issues filling her little red head, and this one probably won't even show up on her radar screen. By the way, if you do it, don't tell me. One of us has to be around to try the case."

"I read you, Johnny Bob."

Tod found the designation of experts on his desk when he returned to the fire station after assisting one of his partners at a hearing for a major client, a rare appearance for Tod on anything other than the Brady matter. The designation was required to name each expert, his or her field of expertise, and a short statement of expected testimony. It included a report and curriculum vitae from each expert. After getting a cup of coffee, he propped his feet up on the corner of his desk and leaned back to learn about the opposition's experts—next to the parties themselves usually the key witnesses in the case. As Tod read down the list, the first experts were routine. He expected to see an obstetrician, a psychologist and doctors from Hermann. When he got to the third page, his eyes widened. He kicked his feet off the desk and gulped at the cup of coffee. *What the holy shit is this?* A geneticist, an embryologist, a fertility specialist, a theologian/philosopher, the obstetrician listed again but this time as an expert in reading of fetal ultrasounds, a professor of fetal physiology, a professor of neurology and pediatrics, a neonatologist and even Reverend Thomas Jeremiah Luther. As to their expected testimony, it was listed as "when life begins."

"Grace," he hollered out the door, "call Jan and get her over here and tell Wayne I need him now." As he waited for Wayne, he stared out the window and pondered. What's going on here? Johnny Bob files a malpractice case and I answer for Dr. Moyo. Then I sue T.J. and all of his buddies, claiming slander. I've proved that the words were spoken. Hell, I have him on videotape. I still have to tie in the organizations and have Walter McDade scheduled for deposition at the end of the week. Aunt Jessie has already given us a road map for his deposition. There's no doubt that calling Zeke a murderer and baby killer is defamatory and his practice has gone to hell.

Then it hit him. The only defense left is "truth." They're going to try to prove what T.J. said is true, and the way they are going to do it is to prove that life begins at some time long before the child is born.

"Son of a bitch!"

The words escaped from Tod's mouth as he flipped to the expert reports. The first was from the geneticist, who had an outstanding pedigree: Harvard, work on the human genome project, nomination for a Nobel Prize. Skipping through three pages of detail, Tod got to the three-sentence summary that concluded that human life began at the moment of conception. Next was the philosopher/theologian. What the hell can a philosopher have to say that is relevant to when life begins? Again, he skipped to the end. According to the expert, it has now been established that ensoulment takes place at the moment of conception. *What kind of Looney Tunes is this? How could anyone possibly be certain of this kind of stuff?* The rest of the reports all reached similar conclusions. Only T.J.'s was a little different. His report proclaimed that life began at conception because his Father told him it was so.

"Objection, Your Honor! Hearsay!"

"Sorry, boss. I got hung up on the phone. Why are you yelling a hearsay objection out the window?" Wayne asked as he strolled into the room.

"Hey, Wayne. Didn't realize I was talking out loud. You won't believe this shit. Take it down to your office and read it. Might as well get Grace to make a couple of copies. No, make it four or five. Soon as Jan gets here, we'll talk."

Wayne took the papers from Tod's hand and left without a word, eager to see what had his boss so agitated. Less than thirty minutes later Jan appeared at his office door. Knowing that she did not need to be announced, she just said hello to the receptionist and walked up the stairs where she found Tod still staring off into space, trying to figure out his next move.

"If I had a camera, I'd take a picture of you. With that puzzled look on your face, it would make a great Christmas present for your boys. They could put it on the refrigerator and look at it every time they get stumped on a homework assignment. Are you ready for me?"

Tod's mind returned to the present as he answered, "Jan, damn right I'm ready for you. Have you seen the experts?"

"Of course. I read the reports as soon as they hit my office this morning. I called over here and found that you were in court. Figured that I'd hear from you as soon as you got back."

Wayne had heard them talking and walked down the hall to Tod's office.

"Here, you and Wayne have a seat. Grace, get Jan some coffee."

They all sat at the table by the window and Tod continued, "So, what do you think? I've been practicing nearly twenty-five years and never saw so many different experts. How can anyone prove when life begins? You ever heard this term 'ensoulment'?"

"Tod, settle down. I've been down this road, at least part-way, a couple of times," Jan interjected.

"Jan, don't we live in a state that says that a fetus really has no rights until a live birth?"

"Tod, I can answer that one," Wayne spoke up. "I checked the penal code before Jan got here. Murder in this state is causing the death of an 'individual.' Individual is defined as a human being who has been born and is alive. So, I don't see how Dr. Moyo can be rightfully accused of murder."

"Wayne's right," Jan stepped in, "as far as he goes. The problem, though, is that we are dealing with a civil case, not criminal. Nobody is accusing our clients of violating the Criminal Code. We're in the civil courthouse and the Civil Practice and Remedies Code provides a cause of action for an injury that causes an individual's death. Problem here is that 'individual' is not defined on the civil side and you know as well as I do that it's not likely that the Texas Supreme Court is going to look to the penal code for a definition in a civil case. As far as I can tell, it's an open question. Texas doesn't currently recognize a cause of action for the wrongful death of a fetus, but we're coming closer every time the Supremes have a chance to evaluate the issue. We're currently in the minority among the various states. At last count, approximately thirty-six states and the District of Columbia permit a claim for the death of a viable fetus. Remember that word, 'viable', and we'll come back to it later. Also, you and I know that we have a Texas Supreme Court that is all Republican and very conservative. If they want to be re-elected, they may have their papers graded by the Christian conservatives. They may flunk the test if they have the opportunity to recognize the life of a fetus and fail to do so. Don't forget that the Republican winds are blowing from the right these days, and they're approaching hurricane force. Well, maybe only tropical storm speed. You get the idea."

"So you're saying that they have a shot at putting on this testimony and proving that T.J. was telling the truth when he called our clients murderers?"

"Well, Tod, I'd say it's a stretch, but only a little one. You know judges. On a close call, they're prone to letting evidence in. I think we have to be prepared to defend on this issue. As a matter of fact, I've already been on the phone to some of my sources this morning. We'll come up with some formidable experts on the other side of the issue, although I'm not sure that I can find us a Nobel Prize nominee."

"You've got less than thirty days, Jan. Can you get it done?"

"You and Wayne take care of the rest of the case. I'll handle the experts. Should be interesting. I'd say that old Johnny Bob just topped your full house with a royal flush. Fortunately, there are a few more hands to play before we see which side of the table the money ends up on. Chalk up one hand to Johnny Bob."

Normally full of enthusiasm, Tod spent the rest of the day rehashing the moves and countermoves that he and Johnny Bob had made in their chess game of a lawsuit. The more he thought of his opponent's latest move, the more depressed he became. It took a victory by Kirk's soccer team that evening to break him out of it. As he drove home after the soccer match, he pondered who was playing a game and who was living life. Kirk or him? The question deserved further analysis on a morning run.

When he arrived at the house, Tod saw the "message waiting" light blinking on the answering machine. It was Zeke Moyo asking that he call as soon as possible. No doubt what the call was about. He had a set of the expert reports delivered to Zeke earlier in the day. After considering postponing the return call until the next day with an excuse that he didn't see the blinking light, he had second thoughts and dialed the number. Zeke picked it up on the first ring.

"Tod, what's this all about? Why do they have all of these experts talking about when life begins? I'm not a murderer. What I did was perfectly legal. How can they claim otherwise? Besides, I'm an obstetrician. I know when life begins. There's no way that modern science can keep a fetus alive outside its mother's womb before twenty-three weeks. Even then it usually takes a miracle along with close to a million dollars."

This time it was Tod's turn to slow down a string of questions and comments. "Zeke, believe me, I understand all you are saying. They raised an issue that, frankly, I didn't anticipate, just like we did to them when we counterclaimed for slander. It's happened to me before and it'll happen again. We'll meet their challenge head on; so, just calm down. Remember, I'm the one who gets paid to handle this case, including the part about worrying."

"Tod, I understand. But when we get together, I still want you to explain in more detail how I can perform a legal abortion and still be accused of murder."

"I will, Zeke. Now, let's both get some sleep. I have another full day with Johnny Bob tomorrow. Hopefully, I'll nail down that T.J. was speaking for his pro-life consortium with our first deposition. After that, Johnny Bob has three clinic personnel scheduled, including the two nurses who were on duty the weekend after Lucy's abortion. By the way, we've got a strong obstetrical expert lined up to support you. He's even one of the editors of your leading obstetrics textbook. He'll come on strong. Good night, Zeke."

52

At ten the next morning, the deposition of Walter Thaddeus McDade was scheduled at the fire station. He appeared at the appointed hour, accompanied by Johnny Bob and Claudia. McDade was a commanding figure and it was not surprising, considering his background. He had served in the Air Force for more than twenty years, retiring in his late forties. He considered a political career, opting instead for the money, taking a job as a senior vice president of an aerospace company. Within a matter of years he became CEO, and he remained in charge until he reached mandatory retirement at age sixty-five. Now past seventy, he still commanded the attention of all in a room when he appeared at the doorway. His job as director of Executives for Life was non-paying. Money was no longer an object for him. As a fervent Catholic, he believed in the pro-life mission. He had served his country, made more money than his next three generations could spend, and it was now time to leave a lasting legacy. If it was humanly possible, he intended to wipe out abortion before he died. The organization was his idea, created while he was still in the aerospace industry. As Fortune 500 executives approached retirement, he quietly checked them out, and if he found their views to be favorable to his cause, he persuaded them to join with him. At the time of his deposition, his organization numbered three hundred and was among the wealthiest in the pro-life movement.

When the deposition started, Tod got to the point. After the formalities were over, he asked, "Mr. McDade, what is the purpose of Executives for Life?"

"It's no secret, Mr. Duncan. We have a mission statement on our Web site. We intend to eradicate legal abortion from our society by the year 2010 and we'll use any means possible. That includes legislation, political activism, demonstrations, protests and of course, the courthouse when appropriate."

"Thank you for your candor, Mr. McDade. I think that we will be able to make this deposition very short. Isn't it true that your organization and the other members of the consortium have chosen to fund a substantial portion of this litigation against my client and Population Planning?"

"Mr. Duncan, I think that has been previously established by Ms. Warren Woolsey. The answer is yes."

"And isn't it also true that Executives for Life and the other consortium members authorized Reverend Luther to speak on your behalf about matters pertaining to this litigation?"

"Mr. Duncan, I'll have to qualify my answer, if I may. It's true that we authorized him to speak for the group. However, we did not preauthorize or give preapproval to all of his messages. I might add, had we been given the opportunity to do so, I personally would not have permitted a great number of the comments that he made."

"Now, can you give me a breakdown on how much each organization has contributed to this cause?"

Claudia interrupted. "Just a minute, Tod. I don't mind you confirming their involvement and that T.J. was their spokesman. I'll concede that it's proper information for impeachment, and you may be even be able to tie T.J. around their necks with that testimony. That's where I draw the line. I'll object to these questions going any further, particularly if you're of a mind to find out just how much each one of these groups contributed to the 'kitty'."

"Understood, Claudia. We'll take it up with the judge if I decide to explore it any further. Thank you for your time, Mr. McDade."

With the deposition over early, the lawyers used the time to talk about the status of the case and remaining discovery.

"Johnny Bob, you're to be congratulated," Tod said. "Not

often that I'm caught by surprise. You did it with your expert designations. I missed out completely on the possibility of a 'truth' defense. Nice move."

"Had to do something, Tod. You out-foxed me with that counterclaim. I had to come up with something. I've got to give Ms. Jackson here the credit. She's the one who actually thought of it and lined up all those experts. You gonna be able to match them?"

"Johnny Bob, you know me better than that. I will match them and I plan to outdo you. Jan's already working on it. While we're on that subject, just how many of those 'when life begins' experts do you actually expect to call?"

"Well, Tod, you and I both know that Ruby ain't gonna let me call all of them. I figure I'll try for four and be willing to settle for two or three."

"That's what I figured. The rest of the reports will make good reading for the media. By the way, the *Chronicle* ran a story this morning, describing all of your experts and their expected testimony. Any idea where they got that information?"

Johnny Bob managed to avoid choking on his water and replied, "Tod, you mean the media has already picked up on my experts? Beats me how they found out. You know we represent about a dozen different organizations and had to supply them with our experts and what they were going to say. I suppose any one of them could have leaked it to the press. A lot of them see this as a holy war and don't feel bound by the rules of engagement as dictated by Judge O'Reilly."

"Tod, if you're going to want to depose our experts, I've got to know pretty quick," Claudia added. "They are all busy people and we may have to chase all over the country to get them done."

"Claudia, I'll make that easy on you," Tod replied. "I don't normally go to trial without depositions from nearly all of the experts on the other side. This case is the exception. You've given me thorough reports, which I appreciate, by the way, and I'll just save my cross-examination for trial. What about you, Johnny Bob?"

"I agree with your position, Tod. As the judge says, this train is close to coming into the station. I'll save my best shots for trial. Let's wind up these fact witnesses, and assuming you give us thorough reports, forget the expert depositions."

After Johnny Bob and Claudia left, Wayne challenged Tod's decision. "Are you sure that's the right way to go? This is a big case that's going to get national publicity."

"I hear what you are saying, Wayne. I have to make the call. With all the experts on both sides, we would end up potentially delaying the trial. We want to win this case. Almost as important, our client wants his life back. We can win it without the expert depositions. Believe me, there won't be any more than the average surprises in this one, even without the depositions."

53

The next day T.J. summoned Claudia and Johnny Bob to his temporary quarters. Johnny Bob let T.J. stew for three days before meeting him in the small attorney-client conference room. The deputy had added one more chair and Johnny Bob's bulk made the room seem half its previous size.

"Glad you two could finally make the time for me," T.J. started the conversation. "I'm usually not kept waiting."

"Well, now, T.J., I'm not usually summoned; so, let's just call it even." He had a headstrong client and had to keep him on a tight rein. Johnny Bob had learned many years ago that there could be only one lead dog on his side in a big trial, and he made damn sure that the client understood he was the one. T.J. would be no exception.

"What's on your mind, T.J.?"

T.J. pushed his chair back and stood with arms folded as he spoke. He wasn't quite ready to give up the lead dog position. "I've read in the *Chronicle* about the list of experts you guys have come up with, and I'm mightily impressed. Claudia, I see that you have even added several since we last talked."

Claudia nodded, saying nothing. This was Johnny Bob's show. T.J. continued, "Frankly, I'm honored to be among such a distinguished list of experts. I feel certain that with my help, we can carry the day."

"Let me make sure I'm hearing you right, T.J. Are you saying that you are now wanting to testify in the trial?"

T.J. looked up at the ceiling as if to confirm that he was getting the right message and then, leaning over, placed his hands on the table so that his face was no more than a foot away from Johnny Bob's nose. "You're hearing me right, counselor. I have been authorized to testify. I would like for you to advise the judge and ask her to release me. I understand you have a nice apartment reserved for me just down the street."

"Hold on there, T.J. I can ask, but you still may not receive. You get what I mean? The judge may or may not let you out of jail before the trial. You'll also have to agree to a deposition and agree to answer all, and I do mean all, questions asked."

"I'm prepared to do so." What T.J. didn't say was that he was satisfied that he had accomplished his purpose in attracting worldwide attention to the trial. He figured that the national media would start drifting into town any day now, lining up lodging, looking for background stories, etc. He wanted to be available for stories of "general interest," that would not violate the judge's order and would put him back in the spotlight where he rightfully belonged.

"Tell you what, T.J. We've got a hearing on a couple of matters before Judge O'Reilly on Friday. We'll take this up with her then. Meantime, don't hold your breath."

ALTHOUGH THERE WAS NO formal announcement of any hearing on the Brady versus Population Planning case, the back benches were half-filled with reporters thirty minutes before the hearing. Judge O'Reilly and Judge David Hardman, the administrative judge of the Harris County court system, were in her chambers discussing logistics.

"David, I've done my best to keep a lid on this thing, but I'm afraid that it's boiling over. You know how much it's already been in the press. You're not going to believe this. I'm starting to get press pass requests. I've never had such a thing in my court. They started right after the *Chronicle* ran that story about the plaintiffs' experts. We may have the modern day equivalent of the Scopes Monkey Trial right here in the Bayou City. The press requests already number over a hundred and we're still a month out from trial. On top of that, I've got a request from four networks and Court TV to broadcast this son of a bitch live." As she spoke, David Hardman noticed for the first time that Ruby was getting a few gray hairs.

"You're the administrative judge. What do you want me to do? And let me add that it'll be over my dead body that we have another O. J. Simpson trial in my courtroom."

"I understand, Ruby. Let's cover the number of reporters and spectators first, and remember that we do have public trials for a reason. We have two options. I can make sure that the Ceremonial Courtroom on the second floor is available. That one will seat about two hundred. The other option is for me to call South Texas law school to see if we can use their auditorium. As you know, it holds about seven hundred and can be configured as a courtroom. Also, they have audio-visual capability, if we want it. How long is your trial?"

"I'll get a better reading on that in about thirty minutes when I visit with the lawyers out in the courtroom. My guess is four weeks."

"Why don't I check with South Texas?"

The South Texas College of Law had come a long way since Johnny Bob went to night school there. It was now housed in a substantial building in downtown Houston about ten blocks from the courthouse. Its auditorium was used as a large classroom and as a place to hold seminars for lawyers. On occasion, Harris County borrowed it for use as a courtroom.

"Now, Ruby, what about the television folks?"

"Frankly, David, I've been wrestling with that issue since the very first hearing on this case. I saw it coming and I've flip-flopped on the question at least a dozen times. I think you said it right. The public has a right to know what goes on in their courtrooms. If this case is going to get national publicity, the public might as well get it straight instead of secondhand from some reporter standing on the courthouse steps."

At nine o'clock, the door to Judge O'Reilly's chambers opened. Even the bailiff was a little shocked to see Judge Hardman stroll out the door. Hardman passed by the bench, nodded to the lawyers seated at the counsel table, shook the hands of a couple of the reporters and left the courtroom. Judge O'Reilly followed him.

"Be seated, ladies and gentlemen. My primary reason for having you here this morning is to determine if everyone is on schedule for our trial that is now just a few weeks away. Any problems?"

Tod answered. "Your Honor, I think I can speak for everyone. We've cut out a lot of potential depositions and we've completed discovery. We're all ready to go."

Johnny Bob was next. "Your Honor, I agree with Tod, but I have another matter to take up that is not on the court's docket this morning."

"No problem, Mr. Tisdale. So do I, but let's take up yours first."

"Your Honor, I have been conferring with Reverend Luther earlier this week, and he has authorized me to advise you that he is now willing to abide by your ruling and will testify anytime, anyplace."

That woke up the reporters on the benches, most of whom started writing furiously. Some whispered among themselves, forcing the bailiff to call, "Order in the court! If you can't remain silent, you will be asked to leave."

"Thank you, Mr. Bailiff. Well, counsel, so you're telling me that the Chosen has decided to talk. I presume that in return, he wants out of jail now, particularly since it's only a few weeks until trial. What do you have to say about that, Mr. Duncan?"

Tod sat back in his chair, then turned and conferred with Jan and Wayne before rising. "Your Honor, Mr. Tisdale and I have concluded that we are through with the depositions in this case. We each plan to duke it out with the experts for the first time here in this courtroom. I don't think that Reverend Luther's decision changes that. Besides being a fact witness, he's now also listed as an expert. I've got his defamatory statements on videotape and I don't need his deposition. We'll abide by whatever you rule."

"Mr. Tisdale, here's my decision. I had previously said that when Reverend Luther was willing to testify, he would be released from jail, but I don't recall that I said when that would occur. He has consistently disobeyed my rulings and I don't feel obliged to ask 'how high' when he says 'jump.' He may be released from solitary today. He will remain in jail until two weeks before trial. If you choose, you are entitled to file a habeas corpus, seeking his discharge. In any case, please advise Reverend Luther that my order not to discuss this trial with the media still stands and will remain in place until the conclusion of the trial. Is that understood?"

"Yes, ma'am. I will so advise the reverend."

The judge continued. "Now, let's take up the matter that I want to discuss that is not on today's calendar. As you are all aware, this case is drawing tremendous publicity, which has escalated in the past few days. By the way, do any of you know how the *Chronicle* got hold of the plaintiffs' list of expert witnesses and their reports?"

Claudia coughed and buried her head as she furiously scribbled on her yellow pad.

"Judge, I certainly didn't do it," Johnny Bob replied.

"Judge, I can promise you that we're not out for publicity in this case and we had no desire to leak that list to the press," Tod added.

"Well, it's water under the bridge and I'm not going to waste my time trying to chase down the culprit. Mr. Tisdale and Ms. Jackson, you might remind your various clients that my order applies to them just as much as it does to the attorneys in this case."

"Yes, ma'am. They have been so instructed. I'll warn them again today."

"The bottom line is that I'm getting requests for press passes for our trial. You can see the size of my courtroom. I couldn't even accommodate the number of reporters that have already contacted my clerk, much less leave any room for the general public. You saw Judge Hardman leaving here before we started. He and I have agreed that we are going to check on the availability of the South Texas auditorium for this trial. Anybody have any problem with that?"

Johnny Bob spoke first. "No, ma'am. That's my alma mater. I've lectured in that auditorium and think that it would be just fine."

"Mr. Duncan?"

Again he conferred with his co-counsel before agreeing.

"The next issue is a little more vexing. I've got requests from Court TV and four networks to broadcast our little proceeding live. What do you have to say about that?"

The judge stopped Johnny Bob before he could speak. "Mr. Tisdale, I suspect I can guess what the position of your clients is on this subject. I want to hear what Mr. Duncan has to say."

This time Tod did not have to confer with anyone. He almost jumped to his feet. "Your Honor, I'll have to object to television in the courtroom. It could impact on the demeanor of witnesses, lawyers and even the jurors. Besides, you've complained about this being a multi-ring circus. If you allow television in the courtroom, you might as well invite those elephants, tightrope walkers and clowns you talked about. There's no reason why the public can't be informed by reporters without a live telecast."

"Thank you, Mr. Duncan. I expected that position and understand it. I, myself, have been anticipating this request for some time now and have been wrestling with it. Our Constitution guarantees public trials and I'm certain that our founding fathers did not anticipate television. I'm mindful of my concerns about the circus-like atmosphere, so this may seem like a hypocritical ruling. However, we lawyers and judges have got to evolve with the times. I've decided to permit video cameras in the courtroom. It will be arranged so that the video will be a single feed—if I'm using my TV terminology correctly—that will be available to any of the media that request it. That's another reason to try this case at South Texas. As you all know, they have an audio-visual control booth at the back of the auditorium. The cameras will be located so that they will not interfere with any witness or lawyer. In fact, I hope that you all will forget that they are there. We are going to have a tight, short trial and if any of you think that you are going to become the next Johnny Cochran, you'd better think again." As she made the last remark, she looked directly at Johnny Bob who managed to suppress a smile.

"Now, do we need to discuss anything else? If not, I suggest that you all start exchanging deposition excerpts, exhibits and so forth. We'll have a pre-trial hearing on the Wednesday before trial. I'll consider motions at that time also. Mr. Tisdale, you should be looking at that list of experts you designated. I can guarantee you I won't let you call all of them. At best, I'll allow two or three on that 'when life begins' issue. By the way, if you choose to file a habeas for Reverend Luther, would you be so kind as to favor me with a copy? You are excused."

The front-page story in the next day's *Chronicle* announced T.J.'s change in status and his imminent release, including a quote from T.J. who pointed out that he could not discuss the upcoming trial. He praised Judge O'Reilly as being one of the most fair, knowledgeable and competent judges in the whole state. Certainly, he was willing to abide by her ruling.

TOD, JAN AND WAYNE retired to the fire station after the hearing. It would be the last time that they would meet in Tod's office because they were going to assemble the war room. Tod summoned Marilyn to join them at the table.

When she arrived, he started giving her orders. "Marilyn, let's get the war room ready. Move all the file materials in there. Set up a second computer and plug in another phone. Then start gathering everything you can find on every one of these experts that they've designated . . . the usual stuff, any articles or books they've written, prior depositions, prior testimony."

"I'm ahead of you, boss," interjected Marilyn. "I moved the file into the war room over the weekend. It's all set up. The depositions are indexed. I've got them loaded onto a laptop computer for use in the courtroom. I've got pads, markers, boxes of yellow stickies, probably everything you guys will need. I do need to add the second computer and find another phone around here to plug in there. It's basically ready for you. As to the experts, I'm working on them and should have what you need in a week to ten days."

Tod smiled at the efficiency of his legal assistant. Every good trial lawyer needed a paralegal like her. By the time of the trial, she would know the case as well as he. She would also keep boxes of evidence, pleadings, briefs and exhibits in perfect order.

"Thanks, Marilyn. Stick around. As usual, you need to know what is going on." He turned to Jan and Wayne. "Okay, give me your take on the hearing this morning."

Wayne jumped in, knowing that if he didn't, he might not get to say anything. "I think the judge did what she had to do. She's right. If we can watch the wars around the world live and in color, folks ought to be able to watch national events just the same. And, guys, in case you've both had your noses buried in discovery and hearings, this is the first big national trial since O. J. tried on the gloves that didn't fit. With the pro-lifers not doing so well elsewhere, like the current United States Supreme Court, from what I hear they're making our little old lawsuit their flagship for an all-out assault on abortion via the courthouse. Expect them to be generating all of the publicity they can. If they can win this one, abortion clinics across the country have to look out. I'm talking lawsuits, not bombs and protestors. Most of these folks on the religious right don't like it when the courts are used to attack tobacco and guns. Abortion is a different story."

"He's right, Tod," Jan joined in. "Grace may not have told you. We are already getting calls from the media, wanting to do 'background' interviews. Like it or not, we've got to play by Ruby's rules. Still, we have got to get our story out to the media, too. Otherwise, we're going to be left at the starting gate when we pick a jury."

With a sigh, Tod agreed. "Okay, call in the makeup department. Let's brush a few of the wrinkles off this face and spray down my hair. In the meantime, let's return to something a little more important, and that's our trial. How are you coming with experts, Jan?"

"No sweat, Tod. Fortunately, my contacts on the pro-choice side are just as good as Claudia's on the pro-life side. You know I've already got a University of Texas professor of obstetrics on board on the malpractice issues. Interestingly, he's added a new wrinkle. He says that if Lucy hadn't thrown up her antibiotic on that first day there's a possibility she might have fought the infection off. It's only a possibility, mind you, and that still doesn't help us with the perforation. At least it raises one possible defense that I suspect the other side hasn't picked up on. It's not Lucy's fault, but Zeke clearly was entitled to expect that she would take her medications. As to the other experts, I'll give you the list along with their resumes in about a week, and assuming you're satisfied, we'll get reports out of them with time to spare.

"Now, the issue is not when life begins. No scientist seriously quarrels with the notion that there is life at conception. As a matter of fact, there's life before conception. How else do you figure those little sperm could swim all that way to find the egg, which also is considered a living thing? The issue is when does a human person come into existence. That will be our issue in this trial, and also one, I might add, that has been debated at least as far back as Aristotle."

Tod and Wayne got wide-eyed at the dissertation and

Wayne spoke for both of them. "Are you telling us that when they listed a philosopher and a priest as experts, they were for real?"

"Gentlemen, as real as life itself. Go read *Roe v. Wade.* You'll find that even the Supreme Court addresses theology and philosophy as they relate to when human life begins," she replied as she reached into her briefcase and pulled out six books. "All of these books are on the abortion debate. Since you guys haven't been involved in it much up until now, I suggest you get to reading. Some of them are pro-choice and some are pro-life. You'll need to know the arguments on both sides. You'll find the debate most interesting, and I might add, most remarkable."

Tod propped his elbows on the table and rested his chin on his intertwined fingers as he asked, "Okay, so there's an argument and I'm going to read those books. At least tell me the answer."

Jan grinned. "That's just it. So far, this dispute is at least twenty-five-hundred years old and there is no answer that will satisfy the pro-lifers and the pro-choice folks. It's like your old high school debates. A logical argument can be made for both sides."

Tod was not often stumped by the science of the issues he dealt with as a trial lawyer. This time his eyes momentarily glazed over and then cleared. "Okay, Wayne and I will do our homework. In the meantime, let's start working on the malpractice claims against our clients. Marilyn, call Zeke and tell him we need some of his time. Matter of fact, we're going to need a lot of his time. See if he and his family can come out to my house on Friday night for barbecue. I want to take his pulse, so to speak, as we get close to trial. Jan and Wayne, if you're available, join us. We'll combine a little relaxation with some beginning discussions about trial. Marilyn, while you've got him on the phone, have him set aside two other days, one in the next couple of weeks and one during the week before trial."

54

Contrary to its reputation, Houston is not always a hot, humid and impossible place to live. In fact, from mid-September through mid-June its climate is close to ideal, particularly the fall months when the days are warm and the nights pleasant. On one of those pleasant nights Dr. Moyo parked his Explorer in front of Tod's house. He and his wife and two girls started toward the front door when they saw activity in the driveway, a one-on-one game of basketball. They watched momentarily before interrupting when the ball flew out of bounds into the adjoining soccer field.

"Good evening, boys," said Dr. Moyo. "Is it okay just to come around this way?"

"Oh, hi, you must be Dr. Moyo. Sure, Dad's in the backyard getting the fire started in the barbecue pit. I'm Kirk. This is my brother, Chris. He's younger than me so I let up on him a little when we're playing basketball."

"The heck you do," Chris shot back. "You haven't let up on me in basketball in three years. You just don't want to admit that your little brother is better than you!"

Hearing the exchange of voices, Tod rounded the corner before Kirk could reply.

"Welcome, Zeke."

"May I introduce my family, Tod," replied Dr. Moyo. "This is my wife, Marian. These are our daughters, Erica and Elissa. They are seven and five."

Marian was an attractive black woman with a definite British accent. Erica and Elissa could have been twins, both shy and obviously going to take after their mother as they matured.

"Can I get you something to drink?" asked Tod.

"I suspect the girls would like a Coke and since I'm out of the obstetrics business temporarily, I don't have to worry about being on call. So, I'll take a beer if you have one."

"Dad, before it gets dark, can we get Dr. Moyo out on the soccer field? I'd like to watch him in goal and see what I can learn before the regional championship next week," Kirk asked.

"Well, son, I didn't bring any soccer clothes or keeper gloves. I suppose that if my wife doesn't mind a few grass stains on my pants, and if you can loan me a pair of gloves, we can work in goal for a little while," Dr. Moyo replied, a look of anticipation on his face.

"You're on, Doc," said Kirk. "I'll get you a pair of gloves."

Wayne and Jan soon joined them, and while the charcoal burned down to an appropriate level, they all pulled up lawn chairs as Kirk and Zeke took turns firing shots at each other in the goal. Zeke kicked balls all around Kirk and each time Kirk missed, he would stop and explain what Kirk might have done differently to stop the goal. Then it was Kirk's turn. Zeke forgot about his age, and previously clean clothes, and took everything Kirk could give him. As Tod watched, he began to understand why, on their first meeting, Zeke had said that his quickness and hand-eye coordination made him an excellent surgeon. After about twenty minutes, Zeke made a time-out sign with his hands.

"I give up, Kirk. You're becoming a fine goalkeeper. I'm an old man and now I must have my beer."

Tod was on the field before he could reach the sidelines, beer in hand.

After hamburgers, beans, potato salad and ice cream, Jan invited Marian and the girls into the house while Tod, Zeke and Wayne remained outside, sipping beer. Tod opened the more serious part of the evening's conversation.

"So, tell me Zeke. How are you doing with all of this? You've been through a lot."

"I have, Tod, and so has my family. All in all, we're doing okay. I want to get this over, the sooner the better. I enjoy emergency work, but that's not where my heart lies. Frankly, after all the publicity in this case, I don't think I could ever rebuild my obstetrics practice. Instead, I've applied at Baylor for a position as an assistant professor in their obstetrics department. My credentials are good enough that I am being seriously considered. I just need to get this abomination behind me."

"Okay, then you've just answered my next question. We'll be going to trial in four weeks, come hell or high water. If you thought this case has had a lot of publicity, you ain't seen nothing yet. The media are going to be swarming all over this town. You might as well warn your neighbors to be expecting television vans parked in front of your house. I don't want you to ever talk to them, but don't be surprised if some enterprising young reporter decides to do a remote right smack in front of your mailbox."

Next, Tod launched into a discussion of what to expect over the next several weeks and then asked Zeke about the reports of the plaintiffs' experts. Zeke jumped into the discussion with a dissertation of the various theories of when life begins, touching on ensoulment and when a life form becomes a human being. He had lectured Tod and Wayne nonstop for forty minutes when Jan called out the back door, "Tod, you better come see this."

Jan and Marian were watching the ten o'clock news while the boys entertained Erica and Elissa with computer games in the den. The announcer had just finished his introduction to a press conference held earlier by the president of the United States when President Andrew Foster appeared on the screen behind the podium in the White House press room, answering a question from a reporter.

". . . as a matter of fact, it's clear that choice for women continues to be a topic that has polarized our society. The recent decisions of the Supreme Court mandate a dialogue on this subject. I hope to bring the pro-life and pro-choice forces together here at the White House to begin the process of seeking a solution to this most difficult of issues. Of course, my administration and I are strongly in favor of the right of a woman to choose what to do with her own body, but there are opposing views. It is for that reason that I am inviting the president of NOW and the Reverend Thomas Jeremiah Luther to meet with me here in two weeks, assuming, of course, that the Reverend Luther is released from jail in Houston by that time. I am in the last few months of my administration. If I cannot bring resolution to this question before I leave office, I certainly intend to start the dialogue by bringing the parties together."

A voice came from the audience. "Mr. President, do you have any comments on the upcoming trial in Houston?"

"Well, I suspect you know that I have opinions myself and they are well known to most of the country. However, I respect the sanctity of the judicial system and am certain that the judge and jury will do the right thing. That's all that I should say about an ongoing judicial proceeding with a trial occurring in a matter of weeks. Thank you, ladies and gentlemen."

"Tod, does this impact on our trial?" Dr. Moyo asked.

"Zeke, everything in the media from now on impacts on our trial. The fact that Luther has been invited to the White House will not go unnoticed by the media and the public. We'll file a motion to keep it out of evidence and will probably succeed. Still, any prospective jurors who watch the ten o'clock news—and that's nearly everyone in this town—are going to be aware of it. Certainly, it increases his stature. We'll just have to deal with it."

DOWNTOWN, JOHNNY BOB AND Bernice had just returned from a play at the Alley Theater when they caught the last of the news. Johnny Bob watched with amazement before proclaiming, "Son of a bitch! How the hell did he pull that one off? The Chosen just made damn sure that he'd be out of jail in a week. I don't think that Ruby wants to go up against the White House. Bernice," he yelled, "this calls for a scotch and a big one at that. I may not agree with everything that old T.J. does. One thing's for sure. He sure knows how to get attention."

The television in the deputy lounge of the Harris County jail was also turned to the news. T.J. and two deputies were watching as the president appeared on the screen. His plans continued to work. Of all of the potential pro-life spokespersons, President Foster had picked him.

"Well, I'll be hornswaggled," said one of the deputies.

"Reverend, would you look at that. You're being invited to the White House. Ain't never had one of our prisoners go from our jail direct to the White House. You reckon you could get us the president's autograph?"

"Don't know," T.J. replied with a sly smile. "I bet I can probably swipe a few White House napkins, though."

In her house in the Memorial area of West Houston, Judge O'Reilly watched the same broadcast and cursed. She didn't like outside interference with anything in her court. While the president never mentioned her trial by name, just the fact that T.J. was going to the White House would have an impact, exactly how, she was not sure. And besides that, now she had to let Reverend Luther out of jail early. The president had just presented him with a "Get Out of Jail Free" card. All she could do was come down hard on T.J. about discussing the trial or anything to do with it. Her last thought as she fell asleep was "Let's get this bastard over." That was not a prayer but a fervent wish.

ON THE FOLLOWING SATURDAY, Tod spent the day mentally kicking himself. He didn't fight his battles in the media, and he recognized that he was being beaten in the court of public opinion even before the trial began. All day, while cheering his sons on in soccer and basketball games, he tried to come up with ways to focus positive media attention on their side of the case or at least on some of their witnesses. Then luck fell into Dr. Moyo's lap.

Zeke was working his seven P.M. to seven A.M. shift on Saturday night when a five-year-old Hispanic girl in critical condition was wheeled into the emergency room, trailed by her mother and two police officers. They lived only a few blocks from the hospital in an area known for drug dealing. The girl had been shot in the abdomen in a drive-by shooting. The bullet was intended for her older brother. Normally, Dr. Moyo would have called Life Flight to transport her to the medical center, but there was no time. Nor was there time to call a general surgeon. Dr. Moyo had no choice but to take her to the operating room immediately. As an obstetrician and gynecologist, his specialty was not gunshots. Fortunately, he was a surgeon and this was a young female. He was confident that he could handle whatever had to be done. The bullet had passed through the body and had severed an artery as it did so. He ordered blood, telling the lab to forget the thirty-minute procedure to type and cross-match. He had no time. He opened her abdomen and exposed the bleeder about the time that the anesthesiologist advised that the blood was available. With a hemoglobin of 7.2, he ordered the blood to be administered, and prayed for no complications. With deft strokes, he stitched the artery, sewed the entry and exit holes, cleaned and flushed out the interior of the abdomen and closed.

As he came out of the operating room, a nurse told him that there was a television team outside the hospital, requesting an interview. Although it was something that he would never have considered before watching the president the evening before, he washed his hands, and intentionally leaving on the blood-soaked scrubs with the mask around his neck, he walked out into the television lights.

"As you know, we are live at the scene at the hospital where a life and death struggle has been underway to save a five-year-old girl. Approaching us is the surgeon who just completed the operation. May I have your name, sir?"

"I am Dr. Mzito Moyo."

"Doctor, please tell us the status of the girl."

"The girl will live. She had a severe wound and lost a massive amount of blood for a child so small. With my operation, she should be fine."

As the camera focused back on the reporter, it was clear that he was listening to something emitting from his earpiece. "Dr. Moyo, my station advises that you may be the same Dr. Moyo who will be involved in the abortion trial in just a few weeks. If I can ask, why are you working in an emergency room?"

"First, let me clarify," responded Dr. Moyo. "I am the same Dr. Moyo. However, it is not an abortion trial. Instead, it is a trial to clear my good name. As to why I am working in the emergency room, I am pleased to be here saving lives. However, your audience should know that I expect to be accepted on the faculty of Baylor College of Medicine in the very near future and I will be teaching obstetrics and gynecology very soon."

Signaling with a wave of his hand that the interview was over, Zeke turned and walked back into the hospital.

As the story was followed the next day, an announcement added that Dr. Moyo was one of two candidates out of an original list of forty-five who were being considered for the position at Baylor.

It was the next week when Judge O'Reilly decided to release T.J. As much as she hated to admit it, she was feeling the heat. Not only was the president summoning him to the White House, but her staff was having to field daily calls from media throughout the country, inquiring as to how much longer the Chosen would be in jail. Once again she summoned the lawyers. She also advised the jail staff to get T.J. out of his prison garb and over to her court the next morning at nine o'clock.

T.J. left the jail accompanied by three deputies. As they stepped onto the street, he was dressed in his white linen suit, off-white shirt and white tie. The sunglasses protected his eyes from the bright morning sun. Although pale, he appeared otherwise none the worse for his stay in jail. The media and cameras immediately surrounded him and the deputies. Microphones were thrust in front of T.J. who only smiled and said "no comment" to each question.

As T.J. arrived at the courthouse, Johnny Bob and Claudia met him at the entrance. The cameras rolled as Johnny Bob shook T.J.'s hand and Claudia gave him a big hug. Then, Johnny Bob waved the media and microphones out of their way as they entered the building. Judge O'Reilly, Tod, Jan and Wayne were already in the courtroom when they arrived.

As they approached the counsel table, the judge spoke. "Good morning, ladies and gentlemen. Please be seated.

Reverend Luther, I am sure you know why you are here. You were jailed originally because you violated my direct orders and refused to answer questions pertaining to matters relevant to this case. I have been advised that you are prepared to answer any and all questions, subject, of course, to objections from your lawyers. Is that correct?"

"Yes, ma'am. That is correct," replied T.J., rising from his chair. "Further, Your Honor, I wish to offer my most sincere apologies to you and this court. I now recognize that I was completely wrong and expect to abide by all of your rulings."

"Very well then. You are free to go. Let me remind you, however, that you are under the same rules regarding talking about this case as are the other parties and attorneys. And I have one additional request for you personally. I clearly do not intend to interfere with your religious freedom, and for that reason this is a request only, not an order of this court. My request is that you refrain from preaching on television until this trial is concluded. I know that you have a national audience, and even though you do not mention this trial, just your presence on television in Houston could have an impact on our prospective jurors."

Fortunately, Judge O'Reilly could not see the eyes behind the sunglasses as they narrowed and glared at her like two lasers trying to pierce a metal barrier. But she could see the facial expression harden and his lips narrow as T.J. spoke. "Judge O'Reilly, I am willing to follow your orders regarding this trial. When it comes to preaching the Word, my orders come from a much higher authority. I will give careful and prayerful consideration to your request. However, I must advise that since it is only a request, I cannot agree to be bound by it. If that means that I must go back to jail, then I am ready to go."

T.J. and the remainder of the lawyers and spectators had no problem seeing Judge O'Reilly's eyes behind her glasses. They also narrowed. She expected her requests to be treated like orders. She had underestimated T.J., and now she was boxed in. Reporters were in the courtroom. To change it to

an order would put her back in the position of being accused
of religious persecution. She had no choice but to let T.J. go.
"Very well, Reverend Luther. Let me encourage you to have
a long, hard talk with your higher authority. If you choose
not to honor my request, I will not hold you in contempt.
I guarantee you, though, it will not sit well with me. Do I
make myself clear?"

Knowing that he had won a round with the judge, T.J.
relaxed and replied, "Yes, Your Honor. You have."

55

Johnny Bob and Claudia showed T.J. around his loft. Like the
others it had fourteen-foot ceilings, hardwood floors and
brick walls, long hidden behind layers of plaster before ren-
ovation. His phones were connected to theirs and he had a
computer that also accessed all of the case files. Like theirs,
the furniture was rented, but it came from a service that provided accommodations for visiting executives and was of a
quality that even Aunt Jessie would appreciate.

As they sat in the living area, T.J. smiled. "Sure beats solitary, and it's even a little nicer than the deputy lounge."

"Okay, T.J., Claudia and I have about two months' worth
of work to do in three weeks. We're going to need a couple
of days of your time. It can wait for at least a week. What are
your plans?"

"My plans should fit right into your schedule. I have a
limo picking me up any time now to take me out to Hobby
Airport where the City's Learjet will be waiting."

"Just a minute, T.J. You mean to tell me you have a Learjet?" Johnny Bob interrupted with astonishment.

"Only a small one. It seats six comfortably and eight in a
pinch. It's good to have something like that available when
one gets a call from the president. In any case, I'm flying to
Fort Worth for a meeting with the City's board. They want

an update on the trial, and I need to review what's been going on there while I've been away. Then, I fly to Washington to meet with President Foster on Monday. After visiting with a few of the pro-life congressmen, I ought to be back here about the middle of the following week. Say about a week from now."

"That'll work. Claudia and I and the rest of the team will be here getting ready for the big show. One last warning, when a judge makes a request, treat it like an order."

T.J. frowned. "I understood Judge O'Reilly's request this morning, Johnny Bob. As I told her, the decision is not mine."

T.J. left the loft. Johnny Bob and Claudia watched out the window as the limo driver opened the door to his car and T.J. climbed into the backseat. As they drove away, Claudia asked, "So, what do you think our favorite client is going to do?"

"Damned if I know, Claudia. Wish I had a phone that would connect to that higher authority. Too bad there seems to be only one line in service, and it's already reserved."

56

T.J.'s meeting with the president went well. Hell, as far as he was concerned, any meeting with the president at the White House could only go well, no matter what the outcome. He bought a new double-breasted white suit, a hundred-dollar linen shirt, a two-hundred-dollar tie, some specially made patent leather white shoes and wore a lapel pin that was the image of a twelve-week-old fetus. Only his sunglasses were not new.

T.J. was chauffeured from his Washington hotel in the longest white limousine he could find. Four District policemen escorted him, two in front and two in back. The policemen were his idea and paid by him, not the White House. As they approached, he was stopped only momentarily to establish that he was the lone occupant of the vehicle before the gates swung open and T.J. was driven to the front of the White House. The Marines stood at attention. Cameras flashed and videos rolled as he exited the limo and waved to the reporters. President Foster greeted T.J. at the entrance. The president asked him to face the media as they shook hands. Certainly, the president didn't want to lose the opportunity for a few pro-life votes for the Democratic Party. Being shown shaking hands with the Chosen on the six o'clock news could only help. Besides, he had gone through the same scenario with the president of NOW only five minutes before.

President Foster, the Chosen and the leader of the National Organization of Women emerged from the Oval Office two hours later. In reality, they had accomplished nothing. There was no middle ground. While there were some anti-abortion advocates who would agree that an abortion to save the life of the mother was acceptable, T.J. did not represent that faction. On the other side, the current leader of NOW would not permit any government intrusion into a woman's right to choose.

The president held a short news conference, flanked on either side by the two adversaries, and smiled as he said how pleased he was with the dialogue. While they had a ways to go, they had made substantial progress for an initial meeting. When asked when the next meeting could be expected, he avoided the issue by pointing out that he was going to be out of the country for the next several weeks and his staff would have to coordinate schedules. Actually, he expected no further meetings. Even with his charisma and powers of persuasion, he knew when to throw in the towel. Let the other two branches of government wrestle with this issue. He would be out of the White House in only a matter of months, anyway.

There was a presidential debate that evening, the third in a series. The race was too close to call. One national poll gave Peter Vandenberg, the Republican candidate, a margin of four points. Another poll gave Herbert Wells, the Democratic candidate and the current senator from South Dakota, a margin of five. Both polls concluded that with the margin for error, it was a dead heat. It would have been like putting two strands of hair under a microscope to find any real difference between the candidates. One of the few issues that separated the two candidates was abortion, and many believed it could turn out to be the issue that decided the presidential election. Like most Democrats, it was easy for Senator Wells. His constituency—women, liberals, blacks and homosexuals—were strongly on the pro-choice side. The one exception was the Hispanic vote. Predominantly Catholic, if asked, most would say they were pro-life. In prior elections, other than Cuban-Americans in Florida, they would have ignored the abortion issue and voted a straight Democratic ticket.

Now there were changes in the wind. Vandenberg was the governor of a state that bordered on Mexico, and he had successfully reached out to the Hispanic population in his state. His stance was carefully crafted so that he stood with one foot balanced precariously on the fence, reluctantly agreeing to an abortion if necessary to preserve the life or well-being of the mother. His generally anti-abortion stance had the potential to attract enough Hispanic voters to carry the election.

The candidates agreed on the debate format. Questions from three reporters. Taking turns, each candidate would have two minutes to respond to the question with the first responder having a one-minute rebuttal. They were forty minutes into the debate when the CNN reporter raised the question. "I think that the country needs to know each of your positions on the abortion question. Would you introduce a bill to outlaw partial-birth abortions as a matter of federal law, and would you go so far as to extend it to a complete banning of abortions of any kind? As a corollary to the question, with an aging Supreme Court, would you insist on nominating justices who hold a specific view about abortions?"

Governor Vandenberg went first. "I consider partial-birth

abortions an outrage and would support any statute that does away with them. The problem is whether such a statute can withstand a constitutional challenge. As to Supreme Court Justices, I am a conservative, and as such, I do not believe in any litmus test for a Supreme Court nominee. I will seek judicial conservatives with philosophies that are like mine. At the same time, I would never nominate them based on their position on one issue; nor would I even permit such a question to be asked. I'm sure the country will agree that position is consistent with conservative principles."

Governor Vandenberg stayed on the fence, balanced carefully on his right foot. Fortunately, the top rail of the fence was wide, with ample room for balancing on one foot with the other one hanging in the air on the pro-life side.

Next came Senator Wells. "Unlike my Republican opponent, I have never straddled the fence on this issue. Abortion is a question to be resolved between a woman and her physician. Under the Fourteenth and other amendments, if the government were to intervene in that decision, it would violate our Constitution. As to the so called 'partial-birth' decision, if a woman has a right to choose, we cannot start down that slippery slope, trying to draw lines between fifteen weeks and twenty weeks; between twenty-nine weeks and thirty weeks. It is the woman's body and, again, I say it is a decision to be made by the woman and her physician. Regarding judicial candidates, I would not ask any candidate to pre-judge a matter that is not before him. However, I can assure America that I will nominate candidates who will think as I do. Last, please note that the pro-choice forces have invited me to join them on the first day of the Brady trial in Houston and I have gladly accepted."

57

On a moonless night, a white four-door sedan turned off the
highway that wound through the small town near the
Louisiana border in deep East Texas. Carefully observing
the posted speed limit, the driver went several blocks before
turning on a street lined with big Victorian houses and giant
oaks. Seeing one with a porch light on, the driver glanced at
a piece of paper to confirm it was the right address before
he pulled into a gravel drive behind an old pickup truck.

The driver turned off the engine and turned to face the
woman in the passenger seat. She was noticeably upset and
he raised his voice in anger as he motioned her out of the
car. Finally, he opened the driver's door, walked around the
car, threw open the passenger door and dragged the crying woman out. As he pointed to the lighted porch, she
slumped her shoulders, wiped her eyes with her shirt-
sleeves and walked up the stairs. Timidly, she knocked on
the door and it opened as the driver got back in the car and
shut his door.

As soon as the woman was in the house, the driver
reached over to the glove box and extracted a flask nearly
full of bourbon. Screwing off the lid, he put it to his lips and
tilted his head as he let at least a third of the whiskey trickle
down his throat. Returning the flask to its place, he spent the
next thirty minutes punching up radio stations that broadcast
from cities as far away as Chicago.

Finally, the front door opened and the woman exited,
slowly walked down the steps and climbed into the front
seat. Before she could even get her seat belt on, the driver
was backing out of the driveway, but not before the driver
noticed an old man with a white beard who followed the
woman out onto the porch. He was wiping his hands with a
towel and as the car started down the street, he too went

down the stairs, squinting to see the license plate on the white sedan. Then he went back into his house and promptly wrote the license on the margin of a piece of paper on his desk.

58

T.J. couldn't resist. Maybe it was his higher authority, or maybe it was the devil that made him do it. But eight days before trial, he returned to the pulpit. He didn't even tell his staff that he would be preaching that morning, and he specifically did not mention the idea to Johnny Bob. While the collection buckets were being passed among the congregation, he appeared backstage and told the assistant minister that he would take over. Dressed in his white satin robe, he mounted the platform and directed the crew to raise it above the stage. The lights dimmed, the curtains opened and the spotlights focused on the platform thirty feet above the stage. As one, the audience gasped and then stood in thunderous ovation as they realized that the Chosen was above them and was going to preach for the first time since he was jailed. The platform made its slow descent, accompanied by shouts and cheers. Three elderly ladies close to the front passed out and were carried to the back of the auditorium. T.J. stepped from the platform and walked to the pulpit. He let the sound thunder over him for what seemed like five minutes before raising his hands and calling for silence. It was quiet when a loud male voice from the back shouted, "Give 'em hell, T.J."

T.J. laughed and replied, "It's not mine to give, brother, but you can bet that's what they are about to get."

That brought a laugh from the audience.

"Now, my friends, it's time to be serious. As you all know, I've been incarcerated in the Harris County jail for several months. I am a defendant in a case that will go to trial there in eight days. I should say that all of you are defendants because the City of Miracles is also a defendant. We have been sued, along with others, for one hundred million dollars because I spoke the truth."

Shouts erupted. The auditorium was filled with voices yelling, "No!" As T.J. called for silence, the same male voice from the back yelled, "That's bullshit!"

This time T.J. did not laugh, but said, "My friend, while I may agree with you, I must ask you to watch your language in the house of the Lord. If you have read the newspapers or watched the news on TV, you are aware that the judge in Houston has muzzled me. I am not permitted to talk about the trial or what will be going on in Houston. I have given her my word and I will keep it. However, each of you knows me to be a man who stands up for his beliefs. My beliefs go beyond that trial in Houston. In fact, my beliefs are so well known that I have only recently returned from the White House where I conferred with the president about the plague of abortion that is upon this land. So, rather than talk to you about the trial in Houston, let me report to you on what I told the president."

Again, the congregation cheered. Most in the audience figured out that T.J. had neatly sidestepped any orders from the judge by offering to report on his presidential meeting. This time the male voice in the back remained silent as T.J. launched into his sermon, condemning abortion and anyone who would consent to or perform such acts. Careful this time not to mention Houston, the trial, Dr. Moyo or Population Planning, his attack was just as vituperative as the ones that had landed him in jail. Abortionists were baby killers. Abortion clinics were murderous temples of the devil. He didn't stop there, but gave equal time to the Supreme Court, calling their opinion that abolished the Nebraska partial-birth statute a decision that could only come from the depths of hell. He closed with praise for any potential national leader that would condemn abortion and castigated any potential national leader that would endorse it. The next morning, T.J. took great delight in seeing that there was a two-point shift toward the Republican presidential candidate in the upcoming election. The commentators could attribute it to nothing other than the Chosen's sermon. T.J. basked in the knowledge that the country recognized his political power.

RUBY ERUPTED AGAIN. ON Sunday afternoon, she called her clerk and told her to get the lawyers in her courtroom at nine the next morning. Having seen *The Miracle Morning Hour,* Johnny Bob was not surprised to get the call. In fact, he expected it, but was he going into the biggest trial of his life with one of his clients sitting once again in the Harris County jail? He immediately put Claudia to work on her computer, researching cases to try to find some law that guaranteed that a civil litigant could take his rightful place in the courtroom.

Tod had taken his boys fishing on Lake Conroe, figuring that it would be the last day he would take off for several weeks. He didn't get the message until he listened to his answering machine at nine that evening. He hadn't even heard T.J.'s sermon and had to call Jan to find out what was going on. When he got the news, he was ready to go to court that night. Whatever Ruby was going to do could only be good for his side.

All of the lawyers were fifteen minutes early. They exchanged pleasantries and avoided talking about the case. At five minutes until nine, Judge O'Reilly strode in from the back of the courtroom.

"Counsel, this is going to be very brief. I lay awake half the night pondering what to do about this situation. Mr. Tisdale, I suppose that your client did not violate my order, but he certainly violated the spirit of my ruling, not to mention a direct affront to my request. I give up. I think it's best that any case, and particularly this one, be tried in my courtroom and not in the media. It was for that reason that I ordered you not to talk to the press. I've never had a case where one of the litigants has, literally, a national pulpit and can apparently impact a national election. Further, I've never had a matter where some of the very issues that may be relevant to our case are also issues of national debate. I'm withdrawing my order."

She stared over her glasses at Johnny Bob as she continued. "It's unfair to Mr. Duncan, Ms. Akers and their clients. Mr. Tisdale, if your client can talk about this case in the guise of discussing national issues, so be it. From this point forward, my gag order is withdrawn. All of you and your clients are free to talk about this case to anyone you choose, and that includes the media. I caution you attorneys that you are still bound by the Disciplinary Rules. I suggest that you read them and try not to stray too far from them. Otherwise, go to it. Personally, I'm not going to sanction any of you for what you say outside my courtroom. Mr. Tisdale, I suspect that your side is already adequately represented with the press. Dr. Moyo and Population Planning may need to level the playing field, and if they choose to do it through their lawyers, as far as I am concerned, they can say whatever they want to whomever they want. Let the chips fall where they may."

For a second time, Judge O'Reilly stormed from her bench and slammed the door to her chambers, leaving five lawyers who were rarely at a loss for words stunned into silence.

Tod and Jan moved rapidly. Trial started in one week. All they had to do to draw a crowd of reporters was make a few calls to announce a press conference in front of the courthouse that afternoon. With trial only a week away, the national media had already assembled. The evening news on each of the major networks started with the press conference. First came Dr. Moyo. Unaccustomed to such a forum, nonetheless, he came across as the caring physician that he was. He read a short statement and then answered a few questions before three women, all of whom had abortions earlier in their lives, told their stories. One was a rape victim, one a victim of incest, and the third was an older woman. The first two said that they would have committed suicide if abortion had not been available from Population Planning. Both were now volunteers at the center. The third woman told of her horrifying experience with an illegal abortion before *Roe v. Wade*. She had complications and was left for dead in a five-dollar motel room, only to be found by the cleaning lady the next morning. She survived, graduated from the University of Texas with a Ph.D. in psychology and was the former lieutenant governor of California. She eloquently made the case for a woman's right to choose.

59

About a month before the Brady v. Population Planning trial, both teams focused on it and little else. Each set of lawyers prepared a battle plan along with multiple contingencies. Lawyers were assigned specific tasks and witnesses. Briefs were prepared on key points of evidence. Strategy sessions were used to debate which witnesses should be called and the appropriate order of witnesses to maximize their effectiveness. The clients had to be rehearsed and prepared for days on end. In a process known in Texas as "woodshedding the witness," the litigants were seated at a table, often with a video camera on them, as their own lawyers peppered them with almost every conceivable question that could come up in the trial. Their answers were rehearsed, their demeanor was criticized, and they were even schooled on when to turn to the jury and smile. The lawyers studied every scrap of evidence. In a case with expert witnesses, they scoured the literature on the experts' subjects until they comprehended it almost as well as the witnesses.

Johnny Bob sent Bernice back to Palestine three weeks before trial. Not that he didn't love her. He had work to do. She understood. She had been married to him for more than thirty years. She still remembered the early days when he would leave home and hole up in a motel on the outskirts of Palestine for days, seeking solitude as he prepared for an upcoming trial. For this one, his team's equivalent of a war room was the living room of the loft shared by Mildred and Sara. It was there that the four of them, Johnny Bob, Claudia, Mildred and Sara, planned their side of the case.

Johnny Bob led the discussion. "Let's remember that we have a plaintiff case to put on. First decision is whether to put on Lucy and her family followed by Moyo and the clinic folks or the other way around."

Claudia spoke up. "I vote for Lucy and her family first. With all that has happened to her, we'll get the jury's sympathy on our side right from the start. Those folks aren't going to like how they abandoned her and almost let her die."

"I agree," continued Johnny Bob, "just didn't want to sway you with my opinion. Claudia, I think you ought to be the one to present Lucy and her mother. I think that your feminine approach will help draw out the emotions that we need from Lucy and her family, as well as the jury. Besides, I think that Lucy will respond much better if you are handling her rather than an old East Texas redneck. We'll talk some more before we decide who will take Aunt Jessie. We want Bo in the courtroom, although I don't see any reason to put him on the stand. He can't add anything that the others won't cover. After that, we'll continue with Dr. Moyo and the two weekend nurses. I figure they'll be well woodshedded so it will take some work to discredit them, particularly Dr. Moyo."

The discussion turned to other potential witnesses, including the Life Flight crew. Mildred was an old hand at these kinds of conferences and while she held no law degree, she had prepared for and helped Johnny Bob try cases for fifteen years. She spoke up. "The judge is going to be pushing us to keep things short. So, I'd leave the crew out and just rely on the lay testimony of Joanna as to what happened before Hermann Hospital. I'd also leave out the counselor at Population Planning. Lucy can talk about what was said. Let them call the counselor if they want."

"Hearing no opposition," Johnny Bob said, "we'll adopt Mildred's plan, at least for starters. Damned if I didn't almost overlook the Chosen. How could I possibly leave him out? Freudian omission, maybe. Sara, get him on down here from Fort Worth. I may have to spend the next week just working with him. Now that the son of a bitch has an even bigger national presence, he's not going to pass up an opportunity to grandstand. I've got to at least try to control him, even though it may be a lost cause. Now comes the big question. If we had our druthers, what kind of jurors do we want? Claudia, you first, since you've been involved in more abortion cases than anyone else."

Pleased to be called on for some expertise that Johnny Bob didn't have, she thought for a minute. "That's a tough one, Johnny Bob. We've got a malpractice case where we want big damages. We've got a counter-action to defend for slander where we want the jury to award no damages and we've got the abortion issue overriding everything. For sure, one size does not fit all. Let's start with categories. Men versus women. I'll go with women on that one and younger rather than older. They are more likely to empathize with Lucy. Your problem there, though, is that a lot of the younger women are going to buy into the pro-choice, a woman's body is her own, yada, yada, argument that they'll hear from the other side. We're going to have to make some individual judgment calls."

Johnny Bob absentmindedly stroked his chin as he absorbed what she was saying.

"As to races, since I'm speaking about my own race, let me be the one to say that abortion is not a big issue in the black community. While there are a few black ministers who come out against abortion, you don't see Jessie Jackson on the picket lines in front of abortion clinics. Additionally, we have a very good black doctor as a defendant. It's a toss-up. I'd be willing to go with one or two carefully selected blacks on the jury. Remember I said carefully selected. Hispanics are going to be condemning everyone in this case. Mostly Catholic, they are going to be against abortion, against the doctors, against the clinics and against a woman who has an abortion. Again, I would think they would be more critical of the abortion clinic than Lucy. All in all, it's a damn tough call. The one thing for sure is that we need as big a panel as the judge will allow. Two or three hundred would not be too many."

"Bottom line, Claudia," Johnny Bob mused, "is that while jury selection is a crap shoot in most cases, it's even more so in this one."

"You got that right, Johnny Bob," Claudia replied, as the meeting adjourned, and each returned to their individual projects.

TWO MILES FROM DOWNTOWN a similar meeting was taking place, this one in the war room at the fire station. Over several hours, Tod's team debated how the trial would go and which lawyers would handle which witnesses. As defendants in the primary case, they had the disadvantage of not knowing for certain how Johnny Bob would lay out his evidence. As seasoned trial lawyers, though, they would have a fairly good idea and worked up contingency plans accordingly. Then, they went through the same analysis regarding prospective jurors as had the other team, ultimately coming to the same conclusion that it was going to be nearly impossible to find jurors who would likely be favorable to them on every aspect of the case.

MEANTIME, THE MEDIA WERE having a field day. Johnny Bob held press conferences outside the courthouse. Tod held his in front of the fire station. One of the networks finally talked Tod into a tour of the fire station and got a video of Wayne coming down the fire pole, even wearing a fire-fighter's hat left over from an old products liability case. That scene was shown on the evening news all over the country. They did a study on Judge O'Reilly and some out-of-state lawyer-commentators pontificated on the legal issues likely to come up and how she could be expected to rule on them. Ruby took note of their learned guesses and vowed to see how often she could rule differently from their guesses without being reversed. Then, she realized that she was falling into the trap of letting the media influence her judgment and mentally chastised herself. Let the media and their so-called experts do and say what they may. She would run this trial just like any other.

BACK IN FORT WORTH, T.J. couldn't take it. The media was in Houston and even though he held press conferences, they had heard what he had to say so many times that only the local papers and TV stations attended. When he got the call from Sara that he was needed in Houston, it was time to make an entrance, and a grand one at that. It only took two days for him to reassemble the faithful and a giant fleet of vehicles for another caravan to Houston.

They planned their route to stay off the interstate highways. His publicity department made overnight buys of radio spots on every small-town radio station between Fort Worth and Houston. The ads encouraged his followers to join the caravan as it came through each town and, not surprisingly, they did. What started off as a few hundred vehicles grew as the caravan passed through each small town. T.J. talked on the loudspeaker mounted on the top of the van, horns honked and a few sirens blared from pickups outfitted for volunteer firemen. The caravan could not be missed as it passed down main streets along the route. The numbers grew. As the caravan approached Hempstead, fifty miles northwest of Houston, the Houston Police Department got a call that there were over a thousand vehicles bound for a rally in front of Population Planning's main Houston clinic. When the caravan approached the downtown Houston exit, the vehicles left the freeway, passed in front of the courthouse and headed two miles out of town to the clinic.

The police had the wisdom to man each intersection as they waved the caravan through. T.J. had his audience. The national media learned they were coming. Once again helicopters circled overhead. National reporters, including the *Washington Post* along with the *New York Times,* the major networks and PBS had been in town for over a week and had exhausted stories of local interest. They were ready for an event, and T.J. gave them one. He double-parked his van right in front of the clinic as the remaining thousand vehicles slowly passed by and searched for parking places. Given no choice as the masses grew, the police blocked off the entire street for four blocks in either direction. Not to be outdone, the bishop of the Galveston-Houston archdiocese joined the throng in front of Population Planning. When T.J. heard the bishop was outside, he invited the bishop into the van. Shortly thereafter, the van was transformed. Maybe it was not the reason that it was called the Miracle Van, yet it was impressive nonetheless. Buttons were pushed and the roof of the van was changed into a twelve-foot-tall speakers' platform. Rails rose from all four sides. A podium, complete with microphone, appeared in the middle. Loudspeakers magically appeared at the van's four corners. A stairway descended inside to the feet of the Chosen. Reverend Luther invited the bishop to join him topside. The crowd had now grown to several thousand and the cheers were deafening as the Chosen and the bishop appeared on the roof. It took ten minutes to calm them down. T.J. spoke briefly. "My friends, I have come to the den of the tiger. I have come to the cave of the dragon. I have come to slay the lion with only my bare hands. I need nothing more for I have God on my side."

Cheers erupted again.

"Also on my side is the Catholic Church." T.J. turned and shook the hand of the bishop. "While my followers and those of the pope may occasionally have our differences, when we are faced with a common enemy, we put aside our differences and unite." He again grabbed the hand of the bishop and, this time, raised it in the air as if they had already won the battle. "We will rally here on Monday morning and march to the trial. On that day let your voices be heard. The nation will be watching!"

As the crowd was breaking up, the CNN camera turned to two reporters covering the trial. "So, John, how do you rate this, the opening shot of the Chosen?"

"Peter, I've got to tell you that I am overwhelmed with the size of the crowd. That he could summon what must be ten thousand people, including the bishop, is amazing. With those comments about lions and dragons and tigers, he obviously sees himself as Sir Lancelot, his armor polished and ready for battle. He and J. Robert Tisdale should make quite a force."

THE CAMERA PANNED TO the crowd as they drifted off and then faded into another crowd, this one a rally for the pro-choice forces. When they learned what T.J. was doing, they decided to do likewise, only they chose the heart of the Houston Medical Center as their site, right in front of Baylor College of Medicine. If a rally had ever been held there before, it was unknown to anyone in attendance. In fact, if the medical center police had known that it was to occur, they would have tried to stop the rally, but it formed quietly and quickly. First, a few people gathered on the sidewalk. Then more filled the parking lots and soon overflowed into the streets to be joined shortly by the media. TV vans and helicopters converged as the press learned about the pro-choice rally not far from where T.J. had assembled his forces. Not as big as T.J.'s rally, it easily topped one thousand.

The location of the pro-choice rally, with the crowd surrounded by medical facilities that were among the finest in the world, was a carefully planned decision. The subliminal message was that abortion was okay. It was taught here. Abortions were done here and, as one speaker said, if it were not for *Roe v. Wade,* these hospitals would be overflowing with victims of back-alley abortions.

A CNN commentator observed, "The effect is dramatic and the message is clear."

60

It was Wednesday morning, five days before trial. Judge O'Reilly had moved her courtroom to the South Texas College of Law Auditorium. She got there at seven-thirty so that she could survey the accommodations and make some decisions. Like most Houston lawyers, she had been there on many occasions, usually for seminars. Sometimes she spoke. More often, she listened to lectures on new developments in law, evidence and procedure. She knew that the occasional trial was held in this auditorium, yet she had never really viewed it as a courtroom. Looking down from the highest row of seats, there were three sections. The middle section looked like it would hold about three hundred people and the two other sections, probably two hundred apiece. Beside her and to her right was the audio-visual booth. Cameras had been mounted on each wall close to the bottom where the "courtroom" would be. She concluded that the participants would soon ignore the cameras and focus on the drama that was about to play out in this hall. She walked slowly down the stairs to the multipurpose stage, now configured as a courtroom, complete with her elevated bench, a witness stand and a jury box—at her request designed to hold fourteen jurors, twelve plus two alternates. In front of the bench were two long tables surrounded by comfortable padded chairs. Against one wall was a screen that could be used as a television or to display exhibits.

As she reached the bottom of the stairs, she turned and looked to where the audience would be. She had told the administrative judge that she would need a two-hundred-person panel. At first Judge Hardman thought she must have been joking. After a short conversation, he agreed with her assessment. They would lose close to half of the jurors at the start because they held strong pro-life or pro-choice views and would certainly not be objective. Until the jury was picked, she would use the first rows in the middle section for the panel and the remainder of the auditorium would be for whomever showed up first, press or public. The press wouldn't like the fact that she showed them no favoritism. The bailiffs would give a number to each person who asked to observe. The number would be surrendered when he or she entered the auditorium. When they were out of numbers they were out of seats. She thanked Southwest Airlines for the idea.

After jury selection, the middle section would be reserved

for the public with the press occupying the two side sections. Ruby tried the judge's chair on for size, twirled around in it once and pronounced it satisfactory. As she surveyed her bench, she glanced at a television monitor, which she assumed was placed there so that she would always know what picture was being broadcast to the rest of the world. As she evaluated the silent auditorium, she contemplated the decisions she had made thus far in this case and the ones that lay before her. She anticipated certain issues and would be faced with them in about an hour. There were the other issues, the evidence and procedural decisions that she could not even anticipate that could, conceivably, make or break the case for either side. In her mind an image surfaced of Ruby in referee's stripes in charge at the Super Bowl, the world's attention focused on the game. She was in the middle with giant, violent men running by her from all directions. When she blew her whistle, they all stopped and stared with rapt attention. Whatever her ruling, it would stand. There would be no instant replay.

The second person to enter the courtroom was an old man. Hobbled with arthritis and needing the assistance of a cane, he was thin, stoop-shouldered, completely bald, and wore wire-rimmed glasses perched on a small nose. Judge O'Reilly knew him personally, as did most of the judges in the courthouse complex. Retired for a number of years, he found his entertainment not from television, sporting events, or the theater, but instead from the live drama of the courthouse. Usually, on Monday morning he would show up in the jury assembly room and visit with the bailiffs who were waiting to escort jury panels to waiting judges. He would circulate among them, asking about the trials that were starting in their various courts. Once he conducted his survey, he would hobble off to the chosen court, find a place on the back row and observe jury selection and opening statements. If he found the trial to his liking, he would be in the back row every day, watching the drama unfold. The local trial lawyers called him by name and respected his opinions about how a trial was going, how the evidence was being received and which side was winning. Tod had tried several cases with him in daily attendance, and almost every day he would sit down beside him and seek his advice.

Judge O'Reilly greeted him as he appeared at the top of the auditorium. "Good morning, Mr. Buschbahm. I am now convinced beyond a shadow of a doubt that I will have the best show in town. You're even showing up for pre-trial. Should I be flattered or worried?"

Mr. Buschbahm smiled and spoke in a soft voice. "Perhaps neither, or perhaps both, Judge O'Reilly. Time will tell. Certainly, I have never had the pleasure of observing a trial with so much publicity. I presume that there will be reporters and such. Is there a particular place where I should sit?"

Judge O'Reilly outlined her seating plans and added, "Mr. Buschbahm, there is no reserved seating for this trial, although, Lord knows, the press wants them. If anyone deserves a reserved seat, it's you. So, if you'll pick your seat, I'll tell my bailiff to make sure that seat is empty each day until you arrive. That'll have to be our little secret."

"I'll not be a blabbermouth, Judge, and I appreciate it. If it's okay with you, I'll just take one of these aisle seats on the back row so I won't have to climb up and down those stairs. My arthritic knees and stairs just don't get along anymore."

The first lawyer in the courtroom, as she now called the auditorium, was Wayne Littlejohn. Tod had ordered him to be there before eight o'clock. First come, first served. As he sat his briefcase down smack-dab in the middle of the table nearest the jury box, he spoke to Ruby. "Morning, Judge. I'm surprised to see you here this early."

"Good morning to you, too, Wayne. I didn't sleep so well last night. Woke up early and decided I might as well get down here to survey the lay of the land in peace and quiet."

"I won't interrupt, Judge. Tod just sent me down here to grab this table. I hereby claim possession of it in the name of all that is right and good, and for Tod Duncan for the length of this trial, however long it may be."

"Hear, hear, Mr. Littlejohn," Judge O'Reilly responded, pleased to have a little levity for the occasion. "According to the unwritten rules of this county and the power vested in me, I recognize Mr. Duncan's ownership of that table for the length of time described. However, I must decline to take judicial notice that it is for all that is right and good. Impartiality must rule the day in my court."

Wayne joined her in laughter, and the judge excused herself to make some early morning phone calls, leaving Wayne to look around and disappear into his own thoughts about the biggest trial of his young career.

Shortly thereafter, the room began to fill. Even though trial was still five days away, reporters and other courthouse onlookers drifted in and took seats. Law students and a handful of lawyers joined them. Claudia arrived ten minutes behind Wayne, and seeing him at his chosen table, she sat her briefcase down on the other and settled into the chair beside him, proclaiming in mock horror, "Boy, Johnny Bob's gonna have my ass. He sent me down here to get that table. I got in all that street construction mess and then couldn't figure out where to park. How come you people didn't fix up your streets years ago? Most cities, they usually put in the streets first and then the buildings come along afterward."

"You got me, Claudia. Some bright guy or gal figured that they would just tear up all of the downtown streets at the same time. Must be for sewers or something. Hope Johnny Bob doesn't get too big a piece of your ass. I was sent down here for the same thing. One of us had to get here first and while I'm a chivalrous guy, I'm not so much one that I'm going to give up my table."

"Well, I'm shocked, but I'd at least expect you to put your coat down if I have to walk over a puddle after one of Houston's afternoon showers."

"That, milady, I would proudly do. So, what's your best guess on how long we'll be here today?"

Claudia replied, "Best guess is all day. We've got a bunch of issues and then we've got to talk about jury selection."

As the two opposing lawyers discussed the events to

come, a reporter approached them. Victoria Burton was in her late twenties, slender with short blond hair, and dressed in a conservative gray suit. While not exactly movie star beautiful, she was not far from it. She introduced herself. "Excuse me, may I join you? I know your names already. I'm Victoria Burton. I'll be covering the trial for Court TV as well as doing some commentary for NBC."

Wayne gestured with his hand, offering her a seat with them. "Please do sit down, Victoria. Just for good measure, let me introduce myself. I'm Wayne Littlejohn and this is Claudia St. John Jackson. How long have you been with Court TV?"

Victoria sat at the table opposite them, laid her leather-bound notebook on the table and responded. "I joined them two years ago. Graduated from Georgetown Law and clerked for two years for the Eleventh Circuit. I had a chance to do this or practice law and chose this. So far, it's working pretty well. If I think I've got a shot at shoving Diane Sawyer or Katie Couric aside, I may stay with it. Otherwise, I may join a law firm in a couple of years. However, if I could trade places with one of you at the counsel table on this one, I'd do it right now."

"Well, honey, they aren't all like this one," Claudia replied.

"Believe me, I know. I've covered some trials that would make taking the bar exam exciting by comparison. Listen, I understand the judge has lifted her gag order. Can I get the two of you on record and in front of the camera from time to time?"

"Victoria, from our side, you know that's gonna have to be Tod's call, and I suspect that Claudia will tell you the same about Johnny Bob," Wayne answered. As he spoke, there was a murmur from the gathering audience as Johnny Bob entered through the doorway at the top of the auditorium, followed by Tod and Jan with their legal assistants close behind. As they approached the floor of the courtroom, Johnny Bob asked, "All right, who got here first and won the choice seats?"

Claudia looked a little sheepish and slumped into her chair as she motioned to the empty table. "I'm afraid that I got stacked up in that street construction, Johnny Bob. That's our table over there."

"Well, that's okay. I suspect I can make myself heard from there. Who's this pretty little lady?"

"Mr. Tisdale, I'm Victoria Burton with Court TV. I was just visiting with these other lawyers. I'd like to have the chance to spend a little time with you, Mr. Duncan and Ms. Akers, just by way of background, and I'd like to get you all in front of the camera from time to time."

Johnny Bob walked over to his table, sat a big briefcase on it and responded, "Victoria, I suspect that the American public is going to see more of us than they want before this trial is over. If they haven't had their fill and if you want an interview from time to time, you can find me. Same probably goes for Tod and Jan."

"All rise." The bailiff and the entrance of Judge O'Reilly interrupted them. Victoria Burton returned to her place in the audience, and Judge O'Reilly told the entire group to have a seat.

"My, my, I've never seen such a crowd for a pre-trial and I understand that the cameras are rolling even today. Are you gentlemen and ladies ready to proceed?"

Johnny Bob was still taking papers out of his briefcase, but he looked up and responded, "Ms. Jackson and I are ready, Your Honor."

"If I may speak for Ms. Akers, we're also ready," Tod added.

"Very well, we'll proceed as follows. I've got a few instructions for everyone assembled. Then, we'll talk about the jury and we'll save Motions in Limine until the last since I know they will take some considerable time. If you folks in the audience would also listen to this, I suspect we'll have a full house every day. I've never presided over a trial where several hundred people will be in the audience. I must insist on absolute silence. That also means that you turn off pagers and cell phones when you enter. If one goes off during trial, it will be confiscated and you can pick it up when the trial is over. Because the audience is so large, once we start in the morning, no one will be permitted to enter until the mid-morning break and the same applies after each break and at lunch. I want to minimize distractions as much as possible and I'm not going to have people wandering in and out like you're at a movie theater. If you leave for any reason, you're out until the next break. Understood?

"I've added an additional three bailiffs to make sure that we keep order in here. Deputy Johnson here is my regular bailiff, and if you look around the room you'll see three other deputies, stationed at various places in the auditorium." Deputy Johnson stood beside the bench. A large, young black man, he had played linebacker for Texas A&M and was now in his third year of law school, taking night classes in that very building. He considered himself privileged to be able to work his way through law school by observing trials, never considering that he would be involved in one like this. While he maintained a solemn countenance beside the judge, he mentally waved to the camera and shouted, "Hi, Mom."

"Now let's talk about jury selection. I've asked Judge Hardman to call two hundred jurors to the jury assembly room in the courthouse complex on Friday. They will be given instructions to be here at nine o'clock on Monday morning. Are you all satisfied that two hundred will be enough?"

Johnny Bob rose to his feet. "Your Honor, having never been to a goat roping like this before, I have no idea. I certainly have no reason to disagree and hope that we can get it done with two hundred."

"It'll be close, Judge," Tod commented.

Judge O'Reilly continued, "I've prepared a short questionnaire for each of the jurors to answer on Friday. We need to know in advance if any juror or a close family member has had an abortion and whether any juror belongs to any pro-life or pro-choice organization. Anyone disagree?" Watching the lawyers shake their heads, she continued, "How long do you need to try this matter? Your estimate, Mr. Tisdale?"

"Judge, Ms. Jackson and I are mindful of the Court's admonition that this will not be another O. J. trial. We think that we can do it in about four weeks."

"I agree, Judge," Tod added. "This is not the first rodeo for me or Johnny Bob. We'll get to the heart of the matter with each witness and will do our best not to waste your time."

"Ms. Akers, I don't want to leave you out. What's your thought?"

"I don't know as much about rodeos and goat ropings as these gentlemen. Of course, I do know about trials and I think four weeks will be enough."

That brought a smile from the judge and a few laughs from the audience.

"Well, I'm sure that at an appropriate time, you can get Mr. Tisdale to expound on a goat roping. Let's go to the limines."

A Motion in Limine is a pre-trial motion that is usually filed by each side in a civil lawsuit. The primary purpose of such a motion is to bring potentially controversial issues to the judge's attention in an effort to get an advance ruling that certain matters should not be brought up in front of the jury. The judge spent the rest of the day listening to the attorneys as they fought over what evidence should be admitted and excluded. Each side had some minor victories and some losses. When the last of the lawyers admitted they had nothing more to say, the judge closed the day. "I compliment all of you for your efficiency. Let's hope that the rest of the trial can go as well. Unless you think of something else between now and then, I'll see you all here at nine o'clock Monday morning. By the way, the jury information cards and questionnaires will be available at one o'clock on Friday."

As the lawyers left the building, a few picketers from both sides remained. Of more interest was the interview that Victoria Burton was doing. The camera rolled as she stood, microphone in hand, beside T.J. who was winding up the interview.

"Ms. Burton, I am confident that we are on the right side

of these issues, not just in this trial, but with the enormous issues facing our country. I am certain that Lucy Brady will prevail. What happened to her shouldn't have happened to a dog in the street. As to the slander allegations against me, I'll tell you and everyone in America that I always tell the truth. I don't need an oath. I don't need to be sworn. I speak the truth. If I were ever to lie, then you should disregard every word that comes from my mouth for I would have violated my sacred oath to my Father, and that's the one that counts."

The interview ended and T.J. joined Johnny Bob, a smug look on the preacher's face.

61

Johnny Bob and Claudia set aside Friday afternoon and evening to study the jury information cards and questionnaires. The information on the cards was basic: name, address, occupation, marital status, number of children, involvement in lawsuits, personal injuries, length of residency in county and, perhaps of most importance in their case, religion. One by one, they went through the cards and attached questionnaires, rating each juror on a scale from one to ten, with ten being their best possible juror. They red-flagged any questionnaire where a prospective juror gave a positive answer about abortion, figuring that Judge O'Reilly would dismiss most of them for cause at the very beginning.

AT THE FIRE STATION, Tod, Wayne and Jan were going through the same exercise. After Tod and his team had gone through the juror cards and questionnaires, Tod turned to Marilyn. "Call Ralph and tell him to give us the works on each juror, including pictures. Tell him we'll need the information on Sunday night. We'll pay whatever it costs to get it done."

Ralph was a private investigator and computer whiz. By Sunday night they would have more information on the prospective jurors than any juror could possibly imagine.

ON SATURDAY MORNING, JOHNNY BOB's preparation was interrupted. He had set aside the day to work with T.J. Fifteen minutes before they were to meet, T.J. called to say that he was expecting an important guest that would delay the meeting. Not normally prone to fits of anger, Johnny Bob slammed the phone down and cussed a blue streak out the window.

The campaign plane carrying Governor Peter Vandenberg, the Republican presidential candidate, had departed Jackson, Mississippi, bound for Albuquerque, New Mexico, when it veered south and landed at Ellington Field outside of Houston. Met by a black limousine, the candidate was escorted by four Houston policemen on motorcycles and trailed by a Suburban occupied by the Secret Service. The small caravan had no trouble navigating the quiet Saturday morning traffic as it made its way to the lofts. The candidate's press people had alerted the media that he would be making a short stop in Houston before flying to Albuquerque. The candidate wanted to discuss his party's platform plank on abortion with Reverend Luther. The trial was imminent. He would not mention it, but he wanted to lend assistance to the Chosen in this hour of need, especially since T.J. had endorsed him for the presidency only the week before. Clearly, the candidate expected to impact the trial in a way that could only be favorable to T.J.

Johnny Bob had been watching the press assemble outside his window for over an hour. Television vans joined the throng. When the noise grew to a low roar, he looked out his window to see a limousine stopping at the curb. Men in black suits opened the back door and Governor Vandenberg stepped out.

"Holy shit!" Johnny Bob watched as T.J. left the building entrance to shake the hand of the candidate and pose for pictures. "Son of a bitch! Does this mean that I'm gonna have to voir dire the jury on who they are supporting for president?" The words were said out loud to no one in particular. If T.J. was going to march to his own drummer, at least he could let his lawyer pick the music.

T.J. and the candidate visited in T.J.'s loft for about an hour and left the building to face waiting cameras and microphones. As T.J. stood beside him, the candidate answered a few questions.

"Sir, what was the substance of your discussions?"

"Frankly, the details must remain private. As you know, the president just recently invited Reverend Luther to the White House to begin a dialogue on one of our most volatile social issues, abortion on demand. Since I expect to be the next president, I was looking for an opportunity to express to Reverend Luther that I wanted him to take the lead in the continuation of those talks after my election. As it happened, I had a few hours between campaign stops and found him available this morning."

"Sir, is there any correlation between the trial that starts on Monday and your stopping by to visit with Reverend Luther?"

With a disgusted look, Governor Vandenberg answered, "None whatsoever. While Reverend Luther and I see eye to eye on the abortion issue, I certainly would not want my presence to interfere with a fair trial. It is the American way that issues like this are resolved in a court of law, and I am sure that justice will prevail. That's all, ladies and gentlemen. I have to get on to New Mexico."

THE EVENING NEWS IN Houston headlined the visit from the presidential candidate and emphasized his alignment with the Chosen on abortion issues. Johnny Bob cussed his client and debated his response if the other side moved for a continuance until after the election. Still, T.J. had violated no rulings from Judge O'Reilly. An argument could certainly be made that he was entitled to continue his national agenda even as the trial progressed. He and Claudia finally decided that if a continuance was requested, he would just leave it to Ruby, whom he hoped would deny such a request. Win or lose, Johnny Bob was ready to get back to the piney woods of East Texas and leave Houston in his rearview mirror.

Tod, Jan and Wayne watched the six o'clock news in silence as they ate pizza at the fire station. When the "T.J. and the Candidate" show ended, Tod switched off the television, and they debated what to do. After an extended discussion, they concluded that most of the strong pro-lifers would honestly admit their opinions and would be stricken by the judge. As to the others, if they were going to try to hide their opinions anyway, nothing the candidate did was going to change anything. Besides, he had a client who wanted the trial over. They decided to ignore the issue.

AT TEN ON SUNDAY morning, T.J. knocked loudly on Johnny Bob's door. He opened it to find his client dressed in white slacks, a white golf shirt and white running shoes. Only his dark sunglasses contrasted with his outfit.

"T.J., do you own anything that isn't white?"

"I think that you've seen me wearing a red tie, counselor. Everything else is white." T.J. beamed with excitement. "Now, tell me, what did you think about our little visit yesterday? I started to invite you down for an introduction until I thought better of it and decided that we didn't want to be so obvious in mixing his visit with the trial. Not very often, is it, that a defendant is paid a call on the eve of trial by the next president of the United States?"

"Come on in, T.J.," Johnny Bob growled as he turned and sat at the coffee table where he had been going over his trial notes. "Just as well you didn't introduce me. I'm a Democrat, anyway. Sit down. We've got work to do. Claudia will be along shortly."

As if on cue, the door opened and Claudia entered, dressed in jeans and a black T-shirt with gold lettering announcing, NEVER TRUST A MAN WHO DOESN'T WEAR BOOTS AND A COWBOY HAT.

Seeing her shirt, T.J. greeted her. "I see my lawyer is becoming a real Texan."

"When in Rome, T.J." She smiled as she poured herself a cup of coffee and joined them. "Nice little show you put on yesterday. Did you invite him, or did he just drift off course somewhere over Louisiana?"

"Let's just say that the Lord works in mysterious ways, Claudia. Do I need to go out and buy boots and a Stetson for trial?"

Before Claudia could reply, Johnny Bob interrupted. "Let's talk about some of the trial issues that involve you. In spite of being a man of the cloth, the jury is going to evaluate your credibility just like every other witness. If Tod can catch you hedging on the truth just a little, he'll blow a little lie up so big that you could drive a fleet of Hummers through. If you don't listen to anything else, hear this good. I can handle about anything in a courtroom except lying. I expect nothing but the truth to come out of your mouth, no matter what the question. Understood?"

"Counselor, how many times do I have to tell you that I always speak the truth? I know no other way."

"Then, let's cover some of the issues that you'll be grilled about at trial," interjected Claudia. "First of all, you didn't heal Lucy, did you?"

"Certainly, I did. I can show you the videotape if you like."

Her exasperation showing, Claudia replied, "Come on, T.J., I've read the medical records. She was fully capable of walking. She just didn't want to get out of the wheelchair."

"Very true, my dear. I don't just heal bodies, however. I also heal the spirit and until I commanded her to do so, she would not walk."

"Then how about giving a little credit to the doctors when you get on the witness stand so the jury knows it was her mind that you were working on, okay?"

"Understood. You should also understand that illness and healing often take place in the mind."

"Okay, let's turn to your comments from the pulpit that got you, your church and the others sued. I don't expect you to retract those statements at this late date. I think that for purposes of trial, the words can be the same. The tone and manner can be soft peddled just a little."

"I don't mind changing how I deliver it, Claudia, as long as you understand that I will never change the message. The doctors who perform abortions, the clinics, anyone who assists or participates in abortion must be condemned to a life in hell."

They worked into the late afternoon with Johnny Bob and Claudia covering T.J.'s relationship with the Brady family and with Aunt Jessie along with the coalition of anti-abortion organizations and T.J.'s involvement in organizing them. They spent the better part of the afternoon trying to teach T.J. just to answer questions and not launch into a sermon with every response. As to the latter, they met with little success. Johnny Bob thought they should just pray for a miracle.

62

Monday arrived at last. Tod, Jan and Wayne were at the fire station early. They had spent Sunday evening sifting through all of the information that Ralph had provided and Marilyn had loaded into the computer. Now they knew whether a juror lived in a house or an apartment, and who lived with him or her. If the juror lived in a house, they knew the amount of the mortgage, and if mortgage payments were late. They knew the number and type of vehicles owned by the juror. They did a credit check on each juror and knew what credit cards he or she possessed along with the balances. They also knew the type of restaurants favored by each prospect as well as where they bought their clothes. If a juror subscribed to magazines, they knew which ones. If a juror had vacationed recently, they knew whether it was in Galveston or Europe.

They knew whether the jurors voted regularly and in which primary. They even had investigators drive by the residence of each juror and discreetly photograph it as well as any vehicles in the driveway. Whether the house was well maintained with fresh paint and a manicured yard, or otherwise could be important. They also wanted to see any bumper stickers on vehicles. With the exception of the pictures, it was all there for the taking on the Internet. Under other circumstances, it might be called snooping or invading privacy. The reality was that there was very little private about anyone anymore. It was a big case, and anything they could learn that would help them identify potential biases of jurors was fair game.

Johnny Bob approached jury selection differently. He had used computers and high-priced jury consultants on several occasions and had determined that they were not worth the time and expense. After thirty-five years of picking juries, he had returned to his roots. He figured that he could size up a man or woman about as well as any computer or psychologist, and relied on his own instincts. His results proved that his instincts were pretty damn good.

On the morning of jury selection, he laid out a dark blue suit, white shirt, a blue tie and his favorite red suspenders. He always wore the same outfit for jury selection. Not that he was superstitious, just that he saw no reason to change a good thing. He also had a reason for wearing his red suspenders other than just to hold up his pants.

AT SEVEN A.M., THE crowd started gathering in the street in front of Population Planning. T.J. was there bright and early, decked out in his usual white outfit, but he had added white ostrich leather boots and a white, broad-brimmed Stetson. He made the additions as a gesture to Claudia and also figured that a Texas preacher decked out in white, including boots and cowboy hat, would look good on national television. As the crowd assembled, T.J. tried to shake each of their hands, thanking them for support. He also signed his autograph, "With love, the Chosen," on everything from a man's business card to a baby bassinet.

At seven-thirty, he used a bullhorn to address the throng that he estimated to be in excess of one thousand. "My friends and faithful followers, it's time to roll out. Before we begin our journey, let us pray." The crowd bowed their heads. "My Father, it has been a long, difficult and tortuous path. Yet, I have always followed where You have led me. I now understand why You let me sleep for so many years and brought me back in this time of crisis. I understand that my primary purpose on this earth is to end the murdering of pre-born children and to put death chambers like the Population Planning center out of business. I understand my mission, and with the aid of Your followers, like those who are assembled here, we will triumph. In Your Holiest of Names, Amen.

"Now, my friends, march with me to victory!"

There were very few people out on the street at seven-thirty in the morning. One man out walking his dog paused, curiosity on his face, as T.J. and his followers marched by. A woman in a bathrobe with her hair in curlers had stepped out of her apartment to get the morning paper and was shocked when a man wearing a white suit and white cowboy hat, walking down the middle of her street, smiled and said good morning. When she saw what was behind him, she forgot her paper and hurried back into her apartment, slamming the door. Most of the people on the street were Houston police officers stationed to block each intersection as the parade passed. The small crowd didn't bother T.J. What was important was that the media had cameras rolling. He had been told that his march was being broadcast live on the network morning shows. People all over the country were watching him as they ate breakfast and prepared for the day's activities. The Chosen was in his rightful place, leading the grand entry as the circus was about to begin.

As the demonstrators finished their two-mile walk, they could see another crowd gathered in front of the law school where each side of the street was barricaded and manned by police officers. The middle lane remained open to separate the protestors and permit police officers to patrol between the two groups. It also permitted access to the building although the lawyers and the jury panel had been advised that a side door would be open as an alternative. As T.J. approached, he saw that the pro-choice forces already occupied one side of the street. As he had promised, Herbert Wells, the Democratic presidential candidate, was with them, standing prominently in front and surrounded by police officers and the Secret Service. Both groups carried signs and had been talking among themselves. A strange thing happened as T.J.'s followers approached. Everyone fell silent. The police escorted the anti-abortion protestors to their side of the street, and as the two groups eyed each other, it was completely quiet. No cheers. No name-calling. No chants. Then Johnny Bob and Claudia arrived. They walked by the side door to the crowded street and made a grand entrance. It was the main event and Johnny Bob was not about to sneak into the building. As they approached, T.J. joined them, causing their followers to erupt in cheers. Boos rang out from the other side of the street.

"Nice hat, T.J.," Claudia commented.

"Bought it just for you, Claudia. Boots, too," he replied as he paused and pulled up one pants leg to show off the white ostrich leather boots.

As they entered the building, Tod, Jan and Wayne rounded the corner and made their way up the center lane. This time the boos and cheers were reversed. When they walked through the metal detectors, Tod muttered, "Is this how the gladiators felt when they entered the coliseum?"

To which Jan replied, "Don't know, Tod, but I damn sure hope we're the lions and not the Christians."

The prospective jurors, identified by badges given to them on Friday, also began to arrive at about the same time. Some found the side entrance and were grateful to avoid the mob. Others went up the center lane between the two groups and were escorted by deputies through the metal detector. Three prospective jurors drove close to the law school, saw yelling masses of people and turned their cars around, never to be seen again. The lawyers found the courtroom packed. The only seats that remained were in the rows reserved for the jury panel. Lucy and her family were already seated in chairs immediately behind the counsel tables.

Johnny Bob greeted his client and her family with handshakes. "What time did you get here, little lady? You all must have left Texas City at the crack of dawn."

"Yes, sir. We did. We didn't know how bad traffic was going to be and didn't want to be late. We've been here since seven-fifteen," Lucy said.

"Well, you just have a seat and relax. It'll be a little while before we kick this thing off."

Tod, Wayne and Jan were sitting at their counsel table. They had their jury lists out and were comparing them to faces of prospective jurors when Dr. Moyo, his wife and two daughters entered the courtroom. Dr. Moyo looked around, not sure what to do. Tod smiled and motioned them down. Then he went halfway up the stairs to greet them and show them to their seats. It had taken Tod nearly a week to convince Dr. Moyo to bring his wife and children to trial, at least for voir dire. His trial strategy called for creating an image of his client as a caring doctor and a strong family man. Tod didn't want the girls to sit through the whole trial. However, he wanted to be able to introduce them to the jury on the first day. As to Marian, she was expected to be at her husband's side throughout the trial. Johnny Bob looked at Dr. Moyo's family and thought to himself that Tod had made a nice move. Nice looking family. Hard for anyone to believe that they would have anything to do with a "baby killer" or a "murderer."

The last of the participants to arrive was Gloria McMahon, the director of the local Population Planning clinic. While she had nothing to do with the incident, it was important that the jury put a human face on Population Planning and hers was ideal. A woman in her late forties, she was trim, attractive and prematurely gray. Additionally, she was well spoken, and if anyone called her to the stand, she could defend the role of Population Planning as well as anyone in the country. Jan greeted her and showed her to a seat behind the counsel table.

The parties and lawyers were assembled. At nine o'clock, they were still missing twenty-five prospective jurors, not a surprise to the lawyers since it was the first day and a new location. Even with a well-drawn map, it was about par for the course. The lawyers bided their time by studying the jurors that were present. With a group of nearly two hundred, it was a reasonably accurate cross-section of the socio-economic and ethnic make up of Harris County. As Johnny Bob eyed them, he figured about 50 percent were Anglo with the balance split between blacks and Hispanics and a few Vietnamese mixed in. As to gender, it was close to fifty-fifty.

At the other table, Jan and Wayne were studying their computer. One by one they would look at a panel member discretely trying to study the prospective juror's demeanor, and then analyze the computerized information they had received the night before.

The lawyers' concentration was broken by the voice of Deputy Johnson. "Counsel, Judge O'Reilly would like to see you in her chambers."

The five lawyers rose as one and followed the deputy through a door behind the bench that led to a small room that had been made into the judge's office. It contained a small desk and swivel chair for the judge and six hardback wooden chairs for counsel. Someone had found a United States flag and a Texas flag to place behind the judge.

"Welcome, counsel, to my lavish chambers. Please have a seat and make yourselves comfortable, if that can be accomplished in those chairs. While we're waiting on the remainder of the jurors, let's see if we can eliminate a few by agreement. I've been through the questionnaires, as I'm sure that you have. I come up with twenty-eight that, near as I can tell, belong to an organization that is either pro-choice or pro-life. Does either side object to the court removing them for cause? I figure that you guys will want to challenge them anyway and I'll have to go along."

Tod spoke first. "Of course, Your Honor, I'd like to keep those who are on my side and I'm sure that Johnny Bob feels likewise. I'm in agreement with the court. At the end of the day, they're going to be gone. There's no point in wasting time with them."

"We agree with Tod, Your Honor," Johnny Bob said. "Let's save our questions for the ones who have a chance of serving."

"Next, according to our questionnaire we have ten women who have had abortions," the judge continued, "and another ten jurors who have a close family member who has had an abortion. Any suggestions?"

"Your Honor," Jan answered, "whether they have a bias or prejudice for or against abortion is probably going to depend on a variety of factors, including their experience. I don't think we can excuse them for cause. I suggest that at an appropriate time they should be called to the bench for a private conference."

"Sounds good to me, Judge," Johnny Bob agreed.

"Aren't we all being polite today," replied the judge with a smile on her face. "Let's see how long we can keep it up. Okay, it's nine-thirty. If we're short a few jurors, let's chalk them up to missing-in-action. You guys and gals ready to get this show on the road? Go on back out to the courtroom. As soon as Deputy Johnson returns, we'll get started."

When the attorneys returned to the courtroom, they barely had time to take their seats before Deputy Johnson commanded, "All rise." Judge O'Reilly followed the bailiff from her chambers, then took the two steps up to her bench where she stood and smiled at the trial participants, the audience and the TV cameras before she asked everyone to be seated. "I'll call for announcements in the matter of Brady versus Population Planning, et al."

Johnny Bob rose to his full height and in his best voice responded, "Your Honor, J. Robert Tisdale for the plaintiff, Lucy Baines Brady. We're ready, Your Honor."

"Thomas O. Duncan for the defendant and third-party plaintiff, Dr. Mzito Moyo. Dr. Moyo is ready to proceed."

"Your Honor, I'm Janice Akers, for the defendant and third-party plaintiff, Population Planning. My client is ready."

"Your Honor, Claudia St. John Jackson, representing Reverend Thomas Jeremiah Luther, the City of Miracles and other third-party defendants. We're all ready."

"Very well, counsel, we shall proceed with jury selection. Mr. Tisdale, you may begin."

Johnny Bob rose, turned to face the jury panel, unbuttoned his coat so that he might grasp his red suspenders with his thumbs and silently looked over the audience. When it seemed as if he would never begin, he cleared his throat and started. "Ladies and gentlemen, we are here because my little lady client, Lucy Baines Brady, is the victim of one of the most horrendous assaults and acts of medical malpractice."

That was as far as he got before Tod bolted from his chair. "Objection, Your Honor. May we approach the bench?" Whether dramatic flair or real, Tod's anger was apparent as he stared at Johnny Bob and back to the bench.

"Approach, please, counsel."

Tod moved to the front of the judge's bench and was joined by Johnny Bob and the court reporter.

"Your Honor," Tod continued. "This is voir dire. That statement may or may not be relevant at time of argument, but it's absolutely improper and prejudicial at this time."

"I agree, counsel. Certainly didn't take long for you two to draw swords, did it? All right, Mr. Tisdale, I don't know how you try lawsuits up in East Texas, but that won't fly in my court. I'll let you make a brief, very brief, statement of the nature of your case as a preface to asking questions. That is all. And the flavor better be plain old vanilla. Save your arguments for later. Do I make myself clear?"

Johnny Bob apologized to the judge and returned to his place in front of the jury panel, acting as if she had just given him an Academy Award for outstanding performance. "This is a medical malpractice case. I expect to prove that my client has sustained serious, permanent and life-threatening injuries from an abortion that was performed by the defendant,

Dr. Moyo, at the Population Planning abortion center down here on Space Shuttle Drive."

This time it was Jan on her feet. "Objection, Your Honor. The Population Planning center is not an abortion center."

"Sustained."

". . . at the Population Planning center where they do abortions. We expect to show that the defendants were negligent and performed an illegal assault on my client. Lucy, would you and your family please stand so that the jury panel can see you?"

Lucy, Joanna, Jessie, Bo and Junior stood, turned and faced the audience. The TV cameras showed a family that was certainly all-American.

"Now, Ms. Jackson here represents Reverend Thomas Jeremiah Luther, the City of Miracles, and a number of pro-life organizations. She has asked me to also explain, as a part of our voir dire that Dr. Moyo and Population Planning have sued her clients because of some remarks that Reverend Luther made from his pulpit on national TV. They claim that such remarks have slandered their clients and are seeking large sums of money from what I will call the pro-life coalition. Reverend Luther, would you stand and introduce yourself to the jury?"

T.J. stood, facing the audience and the TV camera with his broadest smile and said, "Good morning, ladies and gentlemen."

Johnny Bob continued, "To start, how many of you have heard of this case?"

From a panel of now one hundred and sixty-five jurors, one hundred and sixty-three raised their hands. The two that didn't were an elderly Hispanic woman and a young white man with long hair and a longer beard, dressed in jeans, a dirty T-shirt and thongs. Johnny Bob suspected that the Hispanic woman did not speak English very well, and as to the young man, he could only assume that the bridge he must live under was not wired for electricity.

Next came the question that the judge and lawyers expected would wipe out a large part of the panel. "Abortion is going to be a part of this case. We all recognize that many people have strong feelings about abortion, on both sides of the issue. Please let me see a show of hands of those persons who have strong opinions. We attorneys respect those opinions, and let me make it clear, none of us seeks to have you change your minds."

One young lady on the first row raised her hand. Then, a black man on the second row. Next was an older white woman three rows back. The flood followed. Soon about half of the jury panel had a hand raised.

"Thank you, ladies and gentlemen. If you will, please keep your hands up while we write down your juror numbers."

There were eighty-two with raised hands. So that their opinions would not poison the whole panel, the judge required that they approach the bench one by one for questioning. The young woman on the first row, a college student, said that no one could tell a woman what to do with her own body. An older white woman in a blue-and-white polka-dot dress who lived in Pasadena, not far from Texas City, told the judge abortion was a sin. Thirty-five Catholics came to the bench, each to express their opinion that they had been taught since youth that their church condemned abortion. One young man offered the opinion that the only way to save the world from overpopulation was by abortion, that it should be encouraged as a means of birth control. Another twenty-seven women believed that it was a woman's decision and hers alone. There were a few, mostly businessmen, who saw the opportunity to get away from a four-week trial. They mentally crossed their fingers behind their backs as they lied about their opinions on abortion. Four weeks was just too much to give for a civic duty. For some of them, one day would have been too much. It took until the lunch break, but finally all eighty-two had expressed their opinions. The judge excused them all. She expected such a reaction and was actually surprised there were not more. Out of the remaining eighty-three jurors, there had to be a few who had strong feelings but hid them with the hope that they might get on the jury and strike a blow for their cause. The judge could only be optimistic that with such good lawyers they would be ferreted out before the end of the day.

DURING THE LUNCH BREAK, Tod, Wayne and Jan adjourned to an empty classroom that had been reserved for their use where they huddled with their computer and notes while Marilyn went for sandwiches.

"So, what's your assessment, so far?" Jan asked.

"About what I figured. We've got enough jurors left. We'll get it done before the day is over. Boy, Johnny Bob didn't waste any time in taking the gloves off, did he? We'll have to be on our toes every time he opens his mouth. The minute we let our guard down just a little, he'll be aiming a blow somewhere just slightly below the belt. That's okay. I can play that game."

Marilyn came in with lunch, and as they ate their sandwiches, they determined that there were fifteen jurors that they definitely did not want on the jury. It was their investigation that had assisted them in identifying the fifteen.

IN ANOTHER CLASSROOM JOHNNY Bob, Claudia and T.J. were going over their lists as Lucy and her family observed. "Claudia, don't take this personally, but we have too many blacks on this panel. I've got to try to get rid of a few of them."

"Johnny Bob, this is not personal. It's war. I agree. Some of the brothers and sisters are going to start off by putting a black doctor up on a pedestal. As I said before, some of them will be okay. Still, you take your best shot."

Johnny Bob completed his analysis of the jury list and raised his nose up in the air, sniffing like an old hound dog that had just caught the scent of his prey on the wind. "I smell about a dozen that are hiding something. I'll see what it is." The others laughed at the large man in red suspenders, sniffing at the ceiling.

Johnny Bob continued after lunch, this time to a smaller jury panel. They had been moved to fill in vacant seats, making room for a few more spectators and media types who had been standing outside the metal detectors, hoping for a place inside the tent.

"Now, this is a case about medical negligence. Some call it medical malpractice. I know that some people just don't believe in such lawsuits. Let me see a show of hands of those who just couldn't award a verdict against a doctor, no matter what the facts?"

Johnny Bob got rid of ten pro-doctor jurors with that question, including five African-Americans. An inquiry about people who just didn't believe in awarding damages for pain and suffering wiped out five more. When he mentioned that he was asking the jury to award five million dollars in actual damages and one hundred million in punitive damages, five more jurors bit the dust. There were eighteen black jurors that remained after lunch. In evaluating the panel, Johnny Bob reached a conclusion somewhat different from that of Claudia. He preferred to eliminate every black juror possible. He worried that they would not be able to get Dr. Moyo off that pedestal. Johnny Bob questioned each of them in detail and challenged each for cause. The judge excused eight. Then he thanked the remaining jurors and Claudia stepped up.

Claudia made a very short presentation on behalf of her clients. "Ladies and gentlemen, I can be very brief. I represent Reverend Luther, his church and the coalition of pro-life organizations who are being sued by Dr. Moyo and Population Planning. Dr. Moyo and the clinic claim that they have been damaged by alleged slanderous statements made on behalf of the coalition by Reverend Luther. Our defense is simple. If it's true, it's not slander, and we will prove that the words spoken by Reverend Luther were true in every respect."

Claudia returned to her seat. T.J. leaped up to assist her, shaking her hand and beaming as he did so.

Tod came next. Now there were only fifty-seven jurors left. While her face did not show it, Judge O'Reilly was becoming concerned. With nearly two hundred jurors a few hours before, to be down to fifty-seven was a number quite a bit lower than she had anticipated at this point in the trial. The last thing that she wanted was to start this process over.

"Good afternoon, ladies and gentlemen. To refresh your memories after several hours, my name is Thomas Oswalt Duncan. You'll hear me called Tod from time to time during the trial. I represent Dr. Moyo. Doctor, would you and your family stand up?"

Zeke and his family got up and turned to face the jurors. Zeke gave his best Marcus Welby smile. Marian managed a slight upturn of her mouth, and the two girls tried to hide behind their parents. The remaining prospective jurors liked what they saw.

"Dr. Moyo is a Baylor-trained, board certified obstetrician and gynecologist."

Johnny Bob started to object to the bolstering of the defendant on voir dire, then left it alone.

"He is both a defendant in this case and a plaintiff. I see some confused looks on your faces; so, let me explain. He is accused by Mr. Tisdale and his client of failing to use ordinary care in performing an abortion on Ms. Brady. We will prove that his conduct was well above the standards of medical care in this community and he is not legally responsible for the unfortunate complications of the procedure that caused Ms. Brady such problems. Additionally, he is a plaintiff. He is seeking to recover damages to his reputation because of the slanderous remarks of this man, T.J. Luther." As he spoke, he pointed to the man in the white suit and sunglasses.

"Some of you have undoubtedly heard of Reverend Luther. The evidence will show that he and a number of other pro-life organizations have backed this litigation and that Reverend Luther was directed by those organizations to attack Dr. Moyo on national television, not once, but on several occasions. As a result, Dr. Moyo's practice dried up and he has suffered enormous damages, both economically and to his reputation. We seek to recover those damages.

"Since I mentioned Reverend Luther, let's start there. Which of you have heard of Reverend Luther, also known as the Chosen, or the City of Miracles before today?" Tod was not surprised when nearly every hand went up. "How many of you watch his television program, *The Miracle Morning Hour,* on Sundays?"

About twenty hands were raised. The other lawyers quickly wrote down their juror numbers. "Now, who has made a donation to his ministry or subscribed to any of the Miracle publications?" Out of the twenty, there were six who admitted to having done so. It took only a few questions for Tod to disqualify the six. Juror number 134 was Millard Jackson, a middle-aged man who, according to their investigation, both donated to Operation Save-a-Life and subscribed to *The Miracle Magazine.*

When asked about pro-life organizations, he had remained silent, but he raised his hand to Tod's last question. Tod wanted him off the panel. "Mr. Jackson?"

A mousy little man, he sat slumped down in his seat, apparently trying to make himself invisible. Tod decided that Jackson wanted on the jury, and it wouldn't benefit his client. "Yes, sir?" Mr. Jackson replied.

"In addition to watching *The Miracle Morning Hour,* do you donate to the City of Miracles or subscribe to one of its publications?"

"Uh, I occasionally read *The Miracle Magazine,* not very often. My wife is the one who usually reads it."

"Fine, Mr. Jackson. I'm sure it's an excellent magazine." Tod appeared to go to another juror for questioning and Mr. Jackson relaxed.

"Oh, one more question, Mr. Jackson. Do you belong to or donate to any of the pro-life organizations that are involved in this lawsuit?"

"Uh, I'm sorry, Mr. Duncan, but I've forgotten their names. Could you remind me?" Mr. Jackson could feel the trapdoor giving way beneath him. Tod very pleasantly rattled off the organizations.

"Sir, I believe that I may have given some money once to something that sounds like Operation Save-a-Life."

"Isn't it possible, Mr. Jackson, that you have given money

to that organization for the past five years and are actually a member of that group?" Tod continued to probe in a very calm and pleasant voice.

"Well, sir, I guess it's possible."

"In fact, Mr. Jackson, that's the truth, isn't it?"

Knowing he was defeated, Jackson gave up. "Yes, sir. I suppose it is."

Without objection, Judge O'Reilly excused Jackson.

Johnny Bob chalked up one for Tod and mentally smiled at his adversary. This was going to be a battle. Tod then asked about folks who had bad experiences with hospitals or doctors that might influence their objectivity in this case. Four people were excused.

Tod asked to approach the bench. All five lawyers huddled with him. "Your Honor, Mr. Tisdale did not ask any questions of those people who answered the questionnaire about abortion."

"He's right, Judge. An oversight on my part," Johnny Bob agreed. Tod continued, "Your Honor, it's getting late in the day, but we're going to have to call them up to the bench individually. A number of them have already been excused for other reasons, and if my calculations are correct, there are still twelve who have had an abortion or have a family member who has had one."

Judge O'Reilly interrupted, "Then, let's get them up here. I want this jury picked today."

They turned out to be a mixed bag. Of the eight women who remained on the panel and who'd had an abortion, four were still traumatized by the experience. Two continued to have nightmares even though it had been twenty years. The other four had had an abortion, each for a different reason with none of the four having experienced any long-term effects. Each of the four said that under the same circumstances, they would do it again. All eight were excused by agreement. Four jurors had family members who had had abortions. One man had a daughter who became pregnant at fourteen and the family agreed that she should have an abortion. He was excused. As to the other three, a distant relative had had the abortion. They remained on the panel.

Tod's last question dealt with Dr. Moyo's cross-action. When the jury heard that he was seeking large sums of money for damage to reputation, four jurors said that they just didn't think anyone's reputation was worth that kind of money no matter what bad names he was called.

The judge counted up the remaining jurors, confirmed with Tod that was his last question and then agreed to excuse all four. She forgot about Jan who reminded the judge that she had some remarks. Jan's voir dire was brief. She introduced Gloria McMahon, her client's local director. She clarified that Population Planning did much more than terminate pregnancies and, within the constraints of voir dire examination, she painted a carefully crafted picture of a civic minded organization, doing good in the community. Satisfied she had accomplished her mission, she sat down.

The judge then announced, "Voir dire is completed. If my calculations are correct, we have twenty-seven jurors left. Each side gets six strikes; so, with a jury of twelve plus two alternates, we've got one left over. That's a little too close for comfort, but we made it. Since each side is using an empty classroom at lunch, I've made arrangements for those to be your home away from home during trial. You can leave your gear there, and the bailiff will lock them when you're in court. For now, please use them to make your strikes. You've got twenty minutes."

THE ATTORNEYS AND THEIR clients retired to their respective rooms and gathered chairs around a table. Johnny Bob told his clients what would happen next. "We don't really get to pick the jury. The whole process is one of elimination. We started with almost two hundred and are now down to twenty-seven. Again, no picking involved. We can strike any six for any reason."

T.J. asked, "Am I correct that the other side does the same?"

"Again, T.J., you're a quick study. We'll end up with twelve members on the jury panel and two spares in the event that somebody becomes incapacitated, has a family emergency or such. Claudia, give us a brief overview."

"Okay, we've got fourteen women and thirteen men. Among the women, three are black, two Hispanic, eight Anglo and one Asian, probably Vietnamese. Three are fifty years old or above. Five are between thirty and fifty, with six under thirty. As to the men, two black, two Hispanic, and nine Anglo. Ages run the gamut from eighteen to sixty-five. Now let's figure out who we just can't live with and go from there."

IN THE ROOM ACROSS the hall, Tod, Jan, Wayne, Dr. Moyo and Gloria studied the same list. In spite of computers and investigators, and in some cases, jury psychologists and even handwriting specialists, there is very little science to jury selection. Most lawyers have certain rules of thumb that guide them. Blacks are pro-plaintiff unless the defendant is black; Hispanics are emotional and tend to be bleeding hearts; blue-collar workers like to give away corporate money; businessmen and accountants side with the defense; government workers are liberal; Lutherans are conservative. The list could go on and on, but such rules of thumb are as noteworthy for their exceptions as otherwise. With only a short time to evaluate a person and what made that person tick, it was often what Tod called a "wag," a wild-assed guess. Most trial lawyers agreed that jury selection was a crap shoot. No wonder Johnny Bob decided to just rely on his instincts.

63

The bailiff called out the jurors' names and asked them to take seats in the jury box. "Amy Bourland" . . . thirty-ish, white, plump, a third-grade teacher, surprised and delighted to be on the jury, something she would be able to tell her students and grandkids about. She primped her hair just a little as she took the first seat in the box, ecstatic to be on national TV.

"Joshua Ferrell" . . . thirty, black, construction foreman in the daytime, going to the University of Houston at night, studying engineering, didn't have time to be serving on a jury, couldn't figure out a way to get out of it, had a strong temper that he worked to keep under control. At least his company would pay his salary while he served. He could still attend night classes and squeeze in a little studying during breaks and at lunch.

"Roy Judice" . . . fifty, white, mid-level manager for an oil company, married, father of three kids, drove a white Suburban with peewee football bumper stickers on the back, lived in an upper-middle-class subdivision west of Houston and commuted in a van pool to downtown daily, spent all of his spare time coaching or watching his kid's games. Normally would be considered a juror favorable to the defense in a malpractice case. No one could get an accurate read on his feelings about abortion.

"Olga Olsen" . . . her real name and she looked it, sixty, white, probably beautiful in her younger days, now plump from a few too many beers along the road of life, outgoing pleasant personality, worked as a waitress in an upscale diner, divorced, lived by herself, visited regularly by three kids and a bunch of grandkids, had a booth at the local flea market where she sold earrings she made while watching television, expressed no feelings one way or the other about abortion.

"Alberto Marino" . . . twenty-two, Hispanic, assistant manager at a drugstore, single, high school graduate, Latino macho personality, grew up in South Houston and still lived with his parents, engaged to his high school girlfriend. He was Catholic, and Tod did his damnedest to get all the Catholics off the jury. In the end he had to leave Marino. At least he was young and would, hopefully, think for himself.

"Catherine Tucker" . . . thirty-five, white, lived in Memorial, drove a Lexus, husband was a home builder, she sold upscale houses, traveled in some expensive circles, had two kids who appeared to be raised more by a Mexican house-keeper than their mother. Although she didn't express any opinions about abortion, Johnny Bob suspected she leaned to pro-choice. She wasn't a juror that he wanted.

"Samuel Aft" . . . forty-two, white, lean, Marlboro Man look, worried Tod because he looked a lot like Bo Brady, non-churchgoer, worked at the Exxon plant in Baytown, bass boat in his driveway, wife drove a Durango, he drove an old clunker Chevy work truck, coached a Little League team where his twelve-year-old son played shortstop.

"Alfred Totman" . . . sixty-three, black, retired city of Houston bookkeeper, two years of college, old-school black man, smiled at everyone, "yes, sir," "no, ma'am," tall, prob-ably six feet, seven inches, now works part-time as a ticket taker at the Astros games during baseball season, does it so that after the third inning he can watch the game for free.

"Glenn Ford" . . . forty-eight, white, economics professor at Rice, been kidded about his name since he was a teenager, "No, I'm not related to the movie star," round man with wire-rim glasses, wore a white short-sleeve shirt and bow tie for voir dire, lives in Bellaire, ten-minute drive from Rice, kids attend Bellaire High School. Tod figured he would likely be one of "his" jurors.

"Mary Ann O'Donnell" . . . thirty-two, white, lab techni-cian at St. Luke's Hospital in the medical center, married to a radiology technician, sharply dressed in blue blouse and gray pants, lives in upscale apartment complex close to the medical center, took a scuba diving vacation to Belize dur-ing the summer, attractive redhead, drives Mustang convert-ible. Both Johnny Bob and Tod thought that she might think she knows just a little too much medicine. Neither was sure who that would hurt or help.

"Harry Kneeland" . . . fifty-five, white, manager of a Home Depot for ten years, before that worked in construc-tion, belongs to an inexpensive country club where he golfs during the week since Home Depot occupied most of his weekends, non-churchgoing Presbyterian, three grown kids, tan face, aging athlete's body, told Tod on voir dire that he had a twelve handicap, complained that he used to be a seven. Tod hoped he would be the jury foreman.

"Anna May Marbley" ... thirty-seven, black, welfare mother, three kids, already a grandmother, other residents of her tenement apartment included her mother and a nine-month-old grandchild. Tod and Johnny Bob both thought she would be a bench warmer, a juror who would have nothing to say but would just go along with the majority. They would later find out that they were both wrong.

"Alvin Steinhorn" ... first alternate, sixty-five, white, Jewish, bald, known in Houston for radio advertisements for his jewelry store, certainly didn't mind serving on the jury in such a high-profile trial, secretly hoped that he would make the final twelve, smiled every time he saw a camera pointed in his direction.

"Rebecca Dowell" ... second alternate, twenty-two, white, attractive, blond secretary to an oil company executive, part-time student at Houston Community College, grew up in Victoria, a hundred miles south of Houston, moved when she graduated from high school, ran six miles in Memorial Park with three girlfriends at least four times a week. Johnny Bob didn't want her on the jury. As the second alternate, he gambled that she would never see the inside of the jury room during deliberations. Tod hoped she would make it. Surely, she was pro-choice.

"Ladies and gentlemen, will you please stand and take your oath," Judge O'Reilly requested.

As they listened, several had thoughts similar to other ordinary men and women who served on juries. They were becoming governmental officials for a day or a week or a month, maybe longer. They literally held the fate of litigants in their hands, whether it was a murder trial, a business antitrust case, a whiplash fender-bender or a national spectacle like the Brady trial. It was often the highest official calling a layperson would answer in his or her life. While some bitched, moaned and complained about being taken away from jobs and families, judges and trial lawyers would tell anyone that, once they took the oath and were seated in the jury box, they took their job seriously. Most did their best to listen to and watch the evidence, follow the court's instructions, and answer the questions presented to them in a manner that they considered honest and fair. More often than not, they reached a correct verdict.

After she gave them the oath, Judge O'Reilly gave them a rare admonition for a civil trial. "Let me now caution you about the media and the public attention to this trial. You have been instructed that you are to base your verdict only on the evidence that is admitted before you. That's what you see and hear in this courtroom and nowhere else. I have never sequestered a civil jury before, but I have the authority to do so if I think it's necessary. I'm not going to do so now and you are going to be free to come and go and sleep in your own beds at night. The only way that I can allow that is if each of you promise me that you will not read a newspaper, a news magazine or watch TV news or listen to radio news during the trial. In fact, if there is some promo on another program leading into the ten o'clock news that mentions this trial, you must immediately switch stations."

Several jurors nodded their understanding.

"In the event that I find that any one of you has violated my orders, or if I conclude that the media is intruding upon our trial to the extent that it is jeopardizing the litigants' right to their day in court, I reserve the right to tell you to go home, pack your bag, and return here to be escorted to a hotel where you will stay for the duration of the trial. You are now all excused. We will reconvene at nine o'clock in the morning. I suggest that you be here at eight forty-five so that we may begin promptly. When you arrive, the bailiff will escort you to the jury room where you will remain each morning until I request your presence in the courtroom. Good evening, ladies and gentlemen."

T.J. was holding court only a few yards down the street. Surrounded by reporters and facing TV cameras, he had microphones thrust in his face.

"Reverend Luther, what's your assessment of the first day of trial?"

"We are most pleased with how the jury selection went. We certainly have some very fine folks to hear this case. I'm quite certain that they will reach the right decision. After all, they are guided not only by the evidence, but also by the Lord who will be laying His hands on them and infusing them with the Holy Spirit. You might say that He is the thirteenth juror who will lead them."

Another reporter asked, "Are you suggesting that God is somehow involved in this trial?"

"It is not my suggestion, ma'am. It is simply a fact. His presence was there in the courtroom today as I am certain it will be every day of this trial. While this trial is about bringing justice to Lucy Baines Brady, it also has a more important purpose. With God's help, this trial will be a major victory in our crusade to save the lives of millions of God's children. Now, if you'll excuse me, my lawyers tell me we have work to do." T.J. turned to walk away when someone yelled.

"Where'd you get the Stetson, Reverend? Is that something new for the trial?"

T.J. turned and grinned at the cameras. "Matter of fact it is. My lawyer, Ms. Jackson, wore a T-shirt the other day that read, 'Never trust a man who doesn't wear boots and a cowboy hat.' While no one has ever doubted that I speak the truth, I figured that with all of you guys around for a few weeks, I better dress like a true Texan. Hadn't worn boots since my resurrection and I can tell you that they're a whole lot more comfortable now than when I wore them many years ago. See you all in the mornin'."

As Johnny Bob watched the show from outside the crowd of reporters, he commented to Claudia, "Two things I notice. First, ol' T.J.'s damn good with the media. Second, the longer this trial goes, the more Texan his accent is going to become. Folks up in East Texas may even understand him before this thing is over."

"What I like, Johnny Bob, is that if T.J.'s right, we've got the Lord on our side. Make's for a first class lineup, don't you think?"

"You know me pretty well, by now, Claudia. I'll take all the help I can get. Just remember that old saying, something about, 'Praise the Lord and pass the ammunition.' I'll take the Lord on our side, but with Tod Duncan on the other side, you keep passing me the ammunition because Tod won't be fighting with a peashooter. He'll have a full arsenal of weapons, all loaded and pointed in our direction."

As Johnny Bob spoke, Tod was at the other end of the block with Zeke Moyo at his side, facing more cameras and microphones. After Tod had praised the jury and the judge, he said, "Now, my client has an announcement."

"I received a call from the chair of the Department of Obstetrics and Gynecology at Baylor College of Medicine today," Dr. Moyo began. "He advised that the selection process is completed, and upon conclusion of this trial, I will be invited to become a member of the faculty of that institution."

"Dr. Moyo," a reporter interrupted, "is the appointment conditional on your winning this lawsuit?"

"Absolutely not, sir. I have gone through an arduous selection process and it is merely a coincidence that they made the decision today. As a matter of fact, it is my understanding that the chairman did not want to delay the selection announcement to avoid the appearance that it might have been influenced by the outcome of the trial."

"Two questions. First, are you going to accept the appointment? Second, during this trial, what do we call you, doctor or professor?"

"Of course, I will accept the appointment. As to what you call me, doctor and professor are both okay. Or, if you like, Zeke would also be just fine with me."

64

That evening Johnny Bob and Claudia sat in his loft, debating the strategy of trial, particularly the order of their witnesses. "Johnny Bob, I've been thinking and I've decided that it's a mistake to put Lucy on first," Claudia said. "A major trial, national TV, that's no place to put any eighteen-year-old on the witness stand as the first witness. She needs to watch the process for a while. Besides, Joanna and Jessie can tell a very compelling story that should begin to get the jury on our side. Let's save her for later on in the day, or maybe the next day."

Johnny Bob pondered the suggestion as he sipped on a scotch, only two per evening during trial. "Frankly, I liked leading off with Lucy. Even if she's nervous, no harm can be done. Doing it your way is just as good. I'll bow to your feminine intuition. Let's go with Joanna first, then Jessie. With this scenario, I think that I'll want you to take Jessie, too. That means that you'll have to be ready to go following opening statements. Let's put on Dr. McIntosh. Then, we'll put Lucy on center stage. After watching the others, I agree she'll be more comfortable with the process."

OPENING STATEMENTS ARE CONSIDERED by trial lawyers to be of utmost importance. They serve to set the stage for what is to come and provide a road map of expected evidence for the jury. Good lawyers always hope that by the time they complete their opening statement, they will have the majority of the jurors ready to vote for their position. No more evidence needed.

On this Tuesday, the second day of trial, Johnny Bob dressed in a gray suit with a red tie. As he and Claudia approached the law school, the barricaded crowds and media met them. While he had arranged for Mildred to meet Lucy and her family to escort them through the side door, he and

Claudia walked down the center lane between the opposing factions. Cheers still came from one side and boos from the other. On the pro-life side, the crowd started a baseball stadium-like wave, only with this one in a long line rather than circling a stadium. Johnny Bob saluted the pro-life crowd and acknowledged the pro-choice boos with a wave of his hand. Claudia felt more intimidated and merely walked beside Johnny Bob, eyes straight ahead. They ignored the reporters' requests. Perhaps they would have time to answer a few questions at the end of the day. It would become their daily routine.

Tod did it just a little differently. He told Wayne and Jan to take their clients through the side entrance and he took a walk alone through the crowds. Not one to be upstaged for dramatic flair, he gave the appearance of Gary Cooper walking down main street at high noon, the lone sheriff out to meet the bad guys. Tod walked down the middle of the street determined, confident and in control, refusing to acknowledge the presence of the crowd, the police at the barricades or the media. Whatever happened, he was prepared to conquer.

T.J. had to be his own man. Striding down the middle lane, he greeted "his fans" like a movie star going to the premiere of his latest picture. He shook hands with some and high-fived others. He paused for autographs and waved at any camera pointed his way. At Johnny Bob's insistence, the only thing he didn't do in the morning was agree to an interview. If he talked to the media, he was to make it at the end of the trial day, preferably after conferring with his lawyers.

The jurors were directed to a parking lot behind the building where they were met by deputy sheriffs and escorted to yet another door in the back of the building and away from most of the crowds. A couple of reporters found them and snapped pictures. Otherwise, the plan to shield them as much as possible from the crowds and media worked.

To get one of the three hundred seats in the middle section of the auditorium, one had to be in line by four A.M., a line also barricaded and patrolled by deputies that started at the building entrance and snaked around the corner to the side street. Judge O'Reilly correctly guessed that the most fervent on both sides would want a place on the inside. She made sure that tempers didn't flair or that fistfights didn't break out among those who would soon be in her courtroom. So, there were restrictions enforced in this line. No signs. No lapel pins. No discussion of the trial. No discussion of abortion. The only thing she couldn't do was ban reading material, and by the second day, the pro-life forces learned to make themselves known by carrying a Bible. At first they were just family Bibles carried from home. As the trial continued, and the pro-lifers noticed that T.J. always carried one in a gold cover, more and more gold-covered Bibles appeared in the hands of his pro-life supporters. Judge O'Reilly saw the Bibles but knew that the First Amendment tied her hands and did nothing about them.

At eight-fifteen on Tuesday morning, and each trial day thereafter, the doors opened to the spectators and media, with separate metal detectors for each group. Numbered cards were handed to the lucky ones as they walked through the metal detectors. They were directed down the hall to the elevator to the fourth floor where they surrendered their numbered cards at the entrance to the auditorium. Mr. Buschbahm parked in the juror parking lot and entered through the back door. Each of the deputies knew that he had the one reserved seat and at Ruby's direction, they told no one.

As she would sometimes do throughout the trial, the judge assembled the lawyers in her small office at about eight forty-five. As they entered, she said, "Good morning, counsel. I'm pleased you were able to make it here on time, considering the madhouse downstairs. I'm surprised we don't have vendors selling peanuts, popcorn and cotton candy out there. Have a seat and let's discuss what's happening today."

Everyone but Tod took a seat. He leaned up against the back wall, arms folded.

"First, we've got opening statements. I figure an hour per side. Mr. Tisdale, who do you have lined up for the rest of the day?"

"I was going to call Lucy Brady first. Last night, Claudia

convinced me that she needed to get more comfortable with the process before I put her on the stand."

"Good advice from your associate, Mr. Tisdale."

"So, I'm calling Joanna Brady, Jessie Woolsey and Dr. McIntosh who, by the way, will be relatively brief, and then Lucy. That ought to get us through the day and probably into tomorrow."

"Any problems from your end, Mr. Duncan?" asked Judge O'Reilly.

"No, ma'am. I'm ready to get this show on the road."

As Johnny Bob began his opening statement, Judge O'Reilly was mentally on her toes, prepared to bring the hammer down on any lawyer who came close to straying away from what she considered a fair opening statement. The first advocate surprised her. Johnny Bob's commanding presence kept the attention of everyone in the courtroom as he faced the jurors and laid out the case for Lucy. He did so only by describing the various witnesses and what the jury could expect to hear from each. Her story was sad enough that he didn't need to embellish it. Turning to the defense of the actions against the Chosen and the pro-life coalition, Johnny Bob told them that he and Claudia expected to prove beyond the shadow of any doubt that what the Chosen had said was the gospel truth. Life began at conception and anyone who destroyed it after that or assisted in its destruction was correctly described as a murderer or a killer. They would prove it through some of the world's most qualified experts, including one nominated for the Nobel Prize.

Judge O'Reilly breathed an inward sigh of relief. Johnny Bob had spoken for forty-five minutes and did it with no objection. Relaxing just a little, she assumed that Tod would follow suit and merely lay out his case. She relaxed too soon.

Tod rose and made his formal announcement, "May it please the court." Folding his arms, he paced quietly in front of the jury box, up and down, three times, head bowed to the floor, frown on his face, not saying a word. Then he whirled around, pointing a finger at T.J. and shouted, "This man has been accusing my client of murder. Can you imagine how that feels? Having dedicated yourself to bringing life into the world, to be accused on international television of being a murderer, a baby killer? This man and his forces almost destroyed Dr. Moyo's reputation and ruined his life, and we're here to make sure that they don't do it again!"

Johnny Bob leaped to his feet, joined by Claudia, as he sputtered, "Objection, Your Honor. Objection!"

Ruby could have merely sustained the objection and told Tod to move on. Instead, her experience dictated that she exert a little stronger control. "Approach the bench, counsel."

Five lawyers joined her at the bench as she held her hand over the microphone to prevent her words from being broadcast to the world. "All right, Mr. Duncan, that's quite enough. You've been in my court too many times to pull that kind of stunt. Save it for closing argument. Get on with laying out your evidence and nothing more."

As the lawyers returned to their places, she removed her hand from the microphone and in a stern voice announced to the jury, "Objection sustained."

Tod expected Ruby to come down on him for his opening. He had made his point. He had intended to shift the jury's attention away from Lucy and her problems, and to make it clear to them that there was another victim in the courtroom. The judge knew what he had done. As Tod continued with his opening, Ruby reminded herself that the stakes were high. She could not relax for even a moment.

Throughout the remainder of the opening statement, Tod minded his manners. He described Dr. Moyo's credentials, training and experience, letting the jury know early on that his client had been appointed to the faculty of the world-renowned Baylor College of Medicine. He emphasized that every medical doctor who testified would agree that Lucy's post-abortion problems were such expected complications that they were listed in every obstetrical textbook. He lightly covered Lucy's damages and hit hard on her excellent recovery. Then he turned to the slanderous comments of T.J. and

their impact on his client. He closed by outlining the credentials of his formidable lineup of experts who would dispute
the claims of murder hurled at his client and Population
Planning.

When the judge announced the break, Deputy Johnson escorted the jurors out into the hallway and into a classroom.
Because of the configuration of the auditorium, they exited
on the third floor, not the fourth where the spectators came
and went. The area was roped off with a bailiff standing
guard at the end of the hall. Bonding and friendships were
beginning among the jurors, something that nearly always
occurred in a case that would go for more than a few days.

"Boy, that Duncan fellow really got wound up, didn't he?
Thought I was watching a scene from *The Practice* there for
a while," Roy Judice, the suburban football dad, commented
to no one in particular as they entered the jury room.

"Yeah, he was beginning to get under the skin of the
preacher man," replied Joshua Ferrell, the engineering student.

"Wait a minute, gentlemen," Harry Kneeland chastised,
reverting to his role as a Home Depot manager where he
supervised employees. "You know Judge O'Reilly has instructed us not to talk about the case until it's all over."

"Come on, now, Harry," Judice replied, somewhat irritated.
"I wasn't talking about the case, just about the lawyers. Can't
be any harm in that."

The subject was dropped as they all found their way to the
table with coffee, soft drinks, bottled water and donuts that
the judge provided for them each day.

"Hey, Sheriff, we appreciate these donuts. Are we gonna
be able to go out for lunch?" Amy Bourland asked. It was
obvious that the plump schoolteacher preferred not to miss a
meal.

"No, ma'am. Instructions from the judge. There's a deli
down the street and I'm to get your lunch every day and bring
it back. Judge says there're too many people and too many
reporters wandering around. She doesn't want you folks over-

hearing something that you shouldn't. Matter of fact, I've got copies of the deli menu right here. Good news is that the county is buying."

THE ROOMS FOR THE litigants and their lawyers were on the side of the courtroom opposite from that of the jurors. In the one occupied by Johnny Bob and his team, T.J. said, "I'm damn disappointed in you, Mr. Tisdale, damn disappointed. You let Duncan get the best of us and made me look like the bad guy to boot. How come you let him get away with that?"

Johnny Bob didn't take kindly to being chewed out by anyone, especially a client on the first day of evidence. "T.J., let me try to clarify our roles here one more time, in short, simple words that I hope you'll understand. I'm the lawyer and you're the client. I've been doing this for better than thirty years. If I need your advice, I'll ask for it. Trials are like roller-coaster rides. One minute you're at the top and the next you're flying to the bottom, praying that the damn car just stays on the tracks. That's the nature of any trial and the same thing is going to happen in this trial, only the highs will be higher and the lows will be lower. If you can't accept that, I suggest that you just get your ass back to Fort Worth and we'll call you when the jury comes back."

With his last words, Johnny Bob slammed the door behind him, leaving the preacher, Claudia, Lucy and her family stunned.

"Lucy, honey, don't you be worried. Trials are prone to causing tempers to flare," Jessie said.

DOWN THE HALL IN their room, Jan and Wayne were congratulating Tod.

"Great opening, Tod. Best one I've ever seen you do," Jan said.

"Damn sure made the jury understand there's more than one victim in this case," Wayne added.

"Appreciate it, guys. Part of that opening was to get back at Tisdale for those remarks about his client on voir dire, but

like I tell Kirk and Chris, don't stand around admiring your
good shot. You gotta keep moving and be ready for the next
one, particularly against an opponent that's your equal, one
who can also score at will."

65

As the plaintiffs' first witness, Joanna could lay out the facts,
elicit sympathy for Lucy, and was subject to virtually no
significant attack on cross-examination. Claudia took her
through her paces as she covered the areas they had already
rehearsed several times. Touching briefly on her life as a girl
in LaMarque and bypassing the wild side of her youth, she
quickly jumped to Joanna's marriage to Bo, their two children and life together. Junior sat with his sister and dad so
that Lucy's family could be displayed in its entirety. Junior
was a handsome young man in his twenties, dressed in a red
plaid shirt and Dockers. Bo wore a blue, long-sleeved shirt
and slacks. Claudia had carefully chosen a green, very plain
dress for Lucy, one that made her look even younger than
she was. The jury could identify with this family.

Joanna was doing fine when Claudia advised her and the
packed courtroom that they were turning to the events of the
weekend in question. Before Claudia could even ask one
question, there were tears in Joanna's eyes as she took herself back in time. She confirmed that she had had no idea
that Lucy was pregnant. Certainly, she would not have approved of an abortion if she had been asked. No, she didn't
understand why Lucy didn't come to her with the problem
since she had a good relationship with her daughter. The
only thing unusual about the weekend was that it appeared
that Lucy was coming down with a flu that was bad enough
that she missed church on Sunday, something extremely rare
for her. When she described finding her daughter, burning
with fever with sheets soaked with blood, Joanna collapsed

in the witness chair. Tears filled her eyes. Two of the female jurors cried with her and Judge O'Reilly declared a fifteen-minute break. Johnny Bob watched the spectacle unfolding and thought it was not very often that he had jurors crying with the first witness.

Joanna regained her composure after the break, and in a soft, barely audible voice she recounted the ambulance, the Life Flight ride, and her daughter's operation at Hermann. It took more tissue when she told of the doctor advising her that Lucy might not live and her visions of attending her daughter's funeral. Claudia had her describe a typical day in the hospital with Bo, Jessie and the alternating shifts. Yes, she prayed hard, but it was weeks before her prayers were answered. Claudia closed with Joanna's description of how this event changed Lucy's life forever and passed the witness.

Jan conferred with Tod who was seated beside her. She and Tod had discussed what Joanna might say and realized that they could do little with cross-examination. If a witness like Joanna was honest, there was a greater risk of offending a juror's sense of justice and fair play with more questions. After a brief conference, Jan rose and advised the Judge that she had nothing to ask Joanna.

Jessie took the witness stand, dressed in an expensive black suit with a white scarf around her neck and tucked into the front of her jacket. Catherine Tucker, the Memorial housewife and real estate agent, eyed Jessie and figured that the suit must have cost at least twenty-five hundred dollars. Once in her seat, Jessie turned, smiled at the jurors and then turned back to face Claudia, ready for questions. Claudia could not conceal Jessie's wealth. Jessie described the Rivercrest mansion, her late husband's multiple business interests and her donations to the City. Claudia touched briefly on Jessie's stay in Houston while her niece was near death and went into detail about Lucy's slow physical and emotional recovery. Then, she questioned Jessie about that Sunday when the Chosen commanded her to walk. Every eye in the courtroom turned to T.J., who merely smiled and nodded his head in agreement. An admittedly quiet girl before, Jessie described how Lucy had become depressed and had to take three powerful medications. She still lived with her aunt. Her life consisted of television, tutors, counseling, weekend visits with her parents and church on Sunday. Sometimes, Jessie convinced Lucy to go to the City for Sunday evening youth fellowship. On those occasions it was usually Jessie's housekeeper who drove her to the City, waited for her, and chauffeured her back to Rivercrest. In Jessie's opinion, Lucy had peaked emotionally about the time that she began to walk again, and had shown little improvement since.

Tod's plan was to use Jessie to shift the jury's attention to what he had begun to call the plot against his client. He expected Jessie to be honest, and she was. Ignoring Lucy, Jan had Jessie discuss her involvement with the City and the Chosen. Yes, she was a major benefactor of the Chosen. Yes, she served on the Miracle Board, which, she added, was a high honor. Yes, it was Reverend Luther's idea to bring this lawsuit and she was present when it was discussed. She also voted with the board to join with the other pro-life defendants to fund the attorneys' fees and expenses. Reluctantly, she conceded that the purpose of the lawsuit was to bring down Population Planning, and if Dr. Moyo were caught up in its collapse, he would just have to accept such consequences for doing abortions at such a place. Her testimony was direct, businesslike, and brutally honest. The eyes of Alfred Totman and Anna May Marbley, two of the black jurors, hardened visibly as she talked about Dr. Moyo. Claudia's eyes caught Ms. Marbley as she folded her arms and looked down at her shoes when she heard Jessie's testimony.

As the next witness, Dr. McIntosh told of her findings when she operated on Lucy. She described the team of doctors that she assembled to save Lucy's life and the weeks of work they did before she finally awakened. She conceded on cross-examination that perforation and retained fetal parts were known complications of an abortion done by the most skilled hands, adding that it was highly unusual for both to occur in the same procedure. She agreed that physically Lucy could walk when she was discharged from Hermann.

She admitted that when Lucy threw up her antibiotic on that first night, the effectiveness of the antibiotics was compromised. Dr. McIntosh insisted, however, that the bacteria were so potent that probably didn't make any difference. She also confirmed that Lucy's medical bills totaled $385,496.33 for the doctors and the long hospital stay.

AT THE END OF the day, Johnny Bob assembled Claudia, Lucy and her family, along with T.J. for a status conference in their assigned room. The conference was necessary, but of almost equal importance was his belief that the more he could keep T.J. away from the media, the better. Maybe the crowds would be gone and the reporters would be off to some watering hole if they remained in the building for a while.

"End of day two," Johnny Bob announced. "Everybody doing okay?"

T.J. replied, "More important question is what do you think, counselor?"

"Tell you what, let's get Claudia's assessment since she pulled the laboring oar today."

"Well, pardon my French, but I thought we kicked ass. We had the jury crying within the first two hours of testimony. Don't know about you, Johnny Bob, but that's a record where I come from. On top of that, they couldn't even think of a question to ask Joanna here. Jessie was straightforward and didn't hesitate to concede what she had to."

"Jessie's testimony brings up a small concern, Claudia," Johnny Bob interrupted. "When she was talking about Dr. Moyo, a couple of our black jurors didn't look very happy. Since you're our resident expert on the subject, what do you think?"

"I noticed it, too, Johnny Bob, and that can be a problem. Frankly, the brothers and sisters don't like to see attacks on one of their own, particularly by the system that they always have to fight. Still, we've got enough evidence. We'll bring them around."

Johnny Bob turned to Lucy. "Little darlin', you're gonna be first up tomorrow. You ready to go?"

66

During the week before trial, Claudia had helped Lucy buy several new dresses, each one plain and intended to help the jury envision her as a sympathetic young girl. On the morning when Lucy would take center stage, Claudia told her to wear the white dress with blue trim on the sleeves and hem.

"Lucy, introduce yourself to the jury, please," Claudia began. Lucy did as she had been instructed and said, "Good morning, my name is Lucy Baines Brady. I'm from Texas City and I'm now eighteen." She smiled tentatively, and most of the jurors smiled back.

Claudia skipped through her youth, hitting only the high points, because Lucy's mother had already adequately covered it.

"Lucy, how did you get pregnant?"

Silence.

Then, a quavering and soft voice replied, "Ma'am, I was raped by a boy at church."

"If you were raped, Lucy, did you call the police?"

"No, ma'am. We, uh, had known each other for some time, and I didn't think the police would do anything."

"How about your mother and dad, did you tell them about what happened with the boy?"

Tod had been quiet until now. With this question, he rose and in an almost apologetic manner spoke. "Your Honor, Jan and I have allowed quite a bit of latitude to the plaintiffs. However, I must object to anything more in this line of questioning. There is no doubt that Lucy Brady became pregnant. That's why we're here. Her actions and thought processes leading up to her visit to Population Planning are not relevant to any issue in this case."

Claudia understood exactly what Tod was doing. He saw that she was painting Lucy as the victim, a sympathetic figure, caught up in a series of events she could not have predicted or prevented. "Your Honor, I don't intend to belabor this point, but the jury needs to know something about Lucy's state of mind leading up to the abortion. Her decision wasn't made in a vacuum."

"I agree, Ms. Jackson. I'll give you a little latitude here. Make it brief and get to the issues at hand," Judge O'Reilly ruled.

"Yes, ma'am. I'll move it quickly. Lucy, when you thought you were pregnant, did you talk to anyone about it, your mother, your father, anyone?"

"No, ma'am. I learned I was pregnant when I went to the drugstore and got one of those little kits. I was scared and didn't know what to do. I wanted to talk to my mother. Instead, I went to the computer. I read about pregnancy and abortion. The Web site from Population Planning made it seem so simple that I called them. They are the ones that gave me advice."

"How long before you had the abortion did you first talk to someone at Population Planning?"

"Just a few days before, Ms. Jackson. The lady I talked to told me just to come on in whenever I wanted. They could terminate any pregnancy in a couple of hours. I could be back at school in a day or two. I thought about it a few days. Then, I took my money from babysitting and Christmas and caught the bus to Houston on a Friday when we didn't have school. They made it sound so easy."

"Lucy, when you had the abortion, did they explain anything to you about what problems might happen?"

"No, ma'am. Not really. I just talked to a woman named Sylvia and all she wanted to do was make sure that I had enough money. I didn't, and she told me I could sign a note."

"Lucy, do you remember anything about the abortion itself?"

"No, ma'am, not much. I remember that it hurt a whole lot and I cried with the pain."

Dr. Moyo scribbled a note to Tod. *That didn't happen. I never had that happen with a patient of mine.*

Claudia saw Dr. Moyo hand the note to his lawyer and

asked Lucy, "Do you recognize the abortionist?" The last word was said with distaste like she was asking Lucy to identify a cockroach. Lucy pointed her finger at Dr. Moyo and said, "It was that man right there."

Dr. Moyo felt every eye in the large courtroom shift to him and he didn't like the feeling. It was even worse because Marian, his wife, had to endure the moment.

"Lucy, what happened after the abortion?"

"Ms. Jackson, they gave me some pills to take and said I could go to school on Monday. I caught the bus in front of the clinic and went home. I took my pill that night. Then I got nauseated and threw up. I don't know if the pill worked or not. The next morning, after my mother had gone to work, I called the clinic and told the nurse that I was having some bleeding and cramping and thought that I should go back to have them check me. She goes, 'Just take some Advil, and you'll be okay.'"

"Were you worried, Lucy?"

"I was really scared, and they didn't want to help me. Then, the next morning, I had to lie to my mother and tell her I was catching the flu to get out of church." Tears formed in her eyes as she looked at her mother.

Olga Olsen, a mother and grandmother, thought that the clinic better have a damn good excuse for ignoring this little girl.

"I called the clinic back and talked to another nurse. By then the bleeding had stopped, but I was really hot and cramping. This nurse told me the same thing as the first one. Just to take Advil and go to bed. I'd be all right."

"Were you all right, Lucy?" Claudia asked in a low voice, calculated to cause everyone in the courtroom to strain to hear and to pay attention.

This time Lucy broke down and tears rolled down her cheeks. The bailiff handed her a Kleenex box. Judge O'Reilly asked her if she needed to take a break.

"No, ma'am. I'd rather get this over."

Claudia continued. "Okay, Lucy, try to relax. I'll be through in a few minutes. What do you remember next?"

"Nothing, ma'am. Not until I was leaving the hospital. My mother told me I was in the hospital a long time, but I don't remember anything about it. After I was discharged, I went to stay with my Aunt Jessie in Fort Worth because my mother needed to go back to work and couldn't take care of me full time."

"How do you like living with Aunt Jessie, Lucy?"

"It's okay. She has a really big house and I have my own room looking out on the garden."

"Could you walk when you first got there, Lucy?"

"I don't know, Ms. Jackson. They said that I could, but for some reason I just couldn't make my legs move the way they were supposed to. So, I stayed in bed or the wheelchair just about all the time."

"How did you meet the Chosen, Lucy?"

"See, my aunt has been going to his church for a long time and is on the board or something, like she said when she testified yesterday. She made me start going to church with her. Well, she didn't make me. I like church, particularly the singing, and when she said that she wanted me to go with her, I said okay."

"I understand that one Sunday morning, you started walking when the Chosen commanded you to do so."

"Yes, ma'am. He's the one who got me up out of my wheelchair." As she commented about the Chosen, she turned and smiled at him before continuing. "He put his hands on me and I just felt warm all over, a good kind of warm, not like a fever or anything. He goes, 'Lucy, stand up,' and then, 'Lucy, follow me.' I heard a voice somewhere saying that he was a special messenger from God and that I should do his bidding, whatever he asked. So, I stood and walked."

Several of the jurors looked over at T.J., clearly wondering just who this man was. T.J. returned their stares with a look of confidence, as if to say it was just all in a day's work when you're a messenger from God.

Claudia moved on as it was approaching the noon lunch break. She led Lucy through her life since she was healed by the Chosen. She established that it was hardly a life one would expect for a teenager. She was trying to get her GED with the help of tutors that her aunt brought to the house. She saw Dr. Coates three times a week for counseling. In spite of pills for depression and pills to help her sleep, she still had nightmares that caused her to wake up crying nearly every night.

"Lucy, have you been examined by an obstetrician?"

"Yes, ma'am. Several times since I got out of the hospital."

"What has the obstetrician told you about your ability to conceive and bear children?"

Lucy teared up again, answering, "He told me that because of all that happened to me after the abortion, I probably wouldn't be able to have any children of my own."

"And how does that make you feel, Lucy?"

"Like I'm not even sure that I want to live the rest of my life."

"Pass the witness, Your Honor," Claudia said as she received a pat on the back from Johnny Bob for a job well done. Three women jurors were wiping their eyes.

During the lunch break, Tod and Jan conferred about how to handle Lucy's cross-examination. Her testimony had touched several of the jurors, maybe all of them. Jan had to tread gently, but there were a number of points to be made. While she had some reservations, Tod insisted that Jan ask questions about her ability to conceive. Their expert in obstetrics, certainly one of the world's authorities, had studied Lucy's records and was certain that she could have children. Tod wanted to lay the foundation for that testimony, to come at least a week away, maybe more.

Jan started her cross-examination with the positive aspects of Lucy's recovery and life. She was able to walk and use all of her limbs. She was doing well with her tutors and was on track to complete her GED in three months. Lucy had talked about wanting to go to community college and then to the University of Houston. She even volunteered that if she did well in community college, aunt Jessie said that she would pay her way to any four-year college in the country. She agreed that she and her aunt Jessie were going out more and more frequently. They had been to all of the museums and zoos in the Fort Worth/Dallas area and Jessie had begun to take her to the theater every month or so. Because of her love of singing, she particularly liked the Broadway musicals that would come to Fort Worth or Dallas as they toured the country.

Tod watched the jury as Jan was getting these concessions out of Lucy, portraying quite a different version of her life than the one painted by Claudia. She had been able to get Lucy to drop her guard with a gentle, compassionate manner, something he as a male probably could never have accomplished. Jan was scoring with the jury and was down to her final two major points.

"Your Honor, may I approach the witness?"

"You may, counsel," Judge O'Reilly replied.

"Ms. Brady, I'm handing you what we've marked as Defendant Exhibit Number One. Can you identify it as the consent form that you signed before the pregnancy termination?" Jan's decision to refer to her as "Ms. Brady" was as calculated as all of the other decisions made in a trial of this magnitude. Claudia called her Lucy to emphasize that she was still just a girl. Jan referred to her as Ms. Brady to convey the impression that she was an adult, which she was now in the eyes of the law. Jan hoped the jury understood that very little had changed in the year since the abortion other than the celebration of an eighteenth birthday. Certainly, her ability to read, comprehend and make decisions for herself was the same a year ago as today.

Claudia was on her feet. "Objection, Your Honor. Lucy had no capacity to sign that document. Therefore, it's not relevant. It's a matter we discussed when we did the limines."

"I remember, counsel. Bailiff, please escort the jury to the jury room. This is a matter that needs to be taken up outside their presence."

After the bailiff had taken the jurors out, the judge continued. "Let's see if I remember this correctly. The plaintiff signed the form when she was seventeen. Further, in Texas at that time a girl under the age of eighteen could have an abortion without parental consent. Am I getting it right so far?"

"Yes, ma'am, you are," Claudia answered. "Our position is that Texas law is very clear that no one in Texas can be bound by anything they sign until the age of eighteen. There are no exceptions to our knowledge. In fact, even that note that the clinic had her sign was not worth the paper it was written on."

"If I may be heard, Your Honor," Jan interrupted. "If Texas law permits her to consent to an abortion, then inherent in that law must be a duty on the part of the doctor and the clinic to inform her of the risks of the procedure and the duty on her part to give consent after being so informed. In this case, it shouldn't be a hard call. It's not like she was thirteen. She was over seventeen, a junior in high school. No one has suggested that she was not mature enough to understand what she was told."

Judge O'Reilly turned to Claudia. "Is that right, Ms. Jackson? Are you suggesting that she did not have the capacity to understand what she was told or what she signed?"

"No, ma'am," Claudia conceded. "That's not our objection."

"Very well, then. Whichever way I rule, I can see this going up on appeal. I'm going to let this document into evidence. Your objection is noted. Bailiff, call the jury back in."

In the jury room, the talk had turned to Johnny Bob's attire. "You notice that Lawyer Tisdale is wearing something red every day?" Joshua Ferrell, the night student, asked.

"Not today," replied Bert Marino. "Saw him wearing red suspenders the first day and a red tie yesterday, but nothing red today."

"No, man. You're wrong. Look at his boots. They have black bottoms but the tops are red. Look the next time he crosses his legs. Must be his favorite color or something."

Before the discussion could continue, the bailiff knocked on their door and escorted them back to the courtroom. Joshua was right. The tops of Johnny Bob's boots were red.

"Ms. Akers, you may proceed."

Jan approached the witness again and handed her the document. "Ms. Brady, can you read to the jury the name of this document?"

"It says 'Request for First Trimester Abortion.' But . . . but, I didn't read this."

"Ms. Brady, I haven't asked you about reading it yet." As she continued her question, she placed the document on an overhead projector that magnified it several times for the jury to observe on the screen. "Are these your initials beside each one of these twenty numbered paragraphs and is this your signature at the bottom?"

"Yes, ma'am," Lucy answered, not sure what such an admission would do to her lawsuit.

"Ms. Brady, isn't it true that every one of these risks of pregnancy termination was discussed with you before you decided to go forward with the procedure?"

"Uh, well, if they did say any of that stuff, I don't remember it," Lucy answered as she looked down at her hands to avoid eye contact with jurors.

"Thank you, Ms. Brady," Jan responded as she turned off the projector and returned to her seat at counsel table.

"By the way, on that Saturday morning when you talked to the nurse at the clinic, did you tell her about your nausea and throwing up the night before?"

"I don't know, ma'am. I mean, I guess I don't remember. I probably didn't."

"Last question. I don't mean to embarrass you with a personal question, but the jury needs to know. Have you had a relationship of any kind with a boy or man since you left the hospital?"

Lucy sat up straight in her chair and spoke forcefully into the microphone. "No, ma'am. I certainly have not. I haven't even been alone with any man except for counseling."

"Since you mention it, Ms. Brady, who have you sought counseling from?"

"Dr. Frederick Coates, ma'am, and a few times with Reverend Luther on Sunday nights when I would go out to the

City for youth fellowship. Both of them have been trying to help me understand all that has gone on. Without them and Aunt Jessie, I don't think I could have made it this far."

"Thank you, Ms. Brady. No further questions for this witness, Your Honor."

Nodding her head to Jan, the judge turned to Johnny Bob, asking, "Mr. Tisdale, who's your next witness?"

"Your Honor, we'll be calling Dr. Moyo as an adverse witness."

"Do I assume correctly that he will be a fairly lengthy witness, Mr. Tisdale?"

"I expect that with my exam and that of the other side, we'll take at least a day, maybe a little more."

"Then, why don't we quit a little early today and we'll start with him tomorrow. Jurors, let me remind you of my instructions. Don't talk to anyone about this case, not even your spouse. Further, don't put yourselves in a situation where you might see or hear anyone else commenting about this trial. You will decide this case only on what I permit you to see and hear in this courtroom. I'll see you all in the morning."

After Johnny Bob and his entourage had left the courtroom, Tod noticed that Mr. Buschbahm was still seated at the top of the auditorium, obviously waiting for the crowds to clear out so that he would not have to wait for an elevator. Tod bounded up the stairs and sat down beside him.

"So, Mr. Buschbahm, how am I doing so far?"

Mr. Buschbahm thought a moment before replying. "Tod, I'd say you're about even at this point, which you know is pretty fair at this stage of the case. Joanna and Lucy made very good witnesses, but Jan did an exceedingly fine job of neutralizing a lot of the sympathy that the jury had for Lucy this morning. Even-steven is where I put it for now. Dr. Moyo is going to be critical for you."

"I agree, Mr. Buschbahm. I certainly agree. Thanks for your two bits' worth."

Mr. Buschbahm grinned as he ended the conversation.

"Used to be that my opinions were worth two bits, but with inflation, they're now worth two dollars, maybe more."

Tod's crew left the courthouse after most of the crowds had vacated the street. They declined interviews with several reporters and a couple of television crews. Maybe tomorrow. They reassembled at the fire station war room where Grace took orders for Chinese food. Tod and Wayne got a beer. Dr. Moyo and Jan drank Cokes.

Tod propped his feet up on the long table, took a swig of his beer, let the taste and liquid slide to the bottom of his stomach and then said, "Nice job, Jan. No, more than nice. Superb. You cut way into Lucy's damages and even managed to bring her credibility into issue with the consent form."

"I assume that you're going to have Zeke take the jury through the risks of the procedure and the consent form," Jan said. "I think that he can convince them that she's having a rather convenient memory."

The conversation continued about the day's events until Grace returned with the Chinese food. After they had helped themselves, Tod turned to Zeke. "Zeke, you're up in the morning. Any concerns or matters that we need to talk about?"

"I think that I'm as ready as I can be, Tod, thanks to you and Wayne. I want you to be sure to go over the procedure in detail. I have never had a pregnancy termination patient who cried out in pain. And cover the consent form. I know that all of those risks were discussed with her. I also know that I asked her if she had any questions, and she didn't. What should I expect from Mr. Tisdale? He's been very quiet for two days."

"Expect the unexpected," Tod responded. "He'll start off with some question calculated to unbalance and unnerve you. So be prepared for anything. Whatever it is, remember all we have told you. Take your time, be calm, and don't get upset. I'll clean up any messes he creates when it's my turn."

"Tod," Wayne asked, "what's your current thinking about whether to put on Zeke's slander case and his damages now or wait until later?"

"I've got my mind made up. We're going to go full speed ahead on the slander and Zeke's damages. I don't want a day to go by that the jury is not reminded that there are two victims, as Johnny Bob likes to call them. Let's just see who the jury thinks is the real victim at the end of the trial."

67

As the jury assembled for the fourth day of trial, Joshua Ferrell proposed a bet. "All right, I'm convinced that lawyer Tisdale will have on something red today. It'll cost anyone who wants to get in the pot a dollar. You've got to be right about what red item he has on him, and if you're right, you win the pot or split it with anyone else who has the right answer."

"I'm in," said Roy Judice, pulling a dollar from his wallet. "Put me down for a red tie."

"Here's my dollar on red suspenders again," said Olga Olsen, the waitress.

"Red boots," was the guess of Catherine Tucker, the Realtor.

"I think he'll have on red underwear," smiled Amy Bourland, the schoolteacher, as she put her dollar on the table.

"No, Amy, you can't bet on that. What do you want us to do, ask the judge to have him drop his pants in the middle of the courtroom?"

"Okay, then I say a red handkerchief."

As it turned out, Amy won the bet and they would never know that Johnny Bob was also wearing underwear dotted with red hearts, a gift from Bernice for Valentine's Day. He also had a red handkerchief in his coat pocket. After that, the bet became a daily ritual with nearly every juror participating. The pot carried over only one day when Johnny Bob was void of red except for a red ballpoint pen in his shirt pocket, which the jurors missed. Other than the jury, only Johnny Bob knew what was going on in their room each morning. It was a little stunt he had dreamed up years ago to focus more attention on himself and on what he had to say. It always worked.

Dressed in a dark blue suit and wearing his own red tie, Dr. Moyo took the witness stand.

"Good morning, Dr. Moyo."

"Good morning to you, Mr. Tisdale."

Johnny Bob then leaned over his table. "Dr. Moyo, when you were licensed to practice medicine, did you take the Hippocratic Oath?"

Jeez, thought Tod, *he's not wasting any time getting to the short hairs.*

"Yes, sir. I did."

Johnny Bob walked to the projector, turned it on and the screen showed the section of the oath reading, "I will give no deadly medicine to anyone if asked, nor suggest any such counsel; and in like manner, I will not give to a woman a pessary to produce an abortion."

"Didn't Hippocrates condemn abortion nearly five hundred years before Christ was born?"

"Yes, sir."

"Then, please tell this jury why it was that you chose to violate your oath and take the lives of innocent babies?"

Tod leaped out of his chair. "Objection, Your Honor, argumentative!"

"Sustained. Rephrase your question, Mr. Tisdale."

"Be happy to, Your Honor. Tell us why you chose to violate your oath."

Dr. Moyo momentarily covered his face with his hands and then wiped his hands on his pants. Despite all the preparation, he had not anticipated such an attack. "Sir, I did not violate my oath. Not every doctor thought like Hippocrates in his day or today. The oath that I took upon graduation from medical school did not have that exact wording."

"Well, then, tell us what exact wording it did have about abortions."

"I swore that I would maintain the utmost respect for human life from its inception, and I believe that I have abided by that oath."

"Still, you'll concede that old Hippocrates himself admonished you doctors not to do abortions."

"Yes, sir. That's what the words seem to say."

"And, Dr. Moyo, just when did you start killing babies for a living?"

Tod was on his feet like a shot. "Objection! Don't answer that, Dr. Moyo. Your Honor, may we approach the bench?"

"Come up here, counsel." It was clear from the tone of Ruby's voice that she had had enough of the lawyers in this case gallivanting out of bounds. It was going to be hard enough to try this case, avoiding reversible error without such shenanigans. She was going to put a stop to it.

"Your Honor, that question is so inflammatory and prejudicial as to make it impossible for my client to get a fair trial," Tod argued. "I hate to do it after all we've been through, but I move for mistrial."

"Your Honor . . ."

"Mr. Tisdale, you've said quite enough. I'm not going to grant a mistrial. However, I'm putting this on the record so that the appellate courts may have the benefit of my thoughts. Your question as phrased was totally out of line, and if we were not so far along with this monster, I'd grant Mr. Duncan's motion. As for you, Mr. Tisdale, if you wish to get back up to East Texas with your license intact, I demand that you ask questions that do not drip with prejudice. You can lead Dr. Moyo all you want, but only with reasonable questions. I know that you are a wealthy man, Mr. Tisdale; however, I will sanction you with a fine big enough that even you will hurt. The appellate courts can decide if I have been too harsh. In the meantime, the county will have the use of your money if you want to continue in this trial. And, while I have you all up here, the same goes for all of you. Understood?"

The attorneys agreed, particularly Johnny Bob, who returned to his seat, cleared his throat and was about to continue when Judge O'Reilly said to the jury, "You are instructed to disregard that last question. It was highly improper and prejudicial. You are not to consider it for any purpose. Further, you are instructed that our United States Supreme Court has ruled that it is legal to perform an abortion on a woman if she and her physician agree to the procedure."

Strong language, especially the part about the Supreme Court, but Ruby was mad. Let the appellate courts deal with it.

"Dr. Moyo, when you were working at Population Planning, how much were you paid to do an abortion?"

"I was paid one hundred dollars for each one."

"Let's see, you worked there three days a week, didn't you, about four hours a day?"

"Yes, sir. Most weeks."

"How many abortions could you usually do in that time?"

"Usually ten or fifteen, sir."

Johnny Bob walked up to the large pad on an easel and wrote *$1500*. "Well, that means that you could make fifteen hundred dollars a day for just a half day's work. Pretty good wages wasn't it? Forty-five hundred dollars for twelve hours a week?" Johnny Bob knew that there wasn't one juror who made that much working forty or fifty hours a week.

"Sir, I did not ask for that much money. That's what they told me they could pay. You must also understand, after twelve years of study during which I had made no money, I was just starting into a career. Doctors sacrifice a lot in their early years and most feel that they are entitled to make a decent living when they finally are permitted to go into their specialty. May I ask, Mr. Tisdale, how much you earn a year for comparison?"

Tod and Jan smiled as Johnny Bob was caught off guard by the question. The big lawyer replied hurriedly, "What I make is not the issue, Dr. Moyo. How many abortions did you perform while you worked at Population Planning, Doctor?"

Before Dr. Moyo could reply to the question, Tod rose slowly from his chair and addressed the bench, a twinkle in his eye. "Your Honor, I disagree with Mr. Tisdale. I think that the jury would be quite interested in what he makes. I'll certainly tell them what I make in a year if Johnny Bob will do the same. He's the one that raised the issue about forty-five hundred dollars a week being a lot of money."

Judge O'Reilly kept a most solemn face to hide her amusement about the dilemma that Johnny Bob found himself in. Still, she knew that he was right and lawyers' incomes were not an issue in the case. "Mr. Duncan, I'm sure the jury would find both of your earnings quite interesting, but I agree with Mr. Tisdale. Let's move on. Please answer the question, Dr. Moyo."

Dr. Moyo replied, "First of all, I did not work every week. I would estimate that in the four and a half years that I worked there, I terminated approximately fifteen hundred to two thousand pregnancies. I might add, all without incident except for this one."

"Now, Dr. Moyo, let's talk about Lucy Brady. She had some problems following the abortion that you performed on her, didn't she?"

"Yes, Mr. Tisdale. She had a slight perforation and there was some tissue that remained in her uterus after the procedure."

"Tissue, Dr. Moyo?" Johnny Bob bellowed. "Tissue! That tissue was what remained of a twelve-week-old fetus after you got through, wasn't it?"

"Yes, sir, it was, but it was not capable of being identified as part of a fetus. For that reason the pathologist at Hermann merely described it as tissue," Dr. Moyo responded in a subdued voice.

"Now, Doctor, you said that this is the only abortion where you ever had a serious problem. And in this one, you didn't get all of the baby out and even punched a hole in Lucy's uterus."

"If that's a question, sir, the answer is yes. May I explain? The procedure is a blind one and the lining of the pregnant uterus is very thin, which is why a uterine perforation is discussed with the patient as a potential complication."

"Dr. Moyo, let's talk about what you had been doing before you got to the clinic that morning. You had gone two nights without sleep, isn't that true?"

"Yes, sir, I had a patient in an extremely difficult labor. It wasn't exactly two nights. I had slept a few hours two nights before. There's no doubt that I had not slept in more than thirty hours."

"That have anything to do with your performance on Lucy Baines Brady, Doctor?"

"Sir, I've thought about that, and I know it did not. Medical residents of all kinds pull twenty-four-hour shifts, and any obstetrician expects to lose sleep on a regular basis and still perform at the highest level."

"Nonetheless, Doctor, out of all these abortions you performed, this is the only one where you had two major complications. By the way, you could have called in and asked the clinic to find you a substitute, couldn't you, Dr. Moyo?"

"Yes, sir. I could have, and I presume that they would have done so."

"But you didn't because you wanted to make fifteen hundred dollars that day, Doctor. That was more important to you than the safety and well-being of your patients, right?"

Dr. Moyo took a deep and audible breath before replying. "No, sir. My patients always come first."

Johnny Bob expected that answer, but he had made his point. "I'll pass the witness, Your Honor."

It was midafternoon and time for a break. Tod and Jan decided that Dr. Moyo had taken quite a beating. Their plan was just to walk him through his personal and professional life and then regroup. After the break, Tod gave Zeke easy questions. They talked about Zeke growing up in Nigeria, the fact that he was a second-generation physician, his scholarship to medical school in England, his professional soccer career, his submission of applications for residency at some of the world's better medical schools, the reasons why he chose Baylor as a place to study and Houston as a place to live, his marriage to Marian in England, the birth of their two children, and the fact that he passed his board certification exam on the first try. When the day ended, they hadn't touched on Lucy or Dr. Moyo's work at the clinic. Still, Tod had accomplished his purpose of presenting his client as a complete person. The jury did not leave with the impression that Zeke was only an abortionist and nothing more.

At four-thirty, Judge O'Reilly did as Tod expected. "Ladies and gentlemen, let's call it a week. On Fridays I always have a motion docket. So, I'll be back in my regular courtroom at the main courthouse. In a long trial, I rarely get complaints from litigants or jurors about having one day a week off. Gives you a little time to catch up at work or at home. Remember my instructions and I'll see you on Monday morning. Try to be in the jury room at eight forty-five, and we'll start promptly at nine. Have a nice weekend."

After telling Zeke to be at the fire station at ten in the morning, Tod invited Jan, Wayne, and Marilyn to walk the three blocks over to the Four Seasons Hotel for a drink while the traffic cleared. As they left the building, they found T.J., white Stetson in place and gold Bible in hand, being interviewed by Victoria Burton. This time she was doing a story for the NBC *Nightly News*.

"Yes, Victoria, we're pleased with how the trial is going. What happened to Lucy has ruined her life, and I'm certain that the jury feels that way. As to Dr. Moyo, no matter how much perfume you spray on a doctor like him, he still smells like an abortionist. His lawyer can call him a pedigreed pussycat, but the jury will still see him for the polecat that he is."

Tod and the others paused in amazement as they listened to T.J. continuing his attacks on Dr. Moyo. Turning to his legal assistant, he said, "Marilyn, I'll have to buy you a drink another time. Get on back to the station and get the VCR running. We may want to use this next week."

As Marilyn headed toward her car, Victoria Burton interrupted, "Reverend Luther, do you expect to testify soon?"

"Well, Victoria, that's up to Mr. Tisdale and Ms. Jackson. My guess is that my time will come next week. I am eager to get on the stand. As you and your audience know, I have a lot to say about these proceedings. The sooner the better."

Tod and his group walked away. "If I didn't need a drink before, I damn sure need one now. I just hope that Dr. Moyo doesn't watch channel two tonight."

On Monday morning, the trial took another turn that no one could have predicted.

68

Anna May Marbley lived in the Fourth Ward, an old area just barely out of the shadows of the downtown Houston sky-scrapers. Her mother drove her five minutes to the law school each morning at seven-thirty while her children were having breakfast, then returned to get them off to school. Anna May was usually the first juror to arrive. Because she arrived so early, her mother dropped her at the main en-trance in front of empty barricades that awaited the day's crowds, reporters and police officers. She entered through the metal detector and often stopped to visit with the guards who manned the machine before going to the elevator that took her to the third floor. By that time, the deputy had cof-fee and pastries on the table in the jury room. She always got first choice.

On this Monday morning, things were different. Anna May paused only to say good morning to the guards as she took her purse from the metal detector conveyor belt. She went immediately to the third floor and began looking for Deputy Johnson, always the first bailiff to arrive and the one who brought the pastries. Not finding him in the jury room or the courtroom, she sat in the jury room, arms folded and stared at the wall, a grim look on her normally cheery face. Deputy Johnson could see something was amiss as soon as he walked in.

"Anna May, what's wrong with you? You look like you just saw the devil himself."

"I need to see the judge, Mr. Johnson, alone."

Johnson had picked up the coffeepot to take it to the men's room to wash it out and refill it. "Judge won't get here until about eight-thirty. You want to tell me the problem? You got a sick kid? Or maybe a death in the family?"

"Nope. This is for the judge's ears only." Anna May con-tinued to sit with her back to the wall, arms folded as the bailiff made coffee and put out pastries. Soon, other jurors began to trickle in, making small talk and discussing the events of the three-day weekend. Anna May said good morning and nothing else.

At eight thirty-five, Deputy Johnson returned to the jury room, looked at Anna May and said, "Come with me. The judge will see you now."

Fifteen minutes later, Judge O'Reilly summoned the lawyers to her small chambers where Anna May sat facing her. No one spoke until Deputy Johnson closed the door.

"Ms. Marbley, would you please tell the lawyers what you just told me," directed the judge, a solemn and determined look on her face.

"Yes, ma'am." Anna May Marbley did not turn to look at the lawyers, but continued to look straight ahead at the flag of the United States behind the judge. "Last night at about ten o'clock my phone rang. I had just gotten the kids in bed and was talking to my mother. It was a man on the phone. He didn't identify himself and I didn't know the voice. He told me that if I knew what was good for my kids and myself, I'd better vote against that butcher doctor and that murder clinic. He told me not to tell anyone about his call if I valued my life. Then he hung up. I didn't sleep all night. Until this morning I wasn't going to tell anybody. I don't want my kids hurt. But I'm a juror in this case and that makes me an official or something is the way I figure it. So, I decided I had to tell the judge."

"Thank you, Ms. Marbley. You are to be commended for coming forward. Would you step out into the hallway with Deputy Johnson and wait there for a few minutes while I talk with the lawyers?"

"Here's what we're going to do. I'm going to have to sequester the jury. We'll call each of them in here, one-by-one, and quiz them to make sure that there have been no other phone calls. Hopefully, this is an isolated incident. If so, I'll wait until the end of the day to tell them they will be sequestered. We don't want them distracted from today's testimony. A deputy will follow them to their homes where they will have an hour to visit with their families and pack their clothes. Then the deputy will drive them to a yet-to-be-determined hotel. I'll talk to Judge Hardman about the hotel, but it will not be disclosed to the media, or to any of you, for that matter. Not that it won't be found out in a couple of days. All a reporter will have to do is follow the county vans when they see the jurors being loaded into them. Okay, so far?"

Everyone agreed.

"I'm going to have to excuse Ms. Marbley as a juror. I don't see any way that this experience won't impact on her impartiality."

After each of the remaining thirteen jurors were brought to the judge's chambers, and they confirmed that they had not discussed the case with anyone nor had they been contacted by anyone about the case, the judge was ready to start evidence for the week. Her announcement was simple and to the point. She talked to the jury when they were seated. Her words were also for the audience, both in the courtroom and throughout the nation.

"Ladies and gentlemen, Ms. Marbley has had to be excused for personal reasons. Mr. Steinhorn, you are now among the first twelve. Ms. Dowell, you are our one remaining alternate. Mr. Duncan, are you ready to proceed?"

"Yes, Your Honor. May I ask Dr. Moyo to re-take the stand?"

As he did so, three reporters left their seats, determined to be the first to break the story on why Anna May Marbley was no longer on the jury. It was easy to find out where she lived and her phone number, only she refused to talk. Her mother answered the phone and the knocks on the door, saying that her daughter had nothing to say. Anna May Marbley's position would change within twenty-four hours.

"Dr. Moyo, do you still perform abortions for elective pregnancy termination?" Tod asked.

"No, sir, I quit that practice about three months after Ms. Brady's abortion, at a time, I might add, when I didn't even know she had a problem. My obstetrical practice was doing well and I no longer needed the extra income. I should state, though, that I will still do an abortion on one of my patients if the health of the patient is at risk."

"Dr. Moyo, will you tell the jury why you spent several years doing abortions at the Population Planning clinic?"

Dr. Moyo turned and faced the jury, trying to look each of the thirteen in the eye. "First, you must understand that abortions are legal in this country and have been since 1973. I have seen the problems that can result from abortions done by people who are not properly trained medical doctors and under unsanitary conditions. As Mr. Tisdale pointed out, the abortion controversy has been around at least since the time of Hippocrates. Whether we like it or not, for a variety of reasons, women have always chosen to have abortions. If they are going to make that choice, it is my opinion that the abortion should be done by skilled medical practitioners and in a safe environment."

Rebecca Dowell, the young alternate juror, nodded her agreement.

"I, personally, would not do an elective abortion on a fetus beyond eighteen weeks, since I consider that to be close to the time of viability, the time when the child might be able to live outside the womb. In reality, it is probably twenty-three or twenty-four weeks, but I draw the line at eighteen weeks. Now, of course, I no longer do elective abortions."

It was best to concede the obvious and play devil's advocate. "Now, Dr. Moyo, did the money you were paid have anything to do with it?"

"Of course, sir. But given my personal feelings as I have described, and knowing that I was doing nothing illegal, it was a way that I could support my family until my practice was up and going. Remember that if no good doctors performed abortions, they would once again be done in back alleys and motel rooms. Our hospitals would be overflowing with the problems that resulted."

"As to Ms. Brady, did you do anything different from what you did on all the other occasions where there were no complications?"

"No, sir."

"Did she cry out in pain?"

"No, sir. I certainly would have remembered that if it had happened on any of my patients."

"Ms. Akers showed her a consent form where she initialed twenty complications that can result from an abortion. Can those problems occur with any patient even with the best obstetrician doing the procedure?"

"Absolutely, sir. Just read any obstetrics textbook."

"You heard Ms. Brady testify that no one explained anything to her and she just initialed and signed where she was told."

"I know that not to be true, sir. She would have had the procedure and its complications explained to her by the nurse who assisted me. Additionally, I always confirm with my patients that those risks have been explained to their satisfaction before I start the procedure."

Tod shifted gears. "Dr. Moyo, you are also a plaintiff in this lawsuit, are you not?"

"Yes sir. I have sued Reverend Luther here, and twelve pro-life organizations for statements that they made about me."

Tod rose. "Your Honor, at this time we propose to play excerpts from Reverend Luther's sermons where he talks about Dr. Moyo and Population Planning as well as some speeches and interviews that he has done outside his church."

The judge ordered the lights dimmed and the Chosen appeared on the screen. The jurors watched in rapt attention as the clips were shown. With no sermon to lead into the attacks, even in his white satin robe, the sunglasses gave T.J. a sinister appearance as he "called out his enemies by name" and accused Dr. Moyo and the clinic of being murderers and baby killers. In the jury box, Amy Bourland put her hand over her mouth as she watched the attacks. Alfred Totman, the black former city bookkeeper, also appeared to be visibly disturbed. Catherine Tucker refused to look at the screen and merely gazed at the judge. The television clips moved from the pulpit to T.J. addressing the crowd outside the clinic during the week before the trial began. They closed with his interview where T.J. accused Dr. Moyo of being a polecat.

Johnny Bob had not seen the last one and murmured, "Shit!" under his breath. Fortunately for him, only Claudia was close enough to hear. Where was that muzzle when he needed it? How many more clips would there have been if T.J. had not been in solitary all that time? Praise the Lord and Judge O'Reilly, too.

As the lights came up, Tod continued, "Dr. Moyo, how did these words impact you and your family?"

Zeke spoke quietly, a solemn look on his face. "After the first attack, I started having patients cancel appointments. As the attacks continued, I lost so many of my patients that I was forced to shut down my office. I couldn't afford the overhead. I was able to get a job doing emergency room work, but at much less money. I am now making about fifty thousand a year less than I was before I was attacked."

"And how, Doctor, has this affected you and your family?"

"My professional life has been destroyed, Mr. Duncan," Zeke replied. He turned to the jury. "It's hard to put into words how being called a murderer and a baby killer has affected me and my family. It's been devastating. This whole thing is an ordeal that I would have preferred that my family not have to endure. I have been in great fear for their lives and mine since a number of the anti-abortion groups are violent."

"Now, Your Honor, I do have to object. Violence from other anti-abortion groups has no relevance to issues in this case," Johnny Bob cried.

"Overruled, Mr. Tisdale. It goes to his mental anguish claim against Reverend Luther and the other groups."

"But, Your Honor . . ."

"Please be seated, Mr. Tisdale. I have made my ruling."

Tod was ready to wind up. "Dr. Moyo, are you starting new employment at the conclusion of this trial?"

Dr. Moyo smiled. "Yes, sir. I have been accepted on the faculty of Baylor College of Medicine. I would already be there except this trial is taking up all of my time for the next few weeks."

Tod had done what he intended. He had at least put the best face he could on the complications of the abortion and was pleased with the reactions he thought he had perceived from the jury when he showed the attacks on Dr. Moyo. Further, he ended on a high note with Zeke's new appointment.

"No further questions, Your Honor."

"Then, let's take our lunch break. Be back here at one-thirty."

As the rest of the courtroom cleared for the lunch break, Johnny Bob and Claudia remained at their table, heads together in low conversation.

"So what do you think, Claudia? Do we call T.J. after I re-examine Zeke?"

"Johnny Bob, my vote is to get him up there sooner rather than later. I think now is the time. Those clips made him look pretty damn bad. Maybe seeing him live and in person with some of that old T.J. charisma will soften some of those statements. Besides, if his testimony doesn't go well, you've at least got a couple of weeks to repair the damage."

After the lunch break, Johnny Bob took Dr. Moyo on recross. "Dr. Moyo, we're going to discuss the fetus at about twelve weeks, the age of Lucy's baby before you terminated her pregnancy." Johnny Bob was being careful not to stir up an argument since he wanted just to make a few points and move on to T.J.

"At twelve weeks, approximately, is when you terminated the pregnancy of Lucy Brady, correct?"

"Yes, sir."

"At that point in the development of the fetus, the heart had begun to beat?"

"Well, sir, there is electrical activity that could be equated to a heartbeat."

"The fetus had ten fingers and ten toes."

"Correct, sir."

"Brain waves can be recorded?"

"Some might dispute that, sir. Others would agree."

"All of the organs of a human being have been formed, liver, lungs, pancreas, kidneys and so forth?"

"Yes, sir."

"There's even fetal movement at this stage?"

"Mr. Tisdale, there may be some movement, but it's probably not voluntary movement."

"Yet, you say that this is not a human life form?"

Dr. Moyo grasped the witness rail. This time he was the one glaring as he answered. "Mr. Tisdale, what I have said is that at this stage, the life form is not a human being!"

Figuring that he had done all the damage he could with Dr. Moyo, Johnny Bob passed the witness as Judge O'Reilly commanded, "Call your next witness, Mr. Tisdale."

"Your Honor, we call Reverend Thomas Jeremiah Luther."

T.J. stood, buttoned his white coat and walked to the witness stand, carrying his gold Bible in his left hand. Before he could sit down, Judge O'Reilly instructed him, "Reverend Luther, will you please face the bench while I swear you in?"

T.J. replied, "Your Honor, that won't be necessary. I am a man of God and I do not find it necessary to be sworn to tell the truth." Four jurors smiled at his comment as the judge continued. "I respect your beliefs, Reverend, but you, especially, should remember we don't play any favorites in this court. Every witness is to be sworn."

"Very well, then," T.J. responded as he stood at attention and placed his right hand over the Bible in his left.

"Do you solemnly swear that you will tell the truth, the whole truth, and nothing but the truth so help you God?"

T.J. bowed his head as he swore, "So help me God, my Father."

"Please be seated, Reverend. You may proceed, counsel."

"Tell the jury your name and profession, please, sir," Johnny Bob started.

Smiling at the jury, T.J. replied, "My name is Thomas Jeremiah Luther. I am also called the Chosen. I am a preacher and a man of God."

"Reverend Luther, let's get the obvious out of the way first. Why are you always wearing dark sunglasses indoors?"

"Sir, many years ago in a former life I was a resident of the Tarrant County jail," T.J. responded matter-of-factly.

"While incarcerated there I got in a fight with another inmate who threw ammonia and lye in my eyes. I was blinded for a period of time but regained my sight. Some believed it to be a miracle. My eyes were horribly disfigured. Sunglasses make it easier for everyone. I could show the jury my eyes if they would like to see them."

"I don't think that will be necessary, Reverend." Johnny Bob walked T.J. through his seamy early life and rebirth as a Christian. He went into detail about his successful ministry and the building of the City of Miracles. That led to the stabbing years before and his twelve-year sleep.

"Reverend, do you remember anything about the twelve years while you were asleep, if that's the right word to use?"

"Good as any, Mr. Tisdale. At first I didn't remember much, but as my strength and powers were restored, it became clear to me. I was with God during those years."

Jessie twisted uneasily in her seat with those words. She recalled her various one-on-one meetings with T.J. at the Miracle Tower where such a lofty position was never mentioned. The jurors and the rest of the audience were silent as T.J. spoke. Many had looks of skepticism on their faces. Most were caught up in the moment and waited with a sense of anticipation for the next words to come from the man in the witness chair.

"Reverend, just out of curiosity, if I were to ask you to give us a description of God, could you do so?"

Tod considered objecting since he could not find any relevance to this line of questioning, but thought better of it when he surveyed the jury and saw that they wanted to know the answer.

"I could, Mr. Tisdale. I prefer not to do so. There are some things which I feel are better left to the imagination of man. If my Father chooses to reveal Himself, it should be His choice and not mine."

Several people in the audience sighed with disappointment. Even Judge O'Reilly had hoped to hear the answer and leaned back in her chair after the moment passed.

"Understood, Reverend." Johnny Bob made a temple with his hands in front of his chin as he continued. "So, after twelve years, you woke up?"

"I believe, Mr. Tisdale, that the more proper description is that I was resurrected."

Johnny Bob felt uncomfortable with pushing this analogy too far in front of the jury. However, he was stuck and let it go. "Okay, then, you were resurrected. After your resurrection, what did you do?"

"I was fortunate to have a very strong board looking out for my ministry while I was gone. Once I was able, I took my rightful place as the chosen leader of the City of Miracles."

Johnny Bob shifted in his chair, glancing at the jury as he did so. He liked what he saw. The old charisma was coming through on all cylinders, and the jury was buying what T.J was selling. He glanced down at his notes and continued. "Reverend, let's fast-forward a little bit. When did you first meet my client, Lucy Brady?"

T.J. smiled at Lucy as he spoke and she returned the smile. "Lucy's Aunt Jessie, Ms. Warren Woolsey, is a prominent woman in Fort Worth. She's a widow lady whose late husband was actually one of the early contributors to my ministry. When I was resurrected, I learned that she was a member of my board and we became friends. I first saw Lucy sitting beside her in a wheelchair at a Sunday morning service. It wasn't long before I learned what Lucy had been through."

Johnny Bob hoped that he would get the right answer to the next question. "Were you involved in helping her to walk again?"

"Mr. Tisdale, she was physically capable of walking. Her emotions and mind were holding her back. Let's say that on one Sunday morning, I healed her by giving her the strength to overcome the forces that were holding her back."

Johnny Bob smiled to himself as he realized that T.J. had remembered his lessons.

"Reverend, can you heal the lame and afflicted?"

This time, T.J. looked at the jurors and said, "Yes, sir. With God's help, I can."

Tod was watching the jury as they returned T.J.'s gaze. It appeared almost as if the preacher had them under a spell. It was one helluva performance. As he watched, he pondered how he could cross-examine so powerful a personality.

"Now, Reverend Luther, were you somehow involved with my client's decision to file this lawsuit?"

"Sir, I think it was probably my idea. Might I explain?"

Tod made a gesture with his hand, indicating that he had no objection. T.J. might as well say what he had to say now. It was going to come out one way or the other.

"Sir, I was horrified by what had happened to Lucy. Clearly, it was malpractice of the worst degree."

Tod shot to his feet. "Your Honor, I will have to object to that. As far as I know, Reverend Luther doesn't have a medical license and has no expertise to offer such opinions. I ask that his response be stricken and the jury be instructed to disregard it."

"He's right, ladies and gentlemen," Judge O'Reilly ruled. "Evidence of malpractice or negligence, if any, must come from a qualified medical expert and Reverend Luther does not possess such qualifications. That comment is stricken from the record. You are instructed not to consider it for any purpose."

"Mr. Tisdale, let me leave the issue of malpractice for others and just say that I thought that she had been wronged. I encouraged her to bring this lawsuit for another reason, too. When I was resurrected, I was put back on earth with several missions. However, my first and primary one was to end the practice of abortion, first in this country and later in the rest of the world. As I observed what had happened while I was gone, it became clear to me that we who oppose the killing of babies were not going to win the war anytime soon in the U. S. Supreme Court, in Congress or in the state legislatures. We had to open a new battlefront and I chose this courthouse to launch that attack. I hope that Lucy is compensated for her injuries. More important for our cause, I pray for damages against these defendants large enough to put them and others like them out of business for good. Remember, Mr. Tisdale, there are about two million pre-born babies killed in this country every year. Our pre-born babies can't wait for Congress to get off its rear end or for the right president to come along to replace justices on the Supreme Court. We have a holocaust in our own country which must come to an end."

"Now, Reverend Luther, let me bring your attention to one of the major issues in this lawsuit. You know that you, your church and a bunch of other pro-life organizations have been sued because of what you have said outside this courtroom."

The witness's face grew taut and his back stiffened as he rested his hands on the gold Bible in front of him. "I am very much aware of those facts, Mr. Tisdale."

"You saw the video clips that Mr. Duncan here showed to the jury when Dr. Moyo was on the stand?"

"I did."

"Do you want to take back any of those words?"

T.J. turned to face the jury and again looked at each of them before speaking in a voice, low but firm with conviction. "My friends, I stand by every word I said and would not take back one of them. If I were to be found to be bearing false witness, with or without an oath, you should not believe a single word that I speak. I tell you that an abortion doctor is a murderer. The clinics where abortions are performed are temples of death. Anyone who assists or supports the performing of an abortion is just as much a murderer as the doctor who actually kills the baby and also will be condemned to a life in hell."

As he spoke, the jury gave no sign of whether they accepted or rejected what he said. Certainly, though, they listened and considered every word.

"As Matthew said in his gospel," T.J. continued, "'Anyone who breaks one of the least of these commandments and teaches others to do the same will be called least in the kingdom of heaven.' Surely, any person who is even assisting another to have an abortion is violating God's Commandments and cannot expect to enter the kingdom of heaven. I spoke the truth on those television clips and I am speaking the truth now."

Johnny Bob interrupted, "Reverend, how can you be so positive? You know that there are others who believe strongly that there is no life until the baby can live outside the womb."

T.J. turned his gaze back to Johnny Bob and then shifted it to Dr. Moyo, replying, "Sir, I have studied the Bible as much as any man. I have conferred with the world's leading scholars. And I have some experiences that only one other man has ever had. I can tell you in no uncertain terms that life begins at the moment of conception and any person who takes that life or assists in the taking of such a life has killed a human being."

Johnny Bob smiled to himself. T.J. had managed to get God's opinion in the case without actually saying that it was his Father that told him. Strong stuff if it is believed. On the other hand, there may be some jurors who think they are hearing the ravings of a lunatic. The answer, thought Johnny Bob, will be forthcoming in a couple of weeks.

"What about a girl like Lucy who voluntarily decides to end her pregnancy, Reverend? Is she also to be condemned?"

T.J. smiled at Lucy. "No, Mr. Tisdale. Of course not. A forgiving God is not going to condemn a child for being misled by the kind of evil adults who work at such clinics."

Johnny Bob whispered to Claudia, then rose. "We pass the witness, Your Honor."

"Fine, Mr. Tisdale. We'll call it a day," the judge replied. "Ladies and gentlemen, please go with Mr. Johnson to the jury room. I have something that I need to discuss with you."

Murmurs came from the media section. What was Judge O'Reilly discussing with the jury? As they were led out and the lawyers were packing their briefcases, the *Chronicle* courthouse reporter drifted over to one of the other bailiffs. "Hey, Bill, what's going on? What's the judge discussing with the jury?"

"Can't tell you," he replied.

"Come on, Bill, just as background. You know I keep my sources confidential."

"Still can't tell you. I'd suggest that you go out the back to the jurors' parking lot and see what's going on."

In the jury room, Judge O'Reilly had their attention. "You'll remember at the start of this trial that I told you that it was possible that you might be sequestered, checked into a hotel for the duration of the trial. Well, that time has come. I'm not sure how all of you get here each day, but I have thirteen deputy sheriffs with thirteen patrol cars out in your parking lot. One is assigned to follow each of you home if you are driving, or to take you to your house if you came today by some other means. The deputy will give you an hour to pack and explain things to your family. You will be driven to a hotel close to this building where you will stay for the duration of this trial. You'll have breakfast and dinner there. You will be permitted to have newspapers and magazines only after a deputy has read them. Any story about this trial will be cut from such publications. I invite you to bring any books you have from home. They will also be checked by the deputies."

Moans came from several of the jurors.

Joshua Ferrell muttered, "Shit!"

It didn't offend Ruby. "Mr. Ferrell, I know that you are taking night classes. I'll be talking to the dean of the engineering department at the University of Houston to explain your absence. Please bring all of your textbooks and I'll make arrangements for any assignments to be delivered to the hotel. Does anyone else have any significant problems?"

"Your Honor." Olga Olsen raised her hand. "I've changed to the night shift during this trial and have been working from six until midnight. This is going to put a real financial strain on me."

"I'm sorry, Ms. Olsen. This was not something that I really anticipated. There's nothing that I can do about your situation."

Her comment caused Roy Judice to ask, "Then tell us, Judge, why are we being sequestered?"

"It's not a matter that I can discuss with you at this time. It'll have to wait until after the trial."

Thirteen unhappy jurors followed Deputy Johnson out the back door of the building to their parking lot, now filled with sheriff's patrol cars. The *Chronicle* reporter had slipped out the back door and surveyed the scene before the jurors arrived. As soon as he saw the deputies, he figured out what was going on. He continued to observe as a deputy approached each of them and, one by one, they drove out of the parking lot, a sheriff's car behind them. The banner headline in the next morning's *Chronicle* read, "Brady Jurors Sequestered. One Juror Excused."

HER MOTHER SHIELDED ANNA May Marbley from phone calls, until there was one she could not refuse. In the afternoon after the *Chronicle* story broke, Anna May's mother received the call, this one from a reporter for the *Texas Tattler*, the local version of the *National Enquirer*. She listened and then handed the phone to her daughter. the *Tattler* offered ten thousand dollars if she would tell what happened. It didn't take long for the welfare mother to wrestle with her options and reach a decision. She wanted to do her civic duty. She preferred to abide by Judge O'Reilly's instructions. On the other hand, ten thousand dollars might as well have been a million. She could pay off all her bills, buy some new furniture, outfit her kids and still have a couple of thousand left over. When the reporter offered to leave her name out of it and keep it strictly confidential, she told him to be at her house in an hour with a cashier's check.

He arrived as requested, cashier's check in hand. The special edition of the *Texas Tattler* hit the newsstands and supermarkets the following day with its own banner headline, "Juror Threatened. Her Kids Are in Danger."

Deputy Johnson brought a copy of the paper to Judge O'Reilly in her office who frowned as she read article. There was nothing that she could do about it. The story would be in all of the media by nightfall. All she could do was mentally pat herself on the back for the decision to sequester the jury. She would have the bailiffs double their efforts to guard the jury from seeing or hearing anything from the media about the trial.

69

On the evening after Johnny Bob had completed his questioning of T.J., a serious strategy session took place at the fire station. Tod joined Jan, Wayne, and Marilyn in the war room. "Okay, we've got a decision to make. Do we cross-examine T.J. now, or do we save it for when we put on our case? He made a pretty damn good witness, but he might have taken it a little far with all that stuff about 'his Father'."

"Heck, Tod," Wayne replied, "I was kinda interested in finding out what God looked like. Maybe you ought to cross him now on what the devil looks like. Does he really have horns and a tail?"

"Naw," Jan countered. "T.J. would just say that he was always in Heaven and never made it downstairs."

"Well, I'm still disappointed that you didn't ask T.J. what the devil looked like. Heck, for all we know, he might have said, 'Well, to start, she's got long blond hair and a thirty-eight, twenty-four, thirty-six figure."

The group laughed. Jan replied, "You know, I've heard that feminist joke about God being a woman. You're the first one that I've ever heard say that the devil might be a woman."

"Hey, Jan," Wayne added. "Who was it that gave ol' Adam the apple? I submit that's conclusive proof that the devil must be a woman."

Tod cut off the discussion. "Okay, you two. That's an interesting debate. If you haven't noticed, our case has a different one. Let's save the gender of the devil for another day. This is an important decision."

"I know it is, Tod," Jan responded. "You're usually not so uptight. My vote is leave him alone for now. Let's see how the trial goes, particularly Johnny Bob's other experts and try to load up some ammunition for some really good cross toward the end of the case. I've got him pegged as one of those witnesses that starts off well, but the longer he spends on the stand, the less he'll be believed. I think at the end of the trial the jury will see him for the used car salesman he really is."

"Wayne?"

"I agree with Jan. Remember, the jury will have heard from our experts by the time you call him back."

"Marilyn?"

"Make it unanimous, Tod," she replied. "Besides, I'd kinda like to watch him sweat for the next couple of weeks, knowing that you're gonna put him back on the stand."

70

Dr. Moyo and Marian usually arrived at the side entrance to the law school around eight-thirty. Their arrival attracted little attention, but not on this morning. At eight o'clock a small band of pro-life protestors were present, awaiting Dr. Moyo's arrival. They were only six in number and were led by a man in his mid-forties, dressed in the jeans and shirt of a laborer, carrying a rosary in his hands. By eight-fifteen, one of the Court TV photographers walked by and reported the scene to Victoria Burton. Five minutes later, she was interviewing the leader, who nervously fingered his rosary as he talked into the camera. Behind him stood the others in the small group, some with their own rosaries, some carrying gold-covered Bibles, and one with a sign asking God to TAKE THE SOULS OF THE UNBORN INTO HIS HANDS.

"I'm here with George Blanchard at the side entrance to

the law school courtroom. Mr. Blanchard, what is your organization and can I ask why you are not out in front with the other demonstrators?"

"Our small band is called the 'Helpers of God's Children.' Normally we maintain a vigil at abortion clinics—at the death scenes, if you will. We cannot prevent the children from dying. At least when they die, we will be there for them and pray to God for them. For all we know, it may be the only human love they will have on this earth. We want to be there when God's children are put to death. We are also there to let the abortionist and his helpers know that society refuses to recognize or accept abortion. We hope that our presence will give them reason to repent."

Victoria Burton faced the camera. "I can understand such a mission at the abortion clinics. What do you hope to achieve here at the side entrance to the law school?"

"We know that Dr. Moyo arrives here at about eight-thirty every morning. He needs to know we are here and feel our presence throughout the day. If you'll excuse me, I see him coming across the street now."

The camera panned to show Dr. Moyo and Marian crossing at the corner and followed them as they made their way to the entrance. As they approached, the group lowered their heads in prayer. "Hail Mary, full of grace. The Lord is with thee. Blessed art thou amongst women, and blessed is the fruit of thy womb, Jesus. Holy Mary, Mother of God, pray for us sinners, now and at the hour of our death."

The voices were low, but the words distinct. Dr. Moyo frowned as he grabbed his wife's elbow to hurry her by them and into the building. The small group continued to repeat the prayer until the camera quit rolling. As they walked through the halls to the elevator, Marian was visibly shaken. Zeke tried to calm her.

"Those people were regularly outside the clinic. All of us who worked there frequently had to pass by them. We learned to ignore their presence and their prayers."

Her husband's words did nothing to soothe Marian. Zeke

decided that he might have to leave her at home for a couple of days, maybe for the remainder of the trial.

When the judge had taken her place at the bench, Tod announced that he would save his examination of Reverend Luther until he put his witnesses on the stand. That brought questioning looks from both Johnny Bob and Claudia, but they were ready with their next witness.

"Your Honor, before you bring the jury in, I have a matter to discuss with the court and counsel. Mr. Duncan has elected to start the presentation of his plaintiff case against our clients with the testimony from Dr. Moyo. Before I go forward with any more evidence on behalf of Ms. Brady, I'd like to present some witnesses in defense of the charges of Dr. Moyo and Population Planning."

"I agree, Mr. Tisdale, only I remind you that you shouldn't even think about calling that long list of experts. That's not going to happen. Mr. Johnson, bring in the jurors."

As the jurors took their seats, Johnny Bob announced, "Your Honor, we call Dr. Larson Kriegel in defense of the claims of slander made by Dr. Moyo and Population Planning."

As he made the announcement, the doors at the top of the auditorium opened. Dr. Kriegel entered and made his way down the steps to the courtroom. Dr. Kriegel was a tall man in his late sixties. Mostly bald, he had a fringe of white hair and stooped shoulders that probably came from spending much of his life bent over a microscope. He wore a blue checkered sport coat, gray slacks and a red bow tie. Smiling at the judge and jury, he stopped in front of the bench and raised his right hand. It was apparent that this was not his first courtroom appearance. After being sworn, he did not wait to be directed, but moved to the witness stand, where he took a seat, smiled a good morning to the jury, leaned back and waited for Johnny Bob to begin the proceeding.

"Good morning, Dr. Kriegel. I must say that I admire your taste in ties. Do you tie those things yourself?"

The jury grinned at the compliment about the red tie. Olga

Olsen also grinned when she saw that Johnny Bob had a red handkerchief in his coat pocket. She won the pot for the day.

"Mr. Tisdale, tying a bow tie is a simple matter. If you can tie your shoelaces, you can tie this. And, to answer your question, yes, I do tie all my bow ties myself."

Tod could see that this was going to be a long morning. It was bad enough that this guy had world-class credentials. Now he had the jury in the palm of his hand. Tod thought to himself, *Judge, could we take an early lunch break, like nine-thirty in the morning?*

"I called you 'doctor' because I know a little more about you than the rest of these folks in the courtroom. Would you be so kind as to tell the jury about your professional background and credentials?" Johnny Bob's demeanor was calculated to let the jury know that this was a man who was respected as one of the foremost authorities in his field. Dr. Kriegel smiled as he leaned forward and placed his hands on the witness stand in front of him, almost like he was going to peer at an imaginary microscope.

"Ladies and gentlemen, I'll be brief. I got my doctorate in microbiology at the University of Michigan and my medical degree at Harvard. After that I did a residency in pediatrics at Johns Hopkins. I stayed to teach pediatrics to the residents at Johns Hopkins for a number of years before I elected to devote all of my time to the study of genetics. At that time I returned to Boston. I am currently on a leave of absence from Harvard because I am working with a group that is devoting its entire energies to the human genome project. To sum it up, I have been researching and writing in the field of human genetics for more than thirty years."

With Dr. Kriegel's pause, Johnny Bob jumped in, "Doctor, have you received any prizes or awards in the field of genetics?"

"Nothing worth talking about. I suppose you are wanting me to say that I have been nominated for the Nobel Prize for my work on the genome project. I did figure out a way to shorten the time to complete the project by a year or two, and that seems to be important to some people."

Satisfied that he had sufficiently established his expert's credentials, Johnny Bob moved on. "Dr. Kriegel, in your studies, experiments and so forth, and based on a reasonable degree of scientific certainty, have you formulated an opinion as to when human life begins?"

"I have. It's really not one of the more difficult things that I've done in my career. Matter of fact, I can't really take credit for making any discovery on the question. If you have the right kind of microscope these days, it doesn't even take a scientist, just good eyes and a little common sense."

Johnny Bob looked at the jury. At no time during the trial had he found them paying more attention. He wanted to seize the moment. "Please, Doctor, tell us your scientific opinion as to when life for us humans begins and explain how you arrived at that opinion."

"To make it very simple, ladies and gentlemen, life begins at conception. It may be a mouse life, a dog life, a chimpanzee life, or a human life. Whatever the life form, a new life begins when the sperm fertilizes an egg. In the natural process, the egg and the sperm meet in the mother's fallopian tube. It's a little tube of flesh. Once we began to be able to reproduce the process outside the womb, to create test tube babies, the difference was that the sperm and egg met in a glass tube instead of a tube of flesh.

"More importantly, we could then study the development under the microscope. We scientists call the fertilized egg, that very first new life cell, a zygote. The zygote splits into two cells, and that is the first time that we call it an embryo. Over the next several weeks of life, we use various names and then the new human being attains the status of a fetus. I should hasten to add that those various names are really just names science has given to the various early stages of human development."

"Now, wait just a minute, Doctor," Johnny Bob interrupted. "Are you saying that first little old cell is a human being?"

"Exactly, Mr. Tisdale. Let me explain further." The old professor turned to the jury as if he were lecturing a group of biology students. "I should probably explain that scientists have debated the beginning of life for hundreds, if not thousands, of years. Before the advances of modern science, while we might have suspected that human life began earlier, we were pretty much stuck with the proposition that from a scientific standpoint, life began at quickening. That term has been used to mean different things to different people over the years, For my purposes today, consider it the time when the mother first feels the movement of the baby, somewhere between sixteen and twenty-two weeks. For thousands of years, we could safely say that there was a human being inside the womb if the mother could feel it kicking."

"Hold on there, Doctor," Johnny Bob interrupted again. "That woman had to know that she was pregnant before sixteen weeks. If I may be so blunt, she had to have missed three or four periods by then. It sure didn't take a scientist to figure out that she was expecting a baby."

Dr. Kriegel smiled and continued. "Why, of course, Mr. Tisdale, you're exactly correct. However, even early scientists required some scientific proof that there was a human life form in there and not just a blob of tissue. It was for that reason that they chose to wait until quickening to say that there was a human being inside the womb. In just my lifetime, science has now advanced to eliminate any doubt that there is a human life long before the mother feels it kick and, in fact, from the moment of conception. First came the use of ultrasound. Then, in the early eighties a highly advanced microscope that produces fiber-optic images of the fetus inside the womb was developed. Next came the study of DNA. That, by the way, is where I come in. The more we learned about DNA, the more we confirmed what I am telling you."

Dr. Kriegel paused for a sip of water and continued. "If we combine a human sperm with a human egg, we know that a human cell and not a monkey cell is formed. In the DNA from the sperm there are twenty-three parts of the program we call chromosomes. Likewise, in the ovum there are also twenty-three chromosomes. When they meet, all the information necessary to create the new human being is contained in that one cell formed by the uniting of the sperm and the egg. That one cell, that zygote, contains all of the information for a new life, different from any other life that has ever existed before and different from any that will ever occur again. As I said, the zygote soon splits into two cells, then four, then eight and so forth. But that very first cell knew more than the second, and the next two knew more than the next four. The zygote contains all of the information needed to create life. All of this information contained in the DNA molecules from the sperm and the egg are gathered in the new cell that now contains all of the future characteristics of the new human being."

Johnny Bob paused and looked at the jurors to see if all this was sinking in. He saw some understanding from a few and puzzled looks from others. "Doctor, can you give us a little explanation of this DNA stuff? Most of us have read about or seen it talked about on TV. It's not real clear to a lot of us what you scientists are talking about."

"Mr. Tisdale, think of it as similar to a bar code that you see these days on all of the items that you buy at the grocery store. The DNA is the individual's bar code. With our modern science we can look at DNA, whether it's from that very first cell or from some other cell, from, say, an adult, and identify it as coming from one specific individual. Now, don't get confused because the sperm and the egg each have twenty-three chromosomes. The sperm and the egg contain the only cells with that number of chromosomes. All of the other human cells contain forty-six chromosomes. So, when the sperm and the egg meet, fertilization occurs and a new life is formed.

"With that very first cell, there's a new bar code that never existed before, containing forty-six chromosomes, twenty-three from the father and twenty-three from the mother. The DNA in the zygote will be exactly the same DNA as that human being will have as an adult. Not one chromosome different. From the DNA in that tiny cell comes the information that will determine whether the baby is a boy or a girl, has blond hair or brown, has a big nose or small, blue eyes or green, is tall or short. Some things are obviously affected by the environment in which the baby and, later, the child is raised. But the information for the new human being is all there in that cell. It is for that reason that I can say with absolutely no reservation that life begins at conception."

Johnny Bob paused for effect. "Dr. Kriegel, just how certain are you of the opinions that you have just offered?"

"Let me stress that these are hardly opinions. They are scientific fact. As to how certain, Mr. Tisdale, just as I am certain that I came from my mother's womb, am I certain that at the moment of conception, a man or woman is a human being."

Johnny Bob looked at Claudia who nodded her head, confirming that he had accomplished what he had planned with this witness. "Pass the witness, Your Honor."

Tod didn't even wait for the judge to acknowledge it was his turn. As Tod rose from his chair, Wayne reached into his briefcase and took out a small white bowl and placed it on the front of their counsel table. Johnny Bob, Claudia and several jurors noticed what Wayne was doing, but could only wonder what Tod would do next. Having studied Dr. Kriegel, Tod anticipated the strength of his testimony. He had to do something to grab the attention of the jury. As he moved around the counsel table and stood between it and the witness, he removed an object from his coat pocket. It was soon apparent to the judge, the jury, the attorneys and everyone watching on television that he had an egg in his hand. Without saying a word, he held the egg between his thumb and forefinger, then closed his palm around it and squeezed. As the egg shattered and dripped from his hand into the bowl, he asked, "Tell me, Dr. Kriegel, have I just crushed an egg? Or, have I killed a chicken?"

The witness was clearly caught off guard. As Dr. Kriegel pondered the question, Tod took a small towel from Wayne, wiped his hand and prodded the witness. "Come on, Doctor. That shouldn't be a difficult question for a man of your learning and expertise. Let's start off with the basics. If I tell you that the egg came from a chicken, would you agree that it's a chicken egg and not from a duck or an alligator?"

Dr. Kriegel furrowed his brow so that his bushy white eyebrows almost touched before agreeing. "I accept your word on that, Mr. Duncan. That being the case, then I would agree that it is a chicken egg."

The jurors looked back at Tod, who had their complete attention, and waited for his next question. Every seasoned trial lawyer has seen it occur. The jurors get so wrapped up in the repartee between a lawyer and a witness that they appear to be watching a tennis match. Their heads turned to the lawyer for the question and, as soon as the question was out of his mouth, all heads turned to the witness for the answer. Then back to the lawyer again. Tod realized with his grandstand play, he was in one of those moments and wanted to capitalize on it. "Now, Doctor, that chicken egg has all that is necessary to grow into a full-sized hen or rooster. All it needs is a few weeks of warmth in the hen's nest to hatch and then a little time to grow."

Dr. Kriegel recovered, almost as if a lightbulb had gone on above his head, to say, "Whether it is going be a hen or a rooster, or merely an egg, Mr. Duncan, will depend on whether it is a fertilized or unfertilized egg."

Nods from Bert Marino and Amy Bourland, both on the front row of the jury box, indicated that they thought he had come up with a good answer.

"Well, let's assume that it's fertilized, Dr. Kriegel. Did I just kill a chicken?"

Looking slightly chagrined, he could not take a contrary position and maintain his credibility. Dr. Kriegel replied, "In my opinion as a scientist, Mr. Duncan, I would have to say that you just killed a chicken."

That answer brought a frown to the face of Glenn Ford, the Rice economics professor, who seemingly found such an opinion difficult to accept.

Tod had the expert just where he wanted him. "Then,

Doctor, in your opinion, even though this egg has no wings, no feathers, no feet, no beak, not even lungs or a beating heart, I just killed a chicken."

Dr. Kriegel shifted uneasily in his seat. He folded, almost clinched, his hands on the stand before him, and said with a voice that had lost some of its composure, "Yes. Yes, sir. That is my position."

Tod returned to his seat and moved on. Johnny Bob and Claudia had no idea where Tod would go next. "Dr. Kriegel, you know something about in vitro fertilization, don't you?"

"Yes, sir. Some of my former colleagues have done research in that area, and I lent them a hand from time to time."

"Without going into too much detail, would I be generally correct, Doctor, to say that a woman's eggs are retrieved from her ovaries and then fertilization with sperm is attempted outside the womb? If successful, you have created an embryo in the test tube that is then placed in the woman's uterus. If the embryo attaches itself to the lining of the uterus, then the woman can become pregnant."

Dr. Kriegel was eager to jump back into the scientific arena. His voice rose to its former level. "Well, it's a little more complicated than that. For these purposes, that's a reasonable explanation."

Tod was ready to lay his next trap not just for this witness but also for one he expected to see later. "Doctor, let's say that the woman's obstetrician harvested six eggs and they all were fertilized successfully. The couple got lucky and became pregnant with the very first attempt. What happens to those other embryos?"

"Something remarkable can happen, Mr. Duncan. We have known for many years that we can freeze sperm or embryos from animals and carefully thaw them, often successfully achieving pregnancy. With a similar process, we can now do the same with a human embryo. We use nitrogen and take the embryo down to minus one hundred and ninety degrees centigrade. It is not exactly freezing the embryo, although it's often called that. We are essentially stopping the movements of the atoms and molecules in the embryo. We have pretty much stopped time, as far as the embryo is concerned. Later, maybe even a year or two later, if the parents wish to have another baby, we can carefully thaw the embryo and it will begin to flourish and divide once more. We can then use that very embryo to help the couple have another child."

Dr. Kriegel looked quite satisfied as he finished his answer and smiled at the jury.

Tod asked his next question. "All right, Doctor, if, as you say, that embryo is a human being, and can be frozen and thawed out without any damage, then I suppose that would hold true for all human beings. That means we could take my associate, Wayne, here, bring a big old nitrogen can into the courtroom, put him in it, and take him down to minus one hundred and ninety degrees centigrade. I could just leave him there and wake him up in a few months or a few years, whenever I needed his help in another trial. Save me having to pay his salary in between trials, and I wouldn't even have to buy him lunch."

Most of the jurors looked at Wayne, trying to imagine him inside a big can for years and then popping out, ready to go to work. Johnny Bob didn't like where all of this was going and rose, hoping to break Tod's rhythm with an objection. "Your Honor, I object. As near as I can tell, Tod just made a cute little speech, but didn't ask a question."

Judge O'Reilly ruled. "Mr. Tisdale, there may have been a question in there somewhere. I'm not sure. Mr. Duncan, please try to save your speeches for closing argument and just ask questions. Sustained."

"Dr. Kriegel," Tod continued, "I think you understand my point, but let's leave Wayne out of it. Since you have said that a two- or four-cell embryo is a human being and can be frozen, then I assume you have scientific evidence that we can now freeze adult humans and just wake them up whenever we want to, something like what happened to Reverend Luther here. Just take them to a lab, freeze them down and wake them up in twelve years?"

Dr. Kriegel glanced at Johnny Bob, hoping for some help, but Johnny Bob was studying the jury. "Mr. Duncan, while some science fiction writers have proposed what you suggest, at this time, science is not capable of freezing an adult human being and bringing him or her back to life at a later date."

"How about a child? Can you guys freeze a child without killing him?"

"That's never been attempted to my knowledge, Mr. Duncan."

"Maybe a newborn baby, Doctor?"

"No, sir."

"Well, then, how about a fetus, maybe a premature baby, born at twelve weeks, the same age of the fetus when Ms. Brady had her abortion? Why don't we just have a nitrogen can standing by in the delivery room and pop that premature baby that cannot possibly live into the can? Maybe modern science will find a way to save that preemie's life in a few years."

"Mr. Duncan, the only way that we have successfully used this process is with embryos."

Knowing that he had the attention of the jurors and everyone in the courtroom, Tod asked the question that the whole exchange had been leading toward. "Then, Dr. Kriegel, won't you concede that there must be some difference between those frozen embryos and a human being?"

"Mr. Duncan, I'll concede that they are different in that we can freeze embryos without destroying them and we can't do that with a human being at a later stage in life."

Tod had the witness going where he wanted and moved in for his final question. "Maybe, then, Doctor, while that embryo is a life form and has the potential to be a human being, isn't it possible that it might be a day, or a week, or a month, or nine months away from becoming a human being?"

While Dr. Kriegel had testified on several occasions, it was apparent that he had never been confronted with such a line of questions and was not quite sure where to go with it. He searched for an answer and finally his scientific mind gave in. "I suppose, Mr. Duncan, there might be some reputable scientists who might look at data such as you have described and offer opinions that the embryo life form is not yet a human being."

Tod pretended to look through the notes on his desk to give the jury time to ponder what he had just drawn out of the noted scientist. He would never get the witness to change his own opinion that life began at conception, but for Dr. Kriegel to concede that it might be debated in the scientific community was a major blow to Johnny Bob's case. Hopefully, if some of the jurors understood that if it was not an absolute that human life began at conception, then the debate could stretch all the way to the moment of viability, if not birth. Dr. Kriegel looked at Tod as the lawyer rummaged through his notes. The witness wondered what was next. He didn't really expect to be testifying about chickens and freezing adults when he told Claudia that he would help them prove that life began at conception. Finally, Tod concluded that he had done the best he could with a very formidable expert.

"Nothing further, Your Honor."

As the judge called for a lunch break, T.J. was holding forth in the court of public opinion. Ignoring the recommendation of his lawyer to save comments until the end of the day and knowing that most of what went on in the courtroom was out of his hands, he offered his opinions about the proceedings to Victoria Burton and a larger audience. "It's a sad day for our country when our judicial system has reached the basement where such an internationally acclaimed scientist cannot be permitted to offer absolute scientific proof without having his science challenged. It is indeed a sad commentary on those who ignore the fundamental teachings of the Bible. They want to rely on what they call science to refute God's creation yet challenge the overwhelming scientific evidence offered by Dr. Kriegel as to the beginning of life. If anything, the further modern science advances in this area, the more it supports what those of us in the religious community have known for hundreds, if not thousands of years.

I'm certain that the jury saw right through the desperation
tactics of Dr. Moyo's lawyer. We shall continue to carry the
day in the courtroom and in the nation."

It was Claudia's turn after lunch. Johnny Bob had Sebastian Thorpe scheduled to fly in that night to take the witness
stand the next morning. He and Claudia had to fill the afternoon. To do so, they called Nurses Simms and Sylvester, the
two women who took Lucy's phone calls on the weekend after her abortion. While Claudia may not have had the courtroom experience of a J. Robert Tisdale, she could not have
done a better job. Both nurses were nervous as they took the
stand and neither withstood the frontal attack of Claudia St.
John Jackson. Her manner was one of disgust at the treatment
that their client had received at the hands of the clinic and
these two nurses. How could they possibly ignore the cries for
help coming from this innocent young lady? She had begged
not once but twice for help and her pleas were ignored. Claudia was particularly critical of Nurse Simms who took the
Sunday morning call. Using the clinic's own policy manual,
she easily got the nurse to agree that the manual required an
examination if a patient's fever hit one hundred and one degrees. Nurse Simms tried to offer an explanation that Lucy's
description of her condition on that Sunday morning didn't
sound that severe. Because she could only get to the clinic by
bus, she had decided that it would be better for Lucy to sleep
and call back if she had further complications. But she also
had to concede that the policy manual required her to at least
consult with the on-call physician under such circumstances.
By the time Claudia finished, it almost seemed unnecessary to
call a nurse expert to challenge their decisions.

When it was her turn, Jan took each of the witnesses
through their background and experience. The nurses had
practiced for more than twenty years. Each one had worked
in medical center hospitals. Nurse Simms had worked in the
surgical ICU for five years and could recognize the complications of surgery. Responding to Jan's questions, they explained how they had to make judgment calls, based on what
they were told. The question in Jan's mind was whether their

testimony, along with that of the clinic's experts, would be enough to overcome a jury's natural instincts to conclude that, with such a terrible result, someone must have done something horribly wrong. At last she closed the trial day, leaving the jury with the impression that the two nurses were competent.

When the jury was gone, Tod motioned to the group. "Come on team. Let's walk over to the Four Seasons and discuss where we are now, without the benefit of the TV cameras. We need to be strategizing about the next few days. You, too, Dr. and Mrs. Moyo."

As Tod and his group were settling down in the Four Seasons bar, Johnny Bob, Claudia and their clients were assembling in Johnny Bob's loft. As they found seats in the living room, Claudia started mixing drinks. A scotch for Johnny Bob, bourbon for Jessie, a Lone Star for Bo, and a soda for Lucy. "Reverend, what can I interest you in?" Claudia asked.

T.J. grinned. "Well, since I'm around lawyers and not preachers, we'll leave the sacramental wine alone. I'll join Jessie in a little bourbon and branch."

Jessie turned the conversation to the trial. "Okay, you two lawyers, the cameras aren't rolling and the door is closed. So give us a candid evaluation."

"Probably the single most fascinating trial that I've been involved in during my entire career, Jessie," replied Johnny Bob. "I never knew that there could be so many facets to this 'when life begins' issue. The cross-exam that Tod did today about in vitro fertilization, frankly, caught me a little off guard. I'm going to have to get Claudia on the Internet and bone up on it. We've got Dr. Thorpe flying in tonight. Matter of fact, he ought to be here in the next hour. I don't know how Tod can cross a theologian-philosopher on that issue. We better be prepared for some questions coming out of left field."

Jessie brought them back to her question. "I want to know what our chances are at this point. We're all going through emotional hell, particularly Lucy. Is it going to be worth it?"

"I can answer that, Jessie," T.J. declared. "I have it from a very good authority that we are winning and at the end of the day, we will win decisively."

Johnny Bob shook his head at T.J. and took a sip of his scotch before responding, "Jessie, my sources are obviously not as well placed as those of Reverend Luther. I would say that we're about where I expected. We're very strong on the malpractice case at this point. Dr. Moyo is a nice man and did okay, but the jury should know he screwed up. As to the clinic, Claudia pretty well put the britches on those two nurses, particularly the second one. As to our defense of the slander claims, that's a little closer call. Dr. Kriegel is one of the best in the world, but Tod landed a couple of good shots. They weren't knockout punches by any means."

"Did Mr. Duncan's cross-examination surprise you, Johnny Bob?" Jessie asked.

"Not really, Jessie. What you have to understand is that in a trial, the home-court advantage rests with the lawyers, all of them. It's our game and a good lawyer is always going to score some points with any witness. It's the nature of the system. Now, I can encourage you all to drink up. Claudia and I need to get ready for Dr. Thorpe."

71

Sebastian Thorpe, Ph.D., J.D., sat in the witness chair with a thud and a grunt. Only five feet, nine inches tall, his bulk overwhelmed that of J. Robert Tisdale. He had long since quit weighing himself since scales rarely went above three hundred pounds. At a recent carnival, the man who guessed a person's weight in return for a stuffed toy said that he was about three hundred fifteen. His clothes were made for a much smaller man, say one around two hundred and fifty pounds. He couldn't button his coat or the top button on his shirt collar. He was content, instead, to just let his tie hang loosely about two inches below his neck. His one hint at vanity was the way he combed his hair from one side, with the part starting just above the ear so that his bald head was covered with a few strands of brown hair. Fortunately, within less than a minute after he began speaking, most people forgot his appearance and instead became entranced by his words and personality. His voice was deep, like thunder rolling out of a West Texas storm. His smile was infectious, and his blue eyes rivaled those of Paul Newman. He first studied to become a Catholic priest. That was followed by a doctorate in philosophy and a law degree. Now, he was a professor at St. Edwards University in Austin and carried a national reputation in his field, most notably as his various disciplines converged in the area of abortion. Much in demand on the pro-life lecture circuit, he traveled and lectured throughout the United States and several foreign countries. He was willing to go anywhere, anytime to debate the right to life.

Johnny Bob escorted the witness through his background. Thorpe kidded, as he patted his belly, that his most obvious credential was a love of Italian cooking. The jurors smiled. Olga Olsen decided that after the trial she would encourage him to drop by her diner the next time he was in town.

Johnny Bob turned to the matters at hand. "Dr. Thorpe, what can a philosopher and theologian like yourself offer on the question of when life begins? Isn't that just a matter of scientific fact? While you've got a lot of years of education and experience, you really can't say when life begins. Right?"

"Well, Mr. Tisdale, I hope that I can shed some light on the subject. Otherwise, you are wasting the time of the jury and the judge by putting me on this hot seat." He swiveled to face the jury. "While I don't want to tread on the toes of the lawyers, I don't think I will by pointing out that even the United States Supreme Court has recognized the extent of the debate about when life begins. In *Roe v. Wade,* an opinion with which I strongly disagree, the court rightly points out that the debate is one of medicine, philosophy and theology. I might add that they left out science. I suppose that can be encompassed in their use of the word medicine. Science and medicine have certainly aided us in deciding when life begins, particularly in the past two or three generations. But we philosophers and theologians have always been involved in the debate, and what we have to say is of equal importance."

Tod considered an objection to a dissertation on theology, then rejected it in light of the Supreme Court opening that door.

Dr. Thorpe continued to focus on the jury. "We have to start with the premise that there is a God. If any of you don't believe in God, then ignore what I am going to say and just start thinking about what you're going to have for dinner or where you're going to go fishing when this trial is over."

Most of the jurors, even Glenn Ford, nodded their heads, acknowledging that they, indeed, had such a belief.

"Once we concede that there is a God, the next step in our logical analysis is that God has something to do with human life, that he puts us here and he takes us away when our time has come. The question that has been debated for thousands of years is when does he make us a human person. The word 'ensoulment' lurks in the background of all of these discussions. Let me try to give you a shorthand definition of ensoulment. It is that point in life when God infuses the human life form with a soul. It is at that time when the human being becomes a human person. Socrates concluded that the soul exists before it is infused into the body, that the soul is the actual human person. In fact, he called the soul a prisoner of the human body.

"Plato and Aristotle debated the issue twenty-five hundred years ago. It's always remarkable to read their writings about so many subjects and to think that these brilliant men lived so long ago. I'm sure you've also heard something about Hippocrates and what he had to say about some of these issues."

Johnny Bob saw his witness start to stray from the subject matter and he could see the morning being spent in 500 B.C. "Excuse me, Dr. Thorpe, but just how does that all tie into the issue about the beginning of life?"

"My apologies, Mr. Tisdale, sometimes my mind drifts

back to Aristotle and it's hours before I'm back to the twentieth century. Usually, it's a rumbling in my stomach that brings me back. Where was I? Oh yes, I remember. Aristotle actually studied fetuses and came to the conclusion that at first there was a vegetative state, then animal state and finally a human being. His study of embryos led him to the conclusion that what was in the womb became a human being around the fortieth day after conception and that abortion was acceptable up to that time. In our church, St. Thomas Aquinas, one of our great thinkers in the thirteenth century, adopted the teachings of Aristotle and concluded that God infuses the fetus with a soul around the fortieth day. There were other philosophers who decided that there could not be human life without rational behavior. Their opinion was that such behavior occurred with viability, or when the mother could feel the baby move."

"Wait just a minute, Doctor," Johnny Bob interrupted, an intentionally puzzled look on his face. "Are you saying that abortion is okay up to eighteen or twenty weeks?"

"Just hold your horses, Mr. Tisdale. I'm not through yet. These folks need to have a little background on this debate so they can understand why we teachers and preachers have a different idea now. Remember that those folks hundreds of years ago didn't have the benefit of our current science. They couldn't look inside the womb. Anyway, for a while there, Christian theology and canon law fixed the point of animation at forty days for a male and eighty days for a female."

"Did that end the debate in your church, Doctor?"

"Not quite, counselor. By the nineteenth century, our church finally got it right. We Catholics concluded that life had to begin at conception and God must infuse the embryo with a soul at the moment of conception."

Johnny Bob leaned back and scratched his chin as he commented more than questioned. "Took you folks a long time to figure that out, Doctor."

"I'm afraid it did, Mr. Tisdale. We Catholics may move slowly, but we eventually get it right."

Johnny Bob wanted to wind up this witness with a blue ribbon tied around his testimony. "Now, Dr. Thorpe, I know that you're not a scientist, but you mentioned our modern technology. Does that support or contradict your position and that of other learned philosophers and theologians?"

That question got Tod on his feet. "Your Honor, I don't mind Dr. Thorpe offering his own opinions, but I don't think that he can testify for all of the other preachers and teachers in the world."

"Sustained, Mr. Duncan. I suspect that Mr. Tisdale can clear it up."

Instead Dr. Thorpe interrupted, "I think that I can, Your Honor. Clearly, every philosopher and theologian in the world does not share my opinion, and I didn't mean to imply that. It certainly is an opinion that is held by the vast majority of learned men who have studied the subject. As to science, Mr. Tisdale, scientists have now confirmed what we theologians already knew. With the aid of modern imaging that allows us to look into the womb and the studies of fine geneticists like Larson Kriegel, science now fully supports the beliefs that I have just described. Science has proved that there is life at conception and we are now certain that with that life at conception, God has infused that first cell with a soul. It is no longer a matter of debate."

As he finished, he turned to smile at the jury. Six jurors nodded and smiled back at him.

"Pass the witness, Your Honor."

Judge O'Reilly turned to the jury. "Let's take fifteen minutes." As the jury filed out, most of the audience went out into the hallways to find water and restrooms. The lawyers talked among themselves. Johnny Bob encouraged Sebastian Thorpe to stretch his legs and cautioned him to be on his toes when Tod Duncan started his cross-examination. T.J. took the opportunity to shake the hand of the witness, commenting that he couldn't have said it better himself and offered the opportunity to join him at the pulpit during *The Miracle Morning Hour* some Sunday after the trial was over. Wayne left Tod alone to, once more, organize his thoughts before he started cross-examination. Wayne was talking to Jan when he noticed Mr. Buschbahm still seated at the top of the auditorium. Wayne ran up the steps and took an empty seat beside the old man.

"So, Mr. Buschbahm, why aren't you out stretching your legs with the rest? I know you've got a reserved seat."

"Ah, Wayne, my bladder tells me that I should join the others, but my legs vote the other way. As long as I can calm my bladder, I'll just sit here and obey what my old legs are telling me. How did you know I've got a reserved seat? That's supposed to be a little secret between me and Judge O'Reilly."

"It's my supreme power of deduction, Mr. Buschbahm. You're in the same seat every day. And no matter how many others are in the auditorium, your seat is always empty until you get here."

"Very good, Sherlock Holmes. If you don't mind, let me give you a question to pass on to Tod. I find all of this quite interesting, and Dr. Thorpe is a charming man. Tell Tod to ask him what happens to the soul when one of these embryos is frozen for several years."

"Good idea, Mr. Buschbahm. Matter of fact that's a very good idea. Thanks."

Wayne left the old man and walked back down the stairs and sat down beside Tod where Mr. Buschbahm could see him whispering in Tod's ear. Tod nodded, turned to look at Mr. Buschbahm and gave him a thumb's up sign. -

Judge O'Reilly had remained at her bench during the break, visiting with Dr. Thorpe and the attorneys. She took note of the silent communication between Mr. Buschbahm and Tod, wondering what tidbit he had relayed, figuring that she'd learn of it sooner or later. She turned to Johnny Bob and asked, "Well, Mr. Tisdale, we're into our second week. When do you expect to wind up your case?"

Johnny Bob stopped what he was doing and thought a minute. "Judge, after Dr. Thorpe, my main witnesses will be Dr. Ables, our nurse expert, and Dr. Coates. I may read from a couple of depositions. If I do, it'll be brief. Figure another two, two and a half days."

"What about you, Mr. Duncan? Ready to give me any estimates?"

"Judge, between my witnesses and Jan's, we're probably looking at about a week."

"Excellent. We're right on schedule. By the way, I commend you all for moving this case along and managing to ignore the cameras and the media when you're in here. Bailiff, let's get the jury back and get started."

After the jury was seated, the judge said, "Mr. Duncan, you may proceed with cross-examination."

"Thank you, Your Honor," Tod replied. "May I approach the witness?"

"You may."

"Dr. Thorpe, as I understand your testimony, you don't accept the proposition that the human person doesn't really exist until late in the pregnancy."

"Correct."

"Because that very first cell has all of the necessary ingredients to form human life and therefore it must be a human person."

Dr. Thorpe smiled to the jury. "He has it exactly right. It's because all of the ingredients are there that God has chosen to infuse that cell with a soul. You're a very fine student, Mr. Duncan."

Tod walked around the counsel table, walked up to Dr. Thorpe, reached in his pocket and pulled out another object. Although he had no idea what was coming, Johnny Bob remembered the egg and groaned under his breath. Claudia looked on with fascination, having to remind herself that this lawyer was on the other side.

Tod had a very small object, much smaller than an egg. He placed it on the stand in front of the witness and as he turned to walk back to his seat, he asked, "Dr. Thorpe, can you identify this object?"

Puzzled, he answered, "Sir, that appears to be an acorn."

Tod whirled around, and still standing a few feet from the witness, challenged him. "Doctor, why would you call that an acorn? If your reasoning is correct, shouldn't you call that an oak tree? After all, it has all of the ingredients of an oak tree inside it, does it not?"

The priest silently cursed himself for falling into this trap. He should have seen it coming. All he could say was, "Yes, sir."

"Dr. Thorpe, you would agree that if we take this acorn, wait until spring, give it some good soil, some warm sunshine and water, before long, a little shoot is going to appear? If we just wait fifteen or twenty years, it'll become a mighty oak, branches strong enough to hold a child's swing, leaves to provide shade on a hot summer day, one of God's most magnificent creations, worthy of praise from philosophers and poets alike. Right?"

"That's right, Mr. Duncan."

"So, tell me, Doctor, if you theologians insist that we declare one cell in a woman's fallopian tube a human person, why haven't you gotten together and made us start calling that acorn a tree?"

"Well, sir, you would have to plant that acorn in the ground and give it the opportunity to become a tree, wouldn't you?" Dr. Thorpe recovered.

Tod looked at the jury, knowing he got just the answer he wanted. "Exactly, Dr. Thorpe, just like an embryo from a test tube, which would have to be implanted in a woman's womb before it could become a baby. Yet, you say that embryo has a soul and is already a human person, correct, sir?"

Johnny Bob rolled his eyes as his witness searched for a better answer and finally replied, "Correct, sir."

"Well, let's just think about this a minute, Doctor. When that acorn falls out of the tree, it's not alone. It's got a lot of other brother and sister acorns lying with it under that old oak tree. By the way, you'd agree with me that acorns do get ripe and fall from the tree in the autumn?"

"I agree."

Tod was convinced that he was making a significant point with Dr. Thorpe and he assumed he had the attention of everyone in the courtroom until he happened to look at the jury. They were looking past him to the opposing counsel table. Judge O'Reilly was even looking in that direction with a slight smile on her face.

Johnny Bob was using an old trick to distract the jurors from Tod's cross-examination of Dr. Thorpe. As Tod concentrated on his cross-exam, the old lawyer reached into his pants pocket and retrieved a pocket watch. He raised it up to eye level and opened the cover of the antique watch, looked at it, then brought it closer to his eyes and looked again. Next he put it to his ear, the one closest to the jury and listened. He cocked his head and cupped his other hand over the watch, pretending to listen. Bringing the watch down, he started winding the top stem of the timepiece. By then almost everyone in the courtroom was watching him and not listening to the interchange between Tod and Dr. Thorpe. After winding the watch, he listened again and was about to tap it on the table when Tod noticed the distraction.

Tod walked over to Johnny Bob, pulled his left coat sleeve up, revealing his thirty-five-dollar, black runner's watch. As he unbuckled the watch and laid it on the table, he said to Judge O'Reilly, "Your Honor, I believe that Mr. Tisdale needs a little help telling time. This one works without having to be wound."

Johnny Bob looked a little sheepish at having been caught, but thanked his opposing counsel, picked up the black watch, studied its face for a moment and then sat it back down on the table with a smile.

Once again having the jury's full attention, Tod continued. "Let's see, Doctor, before I had to help Mr. Tisdale, we were talking about acorns, I believe. After those acorns fall to the ground, among the things that can happen is that some of the acorns are going to be eaten by squirrels, right? Those squirrels aren't eating oak trees, are they?"

"No, sir."

"Some of those acorns will fall on hard ground and never have a chance to become a tree, maybe even land on a driveway or sidewalk and be crunched under the tire of a car or bicycle. They're not oak trees are they?"

"No, sir."

"Then one acorn gets lucky and lands on some soft soil and over the next six months or so it lies there until spring and a miracle occurs. All of the right conditions converge and a small shoot sprouts from the acorn. Then, if that shoot is not trampled down by an animal or a human foot, it may grow into that mighty oak that I described, right, Doctor?

"Mr. Duncan," Dr. Thorpe replied, "you must understand that I'm not an expert in oak trees. I have a hard time growing a few roses in my garden back in Austin."

Ignoring the witness's attempt at humor, Tod pressed on. "Dr. Thorpe, you would agree with me that what is before you is an acorn, or at most, it is a potential oak tree?"

"Yes, sir. I said from the start that it was an acorn."

"Now, let's leave oak trees aside and go back to embryos. Wouldn't you also agree that a pretty darn strong argument can be made that an embryo in a test tube isn't really a human person at all? It can't possibly become one until it's implanted in a woman's womb, even though, Doctor, it has its very own personalized DNA code, just like Dr. Kriegel told us earlier?"

"Sir, I suppose an argument can be made. I wouldn't agree that it's a strong one."

"And wouldn't you also agree with me that a fertilized egg in a woman's body is not really a human being? It is, at best, a potential human being?"

Dr. Thorpe paused as if troubled by the whole line of questioning, then stared at the ceiling as if seeking divine guidance from above, and finally disagreed. "No, sir. I can't agree with your analogy. Acorns and trees are not the same as embryos and human persons. Our church has been studying this question for two thousand years, and we know we're right."

Tod looked over at the jury. "Just as right, sir, as you folks were when you decided that a male reached viability at forty days and a female at eighty days?"

"Sir, our theologians at that time didn't have the benefit of today's scientific knowledge when they were making those decisions."

"By the way, Doctor, back then did you folks have any women helping you to decide these important questions?"

Dr. Thorpe stared at his feet as he said, "No, sir. Not to my knowledge."

"Earlier, Dr. Thorpe, you talked about all these learned philosophers and theologians who held the same beliefs that you do. You recall that testimony?"

"Yes, sir. I do."

"In fact, there's one religion that's even older than your Catholicism that has a completely different opinion from what you're telling the jury here today. True, Dr. Thorpe?"

The witness nervously fiddled with his tie. "Sir, I'm not sure where you're going with your question."

"Come on, Dr. Thorpe, you know the Jewish position on the beginning of human life, don't you?"

"Well, yes, sir. Now that you remind me, I do."

"Turn to the jury and tell them, then, Dr. Thorpe."

The witness swiveled in his chair to face the jury and in a quiet voice said, "The Jewish religion has always believed that life begins at birth."

"The fact of the matter, Doctor, is that they've even had smart folks studying this question even longer than you Catholics."

"There's no doubt, Mr. Duncan, that the Jewish religion is older than the Catholic Church."

Tod looked satisfied as he continued. "Okay, Dr. Thorpe, I'm moving to a different area now."

Relieved to be off what he saw as a difficult line of questions, the witness asked, "Would you like your acorn back, Mr. Duncan?"

"No, Dr. Thorpe. Let's leave it right where it is. I doubt if it's going to sprout any roots sitting there on the witness box rail. By the way, I'm pleased that you didn't ask if I wanted my oak tree back. Now, let's talk about this thing you call ensoulment. As I understand your testimony, you folks have now decided that God infuses the embryo with a soul at the moment of conception and that's what really makes that fertilized egg a human person. Correct?"

"There's no longer any doubt about that."

"Now, Dr. Thorpe," Tod continued. "You know about in vitro fertilization, don't you?"

Dr. Thorpe paused as he thought about where this lawyer might be going with such a line of questioning. "Yes, sir. We were talking about that a little earlier, and as matter of fact, it's caused some debate within our church."

"Well, I don't want to get into that debate right now. You know that the doctors try to get several of a woman's eggs fertilized in a tube. If they are successful in achieving pregnancy, any extra embryos that are not used are frozen."

Still not sure where all this was going, the witness could only warily answer, "Yes, sir."

Looking at the jury with puzzlement on his face, Tod asked, "When they freeze those embryos, Doctor, what happens to their souls?"

"Beg your pardon, sir?"

"You know, Doctor. You've testified that God puts a soul in that first cell. When it gets frozen what happens to the soul? Does it get frozen? Does God take it back? Does He have a deep freezer up in Heaven where He puts that soul from a frozen embryo until some scientist decides to unfreeze it?"

A dismayed look appeared on the philosopher's face. "Sir, I don't know that I've read or seen anyone debate that subject. You know, in vitro fertilization is a relatively new procedure."

Tod saw that he had the witness on the run. "Does that mean that you folks are going to have to debate that issue for another couple of thousand years before you come up with an answer?"

"I . . . uh . . . don't know, Mr. Duncan."

"Well, how about this. Let's assume that God takes that soul back when the embryo is frozen. If that embryo gets unfrozen, does it get the same soul back or a different one?

Does God tag a soul from a frozen embryo when He sticks it in his freezer so He knows which embryo it comes from?"

Again, shifting his bulk, Dr. Thorpe asked the judge, "Your Honor, these were not questions I came prepared to answer. May I be permitted to refuse to answer this line of questions?"

Judge O'Reilly peered over her glasses at the witness and replied. "Dr. Thorpe, you are not the first witness to be asked questions that came as a surprise. Please answer Mr. Duncan's questions or advise him that you do not know the answer."

"Ladies and gentlemen, I'm afraid that this is an area that has yet to be explored by those of us who do such things. I'm afraid that I cannot answer such questions until I have had a chance to confer with my colleagues and others throughout the world. That may take several years."

Tod smiled inwardly as he continued. "I'm sorry, Dr. Thorpe, but we've promised the judge that we would get this case finished in a couple more weeks. I suspect she and the jurors would prefer not to wait several years. One last series of questions along this line. You would agree that our God is an intelligent, omnipotent God, would you not?"

"Oh, absolutely, Mr. Duncan."

"And you know that for a variety of reasons that even when the human egg is fertilized, way more than fifty percent of those embryos don't make it through to the end of the pregnancy. Some of those eggs don't implant themselves in the womb. There are natural miscarriages and so forth. Some scientists and doctors say the number of actual live births from eggs that are actually fertilized is about twenty percent. You know that, don't you?"

"I'm not sure about your numbers, Mr. Duncan. That's not my area of expertise. However, there's no doubt that there are many natural reasons why a pregnancy is not carried to term."

"Don't you think, Doctor, that since we agree that our God is one smart fellow, that just maybe He would decide that He wouldn't want to waste a bunch of souls on fertilized eggs or on embryos or even a fetus until He's pretty well certain that the fetus is going to become a real, live human being? Maybe at about the time of viability?"

Dr. Thorpe sat in silence. The jury waited for him to answer. Even the reporters in the audience, normally a callous bunch, were leaning forward.

Finally, Judge O'Reilly said, "Dr. Thorpe, you will need to answer Mr. Duncan's question."

Dr. Thorpe slumped in his chair. "I don't have an answer."

With that response, Tod rose and said, "No further questions, Your Honor."

Johnny Bob considered trying to ask a few questions to rehabilitate the witness, but after conferring with Claudia, decided to move on. The jury filed into their room where their deli orders awaited them. As they sat around the table, an obviously upset Bert Marino, the young Catholic juror, said, "It's not right. Just not right for that lawyer to attack a priest. Dr. Thorpe has been working with God his whole life. He's got to be telling the truth."

"Hold on there, Bert," Roy Judice chastised. "He's not stating facts, just opinions and Duncan's got a right to challenge his opinions. That's what he gets paid for."

Alvin Steinhorn, the local jeweler who had just advanced to the status of a regular juror, chimed in, "He's right, Bert. Besides, we're not supposed to be talking about what goes on in the courtroom. Let's change the subject. Anyone see the Rockets game last night?" As the jurors got into a discussion about the Rockets, Bert Marino ate his sandwich in silence.

In the afternoon, Claudia put their nurse expert through her paces. A skilled surgical and intensive care nurse, she had also worked for several years for an abortion clinic. She dissected the care of the clinic, including Nurses Simms and Sylvester, and offered opinions that their conduct was negligent. When her turn came, Jan discredited the expert by pointing out the number of times that the nurse had testified, the amount of money that she made annually by being critical of nurses, clinics and hospitals, and that she worked exclusively for plaintiffs in malpractice cases. Nothing but a hired gun. Annie Oakley in a nurse's uniform.

That evening, Tod's team filled plates with Chinese food at the fire station. As they ate, they rehashed the day's testimony and discussed what lay ahead.

"First of all, Tod, I want to know if you have anything else in your pocket?" Wayne asked.

"Nope, that's it," Tod replied through a mouthful of chow mein. "Pockets are empty. No more parlor tricks. Just plain old cross-examination. Now let's talk about how we're doing."

Dr. Moyo volunteered. "Maybe I shouldn't be the first one to offer an opinion, but I will. I think things are going quite well. I thought that you did a very effective job of pointing out the weaknesses of their two experts, Tod. Unfortunately, I think that Reverend Luther came across quite well. He speaks with conviction and has a very impressive demeanor. I would hope that you will put him back on the stand and do to him what you did to Dr. Thorpe and Dr. Kriegel. As to the clinic, I'm a little worried. The nurses were okay but not great, and the last one had a hard time explaining why they didn't follow clinic procedures. Their nurse expert was very strong. Hopefully, the jury understood she makes her living as a paid testifier."

"You're getting to be a pretty good lawyer, Zeke," Tod replied. "Okay, Jan, they are going to wind up in the next couple of days. Are we ready with our experts?"

"They're ready and will be available on twenty-four hours' notice. They will be in town the night before we put them on the stand."

72

Wearing his red-topped boots that morning, Johnny Bob introduced Phillip Ables to the jury. He was tall, well built, fifty-ish, with curly black hair and a voice that would make Marcus Welby proud. And he was black. Claudia had intentionally chosen a black obstetrician to be critical of Dr. Moyo. Outside the courtroom, she might be a staunch advocate for African-American rights and a leader of their causes, but this was war. If race could help her sway only one juror in the courtroom, she would not hesitate to play that card. Alfred Totman, the retired bookkeeper and an African-American, smiled as he saw Dr. Ables take the stand, not because the witness was black, but because the juror saw a sliver of red under lawyer Tisdale's pants leg.

"I'm Phillip Ables. I'm a doctor and a professor of obstetrics and gynecology at Mid-State Medical School in Ohio. I've been practicing obstetrics for twenty-five years. I've been on the faculty of Mid-State for twenty years, the last ten as a full professor."

Johnny Bob wanted to get one issue out of the way at the very start and asked matter-of-factly, "Doctor, along with delivering babies, do you also perform abortions?"

"Yes, sir. On occasion. I perform pregnancy terminations when necessary to save the life of the mother, but not voluntary terminations. Otherwise, I am obligated to teach the residents the proper techniques of such a procedure."

"Doctor, have you reviewed the records of Lucy Baines Brady's abortion?"

"I have."

"Tell us, please, Dr. Ables, whether the performance of Dr. Moyo and the clinic met the standards of care required in performing such a procedure?"

"If I may, I'll start with Dr. Moyo. First, let me make it clear that I know that Dr. Moyo is a very fine doctor and I understand he is even joining the faculty of the Baylor College of Medicine here in Houston. So, I'm not condemning him as a doctor. In this case, his handling of the abortion just did not meet appropriate standards. I suspect it was because he had so little sleep in the two previous days."

Johnny Bob led him further. "Doctor, please explain how his conduct was negligent."

"I teach my residents the various complications that can occur in this procedure, and all of us have them happen from time to time. However, it's my opinion that one complication can be understood and explained, but with two in the same termination, that, in my mind, shows a lack of attention that rises to the level of negligence. That's part of the reason for the problems that Lucy later developed. The other reasons, of course, are the failure to follow good nursing practices on the part of the clinic nurses which, I understand, you've already heard about."

He then did something highly unusual. The witness turned to Dr. Moyo and said, "I'm sorry to have to say these things, Doctor. However, I must be honest in my opinions from this stand."

Dr. Moyo nodded his understanding and looked away. Satisfied that he had established Dr. Moyo's negligence, Johnny Bob led Dr. Ables into other areas. Doctor, have you examined Lucy?"

"I have, sir."

"Tell the jury, Dr. Ables, will Lucy be able to conceive and bear children?"

Dr. Ables turned to look at Lucy. "I'm sorry to say that based on my exam, the answer must be no."

"Next issue, Doctor, do you have an opinion as to when human life begins?"

"Yes, sir, I do. I agree with most learned scientists that life begins at the moment of conception. I can explain."

"No need, Doctor. We have already had Dr. Kriegel clarify that for us."

"Certainly, Mr. Tisdale, he's one of the best. I'm certain I couldn't add anything to his opinions."

Johnny Bob leaned forward and continued, "Let me get your thoughts on a related subject, Doctor, and that's when a fetus can actually live outside the womb."

"That's an interesting question, ladies and gentlemen. Not too many years ago, we had little chance of saving a baby if it was less than twenty-eight weeks. Now science has advanced to the point that premature babies are saved as early as twenty-three and twenty-four weeks, and even a few can make it at twenty-two weeks. Those are times that are well within the second trimester. Remarkable advancement, if I may say so."

"The point I'm trying to get to, Doctor, is whether there's any end in sight. Is it possible that babies may be saved at less than twenty weeks?"

"Certainly, it may be possible one day, Mr. Tisdale."

Johnny Bob leaned over his table and growled again, "That's assuming of course, that some clinic like Population Planning or some doctor like Dr. Moyo, doesn't get to that fetus, first. Right, Doctor?"

Tod stomped the floor with his feet as he stormed up. "Objection, Your Honor. Argumentative and relevance. We're talking here about an abortion at twelve weeks, not twenty."

"Sustained."

Johnny Bob had made his point. The question of viability was a moving target and the direction of its movement was earlier and earlier in a pregnancy. He passed the witness, not noticing that Alfred Totman stared at him and shook his head at the unnecessary shot at Dr. Moyo. Sitting beside his lawyer, T.J. also didn't notice Juror Totman. Instead, he could only smile at what he perceived as another outstanding performance by one of their witnesses. In fact, the way the case was going, his mind was already drifting off to leading a march on Washington to force a constitutional amendment banning all abortions. It wouldn't take long for Tod to wipe the smile from T.J.'s face.

"Dr. Ables, when you say that you personally perform abortions only when the mother's life is in jeopardy, is it because you have some moral or ethical reason for not doing them otherwise?"

"Correct, Mr. Duncan. I believe that even an embryo is a human life. However, in the interest of complete honesty, I should point out that my institution does have a clinic where elective abortions are performed up to eighteen weeks."

Johnny Bob closed his eyes and cursed under his breath at that last comment. Like every other witness, he had told Dr. Ables not to volunteer information. Surprisingly, Tod did not delve further into the subject. "Dr. Ables, have you had complications when you have done abortions?"

"Certainly, sir. All of us who have done more than a few have had some of the known complications."

"How about your residents? As they are learning to do such a procedure, do they have complications?"

"Yes, sir, more often than those of us who have more experience. I might add, that is the nature of the learning process. However, we always have a senior member of the staff also in attendance with the residents to lend a hand when necessary and avoid any serious outcomes."

"Do these complications include both uterine perforations and retained fetal parts?"

"They do, sir. Retained fetal parts are more common and usually do not require a second procedure. Often, they resolve themselves naturally."

"Dr. Ables, were you negligent when you did an abortion where there were retained fetal parts or where there was a uterine perforation?"

"Sir, I don't recall that I have ever done an abortion where I had a perforation, and I certainly was not negligent if there were retained fetal parts. As I'm sure you've been told, a pregnancy termination is a blind procedure. Sometimes small bits of tissue remain no matter how careful the surgeon."

Tod thanked the witness for his candor. Even Johnny Bob began to relax since Tod seemed to be landing the most minimal of blows to this most credible of experts. He decided that he must remember to compliment Claudia on her selection of experts, particularly this one. That was before Tod made an unexpected shift in his line of questioning.

"Dr. Ables, in looking over your resume, I see that you have done some research and writing on in vitro fertilization?"

That got Johnny Bob's attention. He had heard all he wanted about in vitro fertilization. Every time Tod brought it up, it seemed to create problems for his witnesses. He pushed his chair back and addressed the judge. "Your Honor, it seems to me that we've had about enough talk about in vitro fertilization. This is a case about abortion and slander. Test tube babies have nothing to do with any issue in this case and I object to Mr. Duncan bringing it up any further."

Judge O'Reilly looked at Johnny Bob and asked, "Do I presume that your objection goes to relevance, Mr. Tisdale?"

"Yes, ma'am, it certainly does," the lawyer retorted, glaring at Tod for effect.

"So, Mr. Duncan, what do you have to say about that?"

Tod returned Johnny Bob's stare and replied, "Your Honor, I will be able to tie it up, and I might add this will be the last plaintiff's witness where this issue is relevant to his testimony. I also believe that the first discussion of in vitro came from Dr. Kriegel. They opened this door and that gives me the right to explore other facets of the issue."

The judge pondered and then fixed her sternest look on Tod. "Very well then. I'll let you go a little further, but if you don't show its relevance pretty darn quick, I'm going to have the whole line of questioning struck. Move on."

Tod resumed his seat and Johnny Bob walked over to whisper something to T.J., hoping to distract some of the jurors. Tod continued. "Correct, Dr. Ables? You have done such research and writing?"

"Yes, sir, and I might add, we also have an in vitro fertilization clinic at our medical school."

While Johnny Bob was bent over pretending to whisper to T.J., he heard that answer and whispered an expletive. "Shit, I wish he would learn to just answer the question."

Not that it made any difference, though, for Tod had read about the clinic. It was on the school's Web site.

"Doctor, the jury has heard some testimony about how this is done, so, I don't intend to ask you any questions about the technique. Am I correct, though, that when you have a couple that is trying to get pregnant that you harvest several eggs and often end up with some extra embryos after the mother has become pregnant?"

"Yes, sir. We do. We take those embryos and freeze them for future use."

"And I presume, Dr. Ables, that you take the position that those embryos are human persons?"

"Yes, sir. No doubt about it. Otherwise, when we thaw them out, they could never become a fetus and then a baby."

"Now, Dr. Ables, are you personally involved in that program? By that, I mean do you have patients who go through the in vitro process, achieve pregnancy and then freeze the extra embryos?"

"Yes, sir. I actually developed the protocol at our school and head up the program." With a smile of pride he added, "We've helped hundreds of previously infertile couples."

"How many embryos do you have frozen, just at your facility, Doctor?"

Behind the witness rail, but in sight of several of the jurors, his left leg began to bounce up and down as it often did when he was nervous. From her bench, Ruby O'Reilly looked at Tod as she realized how he was about to make all of this relevant.

"I couldn't say for sure, Mr. Duncan. Certainly, several hundred. Maybe more than a thousand at any one time."

"What happens to those frozen embryos when they are no longer needed?"

Dr. Ables, pretended ignorance. "I'm sorry, counsel, but I don't understand what you mean."

Tod had the witness on the run and was rapidly backing him into a corner where there was no escape. Johnny Bob saw what was coming but kept the poker face of a good lawyer as he stared at the end of his pen. Claudia looked down at her notes and muttered something under her breath. T.J. just stared at the witness, uncertain as to what was happening. Tod pressed. "Come on now, Dr. Ables. When a woman gets pregnant, do you keep the rest of her embryos there forever?"

"No, sir. We can't afford to do that. It's quite expensive and it would serve no useful purpose," the doctor replied, trying to put his best foot forward, yet knowing he was about to step off into quicksand.

"Then what happens to them, Doctor?"

The lawyers and jurors were looking at the witness. Reporters put down their pens. Judge O'Reilly peered over her bench at Dr. Ables, who felt the stares of hundreds of eyes. It was as if they suddenly understood where Tod had been leading this witness.

Dr. Ables realized that he could not sidestep this issue and decided to face it head-on. "Mr. Duncan, it's created a real dilemma for us, a moral dilemma of great magnitude. On the one hand, we've developed a technique to provide otherwise infertile couples with the joys of parenthood. On the other, we have excess frozen embryos. What to do with them? We contact the parents and let them decide. Often they have disappeared and we have to make the decision. At five years, we thaw the embryos and incinerate them."

As the silence filled the courtroom, it was so quiet that the only sound came from the *click, click, click* of the clock.

"In your eyes, Dr. Ables, you have destroyed a life each time you incinerate an embryo, haven't you?"

Dr. Ables lowered his head as he softly said, "Yes, sir. I'm afraid that we have. It's a trade-off that we make in order to provide the joy of parenthood to infertile couples."

"And there's no way to reconcile such an action with your stand on abortion, is there, Doctor? What you've actually decided is that there is at least one circumstance where the benefit to the mother and father overrides the concern for an embryo, what you and Dr. Kriegel and Dr. Thorpe call a human being. Right, Dr. Ables?" Tod's voice was growing louder and he continued before the doctor could answer.

"And if you're correct that an embryo, even a frozen one, is a human life, you've chosen to play God. You intentionally kill that human being, don't you, Doctor? In your mind, that's okay, but you condemn other doctors who terminate a pregnancy of a fetus that's only a few weeks old!"

The doctor gulped and the jurors could see his Adam's apple bobbing up and down as he grasped for the right answer. Finally, he answered, not in the vibrant voice he had on direct examination, but in a broken one that conveyed his now-admitted confusion on the subject.

"Yes, sir. Or maybe I'm wrong when I say that life actually begins at conception. Maybe the human life occurs at a later time. Perhaps one day we'll decide that question once and for all. I can tell you that I think about it every time I sign the order to dispose of even one embryo."

Tod stared at the witness and said nothing.

As the jurors looked back and forth between the lawyers and the witness, Judge O'Reilly broke the silence by asking, "Mr. Tisdale, as I understand it, you are expecting to call Dr. Coates on Monday morning. Will that be your last witness?"

"Other than possible rebuttal, that is correct, Judge."

"All right. Dr. Ables, you are excused." As she spoke, the trance that had possessed the whole courtroom was broken. Chairs creaked. Papers rattled. People coughed. The judge continued. "Assuming that there are no objections, let's adjourn a little early for the weekend. For you jurors, I'm sorry to have to make you cool your heels. The good news is that I think that we can finish this trial in three weeks and not four. Further, I've made arrangements to permit your families to visit."

As the lawyers walked out of the courtroom, Victoria Burton cornered Tod. "Look, Tod, you've avoided me for the whole trial. Nearly everyone else has been on television. I think it's about time for you to say a few words to the rest of the country."

"Victoria, that's really not my style. I try my lawsuits in the courtroom, not with the media."

"How about if I promise you a slot on Sunday's *Dateline*

NBC? I've cleared it with their producer if you'll agree to be interviewed tomorrow morning."

Tod vacillated and finally relented. Maybe it was time for the country to see Zeke as he really was. He didn't think that it would impact on the trial. Perhaps, though, he owed it to Dr. Moyo. Victoria asked to do the interview in the garden behind the fire station in front of the waterfall.

TOD WAS UP AT five A.M. on Saturday morning. The sun was not up and his breath was visible as he started with slow strides, working the kinks out of his legs and trying to get some rhythm in his breathing. At that hour on Saturday morning, the streets were nearly deserted. Tod let the trial play in his head. He had given it all he had. Coming into the last week, he was ready to wind it down. He wanted to spend more time with his boys. As he settled into his stride, his breathing became regular and he adjusted to an eight-minute-mile pace. Reflecting on the trial, he thought about what he might have done differently. He had accomplished all he possibly could with Johnny Bob's experts. Whether it was good enough remained to be seen. Like the fourth quarter of a close football game, for him and Dr. Moyo, this would be the week that counted. If their experts came through and they finished strong, they could win, but if he were asked to place a bet, it would only be a small one—on himself and his client.

When Tod returned from his run, Kirk and Chris were up and dressed in clean jeans, golf shirts and running shoes, their formal attire. They learned about the interview the evening before and wanted to be there just in case the TV lady wanted to talk to Tod's family. Tod shaved and showered, dressed in a blue shirt, khaki pants, and tied on a clean pair of running shoes. Then they were on the road, stopping by the McDonald's drive-through for breakfast. By eight-thirty, Tod and the boys were at the fire station. After Kirk and Chris each had a couple of slides down the fire pole, Tod gave them brooms and ordered them to sweep the garden walks and to pick up any trash. For once, the boys didn't protest. By eight forty-five, Jan, Wayne and Marilyn arrived to watch the taping. In less than an hour the cameras were rolling.

"Tell us, Tod, would it be fair to characterize what's been going on in Houston as this generation's Scopes Monkey Trial? It certainly appears that some of the scenes we've witnessed could have come out of *Inherit the Wind*." Over several months, Tod had allowed such comparisons to run through his mind, and the answer to such a question came easily to him.

"Victoria, there are some similarities, but probably more differences. Yes, the clash between science and religion is at the heart of both trials. In ours, there's no real debate that there is a life form present at the moment of conception. I'm not telling any secrets when I tell you that none of my experts this coming week will disagree with that proposition. The Scopes trial focused the national debate about Darwin's Theory of Evolution on a little town in Tennessee. It clearly was a subject of national interest then. Our trial has abortion as one of its core issues, obviously a subject of continuing national debate. Ours is more complicated since we also have to deal with issues involving alleged medical malpractice and damages."

Tod shifted his answer to lead the interview where he wanted to take it. "Probably the most striking similarity is that both trials have a good man who is a victim of the process. Like Mr. Scopes, Dr. Moyo has done nothing wrong. He's a fine obstetrician and a credit to his profession—soon to be a professor at Baylor. Dr. Moyo has been a victim of a campaign carefully planned by the pro-life movement and orchestrated by T.J. Luther." Tod had decided not to give him the title of reverend. "He's behind the lawsuit and he's the one who has destroyed Dr. Moyo's life with his attacks from his pulpit. The other difference between our trial and that of Mr. Scopes is that Scopes suffered a loss at the end. It was a minor fine, but a loss, nonetheless. Dr. Moyo will not lose this trial. His good name will be restored."

Victoria Burton turned Tod's attention to the coming week

and Tod listed his witnesses. There were only four experts. He did, however, make sure to mention that he was considering calling T.J. to the stand. He sent a message to the man in Fort Worth that his time on the hot seat was not yet over.

ON SUNDAY MORNING, T.J. returned to his pulpit and preached to an overflowing congregation. When the lights dimmed and the spotlight appeared on the raised platform, the congregation stood as one, cheering and applauding as the figure in a white satin robe and sunglasses floated to the floor. He basked in the glow of their adoration for at least two minutes before motioning them to take their seats. His sermon was brief. He summarized his previous series on the Ten Commandments. He alluded to eight of the commandments, spending five minutes apiece on each of the remaining two. His voice rose as he discussed them: "Thou shalt not kill," and "Thou shalt not bear false witness." While he didn't mention the trial, the message was clear. As he closed, he told his audience that he, Lucy, his church and the pro-life organizations needed their support. As would be obvious on Monday, they received his message. Later in the week, he would learn he should have chosen a different topic.

73

Monday brought overflowing crowds. T.J.'s followers filled the area behind the barricades. Not to be outdone, the pro-choice forces had responded to calls from some of their leaders who also had watched *The Miracle Morning Hour.* Once again, the street in front of the law school resembled the stands at a college football game.

Just before nine o'clock, T.J. appeared at the top of the auditorium stairs. He strutted as he descended the stairs, his ears still echoing with the cheers of his followers. He took off his Stetson, pitched it to the middle of the counsel table and shook hands, starting with his lawyers and ending with Jessie, Joanna, Bo and Lucy. He paused long enough to kiss Lucy on the cheek.

Johnny Bob's last witness in the case was a calculated decision. Of course, for a lawyer of his experience, he planned nearly every move for the largest possible dramatic effect. Dr. Frederick Coates was an experienced psychologist. More importantly, he was an experienced testifier, and was not likely to be easily confused by Tod's questions. His testimony would serve to make the jury feel sorry for Lucy, sympathetic little Lucy, the real victim in all of these events that had been unwrapped and put on display. In a trial like this, where the answer to every jury question would be a close call, sympathy could tip the scales in favor of the plaintiff.

As Dr. Coates walked down the stairs, Tod sized him up. He was a small man, of medium build, with brown bushy hair and a beard and mustache that Tod was certain Dr. Coates thought would add just the right touch for a psychologist. He took the witness stand with assurance, and it was justified.

As a forensic psychologist, he was accustomed to courtrooms. Appearances such as this were a frequent part of his practice. As he surveyed the scene and particularly the lawyers, he knew that whatever any lawyer could pitch, he could hit over the fence. Johnny Bob quickly took him through his credentials: bachelors and masters at the University of Texas in Austin; doctorate from the University of Houston; return to his hometown of Fort Worth where he had been in practice for twenty years and, yes, about 50 percent of his income came from working with lawyers. After taking the witness through his credentials, Johnny Bob slowed the pace as he shifted the attention of the witness and jury to Dr. Coates's care of Lucy.

"Now, Dr. Coates, at my request, have you been seeing Lucy Brady as a patient?"

"Yes, sir. She's been under my care for over six months now."

"Would you tell us about her condition when you first

started seeing her, your treatment of her and how she progressed during those early months?"

Dr. Coates cleared his voice and apologized to the judge and jury for the remainder of a cold in his throat. That prompted Deputy Johnson to bring him a glass of water.

"Thank you, deputy. When I first saw Lucy, she was in extremely bad condition. She was suffering from one of the worst post-traumatic stress disorders that I have ever seen. I was seeing her three times a week at her aunt Jessie's house. Although I had read her medical records and she had made a fairly good physical recovery, she was still an emotional wreck. I did most of the talking and was lucky to get a yes or no in response. I knew that she had been talking more with her family and even Reverend Luther, but in her eyes I was a stranger not yet worthy of trust. At first, I was worried that she might be contemplating suicide. I warned her aunt and her aunt's staff to clear the house of any guns and to secure any sharp objects."

"Doctor, did she need a wheelchair after she left the hospital in Houston?" Johnny Bob asked.

"Not from a physical standpoint. I studied her medical records. All of her neurological systems were intact, and while her muscles were weak, she could have walked. It was a further sign of her severe emotional disturbance."

"Now, Doctor, I understand that it was not until Lucy was at a church service with Reverend Luther that she began walking again. Can you enlighten the jury on how that happened?"

"Certainly, I've got to give Reverend Luther credit for getting her to walk."

The jury looked at T.J. who merely nodded in return.

"Reverend Luther did an emotional healing, not a physical one. Whatever he did on that Sunday gave Lucy the motivation to get out of the wheelchair and walk on her own two feet. His touch seemed critical. Since that time, she has felt a real closeness to Reverend Luther. She sees him as the one person outside of her family whom she can trust. He's become almost like a second father to her."

Johnny Bob spent the rest of the morning having Dr. Coates describe each of his visits with Lucy and how she progressed. It was a long process, even laborious. Still, the lawyer thought it was important enough that he was willing to risk boring one or two jurors to make sure they understood the depth of Lucy's emotional distress. After the lunch break he covered Lucy's current condition and her prognosis.

"Mr. Tisdale, Lucy is much improved, but she will never be normal. When we talked her into resuming her high school studies, she would only do so with tutors that her aunt brought to the house. She refused contact with anyone her age, particularly boys. She is dreadfully fearful of doctors and hospitals. I'm just thankful that she has not had a medical problem that required her to see a doctor. If that had occurred, it might have put her back in bed with the covers pulled over her head."

When Dr. Coates mentioned Lucy's refusal to have anything to do with boys, Johnny Bob had to separate her problems caused by the abortion from those potentially caused by the rape.

"Doctor, wouldn't she have had some of these problems even if the abortion had been one with no complications?"

"Possibly, sir. I've counseled young ladies who have had a routine abortion, if I may use that phrase. I have had to help them work through guilt, anxiety, crying episodes, sleep disorders, depression and a variety of other problems. While they frequently have serious consequences from an abortion, with my help, they are usually able to get on with their lives after some extensive counseling. That, unfortunately, is not the case with Lucy."

"Tell the jury, Doctor, what can Lucy expect in the future?"

"Glad to, Mr. Tisdale. She's going to need my counseling for several years. I would hope that in, maybe, three years, it would be down to once or twice a week. For the rest of her life, she's going to have periods of time that will require intense therapy. For example, if she were to become romantically involved with a man and that relationship didn't work out, it could throw her back into a depression like she has just been through. If she has to go into the hospital for any reason, her distrust of doctors is such that a hospitalization could also cause a similar reaction."

"What about childbearing, Doctor?"

"That's probably the hardest thing that Lucy has had to deal with. Your obstetrical expert has told her that it is not likely that she will be able to conceive and bear children. Like most young women, her life plan had included finding a suitable husband and raising a family. That has all changed. In her mind, no man will want to marry her now. She starts crying every time I try to bring up the subject of her infertility. Still, it's important that I continue to try to address that issue with her since, in my opinion, the only way she will come to grips with it is to talk it through."

As Dr. Coates described Lucy, Johnny Bob looked at the jury and found Amy Bourland, Olga Olsen and Catherine Tucker quietly wiping their eyes. Just the reaction he wanted. Johnny Bob wound up his examination of Dr. Coates by offering his past bills into evidence and his estimate of the cost of future psychological counseling. Last, he offered Dr. Coates's counseling records in evidence and passed the witness. Having worked with Dr. Coates before, Johnny Bob expected Dr. Coates to craft his notes so they would be most advantageous to Lucy's case. Not that they wouldn't be truthful opinions, only that the opinions would be slanted to assist Johnny Bob in justifying the largest possible verdict for his client.

Tod took over. His experience told him that he should avoid challenging this witness's opinions. With such a seasoned testifier, all that he would accomplish would be to give Coates an opportunity to twist Tod's questions around and re-emphasize Dr. Coates's opinions. The jury had heard enough of the poor Lucy story. Instead, he turned the jury's attention on Dr. Coates himself.

"Now, Dr. Coates, this isn't your first rodeo, is it?"

Judge O'Reilly smiled.

"I'm sorry, Mr. Duncan," replied the witness. "I'm not sure I understand what you mean."

"I'll clarify, Doctor. You've been working for Mr. Tisdale almost since the time that you got out of school, haven't you? Matter of fact, according to my research, you've been involved in forty-two cases for Mr. Tisdale in the past fifteen years, all of them with plaintiffs who were seeking money damages in lawsuits. Correct, sir?"

"Mr. Duncan, I don't keep such statistics, but you could be right. Mr. Tisdale has asked me to care for his clients on a number of occasions."

"And you also write reports and testify when Johnny Bob calls. When he whistles, you come running, right?"

"I wouldn't put it quite like that. I am available for hire for him as well as other attorneys, sir."

"Speaking of other attorneys, you've testified literally hundreds of times, either by deposition or in trial, always hired by plaintiff lawyers who are out to get money for their clients, correct?"

"Well, sir, if I remember correctly, I did testify a couple of times for defense lawyers."

"That, though, was early in your career, before you began advertising in the plaintiff lawyer magazines, wasn't it, Dr. Coates?"

"Probably true, sir."

"As a matter of fact, Doctor, over three quarters of your income comes from working with plaintiff lawyers, and it's enough income that you have a house in the Rivercrest section of Fort Worth, just a couple of blocks from Ms. Woolsey."

"Well, sir, frankly, I'm very good at what I do. I've been well paid over the years. I might add that my house is not quite as big as Jessie's."

"Speaking of payment, not counting your counseling with Lucy, you've billed Mr. Tisdale twenty thousand dollars, just for your work on this case?"

"Approximately, Mr. Duncan," Dr. Coates replied with a smugness in his voice that gave the impression that he thought he was worth every penny of it.

"No wonder you can afford a house in Rivercrest."

Johnny Bob started to rise to object. Seeing him getting out of his chair, Tod said, "Oh, never mind, Your Honor. I think the jury gets the idea."

It was the end of the day. Johnny Bob conferred with Claudia and then rose. "Your Honor, subject to making sure that all of our exhibits are properly marked and in evidence, Plaintiff rests."

As the jury and the audience left the courtroom and the lawyers were packing up their gear for the night, Jan wandered up to the court reporter's table where exhibits, mainly medical bills and records, were stacked. Not looking for anything in particular, she picked up the records from Dr. Coates and rummaged through them until she stopped at a page near the back. She studied an entry and flipped several pages forward and back, looking for a similar entry. Making sure that Johnny Bob and Claudia were wrapped up in their activities, she motioned for Tod to join her and pointed out the entry that caught her attention. It was one seemingly innocuous phrase: *Saw Dr. Olstein.*

That was it. There was none of the detail normally used by Dr. Coates. Tod confirmed with Jan that the name did not appear elsewhere in the records and told her to write it down. They would defer talking about it until they returned to the fire station. He walked over to Dr. Moyo and told him that something had come up and they needed him with them back at the station.

74

Tod pitched his briefcase into the back of his Suburban. As he pulled out of the parking lot, he called Grace and told her to go down the street to buy a couple of six packs of Budweiser. Next, he called home to check on the boys. Not surprisingly, he heard the answering machine. He left a message that he was out of trial for the day and would be at the office for several more hours. Then, he mused about the mysterious Dr. Olstein.

The name had not come up before, not in testimony, not in responses to discovery, and not in any medical record. They had asked Lucy in her deposition about every health care practitioner that she had seen since the day she was born. They asked similar questions to her mother and aunt. This Dr. Olstein had not been mentioned by any of them. They had subpoenaed the records from Dr. Coates twice, once as soon as they learned that Johnny Bob had hired him, and again a few weeks before they put Lucy under oath in her deposition. Olstein's name was not there either time. The name appeared in the notes of a session between Lucy and Dr. Coates after the deposition and before trial, yet there was no indication as to when Lucy saw Dr. Olstein. It could have been around the time of that visit, months before, years before, or even shortly before trial. Maybe it was important. Maybe it was insignificant.

One thing did strike Tod as such thoughts traipsed through his mind. Lawyers knew Coates to be one who wrote notes that were most helpful to his patients and their lawyers when litigation was involved. This cryptic note was all of three words. Further, Johnny Bob had kept Dr. Coates on the stand for almost an entire day, covering every session he had with Lucy. Yet, on the visit for that particular day, Dr. Coates had not mentioned this Dr. Olstein. Tod's curiosity was piqued.

Gathering in the war room, Tod, Jan, Wayne, Marilyn and Dr. Moyo assessed the testimony of Dr. Coates and the impact of all of Johnny Bob's witnesses.

"Coates didn't surprise me," Wayne began as he passed beer around to everyone except Marilyn who opted for bottled water. "Every one of us could have predicted what he was going to say. He's been singing from the same hymnal for fifteen years. Post-traumatic stress disorder is always one of his favorite diagnoses."

"Yeah, Wayne, I agree," Jan said as she brought the feminine viewpoint into the discussion, "but no one can seriously quarrel with the diagnosis in this case. Lucy went through more than anyone should have to, particularly at seventeen."

"And don't forget that there were at least three of the female jurors who were tearing up when Coates started talking about her not being able to have any kids," Marilyn added.

"Fact of the matter," said Tod, "is that we haven't caught her or anyone on the plaintiff's side in a lie. Every plaintiff lies about something. You just have to find out what it is. When you do, you can win your case because jurors are not likely to give liars any money. Right now all of their witnesses could be in Mother Teresa's choir. The one exception may be T.J., and we don't have anything concrete on him. On the other hand, Lucy's damages are potentially going to be big. Now let's talk about this Dr. Olstein. Jan, tell them what you discovered at the end of the day."

"While you guys were packing up, I went over to the exhibit pile and was just rummaging through Dr. Coates's records when I ran across this name. All the note said was 'Saw Dr. Olstein.' Nothing else," Jan explained. "It's for a visit a couple of weeks before trial, but there's no clue as to who Dr. Olstein is, where he is, when she saw him, or what she saw him for. He could be a chiropractor, for all we know."

"Well, let's start with the assumption that he's a real doctor. Any guesses as to why she saw him? It could just be the flu or a sore throat."

"I'll start the guessing, Tod," Marilyn volunteered. "I don't think that it's something like that. That's not the kind of problem that would come up in a conversation with a psychologist."

"Good point, Marilyn."

Dr. Moyo joined in the debate. "Tod, I've been around you lawyers for months now and I may be starting to think like some of you. That, by the way, may not be such a bad thing. Nonetheless, I agree with Marilyn. I don't think that whatever Lucy saw this Dr. Olstein for will be helpful to her. Otherwise, she and Johnny Bob would have listed him as a witness. At the very least, Lucy or Dr. Coates would have testified about it."

"Okay, Wayne," Tod said, "go get one of those honorary law degrees out of the back closet and write Dr. Moyo's name on it. Just kidding, Zeke, but your analysis may be right. I'll add that if Johnny Bob and Claudia had known about it, they certainly would have had to list him. They're good lawyers and they wouldn't take a chance on hiding a witness, so, I think that we can add to your analysis that Lucy and Coates didn't tell them about this Dr. Olstein. We need to chase him down and we only have a couple of days to do it. I ought to kick myself in the butt for not studying those latest records from Dr. Coates before I let him off the stand."

"Come on, now, Tod," Jan chided him. "No self-flagellation. There's no way for you to have expected that a new, undisclosed doctor would pop up in his records just a couple of weeks before trial. I also suspect that Johnny Bob didn't pick up on that name since they probably thought they already had all of the records of her visits with Dr. Coates. Besides, it may turn out to be nothing."

"Thanks, Jan. I'll put away my whip now. Marilyn, let's get to the bottom of this. Let's try the easy way first. Go get our *Harris County Medical Society Directory*. Maybe we'll get lucky and find that he's in Houston."

Marilyn left the room and returned almost instantly, a large directory in her hand. "Nope, not there. I've looked for a physician with a name of Olstein and also tried Olstien, Olsten, and Osten. Matter of fact, I looked at all of the 'Os' and found nothing. He's not in Harris County."

"Next likely place is Fort Worth. I'll make a couple of calls to some lawyer friends of mine up there. I ought to be able to find one still in the office."

Tod went to the phone and called information in Fort Worth. On the third try to a lawyer's office, he found who he was looking for. After a brief conversation, he turned to the group. "No luck. No Dr. Olstein or anything close to it in Tarrant County."

"If this doctor is in Texas, Tod, I can find him," Zeke said. "I can't do it until the morning. Then, I'll call the Board of Medical Examiners in Austin. They'll tell me if there's someone with that name practicing in the state and the location of his office. I'm not sure what time they open. I'll start calling at eight o'clock."

"Good idea, Doc," Tod responded. "You stay home and start making those calls. As soon as you get something, call Wayne on his cell phone. I'll have him keep the phone on until we start testimony around nine."

The next morning when Wayne got to the courtroom at eight-thirty, he told Tod that he still had not heard from Dr. Moyo. Tod sent him to their assigned room to await the call that they hoped would come before the judge took the bench.

Ever alert for changes in the patterns of a trial, Johnny Bob noticed that Dr. Moyo was missing and struck up a conversation with Tod. "Well, my worthy adversary, you sure did beat up on my witnesses. I only hope that I can return the favor."

"Come on now, Johnny Bob, I scored a few points just like I'm sure you'll do."

"You figure that we'll get this thing over by the end of the week?"

"Good chance, Johnny Bob, particularly if the judge lets us work on Friday and I suspect she will. She wants this one over about as much as you and I."

"What'd you do with your client, Tod? Haven't seen him around this morning."

"Oh, he had to drop a form by Baylor this morning, something to do with his new job. I told him he could be a few minutes late, if necessary."

As he finished the sentence, he saw Wayne motioning to him from the hallway door. Tod excused himself. When they closed the door to their room, Wayne started. "We've got him, I think. Moyo called. There are two doctors with that same last name in Texas. There's one in West Texas. The board says he's been retired for five years. The other is a Dr. Wallace

Olstein. He's a family practice doc, seventy-five years old, still with an active license. Lives and has an office in San Augustine."

"Is that within a hundred and fifty miles, Wayne?"

They had both been to San Augustine for depositions, but neither really paid attention to the distance. All he could recall was that it was a three-hour drive through East Texas and the town was close to the Louisiana border. Now, though, the distance was important because if Olstein was within that distance, they could subpoena him or his records to the trial in Harris County. Beyond that distance, they could do nothing but call him and try to pry information out of him.

"I've already called Grace. It's close, maybe a little over a hundred and fifty miles, but who's gonna measure? I say we subpoena his records. I'll bluff, if necessary."

It took Tod only a split second to make a decision. "Okay, get your ass over to the real courthouse and get a subpoena issued to the custodian of his medical records for anything they have on Lucy Baines Brady. Then, hightail it up to San Augustine and serve the subpoena. I want those records back here by tonight."

"What about just subpoenaing old Doc Olstein himself and getting to the bottom of this in a hurry?"

"No, let's take it one step at a time," Tod disagreed. "I want to see what's in those records first. Get going. I'll call you on your cell phone at the lunch break to see what's up."

Wayne disappeared out the door and ran down the stairs. As he left the building, he saw Victoria Burton going through the metal detector. He tried to ignore her.

"Hey, Wayne," she said. "You're going the wrong way. Has Ruby put things off for the morning?"

"No, Victoria. Tod forgot something back at the office and I'm going back to pick it up. See you later."

Puzzling, thought Victoria. Tod wouldn't be sending Wayne back to the office. That would have been Marilyn's job. Either that or he would have called someone to bring the forgotten item to them. She filed the puzzle away in her mind, took her briefcase and purse from the X-ray belt and waited for the elevator to take her to the courtroom.

Wayne got to his car, placed the cell phone in its cradle, and drove to the old Harris County courthouse. He double parked in his usual courthouse parking lot and left the keys with the attendant. For some reason it seemed that every lawyer in town had to file something or have a subpoena issued. He fidgeted in line for half an hour before getting to the counter where a gum popping eighteen-year-old girl asked what she could do for him. He explained his mission and she began completing the form. The process bogged down when she got to the part that asked for the address of this witness. He didn't know anything other than that the doctor lived and worked in San Augustine.

It was too late to call Dr. Moyo who by now would be in the courtroom. Further, he didn't want to go back to his car where he could make a long distance call. When the clerk refused to issue the subpoena without an address, Wayne did what any good lawyer would do. He made one up. Fumbling in his shirt pocket he pulled out a crumpled laundry receipt, saying, "Oh, here it is. He's at Four-fifty-eight Oak, San Augustine, Texas, 77999."

As Wayne grabbed the subpoena and left the clerk's office, he was relieved that the media weren't around. When he arrived at the parking lot, he paid the attendant, got into his car and made his way to the downtown entrance to U.S. 59, the main highway through East Texas.

THERE WAS ANTICIPATION AT the courthouse. In the jury room, the jurors speculated about Tod's first witness. Alfred Totman got it right when he predicted that it would be an obstetrician. However, Joshua Ferrell won the Johnny Bob pot when he predicted the lawyer would wear his red suspenders. The reporters and spectators also were buzzing as they awaited the command from the bailiff. They, too, were debating Tod's first move. Others were talking about the strengths and weaknesses of Johnny Bob's case.

One of the few spectators who remained silent was Mr.

Buschbahm. He respected Tod's ability and hoped that he could pull a big white rabbit out of a hat and carry the day. He always rooted for the home team, and in this case Tod and Jan headed that team. As he eyed those assembled below him, he saw Dr. Moyo hurrying down the stairs, then noticed that Wayne was not in the courtroom.

The bailiff gave the order and Judge O'Reilly walked briskly to her bench. Once again she surveyed the scene and smiled at the camera. Jan noticed that her hair had taken on a different shade of red sometime during the past two weeks. Turning to Tod and Jan, Judge O'Reilly asked, "Are you ready to proceed with your case?"

Tod answered, "Yes, Your Honor. We'll be calling Dr. David Patterson as our first witness."

By now, the jurors and spectators were accustomed to the procedure. Everyone looked to the top of the auditorium where a bailiff opened one of the doors and the man or woman of the hour entered. David Patterson seemed to belong on the back of a horse on a ranch in West Texas. In fact, raising quarter horses was his passion when he wasn't delivering babies. In his fifties, he was a lean and muscular six feet. His hair was already white and his face was lined with wrinkles. It was the sparkle in his emerald green eyes and deep tan that gave him away as a man who was much younger than his years. As he entered the auditorium, he smiled at those assembled and then took the stairs two at a time. Without waiting for direction, he skipped the last step and planted both feet on the floor of auditorium and said, "Good morning, Judge O'Reilly."

"Good morning to you, Dr. Patterson. If you'll raise your right hand to be sworn, I'll do the honors and then you can take a seat."

Dr. Patterson took the witness stand and, again without being prompted, smiled to the jury box and said, "Good morning, ladies and gentlemen."

"Good morning, Doctor," thirteen jurors replied.

This guy is something else, Johnny Bob thought. He hasn't been asked one question and already has the jurors eating out of his hand. Probably every one of the women on the jury, and maybe even the judge, will be switching gynecologists as soon as this thing is over.

Tod began. "Dr. Patterson, would you tell the jury about your profession, education, training and current employment?"

"My name's David Patterson. I'm an obstetrician and gynecologist. I grew up in Houston. Went to the University of Texas in Austin on a baseball scholarship and played shortstop when I wasn't studying. I really hoped that I would be a major league baseball player, but discovered that while my skills were good enough for college ball, they weren't going to take me to the major leagues. I decided I better look for another career and stayed an extra year in Austin, taking more science courses. With that additional year I was able to get into medical school at Texas Tech. After graduating, I did my residency at the U.C.L.A. affiliated hospitals in Los Angeles. Three years in California was enough and I was ready to come back home. I accepted an appointment as an assistant professor at the University of Texas Medical School. That was twenty years ago. Now, I'm a full professor. I also see private patients along with my teaching."

"Doctor, there's a medical textbook, called *Patterson on Obstetrics*. Is that you?"

"Mr. Duncan, sorry, but I can't take that much credit. My uncle wrote the first edition of that book over fifty years ago. However, I am pleased to say that I am one of the five editors of that text. We update it and put out a new edition every few years. I hope the editorial board selected me as one of the editors because of my abilities, not because of my name."

"Dr. Patterson, I've asked you to review the medical records in this case, haven't I?"

"You have, Mr. Duncan."

"Based on that review, Doctor, was Dr. Moyo's care of Lucy Brady negligent?"

"No, sir. It was not. If I may explain, first of all, Dr. Moyo is extremely well trained in our field. What you have to understand is that medicine is not perfect. There are risks and complications in any procedure that are out of the control of even the best of doctors. What happened to Lucy Brady could have happened no matter who performed the procedure."

"But, what about how sick Lucy got, Doctor? Doesn't that tell us that Dr. Moyo must have done something wrong?"

"Of course not. You can't say in medicine that just because there's a bad result that the doctor did something wrong. If the jury has seen the consent form that she signed, then they know that it contains at least twenty known risks, including severe bleeding, infection and even the possibility of death."

Tod pulled the consent form from the stack of exhibits and took his time in going over the known risks and complications, asking the doctor to explain how each of them could occur without negligence. By the time he got through the list, the judge called for the morning break. Tod and Dr. Moyo disappeared down the hallway to their room as if to go over the expert's testimony. As soon as they closed the door, Tod flipped open his cell phone and punched in Wayne's number. As soon as he heard his phone ring, Wayne knew who it was.

"Subpoena service hotline. We serve subpoenas in the daytime and deliver pizzas at night. How can I help you?"

"Okay, Wayne, cut out the comedy," Tod replied. "Where are you?"

"Got tied up in the hassle at the courthouse, Tod. I'm just barely out of Houston, passing through lovely downtown New Caney."

"You got the subpoena, though?"

"Sure. No sweat. I did have to invent an address for Dr. Olstein before the clerk would issue it. If Dr. Moyo's there, ask him if he got Olstein's address."

After a short conference, Tod returned to the phone. "He says that it's Nine-one-four Bayou Street. Ask directions when you get there. I'll give you a call at the lunch break."

As the proceedings resumed after the break, Tod got Dr. Patterson to explain the importance of antibiotics in preventing infection. He confirmed that the problem that Lucy had in throwing up the antibiotic on the night of the abortion played a very significant role in her subsequent illness.

"Doctor, in studying the voluminous records from Lucy's stay at Hermann Hospital, can you tell the jury whether, in your opinion, Lucy will be able to conceive and bear children in the future?"

"Ladies and gentlemen, I have read every page of those records. While Lucy had a stormy time at Hermann and even came close to death, she made it. Her ovaries are intact. Her uterus appears to be in at least average condition. She, by the way, was quite fortunate that the doctors did not have to do a hysterectomy. I can see no medical reason why she can't get pregnant and have children."

WAYNE ARRIVED IN SAN Augustine a little after noon. He stopped at a service station and asked the attendant how to get to Bayou Street.

"Who you looking for on Bayou Street?" the attendant questioned the tall stranger dressed in a dark suit and yellow tie, certainly not standard attire in San Augustine.

"Looking for Doc Olstein's office. You know him?"

"Sure, son, everyone in town does. He's been practicing here near fifty years. Go up here two blocks and take a right. That's Bayou. He'll be down on the left about four blocks. He's got a house there. His clinic is on the first floor and he lives above it." Looking at his watch, the man continued, "You won't find anybody there now. Doc closes for two hours, sometimes three at lunchtime. He'll either be upstairs asleep or he's gone over to Toledo Bend Lake to see if the bass are biting. His nurse, Cary Ann, goes home for lunch."

Wayne thanked him and followed the directions to Dr. Olstein's office. What he found was an old frame house, two stories, with a wide veranda on three sides. Giant oak trees filled the yard. Their limbs overhung the house, the sidewalk and formed a canopy over the street where they met similar trees from the house across the way. The street in front of the house was deserted, a pretty clear sign that the clinic was closed. Wayne got out of his car, walked up the sidewalk and mounted the stairs to the front door. A small sign on the door read WALLACE OLSTEIN, M.D. Wayne rang the doorbell and waited. No one appeared. He knocked loudly and no one came.

Responding to a rumble in his stomach, Wayne got in his car and started driving. Like every other small town in Texas, this one must have a Dairy Queen. He just had to find it. A hamburger and fries would suit him just fine. Then, the phone rang.

"Hey, boss, I'm looking for a Dairy Queen. You want me to bring you anything?"

"All right. Tell me why you're looking for a Dairy Queen and not serving our subpoena."

"No choice, Tod. I got here at lunchtime. Our favorite San Augustine doctor's office is closed 'til two o'clock. I'm stuck."

"Dammit. I want that record. All right. We're on a lunch break here. Grab your sandwich to go and get back over there. I want you camped on that guy's steps when someone gets back."

"You got it, boss. I'll even leave off the onions so I won't offend anyone around here."

Wayne found the Dairy Queen and in twenty minutes he sat on the steps of the old house, hamburger in one hand and large Coke in the other. It wasn't long before he discovered that there was life on Bayou Street. Probably attracted by the smell of Wayne's lunch, an old black Labrador Retriever moseyed around the corner of the porch and camped on the sidewalk three feet in front of the steps where Wayne sat. He didn't bark. He merely sat and stared at Wayne, occasionally smacking his lips. Wayne slowly ate his hamburger and stared back for about a minute, then succumbed.

"Okay, I'll share my fries with you, but forget about getting any of my hamburger." Wayne was positive that he saw the old dog smile. He pulled the bag of french fries out of the sack and stuck a long one in front of his snout. The dog took it very gently between his lips and gulped. Next please. One at a time, Wayne started feeding him the fries as he finished his hamburger. Down to the last bite, he decided the old dog deserved it more than he did. They shared the remainder of the fries until Wayne said, "Sorry, old fellow. All gone."

The dog remained seated for another five minutes and then disappeared around the corner of the house. "Enjoyed lunch," Wayne hollered after him. "Drop in any time."

Wayne hadn't seen the last of the dog. When he returned, the dog had a Frisbee in his mouth and dropped it at the feet of his new friend.

"Okay, Bowser, I figured you'd be ready for a nap after lunch. If you want to play, you've just found one of the best Frisbee tossers in the whole great state of Texas. Let's just see how good you are."

Wayne launched the Frisbee among the trees and the dog took off, looking as if he had dropped at least ten years from his age as he tracked the Frisbee's flight and leaped nearly four feet off the ground to catch it. Wayne was impressed. Thirty minutes later he said, "Okay, you win. You wore me out."

Bowser seemed to understand as he mounted the steps and curled up in the shade of the porch and promptly fell asleep. Wayne looked at his watch and saw that it was approaching two o'clock. So just where was Cary Ann, anyway? As if on cue, an old Ford Taurus turned into the gravel driveway, driven by a heavyset woman in her late forties. As she got out of her car, she saw Wayne starting to get up from his seat on the steps.

"You here to see Dr. Olstein? I don't remember that he had an appointment at two this afternoon. He's over at the lake fishing. Probably won't be back 'til later on."

"No, ma'am. I'm not really looking for Doc Olstein. Name's Wayne Littlejohn. I'm from Houston and I've got a subpoena for you." As he spoke, he handed her the piece of paper.

"Subpoena for what?" the woman asked with irritation in

her voice as she took it and mounted the stairs to the front door.

"If you're Cary Ann, I suspect you're the one I'm looking for. We just need some medical records on one of Dr. Olstein's patients."

As she unlocked the door, Cary Ann turned and said, "Well, you look here, Mr. Wayne whatever your last name is. Like most clinics, we're accustomed to providing medical records in lawsuits. Folks around here always give us a little notice so I can find the records and have Dr. Olstein look at them before we turn them over. You just call back in the morning and I'll give you a time when you can come back next week and get these records."

Frustrated, Wayne raised his voice. "I'm afraid you don't understand, ma'am. We're in trial in Houston on a case right now. That subpoena actually requires you to bring those records to Houston tomorrow morning at nine o'clock. You can either do that or you can just turn them over to me now. If you don't want to give them to me, I'll see you in Houston in the morning or have a sheriff up here for you in the afternoon. Your choice."

Cary Ann frowned at the young man in front of her and finally responded. "Well, you don't have to get so huffy about it. Come on in. I'll see what I can find. What's this patient's name, anyway?"

Relieved, Wayne replied, "Brady, Lucy Baines Brady. My guess is that she's been here in the last few months, no more than six."

Cary Ann looked at the subpoena to confirm the name and then walked into the next room where there were rows of metal shelves crammed with patient records. It looked as if Dr. Olstein had the first record on the first patient that he ever saw.

"Let's see, Brady, Brady, Brady," Cary Ann said to herself. "Got some Bradys here, but no Lucy Baines Brady. You sure you got the right doctor? There are some others here in town."

Wayne was dismayed as well as dumbfounded. "Cary Ann,

I'm sure this is the right place. Maybe her record is on the doctor's desk or maybe misfiled."

"Not misfiled. I can tell you that. I do all the filing and I don't put files in the wrong place. I'll go look on the doctor's desk."

The nurse returned almost immediately. "Nope, not there. Sorry."

Wayne resorted to pleading. "Look, Cary Ann, if I don't go back to Houston with that chart, I'll get fired. Isn't there any place else to look?"

Cary Ann eyed Wayne, weighing something in her mind. "Well, there are certain procedures that Dr. Olstein does where he keeps the files locked up in a cabinet in his office. I suppose that I could look there. Let me find the key."

She rummaged around in her top desk drawer and retrieved a small key, then disappeared into the doctor's office. She returned in less than a minute with a smile on her face. "Found it. I'll make a copy of the chart. It'll cost you a quarter a page."

Wayne couldn't hide his excitement. "Cary Ann, if you said it was a hundred dollars a page, I'd write you out a check."

"Don't tempt me, young man," she replied. "Twenty-five cents is just fine."

Cary Ann went to the back of the house to a copy machine. Wayne followed her to make sure that she copied every page and paid her two dollars and seventy-five cents. Thanking Cary Ann, he rushed out the door, leaped the five porch steps and landed on the sidewalk, waking up Bowser who barked a good-bye.

As soon as he got to the car, he opened the file and began to read. His eyes grew big and a smile erupted on his face. "Well, I'll be a son of a bitch. Wait 'til Tod sees this."

75

"**Dr. Patterson, I'm J.** Robert Tisdale from up at Palestine," Johnny Bob began in his best country boy manner. "You know about clinics and their procedures, don't you?"

"Yes, Mr. Tisdale, I'm on one of our hospital committees that sets policies and procedures for our obstetrical clinic."

"Tell me, Dr. Patterson, if a woman has an abortion and is complaining the next day of some pretty heavy bleeding and then has a fever of one hundred and one, isn't that a time to start getting worried?"

"Depends, Mr. Tisdale. I'd have to know something more about the bleeding. I'd agree that I don't like a temperature of one hundred and one following an abortion."

"Well, let me be more specific, Dr. Patterson. Wouldn't you agree that in Lucy Brady's case, with what she told the nurse on the Saturday following her abortion and what she told the other nurse on Sunday, wouldn't you have expected the nurses to get her in for a doctor to have a look at her?"

"Not necessarily, Mr. Tisdale. The nurses have to exercise some judgment."

"Well, let me put it this way. Let's assume that it was your daughter, and I'm not suggesting that your daughter would have an abortion. By the way, do you have a daughter?"

"Yes, sir. She's eighteen."

"Just Lucy's age. Okay. Assuming that it was your daughter and she had those same problems that Lucy had, wouldn't you want to have her checked by a doctor?"

Dr. Patterson answered, "I agree that would be the best procedure."

"And that's what should have been done in Lucy's case, right, Dr. Patterson?"

"I think that I would agree, sir."

Score one for Johnny Bob and Lucy. He moved on to his next line of questioning as Jan tried to hide a frown.

"Now, Doctor, as to Dr. Moyo, you know that he hadn't gotten any sleep in about thirty-six hours."

"Well, I think that he might have gotten a little, but not much. I might add that it's common for those of us in obstetrics to lose a night's sleep on a fairly regular basis. We can't always convince babies to be born between the hours of nine and five."

Several of the jurors chuckled when they heard Dr. Patterson's reply, especially the women. Even Ruby smiled.

"Believe me, Doctor, I understand that. I've got kids and grandkids of my own and I appreciate you doctors staying there however long it takes to deliver a healthy baby. You would agree that, like anyone else, when you go without sleep it can affect your judgment and could impact on the co-ordination necessary to do surgery, particularly if it's a blind procedure?"

"We're human, too, Mr. Tisdale."

"Now, I understand your testimony about perforation and retained fetal parts being just something that can happen in one of these procedures, but wouldn't you agree that if a doctor is just dead tired, it could have some effect on his skill level?"

"I suppose it could, Mr. Tisdale. I should add that most of us have gone without sleep for many hours and have been able to perform according to the standards of care."

"Well, let me put it this way, then. Since Dr. Moyo didn't have a baby to deliver at the Population Planning clinic, but only had to do some voluntary abortions, wouldn't it have been the better practice for him just to have them get someone to substitute for him instead of trying to do one of these blind procedures with no sleep?"

"Again, Mr. Tisdale, in an ideal world, that might have been a good idea. I don't know what the procedures are at the Population Planning clinic."

Johnny Bob saw his opening. "That brings up a good point, Doctor. In your residency programs, if a doctor has been up for pert near thirty-six hours with no sleep, what's your procedure?"

"We require them to take at least twelve hours off to get some sleep before they return. I might add, I don't think that's the standard of care among obstetricians."

Johnny Bob had made his point and moved on. He established that the witness chose not to do abortions except in the case of rape, incest or to save the life of the mother. Knowing that this would be the last obstetrical witness, he used Dr. Patterson to confirm that there was not an obstetrician in the case who did abortions for voluntary pregnancy termination. He even elicited from Dr. Patterson that most board certified obstetricians took the same position. With that testimony, Johnny Bob was able to give the jury a very clear message that most really good obstetricians didn't want to dirty their hands with such procedures. Then he quit.

It was near the end of the day and Tod made one more point on redirect examination. He established that *Patterson on Obstetrics* taught that a fetus could not be expected to be viable before twenty-three weeks. It was a nice predicate for what would come the next day.

As the judge recessed the trial, Tod rushed down the hall to their room and called Wayne.

"Hi, boss. I'm bringing you something back from San Augustine that you'll like, and it ain't a cheeseburger."

"What is it?"

"Meet me at the fire station. I'm on the outskirts of Houston and I ought to be there about the time you can make it. I'd rather you see it than me tell you about it."

Tod rushed back to the courtroom, grabbed his briefcase, told Jan and Dr. Moyo to meet him back at the office and ran up the stairs and out the door. Jan and Dr. Moyo took one look at each other and followed.

Wayne was so excited that he met them in the parking lot as they arrived. He hurried them into the war room and closed the door.

"Here, Tod, take a look at this. You ain't gonna believe what your baby blues are reading."

Tod read through the chart and as he handed it to Jan, he exclaimed, "Well, I'll be a son of a bitch."

"Couldn't have said it better myself," Wayne grinned. "Matter of fact, you stole my exact words."

Jan just smiled as she handed the chart to Dr. Moyo and they remained silent as he read it. Then he asked, "I understand what I'm reading. How are you going to use it?"

"Let's get a little more information first. Let me see if I can get Dr. Olstein on the phone. We may have to get him down here as a witness."

The phone rang ten times before an elderly male voice answered. "Dr. Olstein, this is Tod Duncan. I'm a lawyer in Houston. My young associate was at your office today."

"Yes, sir. I think that Cary Ann mentioned something about him."

"We're in a lawsuit down here involving Lucy Brady, one of your patients, and we need your help."

"Son, I'm old fashioned. I won't talk about my patients, particularly with a stranger over the phone."

"Look, Dr. Olstein," Tod continued as he tried to hide the exasperation he was feeling, "this is a malpractice case and my client is being sued for one hundred million dollars."

"Oh, is that right? Well, that changes things a little. Don't much care for these malpractice cases. Let me pull my chart and see what I can tell you."

Dr. Olstein left for a moment and returned to the phone. "Ah, yes. I remember this young lady. How she got to me was a little strange."

Although Tod took careful notes, he wouldn't need them. He would never forget what Dr. Olstein had to say. As he ended the conversation, Tod asked Dr. Olstein if he would be willing to come to court on Thursday morning. The doctor was reluctant until Tod offered to pay him $250 an hour as an expert witness fee. That got his attention and he agreed to be there by ten on Thursday morning.

As Tod hung up the phone, he turned to Wayne. "Sure hope you like that road to San Augustine. You'll be on it again tomorrow. Olstein says he'll come on Thursday. I don't want to take any chances. Get to the clerk's office at eight in the morning and have a subpoena issued for him. Get up there and personally hand it to him before he goes fishing. Oh yeah, put another Dairy Queen cheeseburger on your expense account."

That night Tod could not sleep. The events of the day raced through his mind. He wanted to skip the expert witnesses scheduled for the next day and jump right to the one he now expected to be the last witness in the case. Of course, he couldn't do that, but the idea kept him awake. Besides, he couldn't execute his plan until Dr. Olstein made an appearance. By morning, Tod's adrenaline rush was so great that he didn't even miss the night's sleep.

BACK AT THE LOFTS, T.J. was complimenting Johnny Bob on his cross-examination of Dr. Patterson. The drink in his hand enhanced his ebullient spirit. "Boy, Johnny Bob, I knew that I got me the right lawyer when I called you months ago. You proved it with Patterson. We're gonna get us one big verdict against that clinic and Moyo, too. You think that you've sued for enough money?"

Even though Johnny Bob was feeling pretty good himself, at least about Lucy's case, he knew that he had to bring T.J. down a few notches. "Now, T.J., don't start getting too big for your britches. Tod's got himself two first-class experts tomorrow and Jan's got herself a nurse expert who'll probably do a bang up job of explaining how her clinic nurses did the best that they could under the circumstances. And remember, Tod reserved his cross-examination of you. I expect he'll still put you on the stand."

"Hell, Johnny Bob, bring him on. I can take anything that he can dish out. Besides, that jury likes me. I've been watching their faces and every once in a while, I'll see one of them look at me and smile. That Mexican kid even gave me a thumbs-up sign at one point when Dr. Thorpe was testifying. Remember, I'm a man of God and they know that."

Claudia had entered the room and listened quietly until T.J. had finished. Then she looked squarely at him and said, "You better listen to what Johnny Bob has to say. I'll agree that Lucy's case is looking okay, but these experts tomorrow on the beginning of life are just as good as ours. If we don't carry the day on that issue, you'll end up with a judgment that'll make you wish you had been a little more careful about calling out your enemies."

IN THE STRATEGY SESSION during the evening before, Jan told Tod that she wanted to put her nurse expert on the stand next. After the concessions that Dr. Patterson made, she had to diffuse those issues as quickly as possible. As the morning's first witness, Jan called Robin Dorsey, a rotund, gray-haired lady, probably close to sixty. She had been a nurse for nearly forty years and knew her way around hospitals and clinics as well as any nurse in the country. There were few medical problems or medical emergencies that she had not seen in her long career. She had even worked in an abortion clinic for a couple of years, although that had been more than twenty years earlier. Jan focused on the kind of judgment calls that nurses had to make on a daily basis. Whether it was in the office, at a clinic or in the ICU, nurses had to assess patients, listen to their histories and decide if the problem warranted a call to a physician. She did a superb job of explaining the line that a nurse had to walk between deciding what was best for the patient and not being in a position of crying wolf so often that doctors lost confidence in her nursing judgment.

Sure, a nurse was not perfect. Of course, she was occasionally wrong. But using hindsight as she called it, to judge the ordinary care of a nurse would mean that no nurse could ever make a decision not to involve a doctor. And that was not only unreasonable, but also unfair. As for the two clinic nurses, they had to weigh the information that they had and make a judgment call. The fact that it turned out to be wrong did not mean that they acted below the standard of care. In her opinion they did exactly as they should have with the information that they were provided. She added that if either nurse had known that Lucy had thrown up her antibiotic on the night of the abortion, they probably would have changed their decision. As she passed the witness, Jan was pleased with Nurse Dorsey's performance. She also noticed that

Mary Ann O'Donnell, the lab technician, seemed to be nodding her head in approval.

Johnny Bob covered the same basic points that had previously been made with other experts. Then he quit. He figured that, by this late in the trial, the jurors had already made up their minds on the nursing issue before Jan's expert ever got on the witness stand.

It was midmorning. During the break, Tod glanced at his watch and did some mental calculations. To make his plan work he had to get his next two witnesses on and off the stand before the end of the day. He had to make a few points with his next witness and pass him to Johnny Bob, hoping that he would finish before lunch, leaving the afternoon for his last expert, the medical ethicist.

"My name is Lawrence Crosswell. I'm a neonatologist."

"Would you tell the jury, Dr. Crosswell, what a neonatologist is?"

"I'm a baby doctor, but I specialize in very small babies. Most of my practice involves the care of premature babies and full-term babies who have significant problems."

Tod didn't waste any time in getting to the point. "Doctor, at what gestational age can you reasonably expect a baby to live outside the womb?"

"Ideally, Mr. Duncan, we would prefer for the baby to go to full term, which is considered forty weeks. Of course that is not always possible. A few years ago, we were saving premature babies at twenty-eight weeks. Now we are able to save a few who are born at twenty-three weeks, at a cost, I might add, of hundreds of thousands of dollars. Even a million on occasion."

"Dr. Crosswell, from your experience have you formed an opinion as to when human life actually begins?"

"I have, Mr. Duncan." As he spoke, he turned to look at the jury. "From what I see as a neonatologist, I am convinced that there can be no human life outside the mother's womb until approximately twenty-three weeks. I don't quarrel with my geneticist colleagues who say that there is a life form with the potential for human life as early as conception, but the process from conception to birth is a long road, full of obstacles, even with the best of care. Our statistics show that in the first trimester more than fifty percent of pregnancies are lost for one reason or another. It would not be reasonable or even legal to call those deaths of human beings. If we did, we would have a statistically enormous death rate. As a matter of fact, I am not even allowed to complete a death certificate on a baby unless it is actually born alive."

Tod looked at Jan who nodded, and he passed the witness. The move caught Johnny Bob by surprise since he assumed that, like the other experts, this one would be on the stand for several hours. Johnny Bob directed his cross-exam toward the scientific advances that had been developed, giving the fetus born at twenty-three weeks a reasonable chance of living. Dr. Crosswell agreed that the science was still progressing. He also conceded that, like so many other areas of medicine, as medical techniques were refined, they would almost certainly bring down the cost of saving a young life. Johnny Bob closed by violating the cardinal rule of a trial lawyer, never ask a question when you don't know what answer to expect. He asked the witness if he believed in abortion. He took a chance and it paid off in spades. He got a very strong "No."

As Tod and Jan entered their room, Tod second-guessed himself about his strategy with Dr. Crosswell. He was among the best neonatologists in town, yet he ran him through the courtroom like a cow down a chute. On top of that, it turned out that the doctor was pro-life, a question he had never even thought to ask the neonatologist.

"Tod, don't sweat it. You made the call and it's over. Besides, our nun is going to be gangbusters, and by the time the jury hears the testimony tomorrow, they're probably going to forget everything else in the trial."

"You're probably right, Jan. Let's call Wayne and see how he's doing."

WAYNE GOT TO THE clerk's office at seven-thirty and was waiting when the first employee arrived to unlock the door.

Planting himself at the head of the line, he waited until Miss Bubblegum took her seat behind the counter. After he got the subpoena, he pointed his car north and arrived in San Augustine by eleven-thirty. Not a minute too soon. A fishing rod and bait bucket were leaning against the door. As he walked up the steps, Dr. Olstein came out, locking the door behind him. The doctor was a big man, six feet, four inches tall at least, with disheveled white hair, a white beard and an ample belly. Other than being a little tall, he certainly could have played Santa Claus in the San Augustine Christmas parade. Hell, Wayne thought, maybe he does.

"Dr. Olstein, I'm Wayne Littlejohn. I was up here visiting with your nurse, Cary Ann, yesterday afternoon. I have a subpoena for you to appear in court in Houston tomorrow."

The old man glared at the young one. "Son, that's not necessary. I've told your boss I'll be there and I'm a man of my word."

"I understand that, sir. It's a big trial and we just can't afford to take a chance."

The old doctor's demeanor softened slightly. "Well, I understand it's a big trial. I've been following it in the newspaper and I catch a little bit of it on TV. Didn't realize until yesterday, though, that it involved one of my patients. Guess my memory isn't what it used to be. I'll take your paper. I'll be there. Don't like these damn malpractice cases myself. Gonna put us doctors out of business."

He picked up his fishing rod and bait bucket, said goodbye and headed to an old Ford pickup. After he placed his rod and bucket in the bed of the truck, he backed it out of the drive and drove slowly down the tree-covered street.

On his way out of town, Wayne stopped at the Dairy Queen once more for a cheeseburger. As he ordered, he had a second thought and made it two. After paying, he drove back to the doctor's office, got out of his car and whistled. It wasn't long before his four-legged friend came around the corner of the house. As Bowser approached, Tod took the second cheeseburger from the sack, unwrapped it and handed it to the dog. Two gulps and it was gone. The Retriever looked up at his new friend with eyes that asked, "Okay. Now, how about my fries?"

"Sorry, Bowser, that's it for the day. I'll drop by the next time I'm in the neighborhood."

Realizing that lunch was over, the old dog trotted back around the corner of the house as Wayne got in his car to head back to Houston. While he fastened his seat belt, the cell phone rang.

"SPCA, San Augustine chapter."

"You get him served?"

"Sure did, Tod. Caught him, fishing pole in hand, just before he left his office. He'll be there. If for nothing else, he doesn't like malpractice suits. Look for a big, overgrown Santa Claus tomorrow and that'll be him."

"Okay. Get on back here. We've got the nun on this afternoon and I want you in on the planning for tomorrow."

76

The nun was Sister Mary Ruth Bennett, Mary Ruth Bennett, Ph.D. and Mary Ruth Bennett, M.D. Additionally, she was a very good-looking woman. At five feet, five inches tall, she had short brown hair, blue eyes, the face of a model, and filled out a business suit like an aerobics instructor. She became a nun out of a strong religious conviction. She served on the faculty of Tulane University Medical School as a medical ethicist. While her church didn't like what she had to say on the subject, she had adopted the viewpoint that ensoulment did not occur at conception, but at a much later date. It was for that reason that Tod and Jan had decided she would be their last witness. Last, that is, until the revelation of the previous day. After establishing her credentials, Tod got to the heart of her testimony.

"Oh, one last preliminary question, Doctor. If you're a nun, why aren't you wearing one of those black nun's habits?"

Dr. Bennett smiled at the thought. "I'm afraid that would be impossible for me. It's no longer required of nuns and I don't even own one. Conservative business suits like this one do me quite well."

"Dr. Bennett, we heard from a Dr. Thorpe . . ."

"I know him. He's quite well known and respected," Dr. Bennett interrupted.

"Well, ma'am, he's testified for these folks on the jury. He says that there's no doubt that God infuses the human soul at the moment of conception. Is that a viewpoint that you agree with?"

"No, sir. May I explain?"

"Please do."

"I'm sure that you will all find it more than unusual that a nun would be in this chair, offering the opinions that you are about to hear. Please let me explain. Before I was a nun, I was a woman. As a very young woman, even a little younger than Lucy here, I was raped and became pregnant. Having been raised by a very devout Catholic family, I followed in their tradition. I prayed about what to do about the pregnancy. Some days I think that I must have prayed every waking hour. If God gave me an answer, I didn't understand it. Finally, I had an abortion for all the reasons that young girls make that choice. I was lucky that I didn't have any physical complications from my abortion, but I was overwhelmed with guilt. Two years later I entered the convent. After I became a nun, I asked for and received permission to study philosophy. Then, I obtained a medical degree. During all of those years, I studied everything that I could find that dealt with the beginning of human life and what we Catholics call 'ensoulment.' Deep down, I knew that I was looking for the answer to the question I had carried with me from the day I ended my pregnancy. Had I killed my baby?"

Tod was studying the jurors who were listening to every word his witness was saying. He interrupted, "Dr. Bennett, did you find the answer to your question?"

"If I may, for a moment, answer like a lawyer, yes and no. I concluded, like most scientists, that there is certainly a life form at the moment of conception. Is that life form a baby? I must respectfully disagree with my church's current doctrine."

"Can you explain?"

"I hope so, Mr. Duncan. The Supreme Court probably said it best when they said it was a medical, philosophical and religious debate. The truth of the matter is that no one can really say with certainty. Only God knows for sure. Like so many other mysteries, I think that He has chosen to keep that answer to himself. I know that there are others who say that they speak for God. I cannot accept that."

As she made the statement, she looked directly at T.J. "I have spent my life searching for just such an answer and I can tell you what I have concluded. Others may disagree, but my research confirms that far less than half of fertilized eggs develop into human beings. A large number never attach to the uterine wall. Others detach in the first several weeks or just don't develop and are washed away. To suggest that God has a pregnancy mechanism that is going to naturally eliminate over half of fertilized eggs and embryos, yet say that same God has given them a soul, only to have that human person die an early natural death just does not make sense."

Glenn Ford, the Rice University professor, looked on with agreement.

"Obviously, as a fetus approaches term it has all the characteristics of a newborn baby. While some might say that it is not alive until it breathes its first breath, I would disagree and say that in those last several weeks in the womb, the fetus is a human person. At the other extreme, the zygote and embryo during the first several weeks really have virtually no characteristics that we would ascribe to a human person. The embryo has no capacity for reasoning. The embryo has no self-awareness. The embryo cannot communicate. It really has none of the characteristics of personhood. Is there a life form at conception that is a member of the biological species, Homo sapiens? From a scientific standpoint, the answer must be yes.

"The idea that a distinct person emerges at conception is

not a scientific claim but a moral one. Just as a baby is not an adult, neither can we say that an embryo is a baby. Just as a baby must evolve through a multitude of changes to become an adult, so must that first cell evolve through a series of changes to become a human being. I am convinced that a fetus is not a human person in the first trimester. I am convinced that it is a human person in the last few weeks in the womb. In my opinion, the debate centers between eighteen weeks and twenty-four weeks. At this stage of the development of our knowledge, I cannot be more precise. Have I answered your question, Mr. Duncan?"

"I have a question, Dr. Bennett. How can you be right and all of the priests be wrong?" The voice was not that of Tod, but of Alberto Marino.

Judge O'Reilly immediately stood at her bench. "I'm sorry, Mr. Marino. Our procedures do not permit jurors to ask questions. You'll have to refrain from doing so anymore. I apologize for not making that clear earlier."

Pleased with how this brilliant woman was doing Tod asked the juror's question. "Dr. Bennett, since I can ask questions, I'll ask the one posed by Mr. Marino. How come you're so sure you're right and priests, popes and bishops for two thousand years are wrong?"

"Mr. Duncan, and Mr. Marino, ladies and gentlemen." Dr. Bennett looked first at the jury, then at the audience and last at the TV camera. "I do not speak for my church or for my medical school. I'm giving you only the benefit of my years of study. I disagree with my church on many issues. Remember that my church has not had a consistent position on this issue. Further, the Vatican requires compulsory pregnancy for women. Men made this choice. It is the men in my church who do not permit me or any other woman to become a priest. My church says that regardless of pregnancy by rape, incest, or accident, a woman must remain pregnant. My church encourages freedom of choice, but if the men in my religion had their way, those choices for a woman would be limited to the woman's role as a wife and mother. God selected women to bear the responsibility of childbearing. It seems clear that God has also placed His confidence in women as moral beings. It should be woman, not man, who makes the final decision about whether to bear children. God gave humans free will, the Bible's term for right to choose. It was not 'I give you such a right but you must always choose My way.' God trusted women. Otherwise, he would not have given us the right to choose." She turned to face the jury box and confronted Mr. Marino.

"I might also add, Mr. Marino, that our church, yours and mine, has always waited until a child is born alive before it is christened. Even today there is no movement to christen fetuses in the womb or embryos that are in a test tube. Sometimes, in religion as elsewhere, actions speak louder than words."

Very quietly, Tod asked, "Did you kill a baby when you had an abortion, Dr. Bennett?"

"Mr. Duncan, I had an abortion at about fifteen weeks. After twenty years of thinking about it, praying about it and studying it, I did not. I am at peace with myself."

"Pass the witness, Your Honor."

"Fine, Mr. Duncan. Let's take a break and then we'll hear cross-examination from Mr. Tisdale."

Jan turned, shook Tod's hand and whispered, "Nice job!"

"Thanks. She's a strong woman. Let's reserve judgment until we see what Johnny Bob does with her."

After the break Johnny Bob attacked. "Ma'am, do I call you Dr. Bennett or Sister Mary Ruth or what? See, I'm not a Catholic and I'm a little confused about what hat you're wearing."

"In this secular setting, Mr. Tisdale, probably Dr. Bennett is correct."

Tod smiled.

"Well, Dr. Bennett, I assume from what you have said that you are in favor of abortion."

Johnny Bob got an answer he didn't anticipate. "No, Mr. Tisdale. I'm not in favor of abortion. No one that I know of has anything good to say about abortion, including me."

"Well, then . . ."

"If I may continue, Mr. Tisdale, I was not through with my answer. The only ones who favor abortion are those who have decided for whatever reason that they really have no choice. A woman may need it to save her own life. She may choose it because it's the best thing for her emotional well-being or the financial and social well being of herself and her family. Would any woman rather not be in a position of having to make that choice? Of course she would. Does that mean that she favors it? Absolutely not."

Rarely at a loss for words in front of a jury, Johnny Bob was surprised at her answer. He looked down as he fumbled with his notes.

"Now, you're a religious woman, aren't you, ma'am?"

"That should be rather clear, Mr. Tisdale."

"Wouldn't you agree that you Catholics have had some pretty good thinkers who have been discussing and debating this and other similar topics for a couple of thousand years now?"

"True, sir."

"Yet, you want this jury to throw out two thousand years of debate and carefully thought-out decisions and just accept what you have concluded in about twenty years."

"It's their choice, sir," Dr. Bennett replied. "I thought that I had made it clear that these were only my opinions and not that of my church or my university. I am not permitted to speak for either."

"Even science has advanced in the past several decades so that we now know that first tiny cell has all the DNA from its mother and father to become a complete human being. When your church decided over a hundred years ago that human life began at conception, they didn't even have the benefit of that science. Isn't that true?"

"If that's a question, Mr. Tisdale, I'd agree."

"As I understand it, Dr. Bennett, you're a member of a number of pro-choice groups, aren't you?"

"I am, sir."

"Another word for those groups would be pro-abortion?"

"Not in every case, Mr. Tisdale." The witness suddenly

broke out in a coughing spell. Johnny Bob, ever the gentleman, quickly poured water from the pitcher on his table and took the cup to the witness, who thanked him and continued as several jurors smiled their appreciation at the big man. The witness continued. "What I was saying is that most of those groups do support a woman's right to choose."

"Isn't it true that every time a bill comes before Congress or any state legislature that would limit abortion, you're called on to testify against it?"

"I'm often asked to testify and do so when my schedule permits."

As she answered, Johnny Bob put on his reading glasses and looked down at notes Claudia handed to him. "As a matter of fact, just this year you've testified before fourteen legislative bodies and in every case, I mean every case, you've testified in favor of abortion. Isn't that right, Dr. Bennett?"

"I don't keep up with the numbers, Mr. Tisdale."

Tod saw that Johnny Bob was on a roll now. He was doing a good job of showing the witness's bias. Tod was beginning to think that Johnny Bob would call her a religious maverick or abortion zealot by the time he got to closing argument. Thank God it had turned out that she was not the last witness. He tuned back in to Johnny Bob as he was asking, "Dr. Bennett, you're familiar with the current debate in our country about research on fetuses and stem cells from fetuses that have been aborted, aren't you?"

"Mr. Tisdale, it's not only on cells that have been aborted. The research is also on cells from miscarriages and frozen embryos that have been abandoned."

"In fact, Dr. Bennett, didn't you just recently testify before a congressional committee, advocating the use of cells from aborted fetuses for scientific research?"

"My testimony was more broad than that. That research, by the way, is very important to many people in this country with otherwise incurable diseases."

"Objection, Your Honor. Nonresponsive."

"Overruled, Mr. Tisdale. Please continue."

"And again, Dr. Bennett, your position on that subject is

contrary to that of the Vatican and the entire Catholic Church which condemns such research because it is likely to encourage abortions?"

She spoke softly now. "My position on stem cell research is contrary to most of those in my church."

"Yes, ma'am. One more area, Dr. Bennett, or for this line of questions, maybe it should be Sister Mary Ruth. Now if my Baptist Bible is the same as your Catholic Bible, God has spoken about life in the womb, hasn't He?"

"Some people have interpreted various verses in that way, Mr. Tisdale."

"For example, God spoke to old Jeremiah, not Reverend Thomas Jeremiah Luther here, ma'am, but the original one, and told him, 'Before I formed you in the womb I knew you, and before you were born I consecrated you. I appointed you a prophet to the nations.'"

"That's in the Bible, sir."

"Now, you don't think God would be so dumb as to consecrate Jeremiah as a prophet even before he was born if he didn't think that there was a human life in there, do you?"

"Sir, that verse doesn't say when in the pregnancy that occurred. I can only assume that it must have been late in the pregnancy."

"You don't know, do you? Could have been right after conception, right?"

"Could have been, yes, Mr. Tisdale."

"And if we go to the New Testament, Sister Mary Ruth, Luke told us about John the Baptist and said that he would be filled with the Holy Spirit, even from his mother's womb. Now if God had filled him with the Holy Spirit while he was still in his mama's womb, don't you imagine that he must have gotten around to infusing him with a soul before that time?"

Sister Mary Ruth looked down at her hands, now clasped in front of her on the witness stand rail before looking up and replying, "Probably so, Mr. Tisdale."

"Last, Sister Mary Ruth, you know the Ten Commandments, don't you?"

"Yes, sir. I do my best to live by them and the Golden Rule."

"You know, don't you, Sister Mary Ruth, that God commands us not to kill."

Johnny Bob had done a remarkable job of stripping away her scientific and philosophical garb, leaving her before the jury in a nun's habit.

"Yes, sir. That is God's commandment."

Johnny Bob looked at the jury with satisfaction on his face and turned to the judge. "No further questions, Your Honor."

"Call your next witness, Mr. Duncan."

"If it please the court, I can advise you and the jury that I have only one more witness. Since it's close to the end of the day, I would prefer to put that witness on in the morning."

The judge turned to the jury. "Don't get your hopes up, but we might get lucky and get this to you tomorrow afternoon. Please remember my instructions. I'll see you in the morning."

As soon as they got back to the fire station, Tod threw his briefcase down on the war room table. "Marilyn, go up to my office and get that bottle of scotch out of the bottom drawer of my credenza. I need something more than a beer after today. Make me a tall scotch and water and fix one for Wayne and Jan."

"Wayne's not back yet, Tod. And, Marilyn, make mine a Chardonnay," Jan said.

As it turned out, Wayne had returned to his office. When Marilyn told him the team was assembled downstairs, Wayne managed to come down the fire pole, holding the pole in one hand and a glass of scotch in the other. His landing spilled only a few drops. "Well, Tod, I understand from Marilyn that you got an education on the Bible this afternoon. About time you got some religion."

"Yeah, thanks. With friends like you, why do I even need the Johnny Bobs of the world? And how come you've got scotch and I don't?"

Before Wayne could answer, Marilyn entered with a tray

of drinks. Tod grabbed the glass of scotch and water, downing about a third before coming up for air. "Thanks, Marilyn, I needed that."

"Yeah, boss, but watch it," Marilyn cautioned. "You obviously haven't slept much in two days and I would hate for you to have to ice this cake tomorrow with a hangover."

"Don't worry. Only one. Okay, Wayne, are we set with Dr. Olstein for tomorrow?"

"As set as we can be, Tod. I've subpoenaed him and gave him an advance of two thousand dollars for his time. Short of hog-tying him and throwing him in the trunk of my car, that's the best I can do. He'll be here at ten o'clock. I'll meet him at the metal detector and get him to the fourth floor. Whether I'm with him or not, just have Jan be on the lookout for a giant Santa Claus at the top of the courtroom. You'll be busy with our favorite witness. With a little luck, you may not even have to put Dr. Olstein on the stand."

77

The last day of any trial, civil or criminal, is filled with anticipation and trepidation, usually in about equal parts. The anticipation comes from the hope of victory. The trepidation stems from the possibility that no matter how well things have gone or how hard the parties and lawyers have worked, their fate rests in the hands of twelve strangers.

On this Thursday morning, Tod rose early, dressed and poured a cup of coffee to drink on the way to work. Leaving a note for his boys, he left the house at five-thirty to beat the Houston traffic.

Up at five o'clock, Johnny Bob sipped coffee and reviewed his notes as he prepared for closing argument. He would wear his red tie, red suspenders, put the red handkerchief in his coat pocket and wear his red-topped boots. Let's have a lot of winners today.

A few doors down the hall T.J. smiled in anticipation that Tod would call him back on the stand. As he shaved, he studied the road maps that he had for eyes and wondered where his road would lead after today. Next, he dressed and read the morning *Chronicle* while he flipped channels, looking for news about the trial.

He didn't have to look far. The *Chronicle* headline announced that the trial was likely to go to the jury today. The network morning shows had reporters in Houston, set up outside the law school, reporting on the events of the previous day, especially the testimony of a nun who was on the pro-choice side. T.J. listened as CNN announced that Governor Vandenberg, the Republican presidential candidate, had arrived in Houston the night before and would be behind the barricades with the other pro-life forces. The polls were showing a statistical dead heat. Obviously, the candidate wanted to be where the action and the TV cameras would be. T.J. would make sure that they had a photo opportunity before he entered the building. T.J. placed his white Stetson on his head, careful not to mess his hair. As he walked out the door, he picked up his gold Bible and sunglasses.

The crowds began assembling on the street outside of the building long before dawn. If this was to be the last act of the drama, supporters on both sides wanted to be able to say that they were there when the curtain came down. The various TV and newspaper reporters were interviewing the people behind the barricades.

Back at the fire station Tod met Jan, Wayne and Marilyn. They walked out to Tod's Suburban and drove the ten minutes to the law school. As they parked the car, they were met by a deputy who told them that the crowds were already so big that they were overflowing the ends of the barricades. He escorted them into the building. One last time, they walked between the barricades, game faces on, refusing to acknowledge the throngs on either side of the street.

Johnny Bob and Claudia came in separate vehicles and arrived about five minutes after their adversaries. They also walked, grim-faced, through the crowds with Claudia only pausing to shake the hands of two friends who were behind the pro-life barricades. She whispered to Johnny Bob, "You ain't gonna believe this. Our friend, Governor Vandenberg, is here, surrounded by a bunch of big guys with gadgets in their ears."

Johnny Bob glanced to the pro-life side, replying, "I can believe it. Where else is he gonna find this many cameras and reporters in one place?" Then he laughed and said, "Just goes to show we're an equal opportunity trial. Both candidates feel free to drop in whenever they want their mugs on TV."

Several of the reporters were holding microphones in front of the presidential candidate as cameras rolled. One asked, "You're on the pro-life side of the street. Does that mean that you would encourage the jury to find in favor of Lucy Brady and Reverend Luther?"

Dressed in a blue suit, white shirt and a tie that looked like it was borrowed from Johnny Bob, power red in color, the candidate said, "Everyone in the country knows my stand on abortion. It certainly wouldn't be proper for me to suggest anything to the jury, although I understand that they are sequestered. I'm here to show my support for the young lady and Reverend Luther. As you know, Reverend Luther is a friend of mine and friends should be there for friends."

In her small office behind the bench, Judge O'Reilly visited with Deputy Johnson. "So, did you ever think that we would make it this far without a mistrial?"

"Frankly, Judge, no, but here we are. I want to thank you for letting me be a part of this. I'll be telling my future law partners and grandkids about this for the rest of my life."

"Just the luck of the draw. Some other judge's number could have come up when Johnny Bob filed this, and we'd be back in my old courtroom, trying a fender-bender today instead of playing supporting roles in the biggest courtroom drama to come along in years."

"Now, Judge, I may qualify for a very small supporting role, but you've been the ringmaster in this circus. Without you, this show never would have gotten this far. If I may ask, what are your thoughts at this point?"

"Really only one," Judge O'Reilly replied. "Have I made all the right rulings? Will this son of a bitch stand up on appeal? Well, I suppose those are two, but closely connected. Enough talk. Go check to see if our jurors are here. If they are, let's get ready for the grand finale."

As he rose, Tod spoke the words that everyone had anticipated, "Your Honor, we will re-call T.J. Luther."

As T.J. took the stand, he put the Bible on the rail in front of the witness chair, then placed his hands on top of it. "I'm ready, Mr. Duncan."

Tod took a deep breath and launched what he hoped would be the cross-examination of his career. "Let's start, Reverend Luther, by refreshing the jury a little about your testimony of a couple of weeks ago. We know that you are a man of God and you will tell us nothing but the truth."

"I will, sir, so help me God. As a matter of fact, I just gave a sermon last Sunday where I discussed the Ten Commandments, including one forbidding the bearing of false witness, God's way of commanding that His followers must always tell the truth."

Johnny Bob grimaced behind a big hand that covered his mouth. *Shit,* he thought, *I forgot to remind him again just to answer the questions and not volunteer anything, but it wouldn't have done any good.* T.J. was on center stage in the last act of this drama and he was going to try to take control. Might as well just sit back and watch the fireworks.

"And you are a strong believer that abortion is a sin."

T.J. looked at the jury and replied, "Sir, I believe it's even much stronger than that. The other commandment that I discussed just last Sunday was 'Thou shalt not kill'!" His voice rose on the last four words, almost as if he were behind his pulpit in Fort Worth rather than on the witness stand.

"We've established that this lawsuit against my clients and Population Planning was your brainchild."

"Yes, sir. I've readily conceded that."

"Your reason for doing that, Reverend Luther, was because you have the very strong belief that anyone who performs an abortion is a murderer and a baby killer."

"Mr. Duncan, I used those words only because I could not think of any stronger ones at the time."

Tod rose and walked a few steps to stand beside Dr. Moyo, placing his hand on his client's shoulder as he did so. "In fact, those were the words that you used to describe my client, Dr. Moyo, not just once but on several occasions from your pulpit in Fort Worth where those words were carried by television to the four corners of this world."

T.J. took that as a compliment and a self-satisfied smile covered his face as he answered. "Yes, Mr. Duncan, I have a worldwide ministry and I used those words to describe your client and Population Planning. In fact, I repeated those exact words from this witness stand two weeks ago. I have not changed my opinion."

Johnny Bob had a quizzical look on his face. All of this had been made very clear to the jury. There had to be a reason for rehashing such testimony. However, his years of experience were not giving him a clue.

Tod continued. "As I understand it, you agree that such accusations would be defamatory, meaning they could certainly damage a person's reputation. Your defense is that they are true. Correct?"

"That is correct, Mr. Duncan."

"Now, you've also testified that it's not just the abortionist who is a murderer, but anyone who aids or assists in having an abortion performed is likewise to be cast in the very same light."

"Your memory is very good, Mr. Duncan. I said almost those exact words." T.J. leaned back in the witness chair, legs crossed and hands folded on his knee, a picture of relaxation and confidence. "Those who are found to have aided or assisted a woman in having an abortion and killing her baby are likewise murderers."

Tod paused momentarily to make sure that he had fully

set the trap. "Reverend Luther, on this subject of bearing false witness, I suppose that if you were found to have borne false witness in this trial, you would tell the jury to disregard all of your words. To disregard all of your testimony for you would have been found to have been a liar, not subject to belief under oath or anywhere else."

"Again, sir, I think that I covered that two weeks ago. I'll go one step further and add that if I were to be found to bear false witness in this trial, I would recommend that the jury find against me."

Johnny Bob had laid traps for witnesses often enough to recognize one. He could only hope that T.J. was smart enough to avoid getting caught. What Johnny Bob didn't know was that Tod had just dug a trap big enough for an elephant.

"Reverend Luther, have you ever killed anyone, even in the days that you described when you lived on the dark side of life in Fort Worth before you were born-again?"

So that's where he's going, Johnny Bob thought. He's turned up some crime, maybe even murder that T.J. has hidden all these years. Johnny Bob rose to his feet. "Your Honor, I respectfully object. Whatever Reverend Luther did years ago and before be was born-again is hardly relevant to any issue in this case."

"Sustained."

Tod didn't care that the objection was sustained. He had just thrown that question out as a red herring to get T.J. worried about what he might have on him from that era of his life. Tod switched gears.

"Reverend Luther, do you drive a new white Lincoln Continental?"

"Yes, sir. I do. In fact, a lady in Fort Worth whom I cured of lung cancer gave it to me."

The answer got Jessie's attention. If it was the same Lincoln she knew about, she had been with T.J. when he bought it from one of her late husband's dealerships. While she no longer owned the dealership, she was able to get the car for T.J. at the dealer's cost.

"Does that white Lincoln Continental have a license plate that reads CHOSEN 1?"

"I believe it does, Mr. Duncan. My public relations people secured that license plate for me many years ago."

Having thrown out a couple of softballs, Tod started throwing strikes. "Reverend Luther, have you ever assisted any woman in any way to have an abortion? Let me clarify that. Let's make it since you awakened from your long sleep."

Now the cogwheels were spinning furiously in T.J.'s mind as he replied, "Of course not, Mr. Duncan. Absolutely not, ladies and gentlemen of the jury."

"Reverend Luther, are you familiar with a town called San Augustine?"

"I believe I've heard of it, sir," T.J. replied, his face suddenly feeling flushed.

"Not a very good question. Let me try again. Have you ever been to San Augustine, a small town up in East Texas along the Louisiana border?"

It was an innocuous question to everyone in the courtroom except T.J. Now Johnny Bob knew that he was about to witness a trap being sprung.

T.J. answered, "I . . . I think that I might have been there many years ago, early in my ministry when I was working small towns with the Jerry Abraham tent revivals."

"I mean more recently, sir. Like in the past couple of months?"

"No, sir. Not that I recall."

The jury looked puzzled.

"Oh, and, Reverend Luther, have you ever seen or met a Dr. Olstein from San Augustine?"

T.J. nervously ran his fingers through his hair as he tried to respond with a firm voice. "No, sir. Never heard of him." Turning to the judge, he asked, "Your Honor, I wonder if we might take a break at this time."

Judge O'Reilly was not about to break up Tod's cross-examination. Besides, she was as curious as everyone else in the courtroom about where these questions were leading.

"Reverend, unless it's a real physical emergency, we need to move on."

"It is, Judge."

"Very well. The bailiff will escort you to the men's room. The rest of us will wait here until you return. The rest of you are welcome to stand and stretch. Don't go anywhere. Deputy Johnson, please go with the witness."

T.J. didn't get what he wanted. He had hoped for a fifteen-minute break to confer with Johnny Bob about this whole line of questioning. Maybe he could have found some way to stop it. Judge O'Reilly had foiled that attempt. T.J. followed the bailiff out the door to the men's room where he washed his face and hands. In less than five minutes, T.J. returned to the witness stand.

"Feeling better now, Reverend?" Tod asked.

"I am, sir."

"All right, Reverend Luther, let me get to the bottom of this. Isn't it true that about five weeks ago you arranged for Lucy Baines Brady to go to San Augustine, Texas, where she had another abortion, this time by one Dr. Wallace Olstein?"

Tod could have pitched a hand grenade in the courtroom and it would not have caused any more commotion. The people in the audience, forgetting that they were in a courtroom, were abuzz with conversation. Reporters openly talked into microphones and tape recorders. Johnny Bob glared at T.J., a frown covering his enormous face. Lucy looked down at her hands. Her parents and Aunt Jessie had blank looks on their faces.

At the judge's instructions, the bailiff yelled, "Order in the court!" It took him five times to restore silence in the auditorium.

Judge O'Reilly, using her most stern and judicial voice, said, "There will be no more outbursts like that. If it occurs again, I'll have the entire audience, including the media, removed. This will still be a public trial, only you will be watching it on television." There was an immediate hush among the spectators.

Suddenly, T.J. straightened up in his seat, turned to face the jury and said, "No, Mr. Duncan, I did not."

Murmurs filled the courtroom until the judge banged her gavel. Silence returned quickly. With the silence came a creaking of a door at the back of the courtroom. Jan looked around and whispered to Tod, "Santa Claus has just come to town."

Dr. Olstein had entered. Wayne was with him and directed him to stand at the back of the auditorium where T.J. could clearly see him. The two men stood there, arms folded, leaning against the back wall. With a very deliberate motion, Tod turned in his seat and stared at them. As he planned, the eyes of seven hundred spectators, thirteen jurors, four bailiffs, the parties, opposing counsel and the judge looked with him.

While Tod could not see behind T.J.'s glasses, he was sure T.J. had to recognize the big man with the flowing white beard.

Of course, T.J. saw the man in the back of the building. Trying to calm a racing heart, T.J. looked at Tod and said, "Perhaps I should explain something, Mr. Duncan."

"Perhaps you should explain a lot of things, Mr. Luther," Tod replied. If Johnny Bob could strip Dr. Bennett of her rightful title, then he could defrock T.J.

"After I was able to heal Lucy. To ... uh ... assist her with walking again, I became her counselor. She was seventeen at the time. She had no friends. She needed someone to confide in. I served as her counselor, her preacher and her mentor. She came to our Sunday night youth fellowships. We usually took that time for me to give her counseling. She was an emotionally distraught young lady. As I worked with her over the weeks and months, she began to come around. She was less withdrawn. A smile filled her face once in awhile. She even started talking about her desire to join the Miracle Singers. And it is correct, sir, that I encouraged her to file this lawsuit. While she deserved to be compensated for the damages she had sustained at the hands of these defendants, I also thought that it was important that this lawsuit be a means to bring closure to a very horrible part of her life."

T.J. looked at the jury and saw that he had their attention as he continued in a firm voice. Johnny Bob whispered to

Claudia, "I don't know where this son of a bitch is going, but I don't think we're going to like it when we get to the end of the road. I'm fresh out of ideas. You got any?"

Claudia could only shake her head.

T.J. focused his attention on the jury, certain that he was putting on the performance of his life. Tod's supposition about the bearded man in the back of the courtroom was correct. T.J. recognized the doctor. On the other hand, T.J. figured Dr. Olstein did not recognize him. T.J. had stayed in the car with darkened windows on the night he drove Lucy from Fort Worth to San Augustine. Dr. Olstein was standing on the porch when they were leaving; he could not have seen who was driving.

"During the course of this lawsuit, because of the strength and force of my convictions, the judge incarcerated me in your jail here in Harris County."

Looking at Johnny Bob, he said, "Mr. Tisdale, I know that I was not supposed to tell the jury about that, but they need to hear the whole truth and Judge O'Reilly did put me in jail when I refused to answer deposition questions by Mr. Duncan.

"After I got out of jail, and by the way, after the White House called me to confer with the president, I returned to Fort Worth and received a call from Lucy. She told me that she, was, ah . . . . had, yes, had a relationship with a young man in my church and was pregnant again. She was around twenty weeks along. She asked for my help. She was distraught.

Lucy stared at T.J. in disbelief. As his words sank in, her face flushed and tears welled up in her eyes. Her parents were suddenly sheet white as they looked to her for a reaction. Jessie glared at T.J. with a look that pierced straight through his dark glasses.

"Frankly, I thought she might commit suicide," he continued, hanging his head. "I, ah, I made arrangements for her to have her pregnancy terminated and, ah . . . yes, ah, arranged for the young man to drive her to San Augustine for the procedure. It was against everything that I stood for and believed in, but if Lucy was going to survive, I thought that it had to be done quickly and, obviously, out of the glare of public attention."

From behind Tod, there came a voice, quiet and then increasingly louder. "That's not true." Lucy was on her feet, pointing at T.J. "Liar. You liar! YOU made me do it!" Turning to the jury she cried, "He's lying. He made me do it."

Turning finally to her family, she sobbed and shouted. "I didn't want an abortion. I wanted that baby. He told me that if I didn't have an abortion, we would lose this lawsuit, and I had to have it done. He made me lie about it." She fell to the floor and buried her head in her mother's lap.

Pandemonium broke out. Over the uproar in the auditorium, the judge pounded her gavel. All four bailiffs yelled for order in the court. Johnny Bob and Claudia saw their lawsuit spinning out of control. Tod and Jan merely looked at their notes. In the back of the courtroom Wayne was smiling. On the witness stand, T.J. had turned as white as his linen suit.

As the judge restored order, Joanna wrapped her arms around her sobbing daughter. Judge O'Reilly said to her deputy, "Mr. Johnson, please escort Ms. Brady and her mother out of the courtroom until she is able to regain her composure. Mr. Brady and Ms. Woolsey, you're welcome to go with them if you desire."

Bo joined his wife and daughter as they left the courtroom. Jessie could feel her blood boiling as she continued to stare at T.J. "No, thank you, Judge. I'll stay. I want to hear the rest of this."

Silence instantly blanketed the huge auditorium.

"Mr. Luther, let me see if we can't move this along," Tod continued. "Isn't the whole truth that you were looking for a place for Lucy to have an abortion as far away from Fort Worth as you could find?"

"Yes, sir. I thought it was important for Lucy's sake."

"You found Dr. Olstein who had been doing abortions in deep East Texas for nearly fifty years, even before the Supreme Court said they were legal?"

In a quiet and humble voice, T.J. replied, "Yes, sir."

"You wrote a check to Dr. Olstein on your private account for five thousand dollars to do the abortion at eight o'clock on a Sunday night?"

"We had to have it done in a hurry, sir. The hour of the evening was just how long it took for the, ah, for the young man to get Lucy to San Augustine."

Tod took the opportunity to glance at the jury. They were stunned. They had front row seats at the best soap opera in town. Several jurors were leaning back with arms folded, their body language making it clear that after three weeks of trial, they finally saw the real T.J. Luther. Finally, Tod thought, some of them were beginning to see this man as the snake oil salesman he was rather than the persona of God's man on earth that he had so carefully crafted. He tossed another hand grenade.

"Mr. Luther, isn't it true that you were the one who drove Lucy to San Augustine?"

"Absolutely not, sir. The young man took her in one of our vehicles, a white Chevrolet, I believe."

Tod paused for dramatic effect. "Oh, T.J., come clean for once in your life. Tell this jury the truth! The child Lucy was carrying was really yours, now wasn't it? It was your very own flesh and blood that you were arranging to have aborted, isn't that the truth?"

Again it happened. The courtroom exploded. A few reporters leaped from their seats to be the first to break the story.

Summoning whatever will he had left, T.J. tried righteous indignation. "Mr. Duncan, I'm shocked that you would even suggest such a thing."

Last hand grenade. Tod reached into his briefcase and took out a thin file folder. From the top of the auditorium, Wayne let another smile cross his lips. Tod took one long sheet of paper from the folder, rose and walked over to the court reporter, asking, "Would you please mark this as our next exhibit?"

It became Defense Exhibit Number 19. As was the custom, Tod handed a copy of the exhibit to Johnny Bob and offered it into evidence, identifying it as the medical record of Dr. Olstein on Lucy Baines Brady.

Rising from his seat, Johnny Bob objected in a booming voice, "Your Honor, this exhibit comes as a complete surprise to us. We've never seen it before. Counsel must have known about it all along and hid it from us and from this court. Such conduct not only calls for a mistrial, but demands sanctions against the lawyers for the defense."

"Your Honor," Tod replied in a very calm voice, knowing that he had the upper hand, "if anyone has been hiding the ball, it's Mr. Tisdale and his clients. Even though we asked them to disclose the names and addresses of any doctor who has ever treated Ms. Brady and they listed over thirty, they omitted this one country doctor from San Augustine. And, I might add, that their client, Ms. Brady, also lied from the witness stand about it."

"Further, Your Honor," Johnny Bob sputtered, "this document is hearsay and not authenticated."

Tod was prepared for this objection. "Judge, that man at the top of the auditorium with the white beard is Dr. Olstein. I subpoenaed him here for just this purpose. If there's any question about the accuracy of this document, Johnny Bob is welcome to call him to the witness stand."

Johnny Bob threw out one last desperate appeal. "Your Honor, we need a break at least so that I might have a chance to confer with my client about this previously undisclosed document."

Ruby ignored the request. "The exhibit is admitted. Mr. Tisdale, you may call Dr. Olstein as a rebuttal witness if you think it is necessary. No, you may not confer with your client. I think the jury needs to hear what he has to say about this document without the benefit of your counsel. Continue, Mr. Duncan."

By now T.J.'s eyes were darting about the large room almost as if he were looking for an escape route. He took a handkerchief from his coat pocket and put it back without wiping his brow. Tod gave him the document.

"This is the chart from Dr. Olstein's office that he prepared on the night of Lucy's abortion about five weeks ago. I'm going to show you the back first. I'm not asking you to read the medical portions. If you'll look in the margin at the bottom of the page, would you read to the jury what is written?"

T.J. swallowed and then said, "Chosen 1—White Lincoln."

"Now that's a description of your car and your license plate, isn't it?"

Fumbling for some other explanation and coming up with none, all T.J. could say was, "Well, uh, yes, it is."

"Would it surprise you that, if Dr. Olstein is called to the stand, he would testify that, after receiving a five-thousand-dollar check from a stranger to perform a late-night abortion, as the car left his clinic, he wrote those words in the margin?"

T.J. looked down at the Bible on the rail in front of him, looked up to the bearded man at the top of the auditorium, and clutching his Bible to his chest, said, "I don't know, sir."

"In fact, you were the one driving the car that night, weren't you, Reverend Luther?"

"Uh-huh," the witness mumbled.

"Was that a yes?"

T.J. nodded.

"And, *Reverend* Luther, if we turn to the front of this form, there's a history there that appears to be in Lucy's handwriting. By the way, I'll represent to you that Dr. Olstein has been using this form for forty years and concedes that it's probably no longer politically correct. You see where I'm pointing?"

The witness froze. The blood drained from his face.

"You see that blank where it says 'father' and written in that blank are two letters, 'T.J.' That's you, isn't it, Mr. Thomas Jeremiah Luther?"

This time there was no uproar. No one moved as they waited for the answer. In the silence of the courtroom, Tod walked back to his counsel table where he sat and stared at the witness.

Just as Ruby was about to instruct T.J. to answer the question he took his Bible, got up from the witness chair, walked around in front of the judge's bench and kneeled, facing the jury.

"Let us pray. My Father, who art in Heaven . . ."

78

Jessie stormed from the courtroom. The judge looked at the lawyers in anticipation of an objection. None came. Johnny Bob was stumped. Tod observed what T.J. was doing and glanced at Jan who merely shook her head in amazement. All of their combined years as trial lawyers had not prepared them for this moment. So they did nothing. The court reporter looked up at the judge, her eyes asking if she should be taking this down. The judge nodded for her to keep transcribing. Most of the jurors looked on with disbelief. Mr. Marino crossed himself.

". . . We are all victims of the flesh. From the day that Eve first tempted Adam with the apple we have been sinners. As You told us through my brother, Jesus, if we confess, You will be just and forgive us our sins, purifying us from all unrighteousness. Father, I confess to You, to the judge, to this jury, to the world, and, most importantly, to Lucy Brady."

As T.J. spoke, he looked up at the ceiling, his voice rising to a high-pitched wail. Tears streamed from below his glasses and down his cheeks.

"I can still do Your work, my Father. I ask Your forgiveness and that of this jury. Please forgive me so that I can continue to carry Your message to the four corners of this earth. In Christ's name, I ask Your forgiveness. Please help me God!" As he finished, T.J. prostrated himself on the floor, his head resting on the gold Bible. Silence reigned.

No one moved. Finally, Tod rose and said, "We rest, Your Honor."

Johnny Bob, shoulders slumped, replied, "Your Honor, we have no more questions for this witness." Almost as an afterthought, he added, "And we're through, too, Your Honor."

"Deputy, please ask the plaintiff and her family to return for final arguments," Judge O'Reilly said.

THE FINAL ARGUMENTS WERE brief.

Johnny Bob rose and walked slowly back to where Lucy was sitting. As he put his big hand on her shoulder, she folded her hands in her lap and avoided the eyes of the jury. "My friends, what you see before you is a young lady who is a victim. From the time she met that young man in church until today, she has been guilty of only one thing. She trusted others. She trusted Population Planning. She trusted Dr. Moyo. She trusted Reverend Thomas Jeremiah Luther. It is likely she will go through life never trusting anyone ever again. Yes, she lied from this witness stand, but she was under the spell of a charismatic preacher who repeatedly misled her.

"Did she make some bad decisions in the past year? Of course she did. However, as you deliberate, remember that none of those decisions would have been necessary if Dr. Moyo and Population Planning had only exercised reasonable care."

Addressing Judge O'Reilly, he said quietly, "That's all I have to say, Your Honor."

Tod returned full circle to the first day of trial as he paced up and down in front of the jury box, saying nothing until he looked over at his client. "If you translate Mzito Moyo from Swahili to English, it means 'baby heart.' You see, it was not a coincidence that Dr. Moyo became an obstetrician. In Africa his physician father hoped his newborn son would become a doctor who delivered babies. By now, you know him to be a man of integrity, a man of honesty, a man whose skill and credentials are unsurpassed in this state or any other. On the other hand, you now know that the man in the sunglasses has lied to Lucy, has lied to his followers and, more importantly, has violated the oath he took in this courtroom. He told you from that very witness stand if he did not tell the truth, you should find against him. For once, I believe you should follow his advice. He nearly destroyed my client's reputation and you should punish him for it."

Claudia found herself in a conflict of interest that was not of her making. T.J. would just have to live with her argument as she endeavored to absolve her other clients of any liability. "Ladies and gentlemen, it should be clear that the comments of Reverend Luther were his and his alone. There is no evidence that any of the other pro-life defendants approved or condoned what he said. He alone must bear the responsibility for any damages caused by his words."

Interestingly enough, the last word came from T.J. As Claudia sat down, he rose, faced the jury and said, "I'm sorry."

THE VERDICT WAS UNANIMOUS in part and split in part. In a civil case in Texas it only takes ten of the twelve jurors to be in agreement to reach a verdict.

Silently, the jury filed into the courtroom, some staring at the floor, some staring at the flags beside the judge, others looking somberly at the lawyers and at Lucy and her family. As they took their seats Judge O'Reilly asked if they had reached a verdict..

"We have, Your Honor," responded Glenn Ford, who had worn his red tie and red suspenders for the occasion.

The judge studied the verdict, and announced the result.

"As to the case of Lucy Baines Brady v. Dr. Moyo and Population Planning, the jury finds no negligence on the part of Dr. Moyo."

Tod turned and grabbed the hand of Dr. Moyo.

"As to Lucy Brady's case against Population Planning, the jury finds that the defendant, Population Planning, was negligent and awards Ms. Brady her medical bills only."

Johnny Bob looked down at his boots, knowing that it was a hollow victory at best.

"As to the counter-claims, the jury finds in favor of Dr. Moyo and Population Planning against Reverend Luther and the City of Miracles only. They find that the remainder of the pro-life defendants are not responsible for the words or conduct of Reverend Luther. They award damages to Dr. Moyo in the amount of ten million dollars and to Population Planning in the amount of one dollar. This portion of the verdict is split ten jurors to two."

Zeke sank to his seat and buried his tearful eyes in his hands. Claudia breathed a sigh of relief that her other pro-life clients had escaped, unscathed. Jan smiled. Her client didn't want money, only justice. She considered that Population Planning had received that justice.

The judge thanked the jury and advised them that they could now talk about the case to the lawyers or to the media.

79

Johnny Bob packed his briefcase and turned to Claudia. "I'll tell Mildred just to leave our stuff in the lofts. I'll send someone down next week to pick it up. I'm heading home."

Johnny Bob hugged Lucy and wished her well and did the same with Joanna and Jessie. He shook Bo's hand and started walking slowly up the steps. He had no comment for the reporters who tried to stop him as he bulled his way to his pickup. When he cleared the crowd, his step lightened and he began to walk more quickly. By the time he got to his truck, he thought, *You win some, lose some.* There was nothing he could have done about this one. Besides, he had nearly two million dollars in his bank account back in Palestine. Certainly not his biggest fee by a long shot. Still, not a bad day's work.

He tossed his briefcase on the passenger side of the red box in the bed of the truck and walked around to the driver's side. He opened the refrigerator and dragged out a cold Lone Star tall boy. Popping open the top, he drank it half down. As he got in his pickup and pointed it toward Palestine, a siren pierced the late afternoon. It could be heard on the street in front of the law school.

Judge O'Reilly paused at the doorway of the building with Dr. Moyo, Tod and Tod's team. Tod thanked her for her hard work and a good job in managing the trial.

"Judge, did you hear that siren? Johnny Bob's heading home," he told her.

She just smiled. "How on earth did you find out about Dr. Olstein?" she asked. "Mr. Tisdale is too good and too careful to miss something that would implode his case."

"He's a great lawyer, but he had a holy liar as a client." Tod smiled.

The judge bid them good-bye. "Dr. Moyo, you have a fine group of lawyers."

"Yes, Judge, the finest."

"Look around," Tod said to Jan and Wayne. "This is the scene of what will probably go down as the crowning achievement of our legal careers. We won our case, or most of it. Those medical bills will be covered by the clinic's insurance. But, did we answer the question?"

"You mean the question of when life begins?" Jan asked. "Of course not. I told you on that first day when it popped up in the case there is no answer that is satisfactory for everyone. At least not yet, and maybe never. If you think that our little old pissant trial is going to change the course of that debate, you better take a look at history. We put the debate under a microscope for a few weeks. All those doctors and philosophers and theologians will just take a new look through that microscope. You can bet your last red cent that each of them will see something different. As for those people out on the street, their minds were made up before they got behind those barricades. I'll bet you a dime to a donut that not one of them climbed their barricades and crossed over to the other side because of our trial. Speaking of them, you ready to go face the media?"

"Might as well," Tod replied. "I'd rather find a quiet place and sleep for a few hours until they're gone, but we might as well get it over now instead of later. I damn sure don't want them ringing my phone off the wall and pounding on my door."

Wayne had been quiet up until now. "Come on now, Tod. We're the conquering heroes. Let's go out there like we just singlehandedly won World War Three or at the very least knocked Rocky Balboa over the ropes and into the third row in the fifteenth round."

They were not surprised when they walked out the front door and were accosted by reporters with cameras not far behind. The crowds behind the pro-choice barricades cheered like the lawyers were the Houston Rockets who had just won a championship. The crowds behind the pro-life barricades were silent.

Victoria Burton asked the first question. "Mr. Duncan, it appears that you have vindicated the position of the pro-choice faction. Any comments?"

"Victoria, maybe I better clarify. I wasn't paid to take sides in the abortion fight. I was hired to represent Dr. Moyo in a medical malpractice case, something that I've done at least a hundred times in my career. I was forced to file the counterclaims when the other side tried to destroy my client's reputation. I didn't start the 'when life begins' debate. I mounted the best possible defense for my client."

"The critical testimony in the case came from Reverend Luther when you put him back on the stand. Would the outcome have been different without that testimony?"

"That's for you media folks to debate. Ask Larry King or Ted Koppel. I'm not going to speculate on what might have been."

Not far down the street in front of the pro-life barricades, T.J. talked to a few reporters, still wearing his Stetson and carrying his Bible. His stock had dropped to the point that only the local media were interested in what he had to say, but he continued to put on a brave front.

"Obviously, I'm disappointed in the outcome of the trial. We certainly will be appealing the verdict against my church. I did not intend any malice in my words about Dr. Moyo. I merely spoke the facts."

"Reverend Luther, will you continue your ministry?"

"Of course, young man. My ministry is worldwide. In fact, I'm starting a revival tour of forty cities in twenty countries next month. I can promise you that we will have our usual full stadiums."

"What about Lucy?"

"I'm sorry, sir?"

"I said, what about Lucy, Reverend Luther?"

"Oh, you mean Lucy Brady? I apologize. My mind wandered away from this trial and I was thinking about my future ministry. I'm certainly sorry that she didn't get more money. Is that what you were inquiring about?"

"No, Reverend. Actually, I was wondering if you would comment about your testimony today, your previous relationship with Lucy Brady and the impact of all of these events on this young woman who's a member of your church."

T.J.'s lips narrowed and his face hardened as if he could put the whole episode behind him with a few words. He had more important things to consider. His ministry and regaining his position of power were far more important than any one girl. His voice made that clear when he replied, "I have nothing more to say about Ms. Brady. I answered all the questions about her on the witness stand. She's an adult now. I suggest that you ask her about her future plans. Next question."

While T.J. spoke to the media, Jessie walked Lucy, Joanna and Bo to their car and kissed them good-bye. She invited them to stay at her place until things quieted down. She walked to her Jaguar, opened the passenger door, reached into the glove box and retrieved an object that she placed in her purse. She calmly walked toward the corner where T.J. was being interviewed, nodded to a policeman and crossed to where T.J. rambled on. He had climbed back on his soapbox where he lamented the evils in society with abortion being the worst of all. It appeared he had no memory of the day's events. Or perhaps he was mad.

For Jessie, it didn't matter. She knew what she had to do. This man had lied to her. This man had betrayed her trust. And this man had seduced her niece.

Jessie waited for her chance. A reporter closed his notebook and slid out of the crowd, leaving T.J. exposed. Quietly, very quietly, she removed the pearl-handled pistol from her purse, raised it and squeezed the trigger.

As she raised the pistol and took aim, a reporter standing beside T.J. saw the gun an instant before Jessie fired.

"Gun!" he cried as he shoved T.J., but he was too late. The bullet entered T.J.'s head, not between the eyes where Jessie had aimed, but in the side of the head as the reporter tried to shove him out of harm's way.

Law enforcement officers raced toward them from every direction. Jessie didn't move. Instead, she handed the gun, butt first, to the first officer who pushed his way through the crowd. The shot also brought Tod, Jan, Wayne and Dr. Moyo running. Without hesitating, Dr. Moyo dropped to his knees and began CPR. An officer called for Life Flight. Dr. Moyo continued CPR until the helicopter arrived. It was Captain John Peterson who skillfully threaded the chopper down between buildings.

"Tod, I am going with him to the hospital," Dr. Moyo shouted.

"I suppose you should, Doc. You're the only physician around. It's your call."

"It is my call, Tod. And it's my calling."

Epilogue

Ignoring requests for comments from the media about the sudden turn of events, and admittedly shaken themselves, Tod, Jan and Wayne headed for the Four Seasons bar. If ever they had needed a drink, now was the time. As their drinks arrived the call came from Dr. Moyo.

"Tod, Zeke here. It's not good. The neurologists have examined him and the surgeons are operating now. He will probably live. The odds are about ninety percent that he'll be back in a vegetative state. He has no sign of anything but the most primitive brain function. One of the nurses called someone at the City of Miracles. If he doesn't improve, they'll send an air ambulance when the doctors say it's okay. They've been through this before and know how to care for him."

"So they do, Zeke. Twelve years of experience," Tod replied.

"Tod, Reverend Luther nearly destroyed me, but I would never have wanted this to happen."

"I know, Zeke." Tod paused and asked, "Do you believe in destiny, Zeke?"

"Well, yes, Tod, I suppose that I do. I don't understand."

"Mark it down to destiny. We never know what fate has in store for us, not even T.J. Or maybe it was God who decided T.J. was dancing with the devil."

AGAINST ALL ODDS

"Grow up, Maggie! There aren't any heroes out here. There are only survivors. That's why I'm getting out, while the getting's good."

Tears streamed down Maggie's upturned face as she stared up at the black anger gleaming in his dark eyes. The heart-wrenching sight was more than he could bear.

"Damn you, Maggie." He gathered her into his arms and dipped his head. About to kiss her, his common sense prevailed. He dropped his arms and stepped away from Maggie as if she had a plague—a plague that could destroy him should he surrender to the temptation.

Shaken, Maggie swiped at the tears on her cheeks. "Don't run away, Dakota," she pleaded.

"Maggie, only a fool would take a party of greenhorns into the hills. Your sister can't even mount a horse, much less sit a saddle. You're not much better. You think grit makes up for lack of know-how. Well, it doesn't. Not on the trail. Not one of you people has even considered the possibility that somebody could get hurt or killed."

"We know the risks. It's a chance we're willing to take."

ANA LEIGH

PROUD PILLARS RISING

LEISURE BOOKS   NEW YORK CITY

This book is about a hero.
I dedicate it to my husband
        Don
who has been my personal hero for
the past thirty-eight years of
our marriage.

And, if God choose, I shall but
love thee better after death.
        —*Elizabeth Barrett Browning*

Prologue

Rising abruptly from the flat plains of the prairie like proud pillars reaching to the sky, the wooded slopes of the Black Hills stretched majestically for a hundred miles; the sacred hunting ground of the mighty Sioux Nation, the land which by treaty the White Father in Washington had promised would remain inviolable—the home of the Great Spirit, Wankan Tanka.

A man and a boy stood on a high crag. The steep cliff, barren except for a few scrubby pines, jutted above the wooded ridge it rested upon like a granite altar—sacrosanct and unscalable. Only an intrepid few had ever braved the rugged path to the top.

The boy was just a lad of eight. His bronzed face was fraught with grief, and his dark eyes welled with the tears he stoically fought to withhold. The man slipped his arm around the youngster's shoulders.

"They will rest peacefully," he said, gazing at the nearby heap of boulders, "with the sun to warm their faces and a gentle breeze to ruffle their hair."

"And the Great Spirit, Wankan Tanka, will smile upon them," the boy said proudly.

The man returned his gaze to the sylvan splendor before him. Far below, in the depth of the hollow valley, a herd of buffalo roamed.

"Remember this place always, my son, for if our paths must take separate twists in the road, one day they will cross again at this spot."

Twenty miles away as the crow flies, the peace and tranquility of the ancient hills were being shattered by the ring of picks and shovels as the white man scraped and grubbed the streams and ravines in a relentless pursuit for bits and powder of a gleaming ore—gold.

Chapter One

Margaret Collingswood rode through the park as if all the demons of hell followed in hot pursuit. Green woolen knickerbockers, gathered into a band below each knee, blossomed out like sails on her long legs. The hip-length coat, dictated by fashion to be the proper covering for such sporting apparel when worn by a modest young lady, had been negligently stuffed into the pouch attached to her bicycle. The wind rippled through her simple white blouse, ballooning the leg-of-mutton sleeves, and teased the straw porkpie hat clinging precariously to a disheveled mass of red curls.

The bicycle came to a screeching halt beside her favorite bench, and she jumped off the pedals with the agility of a circus performer (a profession which, at one time, Maggie had considered until her mother threatened to put her in a convent).

She snatched a brown paper package from the pouch and within seconds had ripped off the wrapper. Her eyes glowed with excitement as she sat down on the park bench to savor the latest edition of Beadle's Dime Library.

With eager anticipation Maggie looked at the bold headline, "Buffalo Bill's Most Remarkable Story," and quickly flipped the pages to find the provocatively titled tale, "The Girl Mascot of Moonlight Mine." Her starry-eyed expression became fixed in a smile of serene fascination as she began to read the further exploits of her favorite Wild West hero.

Maggie had become an avid reader of this weekly magazine after she discovered a discarded copy in the park the year before. The writings of Louisa May Alcott, her favorite author, had been quickly abandoned, and she had not missed a single edition of the publication since.

Her eyes devoured each word of the story in the cheap pulp magazine, and a short while later she leaned back with a sigh of contentment; once again Buffalo Bill's unparalleled dueling had saved the day for the beleaguered heroine.

"'Peers to be a pretty exciting story."

Startled, Maggie's glance swung to the speaker, a gray-haired man with a neatly trimmed beard who was sitting on the other end of the bench. Having been thoroughly engrossed in the story, she was unaware of how long he had been observing her. She blushed self-consciously.

"Yes, it is a very exciting story," Maggie said

politely and began to gather up the torn paper scattered about.

"Seems strange a young lady would ever be interested in that big bag of wind, Buffalo Bill."

Maggie was swept with a surge of outrage. Whatever the provocation, nothing could have had such a galvanizing effect on Margaret Collingswood as an affront to her hero. The tossed gauntlet could not go unchallenged.

Maggie's green eyes flared with indignation. Arms akimbo, she primed for battle.

"How dare you say that! Surely, sir, you are not defaming the frontier's most heroic protector and scout, William Frederick Cody?"

The man's blue eyes danced with merriment. Maggie realized, too late, the error of her ways and sank down on the bench with a sheepish grin. "Oh, you're only teasing, aren't you? I must sound very foolish to you."

"You don't sound foolish to me," the man said. "I like your spunk. And I like the fact that you're willing to stand up for someone you believe in."

As he leaned back, casually resting his hands on the solid silver handle of a cane, Maggie studied the speaker with increased interest. He had to be close to sixty. Dressed quite fashionably in a black morning coat and gray homburg, his black-and-gray stripped trousers were sharply creased, and gray spats covered his shoes.

Despite his fastidious attire, Maggie could tell by his speech that the stranger was not from the East. Deeply tanned, the lines creeping from the corners of his eyes attested to long hours spent in the sun and wind. Her instincts told her he came from the West.

"Someday I hope to go to the frontier and meet Buffalo Bill in person."

"There's a lot of space out there, girl. It's pretty easy to miss a man in passing."

Maggie smiled, then her eyes gazed off as she tried to visualize the vastness of her far-away dream. She returned her concentration to the stranger. "Are you from the West, sir?"

"Yes. I've lived there my whole life."

The admission caused Maggie's eyes to gleam with curiosity. "Have you ever hunted bison like Buffalo Bill?"

A twinkle lighted his eyes. "On a few occasions."

"Oh, how I envy you," she sighed. Maggie's enthusiasm mounted. She had never before discussed her favorite subject with someone who had actually lived on the frontier. Although her stepfather had been in the cavalry in Wyoming, for some reason he rarely spoke of the experience. "Then you must have had the opportunity to encounter the noble red man?"

Amused, the old man weighed his answer. "Well, I met my share of redskins, if that's what you mean. Most folks in the West don't look upon Injuns as charitably as you people do here in the East. I never met Buffalo Bill, but I did know Wild Bill Hickock. Matter of fact, I was in Deadwood in '76 the afternoon Jack McCall shot him in the back of the head."

Maggie's young face curled up in commiseration. "Oh, that was such a dastardly deed! When I read of that heroic man's murder . . . I wept."

Margaret surprised herself by confiding in the stranger. Then her thought connected with another tragic event. "General Custer and his gallant troop were massacred the very same year."

The man's eyes suddenly clouded with bitterness. "Yes, and a massacre is something you never forget."

Having experienced this excitement only vicariously through the pages of a pulp magazine, Maggie's eyes widened, brimming with incredulity. "You mean you were there? With General Custer?" She couldn't believe she was actually speaking with a flesh-and-blood hero.

"No, but I once served in the cavalry out West."

This revelation increased her admiration and fueled her imagination. "Oh, if only I were a man. I would run away and join the cavalry, too," she declared fervently.

The stranger chuckled at the idea. "Are you really that anxious to go West?" he asked kindly.

"It's the dream of my life," she declared, then her face quickly saddened. "A foolish dream, I fear. My mother would never permit me to journey there alone."

"Your mother?" His eyes brightened with surprise. "I'd of thought your husband. You must be at least 18 years old . . . aren't you married?"

"Married!" The young girl's vibrant face curled with disdain. "Me, married? I'm never going to get married, if I can help it."

Suddenly realizing she had lingered too long, Maggie rose to her feet. "Well, sir, it has been very pleasant talking to you." She retrieved her bicycle and tucked the magazine into the pouch.

"How come you aren't riding one of those outlandish contraptions with three wheels? That's what I see other young ladies riding," the old man teased.

"Three-wheelers are for beginners or children," she declared with feigned superiority and climbed onto the seat.

"Well, Missy, don't let that horse throw you," he called out good-naturedly.

"Goodbye, sir," Maggie grinned. With a spirited wave she rode off.

The park was located only blocks from her home, and Maggie returned quickly. She rode up the long, oak-lined drive and parked her bicycle on the lawn of the huge, white-columned house. Grabbing the precious magazine, Maggie thought hopefully, *If I hurry, maybe I can read it again before supper.* As she ran up the porch steps, her hat began to slide down her forehead. She yanked it off without breaking her stride, her other hand tenaciously clutching the magazine to her breast.

Maggie stopped abruptly at the entrance to take several deep breaths before opening the thick oak door.

The Collingswood mansion was elaborately furnished with the unrestrained luxury and elegance of rich mahogany cabinetry, Queen Anne chairs, crystal chandeliers, and magnificent carpets from the Orient. This was one of the few houses which could boast the ultimates in modern convenience—a private bathroom and electricity in the drawing room.

She attempted to walk sedately across the

marble-tiled foyer to a massive stairway. However, unable to restrain herself, she began to race up the stairway, taking the steps two at a time in the unladylike manner which was a continual cause of distress to her mother.

Maggie entered her bedroom, tossed aside the hat, and belly-flopped on the bed. Within seconds she was once again absorbed in the novel, only to be interrupted by a light tap at the door.

"Margaret, are you in there?"

Maggie grimaced and put aside the magazine. "Come in, Mother."

Katherine Collingswood swept into the room in a swirl of expensive Chinese silk chiffon and French perfume. The older woman looked stunning at age thirty-six. Other than their green, almond-shaped eyes, Katherine and her eldest daughter bore little similarity to one another. Reed-thin, with flaming red hair, Margaret stood a head taller than her mother and sister. She appeared gangling and awkward beside their petite and curvaceous blonde femininity.

The wife of a diplomat, Katherine Collingswood had the reputation as one of Washington's most renowned hostesses; and the honor of attending one of her dinner parties was surpassed only by an invitation to the White House from President Rutherford Birchard Hayes.

At the sight of her daughter stretched out on her stomach, Katherine's delicate brow rose in censure. "Margaret, will you kindly remove those hideous bloomers and get dressed properly? Peter Brent is joining us for dinner."

19

Maggie sat up, swinging her long legs over the side of the bed. "So what? He's not coming to look at me."

Katherine retained a cool demeanor and picked up the magazine her daughter had put aside. "I don't understand you, Margaret. It would be wise to follow your sister's direction. Next month you will be eighteen years old, and yet you spend hours reading these ten-cent novels instead of using your time to encourage proper young suitors as Diane does. And she's younger than you are."

Maggie humphed in derision. "You mean like Peter Brent! He would bore me to death. He's forever walking around in those stodgy-looking morning coats and trousers; he allows Diane to lead him around as if he's got a ring in his nose; and he thinks he's smart just because he can beat me at archery and lawn tennis. Even Pudge Petrie thinks he's a drip."

"Margaret, Mrs. Petrie wishes you would cease calling Bartholomew by that derogatory nickname just because he's a trifle overweight. His mother feels the name is having a serious effect on his development."

Maggie was too embroiled in her tirade to pay any attention to the censure. "Furthermore, the only reason you and Diane think he's a proper suitor is because his father owns practically everything east of the Mississippi River."

Maggie didn't tell her mother how much the man bored Diane as well. In fact, she had seen her sister and Joseph Wallace bussing in the rose garden the previous week. Maggie rose to her feet.

"Well, stop worrying about me, Mother, because I do not intend to marry any man. And furthermore," Maggie added defiantly, "when I am old enough, I'm moving to the frontier to herd cattle or buffalo on my trusty and faithful steed."

Unperturbed, Katherine Collingswood leaned over to pick up the hat which had been carelessly tossed aside. "My dear child, one doesn't 'herd' buffalo. Bison are wild and roam freely. And you have never ridden a horse in your life."

Katherine patted her daughter's cheek as if Maggie were a child. "Now hurry, dear. You know your father gets upset when you're late for dinner." Katherine paused at the doorway. "Put on your lavender taffeta, Margaret. That dress looks so lovely on you."

A short while later, Maggie entered the drawing room dressed in a clean pair of knickerbockers. She ignored her mother's glance of disapproval. The tall young man with a pleasant-looking face, who sat next to her sister on the settee, rose politely to his feet. "Good evening, Margaret."

"Hello, Peter." Maggie responded disgustedly as she plopped down in a chair. His deep brown eyes, as gentle as a puppy's, seemed to read her thoughts.

After graduating from Princeton the previous summer, Peter Brent had returned to Washington D.C. and fallen in love with Diane Collingswood the first time he laid eyes on her.

His open adoration of the self-centered young girl was a continual subject of gossip. The elite found it incomprehensible that the son of one of the East's wealthiest men tolerated Diane's behavior. She ordered Peter about like a lackey and flirted outrageously with other men in and out of the smitten young man's presence.

Despite her capricious flirtations, Peter Brent remained totally captivated by Diane Collingswood, convinced that some day the young woman he loved would mature into a faithful and dutiful wife. However, Peter lacked his father's enterprise and aggressiveness and was content to endure her domination rather than force the issue of fidelity.

The match met with the approval of both families. Peter's father had become a colossus in industry. Anticipating that the popularity of cycles would spread nationwide, the entrepreneur had wisely gotten into their manufacture and proceeded to train his son in the business. The senior Brent was convinced that one day every house in America would own a two- or three-wheeled cycle.

As a matter of fact, Peter Brent had given Maggie the bicycle she now rode. Although it was not the horse she longed for, Maggie did find pleasure in riding the cycle and was grateful to Peter for convincing Katherine Collingswood to allow her daughter to keep it.

However, gratitude did not make Maggie a willing pawn in Diane's attempts to manipulate Peter.

Maggie smiled secretly when, after dinner, Peter took her sister for a stroll in the garden. Unable to resist the temptation, Maggie followed the couple. She clamped a hand over her mouth to stifle the sound of her laughter when Peter took Diane in his arms. Diane slipped her arms around his neck as she ardently returned his kiss.

"Marry me, Diane. I need you. I have to have you." He grabbed her and began to trail kisses down her neck.

With a light laugh, Diane threw back her head to give him freer access to the slim column. Peter's hands cupped her waist and slid up to her breasts as his searching lips pressed hot, fevered kisses on the exposed cleavage.

Diane slapped his hands away and stepped out of his arms. "Peter, I must insist that you control yourself." She began to return her mussed hair to the proper order.

Her indifference to his ardor was a blow to the young man's pride. "Why do you continue to tease me, to dole out these few kisses? I don't know why I waste my time with you."

Her green eyes narrowed with seduction. "I don't ask you to, Peter," Diane cooed confidently.

"No, but you enjoy driving me to distraction with your kisses."

Diane rose on her toes and pressed a light kiss on his lips. Then, laughing lightly, she strolled away.

Although Peter stormed away disgruntled, both knew he would be back the next day.

Later, Diane came upstairs and found Maggie lying on the bed with her chin propped in her hands, absorbed in her novel. She glanced up over the top of the book as Diane paused at the open door. "Did the toad leave already?"

Diane entered the room and crossed to an ornate chair covered in flowered silk damask, a piece of decorative fluff which Katherine Collingswood insisted upon keeping in Maggie's room over her daughter's objections. Always mindful of proper feminine decorum, Diane sat down demurely, rather than plopping down and flinging her legs over the delicate arm as Maggie was prone to do.

"He went home in a huff because I wouldn't let him kiss me." With a negligent flick of a wrist, her hand brushed the air in a haughty gesture. *"C'est tres ennuyeux.* He is so boring," she elaborated for Maggie's benefit.

Maggie grimaced in disgust. Diane and her girlfriends had the affectation of interjecting French phrases into their conversation. Maggie thought the habit was silly.

The two Collingswood sisters differed in precepts as much as they did in physical appearance. Usually, the two girls were able to maintain a relatively peaceful coexistence, if not one of sisterly intimacy. They were half-sisters, actually; Maggie's natural father had died when she was one year old.

Diane was materialistic, absorbed with her own beauty and her beaux. Maggie, a dedicated "tomboy," was contemptuous of the frivolities which were so important to her sister.

Maggie's world revolved around her daydreams about the western frontier and the role she would play expanding it. Having no interest in suitors or in her own appearance, Maggie did not feel threatened by her attractive younger sister.

"I noticed you don't think Joseph Wallace is boring. Especially the way he was kissing you last week in the garden."

Blushing, Diane rose to her feet in a huff. "Were you spying on me?"

"With all that smacking that was going on, it's a wonder President Hayes didn't hear you in the White House." She raised her voice to a mocking falsetto. "Oh, Diane, I adore you. You're so beautiful. Smack. Smack. Smack." Laughing hilariously, Maggie threw herself back on the bed.

Diane's green eyes flashed with irritation. "I suppose you told Mother and Father. Well, I'll have the last laugh, Miss Sloppy Bloomers. When I have the most lavish house in Washington and a villa in the south of France, you'll still be hanging by your knees from the limb of a tree, reading one of those stupid dime novels." She stormed out of the room in indignation.

Maggie wiped the tears of mirth out of her eyes and reached for her magazine.

The following afternoon Maggie found herself drawn to the park. She hoped to see the old man again. Much to her delight, she found him sitting on the same bench as if waiting for her to make an appearance.

They fell into a comfortable pattern of talking together, a pastime which became a daily ritual. Maggie listened to his stories of the West and began to see the vast magnitude of the land through the eyes of a man who had lived at its mercy. She came to recognize the hardship and conflict in a way of life which previously had appeared to her as solely adventuresome and romantic.

Maggie, in turn, found herself telling him about her mother's relentless insistence that she change her unladylike demeanor. And with tears misting her eyes, Maggie confessed to the old man her most secret fear—that one day her mother would succeed in achieving that goal and Maggie would never get to fulfill her dream of the West.

Like true friends, they did not ask for more than a shared companionship. He was Mr. Smith to her, and to him, she was simply Maggie, a nickname Margaret knew would horrify her mother.

Exactly one week from the day she met Mr. Smith, Maggie returned to the park as usual, after picking up the latest copy of her magazine. This time the old man greeted her with a sad smile. "I was afraid you wouldn't come today. My business requires that I leave tomorrow, and I hoped we would be able to say goodbye."

Maggie was devastated. Mr. Smith had come to mean so much to her in the hours they had shared together. Maggie pulled out a small, white square envelope.

"This is an invitation to my eighteenth birthday party in two weeks. I haven't many close friends, so I was hoping you would be among them."

The old man patted her hand and she saw a glitter of tears in his eyes. "I only wish I could, my dear. I promise you I will be thinking of you that day." His smile was gentle. "A part of me will be with you."

So, for the last time, smiling wistfully, Maggie sat and listened to him talk about the spectacle of buffalo herds roaming the range and the sight of a thundering horde of Sioux galloping across the plains. And the young dreamer wondered if she would ever witness such scenes.

When they said their final goodbye, the old man raised her hand to his lips. "Hold tight to your dream, little one. Don't ever let it go until you replace it with a sweeter one."

Maggie's homeward ride was slow and sad. Already, she felt the loss of her newly found friend.

For the first time in two years, the copy of Beadle's Dime Library remained unopened in its brown paper wrapper.

Chapter Two

With uncharacteristic trepidation, Margaret nervously chewed her lower lip as she stared at the huge mare standing broadside before them. The animal turned its head toward her and, for a long moment, Maggie and the horse eyed each other suspiciously.

"What are you waiting for?" the livery man inquired. "Just put your left foot in the stirrup and swing yourself up." An impossible feat, Maggie thought, and threw a dubious glance at the man. "You told me you've ridden a horse before," he challenged.

"I have," Maggie lied glibly, "I'm just not very good at getting on top of one."

"Just be sure to grab a handful of its withers."

Maggie stood on her toes and placed a firm hold

on the pommel of the saddle. She took a deep breath, put her left foot in the stirrup, and hoisted herself up onto the horse. She felt as if she were going to slide right over the animal's head. The uneasy sensation of sitting a horse turned out to be nothing akin to the secure command she had on her bicycle.

"Here, lady, take the reins." With a dubious scowl, the man impatiently held the leather straps out to her.

Maggie managed a shaky smile, but she was not about to release her hold on the pommel. She reached out tentatively with her left hand and grabbed the reins.

"Hold them loosely and don't pull up on them," he warned. The man goaded his own horse forward. Maggie's stomach lurched when her mare followed.

After a few moments Maggie found herself beginning to relax. Riding a horse wasn't so difficult after all, she reasoned with a cocky smile, and released her grasp on the pommel.

Suddenly, without warning, the horse ahead increased its speed to a gallop and Maggie's mare quickly followed suit. The young girl's right foot slipped out of the stirrup, and she began to slide from side to side. She dropped the reins and clutched the pommel with both hands, hanging on for dear life.

The astounded livery man grabbed one of the flapping reins as her horse raced by him. "Whoa, Strawberry," he called out. The animal halted abruptly. Squealing, Maggie tumbled to the ground and landed on her backside with the wind knocked out of her.

Thanking God she was still in one piece, Maggie sat for a few seconds until she regained her breath. Then, without the least sign of embarrassment, she rose to her feet and brushed the dust off her hands and skirt. "That was most enjoyable, sir. I will return tomorrow for another lesson." Composed, Maggie nodded curtly and walked away, apparently none the worse for her fall.

"Lesson?" the perplexed man called after the girl. "If you couldn't ride, why didn't you say so?" He shook his head in disbelief, but then broke into an amused grin in spite of his annoyance. "Darn fool girl could have busted her head."

Maggie awoke the following morning convinced she would limp the rest of her life. Every bone in her body ached. Wincing with pain, she hobbled to the bathroom and a short while later lowered herself gingerly into a steaming tub and sank gratefully into the soothing water.

Riding a horse was not quite what she thought it would be, Maggie reflected as she soaked herself. She definitely had to change her plans to resume the lessons that morning. It would be impossible to even ride her bicycle today, much less climb up on a horse. She would go to the library and get a book on how to ride a horse. However, if she intended to become a rancher, she would have to bite the bullet and go back to the livery soon. *That's what Buffalo Bill would do*, she told herself. Then her young face creased in a fretful frown. *But not until after my birthday or I'll be hobbling around at my own party*, she reminded herself.

Then, with the typical logic of youth, Maggie concluded her misery was all her mother's fault for being the one who reminded her she had never ridden a horse before.

On the day of Maggie's birthday, Katherine Collingswood engaged additional servants to assist in the preparation of the party. The furniture and the Oriental rug had been removed from the mammoth dining room. A long table covered with an elegant white Quaker lace tablecloth was placed against a wall to hold the punch and numerous cakes being prepared for the occasion.

Throughout the day, as she watched the servants scuttle about doing their duties, Maggie harbored a premonition that something momentous was going to happen. The feeling of expectation had gone far beyond the excitement of a birthday party.

Her feminine intuition told her to expect the most important day of her life.

Despite the pains Katherine Collingswood took to improve her daughter's appearance, there was still evidence of the tomboy in Maggie that evening. Her red hair had been swept high into a chignon on the crown of her head with love curls dangling enticingly around her face. She wore a green voile dress, with full floppy sleeves ruffled at the shoulders and elbows, a style in the height of fashion.

But Maggie hated her appearance as she surveyed herself in the mirror. She looked like a six-year-old playing dress-up in her mother's clothes, a charade Maggie had never considered even as a child. Her breasts were too small for the bodice of the gown, her feet too large for the green pumps her mother insisted she wear, and she was afraid to move her head for fear her hair would come tumbling down to her shoulders. Belligerently, Maggie stuck out her tongue at the image in the mirror.

She would not let anything spoil the most important day of her life.

The folds of the full skirt swirled about her ankles and Maggie tried not to trip as she descended the stairway. When she reached the dining room without mishap, she planted herself firmly against a wall and vowed not to budge from the spot the rest of the evening.

The orchestra, cued and ready to play on Maggie's appearance, struck up "Happy Birthday" as the gathering applauded and sang along. To Maggie's further distress, she saw her mother approach with Pudge Petrie in tow.

"You look lovely, dear," Katherine whispered with pleasure as she hugged her daughter. "Bartholomew has been waiting patiently for the first dance." At Katherine's nod, the musicians began to play a popular Strauss waltz.

"Happy Birthday, Margaret. May I claim the first dance?" the stocky young man said, making his best dancing-class bow. He took her arm and led her onto the dance floor. "You're dressed up early for Halloween, aren't you, Maggie?" he snickered as they began to move to the music.

"Just shut your fat mouth, Pudge Petrie, and don't step on my toes or you'll break my foot," she snapped.

As they moved awkwardly around the floor,

Maggie glowered with displeasure. She hated dancing. Another frivolous convention of Society. In real sports, such as swimming and lawn tennis, she challenged and often bested her male opponent. But with dancing, she had to allow her male partner to lead her around as if she didn't know where she was going, a concept which made no sense to Margaret Collingswood.

The hours passed slowly as each young man, bowing to the demands of parents or hostess, claimed a dance. Maggie's displeasure increased with each partner. Her stepfather noticed Maggie's dejection and invited her to waltz.

"You look lovely tonight, Miss Collingswood," he said gallantly.

Maggie glanced up at him gratefully. "That's very kind of you, Father."

Taylor Collingswood's appearance was the epitome of moderation. He stood a pleasing height to tall and short alike, slender but not skinny. His eyes were set in a square face just wide enough apart to appear intelligent and candid. The hair at his temples was just gray enough to reflect distinction rather than age. His nose was straight, but not long; his jaw was refined, but not weak. A neatly trimmed moustache rested above thin, but not tight, lips.

His dark handsomeness was a perfect complement to his wife's blonde loveliness. They made a striking couple.

Katherine waved at them as the petite woman whirled past in the arms of Peter Brent. "Your mother looks like she's enjoying herself more than you are, honey. Is something bothering you?"

"It's just me. I'm not meant for grand affairs. I'll never be a socially proper woman like Mother or Diane."

"I like you just the way you are," Taylor said graciously. "Don't change to try to fit the likeness of someone else. It may not always be for the better," he added obscurely as they finished the dance.

Maggie felt relieved when there was a pause in the dancing while her cousin, Sheila Delaney, played several selections on the piano. The young woman finished to a rain of applause, and Maggie slipped out to the portico.

Crestfallen, she sat alone pondering her plight. She knew her disappointment was due to her earlier expectations. The day was almost over, and her premonition had not materialized. She had been so certain something momentous would happen.

"Margaret, aren't you feeling well?"

She glanced up in surprise to discover Sheila Delaney beside her.

Maggie and her cousin were close in age, but Sheila was shy and reserved, lacking Maggie's penchant for impetuosity. Katherine Collingswood had often remarked that Sheila had been born an old woman and would never find a man to marry until she changed her mousey ways. A Junior Patron of the Arts, as well as a skilled pianist, Sheila was as engrossed in music, as Maggie was in ten-cent novels. Despite these differences, the two girls liked each other and enjoyed one another's company.

Seeing the compassion in her cousin's eyes, all of Maggie's misgivings began to pour forth with the suddenness of a cloudburst.

"I felt so certain something momentous would happen to me tonight, Sheila, and all that happened was that my mother dressed me up like a circus clown. Mother is upset with me because I never want to get married. Why am I expected to wed just because I've reached the age of eighteen?"

Sheila listened in silence, allowing Maggie to release all her pent-up frustration.

"I want to be the one to decide what I will do with my life!" Maggie declared vehemently.

"There's nothing wrong with that, Margaret. I wish I had the courage to make such a stand." Sheila's eyes glowed with warmth. "I'll tell you a secret. I've always admired your gumption."

Maggie, used to being criticized, was pleased with the compliment. "Are you unhappy with your life too, Sheila?"

"No, not actually unhappy. I have my music. I could never be unhappy as long as I have that."

Maggie sighed in desolation. "I have nothing but my dreams." The conversation had finally reached the crux of her problem. "I am certain about one thing, above all else; I do not want to marry a man like Peter Brent or Pudge Petrie and be forced to settle down, trying to be the perfect hostess, living in the perfect house. I'm like Jo in *Little Women*, I *know* I am meant to do something different with my life."

"Have you thought of pursuing a nursing career,

or becoming a teacher?" Sheila said gently.

"A teacher, perhaps. But I *really* want to go West and become a rancher."

"But I thought you didn't want to get married?" her cousin asked, confused.

"No, not *marry* a rancher, I mean *become* a rancher myself. I want to ride the range, rope steers, and do all the things a rancher must do to survive."

Sheila was openly astounded. "But, Margaret, that's not a proper thing for a woman to do."

"Proper! Maybe it's not proper in Washington, D.C., but it's proper in the West," Maggie asserted, regaining her normal spunkiness. "And I'm going to do it somehow," she added, with a determined shake of her head. "And I don't care who doesn't like it."

Sheila smiled broadly, elated to see good spirits return to her favorite cousin. "And I bet you'll be the best rancher in the whole West."

The two women broke into laughter and hugged one another. Arm in arm, they returned to the ballroom, giggling like schoolgirls.

Later, after the last guest had finally departed, Maggie quickly retired to her room. She was about to climb into bed when one of the servants tapped on her door. "Mr. and Mrs. Collingswood would like your presence in the library, Miss Margaret."

Maggie sighed deeply, pulled on her robe, and prepared herself for another lecture. When she entered the library, she saw Taylor Collingswood leaning over his distraught wife, trying to comfort her. Katherine was ashen; she looked as if she had seen a ghost. A stranger stood uncomfortably by the desk.

"Mother, what's wrong?" Alarmed, Maggie hurried over and knelt on the floor at her mother's feet. "Are you ill?" Katherine's usually controlled features were contorted in distress. She began to sob into the handkerchief Taylor quickly handed her.

Maggie glanced up at Taylor. "What is it, Father?"

"I suggest you sit down, Margaret. We must discuss a matter of grave concern." At the sight of his somber image, Maggie felt an even greater cause for alarm. Taylor Collingswood was not prone to hyperbole. "All right, Mr. Davis," he said. "This is Margaret Collingswood."

Maggie turned her attention to the stranger.

"Miss Collingswood." The man handed her a white business card which identified him as Lionel Davis, Bonded Courier. "As I just explained to your parents, I have been retained by a William Godfrey of Deadwood in the Dakota Territory. He, in turn, is representing a Mr. Samuel Harris. My instructions are to deliver this sealed letter to you on the day of your 18th birthday. I am sorry for the late hour, but I was inadvertently delayed as a result of a carriage accident."

"Samuel Harris?" Maggie glanced in confusion at her mother, who had ceased sobbing and now watched her intently. "Samuel Harris? But that was my father's name."

Davis handed Maggie a packet. "Now if you will excuse me, I can see myself out." He dipped his head politely and hastily departed.

Maggie opened the packet and began to read aloud the enclosed letter.

Dear Miss Collingswood,

I regret to inform you of the demise of your father, Samuel Harris. Mr. Harris left a considerable estate and named you a beneficiary. However, the conditions of his will necessitate your personal presence to claim the inheritance, or the total estate will revert to the remaining heir. Enclosed you will find money to cover your expenses to Deadwood, in the Dakota Territory. Please wire me the date of your arrival, so I can make the necessary accommodations."

Respectfully,

William Henry Godfrey.

Maggie stared down at a white envelope, enclosed in the packet. She saw the name *Maggie Harris* scratched across the front and knew instinctively the writing had to be her father's script. For a moment she tightly clutched the sealed envelope, then slowly released the gummed flap and pulled out a single piece of paper. It seemed to be part of a map. The symbols and markings on the sketch meant nothing to Maggie. She was still too perplexed to perceive its significance.

"Oh, this is a nightmare. I can't believe it," Katherine exclaimed.

Maggie stared incredulously at Katherine. "Mother, you told me my father was dead."

"We thought he was." At the look of incredulity in the eyes of her daughter, Katherine's features softened. "Darling, your father never returned to the post. He was presumed dead. You were only a year old. A short time later, I married Taylor and we came east."

Maggie was stunned. "Post? What post?"

Katherine's glance swung beseechingly to Taylor. "Let me explain, my dear," he interjected. "Margaret, your father was a sergeant under my command. He was sent on a mission to scout hostile Indian movement and never returned."

Maggie was incredulous. "Why did you tell me my father had been killed in an accident?"

"For heaven's sake, Margaret, what difference does that make now?" Katherine declared, irritably.

"What difference does it make?" Maggie knew her mother was not being honest with her. Everything seemed bewildering; she felt betrayed by both parents. The knowledge that her real father had been alive all this time was devastating. Her mind raced with two troubling questions. Why hadn't her father come to see her? The letter obviously proved he knew where to find her. And why had her mother lied about the cause of his death? Even now, her mother had evaded Maggie's question.

Maggie brushed aside her tears and rose to her feet. She wouldn't mourn her father. Had he loved her, he would have come for her. And there was no sense in shifting the blame for his absence onto her mother. "If you will excuse me, I would like to go to my room. I think I've had enough excitement for one night."

"Of course, honey. Go to bed. We'll discuss the matter in the morning," Taylor said kindly.

Maggie paused momentarily outside the door, still stunned by the sudden turn of events. The voice of Katherine Collingswood carried through the door which was slightly ajar. "Well, Taylor, this comes as a surprise, doesn't it? What are we going to do?

"I suggest we go to Virginia and get remarried. The fact that your husband has been alive all this time could cause a scandal damaging to my career."

"But what about his money? As his legal wife, his estate really belongs to me."

"My God, Katherine, let Margaret have her inheritance."

"The letter mentioned another heir. Why should someone else have money which is rightfully mine?"

"I think you know the answer to that, as well as I." The accusation in Taylor's voice added to Maggie's confusion. What had he meant by his remark? She could not bear to listen to another word and ran up the stairway with tears streaking her cheeks.

Sleep came slowly to Maggie. When she finally succumbed to slumber, she dreamed her arms had been shackled and she was sucked into the vortex of a maelstrom where a grasping, greedy mother and an indifferent father swirled around her in the turbulence.

Maggie woke with a start and sat up in bed. She turned on the light, picked up the envelope lying on the pillow beside her, and removed the torn map. Another puzzle in the mystery.

She began to trace the markings with her fingers. A feeling of excitement began to mount within her, transmitted through her fingertips from the ripped piece of paper.

Suddenly, one redeeming aspect about the whole situation, which she had ignored in the confusing events of the evening, sprang to the forefront of her mind. Her long-awaited dream would come to pass—she was going to the frontier!

Chapter Three

"Margaret, get your head in here at once. It is unbecoming for a young lady to lean out a train window," Katherine Collingswood scolded.

"Oh, let the girl be, Katherine," Taylor Collingswood intervened. He had listened to his wife censuring Maggie for the last ten miles. "She's enjoying herself."

"She could get hurt," Katherine insisted.

Maggie sat back and brushed the dust off her gown. "I haven't seen one buffalo, other than that poor pathetic beast we saw at the tent show in Mitchell."

"And it stank miserably," Diane carped. "As much as everything about this horrible goose chase."

Taylor ignored the outburst. His youngest daughter had been complaining as much as his wife. "You probably won't see any buffalo so close to the railroad, honey," Taylor said to Maggie. "The noise would scare them away."

"I hope the monotony and grime are teaching you a good lesson, Margaret," Katherine preached. "You've been filling your head with the nonsense you read in those cheap novels. Now you know what the frontier is really like—boring and dusty."

"And the dust sticks to my face. I hate it!" Diane griped. "I don't see why I had to leave the comforts of Washington, just because of some silly treasure map. This dumb trip is like something out of *Treasure Island. C'est ridicule!*" Diane cast a disgruntled glance at her sister sitting beside her.

"Believe me, any circumstance even remotely associated with Samuel Harris is ridiculous," Katherine scoffed.

Maggie resented the remark and, for the first time since receiving the letter, sprang to her father's defense. "You married him, Mother."

"Don't be disrespectful, Margaret," Taylor Collingswood chided sternly.

"I'm sorry," Maggie apologized. "But Diane never stops complaining. Why did she have to come along with us? I hope things will be different when we reach Deadwood. Maybe I'll meet Deadwood Dick." Maggie reached for her copy of Beadle's Magazine to resume reading about the notorious Deadwood renegade. "His real name is Richard Clarke; Deadwood Dick is an alias. He sounds just like Robin Hood."

Taylor shook his head in disagreement. "Margaret, don't lose sight of the fact that the man is an outlaw, no matter how some writer chooses to paint him."

"Well, so was Robin Hood, and he was on the side of right, wasn't he?"

Taylor frowned and then said severely, "There's nothing righteous about Deadwood Dick. The man is an outlandish scoundrel."

"Who has been glorified in those dime novels you read," her mother added by way of the final word.

Maggie was in no mood for any further lectures and returned her attention to the story. Thus far, the trip had not lived up to her expectations. Even the magazine seemed to have lost some of its previous fascination.

The sound of a rifle blast jolted Maggie out of her reverie. Her glance swung to the window with alarm, then quickly changed to incredulity. Speechless, she stared with mouth agape at the scene unfolding outside.

She saw a squad of United States Cavalry approach the train at full gallop. The shrill whistle of the train sounded in response to a warning shot, and the huge locomotive ground to a screeching halt, jostling the passengers in the connecting cars.

Maggie's eyes glowed with excitement as she watched the rapid approach of the blue-uniformed cavalrymen. Her pounding heart threatened to bludgeon the wall of her chest.

"Oh, look at them, Mother," she gasped. "Aren't they glorious!"

Taylor appeared perplexed as he spied the insignia on the guidon. "The Third Cavalry is stationed in Wyoming. I wonder what they're doing this far east."

When an officer leading the troop raised his hand, the men reined in their horses. He rode ahead to converse with the conductor, who had hopped off the train. Maggie had a good chance to study the men sitting astride their horses right outside her window. Her eyes swept the troop, mounted in two columns, and stopped to rest on a lone rider several yards ahead of the others.

The man wore blue trousers with a yellow cavalry stripe down the side, but rather than the blue shirt worn by the other soldiers, his was made of buckskin. *Just like Buffalo Bill*, she thought wondrously as a chill ran down her spine.

With the front brim of his campaign hat bent up in the favorite style of a cavalryman, she saw a face deeply bronzed, the profile chiseled in high cheekbones and a broad nose.

As if sensing her stare, the rider turned his head. Maggie found herself looking into a pair of eyes so dark they appeared to be black. Thick, long lashes shrouded his eyes, changing his face from severe to handsome.

He returned her stare unwaveringly. Maggie blushed, but there was no glimmer of response in the dark eyes; they remained impassive.

Caught in the act of staring at him, she turned away in embarrassment. At the sight of the two young girls in the window, several of the men in the column doffed their hats and began to hoot. Diane remained poised, but Maggie smiled and waved to them.

"For heaven's sake, Margaret, please stop making a spectacle of yourself," Katherine admonished her.

The conductor climbed back on the train and signaled the engineer. The train lurched forward in spurts and jerks. Maggie could not resist leaning out the window and waving goodbye to the troopers.

His dark gaze still locked on Diane, the lone figure had not moved.

As soon as the conductor entered their car, Taylor Collingswood called to him. "What is the cavalry doing this close to Rapid City?"

"The lieutenant said they are tracking some renegade Indians. Jumped the reservation, they did. Seems as how these redskins got to arguing among themselves and a couple of 'em got killed." The man snickered. "As far as I'm concerned, the murdering savages can all kill each other off. Lieutenant said they were armed and right dangerous."

"Oh, good heavens!" Katherine moaned. "Why did I ever come to this God-forsaken place?"

Maggie voiced the thought festering foremost in her mind since the letter had arrived from William Godfrey. "Greed, Mother." Katherine's glare toward her daughter was withering.

"Now, now, dear," Taylor said reassuringly as he patted his wife's hand. "They're hardly going to attack a train or a city. If I know Indians, they'll flee to the Badlands and hide out."

Maggie picked up her magazine and returned to reading. Her spirits had been considerably buoyed by the sight of the cavalrymen. However, she found concentration on the printed page difficult—her thoughts continually strayed to the soldier with the dark brooding eyes.

An hour later, the train reached Rapid City, which was as far as they could go by rail. The following morning they would complete the trip by stagecoach.

After eating a hot meal, Margaret washed away the grime from the long journey. She retired for the night in the soft bed of a hotel room, her thoughts skipping ahead excitedly to the adventure that lay ahead when she reached Deadwood.

Later, too excited to sleep, she arose and moved to the window. Enthralled, Maggie sat with her head propped in her hands, peering out of the window. Even though the shops were closed at the late hour, the street below bustled with activity. Horses shuffled at hitching posts, and the rinky-tinkle of pianos and boisterous laughter bellowed from the open doors of honky-tonks.

Loud and rowdy, with thirsts to match, cowboys and miners were still arriving in the town, hell-bent for a weekend of hard drinking, gambling, and whoring until their money or gold dust was exhausted. Maggie's attention fell on a floozy walking down the road with the arm of a cavalryman draped around her shoulders. The woman giggled and pretended to slap the soldier's hand away when he reached down and cupped the rounded cheeks of her rear. The two people stopped to kiss. Maggie's eyes, widened with shock, followed the amorous pair until they disappeared into the shadows.

Sighing wistfully, Maggie turned away. She

yearned to be down on the street instead of having to observe the sights from a bird's-eye view three stories above. Her young mind began to flirt with a dangerous thought. Why should she dally upstairs, when there was so much to see below?

She glanced at the bed. Diane was sound asleep. Maggie knew her mother and Taylor were asleep, as well, in the adjoining room. Without further hesitation, she pulled her night shift over her head and quickly donned a shirt and knickerbockers.

Maggie fretted with impatience as she fastened the long row of buttons on her gaiters, and she vowed to buy a pair of boots the first thing in the morning.

She turned her attention to her next problem—concealing her mass of red curls. It would take too much time to braid her hair, but she knew she couldn't pass as a boy with her long hair falling past her shoulders. She rummaged through her trunk and retrieved the touring cap she had won from Pudge Petrie in a marble game. Maggie pulled the cap down over her ears and shoved her hair beneath the woolen covering. After a quick glance in the mirror to make certain all strands of the telltale evidence were hidden, Maggie grinned with satisfaction. The disguise was perfect. No one would guess she was a girl.

She came to an abrupt halt at the door. For the first time, Maggie realized that if she unlocked the door, it would have to remain unlocked while she was gone. Waking Diane to lock the door after her made no sense. Her whiny sister would just make a fuss which would wake her mother and Taylor.

"Feathers and damnation!" she swore, mouthing

Pudge Petrie's favorite curse. Her mind was made up; she wasn't about to turn back now. Her roving glance fell on the means of her escape—the open window.

Maggie stuck her head out and surveyed the situation. She looked down to the street, a formidable three stories below, but saw that the front roof of the hostelry came to a peak just a short distance beneath the window. She swung her legs over the sill.

It was a simple task for Maggie to lower herself down to the roof. She inched cautiously across the sloping roof to an oak tree which stood off the end of the building. Maggie leaped across the gap and grabbed one of the huge branches. For a few seconds she dangled by her hands until she was able to swing her legs onto the limb. As nimble as a monkey, Maggie skittered down the trunk to the lowest branch and dropped to the ground.

Grinning smugly, she brushed off her hands and hurried down the street.

No one paid her any heed as she strolled along, gawking into store windows and the tavern doorways. Nothing was as she had expected. The city abounded with buildings made of stone, when she had expected them to be crudely made of wood. Banks, factories, utility departments, and countless mercantile establishments offered everything from ice cream to Colt pistols.

She didn't see one Indian.

Enthralled with the sights and sounds around her, Maggie wandered farther away from the congested center of the town. Much to her amazement, she encountered whores, standing in the amber glare of oil lamps, who called out ribald offerings of their services to the boyish figure. Blushing, Maggie lowered her head and continued past them without a word.

She stopped at a dry goods store which bore a red, white, and blue sign boasting *Boots And Saddles*. Maggie studied the contents of the window for several lengthy moments. Resolved to shop in the morning, she began crossing the street with the intention of returning to the hostelry.

But the sound of gunfire caused her to spin around in alarm. Whooping loudly, half a dozen cowboys came galloping down the road. The revelers were too liquored-up to notice the figure standing directly in their path. Paralyzed, Maggie stared at the thundering horses bearing down on her.

Suddenly, a strong pair of hands snatched her from the path of the trampling hooves. Startled, she looked up into a pair of dark eyes blazing with anger. "What in hell are you trying to do, kid? Get yourself killed?"

Speechless, Maggie stared up helplessly at the angry man who had rescued her. Her eyes, round with fright, began to fill with unaccustomed tears. Maggie was not a cry-baby, but the man's anger terrified her as much as her brush with death. In all of her eighteen years no one had ever spoken so harshly to her. Her mind seemed as numb as her legs had been seconds before.

In near panic, she shrugged out of his grasp and raced back to the hotel. Breathless from the run, she slumped down and leaned back against the sturdy trunk of the tree until her trembling ceased.

When she regained her composure, Maggie rose to her feet and stretched to grab the tree limb. But she could not stretch far enough. She made several attempts to leap up and grab it, but the branch was decidedly out of reach. Strange. She hadn't noticed how high the limb was from the ground when she jumped down.

The trunk was too big to straddle and shimmy up to the branch, so she continued the fruitless effort of jumping and grabbing at the errant limb.

"Still trying to break your fool neck, huh, kid?"

Maggie spun around in surprise, and found herself face to face with the man who had just saved her. Now in the brighter light and with her mind not frozen from fright, she recognized him —none other than the soldier she had seen from the train window that afternoon.

"Everybody can climb a tree," she retorted. Maggie knew the proper etiquette would be to thank him for saving her life. But he seemed to be laughing at her, and she felt resentment.

"From where I'm standing, it sure don't look like *everybody* can."

He *was* laughing at her. Her eyes flashed with anger and determination. "Well, I made it down this way, so I can make it back up the same way . . . somehow," she added, less confidently.

"What do you intend to do when you get up there? Sleep in the tree?" he asked, amused.

Even though she resented his attitude, conscience began to unravel spite, and Maggie realized she owed the man a debt of gratitude. The situation called for a reserved courtesy. "No, sir, I intend to return to my room in the hostelry. And I do thank you for saving my life earlier." Maggie turned back to the tree, hoping the man would recognize she had nothing further to say to him. She made another useless leap at the hanging branch.

"Have you thought of trying the door?" he drawled.

Exasperated with her futile effort to climb the tree, she swung around and glared at him. "If I use the door, I'll wake my mother."

He threw back his head and began laughing. Maggie gasped in amazement. Even in the shrouded light, his white teeth flashed against the dark bronze of his skin. His handsomeness was devastating. In the past Maggie had pooh-poohed any talk about a man's looks. She scoffed at girls "ohing and ahing" over a man's curly hair or blue eyes. But now her heartbeat quickened as the chiseled lines of his face softened into boyishness. Budding passion melted resolve, completely squelching the fire of her anger.

"It's sure a lot easier coming down than going up." She grinned sheepishly. "Besides, I'd much rather take the chance of breaking my neck then have to listen to Mother pound my ear for sneaking out in the first place."

Before she realized the soldier's intent, he walked over and spanned her waist with his two hands. Effortlessly, as if she were a sack of feathers, he lifted her. Maggie grabbed the limb and swung herself onto the branch.

She flashed a grateful smile at him. "Thanks, mister."

The soldier continued to grin up at her. "Now don't break your neck, kid."

Maggie retraced her route and climbed back unscathed into the window. She waved to the man on the street below.

For a few seconds, Dakota MacDonald stood silently staring up at the figure in the window. He recognized her as the girl who had waved to the troop from the train window. Dakota had a habit of reading a person's eyes. The eyes usually told him all he needed to know about a stranger—a reliable gauge which had helped to save his life more than once. She may have hidden her blazing red hair under a cap, but there was no disguising her green eyes, and Dakota had not forgotten them. He liked the innocence he read in them. He figured the gal had her reasons for running around dressed as a boy—but there sure was no disguising those green eyes.

Her damn mother ought to take better care of her before the kid gets herself hurt, he grumbled to himself. Then he turned and walked away.

Maggie watched the man amble down the street and noticed his smooth, relaxed stride. She slid her hands past her hips to cup the rounded cheeks; the warmth still lingered from his touch. She told herself that the breathless fluttering in her chest was due to the strenuous climb.

Chapter Four

Maggie woke bright and early the following morning. Eager to be on her way, she washed and dressed quickly. To her chagrin, she met her mother just leaving her room carrying soap and towel. Katherine interrupted Maggie's departure.

"Taylor has gone to talk to the military officer here. I want you and Diane to remain in your room, dear, until I am through, then we'll join him for breakfast." She proceeded down the hall to the bathroom.

Diane was still asleep, and Maggie had no intention of twiddling her thumbs in a hotel room. She had several purchases to make. She was down the hall and out of the hotel before Katherine closed the bathroom door.

Heads turned in passing for another look at the

young woman with flaming red hair who strolled purposely down the street dressed in mustard-colored knickerbockers.

When Maggie expressed her needs, the gray-haired clerk in the dry goods store was both understanding and helpful. Within thirty minutes, Maggie emerged re-outfitted from head to toe. A plaid shirt replaced her white blouse, and a pair of jeans, tucked into leather boots, encased her slim hips and long legs. A felt Stetson was set at a jaunty angle atop her mass of red curls.

Maggie left the store, her old clothing tied in a neat bundle. Out on the street, she paused beside a red-and-white barber pole, seized by a sudden impulse. If she had her hair cut, she wouldn't have to spend so much time braiding it. The idea tempted the impetuous Margaret Collingswood. The mass of hair was hot and cumbersome in the summer. No matter what she did with it, her hair always ended up in her eyes—and worse, long hair forever needed washing. The last thought won the debate.

Maggie turned to enter the shop when she heard loud voices coming from an adjoining building. A sign above the door bore the words, *Office of Indian Affairs, Department of Dakota and Department of the Platte*. The door stood ajar, and the din of raised voices came from within. Maggie did not intend to eavesdrop until she recognized the voice of Taylor Collingswood.

Inside the room, the air bristled with hostility. Dakota MacDonald glared at the army officer seated behind a desk.

"Gentlemen, gentlemen, can't we discuss this reasonably?" Taylor Collingswood said calmly, trying to placate the two men who had squared off against one another.

"There's nothing further to discuss," Dakota declared. "I'm not leading any patrol against the Sioux."

The portly colonel banged his fist on the desktop. "What the hell are you talking about? You've been chasing Sioux for a week."

"Murderers—braves who kill their own—yes, any Sioux would hunt them down. But there are many Sioux in the Badlands because they don't want to live on a reservation. If I take an army patrol in there, it will lead to a battle against my own people."

"Do I have to remind you, Sergeant, that you've got white blood, too. As such, you have an obligation to the white man as well."

Dakota MacDonald leaned over the desk, his dark eyes glaring with anger. "Why is it, Colonel Besting, that if I want to talk to your women or drink in your saloons, I'm an Injun, but when some stinking job has to be done, I'm a white man?"

He straightened up, stretching his lean, rangy frame to its full height. "Well, I've done my job. I scouted the Nez Perce, Cheyenne, and Crow for you. But I'm not scouting the Sioux."

Besting jumped to his feet. "Damn it, Sergeant, this is insubordination. I'm ordering you into those hills, or you'll find your ass in the stockade at Leavenworth."

"And I'm not taking any more of your goddamned orders. My enlistment is up at midnight. Lock me up if you want to, but my decision is final."

The colonel sighed deeply and sat back down in the chair. "Oh, get the hell out of here, Dakota."

"You'll find my army mount and saddle in the stable, Colonel." MacDonald turned to leave.

"Dakota." The young man turned back in irritation. "Good luck," the colonel said gruffly.

Dakota MacDonald paused momentarily. His stern visage softened. "Thank you, sir." He came to attention and saluted. Colonel Besting rose to his feet and returned the young man's courtesy.

Margaret had become so engrossed in the conversation, she was caught unawares when Dakota came out the door. For seconds, they stared at each other. She stood motionless, amazed to once again be facing the man with the buckskin shirt who had helped her.

Without saying a word, he walked away.

"Cheeky devil, isn't he?" Taylor Collingswood commented after MacDonald's departure.

Besting picked up a carved humidor from his desk and offered a cigar to Taylor, then withdrew one for himself, biting off the end. "Actually, Mr. Collingswood, Dakota MacDonald is an excellent scout. His mother was a Sioux princess and his father a Scottish trapper. He refused to scout against the Sioux, so we used him in Arizona and New Mexico against the Apache. He also helped to track down Chief Joseph and his band of Nez Perce in Montana in '77. God! That was a bloody campaign. We chased them for four months, over a thousand miles. It was cold, snowy . . . we lost over a hundred troopers." Besting shook his head sadly. "Yes, MacDonald's a damned good scout."

The colonel lit Taylor's cigar and then his own. "You know, Mr. Collingswood, we've had Apaches scout against their own people. The same is true of the Cheyenne, the Kiowa, the Crow, the Nez Perce. In fact, most of the Plains Indians—except the Sioux. They won't betray their own for any price."

He paused and stared reflectively into space. For a moment, Taylor thought the man had ended the conversation.

The colonel drew deeply on his cigar and blew several smoke rings into the air. "You have to admire that kind of . . . nobility, don't you?"

Outside, with renewed interest, Margaret's glance followed the broad back of Dakota MacDonald. The empathy she felt for this stranger was turning into a new and disturbing sensation. A sadness about him grabbed at the strings of her heart. The Colonel's words echoed in her mind. *Nobility.* Yes, he definitely had an aura of nobility. And he was a half-breed. A smile of satisfaction tugged at the corners of her mouth.

She had finally encountered her first noble red man.

A bell tinkled as she opened the door to the barber shop. Two men sat at a table in the corner engrossed in a chess game.

"Take a seat and I'll be right with you," one called out. His eyes remained trained on the chessboard.

Maggie waited impatiently, knowing full well

she would soon have to get back to the hostelry. Finally, she stated firmly, "I would like my hair cut."

The barber turned his head and peered at her over the glasses perched on the end of his nose. "Peers like you're in the wrong place, little lady. The Frenchie at the end of the block does high-falutin' hairdos for the ladies." He returned his attention to the board.

"I'm not interested in any high-faluting hairdo, sir. I just want my hair cut off, and, if you don't mind, I'm in a hurry."

The barber, annoyed by the interruption of the chess game, looked up at Maggie, and this time his eyes scrutinized their object, slowly moving from head to toe and back again.

What in tarnation does this female have in her mind? he thought. He wondered why a young lady with a beautiful face and glorious red hair would be dressed in such an outlandish get-up. As to any woman wanting her hair cut off, surely that was a sin if there ever was one. *She must be daft or part of some Wild West show.*

The barber rose to his feet. "All right, suit yourself, gal. I'll see what I can do." He shook out a white cloth and draped it around her shoulders. "How short do you want this, sonny?" he chortled. His companion at the table joined the chuckling.

Maggie began to feel a gnawing in her stomach, an intuition signaling loss of nerve, but she forged ahead and took a deep breath. "Cut it short to the head," she snapped boldly without flinching.

"Heck, gal, if you want scalped, I reckon some

Ana Leigh

Sioux would be glad to oblige you. Be darn cheaper than paying old Ben here to do it," the man at the table commented.

The two men fell into another round of chortles. *Braying asses*, Maggie thought to herself, and she was tempted to tell them as much. Instead, she clenched her lips tightly, closed her eyes, and listened to the snip of the scissors as the barber began to cut her hair.

The long strands brushed her cheeks as they fell away to her shoulders. When Maggie couldn't bear the suspense any longer, she opened her eyes and gasped at the reflection in the mirror. A mass of short red curls covered her head and hugged the cheeks of her face.

"That's close enough," she cried out. Her hair had been cut shorter than the length fashionable for men. She quickly covered her head with the Stetson, paid the barber and rushed out of the building. When she looked back, she saw both old men shake their heads in disbelief.

Maggie hurried back to the hostelry. She found Diane bent over a trunk, finishing her packing. Her sister turned around when Maggie entered the room. "Where have you been? Mother is just wild with—" Her mouth gaped and her eyes widened in shock when Maggie removed her hat. "Mother!" she screamed. "Mother, come here, quickly!"

Katherine Collingswood rushed in from the adjoining room with Taylor following closely at her heels. "What is it, Diane? What's wrong?"

Diane pointed an accusing finger at Maggie. "Look at Margaret. Look at her hair."

Katherine turned to look at her eldest daughter. The woman's face constricted with horror and she clutched a hand to her head. "Oh, Good Lord, Margaret! Taylor, do see what that girl has done to herself." She staggered back and sank down on the bed.

"I had my hair cut," Maggie responded with belligerence. "What's wrong with that? It's my hair, isn't it?"

Taylor Collingswood looked as shocked as the two women. "Margaret, whatever prompted you to take such a drastic step?" He tried to remain calm in the face of his wife's near-hysteria.

"Because long hair is hot and a nuisance to take care of. I can't be bothered with it. Besides, I'm old enough to decide how I want to wear my hair," Maggie defended herself.

"Thank goodness none of my friends are here to see it," Diane moaned.

"You think I care a hoot what your friends think?" Maggie lashed out at her sister. "If you put all their brains together, there wouldn't be enough to feed a gnat."

Maggie stormed over to the mirror and fluffed up the flattened hair with her hand. Soft waves sprang up to cap her head.

As he watched her, Taylor considered the situation objectively. He had never before seen a young lady with her hair chopped off. But then, Maggie's intelligence, curiosity, and independent behavior had always set her apart from the ordinary girl. The more Taylor studied her, the more he became aware of how much the haircut actually flattered

Maggie. The short curls brushing her face were a perfect complement to his stepdaughter's almond-shaped eyes and high cheekbones. She looked gamin, winsome, yet mysterious and . . . Taylor realized that for the first time he could recollect, that even in the pants and shirt, Margaret looked not feminine, but . . . womanly.

He walked over, cupped her cheeks in his hands, and smiled down tenderly. "You look very lovely, my dear."

Maggie smiled up gratefully at him. "Thank you, Father." She was unaware that this was one of the few times she had reverted to calling him "Father" since the night of her birthday.

Taylor smiled with pleasure and pressed a kiss to her cheek. "Now hurry and finish your packing. We just have time to eat before the stage leaves for Deadwood."

Katherine Collingswood rose to her feet and paused at the door connecting their rooms. She turned back, casting a tragic look at her daughter. "You deliberately do these things to embarrass me, Margaret. I don't understand the reason for your rebellion." She turned and departed like a Christian martyr being led to the lions.

"Well, this time you've really gone too far," Diane snickered. "Your hair! And those clothes! Maybe we can find a tent show that needs a freak."

"If we do, look out. You might end up the main attraction," Maggie retorted. She placed the package of clothing in her trunk and slammed down the lid.

An hour later, Maggie sat in the stagecoach

waiting eagerly as the driver finished loading their luggage on the top. The letters *Cheyenne & Black Hills Stagecoach Line* were neatly painted on the outside of each door. Hitched to the coach, a team of six horses snorted and pawed the ground, as anxious as Maggie to be under way.

Diane sat next to her. Her face registered the perpetual pout she had worn since the day they had left Washington. Hot and disgruntled, their mother sat opposite them.

"Taylor, what is causing the delay?" Katherine asked irritably of her husband, who was seated next to her.

"They're waiting for the mail," Taylor answered negligently.

"I don't understand why we had to board if they weren't ready to depart," Katherine protested.

Diane's pout deepened.

Since returning to the hotel, Taylor Collingswood had appeared preoccupied. Maggie eyed him with curiosity. She knew he was unaware that she had overheard the heated argument between the officer and the disturbing young scout.

And Dakota MacDonald *is* disturbing, Margaret reflected as she recalled the army scout's dark eyes filled with anger and hostility.

"Margaret, you look quite flushed. Aren't you feeling well, dear?" Katherine leaned toward her with a concerned look on her face, previous grievances forgotten. She put a cool hand on Margaret's brow.

"I'm just anxious to get going, Mother. It's been a long trip."

"And it's not over yet," Taylor cautioned. "The terrain ahead is rough and the road will be bumpy."

A bespectacled old man in a vest ambled over with a pouch of mail. "Hey, Charlie, Dan Reever's wife is havin' a baby, so he ain't makin' this run with you."

The driver, Charlie Walters, climbed down from the coach. He took the bag and tossed the mail pouch on top of the stage. "You mean, I ain't got nobody to ride shotgun agin?"

"Better keep your eyes open. Heard a troop of cavalry tracked a band of hostiles to this area," the old man said to the driver.

"Yea, I heard about it."

Walters stuck his head in the window of the stage, and nodded politely to Katherine and the two girls. "Morning. Name's Charlie Walters. You packin' any iron, mister?" he asked Taylor.

Taylor shook his head. "Why, no."

The driver turned away. "Just my luck to get a coachful of Eastern dudes at a time like this," he grumbled beneath his breath. He crawled up onto the driver's seat, removed a wad of tobacco from his shirt pocket, and bit off the end. Walters returned the plug to his pocket and gathered up the reins.

"Hey, Charlie, hold up. You've got another passenger."

Dakota MacDonald approached the coach carrying saddlebags and a carbine.

"Well goddamn! If it ain't Dakota MacDonald! What in hell are you doing here, boy? Did they kick you out of the army?"

"I'm heading home." MacDonald tossed the saddlebags to the top of the coach and opened the door. His gaze swept the occupants of the stage and came to rest on Diane. She smiled, then dropped her eyes demurely. MacDonald drew back and closed the door. "I'll ride on top."

Charlie Walters grinned at the young man. "Set yourself down here next to me. I need someone to ride shotgun, anyway."

Dakota handed his rifle to Charlie and climbed up next to the driver. The old man drew the tobacco out of his pocket and offered the plug to Dakota. "Want a chaw?" When Dakota shook his head, Walters returned the chunk to his pocket. He flicked the reins and the coach began to roll slowly down the street.

Inside the stage, Margaret Collingswood sat with her hands folded meekly in her lap, trembling with excitement.

Chapter Five

"Haw, haw!" Charlie Walters called out, prodding the horses to a faster pace as the stagecoach rumbled over the worn grooves of the road.

Inside the carriage, Katherine Collingswood clenched her teeth each time the wheels hit a pothole. "I swear the man is driving this way on purpose. Taylor, tell him to slow up." She grimaced when she was thrown against the wall of the stage. "I declare, I'll have one bruise on top of another."

Taylor patted her hand. "I think Mr. Walters is just anxious to get to Deadwood, my dear." He gave her hand another conciliatory squeeze and continued his own effort to avoid being unseated when the wheel bounced over a fallen boulder and the carriage began to rock like a cradle in the wind.

Maggie couldn't have been more delighted. She enjoyed every moment of the ride. Being jostled about in a stagecoach fit perfectly into her conception of the Wild West.

The road wound through thickly wooded hills and granite buttes rising like obelisks toward the sky. Maggie gazed out the window, her head bobbing and turning continually as she tried not to miss one iota of the spectacular scenery.

Suddenly, Walters pulled up sharply on the reins. Horses and stage came to an abrupt halt, scattering pebbles and raising a cloud of swirling dust.

With the screech of a banshee, Diane was flung onto the opposite seat, which shoved her mother into Taylor. His hands grasped his wife's shoulders to prevent her from falling, while Maggie landed on her backside on the floor of the coach.

A fallen tree lay across the road. Dakota MacDonald grabbed his rifle and jumped down from the seat. Cursing, Charlie climbed down after him. Shaking his head in disgust, the driver stared down at the obstacle for several seconds.

"'Peers like I'm gonna have to unhitch the team to move it," he grumbled.

"What's the problem, Mr. Walters?" Taylor asked, leaning his head out the coach window.

Charlie spewed a stream of tobacco juice on the dusty road. "Tree's down. Could take a while. You folks might as well climb out and cool your heels." He pointed to the front seat. "Canteen's up front if you're thirsty." The old man turned to Dakota. "How about givin' me a hand, Dakota?"

Fascinated, Maggie watched Dakota MacDonald as he walked over to a tree and leaned his rifle against the trunk. When he turned back to help the driver, Maggie clambered out of the stage and plopped down in the shade of the pines that lined the road. She opened her magazine, but her eyes immediately peered over the top of the page to watch the movements of the handsome half-breed.

Taylor climbed out and extended a hand to help Katherine step to the ground. When he assisted his daughter, Diane descended royally, brushed herself off, and moved haughtily out of the sun into the protective shadows.

Dakota's glance shifted to follow Diane. Maggie grimaced in disgust. *Oh, no. I can't believe he's dumb enough to be falling for her, too.* Disillusioned by her flesh-and-blood hero's taste in women, Maggie returned her attention to the magazine.

The driver and Dakota had just unhitched the team when a figure on horseback stealthily appeared from the concealment of the thick pines. His hat was pulled low over his forehead, and a red-and-white bandana covered his face, leaving two beady black eyes exposed. A pistol in each hand spoke of his intent.

Diane, the first to see him, screamed, whereupon Dakota dropped the horses' reins and reached for the Colt slung on his hip.

"Hold it, soldier boy, and grab some sky," the man ordered. Dakota raised his arms above his head.

Gaping, Maggie glanced at the picture of Deadwood Dick in the open magazine on her lap and saw the same hat and the same scarf worn by the man who held them at gunpoint. However, nothing about the outlaw appeared romantic. A heavy paunch hung over his belt, and the man looked as if he hadn't bathed in months. Maggie mentally excused his slovenly appearance by reasoning that the bandit's life of crime forced him to hide in the hills away from bathing facilities.

"All of you, over there." The masked man waved a pistol, motioning them to the spot where Maggie was sitting.

Taylor put an arm protectively around the shoulders of Diane, who had begun to sob. "Just do what the man says, honey."

"That's right, *honey*," the masked man parroted. "Just do what the man says and nobody'll get hurt."

His glance swept the group and settled on Dakota; the outlaw recognized his greatest threat. "Shuck the gunbelt, soldier boy."

Dakota started to lower his arms. "Hold up," the masked man ordered. "Keep your hands in the air." His glance fell on Maggie. "Hey, kid, get off your ass and unbuckle that belt on him. And don't try anything stupid."

Dakota moved close to Maggie, which brought him within an arm's reach of his rifle. Her body had blocked a clear view of the weapon, and the bandit had not noticed the gun propped against the tree trunk.

As her hands slid to his hips, the outlaw's pistols did not seem as intimidating to Maggie as did Dakota's nearness. The intimacy of removing his gun belt caused her to blush from embarrassment. She couldn't stop her hands from trembling and felt all thumbs as she struggled to release the buckle.

This near to him, Maggie could feel the tension in Dakota's body.

"Hurry up, kid, I ain't got all day," the bandit snarled.

Maggie glanced up helplessly at Dakota, but his steady gaze remained fixed on the gunman. Whatever he thought was concealed behind an impassive mask.

When she finally succeeded in releasing the buckle, the outlaw ordered her to bring the holster to him. He slung the heavy gun belt over his horse. "You the driver?" he asked, turning his attention to Charlie Walters.

"What's it look like?" Casting a contemptuous glare at the bandit, Charlie spat a spray of tobacco juice on the road.

"Carryin' any nuggets or dust?"

"Nothin' but mail and passengers," Charlie grumbled.

The masked man sheathed one of his pistols and pulled out a flour sack. He nudged his horse and trotted over to the other three passengers. "Empty your pockets, dude."

Taylor handed his wallet to the man. "The watch, too," the outlaw commanded. Disgusted, Taylor pulled out his pocket watch and the bandit tossed it into the sack along with the wallet.

"Now you, lady. Let's have that fancy ring on your finger."

Katherine clenched her hand into a fist. "No. I will not part with my wedding ring."

"Lady, if I put a bullet in your hand, it'll hurt a

lot more than it would to part with the ring," he snarled.

"Give him the ring, Katherine," Taylor said authoritatively, aware of his wife's penchant to haggle when she had her mind set.

Katherine began to protest and the masked man raised his pistol. She snapped her mouth shut and opened her hand. "Take it, you cad." Her eyes gleamed as hard and radiantly as the emerald she pulled off her finger. She slapped the ring into his outstretched hand. The man only laughed and tossed the expensive jewel into the bag.

His lascivious leer fell on Diane. "What about you, pretty gal? You got anythin'?"

"No . . . No," Diane stammered. "I don't have anything valuable."

"You've got somethin' under your dress I sure wouldn't mind havin'. I'm willin' to swap your momma's ring for it."

"You vile scum," Taylor exploded. He took a threatening step toward the outlaw and yanked at the reins in an effort to pull the man off the horse.

Diane and Katherine began to scream shrilly. Spooked, the outlaw's horse rose on its hind legs. Taylor fell back and Dakota's gun belt slipped to the ground.

It was the distraction Dakota was waiting for. He grabbed for his rifle.

Horrified, Maggie cried out. "No! Don't kill him." She shoved the gun barrel just as the rifle discharged. The stray bullet grazed the gunman's hand, and he dropped the flour sack.

At the sound of the rifle blast, the horses bolted and the team raced down the road with the harness reins flapping behind them. Struggling to bring his own horse under control, one hand dripping blood from the gunshot wound, the outlaw fired a quick shot at Dakota.

Dakota dived at Maggie to knock her out of the line of fire. By the time he retrieved his rifle and scrambled to his feet, the bandit had disappeared into the thick cover of trees.

"Why the hell did you spoil my shot?" Dakota grumbled at Maggie. "I had a sure bead on him."

Maggie's eyes flared in response to his anger. "I didn't want you to kill him. He didn't mean us any real harm."

Dakota's fierce scowl was enough to make her back away. "That's not the way I read a Colt shoved in my face, kid."

Dakota's displeasure was mild compared to that of her family. All three of them began to verbally harangue her.

Near tears, Maggie tried to explain her actions. "I'm sure he was Deadwood Dick. He's a Robin Hood. He only steals to give to the poor . . . *he doesn't shoot people.*"

Having already expressed his sentiment on the matter, Dakota remained grim and tight-lipped during the family's heated discussion. He silently retrieved his gun belt and strapped it back on his hip, then nodded to Charlie. "I'll get back as soon as I can. You want my rifle?"

Walters shook his head. "No. I've got one under the seat."

The others were stunned when they realized Dakota's intention to leave them. "Good Lord! You're not abandoning us?" Katherine cried out in alarm. "That outlaw could return at any moment and murder all of us."

"Lady, we need some horses." Dakota mumbled in explanation.

"And we have *you* to thank for losing them." The imminent danger having passed, Katherine Collingswood regained her usual arrogance. "If you hadn't fired your rifle, the horses would not have bolted."

"Katherine, the outlaw would have stampeded the horses before he rode off," Taylor said with patient sufferance.

"You don't know that for certain," she persisted. "It's the half-breed's fault we're in this predicament now."

"Ma'am, Dakota MacDonald don't work for the stage line, so he don't have to do what he's doin' for us. I'd be plumb grateful if you'd harness your big mouth," Charlie emphasized loudly. Another spray of tobacco juice fortified his declaration.

Momentarily speechless, Katherine gaped in astonishment. No one spoke to the wife of Taylor Collingswood in such a disrespectful manner. "Taylor, did you hear how he spoke to me? As soon as we get to Deadwood, I want you to report him to his superior."

"Name's Walters," Charlie taunted. "W-A-L-T-E-R-S. Sure hate for you to git the spellin' wrong."

"Katherine, this has been an unnerving experience for everyone concerned. Let's all try to remain calm." However, Taylor Collingswood was not as composed as he would have liked the others to think. He turned in exasperation to his sobbing daughter. "Diane, will you please stop sniffling?"

Diane dabbed at her eyes with a lace hankie, then ran wailing into her mother's outstretched arms.

Dakota had seen and heard all he wanted to of these people. He turned away and began to walk down the road. Maggie chased after him.

"Mr. MacDonald, may I come with you? A long walk would be much more pleasant than listening to my mother's complaints for the rest of the day."

Dakota could understand why the girl didn't want to stay behind, but just making it safely to town would be tough enough without having to wet-nurse a kid on the way. He shook his head. "Sorry, kid. You'll only slow me down. 'Sides, you might take to mothering a rattlesnake," he added with tongue in cheek.

He left her standing in the road. Maggie remained in a pitiful slouch and watched until the tall figure disappeared around a turn in the road.

Dakota had walked for less than an hour when he spied the runaway team standing as docile as grazing cattle along a river bank. It took him a quarter of an hour to untangle the twisted reins, then he mounted one of the lead pair and rode back to the coach.

He saw at once that the situation hadn't changed in his absence. Charlie Walters was sitting in the shade. He had retrieved his shotgun from under the seat of the perch and the weapon now lay across his lap.

The older woman was still complaining to her husband, but the man appeared unperturbed as he sat smoking a cheroot. The kid was sitting against a tree with her face buried in a magazine. Both father and daughter appeared to have closed their ears to the woman's gripes.

The other girl, Diane, now sat near her mother. The younger woman had a pout on her face and her eyes were puffy from crying. Dakota wondered why he had ever thought she was beautiful. Her yellow hair sure had caught his attention, but he noticed she never looked a person in the eye when she spoke and had about as much grit as a rabbit in a snake hole. She needed some of the younger kid's gumption, he thought. His face softened with a rare smile as he remembered the kid scooting up the tree trunk the night before.

Charlie jumped up in relief when Dakota appeared with the team. They quickly disposed of the fallen tree and in a short time were on their way.

A huge gold strike, coupled with its recent designation as the seat of Lawrence County, had turned the tiny settlement of Deadwood into a thriving community. Cleaved in the hollow of Deadwood Gulch, the town had one main street running along the floor of the narrow ravine. Shops, offices, and saloons flourished, squashed together without an inch of breathing space between them. A line of steel rails and a swiftly flowing creek of muddy water added to the congestion in the belly of the gulch.

With only one way to expand, terraced embankments of houses and huts clung to the steep sides of the deep gulch, each wooden platform standing above another, overlooking the roofs of the row below it.

And on either side, the lofty ridges of the Black Hills rose around the town in majestic splendor.

Main Street was crowded with rumpled miners and buckskin-clad mountaineers when the coach finally rumbled into town. Charlie stopped the stage in front of a two-story brick building bearing the name Grand Central Hotel. When they entered the lobby, a balding desk clerk reading a copy of *The Deadwood Daily Times,* glanced up with curiosity. He put the newspaper aside and nodded pleasantly. "Evenin', folks."

"Good evening, I'd like two rooms. Connecting, if you please," Taylor informed him.

The man removed his spectacles and scoffed, "Mister, I couldn't give you two rooms if you were President Hayes himself. We're full up through Sunday."

"Is there another hotel in town?" Taylor asked.

"There's the Miners' Hotel down the block, but it's full up, too. You're plumb loco if you think you'll find a room in Deadwood on a Saturday night."

The screen door slammed as Charlie came in and thumped one of the trunks down on the floor. "Howdy, Wexler. Where's that Chink of yours to give me a hand with the trunks?"

The man shook his head. "Hotel's full, Charlie. I've got no rooms for these folks."

That bit of news did not appear to astound Walters. "Did you hear the stage was robbed?"

"Well, I'll be danged! Anybody hurt?"

"Naw. Dakota MacDonald got a shot into him before the guy took off. Spooked the horses, though. That's why I'm gettin' in so late."

"So, Dakota's back, huh?" Wexler said grimly. Charlie nodded, and for several seconds the two men stood solemnly, ignoring the others. Finally Wexler spoke. "Recognize who held you up?"

Charlie shook his head. "Nope. His face was covered."

Maggie, who had been following every word of the conversation with rapt attention, stepped forward. "I'm sure it was Deadwood Dick."

"Deadwood Dick!" Charlie and Wexler exchanged glances, then both men broke into raucous laughter.

"Taylor, must we stand here all night?" Katherine Collingswood snorted in exasperation. "I'm tired, I'm hungry, and I feel grimy."

Wexler ceased his laughter and scratched the stubble on his chin. "Well, seein' as how the ladies got no place to stay, reckon I could let you folks use my room for the night. I've got an old cot and I can bed down here behind the desk." He cast a circumspect glance at Katherine. "Room's only got one bed, though."

"Oh, Good Lord!" Katherine exclaimed. Aghast, she flung her hand to her forehead in despair.

"One bed," Diane mewled like a child. "Does that mean I have to sleep on the floor?"

Much relieved, Taylor stepped forward. "Thank you, Mr. Wexler, we appreciate your kind offer." He picked up the pen to register and the clerk slapped the top of a small bell on the desk.

An Oriental of indeterminate age and no taller than Maggie scurried out of a nearby room. Dressed in black, loose-fitting shirt and pants, the man wore a pair of thongs on his feet and a straw coolie hat on his head. A long queue hung to the middle of his back.

"Take these folks' trunks to my room," Wexler ordered.

"And there's more on the stage," Charlie added. The Chinaman nodded and shuffled away without a word.

"If you want to go into the dining room"— Wexler glanced down at the registration book— "Mr. Collingswood, I'll have the boy change the bed while you're eating."

"Surely, you don't expect us to eat with all this grime on us," Katherine expounded indignantly. "We'll wait here until the room is cleaned. Then we can freshen up."

"Do what you want, ma'am." Wexler drew a watch out of his waist pocket. "But we quit servin' food in fifteen minutes."

"Oh, Good Lord! Why did I ever come to this God-forsaken place?" Katherine groaned. "Are there no social amenities?"

"Mother, I can't eat with all this icky dust sticking to my face," Diane whined.

Taylor had reached the end of his patience, but he was not one to make a public scene. "Why don't you all sit down and I'll order sandwiches. We can eat in our room."

"And what am I going to sleep on, Father?" Diane queried belligerently.

Maggie could no longer curb her tongue. "On the floor, same as I am." Charlie Walters grinned and winked at Maggie.

Disgusted, Katherine plopped down on a nearby

chair. "Not that one," Wexler called out in alarm. "Leg's broken."

The warning came too late. The chair collapsed under her weight, and Katherine's feet flew up in the air. Amidst a swirl of petticoats and fetching thighs, Katherine Collingswood landed on her rear end.

"Why . . . I've never . . . been so humiliated . . . in my life," Katherine sputtered, trying to lower the folds of her petticoat. Her bonnet was askew, and the skirt of her gown was up around her shoulders.

Charlie Walters covered his mouth to stifle the urge to laugh as Taylor and Wexler rushed to assist the embarrassed woman to her feet. "Taylor, I insist we sue this awful place," she dictated.

Realizing that he could no longer contain his laughter, Walters fled out of the hotel. Maggie wanted to say goodbye to Dakota MacDonald and hurried after the driver. To her disappointment, there was no sign of the reticent scout.

After a lengthy delay, the tired family was finally led to a tiny room at the rear of the lower floor. The women took sponge baths and changed into nightshifts and robes. Then they all settled down to devour a meal of thick roast beef sandwiches and cold milk.

Taylor graciously declined the bed and Diane claimed it at once. He and Maggie each made themselves a pallet on the floor, and the four weary travelers retired for the night.

This has been the most exciting day of my whole life, Maggie thought drowsily, and a contented smile graced her face as she slipped into slumber.

Chapter Six

"Margaret, I insist you wear a dress," Katherine Collingswood demanded the following morning.

Maggie paused, jeans in hand. "But why do—"

"And I will not tolerate an argument," Katherine asserted. "My dear child, you were born a girl. It's high time you begin dressing and acting like one."

Diane's mouth curved into a vain smile. "What would be the purpose, Mother? She would still have a boy's haircut." She pulled a hair brush through her own long golden strands. "Will you help me pin my hair, Mother?"

When Katherine turned away and began to fuss with her younger daughter's curls, Maggie quickly slipped into her jeans and boots. "I'll be with Father." She sped from the room before her mother could voice any further objection.

Taylor Collingswood was not alone when Maggie paused in the door of the dining room. He rose to his feet and waved to her. "Here's Margaret now."

The man to whom Taylor spoke stood up and stared with curiosity at Maggie as she approached the table. Although he was as tall as Taylor, his body was heavier and more muscular. He had a thick thatch of gray hair, and bushy eyebrows dominated his face. Maggie guessed the man to be in his late fifties.

"Margaret, this gentleman is William Godfrey."

"How do you do, sir," Maggie said politely, feeling uncomfortable under the man's continued scrutiny.

"The pleasure is mine, Miss Harris . . . ah, Miss Collingswood."

"Mr. Godfrey is a local banker, dear," Taylor added as he drew a chair for her to be seated.

Maggie smiled nervously at the man, and after an awkward silence, Godfrey commented, "Your father and I were close friends, Miss Collingswood. Forgive me for staring, but you bear a remarkable resemblance to him."

Maggie had never seen a picture of her father. Intrigued, her interest in this man perked up considerably.

"I hope your trip to Deadwood was a pleasant one," Godfrey commented.

"Didn't Father tell you our stage got held up yesterday?"

"Good grief!" Godfrey exclaimed. "I hope no one was injured."

Taylor smiled cordially. "No, none of us is any the worse for the experience, and we even recovered all our valuables."

The conversation ended abruptly with the appearance of Katherine and Diane. As soon as Taylor dispensed introductions, William Godfrey donned his Stetson and shook hands with Taylor. "I will return shortly with a carriage to transport you and your trunks to Sam's ranch."

"A ranch! My father had a ranch?" Maggie's eyes gleamed with the excitement of this unexpected discovery, the fulfillment of her long-time dream—a ranch.

Godfrey nodded. "A horse ranch. Sam Harris raised the best horseflesh in the state." He paused momentarily and smiled down at Margaret. "I think you'll like the Lazy H, Maggie."

"My daughter's name is Margaret, Mr. Godfrey," Katherine sharply reminded him. "Sam Harris called her Maggie, that hideous name, to annoy me."

"My apologies, Mrs. Collingswood." Godfrey nodded politely. "Ladies, enjoy your breakfast."

Katherine cast a critical glance at the back of the departing banker. "He certainly doesn't look like any banker I've ever met, Taylor. And I think he was much too familiar with Margaret."

In an effort to appease her, Taylor patted Katherine's hand. "It was improper, Katherine, but Mr. Godfrey was a close friend of Sam Harris. Perhaps your late husband often spoke of Margaret with him."

"Well, he still had no business addressing Margaret so familiarly. And in public, too." She swung her disapproving glance toward her eldest daughter. "Of course, Margaret, your manner of dress invites such brash informality."

Maggie was only half listening to her mother's complaints. She had heard them often enough to recite the lamentations from memory. Maggie had to admit that her mother might be right about William Godfrey. The way he stared at her was strange. And why would he call her Maggie? Or could Taylor be right? Possibly Sam Harris *had* spoken of her so often to his friend that the nickname just slipped naturally through William Godfrey's lips. Maggie smiled with pleasure. Perhaps her father had cared for her, after all.

Anxiously awaiting the banker's return, Maggie barely touched her food. Her eyes remained riveted on the window. She jumped to her feet as soon as she saw William Godfrey approach in a shay. By the time they joined him outside the hostelry, Godfrey had a buckboard pulled up behind the carriage. "I'll drive the buckboard if you can handle the shay, Mr. Collingswood."

Taylor eyed the pair of spirited-looking black horses harnessed to the rig. "I don't see why not," he replied.

When the trunks had been loaded, Katherine and Diane seated themselves under the carriage's canopy, but Maggie climbed up onto the spring seat of the buckboard. With a flick of the reins, the wagon pulled away. Taylor followed behind with the shay.

Casting a grin at Maggie, Godfrey commented, "I can see what Sam meant. He told me you have a lot of mettle."

Her father's neglect of her still struck a sensitive nerve in Margaret Collingswood. "How would he know? He never knew me."

Her belligerent tone caused Godfrey to glance over at the girl. The man could see a lot of Sam Harris in the resentful expression on her face. She was a scrapper. This wasn't going to be as easy as he had hoped.

"I guess Sam figured a daughter of his couldn't be any other way," Godfrey responded lightly in reply to her feisty comment.

"Only he didn't think I was worth the effort to find out for himself, did he?"

Maggie fell into a brooding silence the rest of the way to the ranch, asking only an occasional question about the sights. After an hour's ride, they reached the ranch.

Her expectations had not prepared her for the size of the ranch house. Maggie's eyes widened in amazement when she spied the long, double-winged log house stretched out before them. "It's . . . so big," she stammered.

"Sam added another wing just before . . . he left," Godfrey said slowly.

A small building, which appeared to be a smoke-house, stood near a large barn and the bunkhouse. Several horses romped in a mammoth corral several hundred yards from the main house.

Katherine Collingswood, just as astounded, gasped as her husband assisted her out of the carriage, "This all belonged to Sam?"

William Godfrey appeared to be well-known to the household staff. An Oriental servant opened the door, nodded politely to the banker, and after a few whispered instructions, scurried off.

Maggie loved the interior of the house on first sight. Roomy and masculine, a stone fireplace occupied one complete wall, and a long dining table framed by a dozen chairs stood at the other end of the large room. Several leather sofas and chairs were dispersed throughout.

Braided oval rugs, scattered over a hardwood floor, which showed signs of a recent polishing with beeswax, added additional warmth.

William Godfrey motioned for them to sit down, then seated himself behind a large oak desk.

Maggie, attracted to a painting of an Indian hanging above the fireplace, walked over to have a closer look. The Indian's hair hung to his shoulders, and two eagle feathers dangled from a plait at the side of his strong, square jaw. The artist had captured wisdom in the dark eyes which seemed to focus on her, penetrating her very soul. Mesmerized, Maggie stared at the face in the painting.

"He's magnificent," she murmured. "Who is he?"

William Godfrey glanced up at the portrait. "Screaming Eagle. An Oglala chieftain."

"An Oglala?" Maggie asked.

"The Oglalas are a tribe of Dakota Sioux," Godfrey added as she returned her attention to the portrait.

The reappearance of the servant with a coffee tray interrupted the discussion. Godfrey quickly offered a cup to Katherine, then added a generous measure of whiskey to Taylor's cup, as well as to his own.

Unable to withdraw her gaze, Maggie remained

entranced by the dignified face in the portrait.

William Godfrey settled down behind the desk and took a deep draught of the liquid. "The ranch house is spacious, and I'm confident all of you will find it much more comfortable than the hotel," he declared. "I regret, however, you'll have to—" Suddenly, the words died in his throat, and the banker rose to his feet, his face creased in surprise.

All eyes shifted to the object of his attention. Maggie spun around, then gasped with pleasure at the sight of Dakota MacDonald framed in the doorway.

"Dakota!" Godfrey exclaimed.

"What in heaven's name is *he* doing here?" Katherine asked, not disguising her contempt.

Ignoring her boorishness, Godfrey crossed to the door and shook hands with Dakota. Then, forsaking formality, he pulled the younger man into his arms and hugged him. "When did you get back, son?"

"Last night," Dakota said succinctly.

Smiling sadly, Godfrey stepped back. "I can't tell you how badly I feel about Sam's . . ." His eyes shifted downward, unable to meet Dakota's pain-wracked stare. "He was my best friend."

"How did it happen, Will?" A deep huskiness edged the younger man's voice. "Yen Ching said you were with Sam when the accident happened."

Godfrey nodded. "Sam spied a herd of wild horses on the northern slope of Twin Buttes and took off after one of 'em. His horse stepped into a chuckhole and stumbled. They both went over the edge of the bluff."

"Was he riding Diablo?"

Godfrey nodded.

Dakota shook his head. "Can't understand it. That black of his was as sure-footed as a mule."

Katherine Collingswood's frigid voice shattered the exchange of grief. "Mr. Godfrey, may I ask why this . . . person . . . is being offered an explanation when my daughter and I are the two people directly affected by Mr. Harris's death?"

Anger flashed temporarily in Godfrey's eyes as he turned to the woman. "I beg your pardon, Mrs. Collingswood, forgive my oversight. This is Dakota MacDonald. Sam Harris's other heir."

"Other heir!" Katherine appeared to be on the verge of swooning. She drew out a handkerchief and began to fan and dab at her brow with the dainty piece of lacy linen. "Are you saying Sam fathered this . . . half-breed?"

Maggie was perplexed. She had heard the Army colonel refer to Dakota's father as a trapper, but Taylor had told her Sam Harris had been a soldier in the Army.

Her gaze lingered on Dakota. If, in truth, this man was her brother, she could understand why she had felt such empathy for him from the first moment she saw him.

Katherine fired another insult. "I don't believe this . . . Indian . . . is Margaret's brother."

Maggie's heart ached for Dakota MacDonald. To learn of his father's death was a tragic homecoming for the soldier, and her mother's insensitivity to his grief was unforgivable.

Godfrey cleared up the confusion as he continued, "Madam, will you let me finish, please? Dakota's father was a Scottish trapper by the name of Angus MacDonald and his mother a Sioux Indian named White Dove. Seventeen years ago, they found Sam severely wounded and they nursed him back to health. The next year, when Angus and White Dove were killed, Sam took their boy, Dakota, and raised him as his own."

Dakota remained unflinching as he listened to Godfrey's explanation. Despite the inscrutable expression on the halfbreed's face, Maggie sensed Dakota's scorn for these people who cared nothing about Sam's death, much less that of his parents. Sam's fortune had been their only purpose for coming to Deadwood.

Dakota's gaze scanned the room and came to rest on her. With a sickening awareness, Maggie realized that his contempt included her. She shook her head in denial. *No. It's not true. I'm not like them,* she silently pleaded.

For a few breathless seconds, Dakota's gaze remained fixed on Maggie, then he turned his head away.

Godfrey called out to Dakota, who had moved to depart. "Dakota, come in and sit down. Sam's will concerns you, too."

"I've got no claim on anything of Sam's," Dakota said. "I'll get my gear and clear out."

"I wholeheartedly concur with your decision, Mr. MacDonald," Katherine interjected, her face twisted in contempt.

Godfrey threw the woman an exasperated look. "Please stay, Dakota. Sam wanted it this way." He withdrew an envelope from his briefcase. "Sam instructed me to give this to you."

Reluctantly, Dakota walked over and accepted the sealed document. Maggie noticed that the envelope was identical to the one she had received from Sam Harris.

Godfrey extracted another paper from his case. "Now that both heirs are present, I'll deliver the will." He cleared his throat nervously and began to read aloud.

"I, Samuel Houston Harris, being of sound mind, do hereby declare this document to be my last will and testament.

"To my daughter, Margaret Ann Harris, also known as Margaret Ann Collingswood, and to my ward, Dakota MacDonald, I leave my ranch, the Lazy H, and all possessions thereon.

"Furthermore, Margaret Harris and Dakota MacDonald are to share equally in the considerable fortune I have amassed in recent years due to a gold strike and shrewd investments. Each heir has been given one half of the map that will direct them to the site of the buried fortune. Should Maggie and Dakota seek the fortune together, I have no doubt they will experience heretofore undreamed-of treasure.

"However, if one party chooses not to seek the fortune, then the entire inheritance, including the Lazy H, reverts to the other heir.

"In the event neither heir wishes to seek the fortune, then the Lazy H and all of my buried

*wealth reverts to my trusted colleague and
executor, William Godfrey."*

"Absurd. It cannot be!" Katherine screamed.

Godfrey paused momentarily to glower disapprovingly over the top of the document.

Utterly astonished, Maggie looked at Dakota, whose face showed no emotion. His eyes stared far off into space as if he had not heard a word. In truth, the reading of Sam's will disgusted him, and his inheritance was of no significance to him. Dakota's thoughts were concentrated solely on Sam, his father and friend gone forever.

Godfrey continued to read.

*"To my beloved wife, Katherine Harris, and
former commanding officer, Taylor
Collingswood, I leave my forgiveness—along
with two return tickets to Washington D.C.*

*"Any interference on the part of Katherine or
Taylor to prevent my heirs from receiving their
inheritance will result in the release of a
document which will be politically and socially
damaging to Mrs. Harris and Mr. Collingswood.*

*"And now, having disposed of my earthly
possessions; I shall muse from aloft on angels,
coyotes, and 'just desserts.'*
Samuel Houston Harris."

"Why, that's blackmail," Taylor blustered.

"How dare that hypocritical reprobate threaten us," Katherine added, her face pinched with anger. "Insanity! Just the sort of thing I'd expect from

Sam Harris. He always had a flair for the dramatic," Katherine ranted. "Taylor, we'll hire a lawyer from the East to have this ridiculous document declared invalid."

The banker ignored her outburst and peered across the desk at Maggie and Dakota. "Are the conditions of the will clear to both of you? If either of you refuses to honor Sam's first request, the ranch reverts to the other. If both of you refuse the last request, the fortune reverts to me."

Dakota leaned back and grinned. "Sam must have been high on coyote juice when he concocted this one."

"He was as sober as a judge," Godfrey denied. "The will is legal and cannot be nullified."

By this time, Taylor Collingswood had regained his composure. "I'm inclined to agree with my wife, Mr. Godfrey. The will is too bizarre to be taken seriously."

Katherine rose to her feet and began to pace the floor. "I was the wife of Sam Harris at the time of his death. Legally, his wealth should revert to me."

Diane, who had uttered barely a word since their arrival, spoke out to contradict her mother. "How could you have been Mr. Harris's wife when you're married to my father?"

Irritated, Katherine turned on her daughter. "Just hush, Diane. This doesn't concern you."

The young girl broke into sobs. "It does too concern me if you and Father aren't married. That makes me a bas—illegitimate."

Taylor rushed to embrace his daughter. "Now, now, honey, this is all a mistake. Of course, your

91

mother and I are legally married." However, he failed to confess to the distressed girl that the remarriage had transpired the day before they had departed for the Dakota Territory.

Maggie and Dakota were forgotten in the uproar of Katherine's shouting, Diane's bawling, and Taylor's officiousness, along with William Godfrey's efforts to placate them all. The whole situation had become too overwhelming for Maggie to comprehend. She glanced at Dakota who had just opened the envelope and was studying a jagged piece of map.

She felt torn between crying and screaming. The whole affair was becoming a circus. Maggie surmised that Sam Harris must be laughing at all of them from his grave. Unable to bear the scene another moment, she dashed from the room.

Maggie raced across the yard to the corral. Breathless, she stopped by the fence and stared for several moments through unseeing eyes at the horses confined within the area.

"Are they always like that, kid?"

Startled, she looked up to discover Dakota MacDonald beside her, casually chewing on a piece of straw. Maggie, embarrassed by her family's actions, remained loyal to them and rallied to their defense. She raised her eyes with belligerent regard. "The trip has been very exhausting for my family, Mr. MacDonald. Being jostled about in a coach and threatened at gunpoint has been a shattering experience for us."

Maggie purposefully included herself as one of them and lifted her head proudly. "I think we are conducting ourselves admirably, Mr. MacDonald."

Dakota hooked a booted foot over a rung of the fence. "Well, if you don't rein up, you're all gonna choke on each other's dust."

A lengthy silence ensued. Maggie stole several sideward glances at Dakota as he stared impassively at the grazing horses. She sensed that he had said his piece and had put the matter out of his mind. Finally, she broached the subject foremost in her thoughts. "What do you intend to do?"

Dakota slowly straightened his tall frame. "Ride out to the north range."

"I mean, what do you intend to do about Sam Harris's will?"

Dakota tossed aside the stalk of straw he was chewing. "Do about it? I've half a mind to go on a treasure hunt." The faint glimmer in his eyes revealed a side to his nature Maggie never suspected. Dakota MacDonald had a sense of humor.

Maggie squared her shoulders, cocked her hat, and thrust up a delicate, but determined, chin. "Well, if you do, you can bet your britches, Mr. Dakota MacDonald, I'm going with you."

Chapter Seven

For several seconds Dakota stared down at Maggie, torn between putting her over his knee or shaking the pesky girl until her brain rattled. Instead, he turned and headed toward the stable.

Determined not to be put off, Maggie followed, running to keep up with his rapid strides. "Remember, Mr. MacDonald, I have the other part of the map."

Dakota stopped and glowered down at her. "You know, kid, you're a real pain in the ass."

Maggie, not easily thwarted, returned the fire. "Please stop calling me kid. Kids are baby goats. And another thing, watch your language in the presence of a lady."

"Lady? That's a laugh. Get smart, kid, take some lady lessons from your older sister."

Older sister! Did he actually believe simpering, whiny Diane was older than she? Maggie thought, astonished. Just because Diane was prettier and dressed herself up like a peacock out for a Sunday stroll didn't make her sister smarter. Oh, men were so . . . *dumb!* How could she have thought he would be different?

Diplomacy was not one of Margaret Collingswood's redeeming qualities. Hands on hips, her emerald eyes flashed as her temper flared. "I want you to know that I am eighteen years old. If you'd bother to look beyond Diane's blonde hair and fluttering eyes, you'd realize I'm two years older and ten times smarter than my sister. I declare, nothing that walks or crawls on this earth is as stupid as a man."

"Then why do you run around dressed like one?" Dakota strode away, leaving Maggie sputtering for a retort.

Dakota could hardly believe the kid was eighteen; he had reckoned fourteen, fifteen at the most. But then, a girl dressed as a boy with most of her face hidden under the brim of a hat—well, her age would be anybody's guess.

By the time Maggie caught up with him, Dakota had already gone into the stable and had begun to saddle a horse. "Just where are you going?" she demanded to the broad width of his shoulders.

Dakota gritted his teeth, swung the saddle over the horse's back, and turned around. He shoved his hat back on his forehead and glared down at her. "Let's get something squared away. I ain't planning on spending the next six months picking your straw out of my hair. So just ride wide of me, kid—ah, *lady*."

Maggie understood the reason for his hostility. He had angered her and she had reacted as nastily as her mother. Feeling contrite, Maggie offered an apology. "I'm sorry, Dakota. I didn't mean to crowd you. I just want us to be friends." She turned and walked toward the house.

As he cinched the saddle girth, Dakota lifted his head and watched Maggie walk away. The kid looked pathetic, the picture of dejection. He could not understand why in hell he should feel guilty, but with a grimace of self-reproach, he called out to her. "Hey, kid."

Maggie stopped and turned her head.

"I'm heading up to the north range. Want to ride along?"

She grinned broadly. "Sure." Maggie ran back to the stable.

"Get me the roan mare. I'll saddle her for you."

Maggie looked helplessly at several horses in nearby stalls and wondered which one was the roan mare. Dakota eyed her quizzically. "You *can* ride?"

Unflinchingly, she answered, "Of course. I just have trouble telling a roan mare from a . . ."—her mind groped desperately for a suitable word—". . . stallion."

Dakota grinned to himself and swallowed the obvious bawdy response. "The one in the last stall."

Maggie approached the tawny horse, relieved to see the mare didn't appear as tall and formidable as the horse she had ridden in Washington. "We're going to be great friends, aren't we?" she whispered.

The mare snorted and regarded her through large black eyes. Maggie's quandary bordered on desperation. She did so want to ride with Dakota but would the horse be of the same mind?

Gingerly, she reached out to pat the animal. When the mare accepted the fondling, Maggie grew bolder. Soon she had forgotten her reason for approaching the animal and stroked the horse with both hands while cooing affectionately in the mare's ear.

"You planning on riding that horse or just talking it to sleep?" Dakota asked, suddenly appearing beside her.

"She's so beautiful," Maggie said, stepping aside so Dakota could saddle the mare. "What's her name?"

"Last time I knew, she didn't have one."

"May I call her Tiger?" Maggie asked.

"Call her anything you want," Dakota said, shrugging his shoulders. "Sounds more like a cat than a horse, though," he added.

Maggie pressed her cheek against the horse. "I know, but she's the color of a big, tawny cat."

Dakota led the two horses out of the stable and handed Maggie the mare's reins. Her mind raced as she tried to recall the instructions in the textbook. Stand close to the horse . . . Face its tail . . . Gather all reins in the left hand . . . Grab a handful of withers . . . She cast her eyes heavenward and said a quick, silent prayer. With a show of bravado, she put her foot in the stirrup and swung herself onto the horse.

"Let me lengthen those stirrups," Dakota said. "Your legs are longer than I thought."

While he lowered each strap, Maggie adjusted to the feel of being in the saddle. She wished she could have had time for another riding lesson before coming to Deadwood. One lesson was not enough to give a person confidence. However, this time the ground did not appear to be so far away. When Dakota finished, Maggie grasped the reins. *Don't jerk them,* she warned herself. She planted each foot firmly in a stirrup and lightly pressed her knees into the horse.

To Maggie's immense relief, the horse stepped forward.

Fortunately, the terrain prevented any fast galloping. Within a short time, she found herself relaxing, and the thousand fluttering butterflies in her chest and stomach settled down.

Maggie became enthralled with the spectacular scenery. Even Dakota's silence did not disturb her. She felt a sense of companionship as they rode side by side.

When he finally reined up and climbed off his horse, Maggie remained in the saddle, watching intently as Dakota got down on bended knee to study the ground.

Dakota stood up and walked over to the edge of the butte. For several moments he stared down at the steep drop. "This is where it happened," he said somberly.

Maggie knew he was referring to Sam Harris's

accident. She dismounted awkwardly and moved beside him. Scattered brush and trees dotted the steep sides of the declivity that ended in a dry gulch several hundred feet below.

Directly opposite and at a deceptively close distance, since the span gaped too wide for man or animal to leap, stood the face of another butte, similar in height and width. Buffeted by freezing blasts of the north wind sweeping across from Canada, the vegetation grew less dense there than on the twin slope.

Maggie stared down solemnly at the gulch between the buttes. A pall hung over the site; not a bird chirped nor a leaf stirred. The throb of her heartbeat seemed to clamor in her ears. Sadly, she turned away.

Dakota tied the horses' reins to nearby shrubs and grabbed a rope attached to his saddle.

"What are you going to do?" Maggie asked at the sight of his grim, determined face.

"I'm going down there."

"You mean climb down? Isn't there a way of approaching from below?"

Dakota shook his head. "Not from this side. We'd have to ride for hours to skirt the bluff." As he talked, Dakota tied the rope firmly to a tree. "I won't be gone long. I just have to drop about fifty feet, then I can make it to the bottom on foot."

Maggie was astonished. "You mean you've done this before?" She walked over for another look at the steep drop.

Dakota pulled his rifle out of the scabbard on his saddle. "Can you handle a rifle?"

Maggie shook her head.

He proceeded to show her how to cock the gun. "If you have a problem, point it in the air and pull the trigger to signal me."

Surprised at the weight of the gun, Maggie cocked the gun once and gave a hesitant response. "All right. I understand." Maggie felt uncomfortable being left alone. She had an uneasy feeling about the place, and the thousand butterflies began to flutter in her stomach again.

She held the rifle firmly as she watched Dakota climb over the side of the bluff and lower himself down the rope. When he reached the end, he grabbed a sapling and cautiously began a zigzag course from scrub to tree until he reached the bottom.

"It doesn't look hard at all," Maggie reasoned aloud. "He even went down standing up." That thought was all the incentive she needed to follow him. Laying the rifle on the ground and without hesitation, she lowered herself over the side.

Dakota was furious when he looked up and saw her begin the descent. *Damn the girl! How in hell could I be foolish enough to bring her with me?* He found himself holding his breath as he watched Maggie move from shrub to tree, stopping at each one to catch her breath and calculate her next move.

Dakota jumped forward to go to assist her when Maggie's foot slipped and she skidded on her rear end for several feet. She quickly regained her footing and continued to navigate her course. Dakota halted, admiration gleaming in his eyes.

The little minx's got more mettle than a she-wolf.

"That was a damn-fool stunt," he barked, hurrying to her side when Maggie reached the bottom.

"I did it, didn't I?" she boasted.

"Yea, and if you'da broken your fool neck, your mother wouldn't rest until she saw mine stretched." Angrily, he strode away.

As she brushed herself off, Maggie's gaze followed the irate young man. Why was he so angry? He didn't really care whether or not she broke her neck. He was just worrying about his own darn neck. Good grief! Did he actually believe Mother would have him hung if I had an accident? Maggie grinned, despite her resentment. *Mother probably would.*

Now that she was down there, Maggie didn't quite know what to do with herself. With her hands on her hips, she watched Dakota examine the ground. "What are you looking for?" she finally asked. "I'll be glad to help you."

"Don't worry about it," he grumbled.

Maggie sat down to watch him. Dakota continued his efforts as if she weren't there, crossing and recrossing the ravine several times. Finally, after what seemed like hours but in truth was not more than thirty minutes, Dakota told her he was ready to leave.

"You said in Rapid City, it's a lot easier coming down than going up. Well, lady, you said a mouthful. Let's go."

The lower part of the climb wasn't too difficult, but the closer they got to the middle, the more difficult it became to maneuver. Maggie stopped several times to draw deep breaths before attempting the next rise.

Breathless, they finally reached the rope with the most tedious climb still ahead.

Dakota took the end of the rope. "You go ahead of me. I'd rather be behind you in case you start to fall."

"You don't have to worry about me falling," she flared. "If I didn't think I could shimmy up the rope, I wouldn't have come down." She leaned back heavily against a tree to rally her strength.

Maggie screamed as the small sapling uprooted and broke loose under her weight. Dakota grabbed her wrist as she started to tumble, falling to his knees in the process. He tried to regain his footing, clinging to the rope with one hand while Maggie dangled from his other hand.

For several seconds, Maggie struggled in panic, her legs thrashing wildly as she swayed helplessly over the deep ravine.

As if she were drowning, her life passed before her, and the ironic possibility that she and the father she had never met would suffer the same fate at the same spot flashed through her mind.

Then the strength in the firm grasp of the hand that held her wrist in a vice dissolved her panic. Instinctively Maggie knew Dakota would not loosen his grip. Dakota MacDonald, no fictional daredevil in a pulp magazine, but her real flesh-and-blood hero, would not let it happen.

Her brain—or could it have been her heart?—transmitted that confidence to her body, and Maggie ceased her frantic struggling.

Not having to fight the pull of her flailing body, Dakota got up and regained a sure footing on the slope. He inched over to the support of a tree and anchored himself. The muscles in his right arm bulged tautly as he began to pull her up.

Finally, Dakota hauled her into the circle of his arm, and a firm band of strength enveloped her waist. Maggie buried her head against his chest and her arms hugged his waist. Breathless, they clung to one another.

Dakota's lungs burned and the sensation in his right arm was like a barrage of needles driven into his flesh. When the pain gradually lessened, he eased his hold on Maggie and looked at her. "Are you ready, Maggie?"

Her name on his lips was a caress to her ears. She nodded, not certain what he expected, until Dakota tied the end of the rope around her waist.

Maggie nodded again, and with a feeble grin began the strenuous climb. Hand over hand she pulled her way up the rope, which seemed to stretch to infinity. Her right arm weakened with each tug. Breathless, she reached the top and collapsed. Dragging air into her tortured lungs, she lay on her back trying to restore her breathing.

"Maggie." The urgent concern in the call jolted her to action. She scrambled to her feet, untied the rope from around her waist, and dropped the loose end down to Dakota.

With a pounding heart, Maggie watched as Dakota began to scale the granite wall. She prayed for his safety. To her, each groping inch seemed a measured heartbeat. Anxiously, Maggie reached out to assist him the last few feet. She broke into a wide smile of relief when Dakota finally reached the summit, climbed over the rim, and collapsed on the ground.

Exhausted, he lay flat on his back. Maggie sat down beside him and pulled off her hat to wipe her brow, now coated with perspiration.

Still breathless, Dakota sat up and stared at her, aghast. "What in hell did you do to your hair?"

"Does it matter?" Maggie asked defensively. Awkwardly, she fluffed self-consciously at the plastered-down curls.

"Not to me." Dakota lay down again. Women were a puzzle, but this one beat all. Why would she cut off that red hair which, if he remembered right, hung all the way down to the middle of her back?

As Dakota turned his head, he caught the glint of a reflection on the opposite hill. Within seconds the flash came again. "Don't move," he cautioned.

Maggie glanced at him, perplexed. "Why?"

"Where's my rifle?"

"Right behind you. What's wrong?"

Dakota inched back until his hand closed around the rifle. "I saw something on the opposite hill."

"Are we in danger?" Maggie asked.

"Maybe. But if someone had a mind to take a shot at us, they had plenty of chance while we were hanging out there. That flash came off a rifle barrel, or I'll eat my hat."

Maggie felt a surge of excitement. "Do you think it's Indians?"

"Can't say, but someone's watching us. Get up and walk to your horse."

As Maggie obeyed his order, Dakota's gaze scanned the hill. He saw nothing among the scattered trees and brush. "Maybe it was just the sun bouncing off a stone," Dakota commented as he climbed on his horse. He could see by her doubtful expression that Maggie didn't believe the explanation any more than he did.

Dakota cast a final backward glance toward the distant butte. Somebody was out there watching them. He'd been an army scout too long not to feel it.

Chapter Eight

When Maggie arrived back at the ranch, a highly agitated Katherine Collingswood was once again stewing over the actions of her eldest daughter. The moment Maggie walked through the door, her mother began to harangue her.

"Where have you been? You're not in Washington now. You just can't go traipsing off by yourself in this wilderness. Why there are wild animals, Indians—and unsavory characters like the one who held up the stagecoach."

"I didn't go alone," Maggie protested. "I was with Dakota MacDonald."

One would have thought Maggie had just confessed to homicide. Horrified, Katherine drew back and threw her hands in the air. "Dakota MacDonald. Good Heavens, Margaret! That half-breed is the very element I am talking about." She shook her head and turned to her husband. "Taylor, talk some sense into this girl."

Taylor tossed his cheroot into a cuspidor by the fireplace. "The young man appears reliable enough to me, Katherine."

The remark raised the woman's ire one more notch. "Go ahead, encourage her disobedience. You always have." Katherine's vexation had turned on her husband. "If you had taken a firmer hand with the girl, she wouldn't be so reckless and headstrong."

"Mother, I wish you would stop referring to me as if I weren't present. Furthermore, I didn't do anything reckless." Maggie was hardly about to tell her mother of her harrowing experience.

"I said *reckless*. You always do as you please, no matter what I say. I am tired of this hopeless struggle." She scowled with displeasure at Taylor. "One woman can't be expected to do it alone without any cooperation." Katherine stormed dramatically from the room.

Maggie wandered over to the fireplace and stared with remorse into the flames. "I'm sorry I got you into hot water, too. Everything I do upsets Mother. Why can't she trust my judgment sometimes?"

Taylor smiled with compassion. "Your mother has your interest at heart, Margaret. She loves you and is concerned about your welfare."

"Dakota and I simply rode out to where my fa—where Sam Harris was killed." With a guilty flush, Maggie realized she had almost let the word "father" slip through her lips.

Talking to Taylor about her real father seemed strange. Taylor was the only father she had ever known. Why should a faceless Sam Harris now intrude into her life, usurping the position of this quiet, supportive man? Maggie's smile was contrite, but not for the reason he suspected.

"I'll always be a disappointment to her, Father. I wish Mother could accept me as I am."

"She will someday, honey." Taylor kissed her cheek and left to console Katherine.

Maggie remained motionless as she struggled with inner turmoil. For the first time in her eighteen years, Margaret Collingswood wondered why she, unlike other women, was inspired by bravery and sought adventure. *I know I can never be the same kind of woman as Mother or Diane. What is within me that keeps me from accepting my proper role in life?*

She glanced up desolately at the enigmatic face in the portrait above the fireplace. For a few seconds she gazed into the dark, penetrating eyes. "You know the answer, don't you, old man."

Maggie's late arrival at dinner caused a new tempest, quite unrelated to her tardiness; she had shed her jeans and shirt for a blue and white gingham gown.

If Maggie possessed a "favorite" dress, this gown fit the description. The ankle-length skirt flared out in a wide flounce below her knees with a blue satin ribbon woven through the top of the ruffle and tied in a tiny bow. A matching ribbon repeated the motif in the flounce at the round neckline of the gown. Her tiny waist was encircled by a blue satin sash tied at the back in a big bow. Cap sleeves exposed the soft curve of her arms and shoulders which Katherine Collingswood insisted had been preserved from freckling only by the diligent application of buttermilk when Maggie was a child.

A vigorous brushing had created an abundance of soft, wavy curls on her head.

No one could have been more pleased by Maggie's feminine appearance than Katherine Collingswood. The woman read the transformation as a gesture of apology on her daughter's part. In truth, Maggie had already put the latest argument with her mother out of her mind.

"Margaret, you look so sweet," Katherine gushed with delight when Maggie slipped into the empty chair next to her sister.

"And very lovely," Taylor commented with a surreptitious wink at Maggie. William Godfrey added his compliment, while Diane rendered a smile of mockery.

Maggie blushed under the rash of flattery. "It's only a dress." She picked up her serviette, placed the napkin in her lap and glanced about in disappointment. "Isn't Dakota going to join us?" she asked when she noticed there was no other place setting at the table.

"Hardly," her mother responded with disdain. Katherine picked up a spoon and began to sip her soup.

"Don't you think it's improper?"

"Improper? To whom? A half-breed?" Katherine's brow was raised in hauteur. "Don't be absurd, Margaret."

Maggie could feel suspicion creeping through

her like the fingers of a flame. "You never asked him to join us," she accused her mother.

"Of course not. Now eat your soup before it gets cold, dear."

Maggie jumped to her feet and threw her napkin on the table. "How could you, Mother? This is Dakota's home. *We* are the intruders."

Too late, Taylor rose to stop her, but Maggie bolted from the room in angry tears. He shook his head in disgust. "You don't give an inch, do you, Katherine?"

Undismayed, Katherine Collingswood raised her serviette and dabbed daintily at the corners of her mouth. "My, this soup is delicious, isn't it, Mr. Godfrey?"

Taylor continued to glare down at her. William Godfrey looked shocked. Diane's eyes gleamed with sudden comprehension and her mouth curved into a smile.

Maggie found Dakota in the stable saddling a mount. Her glance swept the rifle and saddlebags piled beside the horse. "Where are you going, Dakota?" Her voice sounded plaintive, undemanding.

Dakota ignored the question and did not turn around. She grappled for an argument to convince him to stay. "If you leave, you lose your inheritance." She knew he was aware of that fact.

Dakota swung the saddlebags on the horse and began to tie them. "I've got no claim on anything of Sam's. You're his daughter. I'm just a . . ." He turned and the words jammed in his throat.

Maggie's skirt flowed around her in a hazy swirl,

and the dim light of the lantern cast the soft curls of her hair in an auburn glow. Tears shimmered in her eyes.

His gaze slowly traced the graceful line of her neck and came to rest on the rounded swell of her breasts.

As he studied the vision before him, Dakota realized that Maggie, the pesky kid, was actually a beautiful woman. Furthermore, her innocence and unawareness of her beauty enhanced the luster.

"You're just a what?" she asked, prodding him to finish his sentence.

Dakota quickly turned back to the horse and resumed his task. "I was just a stray that Sam befriended."

"You weren't just a stray. Certainly not in Sam's thinking."

Angrily, Dakota spun around to her. "How would you know? You didn't know Sam. Sam *collected* strays. He was a chump to every saddle bum and wounded animal that crossed his path."

Dakota regretted his harsh words when he saw her chin begin to quiver. Maggie covered her ears with her hands. "I won't listen to you. Sam loved you or he wouldn't have made you his heir."

Dakota took the reins of the horse and led the animal to the door of the stable. Maggie followed and grabbed his arm. "Please, Dakota, stay. I know why you're leaving. It's because of my mother. You think you don't belong, but that's not true." Her eyes pleaded with him. "This is your home. I want you to stay. I'm not like my mother and sister."

His face softened with a smile. "You can't

change the world, Maggie. Your mother's no different than most others. I've learned to live with it."

Maggie brushed away the tears streaking her cheeks. "Where will you go?"

"Back to the Army, I guess." Dakota swung up into the saddle and for a moment stared down at her. Her eyes, glistening with tears, looked round as saucers. She seemed so vulnerable that he wanted to get down and take her into his arms.

"Don't let those vultures peck you to death, Maggie," he said grimly and rode away.

Dakota reined in his mount on a nearby hillside and looked back. In the glow of moonlight, he could see Maggie still standing in the door of the stable. Used to be, when the time came to move on, he could ride away from anybody and not look back. Why did leaving bother him now? He didn't owe her anything. *In a short time the kid's sunk her teeth into me like a damn tick that won't let go.*

Dakota watched the slim figure walk slowly across the yard and enter the house. He turned away and prodded his horse to a gallop.

The next day William Godfrey found Dakota passed out in a Deadwood dive with a snoring, naked Oriental woman stretched out beside him.

He shook the woman to wake her. "Get going." He slapped a gold piece into her hand.

Grumbling, the woman pulled on a red silk kimono, ornately embroidered with gold and black snorting dragons, and flounced out of the room.

Godfrey picked up an ewer of water and

splashed the liquid on the face of the sleeping man. Dakota shot up sputtering. At the sight of Godfrey, Dakota draped his legs over the edge of the bed and sat holding his aching head in his hands. "What the hell did you do that for?"

"Christ! This room smells like a saloon," Godfrey said. He opened the window and whipped at the fumes with his hat. "I thought it was against the law to sell liquor to an Injun."

Dakota lifted his head and peered at the man through bleary eyes. The banker's good-natured grin did not help his throbbing head. "They sold it to the white half of me." He rose wearily to his feet and slipped into jeans. "What are you doing here, Will?"

Godfrey eased his frame into a rickety chair, which squeaked under the big man's weight. "Hell, boy, I came to try and talk some sense into you."

"You're wasting your time. My mind's made up." Dakota leaned forward to study his image in the cracked mirror over the dresser. His eyes were blood-shot, his hair was rumpled, and he needed a shave. To add to his misery, his dry mouth felt as if it were stuffed with cotton. He needed a drink, but Godfrey had dumped the whole pitcher of water over his head.

"I think they're right. Indians and liquor don't mix," he said.

William Godfrey regarded the young man reflectively. "Not like you to hit the bottle, Dakota."

"Yea, I know. Last time I got drunk Sam had just hit his strike. The two of us sat up drinking all

113

night." For a brief moment Dakota allowed his thoughts to slip back to a bygone day. Then his eyes clouded. "I'm gonna miss him."

Godfrey's bushy brows rose in query. "I hear tell you're heading back into the Army."

Dakota sat down to pull on his boots. "Maggie tell you that?"

Godfrey nodded. "Why run off to the Army again?"

"It's as good a place as any," Dakota replied. Now fully dressed, he strapped on his gun belt.

"What's wrong with the Lazy H?"

"Too crowded." Dakota slapped on his hat and opened the door. "I need a pot of coffee."

William Godfrey hoisted himself out of the chair and hurried after the young man.

The fresh air helped to clear Dakota's head as he and Godfrey walked down the street to the Miners Hotel. After drinking his second cup of coffee, Dakota felt well enough to order breakfast. Godfrey sipped on a cup of coffee while Dakota consumed a stack of flapjacks and a rasher of bacon.

"You know you're letting Sam down by taking off like this," the banker ventured.

Dakota surmised Godfrey's scheme and wasn't about to jump at the bait. "I don't remember making any deathbed promises to Sam."

"Well, think about Maggie—ah, Miss Collingswood. She doesn't know anything about running a horse ranch. Sam was counting on you to do that for her."

"Yea, and what would happen when the kid finds herself a husband? He'd boot my ass out of there."

"That'd be pretty hard to do when half of the ranch would belong to you," Godfrey argued. "That's why Sam put it in his will."

"Well, he should have had enough horse sense to know it wouldn't work."

Godfrey could see Dakota's mind was set. He decided to try a different tactic. "Ever think of buying out the girl?"

Dakota snorted. "With fifty dollars?"

"My bank will lend you the money, if you want."

"I don't want," Dakota said emphatically. "I'm not tying myself down to a big mortgage for the next ten years."

"Then why don't you run the spread with the kid? You've got nothing to lose."

Dakota got up from the table and threw down a gold piece. "It's a long ride to Rapid City. I'd best get moving."

"Damn it, Dakota, if you won't do it for yourself, do it for Sam's kid."

Irritated, Dakota sat down again. "I'm making life real easy for her. I'm riding out and leaving her the whole spread. That ought to make her mother happy."

"It sure will. With you out of the way, Mrs. Collingswood would be calling the shots. Claims the ranch is hers anyway and she would sell it."

"How could she do that when the Lazy H would belong to Maggie?"

"Maggie's a minor. She's got no money of her own, and she doesn't know a thing about ranching. So what chance does she have fighting her mother?"

Godfrey paused and glanced pointedly at Dakota. "Of course, if you found Sam's treasure, Maggie would be rich." Godfrey grinned. He had Dakota snagged now. It was only a matter of reeling him in. "'Course . . . so would you. You'd have plenty of money to buy out the girl then."

With a suspicious glance, Dakota eyed the banker. "Why are you so damned anxious for us to find Sam's money? You get it all, if Maggie and I pull out."

"Can't spend what I don't have," Godfrey said with a grin. "You gotta find it first. Besides, Maggie doesn't want to pull out. She told me this morning she's all for going on the hunt, if you are. What do you say, son? You got something against being rich, or do you want Sam's widow to get the ranch?"

Having planted the seed, and to avoid overplaying his hand, Godfrey rose to leave. "Sleep on it for a night. We'll talk in the morning."

"I'm not making any promises," Dakota acquiesced. "But I guess one more day won't make any difference."

The two men shook hands and William Godfrey departed, a wide grin splitting his countenance.

Chapter Nine

Dakota topped the rise above the Lazy H and for several moments gazed at the ranch below. His attention became fixed by the figure of Maggie sitting on the fence of the horse corral. Decked out in the familiar jeans, plaid shirt, and a hat concealing her short hair, no evidence remained of the lovely, feminine vision that had appeared in the moonlight on the previous evening.

Maggie's concentration kept her eyes riveted on a ranch hand astride a bucking bronco. When the cowpoke succeeded in riding the mustang to a halt, the sound of her laughter drifted up to Dakota as she clapped with delight.

Dakota prodded his mount and moved down. Maggie turned around at the sound of the approaching hooves, and at the sight of Dakota, she felt her heart leap into her throat. She grinned broadly. "You're back!" Unabashed joy deepened her green eyes to emerald.

Dakota frowned. Although pleased with her reaction, years of oppression had taught him to conceal his emotions. "Only a greenhorn would straddle a fence when they're busting bangtails," he growled.

The smile left her face. Her initial pleasure at seeing him quickly faded with his harsh words. Maggie recoiled, tired of constant criticism. She had been arguing all morning with her mother and Taylor over selling the ranch. Now Dakota had joined ranks with her detractors, habitual nitpickers determined to mend her ways. She lashed out defensively. "I thought you had left for good. Forget something?"

Just as she turned away in a huff, as if to give credence to his admonition the bucking horse tossed its rider and the cowpoke crashed into the fence. Unseated by the jolt, Maggie tumbled into the corral.

Freed of restraints, the horse galloped around the pen. Maggie lay on the ground in its path. Spooked, the animal reared up on its hind legs to trample the latest obstacle in its flight.

Dakota hopped the fence and jumped into the animal's path, wildly shouting and waving his arms. As the frantic animal tried to shy away from this new danger, its foreleg struck Dakota in the head, and with a shriek the animal tumbled to the ground, taking Dakota down with him.

Quickly responding to the accident, several cowhands grabbed the halter of the horse and got the animal under control. Maggie crawled over to where Dakota lay motionless on the ground. Although unconscious, his chest rose and fell in an even rhythm.

"We best get him to the house, Miz Collingswood," one of the cowhands said solemnly.

Maggie felt a rising panic and glanced up at the man. "Will he be okay?"

"Shucks, ma'am, Dakota's got a tough hide. He's been busted up before."

She watched helplessly as several of the hands picked up the unconscious man and carried him to the house.

Dismayed, Katherine Collingswood rose to her feet when the contingent entered the door. "Good Lord, what happened, Margaret?"

"Dakota's been hurt. A horse kicked him in the head."

Katherine was confused. "Dakota? You mean Mr. MacDonald? I thought he had left."

"What does it matter now, Mother?" Maggie voiced in exasperation. "Take him to his room," she ordered as Yen Ching came scurrying out of the kitchen. Maggie and the cowboys followed the Chinaman down the hall.

She paced nervously outside the room while the men undressed and put Dakota to bed. It seemed hours before the door opened. The cowhands doffed their hats and nodded politely as they filed past her and departed.

Yen Ching was just opening a window when Maggie rushed into the room and hurried to the bedside. Dakota remained unconscious, but his color and breathing appeared normal.

"No worly, Missy. He be fine. Mistah Dakota strong wike bull," Yen Ching said with a wide smile.

Maggie needed much more reassurance than the servant's confident grin. "I think we should send for a doctor."

Yen Ching smiled again and bobbed his head. "Doctah come soon." He hurried away when Katherine and Taylor entered the room, followed by Diane.

Maggie watched anxiously as Taylor leaned over to examine Dakota. After a moment, he glanced up at Maggie. "What happened, Margaret? Your mother said Mr. MacDonald was kicked by a horse."

Maggie began to chew on her lower lip to keep from crying. "I fell into the corral. When Dakota jumped in to help me, the horse kicked him in the head."

Taylor put an arm around her shoulders and hugged her to his side. "There, there, honey. I'm sure Mr. MacDonald will be fine. It doesn't appear that he sustained a serious injury."

Maggie could not contain her sobs any longer. Tears began to streak her cheeks. "But . . . but he's been unconscious . . . ever since the ac . . . cident." She wiped away her tears with the sleeve of her shirt. "And it's all my fault."

Taylor hugged her tighter. "Honey, accidents happen. You can't blame yourself."

"How many times have I warned you to stay away from those animals, Margaret," Katherine began. Before she could continue her lecture, Taylor, with a stern frown, cautioned his wife to silence.

120

"There's nothing we can do until the doctor arrives." He took Katherine's arm. "Let's leave the boy alone now."

"Dakota's not a boy, Father. He's a man," Maggie lashed out defiantly. "Why don't you treat him as one?"

"Margaret, you're allowing yourself to become too emotional," Katherine censured. "I suggest you go to your room and rest."

"I'm staying here until the doctor comes," Maggie declared.

"Then get a hold on yourself." Katherine sauntered from the room accompanied by a scathing glare from Maggie.

Taylor paused briefly in the doorway and smiled sympathetically. "I'm sure he'll be fine, Margaret."

Diane waited until her parents had disappeared, then casually strolled across to the door. "I'll be glad to relieve you." She turned back to Maggie with a lascivious smile. "That is, if you want any help."

Maggie's feeling of guilt for causing the accident manifested itself in anger toward her family, who neither cared about Dakota's condition nor concerned themselves with how she felt. No one understood her.

She drew a chair next to the bed and sat down. Dakota's chiseled features were softened in repose. His closed eyelids, concealing the dark, penetrating eyes, emphasized the thick lashes now resting on his cheeks.

"You saved my life again, Dakota," she whispered to the silent figure in the bed. "You're the noblest man I've ever known. And the bravest," she added tenderly, stifling her sniffle. Unable to restrain herself, Maggie reached out and with an awkward motion stroked his bronzed cheek. "Even braver than Buffalo Bill."

William Godfrey had accompanied the doctor to the Lazy H. As the physician examined Dakota, the banker paced the hallway with Maggie. Both bolted to his side when the gray-haired doctor opened the door.

"How is he, Henry?" Godfrey asked.

The doctor shrugged negligently. "A mild concussion. The young man's awake now. He'll have a bad headache for a short time. Whether he wants to or not, I'd advise him to remain in bed for another day."

Maggie shoved past the two men and hurried into the room. At that moment, Dakota tried to sit up.

"What do you think you're doing?" she demanded.

She reached out to shove him back, then quickly withdrew her hands. The sheet had slipped down to his waist, exposing Dakota's bare chest, shoulders, and arms.

"Doctor said you're to stay in bed for a day," Maggie stammered. Inadvertently, her gaze returned to gawk at his naked torso. Wide shoulders sloped down into corded, muscular arms and chest to belie his rangy, raw-boned appearance.

Maggie stared openly, awed by the splendor of his well-developed body. Dakota had the body of a man—not a boy. Unlike Pudge Petrie's flabby, pallid flesh, Dakota's body was beautiful, bronzed —and scarred, like the man himself.

Then she felt an abnormal tightening in the private part of her womanhood, and a shiver raced the length of her spine. The sensation excited her, and she clenched her hands into fists to keep from reaching out to caress him.

Maggie blushed, fearing his penetrating eyes could guess her feelings. She glanced at him and discovered her fears were for naught. Dakota wasn't watching her. His eyes were closed and he was clutching his head.

"Hand me my pants, Maggie."

The curt command snapped her out of her reflective trance. With an emphatic toss of her head, she repeated the doctor's orders. "You are to remain in bed."

This time, she bit the bullet and without hesitation shoved him back. The shock of touching him electrified her. Dakota groaned as his head hit the pillow. "I'm sorry, but you wouldn't listen. I have to consider your welfare."

Dakota opened an eye and growled at her. "Little late for 'sorry,' kid. If you'da listened to me, I wouldn't have a split head."

Maggie flinched under the reminder of her guilt. "Well then, I have all the greater responsibility to make certain you don't get out of bed."

"Just get me my pants," he ordered, gruffly.

"Pants? You won't be needing any pants, young man," the doctor declared as he entered the room with William Godfrey. Before Dakota could object, the doctor stuck a thermometer in Dakota's mouth and grabbed his patient's wrist to take his pulse. After removing the thermometer, he held it up to the light. "Temperature's a bit high, but nothing to worry about. Nevertheless, I'm sorry, Dakota, I want you to stay in bed at least until morning."

William Godfrey leaned over and patted Dakota's arm. "I feel responsible for talking you into coming back, son." Frowning contritely, he eyed the young man. "I sure feel sorry to see you hurting this way."

"If all you *sorry* folks would just ease off, I'd sure feel a lot better," Dakota snarled.

Maggie cringed as Dakota mocked their expressions of guilt and compassion. The redhead riled in defense. "You certainly don't handle pain very well, Mr. MacDonald. Are you always so unpleasant when you're not feeling well?"

"A snake bite or being whomped in the head by a horse will do it every time," he growled. Dakota felt smothered. Next he expected the kid's mother would show up looking 'sorry.' "If you all don't get out of here, I'll show you unpleasant."

The doctor picked up his black bag. "You don't have to ask me twice," he grumbled good-naturedly. "I've got sick folks to tend to. Remember, stay off your feet until morning."

Will Godfrey patted Dakota's shoulder. "Rest, son. You're just a frisky colt fighting the bit."

Maggie couldn't think of anything to say. Besides, she had every intention of returning later whether he liked it or not. With a worried glance at Dakota, she followed the two men.

Several hours later, Maggie opened the door and peeked in. Dakota appeared to be asleep. She slipped into the room and tip-toed over to the bed. Motionless, she stood and watched the even rise and fall of his chest. A tender smile graced her face and, reaching out, she gently raised the blanket to cover his exposed chest. "I can't let you take a chill, Mr. Dakota MacDonald," she whispered lovingly.

Maggie struggled with her thoughts. His presence caused new and strange feelings in her— feelings she didn't understand. She knew he found her to be a nuisance, but she didn't care. She wanted to be with him, near him, touch him. But more bewildering—she wanted him to touch her.

Feeling foolish, she turned away and walked to the window. Outside in the moonlight, she saw her mother and Taylor walking hand-in-hand. Stopping, Taylor pulled Katherine into the cover of a tree. They kissed, their bodies pressed to one another. Transfixed, Maggie watched as her mother's arms slipped around his neck. Taylor's hands slid down and cupped her breasts as the kiss deepened.

Although fascinated, a blush of shame at witnessing the tender moment caused Maggie to turn her head aside. Strange, she had never before visualized her parents as lovers. The discovery came as a shock, an embarrassment. The cause and the nature of closeness between a man and a woman had been a mystery to her. And yet, the feeling of urgency that drew male and female together seemed vaguely desirable.

As she thought about it, an unfathomable wave of longing swept her being, and Maggie wondered if she would ever experience the kind of desire for

a man that demanded the intimacy shared by all
the senses and actions of a loving couple.

Suddenly, Maggie's romantic daydream ended
abruptly. *No, no,* she said vehemently to herself,
shaking her head. *I could never.*

Maggie closed her eyes, painfully remembering
her twelfth summer—the day at the swimming
hole with Pudge Petrie and his cousin, Arnold. She
had put the repulsive nightmare from her
thoughts. But now, the incident appeared before
her, interrupting her pleasant thoughts.

*Maggie didn't like Arnold Cain. A year older than
she and Pudge, the smart aleck always talked about
girls. He tried to kiss her and when she pushed him
away, he began to tease her about not being like the
other girls he knew in Boston. So out of curiosity, she
let him. Before Maggie could guess their intent, the
two boys had her flat on her back, forcing kisses on
her. She squirmed and struggled uselessly as they
opened her shirt and began to run their hands and
mouths over her breasts. Maggie fought ferociously,
cursing and hitting as they slobbered over her. When
Arnold began to pull down her pants, Pudge lost his
nerve and released his grip on her, giving Maggie the
opportunity she needed to break loose. She kicked
Arnold and scrambled to her feet.*

*Pudge ran to save his hide as Maggie picked up a
big stick. She fended off Arnold until the sound of
voices nearby scared him and he too ran for dear life.
Wiping away tears of anger and fright, she quickly
raced back to her room.*

Arnold returned to Boston the following week, but Maggie wouldn't talk to Pudge the rest of the summer.

Maggie opened her eyes and discovered she was clutching the drape with a balled fist. She glanced at Dakota. Would his kiss be just as repulsive as Arnold Cain's or Pudge Petrie's? Her gaze shifted to his mouth and her breath quickened as she studied the firm lips. No, nothing Dakota would do could ever revolt her.

Shocked, she looked down to her breast and realized that the nipples had stiffened into hardened peaks. Swept again by a heated flush, she felt tightening between her legs and had the urge to rip open her bodice to free her aching breasts. She realized that she wanted Dakota to touch them as Arnold and Pudge had done. She *wanted* Dakota to suckle them.

Shamed by the depravity of her thoughts, Maggie buried her flaming face in her hands and sped from the room.

Once in the privacy of her own chamber, she bolted the door and threw herself on the bed. She felt so ashamed. The shocking new sensations confused and frightened her. And they were wicked.

I wish I had never come here. I wish I were back in Washington. I wish I could sit on my favorite park bench reading my Beadle magazine.

With a pitiful sob, she added, "I wish I had never met you, Dakota MacDonald."

Chapter Ten

Maggie purposely avoided Dakota the next day, but their paths crossed when he entered the stable and found her feeding Tiger an apple.

"Looks like you made a friend."

Maggie spun around in surprise. She had been so engrossed with the mare, she hadn't heard his approach. "Oh, it's you." Maggie returned her attention to the mare.

Dakota had long been used to hostile reactions from people, but coming from Maggie, the curt response was a surprise. Without attempting further conversation, he began to muck out the stalls.

His attention soon became drawn to a pile of hay where several apples and a magazine were lying on a blanket. Dakota picked up the periodical and recognized the pulp magazine as the one Maggie had been reading on the stage. After paging through the publication, he shook his head in disgust and began to read a caption aloud, " 'Deadwood Dick, the Robin Hood of the Wild West, Faces His Greatest Challenge From The *Bandit Of the Badlands.*' You believe this hogwash?"

Maggie walked over and snatched the magazine from his hand. "So what if I do? It's none of your business."

His grin changed to a frown. "You're right. It's nothing to me." He returned to the unpleasant task he had begun in the stall.

Maggie regretted her outburst. It wasn't Dakota's fault she was ashamed of the wicked thoughts she harbored. He certainly didn't encourage her attention. Now she had hurt him. And just when he had begun to trust her.

Maggie rested her arms on the door of the stall to watch him. "How are you feeling today? I'm sorry I didn't ask sooner."

"I'm fine," he said curtly, not raising his head.

"I've never thanked you, Dakota, for saving my life. I'm very grateful to you. You didn't have to jump into the corral when you did."

He stopped his labor and looked up, his dark eyes locked with hers. "Didn't have to? That's not for you to say. A man does what he believes he must do."

Maggie sensed his remark wasn't meant as a rebuttal. By now, she knew Dakota well enough to know his philosophy; he lived his life according to his conscience and didn't pass judgment on anyone who did the same.

"Why did you change your mind and come back yesterday?" she asked suddenly. That question had nagged her all morning.

"I decided there are worse things than being rich," Dakota drawled as he picked up the pail of manure and went outside. Maggie followed close on his heels.

Worse things than being rich? Had she heard him right? Her spirits considerably heightened, Maggie dared to ask, "You mean you agree to—"

"Go on that fool treasure hunt," he finished with a grin as he dumped the contents of the pail on the compost pile.

Maggie's earlier avowal to avoid him vanished as she threw herself into his arms—not because of any new and strange sensation, nor because of any sudden womanly self-awareness, nor yet because she thought Dakota must be the noblest, bravest, handsomest man in the whole darn West. Maggie threw herself into his arms because she was so happy, she just had to hug somebody. It was him or the horse.

Her momentum knocked Dakota off his feet, and they both fell into the decaying pile of manure that Yen Ching used on his garden.

Dakota jumped to his feet brushing the foul-smelling fertilizer off his clothing. "Damn it, Maggie! You've done it again."

She looked up at him contritely, then burst into laughter at the sight of his agitated glower. Struggling to control her giggles, she managed to see the positive side. "It could have been worse. You could have gone in face first."

For several seconds, Dakota stared aghast at the girl who must surely be out of her mind. No doubt, the little troublemaker would forever be a menace. But her riotous good humor was infectious, and he couldn't maintain his anger. His face split into a wide grin. "Lady, you're plain loco." He erupted into laughter and offered his hand to help her get out of the muck.

The ranch hands shook their heads in disbelief and gave the pair a wide berth. But Maggie and Dakota walked to the house oblivious of the many curious stares directed at them as they clung to one another, their laughter filling the air.

Katherine and Diane were having tea when the two young people entered the house.

"Margaret dear, come and join us," Katherine called. After one whiff of the pair, however, her smile dissipated at once.

"Mother, what *is* that wretched odor?" Diane complained. Her face curled up in distaste as she glanced accusingly at Maggie and Dakota. "You two smell like a privy." The china rattled on the tray as she slammed down her cup. "And you've ruined my tea." She covered her nose and mouth with her handkerchief and sped from the room.

Katherine's displeasure at the wretched odor echoed throughout the house. The kitchen rattled and clanked and was thrown into an uproar preparing bath water. To escape Katherine's tirade, Dakota grabbed a bar of soap and a change of clothing, then headed for the nearby creek.

Maggie wasn't as fortunate. She had to endure

131

her mother's carping until a bath was prepared. Finally alone in the privacy of the bathroom, Maggie considered the nature of her condition and decided to pamper herself with one of Diane's many bottles of perfumed bath salts.

She lazed in the water until it turned tepid, then vigorously scrubbed her hair to make certain no lingering evidence of the misadventure remained.

Maggie toweled herself and donned a robe. She opened the bathroom door to hasten to her room and ran smack into Dakota MacDonald. A strong pair of hands reached out to keep her from falling.

Startled, Maggie looked up into Dakota's dark eyes. For several breathless heartbeats, their stunned gazes locked as she stood in the circle of his arms. A quiver of excitement raced the length of her spine when his gaze shifted to her body. Her bare toes curled as her senses and nerve ends responded to the exciting perusal. She could feel her breasts swelling and knew the thin robe now clung to the moist curves of her body.

Maggie parted her lips to speak but only a quivering drawn breath slipped past them. A musky male scent tantalized her nostrils, and her fingertips tingled with a pleasant warmth where her hands rested against his bare chest. The pounding in her ears eclipsed her senses until she recognized the sound of her own heartbeat.

She saw that Dakota looked as startled as she. "I think you missed a few spots." His voice breathed a husky, tender caress as his finger traced the row of freckles across the bridge of her nose.

Maggie closed her eyes. The callused stroke left

a velvet kiss on her soft skin. She raised her eyelids to discover a faint smile now softened his face. "But you sure smell good."

"I used Diane's bath salts," she stammered honestly, too guileless to be flirtatious.

Dakota reached out and caught a few strands of her tousled hair. The damp, silken tendril curled around his finger like a clinging vine. "Hair's still wet."

His gaze shifted to her parted lips. Trembling, Maggie held her breath, waiting for his next move. A spark of fire glimmered in his ebony eyes. Suddenly, Dakota dropped his arms, releasing her, and stepped back. Without any further word, he turned away and continued down the hall to his bedroom. Maggie heard a click after the door closed behind him.

Her heart was still pounding rapidly when she returned to her room. Looking around, she found no sign of her soiled clothing. Rather than leaving the room to find her missing boots, and thereby possibly encountering her mother, Maggie donned a blouse, knickerbockers, and her old shoes. As she viewed her image in the mirror, the once favorite outfit looked childish and strange compared to the Western garb she had adopted. She wanted to change, but she had no other style of clothes except her blue gown.

When Maggie finished dressing, she slipped out the rear of the house and started to cross the yard. But she stopped at the sight of her freshly washed clothing beside the dripping jeans and shirt Dakota had tossed over the line. With enthralled delight,

Maggie thought the garments looked quite natural hanging together side by side.

About to don a shirt, Dakota spun around when his bedroom door opened. He was surprised to see Diane Collingswood step into the room. She closed the door and leaned back with a seductive smile.

Dakota lowered his arm and stared at her. Her attempts at seduction were as annoying as Maggie's pestiness. This bored girl meant trouble, and Dakota had no intention of being fool enough to accommodate her. "What do you want, Miss Collingswood?"

Diane's lips pursed into an appealing pout. "I came to apologize for my rudeness earlier." She walked over to him. "You smell much better than you did before." She began to trace her fingertip across his bare chest.

Dakota shoved away her hand. "If you're bored, Miss Collingswood, I suggest you amuse yourself with one of the ranch hands."

A neat row of tiny white teeth appeared when she threw back her head and laughed lightly. "Which one do you recommend?"

Diane took Dakota's grin as a sign of encouragement. She stepped closer. He stood impassively as she ran her tongue across her lips to moisten them.

Dakota wanted to put the little vixen over his knee and spank her, but he guessed she'd probably enjoy it. When Diane slipped her hand along the slope of his shoulders, Dakota tried a ploy he hoped would work. "That perfume you're wearin' sure smells a lot better on your sister."

Diane's head jerked up in surprise. "You can't mean that boyish dolt, Margaret?"

"I sure do. Maybe because she uses it more sparingly. Less smotherin' that way."

Indignant that he would even think to make a comparison between her femininity and Margaret's, Diane dropped her arm and glared up at him. "If you're attracted to anyone as peculiar as Margaret, Mr. MacDonald, you've got a lot to learn about women."

Dakota walked over and opened the door. "Could be, Miss Collingswood. But I'm not askin' for your help in the lesson." He closed the door behind her after she had barely stepped out of the room.

When the door slammed and Dakota came out of the house, Maggie's mood heightened—until she noticed that his arms were full. "What are you doing?"

"I'm moving to the bunkhouse," he declared.

Maggie knew the uselessness of arguing with the man. She watched him stride across the yard, then sighed deeply and entered the house.

Hurrying to her room, she retrieved her segment of the map. The thought of the waiting fortune was minimized by her excitement of knowing Dakota had decided to remain in Deadwood.

Maggie carefully folded the map and tucked it away in the pocket of her pants. Now she had an excuse to seek out Dakota. She hurried out the door. As she hastened toward the bunkhouse, William Godfrey rode up and called to her.

Maggie waved to him and continued on her way. "Hold up, Miss Collingswood," he called out.

Impatient to find Dakota, Maggie waited as the banker climbed off his horse. "How's your patient today?" he said in his usual cheerful manner.

Patient good, patience bad, Maggie thought with agitation, fearful that Dakota would ride off somewhere before she could find him. "Dakota's fine, Mr. Godfrey. He's moved into the bunkhouse, though. I wish you could persuade him to return to the house."

"Leave him do whatever he's comfortable with, Maggie. Dakota's always been a loner. He doesn't cotton to having a lot of strangers around."

"I don't believe that's his only reason for moving out, Mr. Godfrey."

"Wish you'd call me Will, gal." His mouth broadened in an amicable grin. "Or better yet, Uncle Will. Your Pa and I were mighty good friends."

Maggie returned the man's smile. "I'd like that . . . Uncle Will." And she meant it. Maggie liked the new people in her life. Dakota. Sam Harris. William Godfrey. Strangers just weeks ago, they had now become important. Strange how such a brief span of time could challenge so many previously deep-rooted aspects of her life—the identity of her real father, the emergence of her own femininity, and the bewildering awareness of Mr. Dakota MacDonald.

They found Dakota in the bunkhouse and after much cajoling, he returned to the house with them to discuss the forthcoming hunt. Maggie quivered with excitement as she listened to the two plan the trip.

"I intend to join this expedition," Godfrey announced.

Maggie's surprise was evident. "Why would you do that, Uncle Will?"

"As executor of Sam's estate, I feel obliged to go along with you."

Dakota's negligent shrug settled the matter. He drew out his piece of the map and laid it on the table. "Let's see your map, Maggie."

Maggie withdrew the folded piece of paper from her trouser pocket. Their hands touched when she handed it to him, and for an instant his gaze shifted to meet hers before he laid the section beside his on the table.

They huddled over the table. Maggie didn't have the vaguest idea what she was looking at, but the two men appeared engrossed as Dakota traced the route with a long, firm finger.

He's got nice hands, she thought, dreamingly remembering his touch earlier that day.

"The map seems to lead to a cave. See here, where it's marked."

"Think it's a mine?" Will asked.

Dakota shrugged. "Hard to say."

"How long you figure to reach it?"

"I'd guess less than a week. Two pack mules should be enough," Dakota decided after a lengthy deliberation.

Godfrey rose to his feet. "I'll make all the arrangements in town. We should be able to leave day after tomorrow."

"Don't be too sure about that." At the sound of the commanding voice, all of them glanced up to see Katherine Collingswood framed in the doorway. "Why wasn't I consulted about this matter?"

With the bearing of an irate monarch, Katherine swept into the room. "I have something at stake here, as well."

William Godfrey responded to the challenge. "How so, Mrs. Collingswood? Sam Harris's will clearly states that Dakota and Maggie are the two heirs."

Katherine could not be swayed; the set of her shoulders and the fire in her eyes gave evidence of her determination. "I don't care what Sam Harris's will indicates. It behooves me to remind you again, Mr. Godfrey, that *Margaret* is the proper name of my daughter, and Margaret is a minor. As such, I have the responsibility to lay her cards on the table. We will all make this journey together."

"All?" Will asked, confused.

"Myself, my husband, and my two daughters."

Maggie's glance shifted frantically to Dakota. She knew how he felt about her mother. His expression remained inscrutable.

Godfrey began to drum his fingertips on the table and chew nervously at his lower lip. "Please try to be reasonable, Mrs. Collingswood. The trip could be hazardous, especially for someone as . . . delicate as Diane."

Katherine sauntered to the doorway. "My daughter's welfare is my concern. We all go—or Margaret doesn't."

"Can you ride a horse, Mrs. Collingswood?" The

unexpected remark from Dakota came as a taunt, not a question.

She turned around and glared contemptuously. "I was born and raised on the frontier."

"And your husband?"

"A former cavalry officer."

"Your youngest daughter?"

She arched a perfectly plucked brow. "Will have to learn. You'll just have to teach her." Katherine's mouth curved into a smirk. "Won't you, Mr. Mac-Donald."

She walked from the room, leaving the three people staring at her back.

After several days, Diane remained as unskilled at riding a horse as she had been before Dakota began his instruction. Standing alone while Dakota directed her sister, Maggie watched in utter disgust at Diane's ineptitude.

Diane, of course, looked fetching in a split skirt—a green shirt closely fitted over her rounded bosom—and a fashionable pair of shoes totally unsuitable for riding. Her long blonde curls were carefully coifed and tied back with a green ribbon. Feminine and diminutive, especially compared to the towering, masculine presence of Dakota, Diane could not even visualize herself on a horse. Neither could Maggie. But Dakota kept trying.

"I can't do all that with one hand," Diane protested after Dakota explained for the dozenth time how to grab the saddle horn while holding the reins.

"You better learn," he cautioned, "or the animal

will move away from you when you try to mount." His hands spanned her waist as he lifted her onto the horse.

She leaned against him and her eyes gleamed in a seductive invitation. "I guess I'll just have to keep trying to learn." She looked over his shoulder and saw her father approaching. Her mouth puckered into a pout. "Why do I have to do this? Why can't I ride in a carriage?"

"Most likely there won't be trails wide enough for a carriage," he said calmly, displaying exceptional patience with the pampered girl. "Now, let's try it again."

He lowered her to the ground. "Because you're so small, you have to kind of hop into the stirrup with your left foot, then swing your right leg over the saddle."

With dogged determination, Dakota continued the instructions. Finally, after several more attempts, the horse stepped on Diane's foot. She ran bawling into Taylor's arms. "I can't do it, Daddy."

Dakota cast a futile glance at William Godfrey, then threw his hands up in a gesture of hopelessness. "There's no way I can take these women on a trail." He strode away.

Will heaved a resolute sigh and followed Taylor and Diane to the house. Maggie was less complaisant—she headed for the bunkhouse.

Dakota didn't even glance up when Maggie entered. She stood in the doorway and watched him jam clothing into his saddlebags. "So, you're taking off again," she accused him.

He neither slowed his actions nor offered a reply.

When he finished packing, he picked up the bags, grabbed his rifle, and shoved past her.

Maggie followed on his heels.

They reached the stable and Dakota continued to ignore her. He led a horse from one of the stalls and threw a blanket over its back. Even though Maggie understood why a sane person would give up on Diane, her bitter disappointment at Dakota's departure overwhelmed her. Unable to control her emotions, Maggie's frustration boiled over into an unreasonable tirade.

"I thought you were someone special like—like Buffalo Bill or Wild Bill Hickock! But you're not special, Dakota MacDonald. You are running away from a difficult situation just like any . . . *coward*." The word stuck in her throat as she said it.

He spun around angrily. Maggie's hat fell off when he grasped her shoulders, and his fingers felt like talons biting into her flesh. "Grow up, Maggie! There aren't any heroes out here. There are only survivors. That's why I'm getting out, while the getting's good."

Tears streamed down Maggie's upturned face as she stared up at the black anger gleaming in his dark eyes. The heart-wrenching sight was more then he could bear.

"Damn you, Maggie." He gathered her into his arms and dipped his head. About to kiss her, his common sense prevailed. He dropped his arms and stepped away from Maggie as if she had a plague—a plague that could destroy him should he surrender to the temptation.

Shaken, Maggie swiped at the tears on her

cheeks. "Don't run away, Dakota," she pleaded.

"Maggie, only a fool would take a party of greenhorns into the hills. Your sister can't even mount a horse, much less sit a saddle. You're not much better. You think grit makes up for lack of know-how. Well, it doesn't. Not on the trail. Not one of you people has even considered the possibility that somebody could get hurt or killed."

"We know the risks. It's a chance we're willing to take," Maggie snapped, mustering the grit she had often substituted for know-how.

"You sound just like your mother," he scoffed. "You have no idea what's involved. And I know your sister doesn't either. Any prairie dog can see Diane is unfit for the territory."

"Diane? Is she all that's worrying you? Precious Diane might get a smudge of dirt on her face or a splinter in her little finger? You're just like all the rest," she accused him, racked with jealousy.

Maggie started to turn away, but Dakota grabbed her shoulders and forced her to face him. "That's not true, Maggie. I don't want *you* to get hurt."

"There are a lot more ways to get hurt than just falling off a horse. I thought you were different from the others. I believed in you. I believed there wasn't anything you couldn't do. I'm wiser to stick with my magazine heroes."

She shrugged out of his arms and went over to Tiger's stall. The mare nickered a welcome, and Maggie began to pat the animal.

"Your head is stuffed with those damn stories. Lies and fiction. Time you learned a few facts about the *real* West." He opened the stall and began to saddle Tiger.

Surprised, Maggie moved back. "What are you doing?"

"We're going for a ride."

William Godfrey stepped out of the house and watched the two young people ride away. Long after their dust had settled, Will stood deep in thought, drawing on the end of a lit cheroot. Finally he grinned and tossed away the cigar.

"Sam Harris, you're a sly old coyote."

Chapter Eleven

Dakota was silent on the ride to Deadwood. *Stewing in his own juice*, Maggie thought as she cast a sideward glance at the reticent rider. Nearing the outskirts of the town, Dakota's horse went lame. After he climbed down to examine the animal, he grimaced with annoyance. "He's thrown a shoe. I'll have to take him to the smithy."

Maggie dismounted, relieved to hear there wasn't anything seriously wrong with the horse. Having once read a story in which Buffalo Bill had to shoot his horse because its leg had been broken, she feared the same fate could befall Dakota's horse.

"I couldn't bear anything happening to you, gal," she crooned as she patted Tiger's neck.

"You sure have taken a shine to that horse," Dakota said.

"I love her," Maggie declared. "Can I ride her when we go on the hunt?" She glanced up to discover Dakota smiling at her. The rare smile changed his grim countenance into a friendly boyishness, and the transformation startled her. Maggie returned the smile which was too appealing to resist.

Dakota was embarrassed that Maggie caught him off-guard in a smile. His face hardened with a frown. "Who said we're going?" he growled. "And you couldn't take Tiger anyway. She toes out. Liable to stumble on a rough trail."

Maggie could tell he had relented. He was just putting on a big show for her benefit. She grinned broadly, knowing she had won.

"Fussin' over a dumb animal as if it were human . . . you're just like Sam," Dakota chided. He took Tiger's reins and began to lead the two animals.

"Don't you ever become attached to your horse, Dakota?" she asked, walking up beside him.

Dakota shook his head. "Nope."

"Why not?"

He shrugged negligently. "Too easy to lose a horse to chuckholes, wolves—or battle." He answered thoughtfully as if remembering a bygone day.

Maggie's eyes widened in surprise. "In battle?"

"Best way to stop a man. Shoot the horse out from under him."

She drew back abashed. "Oh, how horrible! It's

not the horse's fault you men have to kill one another."

"For a gal hung up on dime novels, you're sure soundin' righteous."

Maggie hesitated, at a loss to defend herself. "Well . . . I like horses."

"You'd do fine with my mother's people."

"Why do you say that?"

"The Sioux consider a strong and spirited horse a great treasure. And they've got a better eye for horseflesh than any white man."

Maggie couldn't decide if the reverence in his voice was admiration for the Sioux or the treasured, strong, and spirited horse he described. "Well, I suspect you've got a lot more of your mother's blood than you're willing to admit."

He chuckled and shook his head. "A man needs two things to stay alive out here—a fast horse and a faster gun."

Maggie stopped abruptly. "I don't believe it."

"Well, it's true. There's not much chance without either."

"No, I'm not referring to what you said. I mean, I don't believe Dakota MacDonald has grinned two times in as many minutes."

Dakota scowled. "Lord, lady, sun's in my eyes. Can't you tell a grin from a squint?" he growled tersely, then continued down the road.

"Say what you like, but that was a grin, Mr. Dakota MacDonald." She followed behind, smiling broadly.

Deadwood hummed with energy. The town seemed as exciting to Maggie in daylight as it had the night she arrived. A general store opposite the smithy immediately caught Maggie's attention. "Darn, I wish I'd brought some money with me," she lamented. "I need to make some purchases."

"Just tell Ben Wallace you're with the Lazy H. He'll put it on the tab," Dakota told her.

The thought had not occurred to Maggie. She jumped eagerly at the suggestion and scurried across the street. After selecting several pairs of jeans, socks, and an assortment of plaid shirts, Maggie was satisfied she had enough clothing for the forthcoming trek into the hills.

The bald-headed shopkeeper peered with curiosity through a pair of spectacles perched on the end of his nose. "Name's Ben Wallace. Heard tell you're Sam Harris's girl," he said as he wrapped her purchases.

Surprised to discover her identity had been town gossip, Maggie flashed her nicest smile. "Yes, sir. My name is Margaret Collingswood."

The man nodded his head reflectively. Maggie began to feel uncomfortable under his intense perusal. "Heard tell there's a passel of you out at the Lazy H spread."

"Just my parents and sister, Mr. Wallace," Maggie replied politely. Obviously, their arrival in Deadwood had created a stir among the local citizens.

"How long you folks plannin' on stayin'?" he asked boldly. Maggie felt he was fishing for more gossip to pass on to the town. She picked up her package and offered a placid smile. "I would imagine until . . . we leave. It's been a pleasure meeting you, Mr. Wallace. Good day."

As she stepped outside, gunfire erupted a short distance away. The sound startled a man crossing the street and he dropped his tote bag. He bent down to pick it up just as a team of horses, spooked by the sound, broke loose from a nearby hitching post and galloped down the street with a wagon careening behind them.

Maggie cried out a warning and grabbed the man's shirt to pull him from the path of the runaways. Several more shots sounded. "H'out of me way, kid," he snapped in speech laced with an English accent. The man dropped his bag again and leaped over some nearby barrels for protection, knocking Maggie down in the process. He crouched behind the barricade.

Indignant, Maggie sat up and brushed herself off. "You might apologize, sir, for your rudeness."

"Well, aye'll be, yer a gal!" he muttered.

The gunfire ceased and Maggie stood up, her worried glance sweeping the opposite side of the street for Dakota. She saw him and the blacksmith calmly watching the excitement.

Relieved, she was about to walk away when the man asked, "H'is h'it safe to come h'out now?"

Disgusted, Maggie glanced down the street. Nothing seemed out of order. "It would appear to be, sir."

The man poked up his head. "'ey, Jim—what 'appened?" he called out to one of the men on the street.

"Just a cowboy shooting at a snake what crawled under a porch," the passing man yelled.

"'old up there, gal," the Englishman cried out

when once again Maggie started to cross the street.

Irritated, she turned back. The pint-sized man stood up, and Maggie gawked at the odd-looking rogue who wasn't even as tall as she. His ill-fitting buckskins, heavily draped with fringe, hung loosely on his skinny frame. The Stetson on his head appeared to be kept from sliding over his face only by a pair of protruding ears. Stringy hair hung to his shoulders, and a long, drooping moustache above his lips added to his comic appearance.

"Couldn't 'elp noticin' yer not from these parts," he said.

"No, sir. I'm from the East," Maggie replied. Despite her romantic vision of a frontiersman, she was hard-pressed to keep from laughing.

"Then aye got just the thing for ya." He began to root in the large pouch. Grinning, he pulled out a black braided pelt. "'ere's a nice souvenir for you to take back 'ome with you."

"Whatever is it?" Maggie asked.

"Why, h'it's a genuine Sioux scalp," he boasted.

Maggie blanched, but before she could voice a protest, Dakota sauntered up to them. The little man cast an uneasy glance at the army scout. "Just you stay h'out of this, Dakota."

"I've got nothing to say," Dakota said, amused. He crossed his arms and leaned back against a post.

"Took the scalp h'off a dead Sioux meself, aye did, h'at the Little Big 'orn," the man continued.

Maggie's eyes widened with interest. "The Little Big Horn? Were you there, sir? With General Custer?"

"Sure h'as aye live and breathe," the stranger said. "This be the scalp h'of h'old Crazy 'orse 'imself. When aye saw that painted savage, aye leaped h'off me 'orse and knocked the 'eathen to the ground. Then aye pulled h'out h'ole Betsy 'ere"—Maggie jumped back in alarm when the man drew a large hunting knife from a sheath strapped to his waist and brandished the weapon in the air—"and lifted the devil's scalp h'as h'easy h'as skinnin' h'a cat."

Maggie had become more than a little suspicious of the man. "I beg your pardon, sir, but from what I read of the battle, Chief Crazy Horse survived the Custer massacre. As a matter of fact, my understanding is that the Indians came out victorious and General Custer's army was destroyed—to a man."

The little man regarded her out of a narrowed eye. "Not all of us, gal."

Now certain the man was an out-and-out liar, Maggie wanted to see the last of him and his treasure. "Well, please put away that hideous trophy. I would never consider purchasing such a ghoulish relic."

"You're making h'a mistake, gal." He reached deeper into the bag and withdrew an arrowhead from the sack. "Now this 'ere's h'a Ute arrowhead from the Battle h'at Milk River." He took her dubious frown for confusion. "Colorado, gal, just last year. Dug h'it out of me leg, aye did, h'after a redskin put h'a h'arrow h'in me. Still got the scar. Wanna see that, too?"

"No thank you, sir. I'm really not interested in any of your souvenirs," Maggie announced.

She turned to depart and the man called out, "Tell you what, gal . . . aye's sell ya me picture. Even put me name on it."

Maggie had no interest in anything the ridiculous little man had to offer. But she tried to maintain her patience in the face of his persistence. "I don't collect autographed pictures, sir."

Dakota chose this moment to intervene. "Bet you'd like *his* picture, Maggie, you being one of his ardent fans and all."

Maggie cast a disgruntled glance at Dakota. He seemed to be having an amusing time at her expense, and he should have realized she didn't want to encourage any further conversation with the annoying little man.

As if reading her thoughts, Dakota explained, "Matter of fact, I brought you to town 'specially to meet Mr. Clarke."

The man doffed his hat. "Me pleasure, gal."

At her perplexed look, Dakota added, "Better known in your world of Wild West tales as . . . Deadwood Dick."

"H'at yer service gal." Clarke made an ostentatious bow. "For h'a loyal fan, such h'as yerself, the price h'of me photo h'includes me h'autograph."

Maggie's mouth gaped open. It couldn't be true. She must have misunderstood. With a smirk of satisfaction, Dakota walked away. She bolted after him, thereby fleeing the erstwhile Deadwood Dick. "The *dead wood* of the Dakotas," escaping through her pursed lips.

"Are you saying that pint-sized, long-winded, lying-through-his-teeth, ridiculous little man is

151

Deadwood Dick?" she sputtered when she caught up with Dakota.

"The Robin Hood of the Wild West," he scoffed.

She raced to keep up with his long stride. "But how . . . I can't believe . . . how could anyone?" She continued to stammer helplessly. "And that scalp?"

"As fake as he is. Makes them 'imself, he does," Dakota mimicked. He glanced back and saw her crumpled expression. "What's this—me lady's idol has fallen at first meeting?" He smothered a grin and restated his belief. "As I told you, Maggie, there are no heroes here in the West."

Maggie stopped to catch her breath and watched Dakota continue on to the smithy. Somehow her disillusionment over her storybook idol was not as shattering as it might had been—after all, she had already met a real flesh-and-blood hero.

She saw the 'I-Don't-Get-Attached-To-My-Horse' Dakota affectionately pat the animal on the neck before he led the horse out of the livery.

Maggie grinned tenderly, then murmured for her ears alone, "You have as much of a false front as Deadwood Dick, Mr. Dakota MacDonald. And furthermore, you're wrong about one thing; I do so know a real hero when I meet one. And he's right here in Deadwood."

As Maggie waited outside the livery for Dakota, her attention was drawn to a sign crudely painted with the words Mount Moriah. An arrow pointed up the steep hill.

"What is Mount Moriah?" she asked Dakota when he joined her.

His glance swung upwards. "Boot Hill," he explained.

"Oh, let's go and see it."

Dakota clearly found the request to be unusual for a young woman, but then again, he realized Maggie wasn't the run-of-the-mill kind of young woman. Besides, she had already started up the hill, so he had no choice but to follow.

Maggie read the markers with interest and stopped by the grave of Wild Bill Hickock. "What a great man. Did you know him, Dakota?" she asked solemnly.

"Met him once when he was marshal in Abilene. Before they ran him out of town."

"Ran him out of town?" she asked, amazed.

"Didn't your dime novels mention that?"

"Who ran him out?" she inquired. Maggie couldn't believe Wild Bill Hickock could ever have been intimidated by anyone.

"Hickock was the kind who shot first and asked questions later. When he accidentally shot his own deputy during a gunfight, the town folk felt they'd had enough of him."

"Oh, my," Maggie sighed in dismay. "I never knew that."

"Another one of your heroes with clay feet, Maggie?" he asked laconically and strolled away.

After the long climb and descent back to town, Maggie was thirsty, so Dakota proposed they eat before starting the ride back to the ranch. Only one table was available in the busy hotel's dining room when they entered. Maggie experienced a new and unexpected pleasure as Dakota put his hand on her back and lightly guided her through the crowded room. The odd couple received more than one curious glance.

Maggie took off her hat and ran her fingers through her hair to fluff up her curls. "The way folks are staring at us, they must think I'm quite a spectacle," she joked.

Surprised to hear Maggie voice a doubt about herself, Dakota regarded her quizzically. "I didn't think you cared what people thought about you."

"I don't . . . usually."

"Then why start now? Besides, the stares are not on your account." It was Maggie's turn to look quizzical. "Some folks don't take to the idea of eating in the same room with a 'breed,'" he mocked.

An overworked waiter interrupted their conversation, rotely spieled the Special of the Day, and hurried away, seemingly oblivious to their order.

"Do you always encounter so much prejudice, Dakota?" she asked.

"More often than not. Though most of the folks here in Deadwood are tolerable . . . about their tolerance."

"I would hope so. This territory is your home. You belong here."

"Seems like that's all I've heard from you since we met."

"Well, it's true. You really aren't going to leave, are you?" she asked. The question had nagged her during the ride to town.

Dakota frowned as he saw the concern in her eyes. "I don't want the responsibility of guiding a group of inexperienced riders into the hills. I sure don't understand why Sam ever saddled me with such a fool arrangement."

"Dakota, the inheritance is my only chance to become independent, don't you see that? If Sam Harris did leave us a fortune, we both stand to gain."

"I might of had a chance looking after one greenhorn, but a whole party . . . well, that herd would be more than I could drive."

"Not so, Dakota. Diane and I are the only two who are inexperienced. As my mother said, she and my father used to live on the frontier."

In her eagerness to convince him, she reached over and covered his hand with her own. "You can do anything, Dakota. I know you can."

Taken aback by her gesture and innocent confidence, Dakota merely shook his head. Fortunately, the waiter brought their food and saved him from voicing a denial.

Maggie began to eat, but Dakota, upset by her blind adoration, sat quietly and studied her. He tried to think of a way to bring Maggie, the naive dreamer, back down to earth.

Hog-tying came to mind. Grinning, he dismissed the idea after imagining the noise from such an attempt would drive the whole country into the hills.

Finally, he thought of a reasonable argument. "I thought you learned your lesson today about bettin' on a blind hand."

"Blind hand? No such thing. Today I learned the difference between truth and fiction," she stated confidently. "That's why I know that if anybody can get us there and back, it's you, Dakota."

She smiled and resumed eating. Distracted, Dakota's gaze shifted to her mouth and watched the fork slide between her parted lips. For several seconds his dark eyes remained riveted on her mouth, his thoughts hidden behind his shuttered stare.

Self-conscious, she lowered the fork. "What are you looking at?"

"Nothing." He shifted his glance and began to eat.

"Is there food on my face?" she asked, dabbing at the corners of her mouth with a frayed napkin.

"Your face is fine," he answered gruffly. Dakota ate the rest of the meal without glancing at her again. "We've got a long ride ahead," he warned when he finished.

The words had barely passed through his lips when he rose and tossed several coins on the table. "I'll get the horses."

Maggie hastily swallowed several gulps of coffee and hurried after him, bewildered by his sudden mood change.

"You could have let me finish my coffee," she grumbled, once outside. "After all, the cost is the same whether you drink it or not."

"I didn't tell you not to drink the damn coffee." He lifted her into the saddle.

Maggie, about to tell him that actions speak louder than words, buried her thought when she saw a man hurriedly approach them waving a yellow envelope in the air.

"Hey, Dakota MacDonald, hold up there." Short and overweight, the man was breathless from running. Dakota waited impatiently for the man, who was the town telegrapher, to catch his breath. "Heard you were in town and wanted to catch you before you left."

"What do you want, McCullough?"

"You got some folks name of Collingswood staying at the Lazy H?"

Dakota nodded, but made no attempt to introduce Maggie to the man. "Got a wire for one of them."

Assuming the important responsibilities of her father's job demanded his attention, Maggie questioned, "Is that telegram for Taylor Collingswood?"

McCullough eyed her suspiciously. "Ain't saying it is and ain't saying it ain't. Who are you?"

"My name's Margaret Collingswood. I suggest you give me the envelope."

"Shucks, lady, I can tell you what's in it."

"That's not necessary." She snatched the wire out of his hand and stuffed it into her trouser pocket. "There is such a thing as privacy, you know." She goaded her horse to a trot.

"Kind of testy, aren't you?" Dakota chided when he caught up with her.

Maggie only scowled at him. Men could be so exasperating. It was fine for him to have moods, but she wasn't entitled to any of her own. Also, her curiosity gnawed at her. She regretted not letting that unpleasant man tell her the message in the telegram. When they reached

157

the ranch, Maggie bade Dakota a hasty good-night.

"I hope you didn't expect us to hold dinner for you," Katherine complained as soon as Maggie walked through the door.

"No, Mother, I ate in town." She handed Taylor the envelope. "This wire came for you."

Taylor ripped it open and quickly scanned the contents. He glanced up with a scowl. "Margaret, will you tell Diane I'd like to see her. She should be in her room."

When the two girls returned, Katherine greeted them with a pleased smile, while Taylor cleared his throat to make an announcement. "My dears, I have some rather surprising news for you."

"What is it, Father?" Diane asked. Maggie had told her about the telegram and Diane hoped the suspicions Margaret expressed were true; Taylor's business would take them back to Washington.

Taylor cleared his throat. "This wire is for you, Diane. It seems Peter Brent is on his way to Deadwood."

Chapter Twelve

Dakota was in town the day Peter Brent arrived in Deadwood. Even though he had had a long, arduous journey, Peter stepped off the stagecoach looking unruffled, with nary a smidgen of dust on his impeccable clothing or on his perfectly blocked gray homburg. Despite the influx of Easterners, Dakota sensed that this particular newcomer must be the Collingswoods' anticipated guest.

Dakota watched the young man look about with curiosity at the bustling town teeming with buckskin-clad mountain men, miners, and mule-skinners. When Brent made a beeline for the nearest saloon and disappeared through the swinging doors, Dakota uncurled his long frame and sauntered after him.

For several seconds, Dakota stood in the entrance adjusting his sight to the dingy, smoke-filled barroom. He saw several grim-faced poker players around a table in the corner engrossed in their card game. A group of noisy cowboys and dance hall girls were whopping it up at one end of the bar. Further scanning the room, his eyes rested on four riders from the Circle C, seated around another table. One of the four was Rafe Catlin, son of the owner of the ranch bordering the Lazy H.

Joseph Catlin, owner of the Circle C, had been a marshal in Texas before coming to the Dakota Territory. He had fought Indians, outlaws, and the relentless forays of nature to defend his land and build a spread.

A big man with a heavy paunch now hanging over a once slender waist, his dark hair had long since turned to gray. Catlin had a deep and gruff voice, each word sounding as if his tongue were coated with coarse-textured sandpaper. He was tough, he was powerful, but he was a fair and honest man.

The antithesis of his father, Rafe Catlin was a spoiled and shiftless young man who continually got himself into one scrap after another. It was widely circulated by the town grapevine that Rafe had a mean streak as wide as the stripe on a skunk's back. Further, he enjoyed bullying or starting a fight for any reason—or for no reason.

At the moment, the rebellious young man's sullen eyes focused mischievously on Peter Brent, who was sitting alone at a nearby table drinking a glass of sarsaparilla.

"Hey, dude, ain't you feared that sassy parilla be a might too strong for you?" Catlin jeered.

The unexpected taunt took Peter by surprise. "I beg your pardon, sir. Are you addressing me?"

Rafe's chair screeched loudly on the wooden floor as he shoved away from the table. Ambling over to Peter, he fired a second insult. "You see anybody else here drinking that baby pee?"

Several loud snorts of laughter emanated from Rafe's men, while the cowboys at the bar ceased their raucous banter and stopped to listen. The floozies, variously draped around the men, waited with avid interest as their painted eyes glowed with pent-up excitement. Even the poker players ceased their game when they sensed an approaching ruckus.

The bartender began to nervously swipe the bar with a grimy rag. "Leave him be, Rafe. He ain't hurtin' nobody."

Peter lowered his glass to the table and looked up at the belligerent intruder. "Strangers had best allow me to mind my own business, sir." He tossed a coin on the table and started to rise.

The veiled threat escaped the wit of the over-confident Rafe; he shoved Peter back down. "Not so fast, Fancy Pants. Gulley, bring me that bottle."

One of the men at the table picked up the bottle of whiskey they'd been sharing and handed it to the rancher. Rafe dumped the remainder of Peter's drink on the floor and filled the tall glass to the brim with the hard liquor. "I figger every pansy dude oughta try a man's liquor at least once in his short life."

"No thank you," Peter said. Dakota casually leaned against the door, surprised to see the young Easterner not the least bit intimidated by Catlin's bullying. "Now if you'll excuse me," Peter said undaunted.

Once again he started to rise, but Rafe shoved him back. "You ain't goin' no place until you drink up."

"Sir, since there are ladies present"—The remark brought a series of giggles from the women at the bar—"I suggest we finish this discussion outside on the street."

Rafe had a fair reputation with a gun, and he was amazed at the guts of the Eastern dude. His face curved into a sneer. "I don't think you know what yer saying, Fancy Pants."

This time he allowed Peter to rise. Dakota stepped aside as the two men pushed past him, followed by the curious and excited throng from the saloon.

Once out on the street, Peter removed his homburg and jacket. He handed the spotless duds to Dakota, who happened to be standing the closest to him. "Would you be kind enough to hold these for me?"

Turning to Rafe Catlin, Peter struck a boxer's posture, with arms crooked and hands clenched into fists. "I should warn you, sir, I am a pugilistic champion from Princeton, Class of '79."

Rafe looked baffled. "What in hell are you talkin' about? Whar's yer iron, fool? You ain't packin' no iron."

"Iron? Of course not," Peter said aghast. "Brass knuckles would be unsportsmanlike."

"A gun, Pansy, whar's your gun?" Rafe snarled in exasperation.

Now it was Peter's turn to be confused.

"Whyever would I need a gun? Disputes between gentlemen are settled with fisticuffs."

"Fisticuffs? What in hell are fisticuffs?"

"Your fists, sir," Peter said.

"Listen, dude, you called me out. So you'd better strap on some iron pronto or I'm puttin' lead into yer gut right here and now."

Dakota saw the time had come to intercede before Catlin shot the young man to save face. "I think Princeton here can take you, Catlin," Dakota taunted.

The angry man glared at Dakota. "You got a stake in this fight, MacDonald?"

Dakota shook his head. "Nope, I just think the kid's a lot easier to like than you are. And I'm sticking around to make certain you don't have your bootlickers gang up on him, 'cause I'm guessin' the kid can beat the shit out of you, 'less you figger to weasel out now."

The bully's malevolence turned on Dakota. "You callin' me yellow, 'breed?"

At Rafe's question, the crowd stepped back to give the two enemies a wide berth. However, Peter Brent, ignorant of the ways of the West, did not recognize the exchange of insults as a deadly challenge. He thought the lanky stranger had merely spoken out in his behalf.

Peter innocently stepped between Dakota and Rafe. "I appreciate your intercession—Mr. MacDonald, isn't it? But I can handle this situation myself."

Dakota's steady gaze never wavered from Rafe's angry glare. "Anytime you feel lucky, Catlin."

Rafe had backed himself into a corner. He knew

he could not out-draw Dakota MacDonald. Better to skin out now and get the hide of the 'breed later. With a venomous snarl, he spun on his heels and stormed away.

Disappointed that the anticipated clash had fizzled, the crowd dispersed when Catlin's men followed Rafe down the street.

Mystified, Peter Brent took his coat and hat from Dakota. "Thank you for your—encouragement, Mr. MacDonald, but interest in the fight seems to have waned. However, no one had cause for alarm. I would have made certain not to hurt him seriously had the bout occurred."

Dakota stifled his grin at the confidence of the Princeton pugilist. The young man would never realize how close he had come to being shot by Catlin. Nevertheless, the kid was no coward. "Your name Brent?"

"Why yes," Peter replied, surprised the stranger would know his name.

"Name's Dakota MacDonald."

Peter extended his hand. "It's a pleasure to meet you formally, Mr. MacDonald," he said with a pleasant smile. "Peter Brent here."

Dakota felt awkward shaking hands with the stranger. "Perhaps you can help me, Mr. MacDonald. I'm looking for a family by the name of Collingswood, Taylor Collingswood to be exact. Do you know where they are residing?"

Dakota nodded. "You'll find them at the Lazy H."

"Is that a hostelry?"

"Just come with me. We'll rent you a horse." He started to walk toward the stable, then remembering the greenhorn crowd he had been dealing with, Dakota swung around with a suspicious scowl. "Can you ride a horse?"

"I was captain of the Equestrian Club at Princeton," Peter responded with self-assurance.

I should have guessed as much, Dakota thought with amusement. He continued on to the stable shaking his head and cursing Sam Harris for ever leading him into this patch of locoweed.

Taylor Collingswood lowered the letter in his hand and glanced across the room at Katherine, her blonde head bent intently over the needlepoint she was stitching. For several moments he sat watching the graceful motion of her hands as she moved the needle in and out of the fabric. This domestic pastime seemed so unnatural to her sophisticated ways, yet it was one Katherine enjoyed. She never kept any of the finished pieces, always donating them to hospitals or orphanages.

A loving smile crossed his face. How lovely she is, he thought proudly. More beautiful, if possible, than on the day he first saw her . . . *dancing in the arms of Sam Harris*. His eyes deepened in reflection.

"Bad news, dear?"

"Ah . . . what?" he asked, jolted out of his reverie.

"The letter you received from Washington. Is it bad news?" Katherine repeated. "You look so glum."

Taylor shook his head. "No, it's not bad news at all. President Hayes has accepted my resignation from the Board of Indian Affairs."

The information came as a surprise to

Katherine. She glanced at him in astonishment. "You didn't tell me you were going to resign. Does that mean we'll be leaving Washington?"

"Possibly." He crushed out his cigar in a nearby ashtray. "How would you welcome becoming a minister's wife?"

Her green eyes opened in shock and she cast aside the stitchery. "A minister's wife!"

He chuckled warmly. "The President has offered me the post of Minister to France."

With a squeal of pleasure, Katherine rushed over to him and plopped down in his lap. "France! Oh, Taylor, is it true? Just think—Paris, the Louvre, Notre Dame. All those lovely Paris fashions." She threw her arms around his neck. "Tell me you'll accept the post," she exclaimed like an excited schoolgirl.

"Does it mean that much to you, dear?"

Katherine composed herself and resumed her usual hauteur. "France would be a superb social and educational experience for the girls. With Diane's beauty, she would flourish and be duly appreciated by the European aristocracy. Besides, she could use a European education, and we could enroll Margaret in the Sorbonne. Her fine mind is being wasted—" Taylor's sad smile caused her to stop her rambling. "What is it, Taylor?"

"Katherine, can't you see that Margaret has found contentment right here? She would be miserable in France."

Katherine rose from his lap and moved to the window. Agitated, she began to toy with the curtains. "The girl doesn't know what she wants.

Besides, this wilderness is no life for a young woman. I'm her mother. I know what's best for her."

She stopped talking and peered out the window at the two men who had just ridden up to the house. "Good heavens, it's Peter Brent!" Katherine turned back in delight. "Taylor, Peter has arrived."

As Peter dismounted, Taylor and Katherine came out of the house to greet him. "Peter, what a pleasure to see you," Katherine gushed. Clasping his arms, she offered her cheek.

Peter kissed her and exchanged a handshake with Taylor. He glanced over Taylor's shoulder for a sign of Diane. "Diane is well, I trust? And Margaret?"

Katherine linked her arm through Peter's and began to lead him to the house. "Of course, dear Peter. Diane's napping at the moment."

Dakota was about to lead the horses away to the stable when Katherine called out to him. "Mr. MacDonald, take Mr. Brent's luggage to the end bedroom."

Taylor glanced at Dakota. The older man smarted, embarrassed by Katherine's insensitive treatment of the young man just because he happened to be a half-breed. Dakota owned the ranch as much as Margaret, but Katherine treated him as if he were a hired servant. Even the room Katherine designated for Peter, in truth, belonged to Dakota.

Taylor smiled apologetically and picked up Peter's valise. "That won't be necessary, Dakota. I can do it."

Dakota nodded and led the horses to the stable. Whatever his thoughts, they remained hidden behind his shrouded eyes.

Once inside the house, Katherine poured Peter a cup of tea. "If I remember, you take no lemon or sugar."

"Would you like something a bit stronger, son?" Taylor asked.

"Tea's fine, sir," Peter responded. He began to walk around the room, studying the various pictures and artifacts as he sipped from the cup.

Katherine watched nervously as he stopped often to stare intently at one object or another. "I must apologize for these primitive accommodations, Peter."

"On the contrary, Mrs. Collingswood, I find this place quite extraordinary." He picked up a vase. "Sixteenth Century, I'd guess."

Katherine cast an uneasy glance at Taylor, hoping for her husband's help. She fidgeted, anxious to know Peter's reason for coming to Deadwood. "And how were your traveling conditions?"

Peter returned and sat down. "Actually, not the best. I found the trip long and tiresome." He put aside the teacup. "But I hope it was not for naught."

Katherine felt her quickened heartbeat and heaved a silent sigh of relief. Finally, he appeared ready to divulge the purpose of his visit. She had to admit that Margaret had been right about the man; Peter Brent certainly could drone on, tedious to the point of exasperation.

"I am sure you are curious as to why I followed

168

you to the Dakota Territory." Katherine's face remained frozen with an expectant smile as she waited for him to continue.

"That thought certainly has crossed our minds, son," Taylor responded when Peter appeared to be actually waiting for a reply to the rhetorical question.

The young man cleared his throat. "Mr. and Mrs. Collingswood, I would be most grateful if you would grant me permission to ask Diane for her hand in marriage."

Katherine's eyes glowed with a rapacious gleam as she rose and began to nervously flit around Peter like a butterfly. "Of course you have our permission," she gushed. "Doesn't he, Taylor?" Her recent decision on the need for Diane to have a European education was quickly abandoned at the prospect of her daughter's wedding the son of a wealthy industrialist—one of the nation's richest. She put her hand on Peter's shoulder. "We'll be proud to have you as a son," she declared with genuine feeling.

Taylor grasped Peter's arm and shook his hand. "I think this occasion calls for something stronger than tea." He crossed to the table and poured a glass of sherry for Katherine and a shot of whiskey for himself and Peter.

"Actually, sir, we may be celebrating prematurely. I still have to win Diane's acceptance," Peter reminded him.

"Oh, my dear," Katherine cooed. "How could you doubt her affections?"

Based on Diane's past attitude toward him, Peter

had good reason for doubt. He was too much a gentleman, however, to discuss such private conjecture with Katherine.

Peter's father, being a man of strong action, had advised his son to "make things happen"—not to sit back and "wait for them to happen." Peter took this recommendation to heart and had come to plead his cause, doubts notwithstanding.

Unbeknownst to her parents, Diane had arisen from her nap and was about to join them when she heard the voice of Peter Brent. Desiring to make a grand entrance, she hastened back to her room and changed her simple red-and-white gingham dress for a sheer gown of white lawn with a satin underskirt.

When Katherine looked up and saw her daughter, she nudged Taylor, and the eager parents made a hasty exit in order to leave the young couple alone.

The love-smitten young man looked with adoration at the approaching angel in the beautiful white gown. Her hair was brushed into a golden cloud which swept her shoulders. Dazzled by the vision, he moved toward her.

"You're looking well, Diane," he murmured, pressing a kiss to the dainty hand she offered.

"Why, Peter, what a surprise!" she exclaimed, as if he had dropped in for a brief visit on a Sunday afternoon. The casual greeting showed little excitement and less appreciation for the fact that he had traveled over sixteen hundred miles by rail and stage to see her.

Peter was disheartened—but not deterred.

"May I offer you a cup of tea?" she asked, stepping past him.

"No thank you. I've already had one," he replied curtly.

"Perhaps a lemonade?" she asked with a coy smile.

"I didn't come all this way for refreshments, Diane."

A perfect brow curved provocatively. "What did you come for, Peter?" Her eyes were wide with innocence. No one was more aware than Diane of Peter's affection and fascination for her. That he had made such a long journey only added to her oversized vanity.

"To tell you I love you, and I can't live without you." He pulled her into his arms and forced a kiss on her.

In truth, Diane enjoyed Peter's kisses, but she derived a greater pleasure from taunting and frustrating him by refusing to respond to them.

Now, to relieve her boredom as much as to stoke his ardor, Diane offered no resistance and a light response.

Elated, Peter could barely contain himself. The enamored young man slipped a hand up to her breast.

"Now, Peter, you mustn't take such liberty," she teased as she stepped out of his arms. Diane walked over to the settee and sat down. He quickly followed.

"Aren't you glad to see me?" Peter asked, his hopes quickly dashed.

"I'm always pleased, Peter. Why would you think

anything to the contrary?'' She picked up a cookie from the tea tray and took a dainty bite.

Peter was beginning to suffer the sinking feeling of inadequacy she always managed to provoke in him. He groped in his pocket and produced a small jeweler's box. "Beloved, I am asking you to do me the honor of becoming my wife."

Peter opened the box and thrust it at her. In a bed of white satin nestled the largest emerald she had ever seen. Diane was speechless.

"You know how much I love you," he declared fervently. "I can't live without you."

Diane wanted to try on the ring so badly her finger itched. The stone was even larger than her mother's. Much larger. She knew her friends in Washington would be envious when they saw the ring.

"Will you, my love? Will you?" the ardent young man continued to plead, taking her silence for hesitation. "I promise to love you the rest of my life."

"Oh, yes, Peter," she whispered.

Excited and nervous, he removed the ring from the box and slipped the emerald on her finger.

The costly jewel had found a permanent niche.

Overwhelmed, Diane lifted her hand to admire the sparkling stone which glittered on her finger. "Oh, yes, Peter," she repeated breathlessly, her eyes a glowing rival to the precious gem on her hand.

Peter drew her into his arms. This time her response was considerably more ardent.

Chapter Thirteen

"Hush, I can't hear what they're saying," Katherine scolded her husband as she stood with her ear pressed against the wall.

Taylor was disgusted with her actions. "Good Lord, Katherine, will you listen to me and come away from that wall? Leave the youngsters in privacy."

She continued to ignore his request. Suddenly, she waved her hand to silence him, her head raised attentively. "Good Heavens! Margaret has just walked in on them. That girl's timing was always the worst," she whispered in a voice laced with false annoyance. Katherine's face altered with a cunning smile, and she dramatically adjusted her hair. "I suppose we'll just have to join them."

When Maggie entered the room, Peter jumped hastily to his feet, his complexion deepened in a blush.

"Well, hello, Peter," Maggie exclaimed. She had not seen him arrive and his presence took her by surprise.

"Ah . . . hello, Margaret," he stammered, trying to shield Diane from Maggie as the younger girl arranged her disheveled clothing.

"I didn't know you were here." Maggie bent her head and tried to see around him. "Is something wrong, Diane?"

Now properly arrayed, Diane rose to her feet. "Look, Margaret. Look what Peter gave me. We're engaged to be married." She flaunted the hand bearing the huge ring in Maggie's face.

Maggie stared at the enormous stone. The precious gem looked large and burdensome on Diane's tiny hand. Considering that her laggardly sister was incapable of carrying even the lightest package, Maggie wondered how she would be able to walk around toting that heavy load.

"It's quite . . . ostentatious, isn't it?"

Maggie chastised herself immediately for uttering the petty remark. Peter and Diane were actually a perfect couple. Her sister was destined for a life of wealth. Although the pretentious arena of the rich held no appeal to her, Maggie realized that she had no right to diminish the joy of the couple by a display of spitefulness on her own part.

She hugged Diane and kissed her cheek. "I'm so happy for you. And you too, Peter," she added, offering him a hug as well.

Now feeling awkward, she linked her hands

together in front of her and began to see-saw from one foot to the other. "So . . . when is the wedding day?" she questioned, grinning at the pair like the Cheshire Cat from Wonderland.

Always attuned to an entrance cue, Katherine Collingswood swept ceremoniously into the room. "Did I hear someone say 'wedding day'?"

A stream of honey-coated words began to gush forth in Katherine's dulcet tones. "We shall have a party at once to celebrate the engagement."

"Don't you think it would be wiser to wait until we return to Washington?" Taylor advised.

Her imperious glance fell with condemnation on her husband. "Of course we'll have one then, the likes of which Washington has never seen. But social amenities must be upheld, even in this God-forsaken part of the world."

Recklessly, Maggie picked up Taylor's argument. "Mother, we don't even know anyone here except Uncle Will and the ranch hands. And you don't talk to the hands," she added to enforce her point.

Katherine's familiar disapproving glare fell once again on her eldest daughter. "I do not believe this matter concerns you, Margaret. I shall contact Mr. Godfrey and have him give me a list of the leading citizens of the community."

Katherine's thoughts were already so preoccupied with plans for the coming fête that she neglected to even glance at Diane's engagement ring. Injured by the oversight, Diane began to whine. "Mother, you didn't even look at my ring."

Katherine quickly covered the faux pas by rushing over to Diane, taking her youngest daughter into her arms. "I can't bear the thought of my . . .

175

baby . . . getting married." A tear appeared in her eye as she took Diane's hand in her own.

"My God!" she exclaimed suddenly, registering astonishment at the size of the ring. Then a glimmer of resentment flickered momentarily and her eyes narrowed as she realized that the emerald was larger than her own.

Amidst exclamations, oh-ings, and ah-ings, Maggie continued to pursue her argument. "I think you should all return to Washington. Dakota won't like it if we delay the hunt any longer."

With regal disdain, Katherine drew up every one of her sixty inches. "*Dakota* . . . won't . . . like . . . it?" The frigid scorn in her voice matched the icy gleam in her eyes.

Too late, Maggie realized that she had uttered the worst possible thing she could have said. She wanted to bite her tongue. Her mother's resentment of Dakota was already obvious; any condescension to him would only increase her prejudice. "Mother, the hunt will merely delay your return to Washington. Shouldn't you begin planning the nuptials at once?"

The air was taut with Katherine's displeasure. "Margaret's right, Katherine," Taylor interjected. He smiled cheerfully, attempting to ease the growing tension. "Have you two lovebirds had time to set the wedding date?"

Peter had followed the tense conversation between Maggie and her mother with mounting interest. Intrigued, he asked, "What is this about a hunt?"

"Oh, Peter," Diane tittered, "you won't believe

what has happened here. There's a crazy will and we all are going to hunt for a buried treasure. *C'est ridicule!*"

"The will didn't say anything about you going along," Maggie flared out defensively. "That's Mother's idea. If Mother insists upon going—"

"Yes, Mother insists upon going," Katherine announced, still angry.

Maggie tried to hide her disappointment that her mother was firm in her determination to go on the hunt.

"Will someone please explain what you're talking about?" Peter requested.

Always the arbitrator, Taylor stepped in. "Yes, Peter. Certainly. You see, Sam Harris was Margaret's real father, and Margaret is named a beneficiary in his will provided she accompany the other heir on a hunt to find where Mr. Harris has buried his fortune. It was our intention—"

"*Is* our intention," Katherine corrected him.

Taylor cast her an impatient look. "It is our intention to accompany Margaret and the other heir on the hunt."

"And who is this other heir?" Peter inquired.

"You've already met him. The young man who accompanied you from Deadwood."

"You mean Mr. MacDonald?" Peter appeared surprised. "This turn of events is all quite interesting and exciting, I must say. If you have no objection, I would like to join you. The whole idea sounds like a grand scavenger hunt to me."

Maggie groaned inwardly. Peter Brent had been her last hope. Had he insisted on returning immediately to Washington with Diane, her mother might have weakened and decided to return with them. Now her hopes were smashed.

Dejected, she slumped down on the settee.

With Peter's affirmative vote, Katherine saw that she had won the issue, and her spirits soared to their former heights. "Now that we have the matter settled, let us get on to the plans for the engagement party."

Maggie picked listlessly at the food on her plate as Katherine continued to discuss the party plans throughout dinner. Unnoticed, she finally slipped away when the meal was finished, leaving the four heads still huddled together, unaware of her departure.

She wandered down to the stable and entered Tiger's stall. The mare snatched the apple Maggie offered her and the dejected girl watched the horse chew the piece of fruit.

"You don't have a care in the world, do you, girl?" she whispered as she patted the mare on the head.

"You're sure looking glum. Aren't you happy with your house guest?" Dakota seemed to appear from nowhere, leading a horse.

Maggie turned around with a sigh. She might as well break the news to him and get it over with. "No. I mean, Peter's okay. But he and Diane got engaged today."

"Is that what's stickin' in your craw?" he asked as he unsaddled the animal.

"Not really, except I know you're not going to like what I have to tell you." Maggie took the reins and wrapped them around a nail on the wall.

Dakota shrugged, picked up a handful of straw and began to rub down the horse. "Reckon it won't change anything whether I like it or not, so fire away."

"Peter Brent intends to come with us on the hunt for Sam's treasure."

Dakota saw no reason to be upset by this news. "Don't much matter to me. Kid's a greenhorn, but he can handle a mount better than most of you."

Maggie worriedly glanced up at him. "Well, that's not the worst of it. My mother is giving Peter and Diane an engagement party before we go."

Dakota slapped the horse on the rump and the animal trotted into the stall. "When's she planning on doin' that?"

"Sunday. I was hoping they would all just pack up and go back to Washington, but my mother had made up her mind."

Maggie helped him toss hay into the horse's stall. "She don't strike me as the kind that turns tail once she sets her head to something," Dakota remarked.

Maggie glanced up with regret. "Do you mind very much, Dakota? I know you're only doing this for my sake, and Mother's making things so difficult for you."

"Don't worry about it, Maggie. Charlie spotted a herd of wild mustangs in the hills. I'll use the time to take a crew out and try to round them up."

Her mood lifted. "Can I go with you?" she asked eagerly.

"No place for you. The trail's rough, and we'll all have our hands full."

When she started to protest, he shook his head. "I mean no, Maggie."

She knew it wouldn't pay to argue. He was as bull-headed as her mother. "How come you're raising horses instead of cattle on the Lazy H?"

Dakota's teeth flashed in a grin. "Thought you liked horses."

"Oh, I do. I love them. I just always thought of the West as having cattle ranches."

"Learn that from your dime novels?" he asked flippantly. She tendered a foolish grin and nodded.

"Well, I don't know of a better place for breeding horses than the Dakota Territory. Best horseflesh in the country. The altitude and hills develop their lung power and endurance and strengthen their legs. Plenty of water and good grazing. Grass cures fast on the stem, better than hay."

Maggie listened, entranced. His love for the hills showed in the husky drawl of his voice. "Is there anything you don't know, Dakota?" she asked when he finished.

Dakota blushed and shoved his hat to the back of his head. "Know enough to know that if a man gets to thinkin' he has nothing more to learn—he's just beginnin'." He dipped his head. "'Night, Maggie."

Maggie's worshipful gaze followed him to the bunkhouse.

At dawn the following morning, Dakota and several of the hands rode into the hills. Since Maggie had no part in the party arrangements, she wandered about aimlessly for days thereafter, waiting for Dakota's return.

Her heart jumped to her throat the day the crew

returned to the Lazy H driving several wild horses. Maggie rushed down to the corral. But there was no sign of Dakota among them.

"Said he'd be along later," one of the wranglers told her when she asked about Dakota. The man hurried away to help pen one of the friskier colts.

Disappointed and bored, Maggie went to the stable and saddled Tiger. Minutes later, she was riding north. She didn't know where she was going, but felt anything would be better than staying around the ranch in the midst of her mother's frenzied party plans for guests none of her family had ever met.

Maggie chose the trail to the Twin Buttes. As she rode along, she soon put aside her troubled thoughts. Now, being a more accomplished rider, she relaxed in the saddle and enjoyed the spectacular landscape.

Suddenly, as she reached the top of a steep hill near the buttes, Tiger's hind hoof caught in a chuck hole hidden by scattered rock. In a tumultuous flurry of bucking and thrashing, the animal reared up on its hind legs again and again, kicking up stones and a cover of dust as its forelegs pounded down on the rugged terrain.

In utter panic, Maggie threw her arms around Tiger's neck and screamed amid the horrible sounds of fright emanating from the trapped mare. She hung on for dear life until at last Tiger's hoof jerked free from the hole.

But the tortured leg of the horse had been broken, and as the hind legs hit the ground for the last time, in a frenzy of pain the animal scrambled, lurching forward in uncontrolled momentum, and tumbled over the crest of the hill. Still hanging on to the neck of the horse, Maggie's right foot flew out of the stirrup but her other foot held fast as Tiger's weight dragged them fifty feet down the hill. When fallen horse and rider came to a halt, Maggie's legs were pinned under Tiger.

Maggie lay breathing heavily for a moment. She slowly moved her head and then her arms. Gingerly leaning on her elbows, she sat up half way. While scraped and bruised, she felt no major pain.

Shaky and stunned, she said in a frightened voice, "Tiger, old girl, looks like . . ." Suddenly stopping, Maggie gasped in horror as she stared at Tiger's motionless head. The animal's bulging eyes protruded grotesquely, staring out at nothing.

"No, Tiger, no!" she cried out, grabbing and pulling on the animal's hide as if prodding would stir the horse to motion. But the awakening would never come, for the beloved mare's neck had been broken.

Maggie unleashed a stream of heartrending tears. In sheer anguish, she clutched at the dead animal over and over again, calling out the mare's name and begging Providence for the impossible.

Finally exhausted, her sobs abated.

Desolate and broken-hearted, Maggie tried to move her legs but found she had no control of them under the weight of the horse. Again and again, she pushed at the dead mare with her hands while trying to move her body backward, but to no avail.

Now for the first time, the seriousness of her

situation began to dawn on her. Trapped under Tiger's body, with night rapidly approaching, no weapon, no protective clothing, and no one mindful of her whereabouts, she was in serious danger.

During the first few hours, she desperately called out for help, but as nightfall descended, her cries grew feeble. Finally, she gave up. Her legs had become numb, and any attempt to move caused excruciating pain.

The hard, unrelenting body beneath her hands grimly reminded her that her beloved Tiger was dead. Maggie slumped against the mare, unleashing a fresh series of sobbing until, eventually, she cried herself to sleep.

But her deep sleep soon deteriorated to a dream of fear and panic—a nightmare in which she frantically tried to run from an unseen terror, yet her leaden legs would not allow her to advance one step.

Then mercifully, the wail of a coyote jolted Maggie awake. Despite a bright moon, she saw the hillside sheathed in dark shadows cast by the tall pines.

Tiger's body had begun to feel like cold stone. Maggie trembled from fright and the raw night air. Each shadow seemed to hold an unseen danger. She had no idea how long she had slept, or how long she had been on the hill. Surely, there must be search parties looking for her. Dakota would find her, she told herself over and over. She resumed her shouts for help, until her voice became too hoarse to call out.

The cries of coyotes sounded ever nearer to the

terrified girl, and the forest seemed alive with sounds and movements. Her glance continually swept the darkness for any movement; her senses remained alert for the faintest rustle.

"Hurry, Dakota. Please hurry." she prayed tearfully.

Chapter Fourteen

Dakota sat gazing at the magnificent animal in the ravine. The black stallion was drinking from a shallow stream which flowed from the rocks above to the gully below. For days he had chased the animal across the boulder-strewn hills trying to get a rope on him.

Now that the stallion was only a rope's length away, Dakota no longer desired to fetter the splendid beast. "You win, boy. Go free," he whispered.

Dakota rose to his feet and tucked a sketch pad into his saddlebags. Then he swung up into the saddle.

He turned back for a final look at the stallion. The horse raised its head, and for a moment rider and animal stared at each other. Then the horse nickered, tossed its head, and trotted away. Dakota turned his horse toward home.

Taylor Collingswood met him at the stable. "Is Maggie with you?" he asked, distressed.

Dakota felt his gut tie into a knot and he glanced at Tiger's empty stall. "How long has she been gone?" he asked succinctly.

Taylor could only shake his head. "We're uncertain. One of the men remembers talking to her about noon. No one saw her ride off."

"I'll get the men out looking for her." Dakota glanced worriedly at the sky. "Sun's gonna set soon."

Katherine came hurrying over to them as soon as she saw Dakota. "Was she—" Taylor shook his head and put his arm around her shoulders. "No, dear."

Katherine burst into tears and buried her head against her husband's shoulder. "Something's happened to Margaret. I can feel it."

Dakota had the same feeling. After a few short instructions, the men separated into small groups and headed out in several directions. Dakota remained behind.

Frantic with impatience, Katherine watched him as he studied the ground intently. "What is he doing? Why doesn't he go and look for Margaret?"

"The man knows what he's doing, dear. Colonel Besting told me that Dakota is one of the best scouts the army ever had."

They both looked up hopefully when Dakota climbed back on his horse and rode over to them. "Once the sun sets, get a big fire going out here and light up everything that'll burn. If she's lost, maybe she'll be close enough to see the light."

Taylor nodded in eager compliance. "Yes, Dakota, I understand."

Dakota turned about and began to ride away, his steady gaze never wavering from the trail.

Maggie fell in and out of fretful dozing, always with the name of Dakota on her lips. Once again her head snapped up in alarm at the sound of thrashing nearby. Her gaze darted in that direction, and her breath caught in her throat as she peered through the darkness. The pounding of her heart was a drumming in her ears, and, petrified, a whimper slipped through her lips when she discerned a huge shadow moving toward her.

Paralyzed with fright, Maggie opened her mouth to scream, but the sound froze in her throat as the shadowy form moved into a patch of moonlight. It was Dakota.

A tear slid down each pale cheek. She stared up at him, her eyes round and moist in the moonlight.

"I knew you would come," she said in a hoarse whisper.

He knelt beside her, his arms a warm mantle as he gathered her to him. Maggie slipped her arms around his neck and buried her head against his chest. "I was so scared, but I knew you would come. I knew you would find me," she sobbed.

Dakota listened in silence, allowing her to spend her tears. Sniffling, she whispered the dreadful certainty already evident to Dakota. "Tiger's . . . dead."

Maggie remained in his arms, feeling his lean strength absorb the pent-up distress from her body.

"Can you move your legs, Maggie?" he asked when her tears finally subsided.

Maggie shook her head. "I could at first, but I can't now. They're too numb."

"Then they aren't broken?" he asked, relieved.

"I don't . . . don't think so," she stammered.

Dakota released her and removed his jacket. He slipped the garment over her shoulders, pulled her arms through the sleeves and buttoned the coat. His body heat lingered in the folds of the fabric, warming her more than the heavy buckskin.

Dakota rose to his feet and removed a rope from the saddle of his horse. Kneeling down beside her, he clasped her hands. "Maggie, I have to get the mare off you now. Do you understand?" She nodded numbly.

Broken-hearted, Maggie watched as he looped the rope around Tiger's head. Unbeknownst to Maggie, tears started to streak her cheeks. Dakota climbed on his horse and began to move away, slowly dragging the heavy carcass off her.

Maggie turned her head aside, unable to watch this callous treatment of the animal she had grown to love. When the burden had been removed, a stabbing pain raced the length of her legs from toe to thigh as the numbness began to wear off.

Dakota returned and knelt down before her. He gently grasped the calf of one leg while the fingers of his other hand gingerly probed the ankle. Cautiously, he traced the length of her leg, checking for a break. Satisfied, he examined the other leg.

His hat had fallen off and Maggie's gaze rested lovingly on the dark head, bowed in concentration as he worked over her. She wanted to reach out and tenderly caress him, but she forced herself to sit quietly while he continued his examination.

Finally, with a husky tremor, she asked, "How did you know where to find me?"

Dakota raised his head and she met the full magnetism of his overpowering eyes. "Tiger's trail was easy to follow, Maggie. Her toes point out." Left unsaid was his previous warning about that very fact.

He stood up, drew his Colt and fired two shots into the air. The sound shattered the silent night like a crash of thunder. He waited thirty seconds, then fired two more. When shots immediately sounded from several directions in response to the signal, Dakota sheathed his weapon.

"What did you do that for?" she asked.

"The first two shots were to let the others know I found you, the last two to tell them you're okay." To her surprise, he was frowning. "Damn it, Maggie, you were foolish to ride off by yourself. The whole crew is out looking for you."

Maggie wanted to burst out crying again. She knew how foolish she had been. Tiger was dead because of her rash behavior. But she didn't want to listen to his angry censure; she only wanted him to say the words she longed to hear—that he loved her. This astounding revelation made her gasp with shock.

Yes, it was true. She wanted Dakota to tell her he loved her, the way she'd heard Peter tell Diane.

Maggie forced back her tears and turned her

head away from him. "I'm sorry to cause everyone so much trouble."

She sensed his nearness as he bent to one knee before her. His fingers forced her head around to meet his stare. Maggie could see the deep anxiety that filled his eyes. "Will you ever stay out of trouble?"

For a moment, they looked into each other's eyes, their lips only inches apart. Maggie held her breath and felt her body begin to tremble. She shifted her eyes downward, too shaken to reply to his question.

Dakota stood up and stepped away from her. "I don't think we should try to move you right away. I'll build a fire and we'll stay here for a while."

Maggie had her emotions under control by the time Dakota finished gathering firewood.

She watched him remove his rifle from the scabbard on his horse. "I suppose you would like to shoot me with that rifle for all the trouble I've caused you."

For a moment his dark eyes flashed. "I would have, if you'd broken your leg."

The joke backfired because it reminded her of Tiger's tragedy. Seeing her begin to tear up again, his jaw shifted into a grim line. "Guess I better leave the joke-making to the folks who know how." He returned to the task of building the fire.

Hot coffee and beef jerky soon had a healing effect on Maggie. Within an hour, she felt like a new woman as she stretched out next to the fire bundled up in a blanket.

The wind began to howl about them, and unconsciously Maggie moved closer to him. "Does the wind always make so much noise? It sounds frightening."

Dakota lifted his head and gazed up at the stars. "Summer's soon ending. You should hear the wind in the winter. Sometimes it doesn't stop blowing for three or four days at a time. Drives snow through every crack it can find."

"You love these hills, though, don't you?" she asked perceptively.

"They were the sacred hunting ground of the Sioux." The tone in his voice was reverent.

"Were? Did the Sioux abandon them?"

He laughed grimly. "Abandon? Never. They died defending the hills. Now they're destroyed. Soon the hills will be too. You can't keep taking something out of the land without putting something back."

Maggie's heart ached for Dakota as she saw him struggle with his thoughts. "It's all been destroyed. A culture as old as the hills. Screaming Eagle said it would come to be."

"Screaming Eagle," Maggie exclaimed, remembering the magnificent face in the portrait over the fireplace.

"My grandfather. He was a Sioux shaman. He saw the end in a vision. Now they're all gone. Grandfather . . . my parents . . . my Mother's people. Even Sam."

"Everyone you ever loved," she said sadly.

Dakota looked up despondently. "Didn't I warn you, Maggie? Don't get attached to anything. You'll only lose it in the end."

Maggie tucked her hands under her head and lay watching Dakota stare sullenly into the fire. She knew he was hurting. He was the strongest man she had ever known—and yet, he was so vulnerable. As she lay engrossed in her thoughts of Dakota, Maggie's eyes slowly drooped and she soon drifted into slumber.

This time she slept peacefully.

Dakota rose to his feet and stood looking down at the sleeping girl. In the glow from the fire, relaxed in slumber, Maggie's face showed the bruises and scrapes she had suffered on her fall.

"You're a real little trooper, Maggie Collingswood," he whispered softly. "Sat up half the night alone in these hills, pinned down by a dead horse, and don't care a hoot about your own aches. Just the dead horse.

"You got more mettle, Maggie, than most men I know."

Streaks of pink and gray painted the horizon when Dakota nudged Maggie awake. "I think we best head back, Maggie."

She sat up, rubbing her eyes. When she stretched her arms, Maggie drew back with a grimace of pain. Ignored in the tragedy of losing Tiger was the toll taken on her body when she rolled down the hill.

Tiger, Maggie thought sadly. Her glance swung toward the animal. To her surprise she saw the spot now heaped with boulders and rocks. Dakota had buried the mare while Maggie slept.

Her tortured glance was fraught with grief when she looked at Dakota. "Thank you," she said softly.

Embarrassed, he turned away. "It'll keep the buzzards off her."

"Is it customary for one to speak over a horse's grave?" she asked solemnly.

Dakota half smiled and picked up the blanket Maggie had tossed aside. "Not to me. But I don't put it past you, Maggie."

Maggie walked over to the heap of boulders and for several seconds stood with her head bowed in a silent prayer. Dakota was waiting astride his horse when she finished.

"Ever ride double before, Maggie?" He reached down and swung her up behind him. She looped her arms around his waist. Neither spoke on the ride back—Maggie deep in gloom, Dakota his usual reticent self.

Having been up most the night searching for her, the ranch hands were still asleep when the pair returned to the Lazy H. Dakota stabled the horse and Maggie slipped quietly into the house.

She wanted to sink her aching bones into a hot bath, but she knew she would disturb the household at such an early hour. Instead, Maggie changed into her night dress and climbed into bed.

Surprisingly, she quickly became drowsy. Forcing thoughts of Dakota and the accident to the back of her mind, Maggie fell asleep.

Bright sunlight streamed through the bedroom window when she opened her eyes. Her mother was standing silently by the bed, gazing down at her.

"How are you feeling, dear?" Katherine asked kindly.

Surprised not to hear censure or scolding,

Maggie smiled. "Fine, Mother. I just ache a little."

Katherine reached out and gently traced Maggie's cheek with her finger. "Your face is bruised. I've told Yen Ching to prepare a bath for you."

"Thank you." This gentle consideration from her mother left Maggie at a loss for words.

Sensing her daughter's confusion, Katherine squared her shoulders, flashed a quick smile, and walked to the door. "Hurry, dear. Remember, Diane and Peter's engagement party is today."

When Yen Ching tapped on her door to tell Maggie her bath was ready, she grabbed her robe and limped to the bathroom. Maggie sank down gratefully into the tub, laid her head back on the rim, and closed her eyes.

The soothing hot water began to work its healing powers on her aching bones and flesh. When the door opened, Maggie raised her head and sat up. Diane stood leaning back against the door.

"I heard you spent the night alone in the hills with the silent warrior. Maybe it wasn't so dumb of you to ride off and get lost after all," she taunted.

"I wasn't lost," Maggie snapped. She thought Diane could show enough concern to ask how she was feeling.

"You could have spoiled my engagement party," Diane blurted out when she realized Maggie wasn't going to volunteer any more information.

Exasperated, Maggie leaned her head back and closed her eyes again. "Maybe I still can."

"You're just jealous because I'm engaged and you're not." Diane thrust out her hand. "I bet *you'll* never have a ring as big as this one."

Maggie opened her eyes. "Get out of here before I hit you with a wet sponge."

"I'm going to tell Mother what you just said," Diane sulked. She slammed out of the room in a huff.

Once again Maggie relaxed, closed her eyes, and grinned. She was beginning to feel better already.

Chapter Fifteen

The Lazy H, bedecked in colorful lanterns, streamers, and flowers by the wagonload, had taken on a magnificent aura, the likes of which the heretofore bachelor-oriented abode had never seen before.

With the rugs rolled up and the furniture toted away, a lavish buffet was being prepared under the supervision and vigilant eye of Washington, D.C.'s most successful hostess—Katherine Collingswood.

Though the Eastern family was known by most of the expected guests only by hearsay, the charming personal note on each beautiful, ornate invitation made the affair impossible to resist. And Katherine was determined that every detail would be perfection.

A harried Yen Ching raced around the kitchen

wielding a meat cleaver at least half his size. The bevy of cooks hired for the occasion cast fretful glances over hunched shoulders wondering if he intended to use the broad knife on the slaughtered calf, woefully stretched out on the cutting board, or on the diminutive Mrs. Collingswood who followed on his heels issuing one last-minute instruction after another.

At noon, the first carriages began to arrive. Arrayed in their finest, local politicians, ranch owners, and the socially elite of the area paraded through the bowered trellis in curious anticipation.

Looking like an ethereal vision in a gold silk-taffeta gown, Katherine Collingswood stepped out on the arm of her husband to greet her guests.

Once inside, the invited, duly awed by the lavish preparations, soon unwound, dancing to the lively offerings of ten professional musicians, chatting enthusiastically with old friends and strangers alike, drinking toasts of imported wine, and partaking of the sumptuous banquet table. All were delighted with the charm and dazzled by the beauty of Diane, the star of the show and truly her mother's daughter.

In a green voile gown, which bared creamy shoulders and clung to her rounded curves, Diane resembled a princess in a fairy tale. A woven band of tiny pink and white tea roses ringed the crown of her head, and her long blond hair, brushed to a golden sheen, hung past her shoulders to the middle of her back.

Unnoticed, Maggie stood aside, almost an observer to the celebration. Against the dazzling blond beauty of her mother and sister, Maggie felt nondescript in her blue-and-white gingham gown.

With hair slicked back and shiny, the Lazy H ranch hands, each dressed in his best bib and tucker, were all in attendance. Maggie continually scanned the crowd for the sight of Dakota. In the evening, her heart seemed to skip to the beat of the music when she finally caught a glimpse of him standing in the doorway.

Dakota had changed his blue cavalry trousers and buckskin shirt for black pants and vest. His dark handsomeness was enhanced by a white shirt tied at the neck with a black string tie. But by the time Maggie crossed the crowded room, he had disappeared.

The men of Deadwood had never seen a woman as lovely as Diane. The belle of the ball flirted outrageously with each of her dancing partners. Her lively green eyes flashed provocatively as she whirled around the floor. Rafe Catlin, especially smitten with her, continually cut in on Diane's dancing partners. Had Diane known of Peter's near fight with Rafe, she would have encouraged the young rancher's attention even more.

Rafe's attention and Diane's flirtations did not go unobserved by her fiance, who stewed on the sidelines watching Diane spin past him in the arms of one dazed male after another. As the evening lengthened, Peter's irritation increased.

In Maggie's eyes, the party dragged on interminably, and she wondered when it would be permissible to go to her room and get away from the isolation she felt. Desolately, she wandered outside to be rid of the noise. Dakota had remained aloof from the crowd and had particularly avoided Maggie during the evening. But she had seen the wishful look on his face as he watched Diane glide gracefully on the dance floor, and she knew he wanted her sister the way every other young man in the room did. He didn't care about the existence of Margaret Collingswood.

A tall pine forest lined the rear of the house. Maggie wandered among the trees, deeply breathing the air filled with aromatic pine to rid her nostrils of the acrid cigar smoke which filled the ranch house.

She stopped wandering at the sound of approaching voices. Maggie had decided to turn back to the house when her sister came into view. Peter followed angrily behind Diane and grabbed her arm.

Maggie stepped deeper into the shadows, hoping they would pass by. She did not want to explain why she was out there alone among the trees, yet she didn't want to spy on them. Funny, she thought with a stab of guilt, she had often followed them just to do the very thing she now found so shameful—peeking at them from the bushes like an obnoxious snoop. That immature child was gone forever.

Maggie was about to step forward to announce her presence when Peter pulled Diane into his arms.

"All evening I've watched you throw yourself at every man at the party," he accused her.

She smiled wickedly. "Does that bother you, Peter?"

"You know it does."

Diane giggled and slipped her arms around his neck. "But Peter, I was only having fun. You want me to have fun, don't you? You know you're the only man I truly care about."

"Then prove it to me now," he murmured. He covered her mouth with a fervent kiss. "I love you, Diane. I love you," he groaned, raining kisses down her neck. Peter buried his mouth in the firm, rounded cleavage of her breast.

"Oh, Peter, you mustn't," Diane protested with a wicked giggle.

"We're engaged now," he pleaded. "Please, my love? I've waited so long." His hands grappled for her breasts and she moved closer, wantonly pressing against him. Peter pushed the gown past her breasts and drew one of the taut peaks into his mouth.

Diane closed her eyes and threw back her head in rapture. "Well, maybe this one time," she said breathlessly.

Transfixed, Maggie watched the pair. *Stop him. Don't let him ravish you*, she raged silently, stunned by her sister's capitulation.

Diane began breathing in short gasps when Peter suckled her breasts. She offered no resistance as he lowered her to the ground and trailed kisses to her breasts. When his mouth closed over a taut peak, her groans grew louder.

"You're so beautiful, my love. I want you. If only I could have you now."

Diane began to writhe beneath him and pulled him down across her.

Maggie wanted to cry aloud. To run. Afraid to move for fear of being discovered, she closed her eyes and covered her ears to shut out the sight and sounds of the couple on the ground.

Her body felt aflame, her head ached, and tears streaked her cheeks.

Stop it. Stop it. Stop it, she screamed silently. Maggie wallowed in shame, knowing she was not only crying out against them, but also against the wickedness of her own desires. She wanted that couple on the ground to be her and Dakota. She wanted Dakota's mouth and hands on her.

A scream of hysteria mounted within her. She had to get away. Desperation gave her the courage to run, and Maggie dashed away into the darkness.

Alerted, Peter raised his head. "Did you hear something?"

"Nothing," Diane moaned in the throes of passion. She reached up and tried to pull him back. "Don't stop now, Peter."

The young man stood up and pulled her to her feet. "Forgive me, my love, for taking such liberties. Thank God we stopped before—"

"Whatever do you mean?" Diane asked indignantly. "Come now, Peter. I wouldn't be the first. Don't you think I'm aware of the girls who followed the Princeton star?" She loved to taunt him.

"Everyone knows there are two kinds of girls, Diane. And they were the other kind." He clutched her hand fervently. "I revere you too much, beloved, to think of misusing you before we are man and wife."

"Oh, poppycock!" Diane snapped. Disgruntled,

she stormed away from the stodgy prude and wondered how she would ever bear being married to him.

Unintentionally, Maggie fled to her one heaven of solace, the stable. She ran to Tiger's empty stall and cowered in the corner like a felon fleeing in the night. She remained huddled in the seclusion of the stable, suffused in shame and guilt as her body shook with sobs.

Katherine and Taylor were bidding goodbye to the last departing guests when Maggie finally returned to the house. She sped down the hallway to her room and crawled under the comforter. But shame prevented sleep.

The next morning Maggie was silent at breakfast. She could not force herself to even glance at her sister or Peter.

Katherine and Diane monopolized the conversation, discussing the success of the party, so Maggie's reticence went unobserved by everyone except Taylor.

When the chatter of the two women slowed enough to get a word in edgeways, Taylor posed the question to her. "Aren't you feeling well, honey?"

"Just a headache, Father," Maggie replied.

Alerted to her eldest daughter's condition, Katherine got up and placed a hand on Maggie's brow. "Are you running a fever?"

All eyes were now on her. Under this unwanted attention, Maggie cringed as if they would be able to read the reason for her guilt. "It's nothing, Mother. Really. I just have a headache."

"I hope you didn't catch something during that

unfortunate . . . experience the other night."

Diane simpered over the top of her tea cup. "Yes, Margaret. You've never told us what happened during that . . . experience."

Near to bursting out in tears, Maggie threw down her napkin. "I've told you, I just have a headache. It's probably due to the loud music last night."

Katherine returned to her seat at the table. "Well, your sister certainly doesn't seem to have suffered any ill effects from it. Diane, dear, I can't remember when I've seen you look so exhilarated. You're positively glowing. Don't you agree, Peter?"

Peter Brent blushed. "Diane always looks lovely to me, Mrs. Collingswood."

Katherine beamed with pleasure. "You're such a charming boy, Peter. You always say the right thing." Katherine bestowed a pleased future-mother-in-law smile on him. "As a matter of fact, you look very refreshed yourself. It appears both of you must have passed a pleasant night."

Diane tittered insipidly behind her napkin, then turned to Peter with a sly smile. "Did you pass a pleasant night, Peter? I do hope your dreams were of me."

Peter's blush deepened. Seeing it, Taylor interceded in the young man's behalf. "Now, now, ladies. Can't you see you're embarrassing the lad?"

Maggie had heard all of the inane conversation she could bear. She rose to her feet. "May I be excused, Father?"

"Of course, honey, Go to your room and try to rest."

Returning to her room, Maggie took her father's advice and climbed back into bed. This time she fell asleep and did not awaken until late afternoon.

There was no sign of her parents. Diane and Peter were near the corral with Dakota, who was trying to give Diane another riding lesson.

Despite Peter's presence, Diane continued her flirtatiousness with Dakota. She didn't miss one opportunity to put his arm around her. Several times the bold girl brushed her breasts against him, then offered an alluring smile when she knew he was aware of her attempt.

Maggie steamed, revolted by her sister's actions. The sight of their bent heads together, or Dakota's hands on Diane, wrenched at Maggie's heart. Having witnessed how Peter lusted for Diane, Maggie could not understand how he could tolerate this flirtation with another man.

But the most heart-breaking fact was that Dakota made no attempt to stop the wanton girl's actions.

The yearning on Dakota's face when he watched Diane at the party burned vividly in Maggie's mind. Perhaps it was just as well she had seen the truth when she did, Maggie thought, or else she would have continued to make a fool of herself by following him around and throwing herself at him in the vain hope that one day he would grow to love her. Desolate, unable to watch for another moment, Maggie turned away.

She walked over to the corral fence and hopped on it. Several of the hands were working the wild horses from the recent round-up. The smell of singed hair permeated the air, and Maggie realized they were branding the horses as well.

She watched as they took the reins and jerked one of the horses to the ground. Several of the wranglers held down the animal as another put the hot poker to the animal's haunch. Maggie covered her ears to shut out the sizzling sound.

"It doesn't hurt them that much," Dakota said, suddenly beside her. He hopped up on the fence.

The riding lesson must be over for the day, Maggie thought belligerently. "How would you know? Are you a branded horse?" she snapped, venting her frustration on the man responsible for it.

His crooked grin gleamed brightly. "Well, not exactly. But I have been called the part of the horse they're putting that iron to often enough."

She ignored the quip. "I think it's cruel. There must be a more humane way of doing it."

"Well, if there is, nobody's thought of it yet."

Dakota studied the distress etched on her face. Something a lot deeper than branding a horse must be bothering Maggie. He wondered if she was still fretting over Tiger's death.

"Why do they always put the brand on sideways?" she asked. "As long as they're doing it, why not do it right?"

Dakota threw back his head in laughter. Maggie couldn't help smiling. Simple laughter was foreign to the taciturn and grim man. Even if she was the brunt of his amusement, Maggie enjoyed seeing him cheerful for a change.

"The *H* on the iron is lying on its side. That makes it a lazy *H*. Get it?"

Maggie's eyes widened with comprehension. "Oh, of course, the Lazy H. Why didn't I guess that?" She climbed off the fence. "I've been pretty dumb about a lot of things around here."

His gaze lingered, following her long, smooth stride as she returned to the house. He liked the way she walked—straightforward, just like her nature. Then his eyes shifted to the way the jeans hugged her hips and long legs. Dakota grinned. He liked that about her, too.

The smile left his face when he caught a glimpse of Diane slipping off in the trees behind the house. He wondered what she was up to now. Brent was a fool for ever getting tangled up with her.

He climbed into the corral but couldn't put thoughts of Diane aside. Last night at the party he had watched the little harlot flirt with every guy who met her eyes. But those rounded curves and golden hair of hers couldn't hold a candle to Maggie's beauty. Maggie was all woman, even in plain jeans and shirt, with a hat pulled down over her auburn curls.

He glanced back to the house just as the object of his musings disappeared into it. *Yep, all woman,* Dakota reflected. *And too innocent to guess just how much woman she really is.*

Diane was Brent's problem, not his. It wasn't his business. Horses were.

Diane hurried through the woods, casting furtive backward glances over her shoulder. After a short distance, she stopped at a leafy copse and waited anxiously, uncomfortable alone in the mammoth forest. Last night, the daring tryst had seemed exciting, but now her courage faltered and she regretted her rash promise. Diane was about to bolt when a pair of hands grabbed her from behind and lifted her off her feet.

"Gotcha." Laughing, her abductor put her down.

"I swear, you almost frightened me to death, Rafe Catlin," she scolded.

"I thought about you all night, baby." He pulled her roughly into his arms and kissed her, grinding his lips against Diane's until she opened her lips and his tongue slipped into her mouth.

Breathless, Diane shoved him away. Her eyes flashed coquettishly as she leaned back in his arms. "My goodness, Rafe Catlin, control yourself. I don't like being mauled."

"Like hell you don't. You love it."

Diane giggled and smiled seductively into his gleaming eyes. "I swear I don't know why I ever agreed to meet you. I had best return before my mother and father become suspicious."

"Where's that fancy-pants boyfriend?" he grumbled and began to nibble on her neck.

"We had a quarrel and he went to his room."

Rafe snorted in derision. "Why don't you marry me? If you was my gal, you'd be in that bedroom with me, not out here in some other guy's arms."

"Marry you?" she scoffed.

"Why not? My pa owns the biggest spread in the Dakota Territory. I can give you anything Fancy-Pants can—and a whole lot more." He leered suggestively.

"Do you think I want to live on a ranch the rest of my life?" Diane mocked. "You must think I'm as crazy as my sister."

His hand cupped her rounded derriere. "No, baby, you're sure nothin' like that skinny-assed sister of yours."

When he attempted to slip her gown off her shoulders, Diane shoved his hands away. "Rafe Catlin, remember your promise. You said you wouldn't try to take liberties with me."

"Sure, baby." He crushed her mouth in another bruising kiss, driving his tongue into her mouth.

Diane pressed her hands against his chest. Her eyes flashed like green jewels. "I swear you're part animal," she teased breathlessly.

Rafe laughed. "Same as you, baby. Knew it the first time I laid eyes on you. That fancy-pants dude of yours ain't got the first notion what a gal like you wants."

"He is an old prude," she giggled. Rafe continued his assault with passionate kisses until Diane was breathless. Once again his hands moved to her breasts, this time succeeding in lowering her gown. Rafe's eyes ravished the pink-tipped breasts.

Diane's eyes narrowed into slumberous slits. "You're wicked." Unconsciously, her lips parted and her tongue laved her lips as she waited, expectantly, for him to continue.

Rafe dipped his head and began to suckle her breasts. When she closed her eyes in rapture, he tried to pull her gown past her hips.

Diane opened her eyes and shook her head. "No, you mustn't do that."

His mouth smothered her words beneath a moist kiss. Rafe raked her mouth with his tongue, driving in with hot, piercing stabs until she groaned with passion. He lowered her to the ground. "I know something you're gonna like a lot more, baby," he whispered.

His tongue lapped at her breasts as he slipped his hand under the skirt of her gown. Before Diane could guess his intent, she felt his hand close over her sensitive womanhood. "No! You promised. You mustn't." She sat up and shoved him away.

Rafe laughed aloud. "Ah, come on, baby. You liked that, didn't you? Bet Fancy-Pants never did that to you."

Diane felt degraded under his lecherous smirk. "Of course not. Peter's a gentleman." She tried to pull up her gown.

Rafe threw back his head and laughed as he pushed her back down. "A gentlemen. You don't want no gentlemen." He squeezed her chin in a cruel grasp and ground his mouth on hers. "You want a man who's wild like me. That's what gets you all excited, ain't it, baby?"

A tremor of fear swept her spine and her heartbeat quickened as she stared up into his feral eyes. "Don't talk like this, Rafe. You're frightening me. I'm going back." She struggled to rise to her feet but he would not release her. "Let me go."

Diane began to panic. Rafe was not Peter. Too late, she realized she could not control him. Mesmerized with fear, she watched him like a frightened animal.

His face twisted into a cruel sneer as he got to his

feet and opened his trousers. "You want some more, don't you?"

She shook her head and began to sob. "No, I want to go back."

"You can go back once you make me feel good, baby," he growled. Her eyes widened in shock and horror at the sight of the engorged organ in his hands. "Let's get rid of all those clothes," he muttered salaciously. "I've been real good to you. Made you feel real good, didn't I? Now, what's good for the goose is good for the gander."

"No. Please. Let me go," Diane whimpered when he began to pull her gown over her hips.

Suddenly, as he reached for her, Rafe was yanked from behind and flung to the ground. "You bastard!" Dakota MacDonald glared down at him. "Diane, get dressed and back to the house," he ordered.

Nearly hysterical, Diane began crying. She hastily pulled on her dress and ran.

"You got no call to butt in, MacDonald. I'm only givin' her what she's been askin' for." Rafe got to his feet. "Or maybe you're mad 'cause I'm jumpin' your claim." He grinned lewdly. "The little tart's got plenty for both of us."

Dakota smashed his fist into Catlin's face, knocking the man off his feet. "Get the hell out of here."

Dakota turned to walk away and Rafe dived at him. For several moments the two grappled, exchanging punches. Both men were tough and hardened from years of arduous work wrangling horses. Finally, Dakota landed a blow that sent Rafe sprawling on his back. Defeated, the rancher lay with blood seeping from his nostrils.

Dakota stood above him, his hands still clenched into fists. "Now get on your horse and get out of here. If I see you again on the Lazy H, I'll put a bullet in you."

With a cold and unwavering stare, Dakota watched as Rafe lumbered to his feet and staggered to his horse. Catlin pulled himself into the saddle, his eyes black with hatred as he stared down at Dakota. "They'll be another time, 'breed." He spurred his horse and galloped away.

Maggie was gazing out of her bedroom window when her sister came hurrying out of the woods. Maggie saw Diane stop and arrange her disheveled clothing, then wipe the tears off her face.

Diane and Peter must have had another quarrel, Maggie thought to herself. *Or maybe they were—* With a blush of shame, Maggie recalled the passionate scene she had witnessed in the woods between the engaged couple. The memory dredged up her own feelings of guilt over her hidden longing for Dakota.

She was about to turn away when Dakota followed Diane out of the trees. Maggie froze. She felt a sickening sensation in the pit of her stomach as she noted the haste and emotional state of the pair; everything about them bespoke duplicity. Her worst suspicions had been confirmed.

Unaware that they were being observed, for several seconds the two people stared at one another. Then, without a word, he walked away.

Moments later, Maggie saw him ride off in a flurry of hoofbeats. Inconsolable, she turned away from the window and flung herself on the bed. Her heart felt near to bursting.

Chapter Sixteen

William Godfrey had been quietly talking to Melissa Pickett, the wife of the Presbyterian minister, when suddenly Dakota burst through the doors with the ferocity of the James gang about to hold up the bank. Startled, Mrs. Pickett dropped her reticule full of the donations from the Sunday morning service and threw up her hands as the coins clanked and rolled across the floor in all directions.

"Lord of Mercy," the nervous woman exclaimed. "Why it's nobody but Mr. MacDonald," she added, clamping her hands to her hips when she recognized the intruder. "See here, young man, what cause do you have for scaring a body so? Crashing in here like a drunken Ind—" Flustered, the pious Mrs. Pickett fortunately remembered her calling before finishing her ill-begotten thought.

The embarrassed banker and the teller scrambled to pick up the scattered money while Dakota remained near the doorway looking formidable and agitated.

Clasping her hands before her, Melissa tried to reclaim her saintly demeanor and sallied forth on a mission of salvation. "Young man, the Good Lord is looking to see you spend your time in church rather than rousting about, frightening innocent people."

Impatient, but goaded to reply, Dakota tipped his hat. "Your pardon, ma'am, no harm intended," he apologized in haste. He bent down to help with the coin collection.

After all the money had been retrieved, Will accompanied Melissa to the teller's cage, comforted the woman with a few pleasantries, and wished her a good day. Getting back to Dakota, he grinned. "Good thing you're known in these parts, Dakota, or you'd be likely to get yourself shot busting through the door of a bank like that."

"Gotta talk to you, Will."

Godfrey motioned to his office and followed the agitated young man. He closed the door and sat down behind a large oak desk. Knowing Dakota well, Godfrey shrewdly guessed something was seriously amiss. He picked up the bottle on his desk. "Whiskey?" Dakota shook his head.

Putting aside the liquor, Godfrey leaned back in his chair. "Well then, spit it out, son. What's stuck in your craw?"

Dakota planted his hands firmly on the desk and

leaned across at Godfrey. "Are you sure that fool will of Sam's is air-tight?"

"Tighter than a whisker on a cat's chin," Will drawled. "Drew it up myself." He eyed Dakota curiously. "Why? Did you change your mind about wanting Maggie to inherit Sam's wealth?"

"No. Just wanted her to get it without having to go on that damned treasure hunt."

Will frowned. "Something happen out at the ranch?"

"Nothing I want to talk about."

Will reflected on the young man's words as he watched Dakota pace the floor. "You and Maggie have a falling out?"

"No. Matter of fact, she's been behavin' herself real fine since her accident."

Perplexed, Godfrey stared at Dakota. The young man's face was inscrutable. "You think the experience affected the girl too much?" Will asked.

Dakota shook his head. "Nope. When I found her that night, she seemed only broke up about the dead horse, not about herself. Maggie's got a lot of Sam's grit. Something else sure is botherin' her, though."

Will leaned forward with interest. "What do you think it could be?"

"How in hell would I know?"

The boy seemed too defensive, Godfrey thought, certainly out of character for Dakota MacDonald. Whatever ailed him, Will knew that Maggie was part of it. He smiled to himself with satisfaction for having guessed something must be abrew between Dakota and Maggie.

"Right now the Lazy H is a powder keg about to blow sky high. I guess we better get this damn treasure hunt over with and ship those people back East where they belong," Dakota declared.

"Ship Maggie back too?" Will asked slyly.

"Damn it, Will! Stop prodding me. I told you the trouble has nothing to do with Maggie. What Maggie does is her own business. Mine is to find Sam's fortune and see that she gets it." He returned to lean over Will's desk. "I'm bringing them all to town tomorrow to get outfitted. Did you get the pack mules?"

Godfrey nodded. "Two of them, just as you said."

"If you're still planning on coming with us, be ready to leave next Monday morning. Give you a chance to go to church on Sunday and pray." Dakota grinned derisively. "This little expedition's gonna need all the help it can get." He turned and departed as quickly as he had arrived.

Will stood in the doorway and watched Dakota ride away until the tall horseman disappeared from his view. The banker emitted a low whistle. "Haven't seen you this rattled, son, since the day Sam forced you out of moccasins and into shoe leather." Will grinned. "You fought the bit just as hard that time, too."

Dakota had one more stop to make before heading back to the Lazy H. The blacksmith put down his heavy hammer when Dakota rode up to the livery stable. "Is she ready?"

"Yep. Got her all shod," the smithy declared. He went into the building and led out a roan mare. The man patted the horse appreciatively. "She's a

215

real beauty. Good legs, deep chest. Ain't seen an apron-faced mare like this in a long time," he murmured, rubbing the large, white blaze on the horse's forehead. "Got a couple of offers while I was shoeing her, if you're interested in selling her."

"Nope. She's not for sale," Dakota said.

"Where'd you get her?" the man asked.

"In the hills, running wild with a black stallion." Dakota paid the blacksmith, nodded goodbye, and led the horse away.

On the ride home, he wondered what Maggie's reaction would be when she saw the horse. She was still grieving over Tiger, and he couldn't bear to see her so sad—as if she had lost her best friend. *Guess she figures she did,* Dakota reflected. But it was just like getting tossed by a bronco, he reasoned. The only thing to do is climb right back into the saddle.

Dakota felt the new horse would help. He had roped and broken the mare himself, not trusting the job to any of the other hands. He wanted to make sure the horse wouldn't be mistreated or turn mean. The mare turned out to be right smart and took to the bit quickly. Maggie wouldn't have a problem handling her.

The hour was late when he arrived back at the ranch. He fumbled in the darkened stable until he found a lantern, then led the mare to Tiger's empty stall. After watering the horse and tossing some hay in the stall, Dakota stepped back like a pleased kid planning a surprise. His usual taciturn face broke into a smile. Tomorrow morning Maggie would discover the horse herself. He hoped the surprise would pick up her spirits.

When he turned to unsaddle his own horse, Dakota discovered that the black gelding had trotted out of the stable. Stepping outside, he saw no sign of the animal. A cloud passing over the moon had covered the yard in darkness, and Dakota could only see a short distance ahead.

I bet that fool horse headed for the sweet grass, he guessed. Dakota crossed the yard in pursuit.

Meanwhile, sleep eluded Maggie; she was too depressed. The walls of the room seemed to shrink and close in on her. Wishing to escape the small confines and her edgy feelings, she quickly pulled on her jeans and shirt.

The darkened house seemed very still as she padded barefoot down the hallway. Maggie wandered outside and took a deep breath of the night air. Through the blackness of the yard, she noticed a faint glow from the stable.

"Who left a lantern burning?" she grumbled. Listlessly, she walked down toward the stable to extinguish the light, her thoughts still dwelling on the painful scene which had haunted her all day and evening—Diane and Dakota coming out of the woods.

Even from the distance of her window, Maggie could see her sister's anger at him. Obviously, Dakota had tried to take liberties with Diane and she had refused him.

Considering the way Diane had thrown herself at Dakota the past few days, Maggie could not blame him. But it broke her heart to realize how much Dakota wanted Diane.

Oh, how she had let her own feeling for him show the many times they had been together. Obvious, loving adoration. And yet, Dakota had never even attempted a kiss. He merely tolerated her, but he absolutely yearned for Diane.

Diane, who was everything Maggie knew she could never be.

She entered the stable and approached the lantern, then stopped abruptly at the sight of a tawny horse in the familiar stall. "Tiger!"

She rushed to the stall, only to draw back in despair. No. This horse was not Tiger. Tiger was dead and she was responsible.

Flinging herself face-down on a nearby pile of hay, Maggie unleashed a torrent of tears. She had never been so unhappy, felt such despair. Everything was lost to her. Everything but the reality of her misery.

Oh, to be the girl she once had been, in an innocent world of bicycles, ten-cent novels, and dreams of the West!

But Maggie knew her old world had been destroyed—shattered by wanton thoughts of Dakota MacDonald. Unattainable fantasies about Dakota. Dakota. Always Dakota.

But Dakota had his own dreams. Dreams of golden hair. Of rounded curves and a diminutive, feminine girl.

"I wish I were everything I'm not." The anguished words slipped past her lips.

Then, without a sound, the awareness of his

presence penetrated the abyss of her despair. Maggie raised her head.

Dakota sat down beside her, his overpowering dark eyes fixed on her upturned face. Having heard her self-reproachful words, he whispered gently, "Why would you want to be anything but what you are, Maggie?"

She faced him with pure innocence glimmering through her tears. "Because I want to please you, Dakota."

Her green eyes glowed like emerald pools. "I wish I were tiny and feminine like Diane. I wish I had long blond hair. I wish I were as womanly—"

Before she could finish, Dakota pulled her into his arms. His mouth covered hers, and instinctively Maggie parted her lips beneath the firm pressure.

His grasp tightened, drawing her closer, and she trembled against the hard outline of his body. "Maggie. Maggie," he groaned harshly, as if driven against his will.

Maggie opened her eyes and gazed with wonder into his brooding stare. She smiled, her love spilling over her cheeks in unrestrained tears of joy.

This time his kiss was more demanding. She responded openly, mindful only of him and the ecstasy of his kiss.

He slid his lips to her ear. "Sweet innocent. Sweet, sweet innocent."

She felt on fire, lit by a flame that engulfed her and ignited her body with ecstatic desire. "Dakota." She breathed his name in mounting excitement and grasped at him eagerly. "Don't stop," she pleaded. "Please don't stop."

"I couldn't, if I wanted to," he rasped hoarsely. His lips covered hers, unleashing the passion he had fought to control for the past weeks.

Maggie watched the shifting passion on his face as he opened the buttons of her shirt. He slipped off the garment, and then her other clothing, until she lay naked.

Conscious of her slim body, she wondered how she must appear to him; her breasts were too small, her legs too long. She had no curves, no womanliness. Fearing his disapproval, she blushed as his smoldering gaze swept the length of her.

Her anxiety caused a sudden downward shift of her eyes. Dakota reached out and cupped her breasts, his callused thumbs toying with the taut nipples. The sensation was exquisite and Maggie gasped, her eyes again meeting his.

"Sweet heaven, Maggie, you fill my hands," he groaned and lowered his head.

Her breasts swelled beneath him as his tongue teased the sensitive peaks, then his mouth closed moistly around a nipple. A tremor raced the length of her spine.

Dakota raised his head and covered her mouth with his own, slipping his tongue through her lips. The sensation caused her to arch against him and he responded with a slide of his warm hands across her stomach. She sucked in her breath as an erotic feeling, like a coil being slowing wound, invaded the most private part of her body. She didn't know what to do, afraid her movements would interfere. The coil tightened and tightened.

Dakota dipped his head to her breasts and his

mouth began a sensuous torture. Her incessant groans became a rapturous cry when his roaming hand found the nucleus of the coil. The spring snapped, releasing a burst of divine sensation throughout her. Maggie started to shudder under waves of mindless tremors.

Dakota held her in his arms until her rapid breathing eased. Then he kissed her, and she felt the quickening within her begin again.

He pulled away and she reached out to him in protest. He knelt and removed his shirt. The wide, muscular brawn of his shoulders and chest was as magnificent as she had remembered.

They knelt face to face, only inches apart, and gazed into one another's eyes.

Maggie caressed the broad shoulders, curving her hand to follow their slope into his firm, muscular chest. In silence, he allowed her to explore. Gingerly at first, her touch soon grew bolder and she began to play with his nipples. A quick intake of breath broke his silence, and Maggie's eyes widened in surprise at their sensitivity.

Curious, she licked the tip of one nub and felt the sudden rapid surge of his heartbeat. Fascinated, she licked the other nipple. Dakota's breathing intensified.

Maggie shifted her glance up to his. Watching her intently, he remained motionless, his eyes inviting her to continue.

Maggie dipped her head and took the nipple into her mouth, just as he had done to her. His hands clenched her shoulders and a faint sheen began to glisten on his bronzed chest and shoulders.

Dakota moved away to remove his boots and trousers. When she would not—could not—look at his male organ, he took her hand and curled her fingers around it. He felt hard, hot. The organ pulsated in her hands.

She grasped the thick tip of him. "Gently," he cautioned and she eased her hand.

Dakota covered her hand with his own and ran them both the length of the shaft. The strength and the feel of him excited her, and his mounting arousal intensified hers. Pushing her back down, he lowered his head to claim a breast. Her hand increased its rhythm as her fevered body throbbed.

Dakota slid his hand to the opening between her legs and cautiously probed the velvet chamber. Maggie's breath became ragged gasps. She could no longer think or direct her actions.

"Maggie, this is going to hurt you," he whispered. "But only for a few seconds." Although she heard his words, she did not understand, and she was beyond caring.

He raised himself up and drove into her. The thin membrane tore, and the exquisite sensation became a painful impalement.

Maggie cried out, but his mouth closed over hers, smothering the sound.

Now, linked together, his roaming hands reignited the rapturous ecstasy. As their tempo escalated, moisture glistened on the taut cord of his arms and neck, strained by the force of his driving impetus.

The same compelling force ravaged her time and time again until she felt a glorious release at the instant his body erupted in rapid convulsions, and his hot liquid filled her for the first time.

Maggie had never known such a sublime moment.

Dakota lay back and closed his eyes. His chest rose and fell in a rapid rhythm as he fought to regain his breath. Maggie lay beside him, her gaze worshipping his chiseled profile.

Dakota opened his eyes and turned his head. "God, Maggie, don't look at me like that."

He rolled over and cupped her face in his hands, staring down into the full measure of her love. "I'm not deserving of it. I'm no better than that bastard, Catlin." Still, he was helpless to resist her, and he lowered his head to gently press a kiss on her lips.

Maggie slipped her arms around his neck. "What are you saying? Who is Catlin?"

"No one who matters." She closed her eyes and he placed a kiss on each of her eyelids. "Maggie, I'm sorry. I didn't mean for this to happen."

The sanctity of the moment began to fade. Maggie's eyes opened in tormenting doubt. "Why? Because I'm not Diane?"

A glimmer of incredulity flickered in his dark eyes. "Is that what you believe?"

"I'll believe anything you tell me, Dakota," she answered with unwavering trust. "I love you."

He sat up hurriedly and began to dress. "Don't say that. Don't say that ever again. Get dressed, Maggie."

She sat up, stunned by his sudden shift of mood. Maggie grabbed his arms to stop his motion.

"What's wrong, Dakota? Please tell me. Talk to me. Don't withdraw behind that mask of yours. Not now. Not after what we've just shared."

He grasped her shoulders, his fingers biting into her bare flesh. "You're naive, Maggie. Your head's been full of foolish dreams from the time you got here. How many times have I told you there are no heroes? Stop trying to make one out of me. Next Monday, we'll go on that hunt. When we get back, I'm riding out for good, and there'll be no stopping me then."

Numbed, she listened in silence to his callous, emotionless words. "I don't want your love, Maggie. I can't return it. I won't return it. I warned you not to get attached to anything. You only lose it in the end. Do you understand?"

Yes, she understood. Now she understood what he had been telling her from the beginning. All this time she had been torturing herself with self-doubts. Her femininity. Her feelings. All for nothing. None of these things were important to Dakota because they wouldn't matter in the end. He would not be there.

Dakota did not become attached to anything because he wanted to avoid commitment—to give it or to receive it.

Maggie turned away and dressed hurriedly; this time her face wore the impenetrable mask. "Where are your boots?" he asked, when she walked away. "You'll cut your feet."

Maggie turned around and stared at him. "Don't worry about me, Dakota. My wounds heal quickly."

With head up and shoulders erect, she walked back toward the house, unaware of the eyes watching her from the concealment of the trees.

Nearing the house, Maggie had an odd feeling, as if someone were staring at her. Her glance shifted toward the wooded fringe. Something or someone was out there. She opened her mouth to cry out to Dakota, but pride overcame caution. It was probably just an animal.

Maggie hurried into the house and slammed the door behind her.

Chapter Seventeen

After a restless night, Maggie had to rally her convictions before facing Dakota again, so she elected not to accompany the party going to Deadwood. Katherine gave Diane last-minute instructions, and she and Taylor remained behind as well.

As she watched her sister ride off with Dakota, Maggie was able to view the situation objectively. Dakota didn't have any more feeling for Diane than he did for her. Dakota MacDonald did not allow himself to care for people.

However, no matter how much Maggie tried to rationalize, Dakota's rejection still hurt. It wasn't the despairing, self-incriminatory hurt she had been suffering, but a dull ache in her chest where her heart had once been.

Strangely, despite all her previous secretive and

shameful misgivings on the matter, Maggie felt no guilt about surrendering her virginity to Dakota. Those few moments in his arms had been the most exquisite she had ever known. Nothing could ever take that memory away from her.

She had grown up. She was a woman now in mind and body. And Maggie had come to know just how painful growing up could be.

Hindered by the memory of the previous catastrophic evening, a great deal of time elasped before Maggie remembered the presence of a tawny horse in Tiger's stall. Secure in the knowledge that Dakota was safely out of the way, Maggie hurried to the stable.

Human beings were still a threat to the animal, and the mare shied away when Maggie tried to pet her. "I won't hurt you," Maggie cooed. "What's your name, girl?" The horse began to gentle under Maggie's touch and accepted the apple offered her.

"I used to have a horse just like you except for the patch." Maggie stroked the white blaze on the mare's forehead. "If you were mine, I'd call you Blaze," she murmured to the animal.

Her one-sided conversation was interrupted when one of the ranch hands came in for a bucket of fodder. "Billy, whose horse is this?"

"I reckon it's yours, ma'am. Dakota roped and broke it for you himself. Maybe he figgered to replace your lost mare."

The information came as a surprise to Maggie. Dakota was so secretive about his actions, she had never suspected what he had been up to.

When the wrangler departed, Maggie returned

her attention to the horse. "So . . . you're going to be mine," she said, pleased. "Well, don't think you and I are going to get attached to one another. Remember, we ladies had the same man for a teacher. First he got us to trust him, then he got rid of us." She rose to her toes and whispered in the horse's ear, "Doesn't believe in commitments, you know."

The mare, soothed by the sound of her voice, continued to regard Maggie with clear, trusting eyes. "Mr. MacDonald's probably told you that he doesn't form attachments. Of course, when he sneaks off and replaces my lost horse, it's good cause to give a person second thoughts." She winked at the horse. The mare blinked back.

"Ever been in love, Blaze, or are you too young for that kind of nonsense?" Maggie asked. She stepped back for a wider look at the animal. "Just how old are you anyway?"

The mare snorted and tossed her head. Then a shiver ran the length of the animal from top to bottom, akin to a dog shaking off water.

Maggie's eyes glowed with merriment. "Well, I'm sorry if I offended you with such a personal question. I was only trying to make conversation."

Her step was lighter as she left the stable a short time later with a promise to return.

Diane's tiny foot tapped an impatient staccato on the wooden walk as she watched Peter tie the large package to the saddle of his horse. "I don't understand why we didn't bring a buckboard."

"Dakota said you needed the riding experience.

That's why we came on horseback," he said.

Exasperated, she put her hands on her hips. "Well, just how are we supposed to get all these packages back to the ranch?"

"Dakota said that whatever we can't carry, Mr. Godfrey will bring later."

Diane's mouth pursed into a pout. *"Dakota said, Dakota said.* Is that all you can say?" Having been caught with Rafe in the woods, Diane felt deep resentment toward Dakota. "I don't see why we have to do what *Dakota* says."

Satisfied the packages were secure, Peter turned to offer an explanation. "Because he's in charge of the expedition. My father has always emphasized that good leadership is the crux of every successful operation. Dakota has the knowledge and skills to ensure such authority. I'm comfortable with him as our commandant."

"That's your problem, Peter," she carped. "You're comfortable with anyone making a decision for you. That way, you don't have to make one yourself."

"An unjust assessment, my dear Diane, and most unkind."

"Well, *my* father always insisted that if diplomacy doth fail, then the truth must prevail." She looked like a spoiled, petulant little girl.

Since 'diplomacy' was simply not Diane's forte, Peter found the remark amusing. She had been complaining about one thing or another from the moment they left the ranch. While Dakota had listened to her griping in silence, he had left the couple on their own as soon as they reached the town. Now Peter had to bear her ill-tempered logic alone.

Peter sighed in resignation. Since his arrival from Washington, he had had ample opportunity to observe how much Diane embraced many of her mother's characteristics.

A long, low whistle sounded from a trio of cowboys lounging against a nearby building. When he glanced in their direction, Peter saw Rafe Catlin among them. The men were whispering and laughing together, and it became obvious from the lewd leers in her direction that Diane was the object of the conversation.

With a mocking smile, Rafe doffed his hat. "Afternoon, Miz Collingswood. You're looking a might pur-r-r-r-ty today. Ain't she, boys?" He nudged the man next to him. Grinning wolfishly, the men nodded in agreement.

"I was just commentin' to the boys here, I bet every inch of you is as purty and pink as that purty, pink face of yours. Is that true, Miz Collingswood?"

Diane blushed and hung her head, but Peter walked over to the group and stood before Rafe. "Where I come from, Mr. Catlin, we do not address a woman with such disrespect. I suggest you apologize to Miss Collingswood at once."

"You said *address*. You mean *undress*, don't you?" Rafe smirked.

Before Rafe could move, Peter grabbed him by the shirt front and delivered a smashing blow that slammed the cowboy back against the building.

Diane screamed and buried her face in her hands when Catlin's cohort, Gulley Thomas, pulled out his Colt and pistol-whipped Peter on the side of the head. Peter sank to his knees.

Malevolence gleamed in Rafe's eyes as he wiped away the blood trickling from the corner of his mouth. "The dude's gonna pay for this."

However, before Rafe could take a step, Peter pulled him down. For several seconds the two men rolled on the ground, thrashing at one another. Finally ending up on top, Peter straddled Rafe and began to pummel the face of the troublemaker. Once again Gulley raised his pistol and struck Peter on the back of the head. The young man crumbled over.

Rafe shoved Peter's unconscious body aside. "Give it to him again," he snarled, crazed with rage.

Gulley raised the pistol to strike Peter when a shot rang out, and the gun dropped through the scoundrel's fingers. Dakota stood with a smoking Colt in his hands.

"You shot me!" Gulley stared down in disbelief at the blood oozing from his right palm. "You sonnabitch, you shot me."

"Be glad I didn't kill you," Dakota said impassively.

Several people rushed up to them, including Dr. Cooper, who began to examine the unconscious man on the ground. Sobbing, Diane knelt down beside Peter.

Walt Bellamy, the sheriff's deputy, shoved his way through the curious crowd that had begun to gather. "What's the shootin' about?"

"That 'breed shot one of my men," Rafe declared, pointing an accusing finger at Dakota.

"Is he dead?" Bellamy asked, glancing down at Peter.

"I'm the one's been shot," Gulley snarled, disgusted. "Take a look at my hand, Doc."

The doctor looked up with a cursory glance. "Bullet went clean through. Stop in my office and I'll wrap it up. Until then, pour some whiskey on the wound. This young man's head is in worse shape than your hand." He resumed his examination of Peter.

Bellamy cast a disgruntled look at Dakota. "What's yer story, MacDonald?"

Dakota sheathed his weapon. "Thomas was pistol-whipping the kid."

"He's lying, Deputy," Rafe avowed. "Me and the dude there was having a fair fight. Just cuz I was gettin' the upper hand, MacDonald butted in; he and the dude are friends. When Gulley here tried keepin' MacDonald out of the fight, the breed drew on him. Ain't that right, boys?" Rafe's cronies nodded in accord.

William Godfrey, who had hurried over from the bank, arrived in time to hear Catlin's explanation. "I've known Dakota MacDonald most of his life. He wouldn't draw on a man without good cause."

Bellamy scanned the crowd. "Anyone else see what happened?" None of the spectators had witnessed the incident. They all shook their heads. "Whata 'bout you, lady?" he asked Diane.

"Yeah, Miz Collingswood, tell 'em straight. You saw what happened." The underlying warning in Rafe's voice caused Diane to glance up in alarm.

Catlin's slitted stare dared her to tell the truth. Diane knew that if she contradicted him, Rafe wouldn't hesitate to tell a tall tale about their dalliance in the woods.

"Yes . . . he's telling the truth," she stammered. Diane hung her head and shifted her guilty glance to Dakota. His fixed stare remained unchanged.

"This young man needs stitching. Couple of you boys help me get him to my office," the doctor ordered. Gulley and his companion jumped forward at once. After they assisted a dazed Peter to his feet, Diane and the men moved off with Henry Cooper.

"Let's have yer gun, MacDonald," Bellamy declared. "Got no choice but to lock ya up."

Will Godfrey was indignant. "Good Lord, Bellamy. You mean you're locking up Dakota for shooting one of those hoodlums in the hand! Where's Sheriff Richards?"

"Sheriff's in Rapid City. Due back on the mornin' stage. I'm lockin' up MacDonald till then."

"I'll vouch for Dakota, Deputy. Turn him over to me until the sheriff returns. There's no call to put him behind bars."

"Who's wearin' the badge, deputy? You or the banker?" Rafe jeered.

Walt Bellamy was far from the brightest of people. Orphaned at ten by a Sioux raid, he had stopped schooling and drifted from one odd job to another until two years before when he became the deputy sheriff. Bellamy loved the position, and the tender-hearted sheriff overlooked the man's shortcomings to allow him to keep the job.

Despite the fact that Rafe Catlin continually got into one fracas after another, Bellamy's hatred for Indians, coupled with the knowledge that Rafe Catlin was the son of the most powerful rancher in the territory, proved to be enough persuasion for the gullible deputy.

"Give me yer gunbelt, MacDonald," he ordered in a gruff voice.

"Sorry, son," Will said solemnly as Dakota unstrapped the belt and gave it to the lawman.

With Dakota's weapon safely in hand, Bellamy bravely drew his own Colt and pointed the pistol at his prisoner. "Let's git goin'."

"Put that gun away," Will demanded. "It won't be necessary. The man's already surrendered to you." Helpless to prevent the injustice, Will followed the two men to the jailhouse, then hurried over to the doctor's office.

The jail consisted of two rooms, one an office containing a desk, chair, and a corner cot. A heavy iron door opened into a back room, which held two small cells.

Both cells were empty until Bellamy shoved Dakota into one of them. "Git in there and don't be causin' any trouble." He slammed the door and turned the key. "Got the whole place to yerself," he snorted as he returned to the office, locking the iron door behind him.

The deputy plopped down in the chair, put his feet on the desk, and closed his eyes. He was snoozing when Godfrey returned to the jail and woke him up a short time later.

"Well, now, if yer gonna hang around here all afternoon, I guess I'll hafta pin a badge on ya, so's I kin go home," Bellamy snickered.

"I would like to talk to your . . . prisoner," Will informed him coldly.

Bellamy tossed Will the keys. "Don't open his cell. Ya got five minutes." He pulled his hat over his eyes, leaned back, and resumed his snooze.

Dakota was stretched out on a narrow cot when the banker came in. At the sight of Will, he got to his feet. "How's Brent?"

"Doc took some stitches. Said he'd be okay but wanted to keep him here tonight. I'm taking Diane back to the ranch. She's waiting outside in the buckboard. 'Case you're wondering, I put up your horses in the livery for the night. Is there anything I can get you before I go?"

Dakota shook his head. "I appreciate what you're doing." Will hesitated, feeling as if he were abandoning Dakota. "Seth Richards is not the damn fool that Bellamy is. As soon as he gets back, I'll get you out of here, son."

"Well, if the sheriff does get back tomorrow morning, I figure there's no reason why we still can't leave as we planned."

Godfrey reached through the bars and the two men shook hands. "I'll see you first thing in the morning."

Bellamy was snoring when Will came out. He tossed the keys on the desk as he left.

Chapter Eighteen

Maggie was sitting astride Blaze, exercising the mare, when Will and Diane returned to the Lazy H. Seeing Will driving, and no sign of Dakota or Peter, Maggie knew there had been trouble. Katherine and Taylor had the same thought, for they were outside by the time Will reined up the buckboard in front of the house.

As Maggie dismounted, Diane jumped down from the seat and rushed past her into Katherine's arms. "What is it, dear? Where's Peter?" Her worried glance swung to William Godfrey.

His grim countenance did nothing to alleviate her fears. "'Fraid I've got some bad news, folks."

"Good Lord, it's Peter, isn't it?" Katherine exclaimed. At the identical moment Maggie cried out, "Something's happened to Dakota!"

The worried and besieged man didn't know which woman to respond to first. Taylor saved him by stepping forward and taking Godfrey's arm. "Let's all go inside and you can tell us what's happened."

Once seated on the comfort of the settee, Will broke the news to them. "Peter got involved in a fight with some men from the Circle C. When one of them pistol-whipped the boy, Dakota shot the fellow in the hand. Peter's at the doctor's now. Doc said he'll be fine in the morning, but . . . Dakota's in jail."

"In jail!" Maggie was aghast.

"Deputy locked him up for using a gun. Soon as the sheriff gets back, I'll get him out."

"Are you certain there's nothing seriously wrong with Peter?" Katherine asked, alarmed. "I'd never forgive myself if anything happened to that dear boy."

"Me either," Diane blubbered into her mother's shoulder.

"Doc took a couple of stitches. Said he'd be fine in the morning," Will reassured them.

Maggie still did not understand the series of events. "I don't see why Dakota's in jail if he was only trying to protect Peter."

"Because that deputy is a fool," Will said, "and if he did have any sense, he'd be downright dangerous."

Taylor stood with his hands clasped behind his back and stared out of the window as Will continued to fill them in on the details of the situation. He turned back to the troubled group. "Well, it appears there's nothing further any of us can do today. Mr. Godfrey and I will clear up this matter in the morning."

"Oh, but in the meantime, it's fine if Dakota sits in jail," Maggie spouted in a burst of temper.

"Margaret," Taylor said patiently, "Mr. Godfrey has explained the whole story. We're dealing with local politics here. If the sheriff doesn't return by tomorrow, I'll send a few telegrams. I'm certain that with my connections in Washington, we will get Dakota released and this matter fully resolved." He offered his characteristic, placative smile. "I'm sure you can use a drink, Will."

He was about to move away from the window when he stopped, pushing the curtain aside. "What's this? Look's like we're getting another visitor."

Godfrey came over to the window and peered out to see the approaching rider. "Why that's Dave Hutchins, one of the tellers at the bank." Godfrey hurried out the door, followed by everyone in the room.

The new arrival appeared to have ridden hard; his eyes were bright with excitement as he hopped off his sweating horse. "I was told you headed out here to the Lazy H, Mr. Godfrey, and I tried to catch up with you. I overheard something in town while I was standing at the bar of the Pink Palace, just having a drink. I usually don't eavesdrop on people, but when I heard them mention Dakota MacDonald, I thought you would want to know."

Hutchins was known for digressing during a conversation. Godfrey tried to hurry him along. "I appreciate your effort, son, but get on with it."

"Well, Rafe Catlin and four of the Circle C riders"—his mouth grimaced in disgust—"Gulley Thomas among them, were standing next to me with their heads together. They're up to no good, Mr. Godfrey."

"Yes, yes. And?" Will began to mop impatiently at his brow.

"Will you please tell us what they said?" Maggie butted in. She wanted to physically shake the words out of the man.

Offended, Hutchins looked at the girl. "Rafe told the others they'd be settling the score with Dakota MacDonald tonight."

"I thought you said Mr. MacDonald is in jail," Katherine remarked to Will.

"That's not worth a hill of beans with the deputy we've got. I'm getting back to town." Will headed for the buckboard.

Without thinking twice, Maggie knew what she was going to do. She ran into the house to grab her hat. Taylor followed her and stopped the girl. "I think you should stay out of this, Maggie. There could be trouble. I'll go back to town with Godfrey."

"Father, I plan on building a life in this territory. Whatever happens to Dakota affects the Lazy H, too. I belong with him now."

He saw the determination in her face and for several seconds hesitated, torn by his concern for her safety. Finally, he took her in his arms. "I guess you're right." With a poignant smile, he looked down at her. "You've grown up quickly, Margaret."

Tears glistened in his eyes as he hugged her. "We've lost the old Maggie, haven't we? You're not our little girl any longer."

Maggie stepped back and smiled at him through the tears misting her own eyes. "Don't you mean your little *boy*, Father?" She kissed his cheek.

Taylor cleared his throat and slipped an arm around her shoulder as he led her outside. "Well, if I were owner of this spread, I'd take a few ranch hands to town with me."

He winked and grinned. "Thank you, Father. I love you." Maggie kissed his cheek again, ran over to Blaze and quickly mounted the horse.

She rode down to the stable, where she found two of the hands cleaning the stalls. "Where's the rest of the crew?"

"They're all up on the north range, Miz Collingswood. Fencing has to be put up for the winter."

"Dakota's in trouble. He's been put in jail, and I need your help."

Without hesitation, the two men dropped the shovels and strapped on their gunbelts. Within minutes, the two had mounted and were headed for Deadwood with Maggie riding between them.

An hour past sunset, Rafe Catlin and four of his men sauntered into the jailhouse. They found Bellamy slouched in the chair, boozed out and asleep. Rafe roughly slapped the sleeping man's feet off the desk.

The deputy sat up and yawned as he scratched at the stubble on his face. "Whataya doin' here, Rafe?"

"Just came to talk to the breed." He picked up the ring of keys from the desk. "Ain't it about time you made your rounds, Deputy?"

Still in a stupor, Bellamy stumbled over to the window. Squinting, he peered out. "Well, I'll be goddamned. Reckon yer right. Sun's set already."

"Have a drink while yer at it." Rafe smirked and flipped him a coin.

Bellamy snatched the coin from the air and grinned with pleasure. "Gee, thanks, Rafe. Don't mind if I do." He picked up a rifle. "Don't forgit to lock up afta ya."

Finding Dakota asleep when they entered his cell, they yanked him to his feet. He tried to struggle, but there was no place to move in the tiny cell. Shoving him back against the wall, two of the men held his arms above his head.

With undisguised malice, Rafe Catlin grinned at his captive. "Shoe's on the other foot, ain't it, Breed?" Held upright with his arms pinned against the wall, Dakota could not defend himself from the blow Rafe delivered to his stomach.

Dakota gasped as the air went out of him, and he doubled over feeling his body had been cut in half. Rafe smashed him with an upper cut on the jaw that slammed Dakota's head against the wall. Pain pierced his head as he felt and heard the bone crunch in his nose. The brute continued to deal several more blows to Dakota's face and stomach, until blood trickled from the beaten man's nose and the corners of his mouth; he could barely breathe. Blood from a broken gash on his forehead streamed into his eyes, obstructing his vision.

Puffing heavily from exertion, Rafe stepped back. "Give him more of the same," he snarled. "Make the bastard beg for mercy."

Another one of the men picked up the assault. Soon Dakota was beyond resistance, his arms and legs limp and his head slumped on his chest, swirling in a semi-conscious state which blocked out every sensation except pain.

The man finally stopped his blows and stepped back. "He ain't gonna beg, Rafe." He waited, his chest heaving and his hand clenched in a fist covered with Dakota's blood.

"All right. Let's get out of here before that fool deputy comes back," Rafe ordered. The two men released their prisoner and Dakota, still conscious, crumpled to the floor.

Gulley Thomas pulled out his Colt. "I've got a score to settle, too," he growled. "Hold out his hand."

"Make sure that shot don't go wide," one grumbled as he lifted Dakota's wrist. Dakota's body jerked spasmodically when Gulley fired a shot through the hand of the helpless man.

Rafe walked over to the slumped figure and grabbed a fistful of hair. He jerked up Dakota's head and leered down into his face.

"Get out of this territory, Breed, or next time you won't be so lucky."

Dakota had not issued a sound throughout the beating, but he rallied the thin shred of his remaining strength. "You should have finished the job, Catlin."

Rafe, too reckless to grasp the ominous warning, sneered and spat in Dakota's face.

Laughing, the men trooped out. "Don't forget to lock up, boss," Gulley snickered and tossed the keys on the desk.

Rafe Catlin and his men had left Deadwood by the time the riders from the Lazy H rode up to the jailhouse. Bellamy, stretched asleep on the corner cot, jumped up in surprise when the party thundered into the room demanding to see his prisoner. The deputy looked bleary-eyed at the strangers, William Godfrey being the only man he recognized. Trying to exert authority, he crossed his arms and barked, "It's too late for visitin'."

Taylor Collingswood began to recite legal statutes to the illiterate lawman, and his words and commanding presence easily intimidated the perplexed deputy. Dropping his arms and grumbling under his breath, Bellamy shuffled over to the desk for the keys.

When Bellamy unlocked the outer door, Maggie could see Dakota laying in a heap on the floor. She cried out and ran to the cell.

"Go get Doc Cooper and hurry," Godfrey ordered one of the ranch hands. He turned his full fury on the deputy. "My God, the boy has been beaten senseless. He could be bleeding to death." His hands clenched into fists. "I'll have your hide for this."

Shocked by the prisoner's condition, Bellamy looked near to tears. "I dinn't know he wuz hurt. He wuz okay when I left on my rounds."

His hand shook so hard that Bellamy fumbled

clumsily as he tried to unlock Dakota's cell. When he finally succeeded, Maggie brushed past the bumbling deputy and knelt on the floor. "He's still breathing, Father," she said, relieved.

"Careful," Taylor cautioned as she laid Dakota's head on her lap. Maggie looked up, tears streaking her cheeks. "He's bleeding everywhere."

The sound penetrated the barrier of blackness and pain. "Maggie." The word came out in a rasped whisper. Dakota opened his eyes.

He tried to see through a haze that shifted from black to gray, then to an obscure image. Dakota blinked several times and the image finally took shape. It was Maggie's face.

"Don't try to move," she told him, forcing a smile.

William Godfrey knelt down beside her. "Doc Cooper will be here soon, son. Who did this to you?"

"Never mind. I'll handle it," Dakota said. He tried to sit up but fell back with a fresh shock of pain. "Damn! I think my rib's busted."

"Then just lie still," Maggie scolded. Dakota tried to smile, but the effort only made his split lip begin to bleed again.

Henry Cooper rushed in, pushing through several people helplessly standing around.

"You're busted up pretty bad, Dakota," he said after a cursory examination. "I have to get you to my office." He motioned to the grim-faced men who were watching. "Let's get him on that cot, boys, and we'll carry him over."

Dakota would have none of it. He forced himself

to sit up. "I'll get there on my own. Just give me a minute to get my legs under me."

Frustrated, Maggie watched him struggle to his feet, brushing aside offers of help from anyone. Slowly, but unaided, Dakota walked out on his own power. Taylor put his arm around Maggie's shoulder and they followed the others.

Will's wrath erupted against the pallid and shocked deputy, who continued to express his innocence. "I dinn't know. I swear, I dinn't know he wuz hurt."

"Who did this to him?" Godfrey demanded.

The deputy stammered, afraid to tell. The name of Catlin carried too much weight in the territory to make an enemy of Rafe. Bellamy hung his head. "I . . . I . . . don't know. I didn't see nothin'." He looked up pleadingly at Godfrey. "I swear, I dinn't. I'd of stopped 'em, if I had."

Will's eyes were cold with contempt. "Well you sure as hell know who did it. Rafe Catlin and his boys beat Dakota near to death, didn't they?" Bellamy hesitated. "Didn't they?" Will demanded.

"Could be, I reckon. They wuz here when I went on my rounds. Rafe said he jist wanted to talk to MacDonald." Bellamy sat down and began to sniffle. "I dinn't know they wuz gonna hurt him. Had I know'd, I wouldn't of let it happen. I'm a lawman."

Disgusted, Godfrey stormed away to catch up with the others.

Chapter Nineteen

"I suggest you boys all go and have a drink," Doc Cooper announced outside his office. "There's nothing any of you can do until I patch him up." Then he turned to Maggie. "I'd appreciate your giving me a hand, Miss."

When it appeared none of the men was going to budge, Taylor started to herd the group toward the nearest saloon. "Let's listen to the doctor. Come on, boys, I'm buying the drinks." The men were easily persuaded. Taylor added a final word to Maggie. "Honey, let us know as soon as the doctor finishes."

When they entered the small office, Maggie was surprised to see Peter asleep in a corner bed. In all the excitement over Dakota, she had forgotten about Peter Brent's injury. Undisturbed, the young man slept on blissfully.

The doctor pointed to a long table in the center of the room. "Climb on that table over there, Dakota, if you can."

Dakota sat down on the examination table, his long legs dangling over the edge. "Appears as if there's nothing wrong with your legs," Cooper remarked. Dakota didn't answer. He ached too much to be sociable.

"Young lady, I want you to fill this basin with water. You'll find a clean cloth over there in the drawer." Maggie quickly complied as the doctor began pulling instruments out of a cabinet.

He put the instruments in a metal tray and poured disinfectant over them. "Get that shirt off him, then start sponging the blood from his hands and face. Can't tell what's under it."

Maggie tried to remain detached as she unbuttoned Dakota's shirt. However, she felt his steady stare and could not look up to meet his dark eyes. Gingerly, she eased the shirt off his shoulders and down his arms. As she did, Maggie was inundated by memories of the previous night and the feel of those shoulders and arms beneath her fingertips.

The doctor's order to Dakota jolted her back to the present. "Lie down while I check your ribs."

She watched as the doctor carefully probed the tender rib cage. "Think you're lucky, son. Can't tell positively, but no ribs appear to be broken. By tomorrow, you'll be able to tell for sure. I'll bind you to ease the pain, just in case."

He helped Dakota to sit up and then wrapped several yards of gauze around him. "It will be painful for you to breathe, so you can't be busting any mustangs for a while."

Maggie couldn't avoid making eye contact with Dakota as she sponged away the blood from his face and head. He sat motionless and, as usual, expressionless. He was in pain, but whatever he felt or thought remained hidden behind the mask.

The squat figure of Doc Cooper blocked her sight of Dakota as the physician examined his patient's head and face. "Can't do much for your nose, son; afraid it's broken. But I'll put a couple stitches on your head here." Within minutes the doctor completed the task. "You can put his shirt back on him now," he said to Maggie.

As she held up the garment, Dakota slipped his arms back into the sleeves. "I can do that," he murmured when she began to button the shirt. They were the first words he had spoken since entering the room.

He made a feeble attempt with his wounded hand, then dropped it and struggled left-handed. "Let's see that hand of yours," Cooper declared.

Somberly, the doctor examined Dakota's hand. "What is this? A bullet wound?" Dakota nodded and Cooper shook his head in disgust. "As long as you boys keep putting holes into one another, guess I'll have to keep patching you up. I'll clean it out and see what we have here. This is going to hurt."

Maggie flinched when the doctor poured disinfectant into the wound. Her gaze locked with Dakota's in an outpouring of love and sympathy. She wanted to hold him, just to let him know she was hurting, too.

The doctor picked up the forceps from the tray and carefully probed the wound. Maggie's eyes must have registered her emotional upheaval. "It's not any worse than branding, Maggie," Dakota murmured, reminding her of their conversation the previous day.

Dr. Cooper took the instrument out of the wound and examined it. Maggie cringed, but Dakota leaned forward to get a closer look. "What did you find, Doc?"

"Well . . . it appears the bullet glanced off the third metacarpal and this here is a shattered fragment."

"The third what?" Dakota asked.

"Bone," the doctor answered as he continued to examine the wound. "Let me see you move your fingers." Dakota slowly moved each finger. "Well, I'll be damned. You got enough luck for a whole tribe. Far as I can see, this will mend if you keep it clean. Take awhile, though."

Cooper began to wrap Dakota's hand in gauze. "Here, young lady, finish this for me," he said to her, handing Maggie the roll.

Looking at Dakota's battered face and body was almost more than Maggie could bear. She shifted her eyes downward and knotted the ends of the bandage, then quickly stepped away when she had finished.

"You boys have kept me busy tonight," Cooper said. He poured water into a basin and began to scrub his hands. "Got a problem where to put you."

"He can have this bed, Doctor." Unobserved, Peter Brent had awakened. He rose to his feet.

"Not necessary. I'm going back to the ranch," Dakota said.

Doctor Cooper grimaced. "I figured you'd say that. It's a long ride, Dakota."

"I know how long it is." Dakota dug into his pocket and handed the man a coin. "Thanks for patching me up, Doc." He put on his Stetson and walked out the door.

"Wait for me, I'm going back with you," Peter called to him. He stopped to grin at Maggie. "It looks like a lot's been happening while I've been asleep."

"I wash my hands of both you," Cooper snorted. "You two crazy fools can do what you want. Me, I'm going to bed." Then, with a second thought, the doctor hollered after Dakota. "Mind you . . . no infection . . . keep it clean."

Maggie shrugged helplessly and threw her hands in the air. "I can't do anything with them, Doctor. Thank you for all of your help."

"You see that Dakota gets to bed, Miss Collingswood. And, young lady, thanks for your help. You're a good nurse. If you're ever looking for work, I can use you."

Embarrassed but pleased, Maggie smiled and ran after the two men.

As they sat in the Pink Palace, no one could convince Dakota to remain in Deadwood for the night. Finally, in defeat, the two Lazy H hands were sent to the livery to get the horses that had been left there earlier that day.

Nevertheless, Will continued with the effort to

change Dakota's mind. "You should rest tonight. Come home with me."

Dakota shook his head. "I'm finishing my drink and heading back."

"Stubborn as ever," Maggie commented to herself.

Dakota put his glass down and glanced in irritation at her. "What did you say?"

"That you're a stubborn jackass." Maggie snorted in disgust.

Every bone in his body ached. He felt mean and ornery, in no mood to take her sass. "What in hell are you doing in this bar, anyway?"

Maggie glared defiantly at him. "What do you expect me to do, stand outside the door waiting for you?"

His irritation redirected toward the obstinate girl, Dakota forgot about his wounds and shoved his hat back on his head. He flinched with pain from the effort. "This is no place for a woman."

In the past week, this man had put her through hell. Maggie felt that if anyone had the right to be angry, it was she. "I've got as much right to be in here as you do," she snapped right back.

"Which is no right at all. Indians aren't allowed liquor, so your argument's not worth spit in the wind," he groused.

"Then why are you here? I swear, Dakota Mac-Donald, you go around breaking the law for the pure pleasure of it."

Taylor cleared his throat. "It's a long ride home and an even longer trail into those hills. I don't think you two should start quarreling with each other now." In truth, he was enjoying the spat between them as much as Will Godfrey, who grinned from ear to ear as he listened.

Peter Brent appeared to be the only person who took the quarrel seriously. He looked genuinely distressed.

Petulance drove Maggie to a bolder tack. "As a matter of fact, I have decided that as long as I'm here, I'm going to have a drink." She lifted her chin defiantly and motioned to the man behind the bar. "A drink of whiskey, please."

The disapproving bartender poured the liquor, walked over to their table, and put down the drink in front of her. "Last woman who ordered a whiskey in my place was Calamity Jane. And she weren't no lady."

Maggie regarded the man with one of her classic glares. "Well, sir, in my short stay to date here in Deadwood, I have observed that the citizens of this town spend a considerable amount of their time judging other people's actions rather than looking to their own and, furthermore, minding their own business. Therefore, when I want your opinion, sir, I will ask for it."

The barkeep walked away scratching his head, unsure of what she had said, and the four men at the table watched in astonishment as Maggie raised the glass to her mouth and gulped down the whiskey in one swallow. As the acid sting shot up to her eyeballs, Maggie opened her mouth and frantically gasped for breath.

Both Taylor and Godfrey looked on speechless, while Dakota's dark eyes became charged with anger. "What in the hell are you doing?"

Again, Peter Brent responded with an opposite reaction by staring at Maggie in sheer admiration. "Miss Margaret, that was awesome. Truly awesome."

Maggie thought she would never be able to speak again. How could they just sit there watching when surely everything from her eyes to her vocal chords was on fire?

Taylor finally took pity and leaned across the table. "Are you all right, Margaret?"

"I'm . . . I'm . . ." She cleared her throat. "I'm fine." Her voice had lowered an octave.

"Reckon we better get her out of here before we have to carry her out," Dakota grumbled.

About to rise, Dakota's attention became fixed on the stairway. Gulley Thomas was coming down the stairs, after visiting one of the upstairs rooms, and whispering into the ear of a giggling floozie.

Dakota slid his hand to his hip, remembering too late that his gunbelt was still at the Sheriff's office. "Give me your gun belt, Will." He never took his eyes off the figures on the stairway.

Unaware of Dakota's presence, Thomas and the blonde on his arm stopped at the bar. Will turned his head to see the reason for the strange request and immediately guessed Dakota's intent. "Think, man—you're in no condition for a fight."

"Give me your belt, Will," Dakota repeated with deadly calm.

"You're not giving it to him!" Maggie exclaimed in disbelief when Godfrey unstrapped the heavy belt and slipped it across the table. "He's going to get himself killed."

Dakota awkwardly strapped on the belt, then

checked the chamber of the gun. He flexed his hand several times in an effort to ease the stiffness. "The rest of you clear out of here."

"I'm staying," Will replied. "Mr. Collingswood, take Maggie and Brent out of here."

Peter was offended by the implication that he belonged to the class which needed protection. "I intend to remain. I'm not a child, Mr. Godfrey."

Maggie echoed the sentiment. "Nor am I."

"Get the hell out of here, Maggie," Dakota growled.

She stood adamant. "I'll leave when you do."

"Haven't you any control over her?" Dakota snapped at Taylor. He could feel his strength waning.

"Maggie has always been her own person. I can only guide her, not lead her," Taylor answered.

"Get out, Maggie." This time the tone of Dakota's tacit command shattered her resistance. Frustrated, Maggie rose to leave. "All of you," Dakota added.

"Damn it, Dakota—" Will Godfrey stopped in mid-protest.

Laughing, Gulley had turned around. His smile froze at the sight of Dakota. The gazes of the two men locked on one another—Dakota's steady and unrelenting, Gulley's one of terror as he faced certain death.

Taylor pulled Maggie protectively into a corner as Peter and Will stepped away from the table. Not a word had been exchanged between the two enemies, yet the small room was suddenly immobilized by tension. All eyes were on the two adversaries.

Like a trapped ferret, Gulley's fearful glance darted around the room as he sought an ally.

"They're not here, Gulley. You're on your own," Dakota said calmly.

"I—I got a bum hand." Gulley held up his bandaged hand.

Dakota grinned and raised his own hand, swathed in gauze. "Looks like a fair fight."

A sheen of cold sweat began to dot Gulley's forehead. "It wasn't my idea. It was Rafe Catlin's."

"You put the bullet through my hand," Dakota said unrelenting.

The cowardly bully raised his hands in the air and began to back away. "I ain't gonna draw on you, Dakota. You can't make me."

It was obvious to all that Gulley wouldn't defend himself. Dakota's hands were tied. "Then start riding and don't stop 'til you're out of the territory. The next time I see you, I'm going to kill you."

Gulley half ran, half stumbled to the door. Suddenly, without warning, he spun and drew his gun. With the speed of lightning, Dakota's Colt cleared the holster. He fanned the hammer of the gun with his left hand and put three shots into the treacherous gunman before the coward could get off a shot. Gulley was dead before he hit the floor.

Walt Bellamy lurched through the doors of the barroom with a drawn pistol. He saw Gulley's body, and the deputy blanched at the sight of the Colt in Dakota's hand.

"Gulley drew first and tried to gun down Dakota, Deputy," Will Godfrey informed him. "We all saw what happened."

Dakota sheathed the weapon and unstrapped the

belt. He returned it to Will and walked to the door.

"Where do ya think yer goin'?" Bellamy asked.

Dakota turned back to the deputy. "Tell the sheriff he can find me at the Lazy H." He walked out the doors.

Still huddled in her father's arms, Maggie remained stunned by the savagery she'd witnessed. Everything about the evening had convinced her of one fact: nothing she had read in her Beadle's Dime Library had prepared her for this night's violence. Life in the Wild West was not as romantic as she had once thought it to be.

Chapter Twenty

Near dawn, a tired and quiet group returned to the Lazy H. The long ride from town had taken a heavy toll on Dakota. Now, weak and stiff, he could barely climb off his horse.

The painful effort was not missed by Taylor. He walked over to Dakota and took his arm. "I think you would be more comfortable here at the house. Margaret, please take him inside so he can get some rest." Dakota accompanied her docilely, too tired to offer any resistance.

As soon as they entered, Katherine hurried into the room and rushed into Taylor's arms. "I've been so worried about you." She turned to Peter and pressed a kiss to his cheek. "I'm so glad to see you back safely. Diane has been frantic with worry. The poor girl has finally fallen asleep. We were all so upset when we heard about the trouble in town. How is your head, Peter?"

The night's events had left the young man feeling quite subdued. "I'm fine, Mrs. Collingswood." He nodded politely. "If you don't mind, I think I'll retire."

As Maggie started to assist Dakota down the hallway, Peter hurried over to them and put a hand under the injured man's elbow. "Here, let me help you."

Katherine raised a brow in query. "Where are you taking him?"

"To his room. I insist that Dakota remain here until he recovers from his wounds," Taylor informed her.

A reserved, straight-line smile appeared on Katherine's mouth as her glance of admonishment swept her husband. "But Taylor, Peter is occupying Mr. MacDonald's former room."

"Dakota can have my room, Mother. I'll sleep with Diane," Maggie quickly interjected.

Taylor sighed, relieved to see the issue easily resolved. "It appears Margaret has the situation well in hand. Shall we retire, my dear? I, for one, am exhausted. This has been a long day for all concerned." He took Katherine's arm and hastily escorted her away before she could voice another objection.

Once inside the bedroom, Maggie lit the lamp while Peter helped Dakota to the bed. "I'm thirsty," Dakota murmured.

"Right on it, old man." Peter left the room and returned with a glass of water.

After taking a sip, Dakota grimaced. "This what Princeton boys favor?"

Peter chuckled at his own lack of consideration. "Well, perhaps a dram of whiskey could be considered medicinal."

"I'll get it," Maggie offered and hurriedly left the room. When she returned, she saw Dakota lying in bed under a blanket with his eyes closed. Peter stood nearby holding Dakota's boots and pants. "Thank you, Peter," she whispered, and then, so Dakota could not hear, she mouthed the words, "I'll take those." She put the glass on the bedside table and left the room with Dakota's clothing.

Within a few minutes, she came back carrying a pillow. "Do you need me for anything else?" Peter asked indulgently. When Maggie shook her head, Peter bade her goodnight and hastened away to catch up on his own sleep.

Feeling awkward and keenly aware that they were alone, Maggie began to rummage through the chest of drawers. "I'll be out of here in a minute."

As she collected her nightgown and robe, Maggie glanced over her shoulder and saw Dakota struggling to drink the whiskey. She hurried to the bed.

"Let me help you." Dakota lay back and, after fluffing the extra pillow, she put it under his head to enable him to gulp the liquor down in one swallow.

"Fastest cure known to man. Thanks, Maggie. I'm sorry about putting you out."

Maggie glanced at him to discover he was staring

at her. "This is your house, Dakota." She dropped her eyes. "I have noticed you don't allow others to shove you around. Why do you put up with such rudeness from my mother?"

When he didn't reply, she shifted her glance back to him. His eyes were closed. Maggie turned to extinguish the lamp, but Dakota reached out and grasped her hand.

"Maggie, I want to explain about last night. I never wanted to hurt you."

She blushed and looked down at a face bruised and battered from the savage beating. His dark eyes were unguarded, wounded and vulnerable. "I understand." Her knees felt weak from his nearness, and she turned her head away from the piercing gaze. "I'm not blaming you, Dakota. It was my fault. I threw myself at you."

"You were an innocent, Maggie. I knew what I was doing."

Forcing a smile, she turned her head and looked at him. "Well, I'm not an innocent any longer. And as I told you, my wounds heal quickly."

He stared sadly at her. Just a short time ago she had been so young, her green eyes filled with such trust and idealism. Maggie was a woman now— her purity replaced by disillusion. And Dakota knew that he was responsible.

"Some wounds leave deep scars, Maggie."

His grasp loosened, and his hand fell away. Maggie realized that he had dropped into slumber. She unfolded the comforter and put it over the blanket. For several moments, she remained at the bedside and stared down at the sleeping figure before she reached out and gently traced a finger along his swollen lip. "And your wounds lie deep, don't they, Dakota?"

Maggie did not feel ready to confine herself in a darkened bedroom, so she picked up the lamp and went to the kitchen. After brewing a cup of tea, she sat down desolately at the table trying to decide what to do.

If she remained at the Lazy H, her presence would drive Dakota away, denying him his rightful inheritance. She wondered if she had the fortitude to ride away from the ranch for his sake as easily as he apparently would have done for hers. That decision required more strength of character than she had. But not Dakota. And might his strength of character be the very reason he refused to commit himself to anyone? Only a man of character would be strong enough to hold the cards he had been dealt, as a half-breed and an outcast, and avoid entanglements which would hurt others.

Sighing deeply, she put her cup in the sink and picked up the lamp to return to the bedroom.

As she walked down the darkened hall, Maggie heard a sound from her bedroom. She shook her head in dismay. Had he gotten out of bed?

When she entered the room, she saw Dakota still asleep on the bed, and from his position she could tell he had not moved since she left. Perplexed, Maggie rechecked the hallway but found neither light nor sound coming from any room. No one appeared to be stirring.

Maggie was sure the sound she heard had come from the bedroom where Dakota lay sleeping. She went back in, put the candle on the table and glanced around the room. She became gripped by a feeling of uneasiness. Something was wrong; something was different.

Maggie shivered and crossed her arms to ward off the chill as she went to close the window. She stopped abruptly, stunned by the realization that the window hadn't been open when she went to the kitchen.

Her heart beat rapidly. She wanted to scream for help, but she thought no one would understand her panic about an open window.

She slammed down the window and her frightened eyes surveyed the yard. Bathed in moonlight, the area appeared deserted. The memory of the night she had felt watched from the trees came to mind. She glanced now at the very spot in the trees and caught a glimpse of movement. Or was it her imagination?

The open window left no doubt in her mind that someone lurked in the shadows of the Lazy H. Whoever it was had been frightened away—this time.

Maggie closed and locked the shutters, then sat down on a chair near the bed. She wouldn't leave Dakota alone and defenseless. If someone was after him, they would have to deal with her first.

A sudden bright shaft of sunlight woke Maggie and she sat up. Surprised, she saw her mother at the window. "My goodness, Margaret, why are you sitting in here with the shutters and window closed?" Katherine opened the shutters, raised the window and glanced back in disapproval at her daughter. "Have you sat up in that chair all night?"

Maggie rose to her feet and stretched her cramped muscles. "Just the last couple of hours, Mother."

"You told me you were sleeping in your sister's room. I've been looking for you."

Maggie went to the bed and looked at Dakota. He was still sleeping soundly. "I intended to, then decided I would sit up for a while. I guess I fell asleep."

"This is the last place I expected to find you. We're waiting for you to join us for breakfast. Freshen up and change your clothing."

"Go ahead without me, please. I would like to take a bath."

Katherine appeared indignant. "And how is Yen Ching to do that and serve breakfast, too? You can't expect us to wait for our meal while he prepares you a bath. We've waited long enough already."

Maggie sighed in exasperation. Her mother could turn the most minor issues into major battles. "Then I'll wait, Mother. I can eat with Dakota when he wakes up."

"Very well, Margaret. Do as you wish. You usually do." Annoyed, Katherine departed without a backward glance.

A short while later Yen Ching popped his head through the open door. "Bath weady, Missy Collingswood. Yen Ching bwing bwekfast for you and Mistah Dakota." With his fast shuffle, he scurried over to the bed. The little man looked down at Dakota's bruised face and shook his head sadly. "Poor Mistah Dakota. He no look good."

Maggie moved to his side and gazed sorrowfully

at the sleeping man. "Is there anything we can put on his face to help heal those bruises?" Maggie asked.

He grinned and bobbed his head. "Mistah Dakota show Yen Ching leaf in fowest. Me go find. Leaf heal good." He smiled broadly. "You see, Missy. Leaf heal good." He quickly hurried away.

Maggie gathered together clean clothing for herself and headed toward the bathroom. When she returned a half hour later, Dakota was awake and sitting up. The comforter had been pushed to the bottom of the bed.

"Good morning. How are you feeling?" she said brightly.

He buried his head in his hands. "Like I've been trampled by a bull. Where are my boots?"

Grimacing with disapproval, Maggie answered saucily, "What do you intend to do with boots?"

Dakota lifted his head and cast a disgusted look in her direction. "I intend to polish them. What in hell do you think I intend to do with them?" he demanded. "And give me my pants."

Maggie put her hands on her hips. "No," she answered defiantly.

"Damn!" he cursed. He lay back and threw his arm over his eyes.

"I see that sleep hasn't improved your disposition. I thought snake bites and getting whomped in the head by a horse were the only things that bothered you."

"You can add noisy, pesterin', obstinate women to the list," he grumbled.

"Can I get you anything else?"

"You were easier to like when you were willing to take orders," Dakota barked.

Maggie smiled sweetly. "And you were easier to like when you weren't so free at giving them." Dakota glared at her. Amused at his frustration, Maggie thought that if looks were knives, she would have been pinned to the wall.

She encountered Peter in the hallway on his way to Dakota's room. "How is Dakota this morning?" the young man asked.

"About as pleasant as a cornered rattlesnake spewing venom," she complained. "I'd advise you to proceed at your own risk."

Dakota was still fuming when Peter tapped on the door and entered. "Good morning."

"Peter, where are my boots and pants?"

"Margaret took them, but I don't know where they are now. I heard you're not in the best of spirits this morning."

Dakota settled back against the pillows. "I just want out of here. Away from these troublesome women."

Peter sat down. "Observation has taught me that life is a great deal easier if you don't fight the women in it."

Dakota eyed him judiciously. "Well, it's a damn sight easier if you avoid them altogether." Both men laughed in accord.

Despite his aches and pains, Dakota relaxed. He liked Peter Brent. Through the years, Dakota had learned to recognize a man he could trust, and Brent was such a man. However, Dakota figured Brent still had a lot to learn about judging females.

Peter reached in a handshake. "I didn't get a chance to thank you for coming to my assistance yesterday in Deadwood. I'm sorry you ended up the worse for it."

"I'll be okay in a couple of days. How's your head?"

Peter grinned. "Slight headache, nothing more. Pays to have a rock for a head." He glanced at the door. "Oh, I see you're ready for our ride."

Dakota turned to see who had caught Peter's attention. Diane Collingswood stood white-faced in the doorway. She was clearly shocked by Dakota's condition. Until that moment, she hadn't given the wounded man's injuries any thought. Furthermore, she felt guilty for having lied about Dakota to the deputy. Her face reddened from shame, but Dakota chose not to make any comment.

"How are you feeling, Mr. MacDonald?" Diane felt a grudging admiration for him. Had it not been for Dakota's intervention, Peter could have been beaten just as much.

Dakota nodded, but his thoughts were glum. Too many people were coming in and out of the room. Dakota was convinced he must get back to the bunkhouse. There was no privacy here, and since that irritating pest had made off with his boots and trousers, virtually leaving him at her mercy, he figured he had more freedom in the Deadwood jail.

No sooner had the engaged couple departed then his nemesis strode boldly into the room carrying his saddlebags. Maggie dropped them on the floor. "I thought you could use a change of clothing, so I had these brought up from the bunkhouse. There's a hot bath waiting for you." Standing with hands on her hips, she dared him to voice an objection.

Once provoked, Dakota did not run from a fight. He leaned back, crossed his arms across his chest and studied her. "You gonna wash my back?" he drawled.

Maggie blushed, but wouldn't bow to intimidation. "If you won't allow Yen Ching to do it, I guess I'll have to."

"Well then, let's get started." He began to lower the blanket. Squealing, Maggie rushed from the room.

With a grin of victory, Dakota wrapped the comforter around him and wobbled to the bathroom.

Two days later, Sheriff Richards arrived at the Lazy H accompanied by William Godfrey. Maggie led the men to the bedroom. The steely-eyed lawman was grim as he handed Dakota his gunbelt. "No sense in holdin' on to this 'cause I know you'll only get another one. Ain't arrestin' you for gunning down Gulley Thomas, Dakota. Matter of fact, some folks in town were glad to see the end of him, and Will here says Gulley drew on you first."

Dakota accepted the belt, but remained silent.

Richards grimaced in disgust. "I can see what they did to you, boy, and I ain't sayin' you didn't have good cause to shoot Gulley. But Joe Catlin rode into town yesterday. Figures you'll be comin' after Rafe when you're back on your feet. What've you got in mind, Dakota?"

Dakota's expression remained inscrutable. "Reckon that's between Rafe and me, Sheriff."

"Damn it, boy, I'm tryin' to talk some sense into you. Rafe's his only son. Joe's not gonna let you kill him. You can't take on the whole Circle C."

"Ain't planning to," Dakota replied succinctly.

A glimmer of hope gleamed in the sheriff's eyes. "You sayin' you ain't goin' gunnin' for Rafe?"

"Didn't say that. I said it's between Rafe and me. If Joe's bringing in the Circle C, I can't stop him."

Richards exploded. "You hear me, and you hear me good, boy. I don't care how much lead you and Rafe want to pump into each other—but it better not happen in Lawrence County or you'll be dealin' with me." He turned to leave. "Talk some sense into him, if you can, Will."

Richards nodded politely at Maggie and doffed his hat. "Ma'am." He stormed out of the room.

"Sheriff's right, Dakota. You can't take on the Circle C."

Maggie waited expectantly for the reply. Dakota's thoughts remained unspoken as he leaned back and closed his eyes.

The following day, Maggie was sitting on the fence of the corral when Joe Catlin and a dozen riders from the Circle C crested the hill above the Lazy H. One of the ranch hands below spied them first and let out a loud whistle.

"Take a look at that, will ya?"

Maggie turned her head toward the hill. "Best get to the house, Miz Collingswood." The wrangler fast-tailed it to the bunkhouse to grab his rifle and warn the other hands to do the same.

Maggie ran to alert those in the house. Taylor

and Katherine hurried over to peer out a window when Maggie gave them the news. The riders were moving slowly down the hill.

"Oh, Good God!" Katherine exclaimed. "Don't tell me we're in the middle of a range war." She threw up her hands in dismay. "I can't believe this."

"Calm yourself, Katherine," Taylor said. "I'll go out to find out what they want."

"What *they* want!" Katherine exclaimed, aghast. She grabbed his arm. "Don't you dare step one foot outside. This isn't your problem, Taylor. It's his," she accused and pointed a finger at Dakota, who had just appeared, strapping on his gunbelt. Now, in the face of an imminent gun battle, Katherine had forgotten her previous claim of ownership to the ranch.

"Young man, I do not want any shooting," she informed Dakota. "You get out there and see what those people want."

Dakota had already gone through the door.

When Peter Brent grabbed a rifle to follow him, Katherine was appalled. "Peter, this is not your quarrel."

"I'm afraid you're wrong, Mrs. Collingswood. It was I who started the fight." He hurried outside, followed by Taylor.

Katherine exclaimed, aghast, "Oh, my God, what am I going to do?" She tried to stop Maggie, who had grabbed a rifle to follow them. "You're staying in here."

"The ranch is mine, too, Mother. I have as much at stake here as Dakota."

"And just what do you intend to do with that

rifle? You've never fired one before."

"They don't know that." Maggie shoved aside her mother's hand.

"They'll find out soon enough when the shooting starts," Katherine cried out as Maggie disappeared through the door. She rushed over to the window and peered out. "This is insanity."

Diane began to whimper. "What's going to happen, Mother?"

Fraught with anxiety, Katherine turned in exasperation to her whining daughter. "The damned fools are going to shoot one another."

The remark caused an even greater outburst from Diane. "But Peter is out there."

"So are your father and sister," Katherine snapped.

At that moment Yen Ching rushed in from the kitchen waving his meat cleaver. "No worly, Missy Collingwood. Yen Ching here to save you."

Helplessly, Katherine raised her eyes heavenward.

Outside, Dakota waited as the riders approached. Taylor and Peter stood a short distance behind him. Maggie watched from behind her father. The ranch hands, leaning against the walls of the stable and bunkhouse, were spread out. Despite the casual stance of the men, all their rifles were loaded and cocked.

"That's close enough," Dakota called out when the riders reached the bottom of the hill.

Joseph Catlin raised a hand and his men came to a halt. "Stay put, boys," he ordered in his gruff voice and prodded his horse in a slow gait over to Dakota.

"What do you want, Joe?" Dakota asked.

"Glad to see you up and around, son," Catlin said. When Dakota didn't respond, Catlin removed his hat and wiped the sweat off his brow with the sleeve of his shirt. "Came to say I'm sorry. I ain't proud of what Rafe did to ya."

"Okay, you've said it," Dakota replied.

The big man slammed the Stetson back on his head. "God damn it, Dakota, this ain't easy. Least you could do is offer a man a drink."

"I would, except we don't have enough for the army you brought with you."

Loud laughter erupted from the rancher's barrel chest. "They're just lookin' after me."

Catlin's gaze locked with Dakota's. "I figure decent folk oughta stick together. What with fightin' Injuns and nature, we got enough to do without fightin' each other. Got no quarrel with you, Dakota. Sam Harris and me were good friends. We started our spreads together. I watched you and Sam workin' side by side to turn the Lazy H into one of the best ranches in the territory. Sam loved you. You've always been a fair man, Dakota, even if you are part Injun."

Dakota ignored the lopsided compliment and let the rancher continue.

"My boy's headstrong. His ma and me have spoiled him rotten. I figure once yer back on yer feet, you'll come gunning for him 'cause of what he did to you. It 'ud break his ma's heart to see the boy dead, so I shipped him back East to my sister's. Hope she can pound some sense into him. Told her to get him into that Princeton school."

A crooked grin split the craggy face of the old

man as he cast a glance at Peter and winked. "'Pears to me they run pretty good stock through their pens."

He leaned over in his saddle and extended his hand. "I'm offerin' my hand to you, Dakota Mac-Donald."

Dakota hesitated. Then he reached out and accepted the old man's hand.

The tension spiraled out of the old man like air out of a balloon. Catlin leaned back in the saddle and grinned. "Hell, son, I'm as dry as a toad in the desert at high noon. Kin I have a drink now?"

Dakota returned the grin. "Reckon after the long blast of hot air you've been blowing, we're about ready for one. Come on into the house."

Catlin climbed down from his saddle and followed Dakota. He paused for a moment in front of Maggie. His weathered gray eyes studied her. "Hello, Maggie." She nodded. "Were you gonna use that rifle, gal?"

"If I had to," Maggie said.

Catlin chuckled. "No mistakin' yer Sam Harris's blood. He'd of been might proud of you, Maggie."

Katherine was so relieved when her family returned unscathed that she personally prepared a pitcher of lemonade. Joe Catlin thirstily gulped down the first glass. Then, much to the old man's relief, Taylor generously spiked the second glass with whiskey.

An hour later, Catlin and the Circle C riders rode away. Frowning, Maggie faced Dakota. Time and Yen Ching's poultice had improved his condition, and he looked much better. But Nurse Margaret had not released him from her care. "I hope you intend to return to bed."

"I've seen all of that bed I intend to." Then to her complete astonishment and shock, he leaned over and whispered into her ear, "Unless you're in it, Maggie."

Her mouth gaped open and her eyes rounded. With an outrageous grin, Dakota shoved his hat to the back of his head. "Don't you reckon it's high time we have us a treasure hunt?"

Chapter Twenty-one

"Doesn't matter who says what. We go tomorrow or not at all." Dakota walked from the library, through the dining area, and out the front door. The Collingswoods and Peter were startled by the only words Dakota had spoken in an hour. The trip had already been delayed a week to make certain Dakota was sound enough to travel. Having heard part of the after-dinner conversation from the library, Dakota had had his fill of talk, especially concerning his health.

"Well, I never!" Katherine exclaimed. "Just how are we going to tolerate that man's rudeness all the way up into those hills?"

Maggie quickly defended Dakota. "He's not rude, Mother. He just wants to get going."

"Yes, that's it exactly," Taylor concluded. "I've watched Dakota working in the stable the last several days. He appears to be fine now and not at all favoring his hand. I think we'd best do as Dakota says and leave tomorrow."

"Best do as Dakota says," Katherine mimicked her husband.

"Mother, do I really have to go?" Diane whined.

"Of course you have to go. Whatever are you thinking, Diane?"

"I hate riding a horse. And we'll be camping outside for days or weeks. I hate camping, and I hate to get dirty. I can't see why we don't all go back to Washington and let Margaret find her old treasure chest if that's what she wants to do."

"Diane, please. Don't be ridiculous." Katherine's impatience signaled the end of Diane's objections for the moment.

"Come on, Diane. The trek will be a lark," Peter said as he offered a hand to encourage Diane out of the chair. "You'll see. Imagine that we will have sun-warmed days and star-filled nights. And who knows—maybe a pot of gold at the end of the rainbow."

"A rainbow only appears after a torrent of rain, Peter." Diane had dampened the rosy picture, but not the young man's spirits.

"Then, 'Come ride with me and be my love,'" Peter misquoted, dramatically closing his eyes and putting a hand to his chest. "For we shall live by the shelter of the tent and the warmth of each other." He grinned infectiously. "Very poetic, wouldn't thou sayeth?"

"Oh, Peter, how you do run on," Diane droned as she got out of the chair.

"'Atta girl. I see thy pioneer spirit overfloweth."
Peter put an arm around her waist and smiled
cheerfully, while Diane put a dainty hand to her
mouth and yawned.

"'Tis best to commence before the dawn
breaketh," Peter continued in his teasing mood.

"Just what does that mean, Peter?"

"Let's go upstairs and pack our things."

"Good idea," Taylor agreed as he took
Katherine's arm.

Once in their room, Katherine asked, "Taylor,
whatever does Peter mean by, 'Imagine star-filled
nights' and 'Living by the warmth of each other?'"

"Oh, you know those college boys, Katherine.
He's just trying to be poetic, making the trip seem
exciting and romantic." Katherine raised a suspicious eyebrow. Smiling to himself, Taylor turned
away. Sometimes, Katherine appeared to have a
short memory.

Dakota had left the house and headed toward the
stable, but he changed direction when he saw Will
on the path to the woods. "Hold up, Will," he
called, running to catch up to the banker. "I've
decided, Will. We go tomorrow. Let's take care of
the mules tonight."

"Why, yes. Sounds fine to me, Dakota. I was
just . . . going to get Maggie a few wildflowers."
Will hastily explained his destination without having been asked. "Care to come along?"

"No, thanks. I'll be in the stable when you get
back."

Later, as they packed the mules, Dakota said,
"I've been thinking about this wild goose chase.

Sam did some wild things in his life, but sending me up into those hills with greenhorns on a treasure hunt beats all. You were Sam's lawyer, Will. Just what are we going to find up there? It seems plain loco to me for Sam to bury a fortune where anybody might come across it."

Busy strapping blankets on a mule, Will shrugged his shoulders and answered without turning around. "Have no idea, son. True, Sam and I were friends for many a year, and I made out his will. But try as I did to change his mind, Sam wouldn't share his thinking on this one." He chuckled fondly. "Didn't cotton to a dissenting opinion on this particular—ah, investment," he concluded as he fastened the strap. "There now. That's done. Be back shortly. Want to take these flowers to Maggie."

The party was unusually hushed the next morning when the group assembled to leave. Maggie sat atop Blaze and watched as Dakota checked the pack mules. She hunched deeper into her jacket in an attempt to ward off the morning dampness. The warming rays of the rising sun had not yet burned away the misty chill, and a cloud of vapor streamed above the circle of horses and mules as they snorted and pawed the ground.

Dakota came over to Blaze and adjusted the stirrups. He glanced up at Maggie. For a moment, their gazes were locked, but the thoughts that lay behind his dark eyes remained a mystery to Maggie.

The rest of the party had mounted and remained silent while he did the same for Diane and

277

Katherine. When he finished, Dakota spoke in low tones to the two hands who had saddled the horses, then he climbed on his mount and they moved out.

By late morning, the warmth of the sun necessitated the removal of jackets. Near noon, Dakota stopped them for lunch. Diane was the first of the subdued group to comment. "I hope this is where we're camping. I've had all the riding I want for one day."

Dakota said nothing, then went over to the pack mules to get the coffee and pot. "We're only stopping here for lunch, Diane," Peter explained indulgently.

Maggie, sitting under a tree, watched and listened. Peter treated Diane as patiently and lovingly as Taylor treated her mother. It seemed to Maggie that beautiful women didn't need to have any common sense—all they needed were the latest gowns and a rich man to pay for them.

She got to her feet, brushed herself off, and walked over to where Dakota had begun to build a fire. "Can I help with something?"

He didn't even look in her direction. "You know how to build a campfire?"

"No," she replied.

"You know how to make coffee?"

"No." Maggie began to feel as inadequate as her mother and sister. Knowing Dakota, she guessed where the conversation might be leading.

He glanced up with a cynical smirk. "Then I reckon you can't help with something." He returned his attention to the task at hand.

"Doesn't mean I can't learn." She stamped away

in a huff, returned to her original spot and sat down, feeling rejected and disgruntled. The man could be impossible.

A short while later, as Maggie sat alone eating one of the biscuits and a piece of the cold chicken Yen Ching had packed, she observed that everyone sat together in pairs—her mother and father, Diane and Peter, Dakota and Will. Everyone but her. Once again she appeared to be the loner, the odd one. This observation increased her discontent so that she was anxious to leave when, a short time later, the journey resumed.

By late afternoon, a steady drizzle began to make the going hazardous. To everyone's relief, Dakota finally called a halt to make camp for the evening. Even in the dry copse of trees, where they stopped, dampness saturated the air, but soon a warm campfire warded off the misty chill.

Two tents were pitched, one for the women and the other for the men. However, Dakota had elected to remain out in the open near the fire.

A full day of riding in the fresh air had a hypnotic effect on the weary travelers. After the evening meal, Peter, Taylor, Katherine, and Diane retired.

The heavy gray clouds above had started to shift eastward, unveiling in the western sky bright streaks of light from the diffused orange ball of the setting sun.

Maggie and Will remained at the fire to chat while they sipped hot coffee. Alone, Dakota had walked a distance toward the sunset and now sat cross-legged on the ground making large sweeps with a pencil on a pad of paper.

"What is he doing, drawing a map?" Maggie asked when she no longer could contain her curiosity.

"Dakota likes to sketch when he has time," Will informed her.

"Sketch? Sketch what?"

"Anything he finds interesting. He's quite talented, really. Recall the portrait of Screaming Eagle that you admired so much?"

Maggie was astounded. She had never suspected that Dakota possessed artistic talent. Of course, she reasoned, he kept it hidden. She wondered how much more about himself Dakota MacDonald kept secreted.

"Will, you've known him all his life, haven't you?"

"Prit near. When Sam brought him here after Dakota's parents died, he was a young lad about ten."

"What was he like then?"

"Come to think about it, he acted different from other kids his age. Older. He was quiet and serious. Didn't join in with the rest of them. Sam worked him hard, but he loved the boy like a son. Reckon they taught each other a lot."

"Why do you say that?" Maggie asked, her gaze straying to the figure sitting alone gazing at a sunset he had seen too many times to count.

"I don't know, exactly. 'Cept Sam had lost you, Maggie, his only child. And Dakota had lost everything, too—his parents, his home, his way of life. So the two of them became family. Sam learned what it takes to be a father, while Dakota learned how to get along in the white man's world. Seems like each found his niche from the love and respect of the other."

While she had been aware of Dakota's background, Maggie felt a renewed wave of sadness at Will's words. Regret for never having known her father and sorrow for Dakota, who had twice lost his family, had haunted her since the reading of Sam's will.

As if sensing her thoughts, Will tugged on her sleeve and said cheerfully, "Perk up, Maggie girl. In a way, old Sam is still looking out for both of you. You'll see when we find his fortune."

"Oh, I'm all right, Uncle Will. But the longer I'm here, the more I think I shouldn't have come to Deadwood."

"And here all the while I thought you were taken with the West." He looked at her out of the corner of his eye. "And just maybe a might taken with Dakota, too."

Maggie was embarrassed by Will's perception, but the outspoken honesty of her nature prompted a quick reply. "Oh, I am, Uncle Will—I mean, I *am* taken with the West. After all, it was born in me. I could live here forever." She shifted her gaze to the fire and nervously poked at the burning wood with a stick.

"And Dakota?" the banker pried.

Maggie tried to avoid a direct answer to his question. "I'm sorry we came out here if it turns out Dakota would lose what Sam intended for him. I mean, he seems perfectly willing to give me the ranch and then ride away without a backward glance. Of course, we could divide our shares in the ranch by selling it. But either way, he loses his home and this community where he is accepted . . . more or less," she added with a shrug.

Maggie stopped fidgeting with the stick in the fire and looked again at Will. She attempted to answer his question more directly.

"I think Dakota is a very interesting person. I do admire his skills and"—she hesitated—"his strength of character."

A smile he could not conceal crossed the banker's lips, but Maggie chose not to notice. Undaunted, she forged on.

"Tell me, Uncle Will, did Dakota go to school?"

"Some, but with all the time it took to build and work the Lazy H, Sam taught Dakota most things. Especially to read and write. 'Course, Sam may have lived to regret the effort." Will smiled and added with a chuckle, "Sam told me once he figured he'd have to give up his liquor and tobacco money to buy the boy all the books he wanted. You do recall the floor-to-ceiling shelves in the library, all full of books?"

Dakota has read all those books? Maggie leaned back on her elbows, looked again toward Dakota's outline framed by the sunset and sheepishly thought about her dime novels.

"No, Dakota didn't have much schooling." The banker concluded his thought. "He was too far behind to begin with, and then, once he learned to read, he was too far ahead."

Maggie sat up and looked at Will quizzically. "And the sketching? Did Sam teach him that, too?"

Will chuckled. "No, Maggie. Dakota brought that with him. Seems like talent gets born with the soul, and it's gonna bust out no matter what the circumstances—even from a poor Indian boy," he added wistfully.

Will looked to the west and saw Dakota returning to the campsite. The light had begun to fade. "I think I've had enough coffee for one night." He stood up and stretched. "Better bed down. If I know Dakota, he'll have us moving before dawn." He patted her shoulder. "Good night, Maggie."

Maggie smiled contentedly. "Good night, Uncle Will."

She washed out their cups. A small amount of coffee remained in the pot so she poured a cup and handed it to Dakota when he reached the campsite. "Coffee?" He nodded and took the mug.

"What were you drawing?" Maggie asked.

"Just scribbling." He quickly put aside the sketch pad and sat down by the fire.

Maggie sat beside him. "Dakota, how long do you think this hunt will take?"

He shrugged. "Can't say. Sam's map is so makeshift. The markings aren't clear. My guess would be about a week before we reach the site, but I could be wrong." His glance shifted to her face. "I'm ready to turn back any time you are."

"I didn't say I wanted to turn back. I was just curious."

"Whatever you want, Maggie." As he took a sip of the coffee, his eyes met hers. By the dim light of the flickering flames, his dark gaze seemed more enigmatic than ever.

When she started to rise, the coffee pot dropped through her fingers. Simultaneously, they both reached to pick it up and his hand covered hers. The shock was startling. Despite the passage of many days, the multitude of hours, the myriad of moments, nothing had changed. His touch still thrilled her. For an infinite moment, they looked into one another's eyes, desire flowing undisguised. Then he withdrew his hand. "You better get some sleep now. We're pulling out of here early."

Wordlessly, she continued to gaze at him. She wanted to throw herself into his arms, but pride came to the fore and Maggie's resolve hardened. "Good night." She fled into the tent without a backward glance.

The following morning when Maggie stuck her head out of the tent, she saw a dark and dreary sky overhead threatening a cloudburst at any moment. She was tempted to crawl back into her bedroll, but the smell of coffee and bacon lured her to the campfire.

The tantalizing aroma soon had an effect on the others. One by one, the members of the party straggled out of their tents. Diane, the last one to appear, immediately voiced an objection.

"Are we going to have to ride all day in the rain?"

Dakota glanced at the dark clouds overhead. "Don't look like the storm's moving out."

"Then why can't we find a dry place and stay there until it stops raining?" Diane pursued.

Dakota shrugged. "Up to the rest of you."

The suggestion did not please Maggie. She spoke

out without hesitation against the idea. "As long as we're out here, I think we ought to keep going and get it over with."

Taylor tried to appear reasonable, but it was evident from the slump of his shoulders that he had little desire to continue. "I don't want to ride all day in the rain, but I agree with Margaret; I'd like to get this over with as quickly as possible." He moved over to Dakota and poured himself another cup of coffee. "How far do you think we still have to go?"

"Can't say for sure. If you want, you can all stay here and I'll ride on ahead."

"Not on your life," Katherine exclaimed. "What is to keep you from finding the treasure and hiding it for yourself?"

Her mother's continued suspicion of Dakota only raised Maggie's ire. "Mother, Dakota wouldn't do that." She couldn't believe that, after all Dakota had gone through in their behalf, her mother still harbored negative feelings about him.

However, not about to back down, Katherine continued, "We all go, or we all stay. I think that is the only sensible thing to do."

"Then it's settled." Dakota began to stamp out the fire. "Let's get going."

A short time later, the mules were packed and they moved out.

The threatened rain did not materialize, but the spirits of the party matched the overcast sky. Even Diane and Katherine were unusually subdued. No one objected when Dakota called an early halt for the day.

He rode ahead to scout the area and left the rest of them to set up the camp. While the others tackled the job of pitching the tents under Taylor's supervision, Maggie volunteered her services to Will Godfrey, who had the responsibility of preparing the evening meal. He assigned her the task of making biscuits for their supper.

After getting the instructions, Maggie set about with fervor mixing the flour and shortening, while Will prepared the campfire. By the time Dakota returned to camp, ham and potatoes sizzled in frying pans and the smell of fresh coffee permeated the air.

Dakota walked over to Maggie as she put the pan of biscuits she had prepared on a heated rock to keep them warm. Grinning crookedly, he wiped a smudge of flour off her nose. "You baking freckles for supper, Maggie?"

Thrilled by his touch, Maggie smiled sheepishly. She picked up the pan and said, "No, but may I offer you one of my best efforts?"

Dakota smiled at the comment. Unable to resist voicing the thought which came to mind, he looked her straight in the eyes and whispered, "Seems I remember one of your best efforts being most pleasurable." Maggie blushed and looked down at the pan.

Dakota bit into a biscuit, and with as much teasing as not, yelped, grabbing his jaw. He flexed it gingerly. "'Pears like a mighty good woman can come up with some rather wicked hardtack. Hope I didn't break a tooth." Trying to digest his compliment along with the rebuke, Maggie didn't know which to respond to, and the confusion left her speechless.

Will walked over to the pair. "How are Maggie's biscuits, Dakota?"

"If we run short of ammunition, I reckon we can carve them down for bullets."

A woman of less mettle might have crumpled under such censure, but not Maggie Collingswood. As she watched Dakota's tall figure cross the campsite, Maggie smiled to herself. *Just you wait, Mr. MacDonald. I'll show you the difference between bullets and biscuits.*

When the evening meal was finished, Maggie went down to the river to wash her flour-dusted shirt, and she encountered Dakota. Bootless, with his pants rolled up to his knees, he was standing calf-deep in the water.

"What are you doing?" she called out to him.

"Fishing." He thrust a makeshift spear into the water and pierced a fish.

Fishing had always been a favorite sport to Maggie, and one at which she excelled. She didn't even need someone to bait the hook for her; she loved fishing, squirming worm included. "I never saw anyone fish with a spear," she shouted.

Maggie immediately removed her boots and rolled up the legs of her pants. She waded out to him. "Why don't you use a pole? It's easier."

Dakota's concentration remained fixed. "Could be."

Maggie lowered her head and peered into the water. Suddenly, she squealed excitedly. "Here's one." The fish shimmered off in a flash of silver.

"Quiet. You're scaring away the fish," he hissed.

"What are you using for bait?" she asked, innocently.

"Your biscuits."

"Very funny," she snapped.

Maggie peered down intently into the water and spied some small white pieces on the bottom of the river. She reared up with indignation. "Dakota MacDonald, you ornery, wicked, piece of hardtack. You *are* using my biscuits!" She shoved him, and he went sprawling on his backside into the water.

Maggie turned away to stomp off, and Dakota lunged for her ankle. She tripped and went down on her knees.

"You're gonna pay," he threatened.

She managed to slip out of his grasp and, laughing, splashed through the water with Dakota in pursuit. He caught her just as she reached the river bank and pulled her down.

Now, half-in and half-out of the water, Dakota straddled her and pinned her arms to the ground above her head. As their gazes locked, Dakota released her arms and slid his hands down to cup her cheeks.

"Maggie," he whispered tenderly. He dipped his head and his mouth covered hers.

She slipped her arms around his neck and parted her lips beneath his. They lost awareness of everything—resolves, determinations, noble sentiments.

When breathlessness forced them apart, Dakota covered her face with gentle kisses, then returned to once again draw the sweetness from her lips. Responding to the touch and feel of one another, their passion mounted and his tongue probed, meeting hers.

"Margaret." The call invaded their brief intimacy.

"Margaret, where are you?" The shout was repeated.

Reluctantly, Dakota rose, then reached out a helping hand and pulled Maggie to her feet. With a lingering gaze, the lovers stared into one another's eyes before he waded out into the stream.

"There you are," Katherine Collingswood exclaimed as she and Taylor came into view. Her mother looked at Maggie's sodden clothing. "Good Lord! What happened to you?"

"I fell in the river," Maggie responded curtly.

When Katherine saw the silent figure of Dakota in the water, her eyes narrowed with suspicion. She put her arms around her daughter's shoulders. "Well, come back to camp at once and get out of those wet clothes."

Maggie cast a final look at Dakota. He had retrieved his spear and returned to fishing. Apparently, he had put their few stolen moments out of his mind.

Returning to camp, she donned her nightdress and robe, then hung up her wet clothes on a line strung near the fire. A short while later Dakota came back.

"You left this on the river bank, Maggie." He handed her the shirt she had laundered.

After taking one look at Dakota, Will exclaimed,

"You better get into the tent, Dakota, and remove those wet clothes."

Dakota nodded and picked up his saddlebags. "Have any luck?" Will called out to him as Dakota headed for the tent.

Dakota paused for a backward glance at Maggie. "Not as much as I would have liked." She blushed and began to fidget with the wet clothes. "Got three fish tied up on a line in the river for breakfast," he said, and disappeared into the tent.

When he emerged, Dakota hung his wet clothes next to Maggie's. She couldn't help thinking that the spectacle of their wet clothing side-by-side on a line was becoming a common sight. Maggie watched Dakota pour himself a cup of coffee, then sit down and pull out his sketch pad.

Maggie wasn't the only one interested in Dakota's actions. Katherine Collingswood watched just as intently. Her glance repeatedly shifted back and forth between Maggie and Dakota. Katherine's suspicions were aroused, but she said nothing. Nevertheless, she was not about to retire until Maggie did.

Unsuspecting, Maggie sat chatting quietly with Diane and Peter. Occasionally, she raised her eyes and glanced across the fire at Dakota. Now and then, he would do the same. But neither spoke a word to the other.

Katherine continued her vigil throughout the evening until Maggie finally excused herself and retired. The others soon followed suit.

In a short time, only the lone figure of Dakota remained at the campfire.

Chapter Twenty-two

Unable to sleep, Maggie lay for an hour disturbed by a compelling desire to join Dakota at the fire. Finally, succumbing to temptation, she pushed aside the blanket and peeked out of the tent flap. A short distance from the fire, she saw Dakota stretched out asleep under a tree. Disappointed, Maggie returned to her own makeshift bed.

Sleep continued to elude her. She could still feel Dakota's kiss all the way to the tips of her toes. A fleeting smile graced her face as she lay back and stretched her arms above her head. With every day that passed, Maggie understood a little more about the enigmatic Dakota MacDonald. He wasn't as indifferent toward her as he claimed to be. She could tell his resolve to resist her was weakening.

Before much longer, she would have him admitting how much he cared for her.

Maggie reasoned that, although a new player in this game between the sexes, she had already learned a lot. She soon fell asleep with a smile on her face.

Sunrise was just a faint promise on the horizon when Maggie arose with the same smile. She dressed quickly and stole out of the tent. Not wanting to disturb the sleeping figure near the fire, she moved about quietly at her task. Dakota, awakened by the tantalizing aroma of perking coffee and freshly baked biscuits, sat up, surprised to see Maggie at the campfire. "What are you up to so early?"

"What does it smell like?" She hunkered down beside him holding a mug of coffee and a plate of hot biscuits.

He accepted the mug willingly, but eyed the other offering with suspicion. "Jaw's still sore from the last one," he mumbled. Hesitantly, he took one of the biscuits. "I guess dunking hardtack in coffee oughta soften it up."

"Just take a bite, Mr. MacDonald," she confidently insisted.

Dakota bit into the biscuit. "Not bad," he conceded and popped the remainder into his mouth. "Who made them?" he mumbled as he snatched another one off the plate.

"I did, who did you think? Care to eat your words along with that biscuit you're chewing?"

Maggie's smirk of confidence would have been hard for anyone to swallow; Dakota could not yield graciously. "I've eaten better."

Maggie stood up and with a cocky toss of her curly head smiled smugly. "No you haven't." She sauntered away.

Dakota grinned and sipped the coffee, his steady gaze on her long legs and slim hips snugly sheathed in her jeans. He knew the little minx had managed to burrow deeper and deeper under his hide with each passing day.

When he finished, Dakota went down to the river and retrieved the string of fish. By the time the others appeared at the campfire, pieces of fish sizzled in a skillet. Meanwhile, Dakota had ridden off to scout the trail ahead.

"What are you smiling about, Margaret?" Katherine commented as she poured herself a cup of coffee. "You must have had a good night's sleep. I don't think I've seen you smile in a week."

"Really, Mother?" Maggie inquired. "I hadn't realized." She returned to her thoughts regarding the cherished capitulation of Dakota MacDonald.

Diane launched forth with her usual morning harangue. "I can't imagine what anyone would find to smile about on this miserable trip."

Peter winked at Will Godfrey and offered Maggie a compliment. "I think her good cheer is a testimonial to Margaret's character. What a remarkable capacity she has to enjoy the natural environment. We should all learn by her serene example."

Diane cast a disgruntled glance at her fiancé. "Oh, really, Peter? Perhaps you should consider making this serene outdoors woman your wife, rather than me. You can serenely swing through the trees like an ape the way she does." Diane stuck out her tongue at him.

The men broke into laughter when Peter grabbed the lower limb of a tree and began to swing. He jumped down, beat his hands on his chest and, with the lumbering swagger of an ape, approached Diane. Squealing, she raced off with her serene, apelike lover in pursuit.

Peter caught her and pulled her into the concealment of the trees. He kissed her until she pleaded to catch her breath, then he smiled tenderly into her startled eyes. "I don't want a wife who swings through the trees. I want my wife in silk and ermine, or perhaps in chiffon that clings to her rounded curves. I want a wife whose skin feels like satin and whose hair smells of lilacs in the springtime. I want you, Diane. You may be spoiled, and pampered, and a little shrew, but God help me, I love you. I'm not giving up on you." He kissed her again, and her arms curled around his neck as she clung to him.

Hand-in-hand, they returned to the campfire. At their approach, Taylor slipped his arm around Diane's shoulders and kissed her cheek. "Have a cup of coffee, honey."

Still flustered from Peter's passionate kisses, Diane wrinkled her nose at the offer. "No, I hate coffee. I'd have a lot more to smile about if only I had a hot sip of tea."

Katherine sighed and sat down next to Taylor. "That's the trouble with the West, my dear Diane. The people here have never learned that the only civilized way to begin a day is with a cup of tea."

"Actually, sitting around a fire drinking a mug of coffee rather reminds me of my Army days," Taylor reflected.

"Oh, spare us the reminiscences," Katherine teased. "Aren't we miserable enough?" Her green eyes sparkled with rare good humor.

Maggie was surprised to see Diane join in the laughter that followed and, despite the primitive accommodations, the party shared an enjoyable meal together.

They were breaking camp when Dakota returned. "Maggie, I have something I want you to see. Let's ride on ahead." As he saddled Blaze, he gave Will the necessary instructions to follow them on the trail.

When Dakota and Maggie rode away, Katherine silently watched them. Taylor walked over to his wife and hugged her to his side. "There's nothing to worry about, my dear. Margaret's safe with Dakota."

With a mocking smile, Katherine glanced up at him. "That all depends on what you mean by safe, my love."

"Where are you taking me?" Maggie asked as she and Dakota rode side by side. In truth, she did not care where they were headed; just being with him was a thrill to Maggie. Knowing that he had ridden all the way back to camp to get her added to her feeling of exhilaration. Near to an hour's ride later, Dakota reined up.

Suddenly, Maggie gasped as she beheld the extraordinary splendor of the scene Dakota had brought her to see; a wall of weathered granite spires encompassed a hillside of pine-dotted, rolling grassland upon which a huge herd of grazing buffalo stretched out before them. "Oh, how magnificent," she exclaimed, gazing with wonder. "There must be hundreds of them." Her eyes glowed with excitement.

"I'd reckon close to four hundred. It's a big herd."

They dismounted and sat down in the shade of a pine. The bulky, shaggy animals lumbered past them, undisturbed by the presence of the two people. While her eyes feasted, Maggie had to tweak her nose in distaste.

"Oh, my. They smell worse than horses."

Dakota grinned. "They do that." He stretched out and leaned back on an elbow.

Maggie tucked her knees under her chin and gazed contentedly at the roaming animals. "You know, I once dreamed of 'herding' buffalo." She chuckled warmly. "It's no wonder my parents never believed I really wanted to go West. I must have seemed naive to everyone." She turned her head and looked at him. "Thank you, Dakota, for bringing me here."

"I wanted you to see the herd before the others." For a brief moment they stared awkwardly at one another, neither able to express the heart's tender thought.

Dakota stood up to move away from the temptation of her nearness. "The others should be here soon." He went to his saddlebags and took out his sketch pad.

Maggie smiled to herself, pleased that for the first time she would be allowed to watch Dakota create a sketch. She purposely said nothing so as not to distract him and jeopardize her privilege.

The two sat in comfortable silence as Dakota sketched the panorama until the sound of horses disturbed the tranquil scene. The rest of the party soon joined them.

Peter was the first to comment. "I say, that's a sight you don't see too often," he admitted. "Altogether glorious, indeed. But right now, I'd just as soon see a sign of civilization. A hotel or restaurant would be a treat."

"Oh, how awful. They stink!" Diane complained. "Let's get away from here so I can breathe."

Katherine quickly agreed. "I've seen buffalo before. And if you've seen them once, you've seen enough."

Maggie's gaze met Dakota's in understanding. She now knew why he had wanted her to view the sight with him alone.

By midday, the sky had clouded up for rain, and shortly after noon a steady downpour accompanied by a brisk wind began to pelt the riders.

Dakota had ridden ahead and returned with good news. "There's a small town about an hour's ride from here. You can sleep under a roof tonight if you want to push on."

"Good God! Do you have to ask?" Katherine remarked. She prodded her horse forward. Even Diane was able to suffer the discomforts of the storm in silence when faced with the prospect of a hot bath and a bed at the end of the trail.

The small mining town didn't even have a name, but it did have rooms to let above the saloon—a welcome relief to the sodden travelers. A large oak sign hung on the door with the words *Public-Private-Baths* burned in the wood.

The bartender grinned broadly as Taylor and Peter came through the door, and two women at the end of the bar looked up with interest.

"Howdy, folks. Been traveling long?"

"Long enough in this weather," Taylor replied. "We would like to rent several rooms for the night."

"A buck each, cash in advance," the man informed them. "Got six rooms, but two are spoken for." He glanced toward the two women. "'Course, it's the middle of the week and business is slow. Reckon Sal and Lucy, there, could double up if they had to." Grinning slyly, he leaned over the bar and winked. "'Less you got use for their private services."

Taylor and Peter looked at each other, then back to the proprietor. Taylor cleared his throat and said with quiet disdain, "My wife and daughters will be joining us in a moment."

"Oh, I see," the barman sighed in a disappointed return to reality. Taylor put a twenty-dollar gold piece on the counter and calmly stated his business. "Four rooms will be adequate, and we will be using the bath, Mr.——?"

"Bennett's the name. Bill Bennett," he said as he eyed the money with gleeful greed. "Got the cleanest rooms in the territory."

"Which isn't saying much, I'm sure," Katherine declared, having heard the boast as she entered the saloon with Maggie, Diane, and Will. She cast her eyes around the shabby barroom and stiffened her shoulders as she gazed momentarily at the two women.

"Your sign on the door says Public-Private-Baths." Katherïne closed her eyes and then opened them in a dramatically wide stare directed squarely at Mr. Bennett. "Just what does that mean?"

"Well, it means we got two large tubs, each six feet by six feet and three feet deep. One for men and one for women, more or less. Cost is one buck per head no matter how many of you want to use the tub. So you get whatever you want, public or private, either way." Then he raised his eyebrows and added, "Or both."

Although she had been listening intently, the explanation confused Katherine and her eyes grew wider. "My dear man, if something is public, it is public, and if something is private, it is private. How can anything be *both?*" Katherine accented the last word to point out the absurdity of the little man's logic.

"Think on it, ma'am. One body in a bath is what you would call private. A passel of men in one tub, or a passel of women in the other, that would be public." The bartender hesitated in a trap of his own making; he wanted as much of Taylor's gold piece as he could get, which meant not riling the missus. On the other hand, in his mind, this haughty dame needed educatin'.

As he continued, the male animal surfaced and overcame his greed. "Now, if'n a couple—you and the mister for instance—wanted to share a bath, and maybe even bring along a few friends of your own choosin'"—he paused extending an open hand to indicate the rest of the party—"well, that would be considered a *private* party for the *public*. And that's what I meant when I said you could have *both*." Mr. Bennett accented the last word to prove his point.

He offered a smile of satisfaction for having explained his operation in the most delicate of terms using no foul language, no tasteless detail, and no reference to Sal and Lucy at the end of the bar.

But the lurid implication had sunk in, and Katherine exploded. "Taylor!" she exclaimed in shock. "We are leaving this place immediately, and furthermore—"

"Now, Katherine, pay no mind to this prairie-dog fantasy. Nothing like that is going to take place. We are only here to—"

Fortunately at that moment, Dakota, who had taken the horses and mules to the livery, entered the saloon and unwittingly put an end to further ado concerning the peculiar bathing accommodations. As he dropped his saddlebags on the floor and began to shake off his wet slicker, Bennett eyed the sodden cowboy critically.

"Yer gettin' the floor wet, Breed, and furthermore, I don't sell liquor to Injuns, so git movin'."

The biting remark caught the group unexpectedly. Taylor recovered first. "Mr. MacDonald is a member of our party."

Taken back, Bennett condescended somewhat. "Okay, then he can sleep in the barn."

"I prefer you to offer Mr. MacDonald an apology," Taylor countered to the bartender, whose attitude had become surly.

Bennett's lip curled in a sneer. "You folks must be strangers here. We don't take too kindly to Injuns here in the Dakota Territory. And with good cause. They're murderin' savages."

Maggie primed for battle. "Well, Mr. Bennett, this *Injun* was good enough to serve in *your* military. He is also the owner of one of the largest ranches in the territory."

"Who'd he scalp to get it?" the man scoffed.

"We're still waiting for an apology, Mr. Bennett," Maggie declared.

"Save your breath, Maggie. I can sleep in the livery."

"Indeed you will not." An authoritative voice in Dakota's defense had resonated forth from the most unexpected source.

Katherine Collingswood stepped forward, her green eyes brimming with contempt. "My husband has just now informed you that Mr. MacDonald is a member of our party. As such, we expect you to extend the same courtesy and accommodations to him as you do to the rest of us. Whatever expenses he incurs will be paid for in the same United States legal tender as ours will be. Therefore, inasmuch as we are all wet, hungry, and tired, we expect your immediate compliance."

Katherine's cold and unrelenting bluster affected the startled group as if the frigid blast of a winter storm had blown open the door. Many a foe in the past had felt the devastating impact of her imperious manner; now it was Bill Bennett's time.

301

Overwhelmed, the astonished bartender's mouth dropped open. "Yes, ma'am! My pleasure." He darted out from behind the bar and picked up two of the saddlebags. "Right this way, ma'am!"

Little did Bennett realize that the woman's own misgivings about Dakota had only been temporarily swept aside for the sake of putting the horrid little proprietor in his place. Katherine Collingswood's first duty, after all, was to see to it that no one, much less this sleazy saloonkeeper, would countermand the future Minister to France.

She turned around to her retinue. "Coming?"

Katherine placed a hand on the arm of her husband and, with shoulders squared and head held high, she ascended the stairway with all the regal bearing of Queen Victoria.

Peter nudged Dakota with his arm and winked. Obediently, the two men picked up the remaining saddlebags and started to follow the others up the stairs.

Once upstairs, Katherine directed traffic by assigning rooms—the largest for herself and Taylor, the room next door for Maggie and Diane, the dark room down the hall for Peter and Dakota, and the small room across the hall for Will Godfrey.

Later, after dinner, Maggie and Diane had just taken their nightgowns out of the bags when Katherine entered the room.

"Your father and I have used the bathing facility, which is downstairs in a room behind the bar. He has paid for you girls to bathe next."

Maggie arched a brow wickedly. "Tell us, Mother—we promise not to breathe a word to anyone—did you and Father bathe *privately* or *publicly?*" The two sisters exchanged glances and giggled.

Katherine did not join in their laughter. "Simultaneously, my darling daughters, I in the women's tub, he and Mr. Godfrey in the men's. I advise you get on with this peculiar arrangement and make short work of it. I didn't see anyone else here except those two—women, to whom bathing is probably of the least importance. Nevertheless, do hurry and be sure you use the tub for women."

With that, Katherine marched out as authoritatively as she had entered.

Chapter Twenty-three

In spite of their mother's trepidation, Maggie and Diane headed for the bathroom without any qualms. The accommodation consisted of two large, square wooden tubs separated by a heavy drape running the length of the room. A sign with arrows directing the ladies to the right and the men to the left hung above the door.

Diane produced a bottle of her favorite perfumed bath crystals and poured it into the water. "Wherever did you get that?" Maggie asked.

Diane giggled. "I packed it in my saddlebags. After all, a young woman can't be expected to travel without bath crystals." Then, with the playfulness of little girls, they splashed their hands back and forth in the water until a foam of bubbles covered the surface.

The two girls sank gratefully into the huge tub of hot water. Diane leaned her head back against the rim of the tub and closed her eyes. "Oh, this is divine. I'll never again take a bath for granted. When Peter and I build our home, I'm going to insist a bathtub be installed in every room." A sound from the other partition caused her to sit up.

"Enjoying your baths, ladies?" a voice called out.

"Peter!" Diane exclaimed.

"Right you are. Dakota and I are waiting for you to share some of those sweet-smelling bath crystals with us."

"Dakota's with you?" A hot blush crossed Maggie's face and a tingle crept up her spine at the thought of him on the other side of the drape just a few feet away.

"I swear, Peter Brent, you are wicked," Diane declared. "What would Father and Mother say? Why, we're practically bathing together," she added provocatively.

"Keep those dulcet tones flowing, my love, and we shall be," Peter warned.

Dakota decided to play the game. "If we corral one, no doubt we'll have to rope the other too. What do you think, Maggie—are you game to join us?" Dakota asked.

"I'm thinking if Father hears this conversation, he's going to have the two of you tarred and feathered. Then you will have wasted the dollar you paid for this bath."

Although the girls knew the men were only

teasing them, Maggie felt uncomfortable because she couldn't think of anything she would rather have Dakota do. Well, in truth, she could think of *one* other thing, but being a lady, she could not allow her mind to dwell on such thoughts.

Maggie quickly finished bathing, washed her hair, and climbed out of the tub. She had just put on her drawers and chemise when the saloon's two prostitutes came into the room. They paused at the entrance of the men's partition, posing seductively with their bodies outlined in loose dressing gowns.

"Good evening, gentlemen. We were just passing by and thought it was about time you two wranglers were introduced to the specialty of the house. My friend here is Luscious Lucy and I'm known as Sal the Siren," the blonde one cooed. "You two handsome gentlemen need your backs washed?"

"Reckon so," Dakota responded to the offer by extending a washcloth.

"What say we don't waste time with that?" Sal answered with sincere interest. "Anything you want, big boy. The price is all the same."

Diane's eyes bulged and her mouth curved into a shocked bow. "Well, of all the nerve."

Sal pursed her lips and whispered to the men. "Wait 'til we get rid of the excess baggage."

"What's the matter, honey, you need your back washed, too?" the dark-headed Lucy drawled sarcastically as she sauntered into the women's section.

"If you *didn't* notice, my sister and I are using this tub," Diane informed her.

Luscious Lucy put a hand on a rounded hip,

thrust out the ponderous evidence of her own endowment, and cast a mocking smirk at Maggie's slender figure. "Did you say *sister?* Oh, excuse me, honey, I thought it was your brother." The remark produced an appreciative snicker from Sal, and the two floozies broke into laughter.

Maggie responded immediately to the effrontery. "Watch out, Diane, you're liable to drown if Lumpy Lucy lowers all that fat into the water."

Lucy's eyes flashed with anger. "In case you two royal highnesses *didn't* notice, this is a public bath. My buck's as good as yours, so why don't you haul your two royal high asses out of here." She removed her robe and climbed into the tub.

Diane purred sweetly, "I'd appreciate it if you would wait until I finish my shampoo. I'd hate for this clean water to be sullied by all that black dye in your hair."

"Uh-oh! I think that'll do it," Dakota muttered from the other side of the drape.

He wasn't mistaken. "Why you little bitch! Here, I'll help you finish your shampoo," Lucy fumed and shoved Diane's head under the water.

"Take your hands off my sister," Maggie cried out and leaned over, yanking Lucy by the hair.

Sal immediately joined the fracas by shoving Maggie, and with a great splash, water flowed over the sides of the tub as Maggie plopped into the tub.

Snatching a washcloth, Maggie scrambled to her feet, wound up her best baseball pitch and fired the wet projectile into Sal's face. But when Maggie started to climb out of the tub, Lucy grabbed her by the legs, pulling Maggie back into the water.

Mopping the soapy water out of her eyes, Diane jumped on Lucy's back and shoved the dark head under the water. "I'm through bathing now. The water's all yours.

"Ladies, what's going on over there?" Peter called out. Continued shrieks and splashing answered his question.

"Trouble brewing. Let's get out of here," Dakota said to Peter as the two men climbed out of the tub and pulled on their trousers.

Meanwhile, Maggie scampered out of the tub in pursuit of Sal, who, upon spying Maggie's clothing, slip-sloshed across the floor puddled with water and soap bubbles, snatched up the bundle from the table, and with a jeer announced, "These could use a washing, honey," as she tossed the garments into the water.

"Then you can be the one to wash them, *honey*," Maggie shouted. She shoved Sal, by now a screeching banshee, who flopped on her backside into the water with her legs kicking wildly up in the air as she shouted vile expletives at Maggie. Snatching the soap, Maggie jumped into the water, shoved the bar of soap into Sal's mouth, and shouted, "Your mouth needs washing worse than my clothes." Sal grabbed the soap from her mouth, flung it out of the tub, and with retching sounds and voluminous spitting, fired a second blast of cursing which ended with "—you skinny-assed bitch."

Just then the cavalry charged to the rescue in the form of Peter and Dakota. Peter stepped on the wet bar of soap and slid across the slick floor on his stomach. Dakota attempted to lift Maggie out of the tub with Sally hanging on, tugging at Maggie's legs to pull her back, but lost the tug of war when the weight pulled him off balance and he landed in the tub.

Peter tried to stand up, but the soapy floor made it impossible. Crawling on his hands and knees, Peter reached Lucy, who held Diane's head under the water, and he yanked the naked, dark-haired woman out of the tub.

Eyeing her from head to foot, Peter stammered, "Oops, pardon me, ma'am, but your—ah—doodads are showing." His wide-eyed ogling gave Lucy the chance to sock Peter squarely in the jaw, which sent him reeling toward the partition drape. Peter grabbed the drape, and the whole overhead apparatus crashed to the floor trapping him under the heavy cloth. Lucy pounced on Peter's draped, struggling frame and beat at him with both fists.

Meanwhile, Dakota had managed to secure Maggie around the waist and pulled her out of the tub as she squirmed and shouted to be set free in order to rejoin the battle. Peter managed to stand up halfway and Lucy shoved the draped figure into the tub where Diane and Sal were engaged in an all-out hair-pulling exhibition.

Snarling like an alley cat, Lucy now lunged at Maggie. Dakota had to release his grip on Maggie and step between them to try to separate the two women. Balling her fist, Maggie delivered a right cross just as Dakota shoved Lucy away, and instead of striking the dark-haired floozie, Maggie's punch landed on Dakota's chin, sending him reeling backward. He grabbed her to try to keep his balance but the maneuver was too hazardous on the soapy floor, and Dakota pulled Maggie with him as he fell into the tub.

Shocked, Diane quit the battle when Peter's arm encircled her nude body and yanked her away from Sal. As Sal climbed out of the water, she cursed Diane and Peter with every black oath she could mouth.

Snorting triumphantly, Lucy and Sal clutched their sodden gowns around themselves and sashayed away claiming a victory.

Disgusted, Maggie turned on Dakota. "Whose side were you on? We were doing fine until the two of you came along."

"Will you kindly get your roving hands off me and get out of here," Diane declared to Peter, hiding her body under the soap bubbles.

"I thought this was my reward for coming to the rescue," Peter teased, but he dropped his hold on her.

At that moment, Bill Bennett came hurrying through the door, after seeing Lucy and Sal storm past him dripping wet. He snorted derisively when he saw the four people in a tub afloat with soap bubbles and sodden clothes. "So you thought to pull a fast one on me, huh? Didn't work, did it? Nothing was said about doing any laundry in the tub. That'll be a buck extra from each of ya."

Later that night, long after everyone else was asleep, Maggie stood at the window of her room staring out at the sky. The rain had stopped, and bright moonlight now lit the narrow street below. She smiled, remembering the earlier fight in the bathhouse. How wild it all seemed to her now.

Maggie glanced at Diane, asleep on the bed. During the fracas she and her sister had fought together, not against one another. It was a strange experience, Maggie thought, but a nice one.

She turned back to gaze out the window and her attention was drawn to a man disappearing into the trees. The figure looked like Will Godfrey. *Why would Uncle Will be out so late at night?* Maggie wondered. She reasoned it could only be someone who looked like him. Shrugging aside the question, Maggie returned to bed.

Tongue-in-cheek, Peter fired the opening fusillade the following morning when they were all assembled at breakfast. "Heard tell there was a big fight last night right here in the saloon."

Maggie and Diane lifted their eyes, and for a moment their gazes locked as each girl forced back a secret smile of shared camaraderie.

"Thank goodness I slept through it," Katherine remarked. "I didn't hear a thing." She picked up a strip of bacon and took a dainty bite. "Did you hear any commotion last night, Taylor?"

"Hear what, dear?" he asked, preoccupied with a two-week-old newspaper he had found lying on the bar.

"Taylor, will you please put down that newspaper," Katherine complained in a huff. "Isn't it bad enough we have to eat our meal in a saloon, without you having your head buried behind a paper while we eat? What kind of example are you setting for your daughters and these young men?"

"You'll be glad to hear this, my dear. This article

says that an English baker in New York has created a new muffin that's tasty, flat, and round. He's called it an *English Muffin*."

Katherine passed a plate of hot biscuits to him. "However that muffin may taste, I am sure it will be a welcome relief from these biscuits. Don't they know how to make anything else in the West?"

Taylor folded the newspaper and put it aside. "Now, what were you saying about a fight last night?"

"Heard tell it was a real free-for-all," Dakota volunteered.

"Yep. Men and women alike," Peter added.

Maggie gritted her teeth and cast a scathing glare at the two would-be troublemakers. She tried to change the subject. "Was that you I saw late last night out on the road, Uncle Will?"

Will Godfrey glanced at her in surprise. "Not me, Maggie. Must have been someone else. Soon as I finished my bath, I went to bed. Slept like a log." He picked up the newspaper Taylor had put aside and began to read it.

Peter had no intention of letting the girls off so easily. He resumed the attack. "Must have been a jolly good show. Just think of it, men and women cursing and slugging at each other. I say, Margaret, aren't *you* curious to know what the ruckus was all about?"

Maggie smiled at him through clenched teeth. "Not at all, Peter. You see, I prefer to mind my own business."

"And appreciate those who mind theirs," Diane added demurely as she cast a sweet smile at her fiancé.

"Considering the element I've seen thus far in this establishment, I wouldn't put anything past any one of them," Katherine remarked.

"Well, it sure must have been something to see. What with the ladies scratching and screaming at each other." Peter winked at Dakota. "Heard tell, the ladies even took off all their clothes. Just heard tell, mind you."

"How shocking!" Katherine gasped. "No respectable lady would engage in such a public exhibition." Katherine's hand fluttered to her chest as she preened with pride. "Thank goodness my daughters would never be involved in such uncouth behavior. Margaret and Diane have been raised to conduct themselves as ladies at all times."

"Yes, indeed, Mrs. Collingswood," Peter quickly agreed, sucking in his breath at Diane's firm kick in the shin. "Margaret and Diane are most certainly the couthest ladies at all times."

Dakota figured he had better get out of the place before one of the girls drew blood. "Guess I better saddle up the horses."

"I'll help you," Peter said wisely. Clutching his leg, he limped out after Dakota.

Alarmed at the sight, Katherine grasped her husband's arm. "Look, Taylor, that poor boy is limping. He must have hurt his leg."

"Or put his foot in his mouth, Mother," Maggie grumbled. She pushed away from the table and followed the men out the door.

"Need any help?" Maggie asked when she joined Dakota in the stable.

He grinned. "If I did, I'd sure think twice before

313

askin'. You still mad, Maggie? We were only teasin'."

She smiled sheepishly and slipped her hands into the pockets of her jeans. "Of course I'm not mad."

Dakota shook his head, wiggled his jaw with his hand and grinned. "You throw a mean punch, Maggie Collingswood." He led a saddled horse over to a nearby tree. Maggie saw Dakota hunch down on his haunches and appear to be studying the ground.

She went over to him and watched expectantly. When Dakota rose and went into the stable, she trailed behind him. One by one, he lifted each leg and examined the shoe of every horse in the stable.

"What are you looking for?" Maggie inquired, brimming with curiosity.

"Nothing," Dakota mumbled.

Exasperated, she stamped her foot and put her hands on her hips. "Don't tell me it's nothing. What are you looking for?"

"All right. Come with me, but I don't want you to say anything to the others until I figure this out." He returned to the tree and pointed at a muddy hoof print. "Remember the day we rode out to Twin Buttes together? Well, I saw this same print on the floor of the gulch that day."

"The same print?" she asked skeptically. "How can you be certain it's the same print?"

He pointed to an indentation in the mud. "Shoe had the same slit right here on the iron."

"Well, couldn't that be a coincidence?"

"Lady, I don't believe in coincidence. If a wolf

crosses your path twice, you'd better climb a tree, 'cause it's not *coincidence;* he's got your scent."

Dakota stood up and stared reflectively into the thick pines surrounding them. "Someone's trailing us, Maggie."

Before he could say more, Peter joined them, carrying several sacks. "I've got the supplies you wanted."

Dakota nodded. "Let's get them on the mules."

He stopped for one more glance toward the thick timber, then Dakota followed Peter into the stable.

Chapter Twenty-four

Gray clouds pressed down on the small party as they continued their trek into the hills. Soon a steady downpour made for a completely unpleasant ride. Even the trees they passed under offered little or no protection, and in places several days of rain had turned the ground into a quagmire. When the trail narrowed, coursing between a ravine on one side and scrub trees on the other, Dakota called for them to dismount and walk their animals, rather than continue the hazardous trail on horseback.

"Why are we doing this?" Diane grumbled to Peter as they trudged through the mud leading their horses by the reins.

"I've been wondering the same thing myself," Peter responded.

The young girl brushed the rain off her face. Several blond curls had strayed from beneath her hooded slicker and were clinging to her cheeks in sodden strands.

"You and I have nothing to gain from this. If Margaret and Dakota want some dumb treasure, let them have it."

"They didn't ask us to come along, Diane," he reminded her.

"Yes, it's all my mother's fault. I'm going to tell her, right now."

When she jerked the reins to move ahead, the maneuver caused her startled horse to buck, and the frightened animal skidded off the trail into a slippery patch of mud on the edge of the ravine.

Clutching the reins, Diane screamed as the animal began to slide. Instantly, Peter grabbed her before she was dragged down the hill with the horse. At the bottom, the hapless animal hobbled to its feet. The front right leg hung limply.

The drenched figures stood silently as Dakota cautiously made his way down the steep hill. Reaching the bottom, he gently soothed the frightened animal, then knelt down to examine the horse's leg.

Maggie held her breath, hoping for a miracle, but when she saw Dakota draw his Colt, she turned away. Her tears blended with the rain streaming down her face as the blast of the gunshot rumbled like thunder above the sound of the falling rain.

After several moments, Dakota rejoined the disheartened group, toting the saddle and bridle from the dead horse. Shouting to be heard above the downpour, Dakota answered the unasked question of his bewildered followers. "Only one thing we can do now. I'll have to ride back to that town and buy another horse."

"You want company?" Will asked.

Dakota shook his head. "No, they'll need you here. This heavy rain can't keep up for much longer, but the trail's too dangerous to keep going. Pitch camp in that line of spruce up ahead on the right. I should be back in four or five hours." He climbed on his horse and was gone before any more could be said.

Although the ground was damp, the thick clump of pine trees served as a welcome umbrella over the heads of the rain-soaked travelers. Peter hacked off the branch of a tree and chopped the limb into firewood while Will gathered pine cones and twigs for tinder to start a fire. A smoky haze streamed from the burning green wood, but soon a blaze from the campfire warmed up the snug compound.

When the rain finally stopped and the sun broke through the cloud cover, the relieved travelers moved out of their hastily erected tents. They sat and talked awhile, but then each in turn decided on some activity to help pass the hours.

To busy herself, Katherine took over the cooking chores and began to bake an apple pie. Taylor and Peter left the camp to hunt fresh game with a promise to return with a ring-necked pheasant, while Will Godfrey stayed behind to mend a few torn bridles.

Diane, unable to think of any task and therefore bored as usual, tagged after Maggie, who had taken their muddy garments down to the nearby river. Laundering soiled garments by pounding them on the stones of a river bank was a new experience for both Maggie and Diane. The novelty of the chore soon became a game, and the two sisters vied with each other to determine which was the most proficient at the task.

When all the garments had been cleaned of the muddy grime, Maggie dipped a bare toe into the stream. "Why don't we go swimming?"

"Haven't you been wet enough all day?" Diane groused. "It's a relief to be in dry clothes."

A dimple appeared in each cheek as Maggie grinned impishly. "Yes, but all the men are occupied right now; we'll have plenty of privacy. Who knows when we'll get another chance like this again?"

Maggie stripped down to her undergarments and waded into the water. "The water's warm," she stammered through chattering teeth. She dove under the water and surfaced near Diane. "Come on in. It's not cold if you keep your shoulders under the water."

Diane was not so easily convinced. "How can the water be warm at this altitude? I think you're just saying that to get me in there so you can dunk my head under. You know how much I hate that."

"I won't dunk you," Maggie promised. With smooth, strong strokes, she swam back into midstream.

Diane began to weaken as she watched Maggie. A swim might be fun, certainly a pleasant change from riding a miserable horse. As she began to shed her clothing, Diane vowed that after she returned to Washington she would never climb on a horse again.

Before long, the two girls were laughing and cavorting in the water. When Maggie finally climbed out, she quickly began to pull on her clothing, convinced she would shiver to death before she finished dressing.

Leaning against a nearby tree, a tall figure straightened up and approached her. Maggie saw him coming and grinned, amused that at least *she* was dressed.

"Here, I think you can use this." Peter Brent handed her a towel. Maggie grabbed the cloth gratefully and sat down to dry her hair.

"Peter Brent, what are you doing here?" Diane cried out.

He grinned mischievously. "Enjoying the view." He held up another towel for her to see. "Come on out."

"I can't, I'm only wearing my . . . unmentionables." Her teeth had begun to chatter.

"I've been watching you for the last five minutes, so I know you are only wearing your—er, unmentionables. Very nice and ladylike they are too, I must say. Considerably more than what you wore last night in the privacy of the pub's tub. Remember?"

"I swear, you're never going to let me forget last night, are you?" she fumed.

"It will always be one of my fondest memories, my love. Are you coming out, or am I coming in?" He began to unbutton his shirt.

Maggie jumped to her feet. "If you're shucking your clothes, Peter Brent, I'm getting out of here."

"Don't you dare leave me alone with this vile, uncivilized ape," Diane cried. But Maggie grabbed her laundry and scurried off.

Unable to bear the cold water any longer, Diane climbed out of the river, her wet camisole and drawers clinging to her feminine curves. Embarrassed, she grabbed the towel and covered herself. "I *told* Margaret someone would see us," she said as a blush crept up her cheeks.

The towel dropped through her shaking hands. Peter picked it up and briskly began to wipe her dry. "After we are married, I intend to do this every night, princess."

"Princess says, we aren't married *yet*, ape-man." Diane could not resist pretending indifference.

His movements slowed to become caresses as he ran the towel along the length of her tiny body. Diane shivered; both knew it was not from the cold. He put the towel around her shoulders like a shawl and grasped the ends, pulling her slowly into the circle of his arms until their bodies were pressed together. Diane could feel his hard arousal against her stomach.

Diane looked into his eyes and saw Peter as she had never seen him before. His intensity seemed to come not from passion alone, but also from some unfamiliar strength of purpose. His hands held her with a grip of command.

As if to verify her thought, Peter lowered his head and claimed her in a fierce and dominating kiss. Diane felt the tantalizing warmth of his hands as he slipped the straps of her camisole off her shoulders. She opened her mouth to protest, but the words passed through her lips as a groan when she felt his tongue brush her taut nipples. His moist mouth closed around one and then the other, tugging and suckling until she was consumed by the exquisite sensation. In passionate surrender, she clutched his bowed head to her breast.

As he continued to feast on her swollen breasts, Peter slid a warm palm under the band at her waist and moved down to cup her most intimate passage. His fingers gently massaged and probed the sensitive opening. When her body began to convulse with tremors, he stopped. Then pulling her to him once again, his crushing lips branded her possessively as he drove his tongue into her mouth, and for several moments, he savored her reciprocated passion.

When he released her, Diane sagged limply in his arms. She searched the intense eyes that seemed to bore into her soul. Uneasily, Diane remembered how she had always enjoyed provoking Peter's ardor because she could control him. But now she sensed a reversal had taken place; he was teasing and controlling *her*.

"Why are you doing this to me?"

Peter relaxed his serious expression and grinned. "The law of the kingdom, my lady. Before a knight can wed the damsel of his choice, she must be fairly won."

"Fairly won?"

"Lured away from competing knights, rousing tournaments, and other daring games of the realm."

"Oh, Peter, how you do carry on. I don't know

what you mean." She shrugged out of his grasp and turned away.

Peter continued to press the point in his light-hearted allusion so as not to anger her. "Methinks you do, my love, and me also thinks I had best win the princess soon, 'ere harm befall her."

Although spoken in kindly jest, the meaning of Peter's message did not escape Diane. True, she had once enjoyed arousing men and playing games —but they were harmless flirtations really, and she had always been in control. Then came Rafe Catlin. With him the game had become a night-mare, and only Dakota's intervention had saved her.

Peter had always known of her trivial flirtations, but did he know about Rafe too? She cast a nervous glance over her shoulder at him. "I swear, I don't know what's gotten into you, Peter Brent. It must be the altitude. We never should have come up into these hills." Trembling, she began to pull on her clothing as Peter continued.

"Quite the contrary, my lady. The clear air cleanses the heart and mind—the proper atmosphere for us to begin anew."

Diane looked at him quizzically, and Peter dropped the frivolity. "It's time to shed the games of yesterday—particularly the game in which you expected to marry a rich man who would pamper and take care of you. I was merely a suitable suitor. If our love is true, we need play those roles no more. I love you, Diane, and if we are to be wed, I must know that you love me."

Diane felt justly chastised, ashamed, and remorseful for using Peter as her fool. She reached out to him.

Peter took her into his arms and looked into eyes filled with tears. "What's this, my love?"

"Peter, I . . ." She wanted to ask for his forgiveness but could not find the words.

The plaintive response was the answer he sought. "Ah, Princess." He hugged her tightly, and Diane pressed her cheek against his chest.

When Maggie returned to camp, Katherine was occupied with preparing pieces of rabbit on a makeshift spit. She looked up and brushed aside a strand of hair, leaving a trail of flour across her cheek. "Where is your sister?"

"Diane's still down at the river," Maggie replied, tossing her laundry over a line already strung with wet garments.

"You left her alone at the river?" Katherine exclaimed.

"Diane is not going to tragically fling herself into the water and be sucked into the black depths of a bottomless whirlpool, Mother." Maggie sighed. "Besides, she's with Peter." She turned and disappeared into the tent to change her wet undergarments.

"What do you suppose is keeping them so long?" Katherine remarked when Maggie returned to add her underclothing to the already sagging clothesline.

"Who, Mother?"

"Diane and Peter."

"Ah. Peter said he wanted to admire the view."

"Isn't that a lovely sentiment." Katherine smiled

with pleasure. "Peter's such a sensitive young man." She glanced askew at her older daughter. "It's a pity you won't make the effort to find yourself a young man just as suitable."

Maggie grimaced and rolled her eyes. "As suitable to whom, Mother, you or me?"

She walked over to the fire and watched as Katherine began to wrap a thin slice of salt pork around each piece of rabbit. "Mother, what in the world are you making?"

Katherine raised her blonde head, upon which even the tiniest hair had remained unsullied throughout the earlier downpour. "My dear Margaret, I am attempting to replace this primitive fodder with some creative cuisine."

"Well, speaking of fodder, I better see that the horses and mules are fed and watered."

Maggie headed for the stock but stopped sharply when she saw no sign of Blaze among the tethered animals. "Darn it, girl, where did you stray off to?" she grumbled and began to search for the missing horse.

Unfortunately, in the course of her exploration, every bit of surrounding nature, from a simple patch of wild flowers to the fallen cones of a towering pine, caught Maggie's eye and demanded her closest inspection.

She gasped with delight when she spied the pert white tail of a tiny deer. Nibbling on a leaf, the fawn raised gentle, glossy-black eyes and moved off on wobbling legs so thin they appeared to be on the verge of snapping.

Maggie followed, fearing for the safety of the animal since the young fawn had apparently wandered away from its mother. Smiling, Maggie's eyes brightened with relief when she saw a large doe approach the young deer and nuzzle the fawn possessively.

Her anxious curiosity satisfied, Maggie returned to hunt for Blaze. She looked around in confusion and realized she hadn't the faintest idea where she was, or in which direction to proceed.

She took a deep breath to calm herself and began to search for something that might look familiar. She finally gave up in dismay and further awe for Dakota who could so easily read signs of the terrain.

Having lost awareness of time, she had no idea how much daylight remained. Maggie shaded her eyes and glanced up at the sky. Her spirits sank right along with the setting sun.

Could it be possible that Dakota had returned to camp and was looking for her now? Maggie cupped her hands to her mouth. "Hello," she called out at the top of her voice. She jumped back in fright when her shout flushed several grouse out of nearby bushes. She watched sadly as they fluttered away.

Maggie shouted again and listened hopefully for a response, but this time nothing stirred; the hollow echo of her voice sounded a grim reminder of the vastness of the forest around her.

Frightful thoughts began to fill her mind. She saw herself mauled by a bear, then attacked by a pack of snarling wolves. Soon, in her rampant imagination, the wolf pack became a band of hostile, painted savages.

Seeking a weapon, she picked up a stick and banged it several times against a tree. Satisfied with the sturdiness of her weapon, she decided that aimless wandering might not be the wisest course of action, so she sat down to wait for Dakota to find her—as she knew he would.

Maggie just hoped he would come before nightfall.

The night air at this altitude could be freezing cold, and she knew she would be in serious trouble if forced to remain shelterless in the wild.

With the swift approach of nightfall, the thought of being alone again in the hills stirred up the memory of her terrifying night with Tiger. *But I'm not pinned helplessly under a dead horse this time*, she told herself. She pounded her cudgel on the ground to fortify her conviction. Resolved, Maggie settled down to await the appearance of her rescuer.

A short while later, her optimism had diminished considerably as sinister shadows deepened among the trees. Restlessly, Maggie began to pace back and forth. There was no question in her mind that Dakota would have returned to camp a long time ago, discovered her missing, and begun a search. *So where is he?* she wondered anxiously.

Maggie plopped down on the ground again, crossed her legs under her, propped her elbows on her knees, and sat with her head in her hands and a scowl on her face—the picture of discouragement.

"Dakota MacDonald, what's keeping you?" Her empty stomach rumbled as if an echo to the question.

Desolately, Maggie stared into the face of a boulder formation just a few feet away. The rocky heap rose about twenty feet high, so she decided to climb to the top of the small mound for a better view of the area.

As she started to rise, Maggie thought she glimpsed in the dim light a streak of yellow and brown among the rocks, but when she looked again, there was nothing. Seconds later, a flat head with glittering, lidless eyes poked out from a small opening among the boulders. A long, forked tongue darted in and out of its mouth as the elongated body of a reptile with a tail of horny rings slithered across the surface of the rocks and dropped silently to the ground before her. Maggie screamed in terror and poked at the snake with her long stick to drive it away.

Instantly, the reptile coiled to strike, with its ominous rattle sounding a signal of death. Petrified, Maggie didn't even hear the rifle blast which blew the head off the snake and flung the serpent's body into the air.

Dazed, Maggie remained transfixed—one instant she had faced certain death; a breath later the headless, twisted shape lay lifeless a short distance away.

She began to shiver uncontrollably and raised trembling hands to cover her face, trying to draw breath into lungs which seemed to have lost their capacity to function.

"Are you all right?" Maggie heard the words, but couldn't get any sound except a whimper past her throat.

She felt the warmth of a jacket and Maggie looked up gratefully, expecting to see Dakota. Instead, she found herself looking into weathered blue eyes set in a whiskered face. "You're safe now, gal." Maggie heard a quiver in the old man's voice and noticed that his hand shook as he tucked the coat around her.

"Thank you," she managed to murmur.

"I'd say that was a close call. Ain't you got any more sense than to be out here alone?" he asked with a hoarse gruffness.

With eyes still round and glazed from her brush with death, she looked like a frightened little girl to the old man. He wanted to take her in his arms to comfort her. "I got lost looking for my horse."

"An apron-face sorrel mare?"

Maggie looked up hopefully. "Have you seen her?"

"Found her a short ways back." He pointed to a distant tree and Maggie's heart surged with joy at the sight of Blaze standing between a chestnut stallion and a pack mule.

Blaze pawed the ground to get free and tossed her proud head in greeting when Maggie jumped to her feet and rushed to the mare. A combination of tears and laughter bubbled from Maggie's throat as she hugged the horse. "Oh, thank you," she cried. Brimming with emotion, she hugged the old man as well and kissed his cheek.

"I best build a fire so's you can relax," he mumbled, clearing his throat.

Maggie had time to study the old-timer as she watched him set about collecting dry wood.

Dressed in the common clothing of all the miners she had seen, he wore baggy trousers and a plaid shirt. Shaggy strands of salt-and-pepper hair hung from beneath the battered hat on his head. His face was virtually covered with wooly gray whiskers.

"Do you live in this area?" she asked when he sat down beside her at the fire.

"Right now, I do," he answered.

"Are you a miner, sir?"

His eyes glowed warmly. "Guess you could say that." He got up and shuffled over to pick up the scaly body of the dead snake.

Maggie grimaced. "What are you going to do with it?"

Maggie stared in wonder as he pulled a large hunting knife from his boot. "Skin it, of course. Snake's good eatin', gal. Tastes like chicken."

The old man soon had hot coffee perked and a skillet of beans mixed with hunks of snake meat ready to eat.

"You don't sound like no gal from these parts," he said as he handed her a plate of the hot food.

"No, I'm from the East." She pierced a small piece of the snake meat with her fork and bit into it hesitantly.

The old man watched her warily and grinned with pleasure when Maggie heartily began to devour the meal. "You sure don't eat like those city gals. Got a right good appetite, I'd say."

"Well, I haven't eaten since morning." She offered her plate for another helping.

He ladled out another spoon of beans and tossed a cold biscuit on the plate as well. "'Nother good reason why it's not smart to go roamin' off alone in these hills."

"I know that now. Dakota and the rest surely must be . . ." She shook her head in disgust at herself.

"Dakota?" the old man asked.

"Yes, Dakota MacDonald. I'm sure he is looking for me right now. Do you know him?"

His expression twisted in disapproval. "Ain't he that half-breed army scout?"

Maggie stood up. "Yes, he is a half-breed, sir." Obviously irritated, she shrugged off the old man's jacket. "I am most grateful to you for saving my life, but I think I should attempt to find my camp."

"Cool your heels, gal. I didn't mean nothing," the old-timer remarked. "Ain't no call for you to take on like a she-wolf protectin' her cub."

Maggie sat down again. "I hate to hear anyone disapprove of Dakota just because he has Indian blood. He's the noblest and most courageous man I've ever known. And he *will* find me. He is a superb scout, you know," she said proudly.

The old man nodded. "Yeah, I heard some talk of that before. 'Pears you got more then just a passin' fancy for this Dakota."

"I certainly do. I intend to marry him," she said emphatically. A dimple came into play in each cheek, and her eyes sparkled from the glow of the fire. "Now, all I have to do is convince him."

"So, he's fighting the bit, huh?" Still smiling, Maggie nodded. "Reckon a purty gal like you shouldn't have trouble hog-tying a man once you put your mind to it."

Maggie snorted at his confidence. "You wouldn't say that if you knew Dakota MacDonald. For a smart man, he has some dumb ideas."

She gazed pensively into the fire. "I never thought I would fall in love. I never really understood what it meant, but from the moment I met Dakota, I knew." She failed to see the old man smile and nod in understanding. Drawn deeper into reflection, Maggie added for her own cognizance, "If I were to lose Dakota, I could never love any man again."

The last words echoed in her ears. Startled, she snapped out of her reverie and smiled with embarrassment. "I'm sorry. I must sound very foolish to you."

The old man's eyes were moist. "I'm thinking, if I'd a been as lucky to know true love when I was young, I wouldn't be roaming these hills alone now."

Maggie realized she had saddened the spirits of the kindly old miner. She wanted to cheer him up, but couldn't find the words. They cleaned up the dishes in silence. After he packed them all away on the mule, he handed her a blanket. "Reckon you should try and grab some sleep. If that scout of yours ain't found you by mornin', I'll get you back to your camp."

"Oh, Dakota will find me," Maggie said confidently. She lay back and closed her eyes.

When Maggie awoke to daylight, she saw Dakota and Will standing above her with worried frowns. She sat up and rubbed her eyes. "What kept you?"

"Damn it, Maggie!" Throwing up his hands in frustration, Dakota walked away. He leaned against a nearby tree and began to kick up the dust at his feet.

"Are you okay, Maggie?" Will asked solemnly.

"I'm fine. My friend has taken good care of me."

"What friend?" Will asked.

She looked around in surprise. She saw no sign of the old miner. Blaze was tied to a nearby tree, but the stallion and mule were gone. "Where did he go?" she exclaimed.

"Someone found you last night?" Will said patiently. Maggie could see he only half-believed her story.

"Yes. An old man. He gave me this blanket after he shot the rattlesnake."

"Rattlesnake!" The shout erupted from Dakota.

Maggie nodded. "He found Blaze, and he fed me. After that, I fell asleep." She cast a fretful glance at Will. "But why would he leave without saying goodbye?"

Dakota was too angry to care. "Maybe for the same damn reason you strayed from camp."

Maggie went over to him. "I'm sorry, Dakota."

"Sorry? That's supposed to make it all okay? Why the hell don't you listen to me?" Dakota ranted. "I told you never to leave the camp alone. Damn it, woman, can't you ever obey an order?"

Maggie cowered under his scathing outburst. She didn't realize that his anger was sparked by his anxiety over her disappearance. When he returned to camp and discovered she was missing, he had searched for her all night. He had been tormented by visualizing her in the hands of hostile Indians, or ripped to shreds by a wild animal. Now, overwhelmed with relief at finding her unharmed, Dakota vented his frustration in an outburst of anger when all he wanted to do was take Maggie in his arms and hold her.

"Please don't be angry with me, Dakota," she pleaded. "I didn't mean to stray. Blaze got loose and I went to find her. Suddenly, I found myself walking in circles, so I just sat down to wait for you."

His features softened as he looked into her trusting face. Helpless to keep from touching her, Dakota reached out and twisted one of her soft curls around his finger. "Maggie, there are so many dangers out here. You've got to promise to stay with the rest of the party. Stop depending on me to be around when you need me. I wasn't there last night, was I?"

Recalling those terror-stricken moments when she faced death from the venom-filled serpent, Maggie knew he was right. With love and trust she looked into his dark, tormented eyes. "I promise. I won't go anywhere without asking you first."

Dakota could no longer control his emotions. He pulled her into his arms and hugged her. Her trembling ceased as she relaxed against him. Maggie closed her eyes and her head slumped on his shoulder as Dakota held her in the haven of his arms.

Will managed to find something to look at in the opposite direction.

"You say this was an old man?" Dakota inquired as Maggie rode behind him with her arms wrapped around his waist.

"Yes, and he said he was a miner. He was so kind. I still don't understand why he would leave without waking me."

Will Godfrey rode behind them leading the saddleless Blaze. "A lot of the old men in these hills are hermits. They naturally shy away from strangers."

Maggie leaned her cheek against Dakota's back and thought of what the old miner had said about finding true love. She felt a deeper sorrow just thinking about the poor man's lonely life. Unconsciously, her arms tightened around Dakota. *I'll never let that happen to you, my love.*

Chapter Twenty-five

As the commotion stirred by Maggie's return subsided, everyone ate breakfast. Soon after they broke camp, and despite the late start, Dakota was convinced that with any kind of luck, they would reach their destination by nightfall.

More than one disgruntled look was cast in her direction as she rode along singing and humming lightly to herself. Maggie was the only one in the party who had enjoyed a full night's sleep, and those who had spent the night searching for her, or sat up worrying, were practically sleeping in their saddles as they plodded along. Whenever a halt was called to rest the horses, the precious time was used to grab a much-needed rest.

Each day had carried the riders into higher ground. Maggie continued to be awed by the majestic splendor. Exposed by erosion, ruggedly beautiful buttes and crags rose abruptly amid the pine-clad hills to form steep, granite-walled gulches with rushing streams for floors.

Late in the afternoon, the dusky blue shadows suddenly deepened to murkiness. When large raindrops began to splatter the riders, slickers were quickly donned just as the sky exploded with a thunderclap and jagged bolts of lightning accompanied by the boom of thunder bombarded the earth.

Caught in the turbulence, the beleaguered riders hunched in their saddles and cringed each time silver lightning bolts streaked across the sky.

"Dakota, we've got to get these women under cover," Taylor shouted to the scout riding in advance of the huddled group.

Dakota felt certain they had to be near their destination, but he hadn't seen anything to indicate as much. Visibility had been reduced to only a few yards, and his eyes scanned the terrain for some unusual sign or clue among the trees and rocks.

Then, in a glittering flash of lightning, Dakota thought he spied a gap in the rocky hillside ahead. He brushed aside the rain streaming down his face and peered intently into the blackness, waiting for the next thunderbolt. The violent clap caused his horse to rear up in fright, but Dakota's trained eye remained fixed on the rocks as he brought the horse under control. Outlined in the incandescent glow he saw a large, round opening, possibly the entrance to a mine.

The site appeared to be the location on the map where Sam Harris had buried his fortune.

The drenched party dismounted and crowded into the dark opening. Although shivering and unable to see, they were grateful for a solid roof overhead to protect them from the force of the storm.

"Don't move around until we get some light in here," Dakota warned. He went back out into the downpour and returned with the pack containing the lanterns. After lighting three of the lamps, he surveyed their surroundings.

The dim light cast an amber glow on walls of rock. The chamber appeared to be about fifteen feet wide, forty feet deep, but not more than six feet high. The men had to crouch to keep from striking their heads on the ceiling of the large cavity.

"My, my, the old homestead hasn't changed a bit," Katherine scoffed.

"It's drier in here than outside, Mother." Maggie stretched her neck to look about. "What's that big hole over there?" she asked, pointing to an opening on the far wall.

Dakota got down and peered into an excavation tunnel burrowed into the back wall. "It looks like an exploratory tunnel somebody dug out to look for a vein. It's a very narrow passage, wide enough for only one person to crawl through."

"Is this Sam Harris's mine?" Maggie asked.

"Could have been one of them," Will answered. "Sam staked out several."

Dakota shook his head. "It's not much of a mine.

There are no signs of blasting or digging other than this tunnel. My guess is we're in a natural cave and the tunnel was dug by some hopeful prospector. This isn't where Sam hit his strike, though." Dakota stood up and brushed the dirt off his hands and knees. "Let's get the rest of the gear, Will."

Taylor rubbed his hands enthusiastically. "I have to say this is quite cozy, regardless of who the former tenant may have been. I think we should get a fire going. A hot cup of coffee will set well with all of us."

"Right you are, Mr. Collingswood. Miss Diane, may I assist you with your wrap?" Peter offered a courtly bow and helped Diane remove her rain slicker.

"Well, you are all certainly easy to please. Forgive me if I can't wax eloquent about this drear accommodation," Katherine grumbled.

"Oh, Mother, don't be such a spoilsport," Diane chided. Everyone turned to the girl in surprise. Throughout the trip, whenever Katherine voiced a complaint, Diane could be depended upon to add fuel to the fuss.

Katherine bestowed a formidable glance on her youngest daughter. "Diane, are you feverish?"

"No, she's just cold and wet like the rest of us," Peter said, championing the woman he loved. "Once we get a warm fire started, Mrs. Collingswood, you'll be surprised how much your regard for this dear accommodation will improve."

"According to the map, this is where we'll find Sam's treasure," Maggie reminded them.

That cardinal fact had slipped their minds—

even Katherine's. They began to move around, peering into corners and around rocks as if expecting to find Sam Harris's fortune in plain sight.

Holding hands, Diane and Peter examined the nearest corner. "What's the treasure supposed to look like?" Diane whispered to Peter.

"A bathtub with hot water," he answered, sotto voce.

"I cherish the thought, my love," she gleefully countered in mock imitation.

Dakota and Will returned toting the other packs and dumped them on the ground. It was immediately evident to Dakota what Diane and Peter were up to, and he shook his head in disgust. "What do you people think you're doing?"

Grinning, Peter said, "I can tell you we're not looking for firewood."

"Well, I sure wouldn't poke around without checking out this place first. Never know what might crawl out from under one of those rocks."

Dakota's warning deterred them all, especially Maggie, whose experience with the rattlesnake was still a vivid memory. They quickly regrouped in the center of the cave as Dakota lit a few more lamps.

Will Godfrey thrust one of the lanterns into the entrance of the tunnel. "I wonder how far back this goes?"

Katherine shivered and moved a step closer to Taylor. "I wonder more what's back there; anything could have crawled in."

"I reckon there's only one way to find out." Dakota removed his slicker, drew his Colt, and, grabbing a lantern, he crawled into the tunnel.

"Wait for me," Maggie called after him, but Dakota had disappeared. Before anyone could stop her, she took a lantern and followed on her hands and knees.

The light revealed a long, narrow tunnel with the ceiling and walls shored up by wooden supports. She could hear the scary patter of tiny feet as rodents scurried away, and when she saw two pink eyes glowing in the darkness, Maggie gasped in alarm. "Dakota!"

"It's just a weasel, Maggie."

The long shaft protruded into the bowels of the hill for about seventy-five feet before coming to an end. Dakota sat down, his head brushing the ceiling. "I wish I knew what we should be looking for."

Dakota held the lamp as high as the low ceiling permitted. They saw white symbols painted on the walls, but none of the markings meant anything to him. "If Sam's the one who painted all this, I can't guess what he had in mind."

"Are these symbols a message in Sioux?" Maggie asked.

"Not any I know."

Dakota shifted around her to inspect the other wall. Maggie felt as if she were suffocating in the confined area and was tempted to leave when Dakota suddenly exclaimed, "Maggie, I think I've found something." He pointed to one of the markings on the wall. "Look at this."

Bending closer, Maggie leaned over his shoulder to examine one of the paintings. To her amazement, she recognized a symbol—the familiar, sideways letter H.

"Why, that's the Lazy H brand."

Dakota pulled out his knife and scrapped at the dirt around the letter. "This dirt is loose."

Within minutes he had dug a hole in the wall. Then the knife clinked against a hard surface, and Dakota turned to her with a grin.

He continued to chip away until he pulled a small metal box out of the wall. "Let's get out of here." They grabbed the lantern and crawled back.

Enough dried wood had been found in the cave to get a fire started and, by the time they returned, the cavern glowed with warmth. Everyone gathered around Dakota.

"Whatever is *that*?" Katherine peered at the dirt-encrusted object.

"I think we have found Sam's fortune, or whatever it is he left us," Dakota offered, somewhat bemused by the find.

"What?" Katherine cried aghast. "It can't be so!"

"Doesn't look like a pot of gold to me." Diane echoed her mother's disbelief.

Dakota took out his knife and pried open the box. Inside, he found a small key and two folded pieces of paper. When he opened the first sheet, Katherine, pushing against his arm to see, exclaimed in utter dismay, "Oh my stars, another map!"

Dakota studied the map for a moment, then opened the other sheet and found a letter addressed to him and Maggie. After reading the letter, he handed it to Maggie. Her eyes raced across the scrawled script.

"Well, what does it say?" Katherine asked impatiently. Her green eyes gleamed with avarice. Maggie lowered the paper and handed it to her mother. Katherine began to read aloud.

Dakota and Maggie:

I had every confidence you'd find this, Dakota. I suppose the two of you are wondering why I put you to all this trouble only to find another map. You will soon discover my reason for this peculiar arrangement. Forgive the folly of an old man who loves both of you very much. Be assured, Dakota, you will find my fortune at the end of the trail on this second map. What you find is merely an accumulation of wealth. I'm hoping by now you and Maggie have already found life's real treasure.

Sam

Maggie's glance sought Dakota. She saw him leaning against the wall of the entrance with his back to her, staring outside. She walked over to him and put her hand on his arm. "What does it all mean, Dakota? You hardly even glanced at the map."

"I think I know where it'll lead us." He straightened up with a sad smile. "Sun's out, Maggie."

She looked outside. Sure enough, the violent

storm had passed over, and the colors of the spectrum shimmered in a radiant arc which seemed close enough to reach out and touch.

"Oh look, a rainbow," she cried with delight.

Dakota glanced at the woman at his side. His dark gaze lingered on her young face, aglow with pleasure. He now understood why Sam had sent them on the hunt; the answer had been there all the while. His closed mind had blinded him to reality.

Peter sauntered over and joined the pair. Glancing skyward, he commented, "Quite symbolic, wouldn't you say, now that you two have found your pot of gold?"

"There's a lot more than a rainbow that's symbolic today," Dakota replied. "How about a hand with the horses?"

"Sure thing," Peter said and followed him.

Maggie returned to her parents. Angry from disappointment, Katherine spoke harshly. "Now there, you see, Maggie? Sam Harris always was impossible. Look how he led us all the way up here only to give us another map. He's as confusing in death as he was confused in life . . . an utterly ridiculous man."

"We didn't have to come, Mother," Diane reminded her. "I knew we should have stayed in Washington."

"Dakota does not seem disturbed, Katherine," Taylor interjected. "Calm yourself, my dear. He will lead us to our destination."

"Destination? What destination? According to that silly note we are headed for 'life's real treasure'—whatever that means." Katherine's voice grew louder with her frustration. "You know what I think, Taylor?"

"No, my dear," Taylor measured his words, waiting for the storm to pass. "What do you think?"

"I think Sam Harris had no fortune and this is just another of his fanciful daydreams, purposely calculated to play a horribly cruel trick on us."

"Not so, Katherine," Will ventured to interrupt the tirade. "Sam's wealth is real, all right. I was his lawyer and privy to business."

"Well then, tell me this, Mr. Privy Lawyer; how come Mr. Big Time Sam didn't put his money in the bank like any sensible man? This is 1880 and no sane person would be leaving a real fortune hidden in the hills, requiring days of hazardous travel to find it, to say nothing of tunnels and boxes and keys and notes and—oh, dear God, another map!" Katherine became hoarse as her voice escalated with each word.

"Please calm down, Mother," Maggie pleaded. "We've come this far and I believe in Sam, even if you don't."

"So do I," Will agreed with Maggie. "True, he was a bit eccentric. But he was rich and he did mean for Maggie and Dakota to share his wealth."

"Yes, Sam Harris was eccentric all right. He never knew when he had it good. He was restless, adventuresome, a man easily attracted by nonsense and risky escapades. The fact that he lived through—" Taylor stopped and cleared his throat before he continued. "Well, anyway, this wild goose chase initiated by Sam Harris for some mysterious treasure in the hills, and now yet another map, should be no surprise to us." Taylor put his arm around Katherine. "Let's go outside, my dear, and get some fresh air."

Maggie retrieved Sam's note and placed it in the strongbox. Then she closed the cover and laid the metal box on the floor with the rest of the gear. She would wait until later to discuss the contents with Dakota.

The sunshine brought a lift to their spirits, and although they agreed to spend the night in the cave rather than the tents, a campfire was built outside in the fresh air.

The contents of the metal box were forgotten in everyone's relief over the disappearance of the dark clouds. Dakota felt the storm front had left the area, and they would be looking at sunny skies for the remainder of the journey. The atmosphere amongst the travelers became jovial, and a feeling of camaraderie prevailed throughout the evening as they lingered over coffee.

Peter and Diane had already retired when Maggie decided to broach the subject of the box's contents with Dakota. She tiptoed quietly into the cave so as not to disturb anyone and found the strongbox. Returning to the campfire, Maggie sat down next to Dakota. She opened the metal box, then drew back with a start and exclaimed, "It's empty!"

The others looked at each other, puzzled, and returned their attention to Maggie. "The key and map are missing," Maggie repeated.

"Are you sure you put them back in there?" Katherine asked.

"Of course I'm sure." Maggie cast a helpless glance at Dakota. His expression was inscrutable.

Nervously, Taylor cleared his throat. "This has been a long and tiring day, Margaret. I'm sure in the morning you'll remember where you put the items."

The empty box fell to the ground as Maggie jumped to her feet. "I *know* I put them back in the box, Dakota." She didn't care what the others believed, but Maggie desperately wanted to convince Dakota she was telling the truth.

He picked up the box and stood up. "I'm sure you did, Maggie."

Katherine started to argue. "Maggie, you—" Flinching, she stopped abruptly when a flying object whizzed past Dakota and hit Taylor with a thud. For a second, Katherine stared at the feathered shaft protruding from her husband's shoulder and then screamed as a circle of blood began to stain his shirt. She grabbed at Taylor to break his fall and slumped with him to the ground.

Dakota shoved Maggie down as his Colt cleared the holster.

"Stay low and don't move."

He no sooner spoke than he saw Will struck by an arrow in the leg. But the old man quickly drew his gun and began to fire into the trees.

"What's going on?" Peter yelled from the entrance of the cave.

"Indians. You two okay?" Dakota called to him.

"Yeah." Peter ducked for cover when an arrow

struck the rock above his head. At least he and Diane had good protection, while the rest lay trapped in the open by the campfire.

"Will?" Dakota asked.

"I'm okay," Godfrey replied.

"What kind of arrow?"

"Sioux, I think."

"And Collingswood?"

Will Godfrey glanced over at the two figures next to him. "Can't tell with Katherine all over him. He don't appear to be moving, though. How many you reckon are out there?"

"Not many, or they'd have rushed us by now. You and Mrs. Collingswood start moving to that cave. I'll cover you."

Katherine stopped weeping long enough to declare, "I'll not leave my husband. He's alive."

"You can't do him any good right now, ma'am," Dakota said. He called out in Sioux to the concealed attackers. There was no response. "Well, they're not friendly, that's for sure."

"What did you say to them?" Maggie whispered. Trembling, she lay quietly behind the log where Dakota had shoved her.

"I asked who they were and told them I am of the Oglala Sioux."

Suddenly, two Indians wielding upraised tomahawks leaped at Dakota from the concealment of the trees. Dakota shot one and immediately the other pounced on him. Maggie watched them grapple with each other as Dakota struggled to release the Indian's grasp on his weapon. Powerless to help him, she glimpsed a knife in Dakota's hand as the two men rolled on the ground in a life-and-death struggle.

Horrified, Maggie heard a guttural grunt when Dakota drove his knife into the chest of the savage. To avoid the thrashing bodies, Maggie shimmied backwards right into the path of an on-rushing Indian headed toward Will's back. The savage tripped over her and rolled across the ground. Forsaking caution, she jumped to her feet and screamed as she saw that the warrior was crouched before her, ready to strike.

Her mouth gaped open in silent horror as his lithe body lunged forward. A shattering blast rang out and Maggie stared down into the lifeless eyes of the painted savage at her feet.

Finding its target, one shot of Peter's rifle had saved her life.

Maggie began trembling and Dakota grabbed her hand. "Let's go," he shouted. Crouching, she half-stumbled as they ran toward the entrance of the cave. "Take care of her," he shouted to Peter and shoved Maggie inside.

Dakota crawled across the ground on his stomach. Once in the shadows, he got to his feet and moved silently into the trees with a knife clutched in his hand.

Dodging an arrow, Will dragged himself to Katherine's side. He picked off another Indian who tried to rush the camp. "Get to that cave *now*," Will yelled to Katherine. "I'll stay with him."

Frightened but adamant, Katherine answered, "I'll not leave my husband, Mr. Godfrey."

"Dammit, you're a stubborn woman," Will

grumbled as he slid shells into the empty chamber of his Colt. "I've got six shots left, and you need decent cover if you intend to keep that pretty scalp of yours."

Several moments passed without further attack. "Do you think they are gone?" Katherine whispered.

"We'll soon know. If there are any left, Dakota will find them."

"Unless they find him first," Katherine replied.

Having regained consciousness, Taylor mumbled, "Katherine."

"Sh-h-h-h, my dear," she cautioned. "Lie still until we're sure it's safe."

Suddenly Dakota shouted from nearby, "Don't shoot, Will, I'm coming in." He walked out from the shadows.

Will knew then that the danger must be over, and he relaxed the grip on his gun. "Any get away?"

Dakota shook his head, tossed down a captured bow and quiver of arrows, then wiped off his knife blade on the leggings of a dead Indian lying nearby.

"How many more were there?"

"Two," Dakota replied succinctly. "One was Limping Coyote. These Indians were the renegades I trailed from Wyoming."

Maggie ran from the cave, followed closely by Peter and Diane. They helped Katherine get Taylor to his feet. Peter took his arm and sat him down on a log near the fire.

Dakota regarded the two wounded men grimly. "Which one of you wants to be first?"

"Take Collingswood first. He looks in worse shape then me," Will said.

"What can I do to help?" Maggie asked.

"Get the bottle of whiskey out of Will's saddle-bags."

"Now, how'd you know I brought that along?" Will chuckled.

"You usually do."

"But only for medicinal purposes," Will joshed. "And I wasn't wrong, was I?"

Dakota grinned and patted the old man's shoulder. Maggie could see the deep regard the two men held for one another, and she wiped a tear away as she went to find the whiskey.

Dakota knelt on the ground to examine Taylor's wound. The arrow had pierced the shoulder. When Maggie returned with the whiskey, Dakota had examined Taylor's wound and stood up. Before Taylor could guess his intent, Dakota grasped the shaft of the arrow and pulled it out. Taylor grunted with pain but remained conscious.

"You're fortunate, sir. There was no poison on the arrow."

However, when Dakota took the whiskey bottle and poured astringent liquor into the wound, Taylor yelped with pain. "Now, Mrs. Collingswood, if you'll bandage and get his arm into a sling, I'll take care of Will."

The arrow was embedded in the fleshy part of Will's thigh. Dakota sliced away Will's trouser leg to examine the wound. He cut off the feathered shaft of the arrow, then shook his head. "Don't look too deep, Will, but I'll have to dig it out."

"Figured you would, son. How about handing

me that bottle of rot gut, Maggie gal?"

"Peter, get Will's blanket from the cave and bring along that narrow-blade knife we've been using to cook with."

When Peter returned, the two men tried to assist Will, but he brushed aside their offers of help and limped over to the blanket.

Dakota put the knife in the fire and waited while Will took several swallows of the whiskey. "Reckon I'm as ready as I'll ever be." He handed the bottle to Peter and laid down.

"Hold him still," Dakota warned Peter. The young man took a deep swallow of the liquor, and, setting aside the bottle, he firmly grasped Will's shoulders. "Hope the two of you saved some liquor to clean out the wound," Dakota said.

Maggie slipped her hand into Will's and gave it a squeeze. The old man looked up and smiled at her. "Do what you have to do, son."

Dakota probed the wound with the knife as Will clenched his teeth. Perspiration dotted Will's brow, and his hand tightened around Maggie's in a crushing grasp. Mercifully, he blacked out, and Dakota quickly finished removing the arrowhead.

When Will opened his eyes a few minutes later, Maggie had already neatly bandaged and wrapped his leg. Will smiled, closed his eyes, and slipped back into restful slumber.

The mystery surrounding the disappearance of the key and map was a forgotten issue in the night's excitement.

The rest of the exhausted travelers were soon asleep.

Chapter Twenty-six

The next day, near the end of the morning meal, the sound of approaching horses startled the small group. The men reached for their weapons, but were greatly relieved to see a patrol of United States cavalry ride up to their camp. The officer leading the patrol recognized Dakota immediately and greeted him with warm regard. "Sergeant MacDonald."

"I'm no longer in the army, Lieutenant Scott, remember?" Dakota replied.

The officer grinned and climbed down from his mount. He offered his hand. "How have you been, Dakota?"

They shook hands. "Fine, sir."

"What might you all be doing up in this wilderness?" Scott asked, particularly eyeing the women with curiosity.

"Well, I reckon we're . . . prospecting, you might say," Dakota answered, amused at the officer's quandary.

"I should warn you, we've trailed hostiles into this area."

"Yeah, we know. But you don't have to worry about them any more."

Realizing what must have happened, Scott smiled. "Limping Coyote with them?"

Dakota nodded. "Yup, with the same band we trailed here from Wyoming."

"Wonder why they didn't head for the Badlands."

"No welcome for them there. The Sioux don't take kindly to killing among their own people."

"Colonel Besting will be glad to hear the news. I'll wire him as soon as we get back to Deadwood."

"Taylor Collingswood, Lieutenant," Taylor said cordially, stepping forward to introduce himself. "Can we offer you and your men some breakfast?" Maggie anticipated the extended courtesy and had already put another pot of coffee on the fire.

"We've had morning mess, but coffee would be appreciated, sir." Scott turned to his squad. "Dismount." The troopers climbed off their horses and moved to the fire.

The lieutenant noticed Taylor's arm in the sling. "Hope your wound isn't serious, sir."

"It's more inconvenient than painful," Taylor remarked to the young man.

The presence of the military unit comforted the whole party. Soon the previous night's scare seemed more heroic than terrifying, and the men of the patrol eagerly listened to the details of the attack. After a short period of coffee and conversation, Lieutenant Scott examined the bodies and had the troopers dispose of them. Maggie ended up making another pot of coffee and several pans of biscuits before the unit finally mounted up and rode away.

With the threat of danger behind, the mystery of what happened to the map and key returned to haunt the small group. After a fruitless search for the missing contents of the metal box, the frustrated members of the party packed up to move on. But they had become suspicious of one another.

Suspicion caused tension, and the once-shared camaraderie began to erode.

Maggie's idealism was severely tested by the theft. She loved and trusted every one of the six people she was traveling with, yet one was a thief willing to steal that which rightfully belonged to her and Dakota.

As they rode away from the cave, Maggie pondered the mystery. She hoped Dakota had taken the contents of the box.

Deep in thought, an outburst of laughter drew her attention to Diane and Peter riding side by side. Maggie wondered why Peter seemed so light-hearted—as if a heavy burden had been lifted from his shoulders. Would he have destroyed the map just to end the treasure hunt and hurry Diane back to Washington?

Maggie's glance next moved to her mother. Katherine's mien was serious and self-absorbed as she rode stiffly at her husband's side. Katherine had made no secret of her belief that Sam Harris's fortune belonged to her, and she would certainly have no qualms about cheating Dakota—but would she cheat her own daughter too?

Maggie considered the possible involvement of Taylor. Although he had been like a real father to her, Maggie wondered if he might have taken the map to placate her mother.

Dakota slowed the pace of his horse. All day he had been unconsciously hurrying to ride clear of the party. Except for Maggie, he wanted to avoid the rest of these people whose lives revolved around money and power; Dakota MacDonald had no desire for either.

Deadwood would be a welcome sight to him.

Later that day, after they had set up their camp-site for the night, the first outburst occurred when Taylor, provoked by suspicion, confronted Will as he was returning to camp.

"Where have you been?" Taylor demanded.

"In the woods relieving myself," Will responded.

Will started to pass by when Taylor grabbed his arm. "I don't believe you. You've been gone for an hour."

Will knocked Taylor's hand aside. "Take your hand off me, Collingswood. I'm not accountable to you."

"I'm concerned about the missing map and key. I think you're responsible," Taylor accused.

"Responsible? That's funny coming from you, Collingswood. From what I hear, you are responsible for a few things which would put a bad light on a man who plans to take a diplomatic post."

"You're just trying to throw the suspicion off yourself by accusing me."

"I didn't accuse you. You're the one doing the accusing," Will replied. "Although I wouldn't put anything past Katherine."

Indignant, Taylor answered angrily, "You keep my wife's name out of this."

Will's face twisted in a smirk. "*Your* wife's name? Don't you mean the name of Sam Harris's wife?" Taylor looked as if he were startled by Will's affrontery. "No need to look so surprised, Collingswood. I know the truth. Sam told me the whole story a long time ago. I suggest you don't tell the others any of your ridiculous suspicions about me, or I might be obliged to tell the truth about you and Katherine. Then we'll see which of us the others decide is the honest man. So put it to rest, Collingswood." Will walked away without a backward glance at Taylor.

But Taylor couldn't put the matter to rest. He was too much of a snob to let the small-town banker threaten him. Taylor seethed throughout the evening meal, casting disgruntled looks at Will until his attitude became apparent.

Finally, Will faced the man. "I told you to put it to rest, Collingswood."

"Put what to rest, Taylor?" Katherine asked.

"Nothing, dear. Nothing at all," Taylor offered hurriedly.

"Taylor, you've been scowling at Mr. Godfrey all evening. Now don't try to tell me there isn't bad blood between you. Why don't you tell me what's wrong? Maybe I can help."

"I don't think he wants you to do that, Mrs. Collingswood. May not be too flattering."

"Flattering to whom, Mr. Godfrey?" Katherine ventured.

"To you, ma'am, and the minister there."

Katherine recoiled abruptly. "Would you be kind enough, sir, to explain what you mean?"

"Katherine, I told you it's nothing." Taylor grasped her shoulder to draw her away, but Katherine brushed aside his hand. "What is Mr. Godfrey referring to, Taylor?"

Taylor cast an irritated look at Will and decided he could no longer conceal his anger. "Apparently, Sam Harris filled Mr. Godfrey's ears with some cockamamie story about our past."

Katherine turned to Will with ire in her green eyes. "I am surprised, sir. As a lawyer I would think you would be interested in hearing both sides of a story before passing judgment on the accused. I do stand accused of something, I assume."

Will looked contrite. He had not meant to open this hornet's nest, and he began to shuffle from one foot to the other. "I reckon, ma'am, that's why I was never successful at practicing law."

"Perhaps you should keep *practicing* then, until you learn how to draw conclusions properly, Mr. Godfrey. Surely you have heard of a libel suit for defamation of character?"

His wife's haughty pronouncement prompted Taylor to interject, "Please, Katherine, do not pursue this matter."

"Mrs. Collingswood, I apologize if I've offended you," Will answered to calm the disturbed woman.

"I accept your apology, sir, and I can assure you that there is no shame connected with my past. However, you must be aware, Mr. Godfrey, that circumstances not of one's own choosing often lead one to desperate measures. For that reason, I feel compelled to tell you my version of life with Sam Harris."

Her glance swept the circle of faces and came to rest on Maggie. "I think, Margaret, that you are the most affected by what I have to say."

All eyes were on Katherine as she sat down and began to speak. "My papa had been a schoolteacher in Wisconsin and came to the California gold fields in '49 with big dreams of striking it rich. He staked a claim and sent for us. I was six years old at the time and my sister, Jenny, was five. By the time we made the long trip around Cape Horn, Papa's mine had run out, so he packed us up and headed back East, this time by wagon. We got as far as Wyoming, near Fort Laramie, when he decided to take up ranching. He used the last of our money to buy some stock, promising Mama that someday we'd be rich, with the largest ranch in the territory.

"The first winter Mama died from some kind of lung disease; we never knew what kind because there was no doctor. And the Indians ran off with the cattle."

Her face twisted with bitterness. "Rich! Papa ended up with a dirt farm, grubbing out just enough to feed us. Jenny and I went barefoot because Papa couldn't afford to buy us shoes. When our feet stopped growing, my sister and I shared an old pair of my mother's shoes. Then Jenny died from a snake bite, the year before I met Sam."

Katherine's voice was the only sound that penetrated the stillness of the night as she continued. "I was near sixteen when Sam's patrol rode up to the farm. They had been chasing hostiles. A couple of the troopers were wounded, and Sam asked for the use of the barn while they tended to their wounds.

"Sam was thirty years older than I, but I didn't care. He had a glib tongue and could charm the skin off a rattlesnake. I didn't know anything about men. Papa gave me my schooling, and we never had any neighbors. No one ever came near the farm."

Katherine paused and smiled gratefully at Taylor when he handed her a cup of coffee. She took a sip of the hot brew, then continued with her story. "By the time the patrol was ready to leave two days later, Sam had asked me to marry him. Even though I hardly knew him, it didn't take much persuasion on his part. I wanted to get away from that desolate place so badly, I would have been willing to go with him whether he married me or not.

"So, I kissed Papa goodbye, climbed on the back of Sam's horse, and left with all my worldly belongings—the dress on my back and Mama's old shoes on my feet. As a wedding gift, Papa gave me an old Johnson's Dictionary and a worn copy of Webster's Blue-Backed Speller. He told me that if I learned the meaning of every word in those books, no one could ever call me ignorant.''

Taylor leaned over and gently touched her hand. "Katherine, this is difficult for you. You don't have to continue.''

She shook her head. As Maggie witnessed the exchange between her parents, she realized how much these two people loved one another. She had never thought about that before. Now, knowing the depth of her feeling for Dakota, Maggie recognized in her parents the closeness shared by people in love.

"Well, Sam and I were married as soon as we got to Fort Laramie. In the beginning I was happy. Sam was good to me. At least he never hit me, not even when he was drunk. He even bought me several dresses and a pair of shoes. But Sam Harris was not cut out for marriage, and when he wasn't away on patrol, he caroused with his friends. What he didn't gamble away, he spent on liquor.

"Life on the post became as lonely for me as it had been on the farm. Aware of the poverty I came from, the other women wouldn't talk to me and I learned a new phrase that wasn't in the books Papa gave me—white trash. That's what those kindly women considered me, and that's how they treated me. The men were just as bad. When Sam was off on patrol, they'd come around, figuring I would be willing to . . .''

For a brief moment, Katherine closed her eyes to compose herself, then cast a fond smile at Maggie. "Then you were born, Margaret. If Sam Harris loved anyone in this world, it was you, honey. As soon as he'd come in from duty, he'd pick you up to hold you and kiss you. He'd walk around the post carrying you and showing you off to people. I guess in all fairness to Sam, he tried to be more of a family man, but before long, he went back to his old habits."

Katherine grimaced, took a deep breath, and continued. "Then the day came when Sam didn't return from a patrol. Shortly after, the Army declared him dead, gave me fifty dollars, and asked me to leave Fort Laramie. They needed the quarters for Sam's replacement. Do you believe it? They thought they had to tell me to get out! Why, I couldn't wait to get away from that miserable hole," she scoffed with a pitiful laugh.

"Did you go back to your father's farm?" Maggie asked.

"No. The farm was gone. Shortly after you were born, I wanted Papa to see his granddaughter, so I persuaded Sam to take me out to the farm. Papa was dead—killed by Indians. Nothing was left. The house and the barn were burned to the ground. Sam figured it must have happened months before. So we buried Papa's remains and put up a marker," Katherine said without any show of emotion.

Despite Katherine's show of bravado, Maggie's heart ached as she imagined the desperation her mother must have felt at being left alone with an infant and no place to go. "Well, war had broken out in the East, and Taylor was reassigned to Washington. He was in command of the patrol that escorted the stagecoach when I left Fort Laramie.

When we reached Independence, Missouri, we were married."

"I imagine the whole experience must have been very painful, Mother," Maggie said solemnly.

"Well, it's long over with and forgotten until now." She glanced deliberately at Will. "I didn't take the key and map, but whatever fortune Sam Harris has left, I feel it is rightfully mine. It's small payment for that nightmare of a marriage I suffered with him."

Leaning against a tree, Dakota had remained silent throughout the narrative. He tossed out the coffee that had cooled in his cup and walked over to pour himself a fresh cup. "Ever stop to think, Mrs. Collingswood, that your scalp would be dangling from the same coup stick as your father's, if Sam hadn't married you?"

Angered, Taylor jumped to his feet. "That is an insensitive remark, MacDonald." He slipped an arm protectively around Katherine's shoulders.

"I guess you figure you've got a right to be real upset with Sam, Katherine," Will Godfrey said from his seat near the fire. "He freed you from an existence you hated and saved your life doing it. And if it weren't for him, you never would have met the rich husband you've got now." His mouth curved in a sardonic grin. "Yep, that Sam Harris was sure a low-down polecat, all right."

"I wouldn't expect the two of you to understand," Katherine snarled at Will and Dakota. Her eyes flashed with contempt. "Small men can only venture small-minded opinions."

The insult, following the white-wash of her story,

goaded Will to reveal more than he had intended. "Could be you're right, Katherine. But I was hoping you would tell Maggie the whole story."

"The whole story?" Katherine asked. The previous scorn in her voice had become edged with wariness.

"That you were carrying Taylor Collingswood's unborn child the day you rode out of Fort Laramie." Having fired the cannon, Will turned on Taylor. "And you deliberately sent Sam on a suicide mission because he knew you were having an affair with his wife."

Shocked by the incredible accusation, Maggie and Diane both looked to their parents for a denial. Taylor's face bore a worried expression, and Katherine sat with her head bowed, apparently unable to look at either of her daughters. Taylor moved behind Katherine and put his hands on her shoulders in a gentle squeeze to comfort her. "My dear, we always knew the truth would come out someday."

"Then I was the unborn child Mother was carrying?" The question had come from Diane. Maggie glanced at her sister. Peter had his arm around Diane, hugging her to his side.

Taylor Collingswood's eyes pleaded for understanding as he faced his daughters. "Yes, Diane. But you both deserve to know the whole story. What Godfrey said is true, girls. Your mother and I fell in love while Sam Harris was still alive."

Maggie sat stunned as Taylor began his narrative. "I shall never forget the day Sergeant Harris returned from patrol and I saw Katherine for the first time. She looked so incredibly young and beautiful. But I allowed myself to think the same about her that the others did."

Maggie struggled with anger; she felt betrayed by these two people whom she had always trusted. Whatever petty squabbles there had been about her mother's snobbery or lack of compassion, Maggie had never doubted the integrity of either of her parents. "And just what were you thinking, Father?" she asked accusingly.

"That Katherine was—ah, easy." Taylor stammered and hastened to explain, "I mean, some girls of great beauty who come from poverty are not respectable. Folks thought Katherine married Sam to get respectability." He felt the stiffening of the shoulders at his fingertips. Once again, he squeezed gently to offer his wife the confirmation of his love. "Then, when I saw how your mother was ostracized, I began to feel sorry for her, especially when Sam didn't do anything to defend Katherine or improve the situation. She was so young, not any older than you are now, Diane.

"As a bachelor officer, I couldn't show any interest in the wife of a non-commissioned officer. It would have just increased the talk about Katherine. Then, when the husband of my laundress was transferred, I took the opportunity to ask Katherine if she would like to replace the woman. The arrangement allowed me to talk to Katherine without causing tongues to wag. The better I came to know her the more I came to see how unjustly she had been treated. Katherine was so lonely, and before I could stop myself, I fell in love with her. We began meeting secretly. Had our affair become known, the scandal would have ruined my military career."

Dakota had heard enough. He sensed that Taylor was telling the truth, and he couldn't figure out why Will had forced these people to dredge up the secrets of their past. He glanced at Maggie and saw the anguish in her proud young face. Diane's head was buried in Peter's shoulder. The confessions of their parents had hurt both of them. Frustrated, he grabbed his sketch pad and moved a short distance away.

However, Taylor continued with the account. "For several months, the Sioux had been raiding the ranches near the Fort, but with winter approaching, we knew the Indians would set up a camp until springtime. We figured if we could surprise them in their winter encampment, we could put an end to the raids once and for all. My commanding officer decided that one man acting on his own had the best chance of scouting the camp unobserved.

"Only two men at the fort were experienced enough to carry out such a mission—Sam Harris and Corporal Ryker. I felt Harris was the most qualified of the two. He had been at Laramie for six years and knew the area like the palm of his hand. I recommended him.

"When I told Sam the mission was voluntary and he could refuse if he wished, I remember he looked at me and asked, 'Mind telling me why you picked me?'

"He laughed when I told him he was the most

qualified non-commissioned officer on the post. 'No that's not the reason,' he said. 'You're sending me 'cause you're hopin' I won't come back. I ain't touched Kate in months, and when that bun in her oven finishes bakin' and pops out, we both know it's gonna be wearin' lieutenant bars, not sergeant stripes.' But despite his accusations, Sam was Army, so he went.

"When he failed to return by the designated time, I took out a patrol. We found his dead horse riddled with Sioux arrows and dried blood over the saddle."

Taylor turned anxiously to Maggie. "That's the way it happened, Margaret."

Katherine reached for his hand. "Taylor, they won't believe you any more than those bigoted fools at Fort Laramie would have."

"All I care about is whether the girls believe me." He walked over to Maggie and grasped her shoulders. "I swear to you, honey, I didn't have any other motive for picking Sam Harris for that mission."

His sincerity was too genuine to be denied. "I believe you, Father."

Tears glistened in Taylor's eyes as he hugged her. "I love you, Margaret. You're as much a daughter to me as Diane. I would never do anything to hurt you."

His jaw hardened grimly as he turned to Will. "I know our past looks suspicious, Godfrey, but I'm telling you the truth. I wouldn't take Margaret's money—not even for Katherine's sake."

Katherine had more to say on the matter. "And

that key and map didn't just walk out of here on their own. How do we know you're not the one who took it?" Katherine challenged. "Or what about him?"

Dakota glanced up from his sketch pad to discover an accusing finger pointed in his direction. "Lady, keep me out of this trial, 'cause I've got no intention of testifying."

Still stewing over his recent exchange with Will, Taylor picked up Katherine's challenge. "Yes, what about you, Godfrey? I caught you sneaking back into camp tonight. What were you doing out in the woods? Burying the key and map?"

"I wasn't sneaking back into camp," Will declared. "I already told you I went out there for the same reason the rest of you do."

Listening to the exchange, Maggie immediately recalled the night when she thought she had seen Will disappear into the trees. He had denied it then, too. What could he be up to? Could this kindly old man be the thief?

Maggie didn't want to believe Will was the guilty party any more than she wanted to suspect her own parents. But someone had taken the key and map.

"Furthermore," Taylor declared as he continued his accusation of Will, "you stand to gain if Margaret and Dakota don't find Sam Harris's fortune. It would be easy for you to just wait it out, Godfrey, until all the smoke clears, and then claim the fortune for yourself."

As Dakota resumed sketching, his eyes swept the people around the campfire. Maggie looked hurt and confused. *Damn these people*, he thought, considering the possible guilt of each. Dakota felt Maggie's stepfather had no reason to covet Sam's fortune, unless the hen-pecked man had stolen for his wife's sake.

Dakota's gaze moved to Peter Brent, who sat with his arm around Diane. These two seemed above suspicion. Neither had any interest in Sam Harris's fortune. *Or did they?* Brent's concern for Diane's welfare was evident. Would he deliberately destroy the key and map to end the hunt, hoping for a fast return to Washington?

Katherine Collingswood sat staring into the fire. She hadn't made a move toward Maggie. Why was she avoiding looking her daughter in the eye? Was she embarrassed about these revelations of her past, or had the woman stolen the key and map? Dakota figured Katherine Collingswood wasn't the kind to apologize for past actions, so he ruled out embarrassment. That left only guilt. Would Maggie's own mother try to steal from her?

If not, the only remaining suspect was Will Godfrey. But Will had been Sam's best friend. Wouldn't he want to carry out Sam's final wishes?

Peter Brent was as disgusted with the situation as Dakota. No one had accused him or Diane of taking the map and key. But the arguing and unhappiness he had witnessed this evening were foreign to his nature. He could no longer bear the quarreling and suspicion, and for Diane's sake, he decided to make his feelings known.

The young man rose to his feet. "The hour is late, my friends, and I have no doubt that whatever happened to the map and key will come to light sooner or later. But for now, nothing can be resolved by the discord and painful confessions I've heard this evening. I just can't understand how people who love Diane and Margaret could subject them to such bitter wrangling and cruel airing of family . . . misfortunes," Peter diplomatically but firmly stated.

"I always did think raking up the past—and brooding about things that we can't change—was a waste of time. And as for squabbling over Sam's fortune—well, I didn't know the man, but I doubt he had all this trouble and interference in mind for Margaret and Dakota."

Peter took Diane's hand and pulled her to her feet. "If the rest of you want to fight over Sam Harris's fortune, so be it. As for myself, I intend to return to Washington with Diane as soon as we can wend our way back to Deadwood." He looked down lovingly at Diane and squeezed her hand. Hers was the only approval he needed.

Katherine did not bow easily to outsiders' demands. "I believe you are overstepping your bounds, Peter. You are only Diane's fiancé, not her husband."

"Mrs. Collingswood, apologies are certainly in order if I have offended you and Mr. Collingswood. But I love Diane, and her happiness is my foremost consideration. To that end, we are going back to Washington where her best interests will be served. I believe your interests have been served long enough."

Peter had laid his cards on the table. He turned

to Diane. "Are you willing to come with me, Diane?"

Defy her mother? Diane had never done so before. Maggie waited breathlessly for her sister's response, knowing full well that she herself had always been the rebel, not Diane. Spoiled and pampered, her sister had remained completely under their mother's domination. Peter's challenge to Katherine's authority would set the course in their marriage. Peter had laid down the ground rules, notifying his future mother-in-law that he had become the decision maker in Diane's life.

In Washington, Maggie's opinion of this rich man's son had never been high. Since his arrival in Deadwood, Peter had demonstrated strength and courage, qualities which had never surfaced in the capital. Maggie had developed a new-found respect for her future brother-in-law.

Diane had experienced a similar reassessment of Peter Brent since his arrival. From the time he had faced off with Rafe Catlin to this moment of confrontation with her mother, Peter had given her much food for thought.

Her eyes now gleamed with admiration. The man facing her parents was no namby-pamby. He was everything a young girl dreamed about—handsome, brave, exciting . . . and rich. And he loved her! Remembering his actions at the river, a shiver of excitement rippled down Diane's spine.

"Yes, Peter, you are right. I will go with you," she answered docilely.

Katherine's green eyes glinted with anger.

Crossing her arms, she began to pace back and forth in front of the fire. "Well, it appears that both of my daughters suffer from the same malady—a short memory and a lack of gratitude. How easy it is for the two of you to abandon principles and respect for your parents to pursue your own pleasures."

"Mother, that isn't true. Diane and I love and respect you and Father. Nothing said here tonight changes that regard. But we're entitled to seek our own happiness."

Katherine Collingswood was used to having free reign over matters concerning her daughters. *How dare they defy her? How dare they challenge her motives? What did these pampered children know about the real world? About having just enough food to take the edge off your hunger? What did they know about the mortification of doors slammed in their faces? Malicious whispers behind their backs because their parents were dirt farmers?*

Defiance. Ingratitude. Disrespect. This was their thanks for all her sacrifice.

Backed into a corner of self-righteous indignation, Katherine struck out viciously at the most visible source of this rebelliousness—Maggie.

"Seek your own happiness, indeed! Like a harlot?"

The slur brought Dakota to his feet.

"Didn't anything I said tonight get through to you?" Katherine raged. "I saw to it that you had the proper upbringing, which I never had. That no one could ever call you white trash, like they did your mother. I tried to make a lady of you. And for what? So you can lust with that half-breed on a buffalo robe like some Indian squaw?"

Stunned, Maggie gasped in shock at the malevolent indictment. Compelled by a desire to protect her from this verbal abuse, Dakota slipped his arm around Maggie's shoulders. "I'm taking you out of here, Maggie." He glanced at Peter. "We're pulling out at dawn and you're welcome to come with us."

Peter nodded. "Come on, sweetheart, we'd better get some sleep."

Dakota still had some final words for Katherine. There was no emotion in his voice when he addressed her. "Mrs. Collingswood, I hope you find the treasure you're seeking, but you're going to have to do it without my help."

In their seventeen years of marriage, Taylor Collingswood had rarely lost his temper with his wife. However, the attack on Maggie incited him to anger. "I think you've said enough, Katherine. Too much," Taylor declared. "I suggest you apologize to Maggie at once." He took her arm. "The treasure hunt is over. As soon as we reach Deadwood, we'll return to Washington."

It appeared to Katherine that no one understood how difficult the evening had been for her. She had bared her soul, reliving painful memories and events she had long put behind her—only to be rewarded with recriminations and ingratitude.

She raised her head with stately dignity. "Very well, as you wish, Taylor. I apologize to all of you."

Katherine walked to her tent.

Chapter Twenty-seven

Maggie could not fall asleep. The whole evening had been too disturbing to her. Was Sam's fortune worth all the bad feelings developing among them?

Restless, she shifted to her side trying to get comfortable. The new position gave her a chance to see out through the tent opening. A bright moon shone overhead, and as she lay gazing at the tranquil stars glowing above, Maggie could feel her tension easing.

Her eyelids were drooping when she glimpsed a shadow moving across the outside of the tent. She was instantly alert and waited until the shadow moved away. One of the men must have gone into the woods to relieve himself. When thirty minutes passed and no one returned to camp, she became engulfed with curiosity, wondering if the mysterious shadow could be another piece of the puzzle concerning the missing map and key.

She stole to the entrance of the tent and poked out her head. Dakota was lying near the fire. Maggie stepped out and peeked into the other tent. Peter and her father were sleeping soundly; Will Godfrey's bedroll was empty.

She hurried over to Dakota and knelt down beside him. "Dakota, Will's been gone for over thirty minutes."

"I know," Dakota replied tersely. He sat up. "Saw him go, and I've been waiting for him to come back."

"Do you think anything could have happened to him? Maybe there are still hostile Indians or something."

"No, I don't think anything has happened to him. Will knows how to take care of himself." There was a tinge of anger in his voice.

"Do you think Father's right? Could Will have taken the key and map?"

"I'd hate to think so. Will's not a greedy man. He must have a good reason, if he did."

"Maybe his bank's in trouble and he needs the cash," Maggie suggested. She shivered, and Dakota got up and put another log on the fire.

"Couldn't say," he muttered.

Maggie could see that Will's suspicious actions were eating away at Dakota. "I know you've been friends for a long time, Dakota. Did Will know Sam Harris while your parents were still alive?"

"No. Sam and I met Will the summer I turned ten. We had come to Yankton to sell furs. Sam had to fight almost everyone he met because of me. People thought I was his son and called him a squaw man. Sam didn't do anything to change their minds, but he wouldn't walk away from a fight either."

Maggie sat down on a log closer to the fire as Dakota continued. "One night, about a half-a-dozen drunken cowboys were giving us a rough time. Sam was tough, but he couldn't handle all six at once. They beat him up pretty bad, then a couple held him down while the others had their fun with me. They'd dunk my head in the horse trough until I'd almost drown. After the third or fourth time, Will came along, saw what they were doing, and put the drop on them."

Another scar, Dakota, Maggie thought compassionately. *How many more are there?*

"Will had been a lawyer, but there wasn't much call for one in Yanktown, so he'd given it up and had gone into the freight business. He had a government contract to haul freight to Fort Meade. Offered Sam a job."

Dakota sat down beside her, apparently finished with his story. But Maggie wanted to hear more. "Well, what happened then? When did Sam go into ranching?" she prodded.

"You sure you want to hear all this?" Dakota asked.

"Of course, I'm sure." Maggie eagerly waited for his next words. Besides, it gave her an excuse to sit beside him at the fire.

"It wasn't long before Sam and Will became partners. By the following year, the line had grown. My mother's people knew Sam, so they never bothered any of the wagons. But Sam wasn't cut out for that kind of routine. He quit freighting and staked a claim. Soon he used up his money, but Will kept staking him. Sam took to ranching then, but always kept looking for the mother lode. He finally got lucky and struck it rich."

Dakota tossed another log on the fire, and Maggie sat warm and contented as she listened to the low, pleasant timbre of his voice. "In '76 when Deadwood sprang up, Will decided he had enough of freighting. He sold out and opened the bank." Dakota shrugged. "That's about the time I joined the army."

But a chronicle of a succession of events does not recount the depth of feeling in a relationship, so Dakota added decisively, "Sam and Will trusted one another. More important, they liked one another. They were closer than most brothers. I never heard either of them say a cross word to the other. If Will took the key and map, I reckon he's got more right to Sam's fortune than any of us."

Dakota stole a lingering look at Maggie, who appeared to be deep in thought. "You'd best get some sleep now, Maggie. It'll soon be dawn. We've got a long ride ahead of us."

Maggie studied his handsome profile, solemn in the glow from the fire. "We still don't know where Uncle Will has gone, do we?"

"I trust him, even if nobody else does." Dakota began to look through his saddlebags.

"What are you looking for?"

"A clean shirt. I've got blood on this one, and the smell might attract uninvited company."

While Dakota changed his shirt, Maggie picked

up the sketch pad, which had been pulled out of his saddlebag with the shirt, and began to leaf through the pages.

The variety of sketches reflected Dakota's sensitivity; there were many scenic drawings of the Black Hills, a picture of several soldiers huddled around a pot-bellied stove warming their hands, a young lad in a cavalry uniform holding a guidon.

She stopped, pleasantly surprised and honored to see a sketch of herself sitting by the fire. Dakota had caught every detail of her face. She glanced up to discover his dark gaze watching her intently, as if fearful of her disapproval.

"The picture of me is lovely, Dakota; I wish I were this beautiful."

"As they say, beauty is in the eyes of the beholder, Maggie." Their gazes lingered, drawing them deeper into one another's souls. Maggie waited expectantly, but Dakota said nothing. She forced her eyes back to the page. Uneasy under his stare, Maggie started to close the book. "I'm sorry, I didn't mean to pry. These drawings are superb."

"Just something to do to pass the time."

"Would you mind if I looked at the rest?" When he appeared to be uncomfortable, Maggie wondered if he was embarrassed.

Dakota shrugged and sat down beside her. "Go ahead."

Maggie's breath caught in her throat at the drawing of a horse. "Oh, this is magnificent!" Dakota had captured the animal's spirit and stateliness with a few discerning strokes of charcoal.

She stopped leafing to study a picture of a young

Scot, bearded and wearing a tam-o-shanter. On the opposite page was a beautiful young Indian woman. Maggie looked at Dakota quizzically.

His shoulder brushed hers as Dakota moved closer to see what had caught her attention. "My parents."

Maggie was astonished. Dakota's parents had been dead since he was a child. Yet, he had drawn vivid images from memory. "What a beautiful tribute, Dakota. You must love them very much."

Stimulated by his nearness, Maggie's heartbeat quickened. He was so close, his mouth just inches from hers. She knew she only had to lean forward to be in his arms.

But pride stopped her. Maggie wanted Dakota to make the move, a sign that he wanted her as much as she wanted him. *Him and his damned control!*

Hastily, Maggie returned her attention to the sketches, her hand shaking as she turned the page. For a moment, emotion blinded her from seeing anything other than the blurred face of a man. She flipped the page, then a sub-conscious awareness caused her to turn back.

Maggie studied the drawing. "Oh, you've met him!"

Dakota glanced at her in confusion. "Met who?"

"The man in this picture—the one who saved my life." She glanced askew at him. "You know, the old miner in the woods."

Dakota watched her with a peculiar stare. "Maggie, look carefully at the sketch. Are you sure that is the man you met the night you were lost?"

She restudied the face in the drawing. "Yes, I'm

certain he's the same man. Why do you ask?"

Dakota didn't answer, but dug in his saddlebags until he found his charcoal pencil. Maggie watched him quickly sketch the same face, this time without whiskers. As the drawing took shape, Maggie saw a resemblance to a familiar face.

"Add a beard and a homburg." Their heads were bowed together over the drawing pad as Dakota's hand moved swiftly across the page. When he finished, they turned face to face.

"Mr. Smith," Maggie said, bewildered.

"Sam Harris," Dakota responded.

They stared at one another in disbelief.

"Who is Mr. Smith?" he asked.

"The friendly gentleman I met on the park bench in Washington."

"You mean *Sam Harris*, the friendly gentleman on the park bench. Sam Harris is alive."

A momentary gleam of pleasure flashed in his dark eyes, then his expression clouded to anger. He jumped to his feet. Agitated, he grasped her shoulders and pulled her up. "Dammit, I should have figured it out sooner, Maggie. Will's mysterious disappearances, the horse with the cleft hoof, the disappearing old miner. Sam's been trailing us all along."

Maggie was still baffled by the startling disclosure "Which means Sam Harris faked his own death. Why would he do such a thing?"

"I can't tell you, but I bet Will Godfrey can. I'd stake my life he's with Sam this very moment."

"You'd lose that bet, son. I left him a good half hour ago." Dakota and Maggie looked to see that

Will Godfrey had returned to camp. "Took you long enough to figure it out."

Dakota's face hardened to anger. "Why did Sam ever pull a fool stunt like this? Maggie could have been killed."

Will's eyes shifted downward in guilt. "I'll let Sam explain it all when we get back to Deadwood."

"I think you'd better explain it all right now," Dakota insisted.

"I'll tell you this much—I took the map and key for safekeeping and gave them back to Sam. He can be the one to tell you the whole story."

"Oh, I intend to get his explanation," Dakota said through gritted teeth. "He'll have a lot of explaining to do when we get back."

"He's already headed back to Deadwood. I think we should keep all this under our hats until we get there," Will advised.

"Why? Afraid the others will string you from the nearest tree for your part in the scheme?" Dakota taunted. "Dammit, Will, you're as crazy as Sam for going along with it."

Will looked sheepish, but did not deny Dakota's allegation. He glanced in relief at the eastern sky. "Sun's up. Let's get breakfast going and be on our way."

"Guess I can't beat the truth out of you." Disgusted, Dakota spun on his heel and stormed away.

Will glanced at Maggie, who had not said a word throughout the whole argument. Her accusing look told him she agreed with Dakota.

"I'm sorry about all this, Maggie," Will said.

"Sorry? I am sorry for you and Sam. You must

both be crazy, just like Dakota said." Unable to meet the condemnation in the young girl's eyes, Will turned away and moved to the mules for ingredients to prepare breakfast.

After the party had been riding for several hours, Dakota reined up on the muddy river bank and climbed off his horse. He hunkered down and viewed the opposite bank, idly tossing pebbles into the water of the same river in which they had romped and fished previously. Under normal conditions, the river was difficult to ford, and now the recent rains had swollen the banks to overflowing; debris flushed from the hillsides swirled in the swift current.

Will Godfrey rode up beside him and leaned across his saddle. "What have you got in mind, son?"

"This is the narrowest part of the river. We could save a couple days' traveling time if we crossed it." Dakota picked up a stick and began to draw lines in the mud. "Deadwood is due east, and we have to follow the river to skirt the canyon. But if we cross the river here and bypass Deadwood, we can head overland directly to the Lazy H, which would only be a day and a half's ride."

"Why didn't we use that route to begin with?" Maggie asked. She had ridden up and overheard the whole conversation.

"When we started out, I didn't know where Sam was leading us. I'd have thought he would have mapped out this shorter trail. Seems like he wanted to drag out the journey."

Dakota stood up, tossed a final stone into the river, and reached for the rope on his saddle. "Get me that clothesline we've been using. Reckon we'll need about a hundred feet."

Will went to the mules and returned with several pieces of rope. Dakota quickly tied the ends together to form one length. "I'm going to run a guide line across the river."

"Current looks pretty strong," Will remarked as Dakota tied one of the loose ends of the rope to a tree and the other end to his saddle. "You figure the women can handle it?"

"If they hang on to the rope," Dakota replied. "Horse does all the work."

Dakota mounted and waded into the water. The rest of them watched in silence, the sound of the rushing water a steady drone in their ears.

Near midstream, Dakota felt the horse lose its footing and start to swim. He wrapped the reins around the saddle horn and slid off the animal, making sure to stay clear of its thrashing legs. Paddling alongside the swimming horse, he held on to the stirrup and let the powerful stallion pull him. When the horse touched bottom again, Dakota slid back into the saddle, retrieved the reins, and waded to the river bank.

He tugged at the long rope, pulling until the line stretched tautly across the river. Then he wrapped the loose end several times around the trunk of a sturdy tree and tied a firm knot.

Dakota cupped his hands to his mouth and called out to the opposite bank. "Will, you come first and bring the mules with you."

Will checked the oil cloths protecting the packs, then looped the reins of the mules around his saddle horn and waded into the water. When the mules lost their footing, the burdened animals flailed frantically until instinct overcame panic, and they started to paddle behind the horse swimming ahead of them. Will reached the opposite bank without a mishap.

Dakota was mounted and waiting for him. "I'm going back now. I'll send Collingswood first, then the women. Best to keep a couple men on each side of the river in case of trouble." He rode into the water. This time the crossing was easier because he had a firm rope to guide him.

Once he joined the others, Dakota motioned to Taylor. "You're next. Think you'll need help because of your arm?"

Taylor freed his wounded arm from the kerchief supporting it. "I'd prefer to try without being encumbered by this sling." He flexed his hand several times to get the circulation moving strongly.

"Be careful, dear," Katherine warned when Taylor mounted his horse.

He smiled and reached down to clasp her hand. "I'll be waiting for you on the other side," he said with a meaningful glance. Katherine stood on the bank and watched as he led his horse into the water.

"You're next, Mrs. Collingswood." Dakota helped her to mount. "Let the horse do all the work. It'll get you across. Hold the guide line with your left hand and the saddle horn with the other.

When the current hits, you'll feel like you're being jerked out of the saddle. Hug the horse with your knees and hang on."

Katherine peered down at him from her lofty perch. "And if all that fails, Mr. MacDonald?"

"Then you best start swimming, ma'am."

Taylor was nearing the opposite bank as Dakota led Katherine's horse to the river. "You didn't mention how cold this water is," Katherine complained as she moved deeper into the water.

"Don't pay that any mind, Mrs. Collingswood. It gets a lot colder near the middle," Dakota called after her.

He moved to help Diane. The young girl had turned pale with fright. "Diane, you're next."

"I don't want to go. I'm afraid. What happens if I fall off the horse?" she said, near tears.

Peter wore a grave demeanor when he moved to her side "I'll take her over. We'll ride double."

"Too hard on the horse," Dakota warned.

"The two of us probably don't weigh as much as Godfrey," Peter argued.

"Soaking wet, you do. And you can't hold on to the line and Diane too. The current will force you out of the saddle."

"Dakota, Diane can do it; she just needs some moral support. I'm not going to let her try it alone. She's too scared." He flashed a dapper grin. "Besides, I'm an accomplished horseman. Are you forgetting Princeton? The Equestrian Club? Remember?"

Dakota knew when to fold in a card game; Peter was going to stay in the pot no matter how high the betting went. "Well, watch that current," Dakota warned. "Tie her mount to yours. If you're lucky, when you fall off your horse, you might be able to grab hers before the current grabs you."

"You are a comfort, old man." Peter climbed into the saddle. "Put her in front of me." Dakota lifted Diane onto the horse and Peter encircled her with his arms. "Come on, sweetheart, we'll make this ride together. If we accomplish this act successfully, my love, we'll ride off and join a circus." He goaded his horse into the water; Diane's mare was tied behind.

Maggie chewed nervously at her lip as she watched the horse slide into the water. "Can they make it?"

"We'll soon find out." Dakota's face was as grim as his voice. The people on the opposite bank watched the pair in the water just as anxiously.

"No matter what happens, hold tightly to the rope," Peter cautioned as the force of the water pulled at them.

"I'm scared, Peter," Diane whined.

"Look, sweetheart, we're already half way across."

Suddenly, the head of the horse bobbed under water. Diane screamed and released her hold on the rope. Peter tightened his grip around her waist before Diane could be swept away, but the move unseated him and the two slid into the water. The other horse passed them as Peter struggled with Diane.

Peter had not exaggerated his swimming skill. He fought current and the panicked girl grappling him around the neck until he was able to grasp the rope.

"Grab the rope with both hands," he yelled. Diane reached out in desperation and clutched the rope as the river endeavored to swallow her.

"Slide your arms around my neck and let me do the rest," he said calmly. Once again Diane clutched him around the neck, almost pushing the two of them under the water.

He pressed her back against the guide line, her body in the circle of his arms. Treading water to keep them from being pulled into the current, Peter began to inch sideways along the rope.

"Don't . . . don't let go of me," Diane pleaded.

"Don't you let go of me, sweetheart. You're doing fine. Just a few more yards."

He sighed gratefully when his feet touched bottom, but he continued to inch along with her. When the water was waist high, he scooped Diane up and waded to the bank, where helping hands reached out to assist him.

Diane wouldn't relinquish her grasp around his neck.

Exhausted, Peter sank to the ground with Diane still clinging to him. Katherine and Taylor sat down beside the pair, wanting to hug their daughter in their arms; but the loving couple remained cleaved to one another.

Silently, Will Godfrey got a blanket from the pack, wrapped it around Peter, and patted him on the shoulder. Then Will walked away to watch the next crossing.

On the opposite bank Dakota and Maggie relaxed when they saw Peter stagger out of the water. "Are they okay?" Dakota shouted across the water.

Will waved. "They're both fine."

Now that the crisis had passed, Dakota turned to Maggie. "Well, Maggie—"

"I know, I'm next," she said, resigned. Maggie climbed on Blaze and leaned over to pat the head of the mare. "We're gonna do this, girl."

"Remember, a handful of rope and a handful of saddle horn."

"And if I fall off, I should tread water until you come and pluck me out."

"It's not a laughing matter, Maggie." She had already moved into the water. "Be careful," he shouted.

Without turning her head, she lifted a hand and waved in acknowledgment. When Dakota saw the gesture, he called out in frustration. "Dammit, Maggie, don't let go of that guide line."

He climbed on his horse to follow and suddenly called out, "Maggie, look out." A mammoth clump of debris was floating downstream directly at Maggie. The ponderous mass appeared to be the top of a tree broken off by a lightning strike.

The people on the opposite bank had spied the danger as well and were on their feet shouting warnings to her.

Maggie twisted around in time to see the approaching tree trunk. She tried to turn Blaze, but the current was too strong. The heavy trunk come down on her, snagged the guide line and snapped the rope as if it were string.

She tried to duck, but an outstretched branch hit

her on the head and knocked her into the water, where she was immediately caught by the swift current. When her head bobbed out of the water, Dakota kicked his horse and galloped ahead to intercept her.

Mud splattered through the air as Dakota raced along the water's edge, jumping the animal over the rubble and logs that lined the river bank. Peter Brent and Will Godfrey thundered in pursuit on the opposite shore, a considerable distance behind Maggie, who floated in the swirling water like the other pieces of debris.

Dakota got the stroke of luck he needed when the river took a turn ahead of him. He cut diagonally across the curved tract bordering the river and leaped off his horse. Tossing aside his hat and gunbelt on the run, he dove into the water. Dakota swam with strong, smooth strokes and reached midstream in time to grab Maggie when she floated around the bend of the river. He managed to keep her head above water and swam back to the river bank.

His lungs felt near to bursting when he finally succeeded in reaching water shallow enough to stand up and carry Maggie's limp body out of the river. Once on firm ground, he flipped her over and began to pump the water out. Within a few seconds, Maggie was gagging and spitting up the river water she had swallowed.

She began to shiver uncontrollably, partly from cold and partly from reaction to the frightening experience. Dakota wrapped her tightly in the blanket of his bedroll. The cover was an added warmth, but her shivering would not subside.

"Is Maggie okay?" Will shouted from across the river.

"Yeah. She'll be all right. I'll get her back to the crossing, but we're not going to try to ford it anymore today."

"Bl—Bl—Blaze?" Maggie stammered. Her teeth were chattering violently and she could barely mouth the question.

"Did Maggie's mare make it across?" Dakota called out to Peter and Will.

The two men's spirits lifted when they heard she was alert enough to ask about her horse. "The mare's fine," Peter shouted. "Tell Maggie I'll even sing the little darlin' to sleep if it will make her rest easy."

Maggie heard the light flippancy, but felt too miserable to acknowledge the remark.

"I've got to get a fire going to dry you off," Dakota said as he strapped on his gunbelt.

He picked Maggie up and carried her to his horse. Dakota sat her sidesaddle, then climbed up and pulled her against him. She snuggled her head against his chest, and his arms closed around her as he gathered the reins.

Dakota rode until he was opposite the campfire on the far bank. After dismounting, he lifted Maggie down and placed her gently on the ground. "You get out of those wet clothes while I build a fire."

"I haven't anything else to put on," she said.

Dakota would have liked to challenge the inane remark just to get a rise from her, but Maggie looked so pathetic and miserable he didn't have the heart to chide her even in jest.

"Maggie, just wrap yourself up in the blanket until your clothes dry," he said kindly.

Dakota began to gather wood and by the time he returned, Maggie had removed all her clothing and sat huddled in the blanket. He struck a spark with a flint, and soon a welcome warmth began to ward off the chill. Dakota pulled off his shirt and boots, laying them beside Maggie's garments to dry at the fire.

The shadows of night crept in to mask the earth in a black veil. Overhead tiny stars glimmered with a pale glow in the far reaches of the firmament as dark clouds drifted across the face of a diffident moon.

Maggie sat relaxed, soothed by the comforting lullaby of the night—the pop and crackle of the log on the fire, the steady chirp of crickets, and the occasional trill of a pheasant calling to its mate.

Across the river she could see the glow from the fire of their party, but here there was only Dakota and the darkness of the night. Her heart began pounding with the excitement of being alone with him.

Maggie's eyes rested on the wide expanse of his bare shoulders and taut muscles as he added another log to the fire; her hungry gaze followed the smooth, sleek line of his chest gleaming in the glow of firelight.

Dakota had purposely forced himself to stay busy to avoid looking at Maggie. He knew the rein on his control was fragile and could snap at any time.

He had come so close to losing her.

His arguments for leaving her were still sound, he told himself. Maggie deserved a better life than she could ever have with him. His intention to ride away, to leave her when the hunt was over, had been genuine.

But a short time ago, that decision had almost been wrenched from his hands; for a few frightful moments, there were no choices. Maggie had almost drowned. In those desperate moments as he raced along that river bank, one thought had prevailed—he couldn't bear to lose her.

With a guilty start, Dakota was struck by the truth.

In those moments, as he raced along that river bank, his concern had *not* been for Maggie, his concern had been for himself. *He couldn't bear to lose her.*

Dakota slowly raised his head and looked at her.

Chapter Twenty-eight

Maggie's round, trusting eyes met his probing stare. For several seconds their gazes locked in man's ageless message to woman. She blushed under the evidence of his naked passion, knowing he could read the instinctive response in her eyes.

As he rose to his feet and approached her, she could hear the rapid pounding of her heart and knew that beneath the blanket she clutched so tightly, her chest was heaving from the exertion.

Dakota stepped before her. "Maggie," he whispered in a husky plea of supplication.

He reached out to her and she put her hands in his, the blanket sliding off her shoulders as he drew her to her feet. Trembling, she stood before him.

Suffused in passion, his covetous gaze swept her slim nakedness, now shimmering in the glow from the fire. Dakota sank to his knees and his arms encircled her. Pulling her to him, he pressed his mouth against the smooth, flat plane of her stomach.

Ignited by his touch, passion surged through her, overpowering in intensity. Maggie arched her body firmly against the heated moistness of his mouth and braided her fingers through his dark, thick hair.

Driven by a need to taste more of her, he trailed his lips down her body, pausing momentarily to allow his tongue to sample and toy with her navel before moving lower to the junction of her legs. His mouth closed around her, and his tongue probed the intimate chamber.

Her body climaxed with convulsive tremors as her hold on reality shattered with an implosion of exquisite sensation. When the spasms ceased, she opened her eyes to discover Dakota had risen to his feet. He cupped her face in his hands and placed a tender kiss on her lips, then moved his mouth on hers as the need to possess her increased the tempo of his loving.

Murmuring expressions of love, he nibbled and kissed, covering her face, her eyes, her mouth until he slipped a warm hand up the slender column of her neck. "Maggie, I've wanted you for so long."

The husky admission renewed her passion.

Swaying into the powerful brawn of his body, she embraced him and drew him to her slender curves. His mouth returned to claim hers, and her tongue danced erotically across the roof of his mouth in response to the provocative pressure.

Stifling a groan, he stepped away to shed his jeans, then lowered her to the ground.

She craved the return of his lips. Her slender fingers grazed his cheek as they tipped his mouth to hers and her lips opened to his probing tongue. The intense persuasion of his kiss alerted her senses to the taste, the scent, the feel of him straining against her.

They breathed together as one—drawing the breath of their existence as one.

When had there been even a moment of her life without him? she marveled.

When had his life ever had purpose without her? he questioned.

She dipped her head to his glistening chest, tasting the fine film of perspiration coating the muscular plane. She felt the pounding of his heart beneath her lips as the urgency in his powerful body escalated.

His control was tenuous. He shifted and slid his mouth to her breasts, laving the turgid nipples until his mouth closed around them, tugging, suckling. Maggie groaned, shimmering and undulating under the marauding mouth that pillaged her senses.

When Dakota redeemed her mouth and slipped his tongue into the moist sweetness, Maggie flung her arms around the corded column of his neck. She could feel his muscular back at her fingertips, his strong thighs pressed to hers, and in his heated shaft the promise of what was yet to come.

He slid his hand to the core of her womanhood. Her response was instantaneous; she arched her back, thrusting her breasts to meet his descending mouth. He suckled voraciously, while his fingers caressed the very source of her sex.

Finally, his firm hand splayed her spine, cupping the cheeks of her derriere to pull her to his loins. Dakota drove his hardened shaft into her and moaned when she gripped and tightened around him.

They rode together to a tumultuous release, cutting off each other's rapturous cries with a soul-melding kiss.

Maggie was awakened the next morning by the sound of Dakota shouting to Will across the river. "Go on ahead without us. I'm not going to risk crossing again. We'll take the long way home." Maggie got up and ran to stand beside him.

"With only one horse?" Will called back.

"We'll ride double. With any luck, we should make it there by Saturday."

"Good luck," Will shouted.

"Same to you. I'm counting on you to get them all back safely, Will," Dakota hollered.

"I'll do my best, son. You take care of Maggie."

Waving goodbye to the figures on the opposite bank, Dakota and Maggie watched them ride away.

He pulled her into his arms and kissed her. "Ready to get started?"

"With what?" she asked with a wicked gleam.

The innuendo was all the encouragement Dakota needed. He took her hand and drew her back to the blanket.

* * *

A bright sun blazed high overhead when Dakota finally began to saddle his horse. Maggie stood beside him, dutifully handing him each item as needed.

"What are you doing with these?" she asked, picking up a bow and a quiver of arrows.

"Took 'em off one of the Indians that attacked us. They might come in handy, since I'm low on bullets." He tied the weapons to the saddle, mounted, then reached down to help Maggie swing up behind him. A nudge of his knees, and the horse moved forward.

Maggie slipped her arms around Dakota's waist and pressed tightly against him. "Keep that up and we're not gonna get too far today," he warned.

"This didn't seem to bother you before," she innocently remarked.

"Yeah, it did. I just wouldn't give you the satisfaction of knowing how much."

The bow bumped against her leg and Maggie moved it aside. "Actually, I can use a bow and arrow if need be. I happen to be an accomplished archer."

"That right?"

"Matter of fact, I *excel* at archery," she boasted.

"That so?"

The responses were too succinct even for the taciturn Dakota MacDonald. Maggie could not leave his reticence unchallenged. "You don't appear too impressed, Mr. MacDonald."

"Ever try hitting a moving target?"

"Well—not actually," Maggie stammered.

"Reckon you're lucky then."

"What do you mean?" She braced herself for the worst.

"There ain't too much out here that don't move 'cepting a tree. Can't say there ain't plenty of those. You oughta be able to shoot down a lot of 'em." A smile tugged at the corners of his mouth.

"Oh, you think you're so smart." She began to tickle his sides.

Dakota broke out into rollicking laughter, squirming and jerking to evade the havoc rained upon him by her roving fingers. "Damn it, Maggie, stop it. You'll get this horse to bucking."

She stopped pestering him and settled back contentedly. "So the stalwart scout has an Achilles' heel; Mr. Dakota MacDonald is ticklish."

"You saying you're not?"

"Right. I'm not saying," she giggled, deliberately rearranging his words.

"Well, when I don't have my hands full of horse, I'm sure gonna find out, lady." Maggie smiled and hugged him.

She could hardly wait.

They rode until dusk, then halted to make camp. As Dakota was building the fire, he lifted his head, listening intently.

"What is it?" she asked, fearing the worst.

"There's a partridge chattering out there."

He picked up his rifle. "Sounds nearby. We could use something under our belts besides beef jerky. I shouldn't be too long."

There weren't too many ways for Maggie to occupy herself while he was gone. She gathered more firewood, laid out the blanket for the night, and watered the horse.

When she heard the rifle shot, Maggie crossed her fingers, hoping he had been successful. She lay back on the blanket to await his return and closed her eyes.

Maggie couldn't have been asleep for more than a few minutes, but when she awoke she saw three Indians, two on horseback and one on foot, come out of the woods. Petrified, Maggie glanced around for a weapon. The bow was the nearest thing. Her hands shook so much, she could hardly string the arrow.

"Don't come another step closer." Despite her fear, Maggie stood steady with the arrow pointed at the heart of the Indian on foot.

"Lower your weapon, Maggie." Dakota suddenly appeared beside her. She had not heard him approach, but her eye remained fixed on the Indian.

Dakota raised his hand in a sign of welcome. "Greetings, White Buffalo."

"So, Dakota MacDonald, you greet your brothers with the raised bow of a woman warrior," the Indian asked.

"Maggie, lower the bow. If they intended to harm you, you'd be dead by now."

For several seconds, Maggie hesitated, remembering the attack on their camp. She finally lowered her arms.

"Come sit and join us, my cousin. Many summers have passed since we last met, White Buffalo. What of your family? My aunt, Bright Star in The Sky, is well, I hope."

"My mother died with my father, Great Bear, at the Little Big Horn," the Indian said.

"And your brother, Wolf That Walks?" Dakota feared the response; his cousin's very absence answered the query.

"Fell, too, at my father's side."

"Their deaths fill my heart with sorrow."

Dakota grieved, recalling the gentle woman with beautiful brown eyes, her husband, the proud warrior, Great Bear, and his young cousin, Wolf That Walks. After the death of his grandfather, they were his only blood kin, and he had always shared their lodge whenever Dakota visited their village. Painfully, he recalled the many times when, as young boys, he and his two cousins had hunted and fished together, or sat in their grandfather's lodge listening to the chief's many tales of the early Sioux.

"You and my brothers have journeyed far, White Buffalo. Crossed many rivers." Dakota held up the pheasant he had just shot. "Share this meal with us."

"It is not safe for us to linger. The sound of your rifle brought us, and it may bring others. We will leave. Our journey is still a long one."

"Are you going to the Badlands?"

White Buffalo nodded. "There we will join others of our people."

They had no weapons for their protection in the wilds; everything they owned had been confiscated when they were put on a reservation. Dakota handed his rifle to White Buffalo. "Take this, my cousin. There are but a few shells remaining. I hope you will not use them on any of my white brothers."

Humbleness did not come easy to White Buffalo, but the proud warrior's gratitude was evident as he accepted the weapon. "I make you that promise."

"And take my horse." Dakota did not wish to embarrass his cousin by seeming to offer charity. "Your news has saddened me, my cousin. My heart is now heavy with grief, and the animal can not carry the burden."

"You are a loyal son of the Oglala, Eye of Eagle." White Buffalo addressed Dakota for the first time by his Indian name.

The two men clasped one another's arms. "May the Great Spirit, Wankan Tanka, ride with you and my brothers, White Buffalo."

The warrior swung up on Dakota's stallion. He glanced down at Maggie, who stood silently, still holding the bow.

"You are the woman of Dakota MacDonald?" he asked.

Maggie lifted her head. "Yes, I am his woman," she said proudly.

White Buffalo shifted his piercing eyes to Dakota. "You have chosen well, Eye of Eagle. She will fill your lodge with many brave warriors." Maggie blushed.

Recovering her composure, Maggie handed him the bow and quiver of arrows. The Indian examined a feathered shaft, then his glance shifted to Dakota. "These are the arrows of a Sioux."

"Limping Coyote."

The two men's gazes locked in understanding. White Buffalo said nothing, nor did the expression on his face alter. He gave the weapons to one of the other riders, then with one final look at Dakota, the three Indians rode away.

Tears glistened in Maggie's eyes as she watched the riders until they disappeared. "It's all so unfair. So much land for everyone, yet not enough. Their homes, families, their way of life—all gone. They've lost everything."

"Not everything, Maggie. They still have their dignity."

"It's all so tragic."

"Don't pity them. They don't want your pity."

"Pity?" Maggie shook her head. "I don't pity them; I salute them."

Dakota lay beside Maggie with his head cradled on his propped arm as he leisurely stroked her hip. She was sleeping after their love-making, and her dark lashes rested on her cheeks. He pressed a kiss to each closed lid. The gentle persuasion coaxed her awake. She opened her eyes and smiled. Her lips were swollen from his kisses; lowering his head, he traced his tongue around the outline of her mouth to soothe them.

He lay back, and Maggie shifted, placing her head on his chest. "What's the matter? Can't you sleep?"

"I guess seeing White Buffalo today stirred up a lot of memories."

"What was your childhood like, Dakota? Were you happy?"

"I can't imagine a better life. The Sioux were at peace. We'd spend the summer with my mother's people, and I'd play with my cousins. In the winter here would just be my parents and me, snug and secure in our cabin."

"And what were your parents like?" she asked, turning on her side so she could see him.

"My mother, White Dove, was tiny. A young boy never stops to think about his mother's beauty, but I realize now that she was very beautiful. Father was tall, with red hair and a red beard." Dakota chuckled warmly. "That red beard caused more commotion among my mother's people than anything else about him."

Maggie smiled as his chiseled profile softened with nostalgia, and she clasped his hand. "I know what they looked like from your sketches, Dakota, but that doesn't tell me what your mother was really like."

"Shy. Her touch was gentle. And I remember that no matter how much mischief I got into, she was never angry with me. Father was a big, soft-spoken man, fair and honest. He'd been born in a coastal village of Scotland near the Isle of Skye. Always said we'd go back there some day, so I could see how blue the sky could really be. He'd left his village when he was eighteen and came to Canada, from there to Wyoming. He camped among the Sioux, met my mother, and they were married."

"And when did Sam come into the picture?" she asked.

"It was the season the Sioux call The Moon of Falling Leaves. I was nearing the end of my seventh summer and we had been visiting the village of my mother's people. The Sioux were moving to their winter camp, and we were returning home so my father could lay his traps before the heavy snows.

"We found Sam badly wounded, barely alive. Father thought Sam would not survive, but we took him to our cabin to try to help him.

"My mother nursed him the whole first winter. Sam's wounds were slow to heal, and he caught pneumonia. When spring came, Sam was still too sick to travel. Father took the pelts to Fort Laramie and came back with the news that Sam's wife was gone. Nobody knew where.

"By the time summer arrived, hostilities between the Sioux and the Army were so bad that we didn't visit my mother's people. We couldn't leave Sam, and we didn't dare take him with us. He wouldn't have been welcomed."

Maggie lay contentedly, listening to the husky timbre of his voice, visualizing the confusion the young Dakota must have felt.

"One day Sam and I went fishing, and while we were gone a band of Crow raided the cabin. They killed my father and mother. After that, Sam and I just kind of stayed together. I didn't know where I belonged. I loved my mother's people, but I couldn't war on the white man. Sam was white; my father had been white."

He paused and she encouraged him to continue. "So what happened then?"

"I'd go back to visit my grandfather and cousins whenever Sam went looking for you and your mother. After a couple of years, he just gave it up and decided to come to Deadwood. That's when we met Will. You know the rest of the story."

"Did you love Sam, Dakota?"

"I never really understood what the word meant to white people, Maggie. Your meaning is different from an Indian's. Some of you say you 'love' chicken, or you 'love' a certain book. Never made sense to me that you could love a chicken and book in the same way you would love another person. So if you're asking me, did I love Sam more than chicken and reading, I'd say yeah."

"And me, Dakota? Do you love me?" she asked softly.

"That's when it gets real confusing, 'cause I sure feel different toward you than I did toward Sam."

"Well, you're supposed to. It's a different kind of love. A man and woman fall *in love* with each other. That's much different from just loving someone. I love my parents, but I'm *in love* with you."

"Well, if being in love means, you're always on my mind and I want to be near you all the time, to hold you, to kiss you . . . then I reckon I'm *in love*."

As his hand gently swept her hip, Maggie lay back with a contented sigh. "I *love* the feel of your hands."

He began to blow lightly at an errant curl on her cheek.

"I know." He found a new target and his warm breath ruffled the hair at her ear.

"Oh, just how do you know?"

"I only have to ride a horse once to know how it takes to the bit."

"A horse!" She sat up indignantly. "Are you comparing me to a horse?"

He pulled her back down to his side. "I'm no poet, Maggie. I don't know the words to tell you what you mean to me."

She lifted her head and looked into his dark eyes. "Sometimes, words aren't necessary. You have your own way of saying it. Just in the way you look at me, you make me feel loved."

His gaze worshipped her and he slid his hand up the column of her neck. "Am I saying it now?" he asked huskily.

"You're saying it now," she whispered softly as he drew her lips to his.

Chapter Twenty-nine

They awoke to sunshine. The rain that had fallen lightly during the night had moved out of the hills. "How far do we have to go?" Maggie asked when they were ready to leave.

"If I remember, there's a trestle about five miles from here. Every morning the train from Deadwood makes a run up to the mine for a gold shipment. If we can reach that track in time, we could hitch a ride back to town."

Maggie's good-natured grin was as warm as the elusive sunshine. "Then let's hurry. The thought of sleeping in a bed tonight isn't that unpleasant."

"You saying you've had enough of sleeping out under the great outdoors?" Dakota teased. "Tired of the primitive life already?"

"As I recall, the Lazy H offers a hot bath and a

soft bed. I enjoy your company, Mr. MacDonald, but right now those two items hold a much greater appeal to me."

Dakota grabbed her, hugging her to his side. "You do care about material things? Here you had me believing you were different from your mother and sister."

Maggie smiled as she looked at him. All the tautness had left Dakota. Secure in the glow of her love, he seemed relaxed and happy, no longer trying to deny his feelings for her. *This is how it will always be between us.*

"I am relinquishing my bicycle and Beadle magazines for you; I draw the line at giving up my hot bath."

Laughing together like children, they trudged along hand-in-hand in the sylvan wilderness, following the river into the floor of a canyon walled with a smooth face of unscalable granite.

Their laughter faded as soon as they reached the foot of the trestle and looked up—the bridge was gone.

The river cleaved a passage between the two rock walls which had once been linked by a fifty-foot length of railroad track, a hundred feet above the raging river. Recent torrential downpours and swollen waters had caused the middle section of the trestle to collapse. Now only the side pilings remained, swaying unsteadily in the raging river as they clung tenuously to the sides of the chasm.

Dakota eyed the sagging framework. "I was figurin' on climbing the trestle to get above and flag down the train. We can forget that idea. With that middle section gone, it'll be too dangerous. Looks like the side sections are going to fall too, at any moment. Hope the train engineer is alert when he comes around that curve above."

"Wouldn't they know the bridge is out?" Maggie asked.

"Not necessarily. It could have happened last night."

"We should try to warn them!"

"I doubt anybody could see us down here in the canyon. There's nothing we can do except backtrack. Maybe we'll find a way to get up there before the train arrives."

Dakota glanced back for a final look at the ruined structure and did not see the trap concealed in the grass at his feet. The teeth snapped around his ankle like the jaws of a shark, and yelping with pain, Dakota dropped to his knees and clutched at the metal vise on his leg.

"Dammit!" he cursed through a clenched jaw.

Maggie spun around in surprise. "What happened?"

"Foot's in a trap."

Maggie knelt down to help Dakota force open the jaws, but the trap wouldn't release. Perspiration glistened on his forehead as the pain intensified, but he continued his struggle to free his ankle.

After a while, he slumped to the ground in exhaustion. "It won't budge. The trap's broken."

"We'll pry it open." She began to search for a thick stick.

"Be careful you don't stumble into one of these, too," Dakota warned.

Maggie found a sturdy stick and returned to Dakota. She could see that his eyes were glazed with pain and his strength was waning. Together they wedged the stick into the trap enough to relieve some pressure from his ankle, but not enough to release his foot. Their further efforts were futile, and Maggie knew she had to get help before he lost the circulation in his leg.

In desperation, she glanced at the damaged trestle. Maggie walked over to the foot of the trestle and peered up at the tall framework. Then her face hardened grimly as she reached a decision. "I can climb it."

"No," Dakota shouted. "Don't try. It could collapse any minute."

He knew he was wasting his breath; he had seen that look of determination on her face before. Frantically, he began to struggle with the trap again, but his efforts were useless. The movement only increased the pain in his ankle. "Maggie, I'm begging you. Please don't try it," he pleaded.

"It's the only way. I'll climb to the top and flag down the train."

"You don't even know if they're sending a train to the mine today. For God's sake, Maggie, you're going to kill yourself."

Maggie grinned gamely. "Are you forgetting you're talking to the best tree-climber in Washington D.C.?" She wanted to kiss him goodbye, but she knew if he got a hand on her, he would never release her. "It's our only hope to get help for you.

I love you," she called and turned away.

Dakota lunged to grab her, but the trap held firm. The steel teeth bit into his ankle and the shock of pain caused him to black out and fall to the ground.

The sound of rushing water was deafening as Maggie began the climb. The skeletal structure swayed and creaked, threatening at any moment to tumble into the raging river. Her foot slipped and for several seconds she hung suspended above swirling waters that seemed to leap up to pull her into their depths.

Maggie clutched the corner of a crosspiece until she was able to swing her legs around one of the timbers and straddle the wood. She felt dizzy and closed her eyes. For several moments she sat wrapped around the upright.

She looked at the undulating river below. Her vision blurred and bile rose in her throat. An upward glance showed nothing but beams rising endlessly above her. She calculated that she must be half way up, but couldn't venture a second downward glance to judge her bearings.

Frightened and trembling, she continued the climb. Once again, the weakened trestle began to sway. She wrapped her arms and legs around a beam and clung tenaciously. When the movement eased, she continued to work her way up from crosspiece to crosspiece. Several times her trembling fingers slipped off the wooden joists, but she managed to hold on.

Her arms and legs soon felt rubbery, and she stopped to regain her strength. With the top only a few feet from her reach, Maggie heard the far-off whistle of the train. A renewed surge of energy propelled her to the top.

She took a few precious seconds to draw much-needed air into her lungs, then crawled along the broken track until she felt solid ground beneath her.

With a grateful sigh, Maggie rose to her feet and on trembling legs ran around the curve. In the distance, the train came into view.

The alert conductor spied Maggie on the track. "What the hell!" he muttered. He reached for the heavy rope above his head and yanked the cord of the train whistle several times as a warning. As he tossed wood into the engine, the stoker turned to see what had caught the conductor's attention.

"There's a fella on the tracks ahead." He blasted the whistle again. Maggie made no effort to move.

"You think it's Injuns or outlaws?" the stoker asked.

"Can't tell, but grab your rifle." The conductor threw the lever of the heavy brake. Hissing steam, the locomotive ground to a screeching halt.

Maggie stumbled to the ground and looked up into the barrels of the half dozen rifles pointed at her. She raised her arms in the air. "Don't shoot. I've come to warn you. The bridge has collapsed."

She was surprised when several soldiers climbed off the train, Lieutenant Scott among them. "Why, it's Miss Collingswood." He took her arm and assisted her to her feet.

"May—may I have a drink of water?" she asked. One of the soldiers produced a canteen.

After several sips, she returned it with a grateful

smile. "Lieutenant, I need your help. Dakota Mac-Donald is caught in a trap. Will you help us?"

The young officer nodded. "Where is he?"

"Down below, near the foot of the trestle. I'll show you."

The soldiers and train crew followed her and drew up abruptly, staring speechless at the gaping hole which once had been a trestle. Maggie anxiously scanned the river bank until she spied Dakota. "There he is." Dakota had regained consciousness and waved to her. Maggie returned the sign.

After a survey of the rocky cliffs, Scott shook his head. "Appears the only way we can get to him is with ropes."

"Please hurry," Maggie pleaded. "He's in pain."

"Got plenty of rope on the train, Lieutenant," the conductor commented. "We was taking' it up to the mine."

"Bring it at once. Private Browning, unload one of the horses."

The train crew and one of the soldiers hurried back to carry out the orders. They soon returned with a horse and several lengths of rope.

Maggie waited anxiously as two troopers were lowered over the rocky cliff. When they reached the bottom, the two men hurried over to Dakota and pried open the trap with a crowbar. Dakota hobbled over to the face of the wall and one of the troopers tied a rope around his waist. Up above, Lieutenant Scott ordered the other end be tied to the saddle of the horse.

"Ready down here, sir," one of the troopers shouted from below.

"All right, Browning," Scott ordered. The private climbed on the horse and slowly backed the animal away from the edge of the cliff. Dakota grasped the rope with both hands and braced a foot against the rocky wall when they began to haul him up.

Impaired by a damaged foot, Dakota had to climb using only one leg. The task was slow and gruelling. Several times he grunted with pain when he swung into the wall and slammed his injured leg against the jagged rock.

Maggie threw herself into his arms as soon as he reached the top. The others turned their attention to the duty of retrieving the two troopers from below, allowing the two lovers their privacy.

After several fervent kisses, Dakota held her so tightly that Maggie could feel him trembling. Finally, relinquishing his hold on her, Dakota stepped back. He grasped her shoulders and scowled at her. "You had to be loco to climb that trestle. Don't ever try a fool stunt like that again, Maggie," he growled gruffly.

He pulled her back into his arms, holding her as if he would never let her go. "Didn't I warn you that you can end up dead when you try to be a hero?" His voice was hoarse with emotion.

"I wasn't trying to be a hero." For several seconds they gazed deeply into one another's eyes. "I guess some of you must have rubbed off on me." She smiled tenderly. "Let me tend to that ankle of yours."

"Ankle's okay. Just need to get off it for a moment." He sat down on a boulder and they were soon joined by Lieutenant Scott.

The two men shook hands. "Thank you, sir," Dakota acknowledged.

Scott laughed and hunkered down beside him. "I'd say it's unusual to find you snared in a trap, Dakota. Have you checked your ankle?"

"I'm better off keeping my boot on. I was lucky; the trap was old and rusty so the boot kept the bone from breaking. Gotta say, though, I'm sure glad you came along when you did."

"I imagine you are. I spoke to Mr. Godfrey in Deadwood and he told me to keep an eye open for you and Miss Collingswood."

"Did everyone make it safely back to Deadwood?" Maggie asked anxiously.

"Despite their wounds, your party looked to be in much better condition than Dakota here," Scott commented. Maggie sighed in relief.

"Well, we had some unexpected set-backs, sir," Dakota replied.

Scott had served long enough with Dakota to know the ex-scout had said all he was going to on the subject. "If you're rested enough, we might as well head back to Deadwood."

Maggie grinned. "I've been waiting to hear you say that, Lieutenant."

The arrival of the locomotive chugging backwards into town attracted a great deal of attention among the citizens of Deadwood. When she climbed off the train, Maggie sighted the familiar face of William Godfrey among the spectators. After listening to Maggie's account of the harrowing incident at the trestle, Will couldn't stop hugging and kissing her.

"I'll send word out to the ranch immediately. They've been frantic with worry."

"That won't be necessary, Will. We're heading there right now," Dakota told him.

"Aren't you going to have the doctor check your ankle?" Maggie argued.

"What did you do to your ankle, Dakota?" Will asked.

Dakota grinned sheepishly. "I hate to admit it, but I caught it in a trap. It's not broken, though. That's all that matters. By morning, it'll be fine."

"Well, stay put and I'll get the rig," Will offered.

"I want to come with you. There's some explaining to do."

"There sure is," Dakota said grimly. "I'll get the rig. You stop at the preacher's house and tell him to come out to the ranch first thing in the morning. Maggie and I are getting married."

"Married?" Will grinned.

"Married!" Maggie exclaimed.

Dakota went limping off in the direction of the livery without replying.

"Married," Will murmured. He grinned and shook his head. "Sure wish Sam were here to see it."

"Well, I think you better go and find the preacher, Uncle Will. Mr. MacDonald is a man of action."

Maggie caught up with Dakota, and despite his limp, she had to half run to keep up with him. "You certainly take a lot for granted, Dakota MacDonald. I don't remember telling you I'd marry you; I don't even remember your asking me."

He stopped, turned, and grasped her shoulders. His dark eyes danced with mischief. "You saying you're no longer interested in lusting with me on a buffalo robe like a squaw?"

Her hands fluttered to her chest in mock chagrin as she batted her lashes outrageously at him. "Is that a proposition or a proposal, Mr. MacDonald?"

Dakota grinned and slipped his arm around her shoulders. "That's a promise, lady."

When the carriage rambled into the yard, Katherine, Taylor, Diane, and Peter came rushing out of the door to greet them. After a tearful reunion, Katherine and Maggie entered the house arm in arm.

After relating the events that had occurred after their separation, Maggie left to take a bath. As she lowered herself into the hot, relaxing water, she was convinced that a hot bath must be the greatest luxury a person could succumb to.

She washed her hair, then lay back with her head on the rim of the tub and closed her eyes. Within minutes, Maggie was asleep.

The tapping on the bathroom door awoke her with a start. "Margaret, are you okay?" She recognized Diane's voice.

"I'm fine. Just finishing." She climbed out of the tepid water.

"We've been waiting for you. Dinner is ready."

"I'll be there in a minute." Maggie quickly toweled herself and pulled on clean clothing. After running a brush through her short curls, she hurried down the hall to join the others. She was pleased to see Dakota, clean-shaven and freshly groomed after his own bath in the bunkhouse.

Maggie thought everyone was unusually quiet

during dinner. While they were eating slices of hot apple pie, baked by Yen Ching especially for Dakota's homecoming, Maggie found out the reason for this silence.

Taylor made the announcement that all except Maggie had known from the start of the meal. "Margaret, I must return to Washington at once. There was a wire from the President awaiting me when we arrived back here. We will be leaving on the morning stage."

"All of you?" Each one of them nodded as her glance swept the diners. Her gaze came to rest on her mother. "I guess this is goodbye."

Katherine lifted her eyes. "Dear, after all you've gone through, are you certain you still wish to remain here?"

"Now more than ever, Mother."

"Good Lord, Margaret, don't tell me you still harbor your girlish, romantic concepts about the West?"

"Yes, some. But I belong here, Mother. The man I love is here."

Dakota had said nothing, but Maggie could sense his tension. "Dakota and I are getting married tomorrow."

Katherine lifted her head just as Maggie reached over and covered Dakota's hand. Katherine's expression softened into a smile. The gazes of mother and daughter altered, becoming woman to woman.

"Reverend Pickett has promised to be here first thing in the morning," Will Godfrey said. "I suggest that we clear up some matters before then."

He reached into his pocket and extracted a key.

"Why, that's the missing key!" Taylor declared. He smiled smugly. "So, I was right. You were the one who took the key and map."

"Only to give them back to Sam," Will murmured with a sheepish grin.

"Sam!" Katherine and Taylor exclaimed in unison. Katherine looked apprehensive. "Sam who? Surely, you can't mean Sam Harris; he's dead." She cast an uneasy glance at Taylor.

"Let's all get more comfortable while I explain the whole story."

Will moved to Sam's huge desk. The others followed, seating themselves on couches and chairs while Maggie chose to stand at the fireplace under the picture of Screaming Eagle. Dakota stood a short distance away from her.

With a feeling that she had lived this scene before, Maggie's glance swept the small group waiting to listen to what Will Godfrey had to say. Peter Brent was the only new player in the scene.

"The whole thing began when Sam Harris saw a picture in the newspaper and recognized Katherine and Taylor. He high-tailed it to Washington to meet the daughter he hadn't seen since she was an infant."

When Katherine started to object, Will raised his hand to ward off her interruption. "Let me finish the whole story as I know it."

Will took time to light a cigar. "Sam intended to face Maggie and you, Katherine. He lost his nerve after seeing your fine house and all, and figured he didn't have a right to disrupt Maggie's life. He watched her for several days until he got enough courage to approach her in the park. You know better than any of us what happened then, Maggie."

Tears glistened in Maggie's eyes, and she lowered her head recalling those few days on a park bench with her new-found friend, *Mr. Smith*.

"Sam returned to Deadwood all fired up. He had two goals—to get Maggie to the Lazy H, and to get her and Dakota together. He knew Dakota's enlistment would be up soon, and the boy would be heading home. If he could thrust them together, Sam was certain nature would take its course."

Will paused and took a deep draw from his cigar. "Well, Sam figured Katherine and Taylor would never let Maggie come West just for the asking. Without knowing how long Dakota would hang around Deadwood, Sam figured he didn't have the time it would take to settle the matter in court. He concocted this crazy scheme of faking his own death and planning a treasure hunt to get Maggie and Dakota together."

"Good God, then he *is* alive!" Near swooning, Katherine began to fan herself with a lacy handkerchief. Will ignored her histrionics, as did all the others in the room except Taylor, who got down on bended knee and began to pat her hand comfortingly.

"I wasn't proud of lying to you folks," Will continued. "Especially seeing your grief, Dakota. But I made Sam a promise not to reveal the truth."

With the smile of a wily fox, Will held up the key and unlocked the bottom drawer of the desk. He removed a square metal box. "The *fortune* has been under your noses all the time," he said.

"What fortune?" Katherine snapped, having fully recovered. "As long as Sam Harris is alive, there is no inheritance."

"Not true. Sam has already legally given this ranch and most of his wealth to Maggie and Dakota. No matter what happens between them, the gift is to be divided equally between Maggie and Dakota."

"And *now* what does he expect them to do in order to claim this gift?" Katherine sneered.

Will shook his head. "Nothing. No conditions. No strings attached." He glanced at Dakota and Maggie standing together at the fireplace. "You are two very wealthy young people."

"I for one couldn't be more pleased," Peter Brent announced. He jumped to his feet and pumped Dakota's hand vigorously. "Congratulations, my friend."

"For what?" Dakota declared. He crossed the room and leaned over the desk. "Where is Sam?"

Sadly, Will looked up at the angry young man. "I don't know."

Dakota's balled fist slammed down on the desk. "Dammit, Will, I've had my fill of this. Where in hell is Sam? Where's he hiding?"

The craggy features of Will Godfrey deepened in regret as he shook his head. "I don't know; I wish I did. He gave me the key and cleared out. Wouldn't tell me where he was going."

Dakota read the truth in the man's eyes and returned to the fireplace to resume staring gloomily into the flames. Maggie went over to him and put a hand on his shoulder. His body felt tense beneath her fingertips.

Despite Will's denial, Katherine Collingswood maintained her skepticism. "You lied to us before, Mr. Godfrey. Why should we believe you now?"

"Whether you believe me or not doesn't change anything, Katherine. Sam's gone, and he's signed his assets over to Maggie and Dakota."

Maggie struggled with the logic behind Sam's actions. "But his plan worked. Why would he go away? Why sign his wealth over to us and then disappear?"

"Why?" Will snorted derisively. "If you knew Sam, you'd know the answer to that. He's ashamed for what he put you all through. He realized, too late, that he had made a mistake. Sam never figured to involve the rest of you, or that there would be hostiles in the area—or floods, or snakes—"

"What did he expect with such a stupid plan?" Dakota lashed out in anger.

"He could have stopped the hunt anytime," Taylor interjected.

Will nodded. "He almost did a couple of times."

"That still doesn't explain why he would disappear once the truth was known," Maggie argued.

Will could only shake his head. "He knows you and Dakota are angry with him and don't want to see him again. So he left for good."

Dakota was blind with rage at the danger Maggie had been subjected to because of Sam's scheme. He could not feel any sympathy for Sam Harris.

"And what makes him think Maggie and I want his handouts?"

Will began to show signs of irritation. Angrily crushing out his cigar, he rose to his feet. "Good Lord, man, we all make mistakes. Sam tried to make up for his."

He sat down again and extracted a document from the metal box. "Sam told me to give you this, Katherine. He legally divorced you years ago under grounds of desertion."

A letter accompanied the document, and with a suspicious scowl Katherine opened the folded note.

You'll be glad to hear that I divorced you years ago. I'm grateful for the fine job you did of raising that gal of ours, Kate, so I'm apologizing for putting you through all the rest. But if you weren't so damned greedy, you'd never have got mixed up in it to begin with. I'm wishing you luck and I bear no grudges. Hope you feel the same about me.

Sam Harris

You're still a fine figure of a woman, Katie, my love. Makes me wonder if I did the right thing in giving you these papers.

Katherine shook her head, a faint smile tugging at the corners of her mouth. "The man is incorrigible."

Taylor took the document and quickly perused

the divorce decree. "Well, I'm certainly relieved to see this."

"I'm sure Diane is, too, sir," Peter interjected. His subtlety reminded Taylor that, although his youngest daughter had remained silent throughout the whole exchange, she still was affected by the outcome. Peter clasped Diane's hand protectively and the young couple exchanged loving smiles.

"I believe there is nothing more to be said on this issue. At this time, the wisdom of Sam's actions is purely academic." Taylor was unaware of how stuffy and officious he sounded, for in truth, Sam Harris had already had the final word.

Taylor drew Katherine to her feet. "We should finish our packing, dear. I'm sure with Maggie getting married, there will be too much excitement to attempt to pack tomorrow." As they crossed the room, he added, "Diane, I'll be glad to give you a hand with your packing."

"That won't be necessary, sir. I'll help her," Peter declared assertively.

The positive declaration had an arresting effect on the older couple. Both turned to look back. Diane and Peter were sitting holding hands; Maggie and Dakota were standing together, an inviolable unit.

Taylor tucked a finger under Katherine's chin to raise her gaze to his. "This trip has cost us more than we bargained for, my dear. I think everyone gained a fortune but us; we've lost our two treasures."

Tears glistened in Katherine's eyes as the reality sank in. Taylor pressed a light kiss on her lips, then slipped his arm around her shoulders.

"Now, now, ma'am, you mustn't feel bad," Peter exclaimed. "Look at this way, Mrs. Collingswood; you haven't lost your daughters, you've gained two sons."

Katherine took a long look at the young man grinning like a hyena from ear to ear, then glanced at Dakota, whose bronzed skin was even darker in the glow from the fire. Appalled, she raised a hand to her brow, and uttered in her deepest, resonant, timbre, "Good . . . God!"

Maggie and Dakota were soon left alone. They could not consider retiring for the night. Too much was happening in their lives. This latest move of Sam's was as overwhelming to them as his fake will had once been. Hand in hand, they strolled down to the stable.

Maggie lingered at Blaze's stall, patting the mare as Dakota gazed with adoration at the woman he loved. She turned her head. Smiling, she reached out to him.

Dakota took her hands and slowly drew her with him, backing away until he reached the pile of hay. "I don't want to be apart from you tonight, Maggie."

"Nor I, you," she whispered tenderly.

He lifted her in his arms and his mouth covered hers as he lowered her to their bed of straw.

Chapter Thirty

On the morning of her wedding, Maggie dressed in her blue-and-white gingham gown. The rest of the family walked around with somber looks, completing their packing and loading up the buckboard to depart as soon as the ceremony was completed.

By the time the Reverend Pickett arrived from town, the groom and the rest of the men were nervously pacing outside while Katherine and Diane added finishing touches to the bride.

Tears shimmered in Katherine's eyes as she hung a gold chain around Maggie's neck. "This locket belonged to my mother, and I wore it the day I married Sam Harris. It's fitting for his daughter to wear it at her wedding."

"I shall cherish the locket always, Mother," Maggie said solemnly. Trying to suppress her tears,

Katherine kissed Maggie's cheek and sped through the door.

Diane lingered. "I only have these to give to you." She handed Maggie a pair of white lacy gloves.

"These gloves are your favorite," Maggie said. "I can't take them."

"Well, I'm just lending them to you. I'll expect you to return the gloves when you come to Washington for my wedding." Her chin quivered. "Don't you know it's proper for a young lady to wear gloves on her wedding day?"

The awkward moment lengthened as the two sisters stared at one another, then Maggie smiled gently. "When did I ever do the proper thing?"

"How strange to think you won't be coming back with us." Diane's eyes moistened with tears. "I just took you for granted. I never really thought about the day we would be separated. I guess I always just thought about . . . myself."

Maggie smiled tenderly. "We both were guilty of that fault."

Struck with the full realization that their lives would now follow separate paths, Diane glanced tearfully at Maggie. "Nothing will ever be the same again, will it?"

Maggie reached for her hand. "No, not the same. We've grown up."

Bewildered, Diane asked, "When did it happen? We were just girls when we came here. How can just a few short weeks accomplish what years didn't? Now, we're . . ." She shook her head. "I'm not certain I'm ready for the change."

"We're ready, or the change would never have happened." Maggie smiled at Diane, and for the first time since they were children, the two sisters embraced. Then, brushing tears aside, they clasped hands and stepped outside.

Only a small group assembled to witness the marriage of Dakota MacDonald and Margaret Collingswood—Taylor and Katherine, Diane, Peter, William Godfrey, Yen Ching, and the Lazy H ranch hands.

A gentle breeze ruffled Dakota's dark hair and sunlight caressed the ends of Maggie's curls with golden kisses as the young couple stood hand in hand repeating their vows. Not a dry eye remained among the spectators.

Nearby, in the concealment of the trees, Sam Harris watched the ceremony, his own eyes moistened with tears. In the past weeks he had often stood in the shadows watching the pair, tempted to call out to them. He had not been wrong about Maggie. She lived up to every expectation he held for her. And his scheme had worked; the two people he loved dearly would build a life together.

In retrospect, Sam realized the plan had been foolhardy. He had not considered the danger. Never would he forget those harrowing moments when Dakota and Maggie had dangled from a rope at Twin Buttes. That day, when he started to go to their aid, he had almost revealed himself to them. Perhaps he should have, while they still had forgiveness in their hearts.

Sam grinned when the groom embraced his bride. His wistful gaze fixed on the couple for a final lingering look, then he wiped his tears and slipped away as silently as he had arrived.

After the customary congratulations and wishes for happiness following the simple ceremony, the ranch hands returned to their duties and the family climbed into the carriages.

The stage was waiting when they arrived in Deadwood.

William Godfrey wished the departing voyagers a safe journey back to Washington, then he left the family to their final farewells.

The moment had arrived to face the sorrow of parting. Dakota remained apart from the group to allow Maggie this intimacy with her family.

Peter Brent approached him. "I expect you to be best man at my wedding." He shook Dakota's hand. "Thank you, Dakota . . . for everything." The two men exchanged a meaningful glance.

Other than Sam and Will, who were more like family, Dakota had never had a close friend. He realized that he had one now and he liked the feeling. Dakota glanced at Maggie, aware that Peter's friendship was another of the many enrichments she had brought into his life.

While the two men took their leave, Diane said goodbye to Maggie. "As soon as we set a wedding date, I'll wire you. You promise you'll come home for my wedding?"

"Of course. I wouldn't miss it." After a long hug they separated, and Peter and Diane climbed into the stage.

Taylor took Maggie in his arms and kissed her. For several seconds, he just held her. Finally, reluctantly, he stepped back. "I know you've found happiness here, and I'm happy for you, honey. But, I'll miss you."

Maggie slipped her arms around his waist. "I'll miss you, too, Father. You're going to make a great minister. Write me as often as you can."

Taylor smiled warmly. "I will, honey." He reached out to Dakota for a handshake. "Take care of her, son."

"I will, sir," Dakota said solemnly.

Katherine waited quietly nearby, dabbing at her eyes. Maggie embraced her with a hug. "And you're going to be the loveliest minister's wife that France has ever seen."

Cupping Maggie's cheek in her hand, Katherine smiled lovingly. "No matter what I did or said, I always loved you, dear."

"I know that, Mother." They kissed. "I love you, too."

Katherine turned to Dakota with a scowl. "As for you, young man, I shall never forgive you for doing this to Maggie." Her face softened as she studied the noble features of this man whom Maggie loved so dearly. "You take good care of my daughter."

Then, to the surprise of all, Katherine reached out and hugged him before burying her face in her hankie and stepping into the stage.

Dakota slipped his arm around Maggie's shoulders as Charlie Walters flipped the reins, and the *Cheyenne & Black Hills Stagecoach* rumbled out of Deadwood.

When the coach had disappeared around the curve, Dakota squeezed Maggie's shoulder. "Ready, Maggie?"

She nodded, and they returned to the carriages. "I'll leave the buckboard in town tonight at the livery."

Will Godfrey approached the young couple and handed Dakota a key. "Don't have a proper wedding gift, so I thought you'd like the hotel's private suite for the night."

Dakota glanced down at the hotel key. "This another of Sam's tricks?" he asked suspiciously.

"Sam had nothing to do with this. I thought Maggie would enjoy a change, so I arranged it myself."

When Dakota remained skeptical, Will flared angrily, "Dad blast it, Dakota, this is your wedding night. You ought to make something special of it. Everything you need is in the room."

Dakota stared at the key for several seconds, then glanced at Maggie. Her trusting look told him whatever he wanted to do would be fine with her. He clenched the key in his hand and nodded. "I think you're right. Thanks, Will." He took Maggie's hand and they entered the hotel.

William Godfrey had indeed made proper arrangements for the bride and groom. As they climbed the stairs, the hotel manager called out to them, "Congratulations, Dakota. And to you, too, Mrs. MacDonald."

Hearing the name for the first time, Maggie stopped in surprise. *Mrs. MacDonald. Maggie MacDonald.* The name had a magnificent ring to it. She glanced with pleasure at Dakota and realized that he was savoring the sound of the words himself.

Their gazes locked as both recognized the effect the simple phrase had on each of them. Maggie flashed a dimpled smile at the manager as they continued up the stairway.

The sumptuous chambers of George Hearst, owner of the biggest mine in the territory, occupied the entire top floor of the hotel.

Hand-in-hand Maggie and Dakota explored the lavish suite. Magnificent Oriental rugs, plush sofas and chairs, damask satin drapery, crystal chandeliers, and a gold-plated bathtub were just a few of the luxuries in the opulent suite.

Dakota threw down the key on top of a rich carved mahogany table. He felt awkward and out of his element. "Looks fancier than a bawdy house," he commented wryly.

Maggie had been raised in luxury and was unimpressed with the elegance. Sensing Dakota's uneasiness, she slipped her arms around his neck.

He drew her into his embrace as she kissed him. From the first touch of her lips, his reservations about the room faded. Nothing existed except Maggie.

When breathlessness forced them to part, her eyes gleamed with mischief. Maggie pulled the ends of his tie and dangled the narrow black strip in the air before dropping it to the floor. "We have the whole day ahead of us. How do you suggest we spend it?"

As she began to unbuckle his gunbelt, her green eyes gazed beguilingly into his shuttered stare. "There ain't too many who've dared what you're trying," he warned.

"And what am I daring?" she asked seductively.

"Parting me from my gunbelt," he chuckled.

"Oh, you ninny! You've got no romance in your soul."

She started to shove him away, but he grabbed her and returned her hand to the belt. "Lady, a gun's not a toy. When you reach for it, be sure you draw it."

Maggie's gaze matched the bold audaciousness in his dark eyes. She released the buckle and the heavy belt dropped to the floor. "You know, this will be the first time we make love in a bed."

She could feel his unswerving stare as she opened the buttons on his shirt. Maggie slowly slipped the garment off his shoulders and down the length of his arms. Her eyes seduced his as she trailed her fingertips across the muscular brawn of his chest. Wordlessly he lifted one foot and then the other as she removed his boots and stockings.

What had begun as a game had escalated into a demand. Her heart pounded rapidly. She could sense his mounting passion, the urgency of that fervor an evident bulge in his trousers.

When her hands reached to release his pants, Dakota's control snapped. With a muffled groan he pulled her into his arms. His mouth consumed hers, and, under a barrage of kisses, she burned with an exquisite heat.

"I love you. I love you," she repeated mindlessly as he disposed of her clothing.

He lifted her in his arms, his mouth closing around a throbbing breast. She slipped her arms around his neck and clung to him, cleaved to him, her legs straddling his waist. He impaled her. Maggie cried out his name as they soared to a rapturous release.

Ana Leigh

He continued to hold her. Maggie slumped her head on his shoulder, and returned to awareness of the physical confines of her body.

"We didn't make it, Maggie," he rasped in her ear.

She lifted her head. "We didn't what?"

"We didn't make it to the bed."

She glanced through the open door to the canopied fourposter draped in blue satin. The large bed seemed miles away to her. "It's no wonder," she sighed and returned her head to his shoulder.

"Maggie?" he asked after a lengthy pause. Wearily, she raised her head again. "Are you going to let go of me, so I can put you down?"

"No. I can't move. We'll have to go through life attached together . . . forever."

"Gotta get dressed and take care of the horses. By now those rigs are drawing attention."

Reluctantly, Maggie released her grasp. She felt a sense of emptiness when he withdrew and stepped back. She slipped her legs to the floor and was surprised to discover they could support her.

Dakota kissed Maggie lightly and released her.

She had barely donned her underclothing when Dakota finished dressing and headed for the door. "Wait for me. I'll come with you."

After assisting Maggie into her gown, a risky manuever nearly causing another delay, the newlyweds clasped hands and left their honeymoon suite.

As Maggie waited outside for Dakota, her attention was drawn to a poster tacked to the livery wall. She could barely contain her excitement when she recognized the face boldly exhibited on the placard.

"Look, Dakota," she exclaimed when he rejoined her. "Buffalo Bill is appearing right here in Deadwood. Oh, please, let's go to see him." She was ecstatic when Dakota agreed.

They stopped at the general store to purchase the tickets, then returned to their suite.

Later, as they dined on a delicious turkey dinner complete with sweet potatoes and cranberry sauce, Maggie lingered over a dish of her favorite confection, chocolate ice cream.

"M-m-m-m-m," she sighed, savoring the taste. "I haven't had ice cream since I left Washington."

Dakota was eating a piece of apple pie. "I've never eaten ice cream."

"What! Why not?"

"Just never appealed to me," he answered, popping a forkful of pie into his mouth. "I figure if you take the time to sit down and eat, there oughta be something to chew."

Maggie couldn't imagine anyone resisting ice cream, especially for apple pie. She could have apple pie any day of the week. Scooping up a spoonful of the ice cream, she raised it to his mouth. "Just try this and tell me you don't like it," she insisted.

Dakota sampled the offering. He looked dubious, so she gave him another spoonful, followed by another, and then another. Finally, she just handed him the dish and spoon.

She ate his pie.

Later, Maggie quivered with expectation when

the long-awaited hour arrived to attend the evening's performance. Excitement surged through her when Buffalo Bill first appeared on the stage, looking exactly as he did in her Beadle magazines.

As the melodrama unfolded, the antics and derring-do of the star began to appear ridiculous to her. The theatrical gestures and posturing of the famous scout contrasted dramatically with the nobility and integrity of the quiet man who sat silently beside her throughout the performance. When the production ended, she applauded politely.

"Why, he's nothing more than a swaggering show-off," she voiced with chagrin as they walked back to the hotel.

"He was a great scout once, Maggie."

"Oh, just like Wild Bill Hickock was a great marshal, I suppose," Maggie argued. "Why are you defending him? He's making money by living on his laurels."

"Why not?" He shrugged.

"Why not? That's sure strange coming from you. You're the one who's critical of heroes."

"No man is an absolute hero, Maggie. Men like Cody and Hickock only did what they had to, to survive. Nothing heroic about it."

"Does that include you too?" she asked.

"I've said so all along."

"Well, I can't see you acting out your exploits on a stage," she argued as they entered the hotel. Maggie sighed deeply. "But I suppose you're right."

Dakota stopped abruptly, grasped her shoulders, and turned her to face him. "You mean I can climb down from the pedestal you've put me on?" he said, relieved.

She lifted her pert chin defiantly. "You?" she exclaimed. "What made you think I'd ever put an ornery, thick-headed mule like you on a pedestal? I'm not that naive."

Dakota flashed the endearing grin that she could always feel clear down to her toes. "Sounds to me like the honeymoon's over."

Maggie's eyes gleamed with devilment. "It soon will be if you don't show me more than you have up to now." She picked up her skirt and dashed up the stairs two at a time.

Dakota was about to follow when he became aware of the Reverend and Mrs. Pickett observing them. He smiled and doffed his hat. "Ma'am. Reverend." Then he dashed up the stairway in hot pursuit of Maggie.

She squealed when he caught her on the landing above and swooped her up into his arms. "Now, you're gonna eat those words," he warned. Laughing together, he carried her up the remaining flight of stairs.

Below, the shocked and flustered Melissa Pickett put a hand on her husband's arm. "Charles, you must speak to Mr. MacDonald at once." She shook her head in dismay. "We have to call on the Lord's help to get that young man into a church."

The Reverend Charles Pickett suppressed his smile and a glint of fancy gleamed in his eyes. He patted his wife's hand consolingly. "You're right, my dear, but I think this would not be the appropriate time."

Once inside the room, Dakota tossed Maggie on

the bed. Giggling like children, the two rolled around on the huge fourposter until he succeeded in pinning her down and kissing her.

Maggie slipped her arms around his neck and gave herself up to the kiss. When he raised his head, she laced her fingers through the thick texture of his dark hair and smiled up into his eyes.

Dakota kissed her again, then rose to his feet. Grinning, he pulled her up and they began to undress one another. Their movements were slow and leisurely, each knowing that they had the rest of their lives to love each other.

Dakota laid her gently on the bed and climbed in beside her. He lay back and drew her into his arms. Sighing contentedly, Maggie rested her head on his shoulder.

"I've been thinking about something," she said softly.

"Hope it's the same thing I have in mind," he answered lazily.

"Despite everything, Sam was right, you know."

"About what?" he asked. His hand explored her hip.

"His plan worked. It brought us together."

"Yeah, and almost killed both of us doing it." Dakota rolled over and began to trail kisses down the slim column of her neck.

Maggie continued to pursue her argument. "But how else would we have ever met? Somehow, it doesn't seem fair. We've got each other, the Lazy H, and his fortune. What did Sam get out of it?"

Dakota raised his head. "So you want me to find him."

"Did I say that?" she asked cautiously.

"Sounds like it to me."

Yes it was true. She did want him to find her father. And she knew, if Sam Harris was to be found, Dakota was the man who could do it.

Maggie reached up and cupped his cheek in her hand. For several seconds she gazed into his eyes. "I love you."

Dakota studied her. Maggie was beauty—in soul and body—her capacity for loving and forgiveness as beautiful to him as the short curls on her head and the freckles on her nose. His arms tightened around her. "I couldn't bear to lose you, Maggie."

Her gaze worshipped him. "You could, my love, if you had to, because you're strong. That's why you're a hero to me, Dakota. Not just because you can shoot faster or ride better than other men— but because of your inner strength. You've taken the injustice life handed you and borne it without breaking. I lift my head with pride because I am loved by such a man. I am the woman of Dakota MacDonald."

Her hand caressed his chiseled cheek. "But lose me? Never. I don't have your strength, but like it or not, you're stuck with me forever."

His dark eyes gleamed with adoration as he gazed down at her. "Oh, God, Maggie, I love you. You've made up for every hurt I've ever suffered."

She sighed with contentment, slipped her arms around his neck, and parted her lips to accept his kiss.

Later, as she lay with Dakota's head on her breast, listening to the soft sound of his breathing, her arm tightened around the body at peace beside her, and Maggie's thoughts slipped back to long-ago dreams—dreams of a frontier stretching to infinity, wild horses, thundering herds of buffalo, noble red men.

The frontier was rapidly vanishing. The Beadle dime novels were put behind her forever. But Maggie knew the heritage of the West would remain—the man in her arms was the promise of that legacy.

The romantic dreams of the young girl on a park bench had reached fruition.

Maggie MacDonald had found her hero.

Epilogue

Rising abruptly from the flat plains of the prairie like proud pillars reaching to the sky, the wooded slopes of the Black Hills stretched majestically for a hundred miles.

The lone man stood on a high crag. The steep cliff, barren except for a few scrubby pines, jutted above the wooded ridge it rested upon, like a granite altar—sacrosanct and unscalable. Only an intrepid few had ever braved the rugged path to the top.

The wind, sweeping along the sculpted rim of the canyon, ruffled the old man's thick mane of silvered hair. His gaze remained fixed on the two mounted figures on the wooded ridge below. Tears glistened in his eyes when the riders stopped at the base of the crag.

The bearded countenance split with a wide

smile as he threw back his head and erupted into joyous, unrestrained laughter.

Below, the man dismounted, his jaw set in a grim line as he looked up at the barren face of the crag.

He's up there. I can feel it, he said to himself.

The woman got off her horse and moved to his side. The short hair on her nape bristled when a screech of laughter reverberated through the valley. The echoing shrill sounded more feral than human.

Grinning, Dakota MacDonald looked upward at the granite wall. Then he reached out and clasped Maggie's hand.

NORAH HESS

Best Western Frontier Romance
Award-Winner—*Romantic Times*

DEVIL IN SPURS

In the rugged solitude of the Wyoming wilderness, the lovely Jonty Rand lived life as a boy to protect her innocence from the likes of Cord McBain. So when her grandmother's dying wish made Cord Jonty's guardian, she despaired of ever revealing her true identity. Determined to change her into a rawhide-tough wrangler, Cord assigned Jonty all the hardest tasks on the ranch, making her life a torment. Then one stormy night he discovered that Jonty would never be a man, only the wildest, most willing woman he'd ever taken in his arms.

__2934-0 $4.50

LINDSAY RANDALL

SILVER SWORD

Shunned by the superstitious villagers and condemned by her own father, beautiful, headstrong Mara fled her home at the first opportunity. She little dreamed of the long and hazardous journey northward, or of the mysterious stranger who would join her travels and invade her heart. In his hard embrace Mara succumbed to temptation, tasting ecstasy in the fiery onslaught of his kisses. But their love would be nothing but an impossible dream with the talisman that neither could wield without the other.

__2948-0 $3.95 US/$4.95 CAN

MADELINE BAKER

"LOVERS OF INDIAN ROMANCES HAVE A SPECIAL PLACE ON THEIR BOOKSHELVES FOR MADELINE BAKER!"   —*Romantic Times*

LACEY'S WAY
__2918-9 $4.50

RECKLESS LOVE
__2910-3 $4.50 US/$5.50 CAN

LOVE IN THE WIND
__2893-X $4.50 US/$5.50 CAN

RECKLESS HEART
__2915-4 $4.50 US/$5.50 CAN

FIRST LOVE, WILD LOVE
__2838-7 $4.50

RENEGADE HEART
__2744-5 $4.50

RECKLESS DESIRE
__2667-8 $4.50 US/$5.50 CAN

LOVE FOREVERMORE
__2577-9 $3.95 US/$4.95 CAN

FIREFLY

by STEF ANN HOLM

To lovely young immigrant Kristianna, the virgin Wisconsin land was the perfect place to carve a homestead. But arrogant trapper Stone Boucher disagreed violently. Stone wanted nothing to do with encroaching civilization, yet he couldn't resist Kristianna's passionate hunger. And once she was in his arms, she discovered that Stone was as exciting and untamed as the land itself.

_2983-9 $4.50 US/$5.50 CAN

by ELIZABETH CHADWICK

When Justin Harte looked into Anne McAuliffe's beguiling eyes, his troubles were only beginning. Anne could shoot better than most of his ranchhands, clean a gunshot wound as well as any doctor, and charm a rattlesnake out of striking. She was the perfect mate for him, and her soft woman's body tempted him beyond all reason. But a twist of fate had decreed she could never be his, no matter how he longed to caress her porcelain skin, or burned to taste her pleading lips...

_2976-6 $4.50 US/$5.50 CAN